PERSONALIZED ESPECIALLY FOR Tommy _____

WINNING

A FICTIONAL NOVEL

by

John Carver

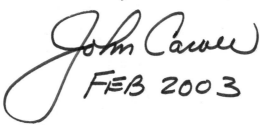

*John Carver
FEB 2003*

HARD TIMES CATTLE COMPANY PUBLISHING

PUBLISHED BY
Hard Times Cattle Company Publishing

The story and characters portrayed in this book
are fictional. The situations and events are purely imaginary.

Book Design and Editor: Ali Fremming
Front Cover Photo: Bruce Gomez
(Original photograph digitally enhanced with goal posts)
Back Cover Photo: 1949 Ranger High School Football Team
"Casey at the Bat": Ernest L. Thayer, 1898

All inquiries for volume purchases of this book
should be addresses to Hard Times Cattle Company Publishing at
P.O. Box 941792, Plano, Texas 75094

Telephone inquiries may be made by calling:
972-669-0707 or FAX 972-690-6585

To my wife Brenda
and my daughter Renee–
Two exceptional women
who know all my faults
and love me anyway.

ACKNOWLEDGMENT

My special thanks to good friends David Hands, Kathy Nepple, Carolyn Potter, Jim and Sara Swinney, Nell Velvin and to my sister Lin Rushing for their help in proofreading my manuscript and for their critical encouragement.

SPECIAL ACKNOWLEDGMENT

The story and characters portrayed in this book are fictional. The situations and events are purely imaginary. However, several of the main characters are real life heroes. Because I wanted to set my story against the background of the incredible Ranger High football season of 1949, Othel Creager, Stubby and Juanita Warden have graciously allowed me to use them as heroes in this novel.

Until 1965, when they sold their interest in the Commercial State Bank and moved to Kaufman, Texas, Othel and Ferrol Creager were two of Ranger's most influential citizens. There were few Ranger residents who at one time or another didn't benefit from Ferrol Creager's presence at the bank. Othel Creager's friendly charisma and her devoted, unselfish work at her church and in community affairs made her one of Ranger's favorite people. The historic Creager House in Ranger has been restored and is now operating as a bed and breakfast establishment.

Ferrol Creager was vice president of the Farmers and Merchants National Bank when he passed away in 1988. Othel lives only a few doors away from the First Methodist Church in Kaufman where at the age of ninety she continues to actively participate in church activities.

Onis Creston "Stubby" Warden was born at Bennett, Texas. After his father died in 1919, Stubby and his family moved to Ranger. Stubby played guard on his high school football team and served as captain. His exploits on the football field are legendary.

After graduating from high school in 1935, Stubby accepted a scholarship to play football for Texas A & M. A year later he married his high school sweetheart Juanita.

Juanita Kimbrough Warden was born in Ranger. She graduated from Ranger High School in 1937. She's a graduate of Clarendon Junior College, receiving her degree while Stubby was coaching at Clarendon High School.

Juanita and Stubby have two children–Marilyn Warden Cundiff, a Librarian for the Dallas Independent School District and Jerry Warden,

Retired Colonel U.S. Army. With four family members—Stubby, Jerry, grandson Mark and granddaughter Kimberlyn—graduating from Texas A & M, the Wardens are passionate and dedicated Aggie sports fans.

Stubby graduated from A & M in 1939 and coached at Clarendon High School until 1942, when he joined the Navy to serve in World War Two. In 1945, he returned from the war and accepted a position as assistant football coach at Ranger High School. Stubby was promoted to head coach in 1946.

Few men have the power and opportunity to influence young people like a football coach. Some coaches handle this responsibility well and still manage to win. Although he was a fierce competitor, Stubby Warden produced winning football teams by insisting on perfection and excellence from himself and from each of his players. Unlike my story, Ranger's limited athletic budget never permitted our coaches to enjoy the luxury of having our games filmed or to have an extra coach to scout future opponents. Most games, our Bulldog players had only a vague idea of what to expect from an opposing team, but no matter what formation the opposition used, Coach always had a solution. He simply made the necessary adjustments, and generally, we then proceeded to beat their socks off. His teams won because of his diligence and because every team member knew his assignment precisely. His football teams were never out-coached or out-classed.

Like every coach, Stubby's Ranger teams had their share of adversity, petty player jealousies and second-guessing, but there was never a young person who played for Coach Warden who didn't respect him or who wasn't a better man for the experience. He never coached a Bulldog football player who wouldn't have willingly sacrificed his body for an encouraging slap on the backside from Coach, or maybe for just a casual nod of his approval.

Stubby had the foresight and genuine good fortune to marry a woman whose warm disposition could smooth over his sometimes coarse demeanor. Juanita Warden's steady, gentle manner has always been a perfect balance for Stubby's fiery, competitive temperament. In her unique, charming and affable way she's been a powerful positive influence on her community.

Stubby and Juanita are retired now. They still reside in Ranger where they are easily the best known and two most respected residents. Stubby was Mayor from 1980 through 1983. Juanita served as Librarian at Ranger Junior College for twenty-four years. They continue to be actively involved in their church, community affairs and volunteer work.

FOREWORD

As a young person growing up in Ranger, there was never a shortage of heroes. Honest, hard-working, family-oriented men like Roscoe Hopper, J.D. Johnson and my father Arlie provided strong male role models who I've often used as examples to pattern my behavior and as reference points when I'm faced with tough moral and ethical questions.

Gentle, considerate, god-fearing women like Vonceil Hopper, Lazelle Johnson and my mother Virginia who were sincerely interested and seriously involved in our youth activities–they were my teachers. Their love and their unwavering faith in me provided me with a sense of self-worth and inner security. Even on my worst days I can honestly say I've never felt alone or unloved.

Teachers and school administrators like H.L. Coody, J.R. "Dutch" Ervin, A.G. Koenig, Helen Hagaman, Lilly Robinson, J.C. Shepard, Lillian Strain, G.B. Rush, Mary Wilson and John Winder–somehow they managed to capture our attention long enough to teach us English, math, science and history so we could compete in a working world after we graduated.

Strong-willed, tough, demanding coaches like Stubby Warden who despised losing–he inspired in each of his players a passion for winning. He also showed us how winning can be achieved with tenacity and perseverance, and by example, he taught us a sense of fair play.

Junior Arterburn, Jimmy Comacho, Raymond Comacho, Dean Elder, Buddy Hamrick, Jackie Hummel, Alvin Langley, Billy Simpson, R.C. Smith, Kenneth Williams, Bill Yung and so many others–their gridiron heroics made them everyone's heroes, bringing glory to their school and making every Ranger resident proud of their hometown.

I've always fantasized about writing a novel. Writing this book has been like creating my own "Field of Dreams." Hope you'll enjoy reading it as much as I enjoyed writing it.

WINNING

A FICTIONAL NOVEL

CHAPTER ONE
THE INTERVIEW

Thursday Afternoon
May 16, 1949

THE CURIOUS WOMAN in the blue gingham dress glances inquisitively at me from behind a paper-covered desk on the opposite side of the room. I'm sure she must be wondering why a young man wearing worn-out blue jeans and a greasy, wrinkled white shirt should be waiting to interview for the head football coaching job. She taps the desk several times with her pencil then goes back to work on the stack of mimeographed sheets before her.

Actually, I'm surprised to be here myself. After graduating from Texas A&M last January, the only job I could find was a temporary coaching position at Gulf State Institute in Corpus Christi. The basketball coach there had resigned in mid-season frustration after being threatened in the dressing room by a drunken player. Gulf State is a junior college which will accept any outstanding athlete without question, not caring whether he's a tough, a thug or a dropout. Being on athletic scholarship at Gulf State usually means you are either too stupid to make college level grades or socially unacceptable at the larger colleges—oftentimes both. I never played basketball in either high school or college. The Gulf State job was not my job of choice, but with a new wife and a child on the way, I was desperate. My basketball team never won a game during my short tenure as coach. I feel fortunate to have completed the season without being hit in the head by a flying beer bottle or having my throat slit by one of my players.

A school bell rings signaling the end of the school day. I hear the noisy chatter of students as they leave their classes and funnel into the hallways, and the banging of metal lockers as students, preparing to leave the building, store their books and belongings. The wall clock above the receptionist's desk says the time is 3:30 P.M. My appointment with the school trustees was scheduled for 3:00 P.M. I was nervous enough about this meeting even before the curious lady seated me here in the principal's office off the main hallway. Students stare at me as they pass by on their way out of the building. My fear of the interview ahead makes me want to bolt down the hallway and out the door with the students.

Without warning, the door to the trustees' meeting room opens. A tall, thin man motions to me. "Coach Warden, we are ready for you. Please come in." My heart beats faster. It's too late to run now.

Entering the room, I find eight men seated solemnly around a long conference table. Each man has a name plate placed on the table in front of his chair. The room is filled with cigar smoke even though a sign above the door declares "No Smoking." I recognize Lucas Masters, the school board president, sitting at the head of the table and G.C. Boswell, the school superintendent, who is sitting in the chair to Masters' right. Masters and Boswell are the only two men in the room wearing business suits. The other men are dressed casually. One of the men wears a khaki work uniform with a name embroidered above the left shirt pocket. The others are dressed in slacks and short-sleeve shirts.

Except for Lucas Masters and the superintendent, the men are all strangers to me. There is no sense of friendliness in this room. This meeting is serious business to each of these men.

Masters speaks first. "Mister Warden, you know why you are here. Tell us why you should be our football coach."

My knees are shaking and my mouth is dry, but I want this job too badly to lose it in the first minute of the interview. I have done my homework. I have an answer for his question.

"Because each of you men wants a winning football team and because I know how to win," I respond, hoping they don't know about my Gulf State record.

Lucas Masters is a seasoned veteran at these board interviews. He's not only the richest man in town; he is also probably the shrewdest and toughest. Masters made his fortune during the Ranger Oil Boom with a slick tongue and a quick mind. In the years since the Oil Boom he has purchased or gained control of almost all the downtown buildings and property. Most of the men around the table are merchants who, one way or another, rely on Lucas Masters for their livelihood. Odds are that Masters has already decided whom he'll pick to be the next football coach. My interview was most likely granted so he could brag to the locals about how the school board tried to find a bright young coach with a new approach but finally settled for someone with more experience and maturity.

I wait impatiently for the next question.

"What makes you think you can produce a winning football team for Ranger High School?" Masters inquires.

"Because I know more about football and football strategy than any other coach you will interview for this job, and because I understand how to evaluate and maximize the talents of your young men."

Masters straightens up in his chair, grinning. This interview with the young coach is gonna be fun. Several other men around the table also begin to smile. Apparently they've seen Lucas in action on previous interviews.

"So, you could've won with the team we had last year. Do you know how many games we won?"

"Yes, we won two, and we lost eight. Four of those games we lost by less than two touchdowns. We averaged scoring only 16 points per game, while we allowed more than 28 points per game. If we had scored one more touchdown and allowed one less, we would've finished with a winning season." I am using "we" very freely–hoping these men will begin to associate me with their football team.

"Are you telling this board you would've fielded a winning team last year if you'd been the coach?" Masters questions, moving me smoothly into a defensive position.

"No, I'm telling this board that with the talent on last year's team, Ranger High would have been district champion, probably could've won bi-district, too."

Every man, including Masters, leans forward in his chair. The interview is progressing even better than they had imagined. This brash young man is truly asking to be cut down to size.

"Well now, young fellow, why don't you explain to the trustees just how you would've performed such a magical trick."

This is the question I have prepared for. During the past week I borrowed last year's game films from the high school. Using a rented projector, I spent countless hours watching each play over and over. I know every player by name, number and position, right down to the team's student manager.

"Buddy Hamrick–Quarterback–'Option Tee' formation."

One of the men sitting behind the name plate reading L. Jackson, who has remained silent until now, speaks up, almost angrily, "That's insane! Buddy is a halfback–has been since seventh grade. Anyway, Ranger plays single wing power football."

The name plate in front of another trustee's chair reads B. Tucker. I gamble that the men are sitting in their designated seats. "Mister Tucker, did you attend the Albany game last year?"

B. Tucker winces, looking at me like I have hurt him. "Son, I have attended every Ranger High football game for the past fifteen years–never missed a game, even on the Friday nights when two of my three children were born."

"Then you must have seen the halfback option pass we tried in the fourth quarter of that game?"

"Of course I saw the play. Didn't do us much good. The pass was incomplete. We were behind by twenty some-odd points at the time."

"Mister Tucker, tell me why the pass was not completed."

"As I recall, our left end Jimmy Ice dropped the ball. I'll always wonder why Jimmy didn't catch that darn ball. It hit him right in the hands."

"Yes, that's always a difficult pass to catch–when the football hits you right in your hands."

I hope my attempt to inject some humor will lighten things up. It doesn't seem to work. Not one of the men laughs at my comment.

"Approximately how far would you estimate that ball was thrown?" I continue.

"Well now, let's see.... We were on our own thirty at the time and ole Jim Boy dropped the ball about the fifteen. I guess that's.... Hey, that ball traveled almost 60 yards in the air!"

"Buddy Hamrick–Quarterback–'Option Tee' formation." I'm beginning to roll. Now, I need to set my lineup.

"Ralph Rogers–Right End– 'Option Tee' formation."

I glance at the name plates on the conference table. I select the tall, thin man who earlier invited me into the meeting. He sits behind an R. Clark nameplate.

"Mister Clark, who is the tallest man on the football squad?"

R. Clark is startled. He obviously wasn't expecting to be singled out like this. Judging from his confused look, it's obvious I have made a mistake. I try to recover.

"Mister Clark, I'm sure you know Ralph Rogers is the tallest man on our squad. He also plays center on the basketball team. And he can run faster than a gazelle. If you would, try to imagine Ralph Rogers jumping high in the end zone to catch a sixty yard pass from our quarterback Buddy Hamrick."

Because of his height, it is very possible R. Clark played basketball in high school and maybe in college. His face brightens when I mention the basketball team.

"Oh, yeah! I can certainly picture that. Big Ralph can sure jump, and he has tremendously big hands," Clark reflects. As soon as he speaks, he realizes he's made an error in expanding on my suggestion. Clark glances around the long table, searching for support. Masters glares at him.

From their expressions it is obvious that several of the other trustees have also seen R. Clark's vision. Now's the time to show them my best move.

"Defense–J.L. Barnes–Middle Linebacker."

This time I turn to G.C. Boswell. "Mister School Superintendent, who is the toughest and strongest kid in high school?"

"No question about it–J.L. Barnes," replies Boswell. "But he doesn't always play fall sports. His dad's a farmer. Keeps J.L. at home working, until his crops are harvested. Most years J.L. doesn't begin attending school until late October. Every year his teachers have one heck of a time getting him caught up with the rest of his class."

In the game films I watched, J.L. Barnes played maybe twenty plays. Even though all his playing time came at the end of games with the losing result already decided, it was obvious J.L. could be a dominating defensive player. For some reason the coaches decided not to play the boy, perhaps as punishment for missing early fall practice, perhaps to keep from hurting some other player's feelings.

I have made a solemn promise to myself–to never make a sentimental or emotional decision which might affect my team's opportunity to win.

I turn to Lucas Masters.

"Mister Masters, you're a rich man. How much would you pay to have a championship team?"

Lucas Masters senses that the discussion has deviated from his intended course. The fun he had planned in embarrassing and ridiculing this young coach has, somehow, never materialized. Masters is now eager to put an end to this pointless discussion and get on with selecting his hand-picked "yes-man."

In spite of his experience at these meetings, Masters has been boxed in by my challenge. He's compelled to respond. I didn't plan to put Masters in such an embarrassing situation, but now I have baited the hook. Masters has no choice. He'll have to strike back.

"Coach Warden, if you are suggesting to this board that we do something illegal, then this interview is over. We will find a coach who can win without breaking the rules. I regret you were invited for this interview."

I've gotta talk fast now.

"Mister Masters, I never mentioned breaking any rules. I only asked how much you would pay to field a championship football team. Are you committed to winning or not?"

Masters is steaming mad now. I have questioned his integrity, and he is anxious to put me in my place.

"Young man, no person in this town has been more supportive of the high school football program. Only last year I personally donated a thousand dollars toward the purchase of new uniforms and equipment for the football team."

"Then, if I could arrange it, you'd be willing to employ a hired hand to help out at the Barnes' farm next fall so J.L. could attend school and play for my football team in September and October?"

It's my team we are talking about now.

Several board members shift about uneasily. They realize that Masters' answer is critical to the continuation of the interview.

My knees are trembling. Even though I'm almost certain that this job, which I want so desperately, will never be mine, I sense I am closer to capturing it than I ever imagined possible. A sharp, sour taste fills my mouth. I feel a terrible urge to spit, but instead, I swallow.

"Are you sure there'd be nothing illegal about such an arrangement?"

"Absolutely sure. Your benevolence would only insure that J.L.

has an opportunity for a good education." I want to add "and insure a winning football season," but I hold back. No point in stating the obvious.

Masters' eyes dart nervously around the room. The mood in the room has changed dramatically. He's losing control of the interview. He had intended to show that this young coach had no experience, no credentials and a losing record, but these men, who he has for so long completely dominated, now appear ready to revolt.

The trustee behind the nameplate reading G. Long asks, "Why should we run an 'Option Tee' offense? What the hell is an 'Option Tee' formation anyway?"

"The 'Option Tee' is an offense conceived by Marshall Robnett, a former 'All-American' football player and now a young assistant coach at Texas A&M. The 'Option Tee' utilizes the same basic alignments as a 'Standard Tee' formation, except the 'Option Tee' provides the quarterback with the advantage of having several options on every play.

"The 'Option Tee' is designed to confuse and open up an opponent's defense. A defensive team is unable to determine whether you intend to run, pass or lateral, until after the play is in progress. The quarterback makes his decision after he reads how the defense is reacting. When you have a smart, quick quarterback who can pass accurately, the offense is extremely difficult to defend against."

"How come we haven't heard about this formation before? Why aren't other high school teams using it?" asks B. Tucker.

"Texas A&M has operated from the 'Option Tee' a number of times in actual games during the past two years. But as you know, Coach Norton, the A&M head coach, has enjoyed enormous success with his double wing offense. It would be a very difficult decision for him to switch offenses, even though he has been most impressed with the success of plays run off the 'Option Tee.' I don't believe you can find a Texas high school coach who knows how to defend against an 'Option Tee' offense."

"Who else knows about this offense?" asks R. Clark. "Are you sure it's legal?"

"Only a few college coaches have used the 'Option Tee' in actual games. The offense requires a smart, quick and very skilled quarterback to execute the plays. Teams which operate from a single or double wing offense usually prefer having a big, strong guy running their offense. While some college teams have switched to a 'Standard Tee,' most college teams still employ a single wing, double wing or some variation of those offenses. Since they don't use the 'Option Tee' offense, most college coaches haven't seriously recruited that type of quarterback. But, to answer your question—yes, the offense is perfectly legal."

Lucas Masters leans over and whispers something to Superintendent Boswell. Boswell nods his head as if to agree.

"Coach Warden, I think the board is satisfied with your interview. Thank you for your time. Would you please wait outside for a few minutes while we consider your application?"

"I'd appreciate your granting me more time to explain to the trustees how I plan to utilize some other team members who'll be returning next year," I argue.

"I'm sorry, Coach Warden, but our time is limited. I believe the board satisfactorily understands the offensive scheme you have proposed," Boswell pronounces firmly, dismissing me like a disobedient child.

I WAIT OUTSIDE in the same chair where I sat so nervously only thirty minutes earlier. The curious reception lady is gone now. The hallways of the school are empty and quiet. I'm alone in the room. My head is light, and I feel dizzy. No matter what the outcome of the interview, I'm satisfied with my performance. I gave them my best shot. Somehow, I avoided talking about my losing coaching experience or my limited knowledge of football strategy, either of which would've doomed me.

MY WIFE'S UNCLE Price Mitchell is the Pontiac dealer in Ranger. Since Pontiac doesn't manufacture a pickup truck, his new car sales are rare. Anyone buying a new passenger car in Ranger will probably purchase a Ford or a Chevy. Price's car business is successful because of his warm personality and his sincere desire to please his customers. He also runs the best auto repair shop in Eastland County.

I'm not sure why Price and his wife Phyliss never had children. Maybe it was because things were so tough for them, scratching out a living during the Great Depression of the '30s. Perhaps the absence of their own children accounts for the way they adopted my wife Juanita and me. Knowing I would be out of work during the summer after my Gulf State experience, Price and Phyliss insisted I come to Ranger and work for the Pontiac dealership until I found a coaching job. Repairing automobile engines is not exactly my thing, but Price keeps me busy changing oil and fixing flats. Phyliss helped Juanita find an office job at the M.E. Moses Store on Main Street. Lord knows, we needed their help. We were close to starvation in Corpus Christi.

It was strictly an accident that I heard about the interview for the Ranger coaching position. One of our customers mentioned it in conversation with Price while his car was in the shop for repair. Price came running to me in the rear car lot, all excited. Would I like to interview to be the head football coach at Ranger High? A few phone calls from Price to some of his influential customers and I was set up with an interview. Price could hardly contain himself. He's never been much of a football fan, but he began making plans to bring his friends and customers to the ballgames–to watch me coach.

Price's enthusiasm was contagious, but I understood from the beginning that my chances of getting the job were very slim, if there was any chance at all. What school in their right mind would hire an inexperienced young coach to straighten out a losing football program?

At Price's prodding and with his help, I made arrangements to borrow last year's game films. I was told to get in touch with Keith Murphy who coaches the junior high team and handles the filming of high school games. Murphy also drives a morning and afternoon rural school bus, five days a week, out to the Alemeda area where he owns a farm.

Murphy is a very busy man. I was able to catch him one afternoon sitting inside his bus, waiting for school to let out.

"Hello. You wouldn't be Coach Murphy by any chance, would you?" I asked.

"Might be? Who wants to know?"

"I do. I mean, my name is Stubby Warden. I have an appointment to interview for the football coaching vacancy. I was told to contact you about borrowing last year's game films."

"I been thinking about applying for that job myself," Murphy replied nastily. "What makes you think they'd hire you? You seem to be a little young and green behind the ears to be looking for a big man's job."

Because of his last name, I had expected him to be of Irish descent with fair skin and light hair. Instead, Keith Murphy was a heavy-set man with dark suntanned skin and dark brown hair. His arms were large and muscular. Murphy's muscles were not the kind obtained by lifting weights in the gym. His muscles came from long, hard hours of strenuous farm work. His hands were hard and calloused, with short, thick fingers. Murphy's scarred knuckles confirmed his reputation about his being quick to fight.

I'd suspected I wouldn't like Murphy, even before I met him. I had heard stories about how he mistreated his young players and about the kangaroo court he had established in his P.E. classes to issue out harsh punishment for even the smallest violation of his rules. His unfriendly attitude toward me only served to increase my dislike for the man.

"Sir, can I borrow the films or not?" I asked. I did not want a confrontation with this man, but it was difficult not to show my feelings.

"Well, son, I reckon, if you'd bring me your mother's written permission, I might be able to loan you the films for maybe a day or so," Murphy teased.

Disregarding his cute remark, I told him, "I'd like to have the films today, not later than tomorrow. I don't have much time to prepare for my interview. Where and when can I get the films?"

Murphy sat up in the driver's seat. "Look here, son! I don't have to take crap off a young punk like you. If you want my cooperation, you better say 'please, Mister Murphy.'"

The conversation was deteriorating quickly. To have any chance at the coaching job, I needed to study those films. I decided to go along. Gritting my teeth, I responded, "Coach Murphy, could I please borrow last years game films?"

The grim expression on Murphy's face slowly began to change to a smile. He'd shown this young smart ass who was in charge of things around here.

"Young fellow, you meet me at the varsity field house tomorrow morning at eight o'clock sharp. I'll have the films ready for you. You have a projector?"

"No." Actually, I hadn't even thought about needing equipment to view the films.

Murphy had to dig me one last time. "Well, you darn sure can't borrow the school's projector. Guess you'll have to hold the film up to the sunlight. Probably do you just as much good that way."

"I'll arrange for a projector. You just have the films ready for me." I was tired of his condescending attitude. I didn't bother to look back as I walked away from the bus. I knew Murphy would be wearing a wide, smirking grin, while he conjured up the story he'd relate to the other bus drivers about the young punk kid who was afflicted with aspirations of being the next Ranger football coach.

THE DOOR TO THE TRUSTEES' meeting room opens abruptly, interrupting my daydreaming. I hear the shuffling of chairs being scooted back away from the conference table and muffled talk as the men adjourn from the meeting.

G.C. Boswell is the first to emerge from the room. He steps quickly toward me. His face bears a sorrowful frown. My stomach churns while my hopes vanish. Boswell, obviously, will not be bringing good news.

"Coach Warden, you gave us a wonderful interview. Our trustees were so very impressed with the way you handled yourself," Boswell tells me, while I wait for him to drive his spike of hurt through my heart.

"The board feels with a little more experience you'll be a very successful football coach. We especially liked your fresh ideas about your new offense and better use of our player's skills."

Several men walk past me on their way out. Only R. Clark stops to shake my hand, then without speaking, gazes down at the floor and walks on. I feel like I am attending my own funeral.

Finally, Superintendent Boswell breaks the news to me. "Stubby, the board has decided to hire Buck Wagner."

His news is like a slap in the face. I can't believe what he's telling me. I didn't know the old coach from Cisco was even being considered for the job. Wagner is a relic who should've retired ten years ago. His Cisco teams haven't been to the state playoffs since before World War Two. If I wasn't hurting so badly, I would burst out laughing.

Lucas Masters is the last to leave the meeting room. As he walks by me, he says, "Tough luck, son. Wish you the best in finding a job. Let me know if you ever need any help."

It suddenly occurs to me that the trustee's meeting was all a farce–a sham. The entire interview process was to lend credence to the preservation of power for this despicable person. He controls the school board.

Those men in the meeting never made this choice. Lucas Masters is responsible for this preposterous coaching decision. He had his "yes man" picked out long before the interviews. Most likely, the school trustees never even bothered interviewing Buck Wagner.

With his man in place, Masters can designate which boy plays and at what position. Yes, his choice for coach is about preserving his power over men who want to see their sons play football for Ranger High.

I PUSH FIERCELY on the front door when I leave the school building. The heavy, metal door swings back hard and rattles angrily as it strikes against the outside brick wall. The force of the early summer heat jars me. Sharp, dry sand particles, carried by the stiff wind howling across the barren campus, sting my face.

I bound swiftly down the front steps to the street, trying to hold back my tears. My disappointment crushes in on me. It's going to be a deadly hot summer.

JUANITA AND I HAVE rented a small two-bedroom house located on Main Street, one block west of the downtown business district. The quoted rent of forty dollars a month was more than we could afford, but Phyliss knows the owner personally. She was able to convince our landlady that we were a nice young couple who would take good care of the place. We finally settled on a monthly rent of thirty dollars, to be hand-delivered to the landlady's house, in cash, on the first day of each month. I suspect Phyliss is secretly subsidizing us with an extra five or so a month to the landlady. If she is helping us, I don't want to know. I have precious little pride left the way things are.

We selected this house because it is close to downtown, close enough for Juanita to walk to her job at the Five and Dime Store on days I can't drive her.

Somehow, in the disappointing events of the afternoon, I have lost all track of time. As I pull the car into the driveway, I'm hoping Juanita will be home from work. I need to talk with her before I return to the shop to tell Price the bad news.

The crunch of my car tires grinding down our gravel driveway prompts Juanita's appearance at the front door. She has been anxiously waiting for me. She runs to the car and kisses me through the window before I can open the door.

"Tell me quickly! How did it go? Did you get the job?" she asks excitedly.

"Not good. They decided to hire Buck Wagner."

"Buck Wagner! Oh, Stubby, that's absolutely appalling. He's not half the coach you are. Why would they pick an old man like him?" she asks, expressing her frustration.

"I don't know for sure, but I believe they had already decided to hire him before my interview."

"Oh, honey, I know how disappointed you must be," Juanita says, wrapping her arms around my waist and pulling herself close against me.

Even in the summer heat my young wife smells clean and fresh. Her soft body seems to soak up and ease my hurt. I squeeze her more tightly.

"Be careful, sweetheart. We don't want to hurt Baby Warden," she whispers in my ear.

"I'm sorry, Juanita. Did I hurt you?"

"No, darling, but the doctor wants me to be very careful. He says there's a lot more risk of losing the first child than with later children," she replies seriously.

"Does that mean you want to have a lot more children?" I joke. I cannot stay depressed for very long around this loving woman. She is the joy in my life.

"Maybe, if you can put up with me being fat and ugly for nine months with every child. Let me have this one first, then we'll talk about it," she replies, taking my question much too seriously.

"You could never be ugly in my eyes, woman. And what do you mean—we will talk about it?" I place my hands on her hips and pull her gently against me, pressing her thighs against mine.

"Mister Warden, you are an oversexed, dirty old man. Come inside, before the neighbors call the police."

She smiles slyly, then turns and strolls seductively toward the house.

FROM OUR BEDROOM I can see the clock in the hallway. The time is six-thirty-two. Price usually stays in his office until around seven. I need to tell him about my interview. If I hurry, I can still catch him.

Juanita is lying sleepily beside me. Our clothes are strewed across the floor, left there as we hastily undressed in heated desire.

"Juanita, I gotta go out for a while. I need to talk with Price."

"Can't it wait until tomorrow? Maybe I should fix you something to eat first?" she offers, halfheartedly.

"No, he'll be anxious. I should get down there before he leaves the office."

I roll out of bed, looking around the room for my clothes. I retrieve my underwear from underneath the bed covers. One shoe is in the hall. I find the other under the bed.

"Shouldn't you take a shower?" she teases. "We could share. I could wash your back and do shameful things for you—things I can't tell my mother about."

I stop searching for my clothes.

"Mrs. Warden, you are a brazen, oversexed pregnant woman. You should be ashamed of yourself for distracting a man from his sworn duties."

"Suit yourself, Mister Warden. I only meant to be helpful. You can bathe alone next time for all I care," she pouts playfully.

I bend down to kiss her softly on the lips. I love the smell of her. The thought of sharing her shower is almost too enticing. If I don't leave now, I won't be able to go.

"Juanita, I love you, but I've got to go."

"I know, my love. I'll wait up for you," she promises.

—————————

PRICE IS LOCKING the front showroom door, preparing to leave for home when I drive into the parking lot. I wave at him. He acknowledges my greeting with a grimacing scowl. I feel guilty for not coming sooner. He has been more nervous and anxious than I was this past week.

"Hey, Price, I'm glad I caught you before you left."

From the expression on his face I can tell he's already heard the bad news. Ranger is a small town, and gossip travels fast.

"I hear they treated you pretty badly."

"Not really. Actually, I believe I did an excellent job of presenting my ideas. I kinda got 'em going with the concept of my new offense and your suggestion about the Barnes' kid."

"I hear they selected old man Wagner. Sometimes I can't believe this town," Price comments. His irritated voice articulates his displeasure.

"Yes, it was a terrible decision—one I'm sure they'll live to regret. But I believe the trustees had already made their choice before my interview. That Lucas Masters fellow seems to run the show. Whatever he says goes. Someone needs to stand up to him."

Price's face pales, like he has suddenly become ill.

"You didn't get into a confrontation with Lucas, did you? I didn't mean for that to happen." There is obvious fear in his voice.

"No, certainly not. I only meant it seems the other trustees didn't have much of a say in the decision to select Wagner."

The subtle fear in Price's voice makes me realize I'm treading on some very shaky ground. Does Lucas Masters have some power over my friend Price Mitchell, too?

"Well, thank goodness you are okay with Lucas. He can be a big help to people he likes," Price advises, showing his relief.

"Price, you know my situation. I can't afford to make enemies with anyone. Hey, you were ready to leave. I'll see you at work tomorrow. I'll give you all the dirty details then."

"Sure. Fine. We can talk some more tomorrow. Listen, Stubby, be careful what you say about Lucas Masters and your interview. We don't need any trouble, okay?" Price says, wanting my assurance.

"Price, I promise to watch what I say. Tell Phyliss hello. I'll see you in the morning."

————————

DRIVING HOME along an almost deserted Main Street I ponder on what power Lucas Masters could have over Price Mitchell. Is there anyone in this town Masters doesn't control?

I try to erase my unpleasant thoughts about today's events by thinking about Juanita. She promised to wait up for me. Maybe she'll still be in the mood for a shower.

CHAPTER TWO
THE SEARCH

RANGER IS ABOUT 75 miles west of Fort Worth. Because the city is almost midway between Abilene and Fort Worth, it is a favorite stop for truckers with loads bound for El Paso or California. Some speculate that the true reason so many truckers stop here is to either bolster their nerves before attempting to negotiate down the steep, narrow, winding grades of Ranger Hill out on Highway 80 east of town or to soothe their nerves after they've made it safely up the treacherous hill. Many local residents make their living in the numerous gas stations near downtown and along the highway.

The Ranger Oil Boom is advertised locally as "The Oil Boom that won World War One," providing the gasoline needed to keep the allied troops mobilized. When the McClesky Discovery Well No. 1 first struck oil in October of 1917, scarcely a thousand persons lived in or around Ranger. Within a month the population had swelled to more than 10,000, and before the year ended in 1918, more than 20,000 persons had taken up residence in Ranger.

Money flowed like the oil from the seemingly ever-bountiful wells. Large fortunes were created overnight, as leases were signed and oil wells were drilled. Jobs were plentiful and wages were high. It was a time of truly amazing events, never to be repeated in such a magnificent fashion anywhere again.

One of the reasons the Ranger Boom was so unique was because of the spectacular wells that were brought in. Oil was often observed shooting as high as 100 feet above the derricks after oil was struck. The enormous oil pool was overlain by natural gas, creating terrific subterranean pressures which were dramatically released when the well's drill bits broke through into the oil.

Many wells were drilled which never hit the oil pool, coming up with nothing but natural gas. Sadly, at the time there was no ready market for natural gas. Many drillers, not realizing the dreadful consequences, simply set fire to the gas escaping from their wells, letting them burn and thereby releasing the pressure on the oil pool. For many years the light from burning gas wells lit up the darkness for miles around Ranger, making it seem like daytime in the middle of the night.

Apparently, the rock formation below the Ranger oil field is very porous. As gas pressure was reduced on the oil pool, the oil was slowly absorbed into the underlying rock strata. The oil became more and more difficult to recover. Finally, the oil played out, and oil speculators moved on to more prosperous territories.

Left behind after the boom were oil workers employed by the handful of companies who maintained the few still-producing wells, merchants with interests they could not sell, the original farming and ranching families and others who decided to stay rather than follow the rigorous life in the new boom towns of Snyder and Andrews. Very little of the vast fortunes made during the boom years remained behind in Ranger.

When Juanita and I arrived in Ranger at the end of April, long after the glorious boom days of the twenties, the population had dwindled down to less than four thousand. After several months of living among the cold, faceless inhabitants in the overcrowded metropolis of Corpus Christi, we were happily astonished at the warm and friendly people we met in Ranger. We both immediately developed a strong love for this town. Up until my disappointing encounter with the school board, it seemed we had found the perfect place to settle down and raise our soon-to-be family.

Tuesday Night
June 25, 1949

IN MY QUEST FOR a coaching job I begin mailing résumés to at least two high school superintendents each day. Every evening, with Price's approval, I use his office to prepare my mailing for the next day.

My résumé is, for obvious reasons, not very long or extensive, but each of my transmittal letters, my résumé, and a mailing envelope have to be individually typed on Price's ten-year-old manual Royal Typewriter. Sometimes, on her slow days, Juanita will type my résumés for that day's mailing on her newer Underwood model at M.E. Moses. Those are the rare nights I arrive home before my wife is asleep.

Tonight we had a late customer. Price was with him in the office until almost eight. It is already dark outside as I roll my first sheet of paper into the ancient typewriter.

The telephone rings. I pick it up and answer, "Pontiac House."

A voice on the line inquires, "Stubby Warden, is that you?"

Immediately, I recognize the caller. The voice belongs to Jerry Lowe, my college roommate from A&M.

"Jerry, it's really good to hear your voice. Where are you?"

"At the moment I'm in College Station, but not for long. Stubby, I've been calling all over, trying to get in touch with you. I finally called the Mitchell house tonight. Mrs. Mitchell told me you'd be at the office."

I wonder where else he might've called. Because of our fragile financial situation, Juanita and I don't have a home phone. I hope he didn't call Juanita's parents. They would've probably hung up on him.

"I've got wonderful news!" Jerry tells me in an excited voice. "I've just been hired as assistant football coach for Cisco High School."

His news rocks me. Cisco is twenty miles from Ranger. How could he find a coaching job right under my nose?

Trying not to reveal my feelings, I choose my words carefully, "Jerry, that's terrific. How on earth did you find a job in Cisco?"

"My new girl friend," he answers. "Her father is president of the Cisco National Bank. She told him I was looking for a coaching job. He called the high school and got me hired."

"Damn! Damn! Damn!" I curse to myself. How stupid can I be? I should have known. With Buck Wagner leaving, there would be a coaching vacancy in Cisco. I've been so busy sending out résumés, I have overlooked the obvious job.

"A new girl friend? How did this happen? You're way too ugly and ornery to have a steady girl friend."

Jerry laughs, "I met her last spring at the TWC dance in Denton. She's beautiful, she's smart, and her dad's a banker. Stubby, I think I'm in love."

"What's to think about? You better marry this girl, before she finds out about your lurid past. Sounds like you've hit the jackpot."

Jerry's jovial mood suddenly becomes somber. I can sense a slight hint of desperation in his voice. "Stubby, she truly is a fine girl, and I have already asked her to marry me. She hasn't exactly said yes, but she didn't say no either. I want you and Juanita to meet her as soon as possible. Maybe you can put in a good word for me."

"Gosh, Jerry, we definitely want to meet her. When can we get together?" I hope he doesn't want to bring her here to Ranger. She sounds like she's the rich country club type. Juanita would be embarrassed to have Jerry or his girl see the way we're living.

"Saturday night, weekend after next. I have to be in Cisco to meet the new head coach. Can you and Juanita meet us at the Cisco Country Club for dinner?"

My guess about his girl is obviously right on the money. After two years of sharing a room with him in the A&M athletic dorm, I know Jerry's type all too well. This new girl will be another of the snooty, empty-headed girls Jerry normally falls for. I'd lay odds that his new girl is a blond. Well, at least this one has a rich daddy.

"Sure, that sounds fine. I'll check with Juanita, but I'm certain we can make it. If I don't call you back, we'll meet you at the country club. Hey, what's your girl's name?"

"Carolyn Sue Ratcliff. Meet us about seven. See you then, good buddy." Somehow hearing Jerry's girl's name further confirms my suspicions about her.

After I hang up, my mind is filled with both envious and happy thoughts. I jealously wonder if "Daddy" has already arranged for Jerry to have his own charge account? I can't wait to see the guy. I need to confide with a friend my own age.

Jerry said the girl's father simply called the high school and arranged for him to get the job. Could her father be Cisco's version of Lucas Masters?

I roll a new sheet of paper into the old Royal and begin to type.

Saturday Night
June 29, 1949

ON MOST SATURDAY NIGHTS Juanita and I walk downtown to the Arcadia Theater to see the latest picture show. The cost of an adult admission ticket at the Arcadia is a quarter. Such an imprudent purchase is a strain on our delicate budget, but Juanita justifies the expense, telling me that we deserve to howl at least one night a week.

In Ranger, there are three motion picture theaters. The Arcadia is on Main Street near the west end of the downtown business district. The Columbia and the Tower Theaters are one block south of Main Street, on opposite sides of Austin Street. The Columbia is open only on Saturdays, showing a double feature "cowboy shoot 'em up." The Tower Theater is located off the lobby of the Tower Hotel, a not-too-nice, three-story residential hotel. Juanita prefers the Arcadia because it is cleaner and more modern. The Arcadia is also cooler, being the only air-conditioned building in Ranger. The movies at the Arcadia are generally recent releases and usually feature the more popular movie stars. Still, I frequently have to resist a strong urge to let Juanita go in alone, while I walk on down to the Columbia to see the two "shoot 'em ups."

As we come out of the movie, we find the theater manager Buford Dinger standing at the street curb with one arm wrapped around a parking meter. The Arcadia is open seven nights a week. In the nine years Buford has managed the theater he has never missed a night of work. He has also gotten drunk on every Saturday night since he became the manager. Although he has been the subject of several Sunday church sermons, most everyone knows Buford is harmless, and actually, a very caring person.

Buford is dressed in his customary solid black suit, white shirt and dark blue tie. A large yellow stain on his shirt collar mars his appearance of being well-dressed. His tie is pulled down, and his shirt collar is unbuttoned. Buford is waving at passing cars as they drive along Main Street in front of his theater.

In spite of its history as a wild and wooly oil town, the city of Ranger is dry. In fact, neither beer nor liquor can be purchased legally anywhere in Eastland County. The closest wet areas are the German communities of Strawn, Mingus and Gordon over in Palo Pinto County, some 30 miles northeast of Ranger. And only beer and wine are sold in the stores there. Nevertheless, Buford always seems to have an adequate supply of whisky for his Saturday night drunk.

"Mister Stubby and Mrs. Stubby, how are you tonight?" Buford inquires, slurring his words as he speaks.

"We are fine, Mister Dinger. We enjoyed the movie very much," Juanita answers. She sounds uncomfortable talking with the inebriated manager but puts on her best face, trying not to seem unfriendly.

"Mister and Mrs. Stubby, I want you to know you can come to my theater any time. I want you to be happy. This town needs more nice young people like you," Buford tells us, swaying back and forth as he hangs onto the meter.

"Well, thank you, Mister Dinger. That is very kind of you. I promise we will come to see your movies every time we can." Juanita's strained voice betrays her. She's not enjoying the drunken conversation.

"I love this town. I love everybody in this town. Mister Stubby, do you still love my town?" Buford asks. He turns to wave at a passing car.

"Yes, I really do like your town, Mister Dinger," I respond, wondering why I should feel so uneasy, talking to a drunk.

The movie manager's mood suddenly changes. His eyes fill with tears, and he begins to sob. "They were mean to you, weren't they, Mister Stubby? They're mean to all of us."

I glance at Juanita. She reaches for my arm. I cautiously move her behind me, not knowing where this is going. Buford steps drunkenly toward me. His knees almost buckle. He clutches onto my arms to keep from falling.

"Mister Stubby, please don't hate my town. There are lots of good people in this town." Buford's breath is heavy with whisky.

Placing my hands firmly on Buford's shoulders, I gently push him upright. He is almost childlike in his drunkenness.

"Buford, I promise you. I still like your town. I have no intentions of leaving. Now, you have frightened Mrs. Stubby. Please apologize and tell her you're sorry."

"Mrs. Stubby, I'm sorry," Buford cries drunkenly, wiping tears from his cheeks with his coat sleeve.

"That's all right, Mister Dinger. I'm sure you didn't mean to scare me," Juanita replies gracefully.

"We need to be on our way home, Buford. Will you be okay?"

"Sure. Sure. I'm fine, Mister Stubby," Dinger mumbles, before he swings himself around and staggers back to his parking meter.

"Okay, we will see you later then."

I take Juanita's arm and start her walking away, up the sidewalk.

"Mister Stubby, you be careful. Don't let 'em hurt you. Don't let 'em hurt Mrs. Stubby," Buford calls from behind us.

I stop and swivel around to look back at Buford, but he's already distracted, waving at another passing car. Why should the words of a drunk cause a cold chill to run up my spine on this warm summer night?

Juanita walks beside me quietly, until we are in the darkness, beyond the light of the downtown street lamps.

"Do you know you are my brave hero?" she whispers softly.

"Ha! Some hero! I manhandled a sweet old drunk."

"Yes. But you did it with gentleness and kindness. Most men would not have been so gentle."

"Oh yeah, that's how I want to be remembered–the gentlest and kindest football coach who ever lost all his games," I laugh, embarrassed by Juanita's loving observation.

We walk side by side without talking for a while, until she slips her small warm hand into mine.

"I wouldn't care if you never win another football game. You will always be my hero."

Wednesday Morning
July 3, 1949

PEARL'S CAFÉ is located downtown at the northwest corner of Austin and Main streets, a few doors east of the Arcadia Theater. The café is a favorite morning meeting place for downtown merchants and oil workers. Men meet there to share the previous day's experiences over breakfast and Pearl's hot coffee. Pearl opens her café promptly at

5:00 A.M. Generally, several men are waiting impatiently on the sidewalk outside her door.

At least one morning during the week I try to sneak away from work at the Pontiac House for an hour or so to find out what is happening in the outside world. Living in Ranger is like being in a news vacuum, sheltered from global events.

Generally, the Arcadia sandwiches in a short-subject news film between their main features, but that news is always several weeks old. The *Ranger Daily Times* is delivered each afternoon to the Pontiac dealership, six days a week. Except for Thursdays, when the paper is filled with grocery and department store ads to entice weekend shoppers, the Ranger newspaper usually consists of six pages of want ads, comics and local gossip about who visited who recently.

Because many of her customers enjoy reading a newspaper while they eat, Pearl subscribes to both the *Fort Worth Star Telegram* and the *Abilene Reporter.* She charges five cents a cup, with one free refill, for coffee that will burn the skin off the inside of your mouth if you take too large a swallow. I have learned to sip my coffee slowly, so I can read through both newspapers before my refilled cup is empty, thereby avoiding Pearl's wrath for making only one purchase.

Entering the café, I am anxious to read the latest news about potential war brewing in Europe. With a college exemption and being married, I have, thus far, been an unlikely candidate for military service. Except for Juanita, I'd be anxious to serve. With two uncles who served in the Navy during World War Two, I should be aboard some gunboat sailing the Mediterranean Sea.

"Good morning, Stubby. How are you today? You want some hot coffee?" Pearl asks, as if she has some other kind.

"I certainly do," I answer, straddling a bar stool and reaching for the stack of newspapers on the counter. "Have you been busy this morning?"

"You wouldn't believe my morning, darlin'. Everything has gone wrong today. First, my cook didn't show up until five-thirty. Then, the Mrs. Baird's breadman forgot to bring my sweet rolls. It's been one thing after another, all morning long. I'm ready to go home, and the lunch crowd hasn't hit us yet," Pearl complains.

"Yeah, some days are like that. But it seems like you get more than your share, Pearl," I respond, trying to sound sympathetic while I straighten out the pages of the newspapers.

"You can say that again, sweetheart. Nobody, I mean nobody, in this town has to put up with what I put up with," Pearl whines while she pours my coffee.

"You do make the best coffee in town though, Pearl. This town would dry up and blow away without your strong coffee to keep it going."

"You'll go straight to hell for lying, darlin'. You know my customers only drink my coffee because it's the cheapest in town. If I raised the price, even you wouldn't come in so often."

"And miss seeing your happy face, Pearl? You can count on me to always be a devoted customer, no matter what price you charge."

Pearl grins and feints, like she intends to hit on me. She picks up a wet cloth and begins to wipe the counter. I sort through the newspapers looking for news about the Berlin situation.

A refreshing breeze from the swamp cooler mounted above the front window gently ripples the pages of my newspaper while it dries my sweat-soaked clothing. The cool air inside the café provides a pleasant relief from the sweltering West Texas heat outside.

The news is not good. Russia's Blockade around West Germany ended in May, but the Berlin Airlift continues because of Truman's uncertainty about Soviet intentions. Occasional conflicts between U.S. and Russian patrols at the East-West Berlin Border add to the tension, but if war develops, the culprit will most likely be Yugoslavia. General Tito is playing both sides against each other. He swears to Russia that Yugoslavia is a communist state while he boasts to the West about being independent of Russian influence.

Naturally, Tito is ready and willing to accept U.S. aid. President Truman has Dean Acheson, his Secretary of State, asking Congress for three million dollars to build a steel plant in Yugoslavia.

If I were President, I bet I could think of a better way to spend three million bucks.

There's talk that Kremlin leaders plan to have General Tito assassinated. If that happens, war is almost guaranteed.

Discouraged by the news, I lay the paper down. If the situation doesn't improve, another war is almost certain. Maybe we can stay out of it. We just finished fighting one war.

"The news from Europe ain't so good, is it, honey?"

"No, it's rather depressing. There's a good chance I'll be drafted if we go to war again. That would sure mess up my plans."

"I'm sorry, darlin'. Here I am telling you about my problems, and you've got your own troubles, don't you? Have you had any luck finding a coaching job?" Pearl asks.

"Not yet," I reply, "but I mail out my résumés every day."

"You keep your spirits up, honey. Something will turn up for you."

"Yeah, I should hear from one of the schools any day." My confident response does not reflect my true belief. With more than seventy resumes mailed, any school wanting me to coach would surely have contacted me by now. Football practice begins for most schools in little more than a month. What school would hire me at this late date?

Pearl steps closer to the counter, speaking softly, so the cook won't hear.

"Well, at least you won't have to coach here in this town. They would've eaten you alive and maybe ruined you forever. You're still young, darlin'. You have a long life ahead. Just thank your lucky stars you didn't get the Ranger job."

"But, I wanted to coach in Ranger. I would love to stay and work in this town. Why would anyone want to ruin a high school football coach?"

Pearl lowers her head and leans across the counter, continuing to speak in a low voice.

"I'm sorry, darlin'. I shouldn't have brought it up. You just forget what I said. I was talking out of turn. You want a refill?"

I gaze down at my empty cup. "No, I really need to get back to work."

Without saying goodbye to Pearl, I put a nickel on the counter to pay for my coffee and walk out the door. Absentmindedly, I step around a small puddle of water on the sidewalk below the water cooler. What makes everyone in this town so afraid?

On my way back to work I decide to call the athletic director at Gulf State to ask for a job.

Saturday Night
July 6, 1949

WAITING IMPATIENTLY IN THE DRIVER'S seat of our 1941 Hudson, I bite my lip and grip the steering wheel tightly. It's a quarter to seven. We'll be late getting to the country club to meet Jerry and his girl.

Juanita and I have been fighting. She is furious about my accepting another job at Gulf State, without discussing it with her first.

Things happened so quickly. On Thursday afternoon I telephoned John Clark, the Gulf State athletic director, to ask about a coaching job. Considering my poor performance last spring, I was surprised when he seemed delighted to hear from me. After a few minutes of amiable telephone conversation, he agreed to see if he could find something and promised to get back to me. This afternoon he called the shop to ask if I would consider teaching physical education classes. A year ago, accepting his offer would have been unthinkable. Now, after a summer of rejection, I jumped at his proposition. I quickly accepted the pitiful salary of two hundred dollars a month he offered and agreed to be in Corpus Christi on Monday, August the 26th, ready to begin work. I was elated. Someone wanted to hire me for a real job.

Juanita emerges through the front door. She's wearing a navy blue maternity dress with a large white collar. The dress is borrowed from one of her M.E. Moses co-workers who recently had a baby. Women seem to belong to an exclusive network which automatically shifts into high gear when one of them discovers she's expecting. Advice about doctors is exchanged, information on pregnancy suddenly becomes available, and maternity clothes magically appear. I cannot imagine a circumstance where I would wear another fellow's clothes, but with women, borrowing clothing is almost a ritual.

Even being six months pregnant, Juanita is deliciously beautiful. Without a word she walks to the passenger side of the car and slips in.

"That dress looks wonderful on you," I say to flatter her, choosing my words carefully.

She turns to me, her dark eyes flashing. "Don't patronize me,

Stubby Warden. I can see I am fat and ugly. If you say one more word, you can go by yourself."

I start to object, then think better of it. She is in no mood to be rational. I start the engine, pull out of the driveway and head toward Cisco.

The silence between us on the drive to Cisco is nerve-racking, but I'm determined not to speak before she does. I don't want to take the risk of setting her off again, not before we meet Jerry and his girl at the country club. There are few men I would fear, even in the bloodiest bar room brawl, but I have learned to lie low when this small package of dynamite gets her temper up.

Carrying the baby she barely weighs 130 pounds, but in a word fight, she can be more vicious than a Mongol tiger. In the arsenal of emotional weapons which women possess for use in combat with the masculine sex, my lady is an expert in using every one.

As we approach the Cisco city limits, Juanita begins to weep softly. She glances toward me with tears flowing down her cheeks and cries, "How could you do it? How could you agree to take a job at Gulf State? You know how we hated living there."

She continues to sob, sulking on her side of the seat until we arrive at the country club entrance. Not knowing what to say, I remain silent.

After I find a parking spot and pull to a stop, Juanita straightens up and begins wiping her tears away. She leans forward and twists the rear view mirror to face her side of the car. She examines her hair and makeup in the mirror.

"I look a mess, but I don't care. No one here knows me, and I'll never be coming back," she grumbles for my benefit.

I do the smart thing. I keep my mouth shut tightly.

The country club building is a long, single-story brick structure with a steep asphalt composition roof. The east end of the building houses the golf shop. Several golf carts are parked in the gravel paved section outside the shop entrance.

Two colonial-style columns on each side of the main entrance support the canopy which extends out over the concrete porch and front driveway. The dining and social rooms are on the west end.

Jerry and a tall blonde girl are waiting on the porch near the front door of the country club. As we approach them, Juanita begins to walk faster, leaving me behind. Then, as we get closer, she runs to Jerry and affectionately wraps her arms around his neck.

"Oh, Jerry, it's so good to see you again," Juanita gushes, raising up on tip toes to kiss his cheek. She hugs him again, very tightly.

"Oh my, is this your girl, Jerry? Hi, I'm Juanita Warden. I've been so anxious to meet you," Juanita tells the tall girl standing beside Jerry.

The girl extends her hand to Juanita. "Yes, I suppose I'm Jerry's girl. I'm Carolyn. We're so glad you could meet us for dinner."

Realizing that Juanita does not plan to acknowledge my presence, I step forward, take the tall girl's other hand and introduce myself. "Hi, Carolyn. I'm Stubby."

Acting a bit confused and looking even more apprehensive about having each of us clutching onto her hands, the blonde girl manages to smile and return my greeting, "Hello, Stubby. I'm delighted to meet you, too."

For a brief second she hesitates, then turns to Juanita. Seeing she has chosen to support the feminine position in our quarrel, I release the girl's hand.

While the girls exchange niceties, Jerry and I shake hands.

"Really good to see you, Stubby. How you been doing?" he inquires.

"Fine," I lie. "You look like you're doing okay. How'd your meeting go?"

Jerry interrupts me. "Why don't we go inside? Our table is ready. We can talk better there."

The girls walk in together ahead of us, talking girl talk. When we reach the entrance foyer leading to the dining room, Jerry motions toward Juanita and asks, "What's going on?"

"We're having a fight," I inform my friend in a low voice.

Jerry grins and nods his head as if he understands.

We make small talk about the hot weather and about country club food while we are being seated. An orchestra begins to play in the large dance parlor adjacent to the dining room. Several couples, who have finished their meal, leave their tables to stroll into the dance area.

Jerry's girl is not at all like I imagined. In spite of the distasteful situation in progress between Juanita and myself, the two women are hitting it off famously.

Juanita turns to tell me, "Carolyn is studying to be an English teacher. She'll be graduating from Texas Women's College next spring."

"Is that so? Carolyn, where do you plan to teach?"

"Where do you think, Stubby? Is there another place in the world as marvelous and wonderful as Eastland County?" she laughingly answers.

The girl is beautiful and witty. I'll bet she's as smart as a whip, too. No wonder Jerry's fallen in love with her.

"There certainly can't be many other places as hot or as dry," I joke back. "Jerry tells me your father is a banker."

"Yes, my father is the president of Cisco National. I really hope you can meet him sometime. You will find him to be a most interesting man," she replies. Her friendly smile vanishes. Her voice has suddenly become very solemn.

"I'd truly like to meet him. I have already had the privilege of meeting many of the important people in Ranger," I tell her sarcastically. Since I have crossed swords with the man who controls everything in Ranger, why shouldn't I meet the man who controls Cisco?

Realizing our conversation is becoming much too somber, Juanita intercedes, "Carolyn, isn't that a wonderful band. Do you and Jerry enjoy dancing? Stubby and I haven't danced in ages. Do you suppose we could dance later?"

While the girls ramble off on a discussion about dancing, I ask Jerry again. "How did your meeting with the head coach go?"

"Very well. Did you know he became the head coach this summer? He's never been a head coach before. He was an assistant at Cisco Junior College last year," Jerry informs me.

"Yeah, that's what I've heard," I reply.

Yes, if he was still an assistant coach, I might be employed. I might be the head football coach at Ranger High. Juanita might not be so angry with me.

"He wants me to take charge of coaching the offense. He's always been a defensive coach."

"Jerry, what do you know about offense? You haven't played on an offensive team since you were in high school. You were a defensive back at A&M. You should be the one coaching defense."

"Yep, I agree," Jerry admits, "but he's the head coach. I guess I'll coach wherever he decides. I didn't want to get off on the wrong foot the first time I met the man."

"But, Jerry, you're not familiar with the latest offensive formations. You don't know about blocking techniques. You've never worked with quarterbacks and tailbacks. How can you teach offensive football to your team when you don't understand it yourself?"

"I'll learn fast, good buddy. I'm gonna do whatever it takes to keep this job. You may not have heard, but it's pretty darn hard to find a coaching job these days. Besides, if I get in trouble, I'll call you and pick that shrewd, offensive-genius mind of yours. You will help me–if I need help, won't you, Stubby?"

"Of course. Absolutely. I'll help any way I can."

Jerry is always so damn positive about everything. This conversation is leading nowhere–except to an argument.

Jerry grins broadly and leans over to whisper in my ear. "And besides, if the dumb bastard doesn't win, maybe they'll be looking for a new head coach next year."

Good old loyal Jerry. I love him dearly, but he'll never change. He can smile and be shaking your hand, while he stabs you in the back. I almost feel sorry for the poor, unsuspecting Cisco head coach.

After an enjoyable dinner, more friendly conversation and a few dances, we say goodnight to Jerry and Carolyn, promising to get together again soon. As we leave the country club building and walk to our car, I wonder if Juanita's harsh attitude toward me has mellowed during the pleasant evening we have shared with Jerry and Carolyn.

"I really do like Carolyn. Jerry would be very lucky if he could convince a girl like her to marry him. Don't you think?" I ask timidly.

"Yes, she is nice. I think I could become very good friends with her. She's very different from other girls Jerry has dated."

I open the car door and hold it while Juanita slides into the front seat. Closing the door gently, I crouch down to her open window.

"Can we be friends again?" I ask. "I love you too much to be fighting with you."

She places her hand on mine. "I love you too, Stubby. You're right, let's not fight any more." She pulls my face through the window and kisses me wetly on the lips.

"But, if you have any thoughts about sleeping in my bed tonight, you can forget about them," she whispers spitefully.

I straighten up, walk around the car and climb into the driver's seat. As I start the engine, I smile slyly to myself and think, "We will see. We will see about that."

———————

Friday Afternoon
July 12, 1949

WHEN PRICE ASKS ME to deliver the Perlstein's Cadillac to their home on Walnut Street, I am delighted. I need a break from the heat inside the shop, where the temperature is hovering at 100 degrees. On the walk back to the Pontiac House I can stop in at Pearl's to check the newspapers. Several customers have voiced their concern about a deteriorating situation in Berlin.

The Perlstein residence occupies a corner lot, facing Walnut Street. Numerous small oak trees crowd the front yard, providing a leafy parasol over much of the well-kept grounds. A long, L-shaped wooden porch wraps around the front of the house to a second entrance at the side.

Although the Perlstein house faces north toward Walnut Street, their garage driveway is off Lula Avenue behind the house. I park the Caddy in the rear driveway and walk briskly around to the front of the house.

Stepping spryly up on the porch, I knock three times on the front door. I wait for a minute or so. When I don't hear anyone moving inside the house, I knock again, this time more loudly.

"I'm coming. I'm coming. Pleeeese be patient," an accented voice cries from inside.

A wide glass panel encased in the front door rattles precariously, while clicking sounds of locks being unlocked originate from the opposite side. Finally, the door cracks open, ever so slightly. "Hello," a raspy voice grumbles from inside. "Who are you?"

"My name is Stubby Warden. I'm from the Pontiac House. I brought your Cadillac back to you. We adjusted the carburetor. It runs fine now. I left it parked in your rear driveway."

The woman opens the door halfway. She is a short, middle-aged Jewish lady, wearing a nightgown and robe. A small towel is clutched in her right hand.

"Thank you, Mister Warden. Do you want me to pay you now?" she asks, wiping her perspiring face with the towel.

"No ma'am, that won't be necessary. Mister Mitchell says to tell you that you can pay him the next time you come by the Pontiac House. He also wanted me to tell you that your oil needed changing. We went ahead and changed the oil and the oil filter. Mister Mitchell says the oil change was with his compliments. There'll be no charge for it."

"Mister Mitchell is a fine person," the lady concedes. "That is why we do business with him. Do you need a ride back? I could put some clothes on and drive you."

"No ma'am. I'd rather walk. I can use the exercise."

"Oh, thank you. It is so hot. I don't believe I could stand to be out in this heat." She raises the towel, dabbing at her face to wipe away her perspiration.

"Yes ma'am. We could certainly use some rain. Your lawn sure looks like it could use some water. Even your flowers and bushes look a little wilted."

Mistaking my casual remark as criticism of her yard, the small woman responds angrily, "Young man, I'll have you know I have always kept a nice green yard. Don't you know I am not allowed to water? Don't you read the newspapers? Only last Thursday the city council proclaimed the city has a severe water shortage. No one is allowed to water their yard, not until it rains again."

"But, Mrs. Perlstein, I didn't mean to...."

"The Mayor says Hagaman Lake is so low the city may have to haul in water from Eastland. My husband tells me the city council is planning to ask our citizens not to bathe more than twice a week," she continues, paying no attention to my pleading.

"Mrs. Perlstein, I apologize. Please accept my apology. I didn't mean to.... I was only trying to be friendly."

"You are a very rude and insensitive young man," she screeches. "You can be sure I will report this to Mister Mitchell." She slams the door, leaving me standing on the porch with my mouth hanging open.

When I reach the Main Street sidewalk, I am still shaking my head, wondering how I could've screwed up the conversation with the Jewish lady so badly. Price will be upset with me. He gives her a free oil change, and I lose her business.

Before I cross the intersection at Sue Street, I tarry to watch the workmen at Art's Tool and Supply load a heavy piece of oil field equipment onto a flatbed truck. In the distance I can see Bulldog Stadium, two blocks to the north. The grass covering the playing surface is lush and green. I count six pulsating sprinklers generously watering the football field.

This is the hottest part of the day, and without a doubt, the most inefficient time to water. Not everyone is as concerned about the water shortage as Mrs. Perlstein.

CHAPTER THREE
THE OFFER

Saturday Morning
July 13, 1949

WHEN I ARRIVED BACK AT the shop on Friday afternoon, Price had left for the day. He rarely leaves early, but
yesterday one of his customers invited him to play a round
of golf. Unable to tell him about my experience with Mrs. Perlstein,
I spent a restless night worrying about Price's reaction when he finds
out I have cost him a good customer.

Normally, Saturday mornings are less demanding at the shop so I
won't come in until after Juanita is awake, and we drink several cups
of coffee together. This morning I leave the house early. I want to
talk with Price before he hears the news from someone else.

When I arrive, Price is inside his office. I breathe in deeply and
knock on his open door.

"Price, you got a minute? I need to talk with you."

He glances up from the papers on his desk and says, "Sure, Stubby.
Come in."

"Price," I begin, "I wanna tell you what happened with Mrs.
Perlstein yesterday."

Price holds up his hand to stop me. An amused smile is scrawled
across his face.

"Stubby, don't tell me anymore. Mrs. Perlstein called me at home
last evening. I understand you don't like the way she keeps her yard."

"Price, honest to God, I never meant to upset her. She took my
friendly conversation about the dry weather and her yard and made it
sound like I was being critical. I tried to apologize, but she slammed the

door in my face. Left me standing on her porch, like I'd been scolded and made to stand in a corner."

Price laughs hilariously. "Stubby, I should have warned you about her. You're not the first man who's lost a piece of his butt to that little lady's sharp tongue. She lit into me once, for commenting on a dress she was wearing. Had me begging for mercy before she was finished. She thought I was insinuating the dress made her look old. She and Mister Perlstein wouldn't trade with me for several months afterwards."

"You mean you're not mad?" I ask with immense relief.

"Of course not, Stubby. They'll be back the next time something goes wrong with one of their Cadillacs. Why do you think I threw in the free oil change? They enjoy being treated like royalty, and neither of them can resist the free perks I throw in from time to time."

"Next time, if there is a next time, Price, I promise to keep my big mouth shut. You can bet I won't try making friendly conversation with that lady again."

Price laughs again. "That might be best, Stubby. Freida Perlstein can be a feisty little hellion—much too ferocious for mortal men like us to deal with."

Then more sternly, Price changes the subject. "Stubby, while you're here, maybe we should talk about your plans. Phyliss tells me Juanita is terribly distressed about your accepting another job in Corpus Christi."

"Price, I've been meaning to talk with you, but it seems there's never been a convenient time lately. Yeah, I have a job offer from Gulf State. As a matter of fact, after all the résumés I mailed out, it's the only offer I do have. The Gulf State job isn't all that attractive, but I can't see as how I have any other choice."

"You know you have a job here for as long as you want. You could stay on, until you find something else."

"Yes, and I appreciate your kindness. You and Phyliss have been wonderful to us. But, Price, I'm a football coach. I'm afraid if I don't take the Gulf State job, I may never get another chance to coach."

"When do you need to be down there?"

"Monday, August 26. If it's okay with you, I'd like to work through Friday the 23rd. Juanita and I don't have all that much to move. We should be able to get everything packed on Saturday and move on Sunday."

"Is Juanita okay with your decision on this? Phyliss says she seems pretty unhappy."

"Juanita has a major mental problem to overcome before she accepts the notion we are moving back to Corpus Christi. But we won't be moving until next month. I'm sure she'll come around."

"I hate to see you leave Ranger. Phyliss and I will miss having the two of you near us. Promise me you won't give up your search for a coaching position. Maybe a better job will turn up."

"That would be marvelous, but I really don't see any other offers coming at this late date. Price, you have work to do. I promise to let you know if anything changes."

———

Tuesday Afternoon
July 23, 1949

WILMA, THE BOOKKEEPING LADY who comes in to do the books on Tuesdays and Thursdays, taps me on the shoulder. "Your wife is on the phone. She said to tell you it's urgent."

Juanita almost never calls me at work. On the infrequent occasions she has called, she has always been careful not to interrupt my work. Generally, she will only leave a message, asking me to return her call when I have time. I put my tools away quickly and rush to the phone.

"Hello. Juanita, are you all right?"

"Stubby, I'm next door at the Creager's house. I need you to come home, right away."

Juanita sounds very calm.

"Sure. But, are you okay?" I ask again.

"I don't want to talk over the phone. Please come home now," she commands forcefully.

All sorts of imaginary disasters race through my mind while I check out with the mechanic working with me and inform Wilma I have to leave for a while.

When I pull into our driveway, Juanita is waiting for me on the porch. She's been crying. Her eyes are red and puffy.

I jump out, slam the car door shut and run to the porch. "Juanita, what's the matter? Are you all right?" I reach out to hold her, but she backs away.

"Stubby, I called my parents today. My daddy is very sick." Her eyes are filled with tears. She begins to cry.

"Gee, I'm sorry to hear that. What's wrong with him?" I question, still puzzled about what is happening.

"Heart attack. They've taken him to the Brownwood hospital. Stubby, I have to go and see him. He may be dying." Huge tears trickle down her cheeks.

"Sure you do. Lemme call Price, and I'll drive you."

"Oh, Stubby, you know you can't come. The sight of you would just upset my parents and family. I have my suitcase packed. The bus for Comanche leaves at three. Will you take me to the bus station?"

"Juanita, I can't let you go alone. What if something happens with the baby?"

"Nothing like that will happen. It's only a two-hour bus ride. Mother will meet me in Comanche."

"I really don't think this is such a good idea. Can we talk about it?"

"No, my mind is made up. I need to get to the bus station. Will you drive me or not?"

"Of course I will. Here, let me load your suitcase."

DURING THE SHORT DRIVE to the bus station we do not speak. Juanita is preoccupied with concern about her father. I worry why she has suddenly developed such a hostile attitude toward me. We are each lost in our own thoughts.

I park across the street from the bus depot. While Juanita hurries inside to purchase a ticket, I grab her suitcase and tote it to the luggage desk to check it in for her.

Inside the bus station the frigid barrier which has sprung up between us grows. We stand together and gaze despondently out the front window toward the street, without talking. After a few minutes a Greyhound bus rolls up to the loading zone and brakes to a stop.

"This is my bus," Juanita ventures, breaking our awkward silence.

"When do you think you might come back?" I ask, unsure of my role in her plans.

"I'm not really sure. Stubby, I need some time to think things out. I may stay awhile. It's been a long time since I've spent time with my family. I'll call you."

"But, what about your job? What about the baby? You aren't taking enough clothes to stay for long," I speak rapidly, trying to give her reasons to return soon. It never occurred to me she might be planning an extended visit.

"I'll call my supervisor at M.E. Moses to explain after I arrive in Comanche. She'll understand. I should get on the bus now. All the other passengers are seated."

A sharp pang of panic shoots through my body. Until this moment, I hadn't considered the possibility that my wife might be leaving me for good.

"Juanita, do you plan on coming back at all?"

"I told you. I'll call you when I'm ready," she answers curtly. Her icy stare rebukes me for continuing to question her intentions.

Juanita kisses me coldly on the cheek, steps through the door and onto the long silver bus. The bus hisses angrily as the driver shuts the door. I stand hypnotized, helplessly watching the bus pull away.

My world is falling apart. My life has hit absolute bottom.

JUANITA AND I MET last summer at John Tarleton College in Stephenville. She had completed her sophomore year and was attending summer school. My coaches at A&M had arranged for me to teach P.E. classes at Tarleton during the summer while I completed courses in history and economics needed for my degree.

We were introduced one Saturday afternoon, a few hours before an early summer get-acquainted dance. From the first moment we met we were both hopelessly in love.

After three years on a football scholarship at an all men's college, my experience with women was rather limited, but I knew immediately this was the woman I wanted to spend my life with. She was beautiful. She was intelligent. She was fun and exciting.

We spent the summer sharing everything. We studied together. We ate our meals together. We held hands and took long walks. We would sit on the campus lawn talking for hours. I had never imagined there were women like her. Every time I began to think I understood her, I would discover another tantalizing aspect to her personality. She was like a lovely rose, so beautiful and so enticing, but surrounded and protected by sharp thorns to prick you when you least expected. It was the happiest summer of my life.

During the fall, when I returned to A&M for my final semester of football and classes, Juanita wrote to me every day. Her letters were tender and loving. The highlight of each day was my trip to the mail room in the athletic dorm.

On the weekends when we played a home game, she and a girlfriend would drive to College Station. At a men's college there was no problem finding dates for her girlfriends.

Twice, I made the disastrous mistake of matching up my roommate Jerry with her friends. Sometimes, I learn slowly.

On Thanksgiving evening, after our game with Texas University, I asked Juanita to marry me. She agreed, but being old fashioned, she wanted me to come to Comanche to formally ask her father for her hand. Things would not go well in Comanche.

Juanita grew up on a large ranch on the outskirts of Comanche. Both her mother and father were born and raised in Comanche County. Juanita's father is a successful cattleman and rancher. He is respected throughout the region for his honesty and fairness. He's also about as hardheaded as a mule and definitely accustomed to getting his way.

Maybe, if we had given Juanita's mother more time to work on her father, maybe, if we had waited until after the holidays, maybe, if we hadn't been so anxious, but no matter what we might have done differently, Juanita's father flatly refused to agree to, or even consider, our getting married. He advised me to get a job and go to work. If Juanita was still interested in me after she graduated from Tarleton, I could come back and ask him again then.

I was devastated. If I hadn't left the house so quickly, I'm certain Juanita's father would have attempted to throw me out.

Juanita and I couldn't wait. We were too much in love to stay apart. On Saturday, January 14, the day after I graduated from Texas A&M, we drove to Oklahoma and were married. Juanita's father has not spoken to her since.

Monday Afternoon
August 19, 1949

TODAY IS THE FIRST DAY of "two a day" workouts for the Ranger High football squad. Like a moth is drawn to a flame, I am overwhelmed with a powerful yearning to drive to the football stadium to watch the players as they begin practicing for the upcoming season.

Each year about this same time, since I was in seventh grade, I have donned my football gear to begin another season of football. A kind of homesickness percolates inside my being, making me long for the pungent smell of sweat and the cracking sound of shoulder pads, as players collide.

It is almost five o'clock when I knock on Price's door. Price is on the telephone. He motions for me to come in. I sit down quietly and wait for him to finish his phone conversation. Finally, he hangs up and grins at me.

"Been wondering how long you could hold out before you came in to ask off. Today is the first day of practice, you know?" he divulges, as if he has read my mind.

"Yeah, I thought I might leave a little early. Maybe drop by the field to watch the old man in action. I might learn something."

"You mean Buck Wagner? You won't learn anything worthwhile by watching that old man. You stick to what you already know."

"There's about an hour of practice left. If I leave now, I may be able to watch them run a few offensive plays."

"Stubby, get out of here, before you give me the fever. See you in the morning."

PROBABLY TWENTY CARS and pickups are parked in the gravel parking lot behind the home side wooden bleachers. I park near the entrance gate and skirt around the bleachers to the south end of the football field.

I'm surprised to find the team practicing on the game field. Most high schools practice on a separate field to save wear and tear on their game field. The grass has been cut very high, perhaps to protect the field from the ravaging of football cleats.

Congregated along the sidelines, several groups of men are observing the practice session. A few of the men, Blake Tucker, Gordon Long and Leo Jackson, I recognize from the trustees' meeting back in May.

The offensive squad is suited out in full pads. They are running offensive plays against a defensive lineup, also in full gear. Buck Wagner and Keith Murphy have positioned themselves behind the offensive huddle.

A huge coach I don't recognize is posted in the defensive backfield. He is obviously upset with the performance of the offense. The offensive team is attempting to operate from a single wing formation. A tall, thin tailback responsible for handling the football seems flustered and confused. When he fumbles a handoff, the huge coach yells an obscenity at him.

One of the men at the sideline strolls over to me. The man is Blake Tucker who participated in my interview with the school trustees.

"Hello, Mister Warden. I'm so pleased to see you again. What brings you out to our practice?" Tucker inquires.

"Football fever. Couldn't stay away. I reckon there must be something contagious in the air this time of year."

"Well, this is the first day of practice. We don't look all that sharp right now, but our coaches will whip the kids into shape," Tucker muses confidently.

"Who is the big guy coaching?"

"That's Sam Aills. He's been an assistant coach here for a couple of years. Coaches our basketball team in the off season."

Two of the other trustees I recognized earlier hear our conversation and walk over to join us. We shake hands.

"Hello, Mister Jackson. Hello, Mister Long. You ready for another football season?"

Gordon Long nods his head affirmatively. "I can't wait for the first game. Looks like we're gonna have one heckava team."

"Coach Warden, I haven't heard. Did you find a coaching position?" Leo Jackson asks.

"No, not a head coaching job. I've decided to go back to Gulf

State. I have a job there, beginning next Monday."

"That's wonderful. I'm relieved to hear you found a good job. I must admit though, I'm still intrigued with the 'Option Tee' formation you told us about. It could be the offensive formation of the future for high school football."

"Yes, my offense will open up opposing defenses and allow more scoring. That should make games more exciting to watch. I believe this group of Ranger players would adapt to my 'Option Tee' offense very easily."

Our sideline conversation is interrupted by loud, profane yells out on the playing field. The big coach grabs one of the offensive linemen by his shoulder pads and drags him bodily to the sideline. When they reach the sideline, the big coach picks up a heavy, sawed-in-half wooden baseball bat and motions for the lineman to bend over. The sound of the bat's impact against the player's buttocks echoes three times across the field.

"Looks like *Jelly* is making an early appearance this year," Tucker advises the other two trustees.

"Yes, with us having a new coach, I was hoping not to see *Jelly* at all this year. Guess that was wishful thinking on my part," Gordon Long laments sorrowfully.

I hang around to chat with the men for a few more minutes, then excuse myself. I have seen all I can handle.

What kind of coach would dress his team out for a full scrimmage on the first day of practice, in hundred degree heat? How can a coach stand by and watch one of his players be beaten with a baseball bat? I shrug my shoulders, reminding myself that these things are not my concern. I'll be leaving for Corpus Christi in six days.

Thursday Night
August 22, 1949

THE FLASHING LIGHTS of the Pontiac sign outside are almost hypnotic as I sit in Price's office, gathering up enough nerve to call Juanita at her parent's house in Comanche. We have not talked since she called me at work the day after she left, to tell me she had arrived safely.

"Number please?" the telephone operator requests.

"I would like to place a person-to-person, long distance call to Comanche, Texas."

"May I have the name and number of the party you wish to call?" the operator inquires.

"Yes, I'd like to speak to Mrs. Juanita Warden. The number is 969."

"Please wait, while I ring."

A high-pitched clicking noise echoes over the line. Eventually, I hear a dull buzzing sound as the phone rings on the other end.

"Kimbrough residence," a voice answers. The voice sounds like Juanita's mother.

"I have a call for a Mrs. Juanita Warden. Will you accept the call?"

"Please hold the line, Operator. I will see if she is available," the voice advises. I hear distant talking and commotion on the other end.

"Hello. This is Juanita Warden."

"You may speak to your party now," the operator advises me.

"Juanita honey, this is Stubby. How are you? How is the baby?"

"We are doing fine, Stubby. The baby is fine." She does not seem particularly delighted to hear from me.

"And how is your father? Has there been any change?"

"We think Dad is out of danger now. The doctors tell us he may be able to come home in a week or so."

"How about you, Juanita? When are you coming home?"

"Mother and I have been talking. We know the doctor here in Comanche, and Mother will be here to look after me. We think it would be better if I stayed here until after the baby is born."

"Juanita, I have to leave for Corpus Christi on Sunday. Please come with me."

"Stubby, you already know how I feel. My mind is made up. I will not move back to Corpus Christi."

"Honey, I can't find another coaching job. You know how hard I've tried. If I don't take the Gulf State job, I might end up an automobile mechanic. Can't you please understand?"

"Stubby, I'm not going! Any further discussion on the subject of Corpus Christi or Gulf State is a waste of our time." Her voice is very stern.

"I've gotta leave on Sunday. Can I come to Comanche and see you on my way to Corpus Christi?"

"The family thinks it best if you don't come now, not with Dad being so sick."

"Then when can I see you?"

"I really don't know. Call me when you get an address in Corpus Christi."

"Juanita, you're my wife. We can't leave things like this. I need to see you and talk with you in person."

"Call me when you get settled in Corpus Christi. I have to go now. Goodbye." I hear a click. The phone makes a dull buzzing sound.

Saturday Morning
August 24, 1949

ON FRIDAY AFTERNOON I said my goodbyes to Price and my fellow workers at the Pontiac House. Later, I drove out to the Mitchell home to see Phyliss. She stood in their driveway, tearfully waving to me as I left. I even stopped in to say goodbye to Pearl while she was closing.

In our two moves since Juanita and I were married, she has always acted as the planner and supervisor. My role was being the designated brainless lifter and toter. This morning I wander aimlessly through the house, from room to room, totally disorganized. This moving task is much more difficult than I envisioned. How could two people accumulate so much junk in such a short period of time? With the prospect of living alone in Corpus Christi, I am pondering over whether to take most of our stuff with me or to simply sort out the essentials and throw everything else away.

The sound of a car turning into my driveway, then screeching to a stop on the loose gravel, interrupts my muddled thoughts.

A voice calls out, "Stubby, are you home?" I recognize the voice as Price. He sounds excited.

I step quickly to the front door and open the screen. "Price, I thought we said our goodbyes."

"Stubby, old Buck Wagner passed away last night. They say he had a stroke and died in his sleep."

"That's too bad," I profess, wondering why he should be in such a hurry to tell me this unpleasant news. "I'm truly sorry to hear that."

"The school trustees have been meeting all morning. Superintendent Boswell called the shop about ten minutes ago. He wants you to meet him at his office across from the high school at two o'clock."

"I'm right in the middle of packing. Why would he want to talk with me?"

"Good God Almighty, son! Can't you see what's happened? They haven't been able to find another head coach. This is the opportunity we've been praying for."

My mind is racing. "But, I promised to be in Corpus Christi on Monday."

"Cut out the crap, Stubby. You know you don't want that lousy piss-ant Gulf State job. Anyway, no one has hired you here yet. Now, get your ass in gear and be at that two o'clock meeting with Boswell."

"Yeah. Sure. I'll get dressed and be there at two," I respond stupidly. This has to be a dream. I'll be waking up any minute now.

"I need to get back to work," Price tells me. "Come by the shop after your meeting and let me know what happened."

When I don't reply, Price smiles broadly. He must realize how dazed I am with this stunning turn of events. He grins and shakes his head in amusement, then returns to his car.

Saturday Afternoon
August 24, 1949

THE SCHOOL SUPERINTENDENT and his administrative staff office in a red brick building referred to simply as the Recreation Building. The building is at the northwest corner of Pine and Marston Streets, directly across from the high school. The building was originally part of another school complex in the community of Tiffin, located some four miles northeast of Ranger. After the Tiffin School disbanded to join with the Ranger School District, the Recreation Building was disassembled and hauled by wagon, piece by piece, to Ranger, where it was reconstructed at its present location in conjunction with a government W.P.A. Program.

Serving the school system as a combination gym, auditorium and office building, the Recreation Building is a bona fide source of local pride. Brick pilasters, which extend above the roof line, protrude outward to divide the exterior walls into equal intervals. Each brick pilaster is adorned with a white ornamental crescent cast into the brick at mid-height. Interlaced within the exterior walls are creative bands of brick coursing and decorative blocks of white stone. A wide, recessed front entrance, which envelopes an outside ticket booth, provides convenient shelter for patrons attending social events held inside.

Construction was completed on the Recreation Building in 1934. Considering the entire building had to be moved here from its original location and the crude equipment available to erect the structure, the building represents an awesome and unique accomplishment.

Most of the building's floor space is dedicated to a small gymnasium, complete with basketball court and bleachers. But, since basketball does not command much attention locally, the Recreation Building is also often used for band concerts, school plays, civic meetings and the annual Halloween carnival.

Inside the front waiting room of the school administrative offices, the air feels crisp and refreshing. Two refrigeration units, chugging away at peak capacity, are strategically placed to achieve maximum cooling efficiency for the three offices. The cool air is a welcome break from the unforgiving August heat outside.

When I enter, G.C. Boswell rises and steps quickly around his desk into the reception area to greet me. He has obviously been waiting for me. Boswell is wearing a short-sleeved white shirt with dark pants. His shirt collar is unbuttoned. His red tie is slightly loosened around his neck. Most likely, this is as casual as he ever dresses in public.

"Mister Warden, it's so nice of you to come on such short notice," he says, shaking my hand.

"Please call me Stubby. Mister Warden sounds much too formal."

"Yes. Well, Stubby it shall be then. Have you heard about our coaching predicament?"

"Yes, I understand Coach Wagner expired last evening. I didn't know him well, but I'm sure his death is quite a shock to everyone."

"I suppose he was a good man, but, as you know, we hired him last May. I didn't know him very well either."

Boswell pauses briefly to demonstrate his respect for the deceased coach, then continues. "But, to get directly to the point of this meeting, the fact of the matter is we are without a head coach. The board of trustees has asked me to inquire about your availability."

"Does that mean you're offering me the head coaching job?" I ask, trying to maintain my composure.

"In a manner of speaking. If you are available, the board would be inclined to give you serious consideration for the job."

"G.C., let's quit playing games. I'm scheduled to be in Corpus Christi on Monday morning, to begin coaching there. I can cancel those arrangements if you are willing to assure me I'll be hired as the Ranger football coach. You need me. I want the job. Do we have a deal?"

Boswell hesitates for a second to consider, then extends his right hand toward me to shake my hand. "We have a deal. I'll see that the board approves your employment."

"How much does the job pay?"

"Three hundred and fifty a month, with a bonus of three hundred for every football game you win."

"That sounds reasonable. I accept the job. I'll be at the football field for practice on Monday morning."

Boswell frowns thoughtfully. "Stubby, there is one more thing."

"What is that?"

"You must meet with Lucas Masters and get his approval before our coaching deal can be finalized."

"Why should I meet with him? Doesn't the school board have the final say on hiring?"

"Not until you have obtained Lucas' blessing. I'm sorry, but that's the way things are. Could you meet with him between practices on Monday—say, two o'clock in the afternoon?"

"Of course, but what will the meeting be about?"

"That will be strictly between the two of you. I will call him and set the meeting up for two o'clock. Please don't be late. Lucas will not tolerate tardiness."

"Don't worry, G.C., I'll be on time."

"One more thing I suppose I should mention, Stubby. Buck Wagner's funeral will be held Tuesday afternoon. You may want to suspend practice that day."

"Can I think on that? I need to see how the news of his death has affected the players."

"Certainly. Please let me know what you decide."

Leaving the superintendent's office, I try to walk calmly and deliberately toward my dirty maroon Hudson. Before I start the engine, I roll up all the car windows. Two blocks away and out of sight of the school offices, I can no longer contain my emotions. I stop the car and raise both arms above my head. I scream, "Whoopee! Yippee! Zoweee!" at the top of my lungs.

CHAPTER FOUR
THE JOB

ON SATURDAY AFTERNOON Price and I celebrated my being hired over a couple of cokes in the alley behind the shop. We ended up laughing like two crazy kids, shaking up the bottles and spewing coke on each other. Then, with our arms wrapped around each other, we both cried like babies.

Most of my Sunday was used to unpack and re-store the belongings I had packed on Saturday. On Sunday evening I called John Clark at his home in Corpus Christi to explain about the Ranger coaching job. He accepted my news graciously. After expressing his disappointment at not having me on his staff, he assured me he could handle the inconvenience and wished me good luck with my new job.

Monday Morning
August 26, 1949

THE VARSITY FIELD HOUSE is an antiquated red brick structure situated at the northern extremity of Bulldog Stadium. Some fifty feet of hand-placed sandstone paving separates the north end of the home side bleachers from the building. The sandstone paving extends from the edge of the bleachers around to the field house front entrance, providing an all-weather walkway. The concrete floor of the field house is some three feet above the playing field. A three-foot high rock wall, wide enough for players to sit on, separates the paved walkway from a burnt-red cinder track which encompasses the grassy field.

Since before daybreak this morning, I've been camped out here. I don't have a key to the front door, so I'm forced to wait on Sam Aills to open up. I jump up to greet him when he arrives.

"Hello," I say. "I'm Stubby Warden."

"Yeah, I've heard. You're the new head coach." Aills' voice is not friendly. He shoves past me to the front door, without bothering to shake my extended hand. He unlocks the door and goes inside, leaving me standing awkwardly on the front walk. I follow him inside.

The ill-tempered coach has assumed a position behind a long work counter while he sorts through a stack of shoulder pads. For whatever reason, he is choosing to ignore my presence. I elect not to force the issue. Placing my hands behind my back, I stroll slowly and very deliberately around the dressing area, inspecting the gang shower, the long metal urinal trough and the unpartitioned toilet bowls.

My experience in numerous conflicts with Juanita, the undisputed champion of emotional combat, has taught me that silence can be a lethal mental weapon. As I closely examine the equipment room, I can sense the big man begin to sweat. His lowered eyes follow my every move.

"You finding everything to your liking, Coach Warden?" Aills asks gruffly, breaking his self-imposed silence.

"Well, I see several things which might be improved, but we can talk about them later. Can we talk about your plans for practice this morning?"

"Whatta you wanna know?"

"Tell me about your practice schedule for today. Do you plan to work on offense, defense, special teams, kicking?"

"I reckon we'll scrimmage the offensive against the defense, just like we've been doing. We generally do some loosening up exercises first."

"Sam, I want you to call me Stubby. We will be working closely together this season. It makes no sense for us to be formal with each other. Whatta you think about Murphy and me taking the offense while you work with the defense on their tackling techniques?"

From my brief observation of the practice session last Monday, I have concluded that Aills' specialty is defense. He leaps at my proposition.

"Yeah, that sounds fine. Our defense needs a lotta work. Our tackling is horrible."

"Sam, I have a few innovations I want to work into our defensive schemes, but I will expect you to take the lion's share of responsibility for coaching our defense. Would you have a problem with such an arrangement?"

"That'd be fine with me," Aills answers. A sly smile creeps across his face. This is not the administrative style he was expecting from a brash, young head coach. To him offense is boring. The real action is on defense.

With Aills returning to his equipment chores, I mosey over to the player's dressing sector. Team members have begun filtering into the dressing room, donning their pads for the morning practice session. I make a point to speak to every player and introduce myself. Many of the young men seem surprised that I know each of them by name.

Keith Murphy arrives after a majority of the players are suited up. I'm concerned about his attitude. Will he have a problem working with the young punk kid who he treated so badly last May? Taking the initiative in mending our relationship, I step swiftly across the room.

"Coach Murphy, you remember me, don't you? Stubby Warden, we met last May." I reach out and shake his hand vigorously.

"Yeah, I remember you. Then you're the new head coach? Well, I'll be damned."

"Coach, could we talk? I'd like to get your opinion on several matters."

"Sure. What is it you need to know, son?" Murphy asks, sounding like a benevolent father.

"Let's get practice started first. Then I'd like to talk with you for a few minutes."

"Sam, can you handle the calisthenic drills while I get with Coach Murphy?" I call across the room. "I wanna have a group meeting with the entire team after you finish."

"No problem," Aills replies.

"Alright, you lazy bums! Get your skinny asses out on the field!" Sam screams to the few remaining players loitering in the dressing room.

MURPHY AND I FIND a shady spot beneath a tree outside the field house to do our talking. Even though it's only a few minutes past seven, the temperature must already be over eighty.

I ask for his opinion about the skills and attitudes of several players.

His answers confirm my doubts about him. His judgement of football skills is poor. He is inflexible, and he is prejudiced against certain players.

Nearing the end of our discussion, I ask, "Coach, how attached are you to the single wing offense we used last year?"

"Well, a single wing is the only offense we've ever used for as long as I've been around. With so many scrawny players, it didn't work too good last year. You got somethin' else in mind?"

"If you would agree, I want to try a new offense. I call it an 'Option Tee' formation. Considering the size and skills of our players, it should work much better for us than the single wing."

"Never heard of it. Don't think I could help much with somethin' I never heard of."

"You're wrong there, Coach. With your experience you can help immensely, working with the offensive line. The blocking techniques we will employ are similar for both offenses. The biggest challenge for the linemen will be learning their blocking assignments for the new plays. You teach an AG class at the high school. I'm confident you can teach ten interior linemen a few basic blocking assignments."

"Okay, I reckon maybe I could handle that." Murphy's answer is less than enthusiastic.

"Coach Murphy, I feel comfortable working with you already. Your support means a lot to me. Let's get over to the team meeting."

MY MEETING WITH THE TEAM is brief. I advise the young men that Coach Wagner would not want his death to affect their goals for the season. I thank them for the opportunity to serve as their head coach and ask them to give me a chance to prove my coaching ability. When I announce my intent to install a new offensive system, my news is greeted with moans, groans and long faces. A show of hands indicates not many boys plan to attend Buck Wagner's funeral. I offer to excuse anyone who wants to attend but decide to hold practice, as usual, for everyone else.

We divide the team into offensive and defensive units. Coach Aills takes the defense. Coach Murphy and I take the offense.

My first official act as head coach is to direct the offensive team to the side lines where I have them shed their heavy jerseys and their shoulder and hip pads. A player's attention span is not very long when he's drowning in his own sweat. Once we are back on the field, I set the offense in a "Tee" formation and begin walking the backfield through the various quarterback options. As the backfield players move slowly through each play, I explain to Murphy and his linemen how the blockers can determine their blocking assignment.

From the other end of the field I hear the now familiar, but sickening, sound of a wooden baseball bat pounding against a player's backside. I glance down the field to watch Aills grab the collar of another player and begin dragging him to the sideline.

Murphy grins at me. "Little *Jelly* is sure getting a workout. Looks like somethin' set old Sam off this morning."

I grimace and try not to show empathy for what is happening at the opposite end of my practice field. What set old Sam off is a young head coach who is much too anxious to get along. A mistake which will not be made a second time.

OUR MORNING PRACTICE ENDS sometime around nine-thirty. We dismiss the team with strict instructions to go directly home, eat a light lunch and lay off eating any sweets. Our players will return this afternoon and be suited out for another practice session at four o'clock.

Almost every Texas high school and college football program begins each new season in mid-August with a two week period during which workouts are held twice a day. To avoid the midday Texas heat, most teams will generally schedule their two practices for early morning and late afternoon. "Two a day" practices usually begin on a Monday and, except for one day off on Sunday, run continuously through Friday the following week.

For every football player, "two a days" are the most dreaded part of the season. At the end of your First Day, you are dog tired. Your weary body yearns to lie down, seeking rest at every opportunity. After Day Two, every muscle in your body begins to ache. After Day Three, even the slightest exertion causes excruciating pain to race through every body cell. On Day Four, your mind becomes numb. You have become a blocking and tackling zombie, mindlessly obeying every coach's command, willing to strike, batter or pound any person or thing you are told to hit. By the end of the first week your mind and body have separated. You glide in semi-consciousness through each practice in a kind of lifeless, suspended state of hurt. Sometime during the second week you reach a point when you commence a slow return to the living. The unbearable pain somehow becomes more endurable each day, as you finally near the end of your football hell.

———————

Monday Afternoon
August 26, 1949

LUCAS MASTERS' OFFICE is near the center of downtown on the south side of Main Street in a second-floor chamber of rooms above Pulley's Jewelry Store. Two large windows open out from his office onto Main Street, giving him a panoramic view of Ranger's downtown business district. He can see everything, from the Texas and Pacific Railroad tracks on the east, to the Arcadia Theater on the west. Possibly, he chose this address so he can sit and survey his kingdom without being observed by the peasants milling below.

My mind is a mess. Sitting here in the Hudson, parked facing the street curb in front of Pulley's Jewelry Store, my thoughts propel wildly around in my head. I have not tried to call Juanita to tell her about the job. This meeting with Lucas Masters could wreck the whole deal. No sense calling her, then have everything blow up in my face. Juanita's mother is Phyliss Mitchell's sister. I'm sure Phyliss has already called to tell them the news. How did Juanita react? With football practice twice a day and the other obligations I'm committed to over the next few days, it's probably better that Juanita is with her family.

The clock in Pulley's display window shows the time is four minutes 'til two. I slide out of the car and head toward the stairway leading up to Masters' offices. Like a good little schoolboy, I mustn't be tardy.

———————

CLIMBING UP THE WOODEN STAIRS to Lucas Masters' sanctum, my hands feel wet and clammy. A chill creeps through my body, as if I am entering some evil and unholy place.

At the top of the stairs is a long, narrow waiting area. This second floor lobby is void of furniture. A bulky, solid black rug partially covers the unpainted wooden floor. Masters' offices are separated from the public waiting area by a dingy wood-paneled wall. Opaque glass windows are spaced at close intervals across the upper portion of the wall.

A sign painted on the glass entry door reads simply "Lucas Masters." I take a deep breath, grasp the door knob and twist. As the door swings open, it makes a shrill, squeaking noise.

Masters' reception parlor contains a secretarial desk, chair and typewriter, but no secretary waits to receive me. On my left are a matching leather couch, chair and a small wooden coffee table. The top of the coffee table is bare, with no magazines or ornaments. The reception room is plain and austere, without the slightest hint of personality or warmth. One picture, a large black and white photograph of a group of men with an oil derrick spouting black oil in the background, adorns the wall above the couch. There is no carpet on the wood floor.

Two office doors open into the reception room. A door to one office is closed, and the lights are off. Not knowing what to expect, I step to the door of the open office. Inside the room I find Lucas Masters behind an antiquated mahogany desk. His back is turned to me as he stares out his window toward the street.

I tap lightly on the office door. "Mister Masters, I'm Stubby Warden. I believe we have an appointment at two."

Masters swings his chair around to face me. "Yes, Mister Warden. Won't you please have a seat?" He makes no effort to shake my hand. I'm glad. I'd hate to offer him my wet, clammy hand.

Although he casts a long shadow in Ranger, Lucas Masters is a medium-sized man, several inches short of six feet tall. He weighs somewhere in the proximity of one hundred and seventy pounds. Around his temples his dark brown hair reveals a touch of gray. The hairline above his forehead has begun to recede. Masters is somewhere in his mid to late fifties. His dark grey business suit, white shirt and solid black tie make him seem much older.

I take the leather chair directly in front of him. "Superintendent Boswell advised me I should meet with you before the school trustees can approve my employment."

"That is correct. There are a few things we must discuss before a final decision to hire you can be made."

"And what do we need to discuss, Mister Masters?"

Masters smiles, leans back in his chair and clasps his hands together against his chest. "Would you mind if we use first names when we talk? My friends call me Lucas. May I call you Stubby?"

"I'd like that," I say, speculating about whom he would consider a friend.

Masters opens a desk drawer, pulls out a sheet of paper and hands it to me. "Stubby, I have prepared a list with names and playing positions of several boys I want you to consider for starting positions on the football squad this year."

The list contains the names of six boys. A playing position is shown opposite each boy's name. Two of the boys are poor athletes. The other names are boys who can play.

I understand immediately that I must agree to Masters' proposal or start looking for another coaching job. That is what this meeting is all about. As my teammates at A&M used to tease about Coach Norton, "It's his way or the highway." With all the indignities I have suffered to be here, now is not the time to stand up for my principles.

Lucas is a crafty old fox, but once before, I had him on the ropes. Maybe there is room for minor negotiation.

"What if I will not agree to play these boys at these positions?"

"I believe the answer to your question is obvious," Lucas growls bluntly.

"Maybe you misunderstood my question, Lucas. What I'm asking is if I might play these boys at a different position other than the one you have shown?"

"For instance?"

"Reed Jones. You have him listed as quarterback. Would you agree to let him play an end position?"

"No. I'm committed to that boy playing quarterback."

His answer bears out my earlier analysis of Masters' involvement in the football program. The commitment he's referring to is, most certainly, some sort of business arrangement–one in which a father is assured his son will start and play, in return for some consideration which will yield a nice profit for Lucas Masters.

"Are there any others where you made commitments as to their positions? Maybe we should go down the list, name by name."

Masters acts surprised that I'm being so helpful. He pulls out another copy of the list. I speak quickly, taking the initiative in the discussion.

"How about Dudley Grey? He's much too slow for a defensive halfback. How about playing him at offensive guard?"

Masters contemplates for a moment. "Yes, I'll agree to that."

Mark one up for me. Grey is one of my poorer athletes. At a guard position I can let him start the game and substitute for him without drawing much attention. Maybe his father will be satisfied with his being a starter and won't complain when he doesn't play much.

"Joel Dorsey. He's not tall enough to play an end position. He has small hands. Can't hold onto the ball. How about defensive half-back?"

"No, he needs to play on offense."

"How about fullback?"

"Yes, that will be acceptable."

Mark two up for my side. In my offense the fullback seldom carries the football. My fullback's main responsibility will be blocking for the ball carrier. With me calling the plays, Dorsey may not touch the ball in a game situation this season.

"Billy Watson. He's plenty big but too slow to play linebacker. How about defensive end?"

"No, I'm committed to his playing linebacker."

We proceed through each of the remaining names on the list. Masters yields to my suggestions on all but Jones as the quarterback and Watson as a linebacker. Within the severe limits of his proposal, I have found myself a few crumbs.

Pressing my luck, I continue.

"Lucas, are you committed to a specific number of downs these kids must play in each game?"

"I will expect each of these boys to be a starter in every game," Lucas replies forcefully, shifting forward in his chair to exert his authority.

"Certainly, I understand. But, do you expect me to play them every down, or will I have some leeway? I need to know exactly what you are committed to with these boys."

Masters seems to be uncomfortable dealing in specific details. He's probably accustomed to making deals on a handshake.

"I want each boy to play at least half of every game."

"Then you'll be satisfied if each of these boys starts each game and plays fifty percent of the time. Can I assume you mean the offensive players play one-half the offensive plays and the defensive players play one-half the defensive plays?"

Lucas considers my question thoughtfully. "Yes, that's close enough to what I mean, except for the Jones kid. He must play every offensive down."

This condition is a real killer. The Jones boy is a good enough athlete, but he's tall and clumsy. He's not the quick-thinking, skilled ball handler I need to operate my offense. I try for another crumb.

"Lucas, I'll need to have another quarterback ready, in case the Jones kid gets injured. Would you agree to his playing less than a full game in the pre-season and non-district games?"

Masters is apparently tiring with the conversation. He has given up far more than he intended. Anticipating an answer I won't like, I back off to give him some room.

"If you want some time to think on it, we can talk about the Jones kid later. You don't need to give me an answer right now."

"Yes, I could use more time to consider that one. I'll get back to you with an answer later."

We stare at each other across his desk for a moment before I realize I have been dismissed. Masters does not offer a handshake as I stand up to leave. When I reach his door, I stop and turn back to him.

"Lucas, one more thing. J.L. Barnes wasn't at practice this morning."

"He never is at practice this early in the season. I thought you understood–his father keeps him home to work on their harvest."

"If I can convince his dad to let him come in for practice, are you still willing to provide them an extra hand to help with their farm work?"

"Stubby, you have a memory like an elephant. Alright, you make the necessary arrangements with J.L.'s father, and I'll take care of the helper."

"Fine. I'll be driving out to talk with Mister Barnes this evening then."

As I turn again to leave, Masters taunts me with one last remark. "Stubby, you haven't asked what my recommendation to the trustees will be."

"No point in asking. I already know the answer," I reply, giving him an imperfect salute.

Lucas is grinning when I walk away.

After I crawl into the Hudson, I drive straight for the field house. I need to shower. Somehow I feel terribly dirty.

Chapter Five
The Preparation

Monday Afternoon
August 26, 1949

GILBERT THOMPSON SUSPICIOUSLY SURVEYS a jumble of clouds drifting overhead while he wanders aimlessly about the stadium parking lot.

Parking my Hudson, I hear someone calling, "Gilberrrrrrt, Gilberrrrrrt."

A slight movement underneath the walkway ramp leading up into the wooden stadium bleachers catches my eye. Squinting my eyes to ward off the bright sunlight, I see three figures hiding in the darkness of the shaded area.

The voice calls again, "Gilberrrrrrt, Gilberrrrrrt."

Gilbert whirls around and gazes more intently toward the sky.

Gilbert Thompson is a big, husky boy, stronger than an ox. Although he can read and write at a level sufficient to attend Ranger High, he is slightly retarded. He speaks in a defined, simple language. Gilbert is our offensive center. He's been a starter since his sophomore year. He is truly a good kid. Foul language in a football team's dressing room and on the practice field is commonplace and can be frequently overheard in conversations among our players, but I would be surprised if Gilbert has ever uttered a curse word of any kind.

Gilbert turns to me as I approach the entry gate. "Coach, did you call me?"

"No, Gilbert. Why do you ask?"

"I heard someone call my name. I don't know who wants me."

Young men can be so cruel sometimes. How could they find it

humorous to torment a gentle, innocent soul like Gilbert?

"Come on Gilbert," I coax, taking him by the arm. "We need to get suited out for practice."

"Yeah, Coach. We need to get dressed."

Gilbert continues to glance back and examine the sky above the stadium gate until we reach the field house.

———————

GRUNTING SOME INAUDIBLE acknowledgment as he labors feverishly behind the equipment counter, Sam scarcely notices when Gilbert and I enter. Aills is tall and heavy-set, standing maybe six foot two. He weighs somewhere in the vicinity of two hundred sixty pounds. His blond hair is beginning to thin, with a bald spot developing across the top of his head. Instead of tanning during the twice a day practices, his fair skin has turned a dull red. His portly body implies that he's soft and flabby, but having watched the way he muscles the players to the sideline for punishment, I have no doubts about his strength. Aills' weakest features are his delicate face and thin lips. When he smiles one corner of his mouth drops down, making it difficult to be absolutely certain whether he is smiling or sneering.

"Sam, if you have a minute, I'd like to speak with you."

"I'm kinda busy. Whatta you need?" he replies without looking up.

"It's important, Sam. Can we talk outside?"

"I got no secrets. Tell me what you want," Aills responds stubbornly.

"Sam! Outside! Right Now!" I have grown tired of being diplomatic.

Sam ceases his equipment repair work. He seems totally surprised by the barbed tone in my voice. I point to the front door and gesture for him to follow me.

When I reach the shade underneath the bleachers, far enough not to be heard by persons inside the field house, I stop and wait for him to catch up.

"What tha hell is so important we gotta come all the way out here? I got work to do," the big coach complains indignantly.

"Sam, I thought we should talk out here, where the players won't hear us. I want you to discontinue your practice of punishing the players by whipping them with the baseball bat."

"You mean *Jelly*? But, that's the way I keep the players in line. Besides, they like it. I tease the kids with it all the time."

"Coach Aills, the matter is not open for discussion. I want all use of the bat to cease, as of right now."

"You mean–no more *Jelly*?"

"I mean–no more *Jelly*."

"The hell ya say! You can't come in here and change the way we do things. One stinking practice and you start throwing your weight around."

"Let's not say things here which we might regret later, Sam. I realize this matter might cause you some embarrassment with the players. I promise you, there'll be absolutely no further mention of the bat by me. I will also see that Murphy keeps his mouth shut. You can handle the discontinuation of spankings with the players in your own way."

I leave Sam infuriated and pouting under the bleachers.

––––––––––

Monday Evening
August 26, 1949

THE BARNES' FARM is some twelve miles west of Ranger on Farm Road 2516, a short distance off the Breckenridge Highway. A bright orange evening sun is disappearing behind the horizon when I identify the Barnes' mailbox and turn off the pavement to drive down a dusty dirt roadway. A large black dog dashes up to bark at the Hudson and run alongside.

The Barnes' farmhouse is an unpainted wood structure, shielded beneath a galvanized metal roof. The house is at least twenty years old. A wide, metal-covered, wood porch extends away from the front of the house. Three wooden steps lead down to a bare and grassless front yard. The front yard is filled with an assortment of various farming plows and equipment, a broken-down tractor and used tires of numerous sizes.

I pull to a stop, parking beside an ancient, faded Ford pickup truck. Light shines through the front windows of the house.

A man dressed in blue overalls appears at the front door as I step up onto the porch. The man is shirtless. The white skin of his chest and shoulders contrasts starkly against his sun-parched face and the dark tan of his arms.

"Howdy, Mister. I saw your headlights coming down the driveway. You need some help?" The man pushes open the screen door and steps to the edge of the porch to spit.

"No, I don't need help. I'm looking for the Barnes' house."

"Well, you found it. Whatta you want?"

"My name is Stubby Warden. I'm the new football coach for Ranger High School. Are you Mister Barnes?"

"Sure am. Clarence Barnes. Most folks call me Buster."

"Mister Barnes, I came out to talk to you about J.L. and his school attendance. I have a proposition I want to discuss with you. May I come inside where we can talk?"

"Mister, there ain't much to talk about. I know what you're after, but I need J.L. here to help with the farm work."

"You haven't heard my proposition yet. If you will allow me to come inside, I believe you'll be interested."

Buster Barnes steps to the edge of the porch and spits again. "Alright then. Why don't you come on inside?"

A long, narrow front room inside the farm house extends from the porch to a kitchen at the rear of the house. Three doors along the right wall open into bedrooms. A pot-bellied metal stove located near the middle of the room is surrounded by a variety of chairs and a flowery cloth sofa. A metal vent pipe extends from the top of the stove up through the ceiling. This room is obviously the central family area.

Smells of supper cooking and clanking sounds of pots hitting pans come from the kitchen. Buster Barnes calls toward the kitchen, "Hey, Maw! Tell Sonny to come up here. There's a man here who wants to talk to us about football." Apparently, J.L. is affectionately called "Sonny" by his parents.

Barnes plops down in a cushioned rocking chair. He motions for me to take a seat on the flowery couch. We wait silently for a moment, until a strapping, muscular young man lumbers in from the kitchen. The young man is also wearing blue overalls without a shirt.

"Sonny, this here fellow is the new football coach. He wants to talk with us about you playing football," Barnes tells his son.

I stand up and offer my hand. "Hello, J.L., my name is Stubby

Warden. It's a pleasure to make your acquaintance."

Buster Barnes begins to rock his chair. "You got the floor, Coach. Tell us about this proposition you wanna make us."

"Mister Barnes, it's my understanding that J.L. will not be able to attend school this fall until after your crops are harvested. You need his help here on the farm. Is that correct?"

"That's about the size of it, Coach. As you can see, we're just plain, ordinary poor folks. Without J.L. helping me, this family would surely starve."

"I'm certain J.L. must be a great help to you, but is there any reason his portion of the work couldn't be done by some other capable farm hand?"

Buster Barnes' reply is sharp and nasty. "You must be a little short on brains, Coach. I just told you we're a poor family. I can't afford to pay another hand while J.L. traipses off to school."

"Buster, please accept my apology, but I believe you misunderstood my question. Let me put it another way. I represent an anonymous benefactor who is genuinely concerned about J.L.'s education and about him playing football. This benefactor is willing to provide you with a full-time farm worker for as long as it takes you to harvest your crops—the only stipulation being that you allow J.L. to begin school on time and play football."

Buster Barnes turns to the giant of a young man sitting in the chair beside him. "Sonny, whatta you think about this offer Coach Warden is proposing to us?"

"Daddy, you know I wanna start to school on time like the other kids. Last year I got so far behind, I like to have never caught up with the rest of my class." J.L. starts to say more, then fearing he might say too much and displease his father, yields to the elder Barnes.

"Coach, can you guarantee this helper will be a hard worker? I don't want to work with no slacker."

I try not to smile. Any worker Lucas Masters would choose to send out here will be so in debt to Lucas, he wouldn't dare slack off.

"Buster, I can assure you that you'll be completely satisfied with any helper we send."

"To be honest with you, Coach, Mrs. Barnes has been after me all summer to let J.L. start to school on time this year. If I can depend on your living up to what you say, we might just strike a bargain."

"You have my word on everything promised here this evening, Buster. If I can have a worker here Wednesday morning, is there a chance J.L. might begin practicing with the football team that morning?"

"Naw, that's a little too soon. J.L. and I are right in the middle of harvesting forty acres of corn. I tell you what. School starts on the Tuesday after Labor Day. You have your man here at six o'clock sharp that morning. We'll see to it that J.L. is in school. He can start practicing football with you that afternoon."

"We have a deal then," I pronounce. "J.L., I'll see you in school a week from tomorrow." I stand up and shake hands with both J.L. and Buster. They invite me to stay for supper, but I make an excuse about needing to be back in town for a meeting.

––––––––––

THE PAY PHONE MAKES a tinkling sound as my nickel drops into the change box. I hear a dull clicking tone on the line.

The telephone operator asks, "Number, please?"

"Operator, I want to place a station-to-station call to Comanche, Texas. The number I am calling is 969."

I haven't been paid since last Friday, my last day of work at the Pontiac House. Anticipating my planned departure for Corpus Christi, most of my pay was used to settle several small debts I owed around town. Now, with only a few coins left in my pocket, I am rapidly approaching a state of impoverishment. Calling station-to-station will save a few cents.

"Please wait, while I ring," the operator tells me.

Clicking noises occur on the line, then a buzzing sound, indicating the phone on the other end is ringing.

"Kimbrough residence," a voice answers. It is Juanita.

The operator interrupts, "Deposit thirty-five cents please."

I insert a quarter and two nickels into the coin slots.

"Hello! Juanita, this is Stubby. I'm calling from Ranger. I didn't make the move to Corpus Christi."

"Yes, darling. Aunt Phyliss called Saturday night to tell us the news. We're so excited. I thought you'd never call. How are you doing?"

"Busier than a barefoot boy standing in a red ant bed. I started 'two a days' this morning. I had to meet with Lucas Masters this afternoon and get his approval before the school would definitely hire me. I wanted to call sooner, but I didn't want to tell you I had the job, then get disappointed."

"Oh, Stubby, you are always so considerate, and I've been acting like a spoiled little brat. Can you ever forgive me?"

"There's nothing to forgive. I love you. I love our baby. And I need you both to be here with me. Juanita, how is your dad? Has he come home from the hospital yet?"

"Yes, Daddy came home Saturday morning. He's doing fine. He's a horrible patient though. It takes both Mother and me to wait on him."

"Are you and the baby okay?"

"Yes, we are both fine."

"Juanita, I want you to seriously consider coming back to Ranger before the baby is born. I miss you terribly, and I need you here with me."

"I miss you too, darling. But, you sound so busy. And Mother really needs me here."

"We finish with 'two a days' this Thursday. My Bulldogs have a practice game scheduled with Breckenridge on Friday night. Do you think I could drive down to Comanche on Saturday? I really need to see you."

"I would like that, but let me talk with mother first. If she has no objections, you can come. She may want to soften things up with Dad. We have to be careful not to get him in an uproar."

The operator interrupts us. "Your time is up. Deposit another quarter, please."

I shove another quarter into the coin slot. It makes another tinkling sound.

Juanita's voice comes back on the line. "Darling, call me Saturday morning. We will finalize our plans to get together then. Good luck on your game. Bye now."

"Goodbye," I say and hang up. A throbbing hurt oozes through my mind. I miss her more now than before I called.

Tuesday Morning
August 27, 1949

AFTER SAM DIRECTS THE SQUAD through a series of muscle
stretching exercises, we separate into three groups. Sam takes the
defense, Murphy takes the offensive linemen and I take the offensive
backfield. I work with the backfield for about an hour, slowly walking
them, then running them, through each of the quarterback option
plays we plan to use in the practice game on Friday night.

Around eight o'clock we suspend practice, allowing the three
groups to break for water. Sam, Murphy and I convene on the sideline. We decide to practice on the kicking and receiving specialty
teams.

During the kickoff drills Murphy stations himself on the sideline,
scrutinizing the receiving team blockers, helping them understand
their blocking assignments. Sam positions himself behind the kicking
team, loping along with them on each kickoff, giving each player personal instruction regarding their coverage routes.

Our place kicker Will Brownlee booms one kickoff after another
to the ten yard line and beyond.

After a half hour of kickoff drills, we set up our teams for punting
and punt receiving. Sam advises that the coaches have been unable to
decide on which player should do the punting, since not one member
of the football squad is able to consistently punt the ball for more than
thirty yards.

We try out several different punters while we painstakingly march
the punting and return teams through their assignments. Finally, in
order to get the ball punted far enough down field to work on our coverage, it becomes necessary for me to take the snaps from center and
do the punting.

For some unknown reason the high school band has elected to
begin their pre-school drills in the open field about fifty yards beyond
the south end goal posts. Ear-piercing sounds of horns, flutes and
drums began to reverberate across the field around nine o'clock this
morning. After a time, it seems each time we gather our players to
explain some aspect of game tactics, the band noise becomes louder.

Jerry Rushing, a freshman halfback, kneels beside me while I try to explain the hand signals we will use to call our various punt return plays. The band noise becomes louder and louder. Several players move in closer, straining to hear me speak.

Grabbing Rushing by the arm, I instruct him to run down to the sector where the band is rehearsing. I tell him to advise the band director that their music is interrupting our practice and to ask the band to please hold the noise down.

In the distance I watch young Rushing conveying my request to the man directing band practice. Rushing starts to run back to the football field, then hesitates and goes back to say something else to the band man.

Jerry comes sprinting back to our huddle to report on his conversation with the band director. "Mister Gans said you can take a red-hot poker and stick it where the sun don't shine."

"He said what?" I ask in amazement, not believing my ears.

"Honest, Coach, that's what he said. I asked him twice to be sure," Rushing recounts. His troubled face displays his dismay at being the appointed carrier of such a vulgar message.

Several of the players begin to snicker.

"The band director don't care much for football coaches," Murphy informs me, making no effort to hide the wry smile etched across his face.

The band starts to play again, much louder than before.

Tuesday Afternoon
August 27, 1949

SINCE THERE ARE VERY FEW PARKS or open play grounds in the city, a favorite gathering place for teenagers wanting to find a pickup game of football is the grassy game field at Bulldog Stadium.

This afternoon, between practices, several young people occupy the field, engaged in a game of Rugby. Unlike the English version, in Texas the game of Rugby is strictly a kicking game. No running is allowed. One person punts the football to the opposing team, whose players try to catch the ball in the air. The player, who catches or retrieves the ball, must then kick the ball back to the other team from the point of catch or retrieval. The game continues until one team is able to punt the football past the other's goal line.

The rugby team defending the north goal is unquestionably superior. They are winning mainly because of a thin, dark-haired boy, who bangs high, spiraling punts which sail for forty and fifty yards, every time he gets an opportunity to kick.

When the rugby game ends, I call to the young man. "Hey there, young fellow. You have a mighty impressive leg. Could I ask your name?"

The young man jogs over to me. His sunburned face is drenched with sweat. Long, wet strands of black hair hang over his forehead, almost covering his eyes. His feet are bare. A pair of shoes with the shoelaces tied together are slung over his shoulder.

"Thanks, Coach. My name is Frankie Jensen."

"Who taught you to kick like that, son?"

"No one. I guess I picked it up playing rugby with the other guys. I like to kick."

"You ever play football, Frankie?" The boy is frail and scrawny. His arms are lean and straight, without tangible evidence of muscle. With his non-athletic build, there is little chance he participates in any school contact sport.

"No sir. I'm in the band. I play the drums, first chair."

"I'm impressed. You must play very well. Have you ever considered playing football?"

"No sir. I'm in the band," he explains, making it sound as if band and football were two separate worlds.

"Look, Frankie. If our football team is to be competitive this year, I need to find someone who can punt the football. If I could arrange for you to march with the band at halftime, is there any chance you would consider kicking for us?"

This skinny kid has never punted in a football practice session, much less in a game situation. Here I am, offering to arrange for him to march with the band at halftime, arrangements which will have to be made with a band director who dislikes football coaches. My grandfather often used an expression to justify similar irrational behavior: "Desperate men are sometimes forced to take desperate measures."

"No sir, I don't believe I could. My dad bought me a new set of drums last spring. He'd kill me if I got hurt and couldn't march with the band."

Digging myself a deeper hole, I ask, "What if I could convince your father? Would you be willing to try out to punt for the team?"

If I convince this kid's father to let him try out and then find he can't handle the pressure of the punting chores, I'll have some mighty embarrassing egg on my face.

"Yeah, I suppose I would, but you'll never get him to agree. My dad can be mighty hard-headed when he gets his mind set on something."

"You leave that part to me, Frankie. How do I get in touch with your father?"

"Jensen's Radio Repair Shop on Main Street, downtown. Everyone in town knows my dad."

"Frankie, let's not mention this to anyone until I talk with your father. We will see how he reacts. Okay?"

"Sure, Coach. You're wasting your time anyway. You'll never get my dad to agree."

Tuesday Evening
August 27, 1949

JENSEN'S RADIO REPAIR SHOP is on the south side of Main Street, almost directly across the street from the Arcadia Theater. When I called Jensen to arrange a meeting, he insisted on meeting here. He explained that he often works late.

The front door of the shop is locked. I knock on the glass. A short minute later Jensen emerges from a back room and comes to unlock the door.

"Coach Warden, please excuse me. I'm on the telephone. Can you wait out here until I finish with my call?" Jensen locks the door behind me and retraces his steps through the shop toward the back room, not waiting for me to answer.

The front portion of Jensen's shop is a showroom/sales area, filled with all sorts and sizes of radios, from AM-FM consoles with record players to tabletop AM models. A matching Maytag washer and dryer are displayed prominently upon a raised platform near the front entrance. Each front store window features a splendid Philco television set, encased in rich, dark mahogany wood cabinets. The television sets face the street to attract the attention of prospective shoppers passing by along the front sidewalk. The rear of the shop is apparently where Jensen does most of his repair work.

Jensen reappears from behind the cloth curtain separating the sales area from the repair shop. "Coach Warden, I'm C.D. Jensen. My son tells me that you and he had a conversation about football this afternoon."

"Yes sir, that's correct. I must tell you–I was quite impressed with Frankie. He is a very polite and likeable young person."

"Coach Warden, what is it you wanna talk to me about?" Jensen is abrupt, anxious to get back to his repair work.

"Mister Jensen, here's the situation. My coaches and I have searched high and low, trying to find a punter among the members of our football squad. We don't have a single kid who can consistently kick the football further than thirty yards. Your son seems to have an uncanny ability to punt the football. Without a reliable punter, our football team has little chance of winning many games this season...." I stop talking, intentionally leaving my argument unfinished, hoping Jensen will pick up where I left off.

"Then you want Frankie to kick for the football team?"

"That is my thought exactly, C.D."

"But, Frankie plays in the band. You can't play in the band and play football. I'm certain that is against school rules."

Ouch! There might be yet another obstacle. In addition to getting the band director to agree, I may need to persuade the school board to reverse some arbitrary participation rule.

I continue with my pitch, trying to sound confident.

"C.D., I'm quite certain he can do both. Being our punter will not require any knowledge of our plays, and Frankie won't be needed to practice with the team, except on Thursdays, the day before our games. He'll be free to participate in band activities on every other school day."

"What about during the games? What about marching with the band at halftime?"

"No problem. Of course we'll want him with us on the field while the game is in progress. Since the band has two other drummers, they shouldn't miss his drums when they play in the grandstands. I can assure you he'll always be allowed plenty of time to change uniforms and perform with the band during halftimes."

"What if he were to get hurt? I've invested a great deal of money in his new drums. He's first chair, you know. His mother and I have been looking forward to watching him march and play his drums. What assurance can you give us he won't be injured?"

"C.D., the player least likely to be injured on the football team would be the punter. Frankie will only be in each game for maybe four or five plays. The chances of his being hurt in a game are very slim. I can guarantee I'll never put him in a situation where he might be injured during practice."

"Will he get a letter jacket if he kicks for the team?"

"Absolutely. If you will allow him to play for us, I will personally fit him for his football letter jacket."

"Coach, could you give me some time to think this over? I really should talk with Frankie's mother before I make a decision."

"Of course, C.D. Can I check back with you tomorrow?"

"You bet, Coach. I'll have you an answer by tomorrow afternoon."

Wednesday Afternoon
August 28, 1949

SINCE LAST SATURDAY AFTERNOON my life has been turned upside down. I've been discovering what life is like–living in the fast lane. Every waking minute has been consumed with football and my new job. There's been no time to visit Pearl's Café and drink a leisure cup of her hot coffee. I haven't talked with Pearl since last Friday when I stopped in to tell her goodbye.

Entering the café, the cool air offers immediate and refreshing relief from the insufferable heat outside. Pearl is at work behind the counter. Her back is turned to the front door.

"Hello, Pearl. I'll bet you never thought you'd be seeing me again so soon."

Pearl swivels around to face me. She raises both hands above her head. "My goodness gracious, Stubby! If you aren't a welcome sight! I hear you got the coaching job after all."

"Yep, and there's nobody who's more surprised than me. I have to pinch myself ever so often, to make sure I'm awake."

"I'm so happy for you, darlin'. You wanted that job so badly." Her voice lowers, almost a whisper. "But you mind what I told you about being careful. There's people you'll have to deal with who'd as soon slit your throat as look at you."

"Pearl, you make it sound like there's an angry lynch mob waiting out there to string me up the first time I make a mistake," I say, scoffing at her concern for me, hoping to lighten the conversation.

"You can joke all you want, sweetie, but the facts speak for themselves. Several of your coaching predecessors have left this town, humiliated, with their tail between their legs. You want some hot coffee?"

Lately, every time she asks me her "hot coffee" question I have this vision of some unsuspecting fool who didn't take her seriously. His cheeks are pooched out, his eyes rolled back and smoke is pouring out of his ears.

Pearl eyes me impatiently while I try to refrain from laughing out loud. "You want some hot coffee, or not?"

"I'm sorry, Pearl. Yeah, I sure would."

Pearl pours my coffee, then remembering something she forgot to do, hikes swiftly toward the kitchen. She and the cook begin some sort of heated discussion while I glance through the newspapers.

In a moment Pearl returns to the front counter. "That shiftless, no-good-for-nothing cook forgot to order pancake batter for tomorrow. I have to think of everything."

Not having anything to add to her comment, I continue to read through the newspaper.

The European situation is getting worse. Russia and Yugoslavia are still at it. Russia accuses General Tito of being a fascist. Tito retaliates by warning Russia to stay out of Yugoslavian affairs. Soviet troops have moved up to the Yugoslavian border. No shots have been fired, but war in Europe could break out any day.

I know I should be worried about the prospect of war, but these days I'm too busy with the problems at hand.

"You want another cup of hot coffee, hon?"

Pearl studies me curiously when I raise my hand up to cover my mouth. I slide the cup toward her, without answering.

"I understand you've been out to talk to Buster Barnes about his kid playing football," Pearl says as she pours my second cup of coffee.

I lay the newspaper down. News travels fast in this town.

"Yes, Mister Barnes has agreed to let J.L. start to school on time this year and play on the football team. I wish J.L. could play this Friday night. We're hurting real bad for a middle linebacker. Breckenridge will probably run us ragged without J.L. to plug the middle of our defense."

Placing an elbow on the countertop, Pearl leans across the service counter. She uses her hand to support her chin, as if she's thinking hard. "Stubby darlin', I don't know a dern thing about football, but I might know someone who could help you out Friday night."

Over the past several months I have come to realize this lady is an amazing fountain of knowledge and information. She immediately has my full attention.

"Whatta you have on that devious mind of yours, Pearl?"

Pearl leans over the counter and whispers softly, "Alfred Steele."

"What is an Alfred Steele?" I ask, amused at her grave demeanor. For someone who could care less about football, she is deadly serious. I'm close to laughing again.

"Alfred Steele is not a what. Alfred is an extremely large young man. His folks moved away from Ranger about two years ago. Alfred stayed behind but dropped out of school to work. I believe he played football through about ninth grade. I hear he was very good. Of course, he's much bigger and stronger now."

Pearl's information intrigues me, but somehow, I can't imagine how the kind of player I need for Friday's game could have been overlooked by a previous coach. With my deficient linebacker situation, her suggestion is definitely worth checking out.

"You really think he could help us, Pearl? Where could I find him?"

"Generally, you can find him hanging around in front of the Gholson Hotel, anytime after seven. Stubby, the poor kid is having a rough go of it. He comes in here hungry almost every morning. I give him the leftovers to eat in the kitchen. I don't know what's gonna become of him come winter. I'm afraid he might freeze to death."

"Pearl, if he has the good fortune to have a friend like you, he can't be in too much danger. Listen, thanks for telling me about him. I intend to try and find him tonight."

Pearl smiles proudly, apparently pleased with herself for helping me with my coaching problem. Convinced that my problem is solved, she recommences her afternoon duties, humming happily while she unloads the pies in her display case onto a large metal tray and totes them into the kitchen.

I swig down the last of my coffee, push the unread newspapers back to the end of the counter and leave a nickel alongside my empty cup. Pearl's suggestion is interesting, but I have work to do. Before I reach the street, my mind shifts to planning the afternoon practice session.

Wednesday Afternoon
August 28, 1949

WHILE OUR PLAYERS SUIT OUT for practice, I pitch in to help Sam sort through a huge stack of dirty practice jerseys, getting them ready to send out to laundry. During the regular season, in order to conserve our limited cleaning budget, we will have our players take their workout jerseys home to be washed by their mothers.

A hysterical, accented voice screams out loudly. "Who deed it? Who deed it? Who deed this terrible thing to me?"

Anticipating that someone has been seriously injured, Sam and I abandon our work and dash into the player's dressing room.

Gilbert Thompson is facing his open equipment locker, pointing angrily at the contents inside.

"Alright! Alright, right now! I want to know who deed this! Who is the practical joker that deed this thing?" Gilbert shrieks.

We inch up slowly to Thompson's locker, not knowing what to expect. On the top of Gilbert's practice jersey lies a large, long, solid segment of human waste. It is an utterly disgusting sight. The poignant smell is sickening.

Like a crazed bull, Gilbert Thompson has reached a state of deranged rage. His face is bright red, and his eyes are rolled back in his head. In his enraged frame of mind, he is mad enough to kill.

"Coach Aills, will you please assist Mister Thompson in properly disposing of this item into a toilet?" I command. I want to defuse the tense situation before Gilbert slugs someone.

Aills swerves to face me in disbelief. From his surprised expression you'd think I had asked him to perform some unnatural act. I wink at him and motion toward the restroom.

Aills glares at me for a few seconds. Then, like an obedient servant, he clasps his nose between the fingers of his left hand and scoops up the jersey with his right hand. In short, delicate steps the big coach strolls slowly to the toilet area. A few seconds later the sound of a flushing toilet echoes through the locker room.

The sounds of laughter cease abruptly when I turn back in the direction of the half-dressed players. I put on my meanest face. "Men, I've had all the ass grabbing and girlish games I'm gonna put up with. One more incident like the one we've just witnessed and each of you had better start praying to God to take your souls, because your lily-white asses are gonna be all mine."

A deathly quiet falls over the dressing room while I stand and stare angrily at the young men. Demonstrating my total disgust, I throw up my hands, stomp out the front door and walk across the sandstone pavement.

When I reach the shade under the bleachers, I begin to giggle. By the time I can reach the darkened region beneath the stadium ramp, I'm laughing out of control. In spite of my sincere concern for Gilbert Thompson, I can't stop my laughter.

Another person comes to join me in the darkness under the ramp. It is Sam. He is grinning from ear to ear.

"How the hell did they get that big a turd into Thompson's locker, and all in one piece?" Sam laughs.

"I can't imagine, but it must have involved one heck of a lot of planning and engineering know-how."

We sit together in the darkness holding our sides–two coaches, laughing hilariously and uncontrollably. Afternoon practice will start late today.

———————

WE SPLIT THE PLAYERS into offensive and defensive teams. Practice this afternoon will be a full-fledged, head-knocking scrimmage–our first real test of the new offense we've worked on for the past two days.

A sharp pungent odor raps my senses as the offensive team huddles. I call the play, "Forty-two, option right."

The ball is centered. Jones, the quarterback, fakes the ball to his fullback who charges into a hole between our right guard and tackle. Watching the reaction of the defensive end, Jones forces him to commit to defending against a possible pitchout to our halfback on an outside sweep. Then he tucks the football under his arm and scampers inside the end for an eight yard gain.

The offense huddles again. The nauseating smell seems to be getting worse. When the wind changes slightly, the stench becomes overwhelming. Several players move back away from the huddle.

Suddenly it dawns on me. Gilbert Thompson, our offensive center, is wearing the contaminated jersey. After our laughing hysterics under the ramp, Sam and I neglected to issue him a clean jersey. Wanting to avoid my threatened wrath, the other players are afraid to mention the smell about Gilbert. Cupping one hand around my brow, I bow my head, trying to subdue the laughter starting to well up inside me again.

"Gilbert," I say, speaking calmly, "come with me. We need to get you a fresh jersey."

Sam squats down in the defensive backfield, covering his face with one hand while Gilbert and I sprint for the field house.

Wednesday Evening
August 28, 1949

LIGHTS ARE STILL BURNING inside Jensen's shop when I park the Hudson at the curb in front of his business. Jensen's front door is locked so I knock on the glass. Jensen instantly emerges from the back room. When he sees me, he waves and rushes to the front door.

"Coach Warden, I thought maybe you'd changed your mind about Frankie," Jensen exclaims as he opens the door.

"Not at all, C.D. I came by your shop about two o'clock this afternoon. The sign on your door said you were out. This is the first opportunity I've had to come back by."

"Yes, I had to run over to Eastland to pick up a washing machine. I'm sorry I missed you."

"No problem at all. Have you reached a decision about Frankie punting for the football team?"

"Yes, we have, Coach. Mrs. Jensen, Frankie and I talked it over this morning at breakfast. We are, naturally, concerned about Frankie being able to march and perform with the band, but we also want to do everything we can to help the team have a winning season. What we would like to propose is to have Frankie do both football and band for two games. If there are no problems, Frankie will continue to kick for the team. If we run into problems, Frankie will quit the football team and participate only in the band."

"C.D., that is a most considerate offer. I will agree whole-heartedly to your terms. Would it be possible for Frankie to work out with the team tomorrow afternoon? I don't believe the band practices in the afternoon."

"If he doesn't have a conflict with band practice, I'll see that he's there."

"Fine then, have him at the football field at four o'clock sharp. Coach Aills will get him fitted into a uniform. I'll clear everything with the band director."

Slipping into the driver's seat behind the wheel of the Hudson, I delay starting my engine, watching Jensen while he locks his front door and turns out his showroom lights.

I wonder what the band director will want to do with his red-hot poker when he learns his first chair drummer is kicking for me.

———————

CRUISING DOWN MAIN STREET, passing the Gholson Hotel for the third time in the past half hour, there is still no sign of the young man Alfred Steele. If Pearl's description is accurate, he should be easy enough to identify.

A striking match flickers to light a cigarette in the darkness of the basement stairway next to the hotel entrance. I slam on my brakes and stop the car. The lighted cigarette silhouettes a shadowy figure huddled at the base of the stairs. Leaving the Hudson parked and running out in the street, I hasten to the top of the basement stairs.

"Alfred. Alfred Steele. Is that you?"

A huge man moves out of the shadows. I cannot see his face.

"I ain't doing nothin' wrong, Mister. Honest, I don't want no trouble. If I'm bothering you, I'll leave."

"Are you Alfred Steele?"

"Yes sir," the voice answers.

"Alfred, my name is Stubby Warden. I'm the high school football coach. May I talk with you for a minute?"

"Whatta you want with me?" Alfred asks apprehensively.

"Come up here, Alfred. Let me assure you; I mean you no harm."

Alfred steps out into the ghostly light of the neon hotel signs. His size is astounding. He is tall and muscular, standing at least six and a half feet tall, and he must weigh two hundred fifty pounds, maybe more. Pearl's assumption is absolutely correct. This young man could definitely be a dominating middle linebacker.

Alfred snuffs out his cigarette and climbs to the top of the steps. When he draws closer, I grit my teeth and try to conceal my revulsion. The young man is dressed in rags. His clothing is filthy. His shirt is torn and his faded blue jeans have gaping holes at each knee. A dirty big toe protrudes from his left shoe. Alfred is truly a pitiful sight.

"Alfred, you hungry?"

"Yes sir," he replies.

"How about my treating you to supper?" I offer. This kid looks famished. Even though I only have a few loose coins remaining in my pocket, somehow I'll arrange to feed him.

"That'd be okay with me. I sure am hungry."

"Fine. Why don't you hop in my car? We can get something to eat while we talk."

The Hudson is parked out in the middle of Main Street. A passing car honks disgustedly at us as it whizzes by.

RANGER HILL CAFÉ is near the eastern outskirts of town at the top of Ranger Hill. The café is open twenty-four hours a day. Most of the restaurant's customers are Highway 80 truckers who brave the infamous hill so fearfully. The café is far enough away from town, so I won't easily be recognized while I discuss my proposition with Alfred Steele.

When we arrive, the café is almost empty. A couple of truckers chatting at the serving counter are the only other customers. A waitress approaches us as we take a seat in one of the six vinyl-covered booths. She hands us a menu and takes our order for drinks. After we each order coffee, I excuse myself and walk to the payout counter.

"Hi there. Are you the manager?" I ask the lady at the front cash register.

"Nope. She's in the kitchen. You wanna speak to her?"

"Yes, could you please get her for me?"

The cash register lady disappears into the kitchen. I hear her shout. "There's a short guy up front! He wants to talk with ya!"

A plump, pear-shaped woman shoves open the kitchen door and walks toward me. Streaks of gray peek through her frizzy brown hair. A greasy apron covers her stained white waitress uniform. She seems upset that I have interrupted her work.

"Whatta you want, Mister?" the woman demands rudely.

"Hello. My name is Stubby Warden. I'm the new football coach of the Ranger Bulldogs. I want to ask a huge favor of you."

The woman's sullen attitude changes quickly. She wipes her right hand on her apron and extends it to me. "So, you're the new coach. I'm so pleased to meet you. My son Eddie plays for you. I'm Louise Phillips, Eddie's mom."

"Yes ma'am. I believe Eddie will be a sophomore this year. He plays fullback for us. He's a fine young gentleman."

"Thank you, Coach Warden. We're very proud of him. You sure seem to know your players."

"Well, Eddie is an especially good kid, and with his flaming red hair, he does stand out a bit. Mrs. Phillips, can you see that young man over in the booth?" I explain, pointing toward Alfred Steele.

"Sure, Coach. I see him."

"That young man is hungry. I'm not sure when he ate his last decent meal. I want to purchase a meal for him, but I am embarrassingly short of funds. Is there any way you might extend credit to me, until tomorrow when I can come back and pay?"

Seemingly in deep thought while she muses over my proposition, the woman wipes her hands on her apron again. She's probably contemplating how the Ranger High football coach could be in such dire straits that he could be in her restaurant asking for a handout.

Her eyes twinkle as she reaches her decision.

"Coach Warden, aren't you something. Coming in here and asking, so politely, for credit," she chides. "You order whatever you want. It's an honor to have you come in and eat with us. There'll be no charge. Please consider your meal to be my treat."

"But, I insist on paying you," I object.

"Your money will not be good in here, Coach Warden, and that's the end of it. You just treat my Eddie right on the football field."

I thank Louise Phillips for her kindness and return to the booth where Alfred is waiting. When the waitress arrives with our coffee, we each order a double portion of chicken fried steak, complete with gravy and french fries. Less than ten minutes pass before the waitress places our order on our table. Alfred wolfs down his plate of food in a matter of seconds.

"Alfred, would you care for another helping?" I ask, acting as if we weren't here on credit.

"No sir. But, I'd like a slice of apple pie. Would that be alright?"

I motion to the waitress and order the pie for Alfred, advising her to supplement the order with two scoops of vanilla ice cream. In my temporary state of prosperity, I can't help but show out a little.

"Alfred, how long has it been since you played football?"

"'Bout two years. I think I was in ninth grade. It's hard to remember. I believe I was in either eighth grade or ninth grade for two years."

My heart sinks. The University Interscholastic League, which is the ruling body for high school sports in Texas, will not allow an athlete to participate in high school sports after they reach nineteen. If Alfred had to repeat several grades, he may be too old to play for us.

With all my fingers crossed, I ask, "Alfred how old are you now?"

"Eighteen."

One hurdle cleared. "When is your birthday?"

"September 6."

His birthday will make him ineligible for the first regular season game, but J.L. Barnes will be on board by then. It may be stretching the rules a bit, but now I can justify Alfred playing for us in the Breckenridge game this Friday night.

"Alfred, would you consider playing football again, for me?"

"You mean for the Bulldogs? Coach, I quit school two years ago."

"Yes, I know, Alfred, but I need you to play one more football game, for Ranger High this Friday night. Would you be willing to play if I arrange it?"

"I don't know. You've been real nice to me and all, but I don't want to start no trouble. I'm gittin' along pretty good. That Lucas Masters and his bunch of crooks can be awful nasty if you get on their bad side."

Alfred's statement shakes me. I abruptly sit up in the booth. The fear in this town extends all the way down to a poor fellow like Alfred. In his beleaguered situation, what could he be afraid of?

"Alfred, if you would agree to play this one game, I'll assure you no one in this town will ever trouble you again. I need you to play, very badly. If you'll help me, I promise things will be much better for you. You certainly can't continue with the way you're living now."

"Alright, Coach. We just met tonight, but I feel like we're already good friends. If you really need me, I'll play for you. But, you gotta promise not to let anything bad happen to me if I do."

I reach across the table to touch his big calloused hand. "Alfred, you have my promise, not only to protect you, but also to be your good friend. We have a deal then. Alfred, I don't renege on my promises. I hope you won't either."

"You can depend on me, Coach."

Louise Phillips emerges from the kitchen while Alfred and I are preparing to leave the restaurant. I introduce her to Alfred and compliment her on the marvelous meal we've just eaten.

As we reach the front door, she calls to me from behind the checkout counter, "Coach, you see that my Eddie gets in the ballgame Friday night."

I turn back to her. "Mrs. Phillips, after the generous hospitality you have extended me tonight, you can count on your Eddie getting plenty of playing time."

In the parking lot outside, I laugh privately to myself. Lucas Masters sells football playing time for huge profits. I'm willing to give it away–for a free meal.

Alfred and I hardly speak during the trip back to Ranger. We are each caught up in our own thoughts. When we reach Main Street, I ask, "Alfred, where do you stay?"

"I been sleeping in the storeroom down in the hotel basement for the past week. I hope they ain't locked it up yet."

"You better come home with me tonight. You need a bath, and I've got an extra bed. I'll fix you breakfast in the morning before we go to practice. Whatta you think?"

"That'll be fine with me, Coach."

All this effort to get two players I need for one practice game. This could be a long, long season. I wonder what Juanita would think about our enormous house guest. Oh, Lord, how I miss her.

CHAPTER SIX
THE GAME

Thursday Morning
August 29, 1949

D O YOU KNOW HOW big his foot is?" Sam Aills asks cynically. "He wears a size fifteen. We'll never find a football shoe big enough to fit him."

"Sure we will, Sam. He has to have shoes. He's gonna play linebacker for us Friday night."

"Well, I'll be damned if I know where to look. Biggest shoe size we have is a thirteen. I even trimmed his toe nails, trying to fit him into one of our shoes. Each of his big toes is a good two inches long."

A visual image of my assistant coach administering a pedicure to big Alfred Steele flashes across my mind, almost causing me to burst into laughter. For Sam's sake I restrain my amusement. The personal atrocities Sam is willing to suffer to keep this team outfitted often astounds me.

When Alfred and I arrived together this morning, Sam immediately assumed a negative attitude about Alfred playing for us Friday night. After sulking behind the equipment counter for a few minutes, his bullheaded brain eventually began to grasp how much Alfred could help his defense against Breckenridge. Now, he is eagerly rushing about the equipment room, using all his skills to get Alfred suited out for our morning practice.

"Don't we have a pair of sneakers we can fit him into? We can't let him play barefooted," I suggest, trying to be helpful.

"Now where the hell would I get a pair of size fifteen sneakers?"

"I don't know. Maybe you could cut the toes out or something."

Sam's eyes light up. "I got it! We'll cut the front end off the pair of thirteens and tape his toes with foam rubber."

"Are you sure that'll work?" I ask, but Sam is already behind the counter rummaging through the shelves.

From some secret nook, known only to him, Sam retrieves a saw. With a few swift strokes of the saw, he cuts off the ends of an almost-new, thirty dollar pair of high-top, cleated shoes. He grabs a piece of foam rubber and a roll of adhesive tape before he hurries into the dressing room.

SINCE WE HAVE A GAME tomorrow night, we decide to scrimmage in full gear, with both the offense and defense operating at full steam. Trying to teach them the new offense, we've been drilling these kids, twice a day, since last Monday. I'm anxious to see how the "Option Tee" offense works against our defensive team when they are totally unrestricted.

In the huddle I call the play. Twenty-three, option left on three.

Hut. Hut. Hut. The ball is centered to Jones. Dorsey, the fullback, takes two steps forward. Jones shoves the football into his midsection and moves along with him behind the offensive line. At the last possible second, after the defense reacts to stop the fullback who plunges into a hole between left end and left tackle, the quarterback withdraws the ball and pitches out to Simpson. Simpson takes the pitchout and runs around the defensive end for a nine yard gain.

With me calling a different option on each try, our offense successfully moves the football for more than forty yards in six plays. Alfred Steele seems confused playing the middle linebacker position. Sam moves in to talk with him after each play, but Alfred has not participated in a single tackle. When we cross the twenty yard line, the offense and defense swap sides, turning around to run in the opposite direction.

Forty-four, option right, on two. Hut. Hut. The ball is snapped. A collision in the middle of the line sends our center Thompson and the right guard Grey, reeling back into the backfield. Dorsey is knocked to his knees and Jones fumbles the ball. A loose helmet rolls by the huddle as the football is recovered by the defense.

Alfred Steele is, apparently, getting the hang of the middle linebacker's job. Sam, resting on one knee in the defensive backfield, is grinning like an old possum.

AFTER MORNING PRACTICE I decide to drive over to Cisco. My curiosity about Jerry Lowe and how he's getting along with the new Cisco head coach can no longer be suppressed. Surely by now Jerry has heard about my being hired as the Ranger football coach, but I'm anxious to tell him in detail how it all happened. There is also a slim possibility they might have a pair of size fifteen shoes I can borrow.

C.D. Jensen whirls into the parking lot as I'm preparing to leave. When he sees me, he jambs on his brakes, throwing up a cloud of dust which drifts over his pickup as he pulls up alongside.

"Coach Warden, I'm so glad I caught you." He sounds out of breath, like he's been running.

"Hello, C.D. What's your hurry all about?"

"Frankie has come down with some sort of stomach virus. He's been puking and throwing up all night. I'm afraid he won't be able to practice this afternoon like I promised."

"Damn, damn, damn," I swear to myself. I'd planned on working Frankie with the punting team this afternoon.

"Gosh, I'm sorry to hear about Frankie. Do you think it could be anything more serious?"

"No, I'm sure he'll be feeling fine by tomorrow, as soon as he throws up whatever is making him so sick."

"C.D., you tell Frankie not to worry about practice. The important thing is for him to get well. Even if he's not well enough to kick, we darn sure want him to march with the band tomorrow night."

"Thanks, Coach. We were worried you might be upset, with the big game coming up tomorrow."

"We can only do what we can do, C.D. If Frankie feels better tomorrow, bring him by the football field, and we'll find him a football uniform. For now, we'll wait and see whether he can kick in the game."

Jensen waves goodbye, guns his motor and tears out across the gravel parking lot, leaving a dense trail of dust behind him. The man always seems to be in a tremendous hurry.

Thursday Noon
August 29, 1949

UNLIKE RANGER, Cisco holds their workouts on a practice field a few blocks from downtown. A combination player's dressing room and equipment building is situated at the west end of the practice field. In a remarkable example of poor planning, someone decided to build the parking lot on the east end of the field, making it necessary to walk the length of the field to get from your car to the player's dressing facility.

A thick blanket of dark green grass covers the Lobo practice field. Neatly striped lines of powdered white lime divide the field into ten yard increments. Silver metal goal posts stand in each of the end zones. A red cinder running track encompasses the practice field.

The front door to an equipment room is open. Clattering sounds of football cleats scraping against a concrete floor originate from inside the room.

"Hello! Is anyone here?" I call out bravely.

"Yeah, who's doing the asking?" a slender young male responds from behind an equipment counter covered with assorted football pads.

"My name's Stubby Warden. I'm the Ranger football coach. I'm here looking for a friend of mine, Jerry Lowe. He's an assistant coach. You wouldn't happen to know where I could find him, would you?"

"Hi, Coach, I'm Bryan Hasslet, the team manager," the young man proclaims amiably. "Coach Lowe should be back any minute. He drove in to town to get some laces for our shoulder pads. You can wait for him in here if you like."

"Thanks, Bryan, I'll do that. You mind if I look around?"

"Help yourself, Coach, but you've gotta promise not to steal any secrets. We play you guys in October, so don't take advantage of our generous hospitality," the student manager replies. He shows me a toothy smile to assure me he's joking.

In addition to being antiseptically clean and freshly painted, the Lobo dressing facility is much more modern than our Ranger dressing quarters. Each shower stall is individually enclosed. The toilets are partitioned to allow privacy from the dressing section. The urinals are single flush, sanitary, white ceramic bowls. Every Lobo player is furnished an individual metal locker, with a door and lock to store his gear. The pads and equipment stored in the lockers appear to be either brand new or in almost new condition. Compared to our facilities in Ranger this place is "Football Coach Heaven."

Jerry materializes suddenly at the front entrance. His arms are loaded with two large paper sacks. He notices me immediately. "Stubby Warden, as I live and breathe, what are you doing here?"

"Thought I'd come over to see how the other half lives," I say, shaking Jerry's free hand.

"Is what I hear true? Did you actually get the football coaching job at Ranger?"

"Yeah, it's true all right. You won't believe everything that's happened to me since I last saw you. If you've got a few minutes, I thought we might talk. I wanna hear all about what you've been up to."

Jerry and I find a shady spot beneath the overhang of the equipment building roof. We sit on the grass while I relate the peculiar chain of events which led to my hiring. I tell him about my meeting with Lucas Masters, my feelings about my two assistant coaches and about Juanita leaving me.

Jerry matches my account of extraordinary experiences with an unusual tale of his own. He tells me about a bizarre situation which has developed concerning the Cisco head coach.

"Jerry, you mean to tell me the head coach doesn't oversee every practice session?" I ask with amazed disbelief.

"That's right, good buddy. He and his wife own this flower shop downtown. Some days he stays down there to help her. Lets us two assistants conduct the football practices. It's like a Chinese fire drill around here, with everybody going in a different direction."

"Have you tried talking to him? Your Lobo team could be in for a rough season if you don't get something worked out."

"With his attitude, I can't see things changing much, even if I was to have a heart to heart with him. Might end up getting me fired. I've decided the best thing for me to do is keep my mouth shut and go along. If we have a bad season, maybe they'll fire him and hire another coach for next year. That might be me."

"You're probably right, Jerry. Keep in touch, though. I'm anxious to see how all this turns out."

"We play your Bulldogs the third week in October. The stinky stuff should have hit the fan by then."

On our walk back into the equipment room I remember to ask Jerry about borrowing some shoes for Alfred Steele.

"He wears a size fifteen? That can't be a person. It must be a thing. Where did you find a player that size?"

"Jerry, you wouldn't believe me if I told you. Right now, he's my house guest. He eats more in a day than Juanita and I did in a week. But he's my ace in the hole for our game with Breckenridge this Friday night. I'm taking extra good care of him until then."

"Come on, Stubby. Let's find a pair of shoes for your own, personal 'live-in' Godzilla," Jerry laughs.

With the help of Bryan, the student manager, Jerry finds an old pair of size fifteens left on the premises by the Abilene Stars, a semi-pro football team which practiced on the Cisco field until the end of July.

We say goodbye, promising each other that we'll get together again soon. On the drive back to Ranger I recollect that Jerry never mentioned a single word about his girl friend Carolyn Ratcliff.

Friday Afternoon
August 30, 1949

PARKED ALONGSIDE THE STADIUM ENTRANCE GATE is the school bus which will transport the football team to Breckenridge. Each player will be responsible for packing and loading his own personal gear. While Murphy and I stuff three heavy canvas bags with footballs, towels, medical supplies and miscellaneous extra gear, Sam recruits several younger squad members to lug the unwieldy bags to the bus and stack them on the rear seats.

Our team bus is the same vehicle Keith Murphy drives to pick up and deliver students on his twice-a-day rural bus route. He will handle the driving. In order to minimize horseplay among the players, Sam will sit at the rear of the bus. I'll take a seat somewhere near the middle.

We coaches will most likely sit alone for the entire trip, since none of the boys want to be teased or accused of "brown-nosing" or "kissing up" to the coaches.

A scorching breeze stirs up a cloud of dust in the parking lot. With the temperature outside hovering above one hundred degrees, our players are anxious to leave. The simmering, still heat inside the bus is suffocating. Even hot air blowing through the open windows will make it seem cooler once the big bus is underway.

Murphy stomps his foot down hard on the bus starter pedal. The bus sputters, emitting a black cloud of smoke from the rear exhaust. The engine coughs and spits, then begins to run smoothly.

Sam makes a final inspection outside the bus to make sure nothing has been left on the ground while I take a head count, confirming that all our players are accounted for. When Sam re-enters the bus, he taps Murphy on the shoulder and gives him a thumbs-up signal. Murphy nods and reaches to pull the lever to close the bus door. The bus engine roars as we lurch forward.

"All aboard the Breckenridge Express," Sam bellows, then ambles down the aisle to find his seat in the back of the bus.

BRECKENRIDGE IS THE COUNTY SEAT of Stephens County. The neighboring city is situated some thirty-five miles northwest of Ranger on U.S. Highway 183. Breckenridge boasts a population of approximately sixty-five hundred, almost twice the number of people who reside in Ranger.

Breckenridge High is classified as a Texas Two A school, meaning that during the regular season they compete against larger schools in an entirely different state classification. Ranger is classified as a Texas One A school.

Although numerous proposals have been offered to make the state football playoff system more equitable, the Interscholastic League presently only recognizes four classifications: City Division schools from metropolitan districts like Dallas, Houston, Fort Worth and San Antonio; Class Two A, which includes Breckenridge and schools of much larger cities like Waco, Austin, Wichita Falls and Lubbock; Class One A, which includes schools from mid-sized cities like Ranger and Eastland, and Class B; comprised of the remaining smaller towns which play eleven man football.

Despite having to compete against much larger schools, Breckenridge is considered a perennial football powerhouse. Breckenridge has advanced into the state football playoffs each of the past three years, losing last year to Wichita Falls, the eventual state champion. It's a well-known secret that wealthy Breckenridge oil men go to great lengths to find good-paying jobs within their city for men whose sons have exceptional football skills. Neither Murphy nor Aills can remember Breckenridge High School ever having a losing football season. Ranger has won only one of the last five games between the two schools.

Since the oil boom days of the mid-twenties, Breckenridge and Ranger have kicked off their football season with a traditional pre-season game, like a kind of ritual marking the end of summer. Somehow, winning the annual game has become associated with the civic pride of both cities. The two schools compete in totally separate football districts during regular season, so local bragging rights are the only interests actually at stake in this yearly practice game. Nonetheless, both the Breckenridge and Ranger football teams and their fiercely loyal fans approach this game with great anxiety.

MURPHY HEADS THE BUS over the brick pavement of Walker Street through downtown Breckenridge. Green and white banners hang from every light standard on both sides of the street. Signs urging their Buckaroos to "Beat Ranger" are prominently displayed in many of the store windows. People along the sidewalks stop and stare at our old yellow school bus as we pass by.

Making a sharp right near the middle of downtown, we catch our first glimpse of towering flood lights protruding above the Breckenridge football facility. We drive a few blocks, then swing across a spacious parking lot. Murphy reduces his speed, swerving to avoid several hazardous chugholes, and parks in an unpaved unloading zone behind the home side bleachers. Our players stumble out of the bus sluggishly; their exuberance sapped by the hot, boring ride.

Buckaroo Stadium is surrounded by a high wooden fence painted in bright green and trimmed in white to match the high school colors. The stadium bleachers are painted with an identical bright green color. At the south end of the football field a huge red and white scoreboard proclaims that Dr. Pepper is delicious and refreshing. The numbers 10, 2 and 4 are vastly enlarged.

Buckaroo Stadium has two separate dressing buildings—one for the home team and one for visiting teams. The visitor's facility is on the opposite side of the playing field from the spot where Murphy parks the bus.

Without even the slightest protest, our players shoulder their gear and grimly begin the laborious trek across the playing field to the visiting team's dressing facility. The mood of coaches and players is strangely quiet.

Friday Night
August 30, 1949

DEAN ELDER, BUDDY HAMRICK AND GILBERT THOMP-SON, our three senior captains, convene with the Buckaroo captains and game officials on the fifty yard line. Despite the hot, dry summer, the grass on the Breckenridge playing surface is green and plush, very much like our Ranger field. Tonight the football stadium is jammed full, filled to capacity with loud and vocal supporters from both cities. This may only be a practice game, but the excited fans don't seem to care.

Both teams and their coaches stand at attention, like sentinels, along the sidelines while the Buckaroo band plays the National Anthem and a local Methodist minister prays for good sportsmanship and for the players' safety. Taking turns, the two school bands play their school songs—first Ranger, then Breckenridge. Many avid fans from both cities wipe tears from their eyes after proudly singing the words.

Out at mid-field the game officials signal we have won the toss. We elect to receive the kickoff. Breckenridge chooses to take advantage of a slight southerly breeze and defend the south goal.

Elder, Hamrick and Thompson come running back to our sideline.

"Coach, their captains wouldn't shake hands. Said they're gonna kick our butts," Elder reports to me in a concerned voice.

"Yeah, Coach. They said they were gonna kick our butts up between our shoulder blades. If they keep talking nasty like that, I think I may get mad at them," adds Thompson.

"You guys shouldn't pay attention to anything that was said out there. Let's play smart defense and execute our offense, the way we've been practicing. I've never heard of a football game being won with words," I tell my three captains, offering them consolation, but wondering why the Breckenridge coach would put his captains up to such uncalled for and unsportsmanlike tactics.

Our kicking team flocks around me. Anticipating the kickoff, fans rise to their feet. The noise from the stands intensifies to a deafening roar. The two school bands take turns, alternately blaring out their loud fight songs, each trying to outdo the other.

"We'll return the kickoff to the left side. Remember your blocking assignments, the way we practiced. Now get out there and make your daddies proud of you."

Breckenridge's place kicker booms the ball to our five yard line where Billy Simpson, our deep halfback, waits to receive. Our blockers set up a wall along the left side. Simpson is brought down hard at our thirty-six.

Our offensive unit charges onto the field. Before the game we selected the plays we would call in this first offensive series. Our first play will be twenty-three, option left.

Keith Murphy comes over and puts a hand on my shoulder. "Stubby, you seen the size of that kid playing opposite Patterson?"

Downfield, I can see the back of a tall green jersey–number 66. The player is Breckenridge's version of our Alfred Steele. He's at least eight inches taller and outweighs our left guard Jim Patterson by probably fifty pounds.

Our first offensive play is to the left. When the ball is snapped, the giant Breckenridge player knocks Patterson into our quarterback for a three yard loss.

"We gotta get somebody in there who can block that big S.O.B., or he'll be in our backfield all night long," Murphy yells to me.

Our next play is to the right side. Jones fakes to our fullback Dorsey, waits until the defensive end commits to the inside, then pitches out to our right halfback Hamrick. Glancing upfield before he has control, Hamrick takes his eyes off the football. Fortunately, we recover for a seven yard loss.

Our third play is to the left side. Again the big number 66 is in our backfield before Jones can handoff. Four yard loss.

"Jensen, get ready," I cry out. "We need a long one, son."

"Yes sir. I'll do my best." I hear from the bench behind me.

Thompson's snap to Jensen is a perfect spiral. Frankie catches the ball cleanly and steps forward to punt. The football careens off the side of his right foot, meandering out of bounds at our thirty-six yard line.

Three running plays topped with a fourteen yard punt; we relinquish the football at the same spot we began our offensive series.

Frankie Jensen runs off the field crying, "I'm sorry. I'm sorry, Coach. I don't know what I did wrong."

"Alright, Frankie, don't worry about it. Get yourself a drink of water. Next time you'll do better."

I grab Jim Patterson by the shoulder pads as he comes off the field. I jerk him around to face me. "Patterson, can you block that big guy, or not?"

Tears well up in Patterson's eyes. "Coach Warden, he's a lot bigger than me."

"Patterson, if you wanna stay in this game, you'd better figure out some way to stop him. I don't care if you have to hold him, tackle him or trip him. You keep him out of our backfield. Do you hear me?"

"Yes sir. Lemme stay in the game, Coach. I promise he won't get by me again."

"Good. I'll talk with Coach Murphy. Maybe we can get Thompson or Hummel to give you some help."

The Breckenridge squad operates from a double wing power formation. On their first play their fullback carries the ball over right guard for four yards. Fighting off three green and white blockers, Alfred Steele makes the tackle.

Sam comes racing down the sideline toward me. "Stubby, did you see that? They got three men blocking on Steele. How could they have figured out about him already? Their coaches must be reading our mail."

Hut. Hut. Breckenridge's quarterback keeps the football, using a power play around right end. With his fullback, halfback and a pulling right guard leading the way, the Buckaroo quarterback gains seven yards and a first down at our twenty-five.

Breckenridge's offense is designed to systematically wear down their opponent's defense with hard, tough power running. In five running plays the Buckaroos score on a power sweep around left end. Three blockers lead the play, leaving our defenders, Charles Williams and Billy Watson, lying on their backsides. The extra point kick is good.

While the officials spot the football for the Breckenridge kickoff, our receiving team huddles again at the sideline. We decide to return the ball down the left side again, sticking with what worked for us earlier.

Our halfback Simpson fields the kickoff. He reaches the thirty-two before being knocked out of bounds.

While the receiving team comes off the field, I confer with my quarterback Reed Jones.

"Reed, let's try number thirty-one. Use a direct handoff to the fullback on the first two plays. On the third play I wanna run twenty-one, option left. Tell Thompson and Hummel to alternate helping Patterson double team that big fellow, number sixty-six. You understand what I want?"

"Sure, Coach. You want me to call thirty-one for two plays. Then run twenty-one, option left. You want Thompson and Hummel to take turns helping Patterson block their number sixty-six."

Jones is a smart quarterback. Damn, I wish he was quicker.

Searching among my players on the bench, I spot the red head I want. "Phillips, get up here!"

Partially because I promised Eddie's mother I would get him some playing time, but mainly because I can't take a chance on Joel Dorsey handling the football, I decide to sub Eddie Phillips for this next series. Eddie is only medium size, but he is tough and chunky. He runs low and hard, making him difficult to bring down.

Phillips runs up to stand next to me. "Eddie, you'll be carrying the ball on the next two plays. I want you to run directly at the number one hole. I want you to run harder than you've ever run in any practice. You keep both legs churning until you're tackled and lying on the ground. Hold the ball tightly with both hands so you don't fumble. You got all that?"

"Yes sir. I understand." I slap his bottom as he runs away toward our huddle.

Hut. Hut. Hut. Jones hands the ball to Phillips who smashes hard against the backs of his blockers, pushing them forward for a six yard gain. Patterson and Hummel shout angrily at the young fullback as they get up and return to the huddle. Phillips points toward me at the sidelines, probably explaining why he ran up the backs of his two teammates.

Hut. Hut. Jones hands to Phillips who dives up the middle for a three yard gain.

On third down Jones thrusts the football into Phillips' mid-section then withdraws it, a split-second before Phillips hurls himself into the line. With the defensive end committing to defend against a pitchout, Jones runs inside the end for a nine yard gain.

Substituting Joel Dorsey back in for Phillips, I instruct him to tell the quarterback to run the option to the right side.

Two option plays to the right net us a total of eight yards. Our situation is third and two.

The field judge calls timeout. He runs to the line of scrimmage and begins an emotional discussion with the Buckaroo defender, number sixty-six. A moment later the referee signals to the Breckenridge bench, requesting assistance for the oversized player who is limping badly.

While the big Buckaroo is being assisted from the playing field, the referee grabs Jim Patterson by the collar and pulls him across the field to our bench.

"Coach, this player is being ejected. He's not to return to the game."

"Why? What did he do?" I ask.

"He bit the Breckenridge player, number sixty-six, on the leg."

"He did what?" I ask again, not believing his words.

"The Breckenridge player's leg is bleeding pretty badly. It appears he will be unable to return to the game. Your team will be penalized fifteen yards for unsportsmanlike conduct."

Since the infraction occurred after the play, we also lose the down. While the officials step off the penalty, I walk over to speak with Patterson who is kneeling on the ground beside Coach Murphy.

"Jimmy, whatever possessed you to bite their player?"

Patterson gazes up at me. His face is smudged and dirty. Several long red scratches are etched across his forehead. A trickle of blood flows from his busted lip. "Coach, he kept stepping on me and kicking me on every play. When he slugged me in the face, I made up my mind to get even. After that last play we were both laying there in the grass, and there was his bare leg, right by my mouth. So I bit it, as hard as I could. I'm sorry I got us a penalty."

"Alright, Jimmy, I guess I understand. Find yourself a seat on the bench. You be our water guy for the rest of the game. Meantime, I want you to study the Breckenridge defense. Maybe you can help us find a weakness somewhere."

After Patterson leaves the sideline, Murphy moves in close to me and whispers, "He's a vindictive little devil, ain't he?"

I can't help smiling as I turn back to watch the game. Our third down play gained four yards. We'll be forced to punt.

With anxious words of encouragement, we send Frankie Jensen in to punt again. This time his punt is for almost sixty yards–twenty yards up, twenty yards down but only nineteen yards downfield. We tackle their receiver immediately after he catches the football. Breckenridge has the ball, first and ten, at their own thirty-six.

Breckenridge moves the football methodically in chunks of four and five yards until they're inside our twenty yard line. Expecting them to continue their hard-running ground game, Sam signals our defense to switch into a 7-3-1–seven linemen, three linebackers with one safety.

Hut. Hut. Their tailback takes the snap, fakes the ball to his halfback, then fires a perfect pass to a green-clad wingback cutting across the wide open expanse between our safety Cunningham and our linebackers who have cheated up, expecting a run. Touchdown. Their extra point try is good.

Sam slams his clipboard to the ground in frustration. With fiery eyes he turns to me. "Stubby, I'm telling you. Somehow they know our signals. They're anticipating every defensive move we make. Somebody over there knew I was changing to a seven-three-one."

Breckenridge kicks off again. Hamrick receives the ball and returns up the left side of the field to our thirty-eight.

With their mammoth number sixty-six out of the game and with Dean Sutton substituting for Patterson at left guard, our offensive team begins to function efficiently. Jones executes the quarterback option beautifully, with a pitchout to Hamrick around the right side. On two option plays to the left with Jones keeping the ball each time, we net twelve yards and a first down. Another option play to the right gains six yards. The quarter ends before we can line up for the next play:

Breckenridge   14   Ranger   0

While the two teams are swapping ends of the field, Max Wade, a reserve defensive tackle, taps me on the shoulder. "Coach Warden, Mister Jensen is waiting down there at the other end of the bench. He wants to talk with you."

Jensen waves his arms to get my attention. Puzzled by his presence at our bench and wondering why my punter's father would intrude while the game is in progress, I leave the sideline to find out what he wants. "C.D., you shouldn't be down on the field. You could get us penalized. And besides, you could get hurt."

"Coach Warden, you gotta take off Frankie's shoes."

For an instant I don't understand what he means, then I realize what he's trying to tell me. "C.D., do you mean you want Frankie to kick barefooted?"

"Yes, he can't kick wearing shoes. He needs to remove his shoes before he kicks."

I remember seeing Frankie barefooted, that afternoon I first watched him punting in the pick-up rugby game. It never occurred to me he wouldn't kick just as well wearing football shoes.

"But, C.D., aren't you worried about Frankie getting hurt? Someone's likely to step on his bare feet."

The seething emotion in Jensen's reddened face causes the white to expand around his eyes. His mouth quivers as he speaks, "You wanna lose this game, Coach Warden? If Frankie doesn't start kicking better, those Breckenridge kids are gonna whip our boys."

"Alright, C.D., calm down. Next time we need to punt, I'll have Frankie try kicking barefooted. You should get back in the stands before one of the officials notices you."

OUR DRIVE TOWARD the Breckenridge goal line continues. A pitchout to Simpson gains five yards and a first down. Hamrick runs eight yards to put the football on the Breckenridge thirty-one.

After a missed handoff goes for no gain, I signal for a timeout. Jones trots over to the sideline while Patterson hustles water out to the players huddled on the field.

"Reed, their halfbacks are moving up to defend against our running game. You think you could improvise a halfback option pass, like the one you and Hamrick tried last year?"

"You mean an option pass, out of a 'Straight Tee' formation?"

"Yes, that's exactly what I want. Pitchout to Hamrick. Let him decide to run or pass. Make sure all our linemen know to stay behind the line of scrimmage."

"Okay, Coach, I understand. You wanna give the play a number?"

"Let's see if it works first. Then we'll decide whether it deserves a number. Now, get back out there. We need to score on this drive."

The referee whistles for time to begin as our team breaks from their huddle.

Hut. Hut. Jones fakes the ball to Dorsey, then moves along behind our line. Jones holds the football until the Breckenridge defensive end gives up on his outside coverage and starts in to make the tackle.

"Lateral the ball!" Murphy screams.

A thunderous popping noise echoes across the field as Jones collides with the Buckaroo defensive end. Somehow, the football emerges to float softly on a low arch to Hamrick. Hamrick tucks the ball under his arm and dashes toward the sideline. Breckenridge's halfback and a linebacker race up to intercept him. Hamrick skids to a stop only a few inches behind the line of scrimmage and launches a long pass, deep into the end zone where our tall right end Ralph Rogers is waiting, all alone. Touchdown. Will Brownlee kicks our extra point.

Breckenridge   14   Ranger   7

Brownlee's kickoff sails to the five. The ball hits the ground and rolls into the end zone. Breckenridge takes a touchback, electing not to run the ball out.

Our defense stiffens. Two power running plays net the Buckaroos only three yards. On third down Alfred brushes away three men blocking on him and meets the Breckenridge tailback head-on at the line of scrimmage. The game officials call time to allow the dazed tailback to be carried from the field.

The Breckenridge punt is short. Hamrick returns the ball to the Buckaroo forty-two.

Hut. Hut. Following behind the fierce blocking of Stiles and Hummel, Jones runs for eight yards. A pitchout to Simpson, an option-keeper by Jones, a pitchout to Hamrick, another pitchout to Simpson and another run by Jones—in five plays we make two first downs.

With the football spotted on the Buckaroo sixteen, I substitute Phillips for Dorsey. I decide to try a similar direct handoff to the fullback again, only this time we'll try the right side, behind Thompson, Grey and Elder.

Taking the handoff, Phillips smashes through the line and past the green-clad linebackers. At the five, Eddie viciously runs over the last Buckaroo defender. Touchdown. Brownlee's extra point try is good.

Breckenridge   14   Ranger   14

A SMALL, FRAIL MAN stands, waiting impatiently, at the end of our bench. The man is impeccably dressed, wearing a crisply pleated, maroon and white band uniform, complete with a bleached-white captain's cap. The man is visually irritated and upset. His dark black, neatly trimmed mustache accentuates the intense anger in his beet red face. His fiery eyes glare at me through thick glasses.

Murphy speaks first, "Oh, Good Lord Almighty, we're in for it! Jensen ain't dressed to march with the band!"

The Ranger band has taken the field, assembling under the south goal in preparation for their halftime performance. Frankie Jensen leaps from the bench and sprints in the direction of the visitor's dressing facility. With the distraction of our touchdown drive not one of the coaches or players, including Frankie, remembered my promise to have him in uniform and ready to march at halftime.

There's nothing I can do except to step forward and take the forthcoming verbal lashing from the band director who hates football coaches.

"Where is my drummer, Coach Warden?" The band director's voice is simmering with anger.

"Mister Gans, please accept my apologies. We'll get him dressed and ready to march with you as quickly as possible."

"That is not good enough, Coach Warden! I want my drummer, and I want him right now! The band cannot perform properly without all our drummers!"

"Mister Gans, I'm truly sorry, but we were driving for a touchdown. The time just got away from us."

"Coach Warden, you don't seem to understand. All these people have come to watch our band perform. Protocol requires the visiting band march first. Now everyone must wait, while my number one drummer changes out of an absurd football uniform. It is humiliating to me. It is humiliating to the entire band." The band director sounds as if he's about to cry.

"Please forgive us, Mister Gans. I can promise you; it won't happen again."

The band director's voice changes to rage. "You can damn well bet your mother's combat boots on that, Coach! What you're doing with one of my band members is illegal and in violation of school rules! I intend to report your actions to the school superintendent!"

"You certainly have that prerogative, Mister Band Director. I was hoping we might work this out among ourselves."

"No way, José!" Gans smarts back to me, before he turns and storms away, throwing up his hands to show his total disgust.

Breckenridge returns our kickoff to the twenty-five. A long Breckenridge drive, consisting entirely of running plays and short gains of three and four yards, eats up the clock. With the football at our eighteen yard line and the Breckenridge quarterback frantically trying to call timeout, the first half ends.

OUR EXHAUSTED PLAYERS line the walls of the visitor's building. Acrid smells of sweat and sounds of heavy breathing fill the room.

Each player finds an unoccupied spot and drops to rest on the floor.

Keith Murphy has helped Champ Pearson, a senior defensive end, remove his sweat-soaked jersey. Murphy and Pearson are engaged in some kind of emergency repair to Pearson's shoulder pads.

Sam strolls slowly around the room, suspiciously inspecting the walls and ceiling of the dressing room. Putting a finger to his lips, Sam motions for me to follow him outside. We meet on the concrete walk near the front door.

"Stubby, I'm convinced they've got a bug in the visitor's locker room."

"Come on, Sam. Don't be paranoid," I laugh.

"This is no joke, Stubby. Those bastards know our defensive signals, and they knew about Steele's position at middle linebacker. They had to been listening when I went through our signals with the defense before the game."

"You got any idea what we can do about it? I don't think it'll do much good to complain to the management."

"You're right about that, Stubby, but we might use it to our advantage later in the game. Lemme see what I can come up with. Meanwhile, watch what you say inside the dressing room. I'll clue Murphy in on our little discovery."

———————

WHEN WE FILE BACK ONTO the field, the crowd noise is even louder than at the beginning of the game. Murphy reports that the fans really got riled up during halftime activities. They were cheering and booing the bands while they marched.

Breckenridge has their choice of kicking or receiving to begin the second half. They elect to receive.

Will Brownlee's kickoff is returned to the Breckenridge twenty-eight. Two running plays and an offside penalty against our defense give the Buckaroos a first down at their forty-one.

Frankie Jensen steps up to my side. He is dressed in full football uniform. "Coach, I wanna check in with you. I'm awfully sorry about the problem with Mister Gans. I should've been dressed and ready to march. My dad and I explained to him that the delay was not your fault."

"Frankie, are you sure you want to be here with the football team? The band director sounds like he plans to cause a big stink about your playing with us. It could hurt you with the band. I wouldn't want that to happen."

"Coach, if Mister Gans wants to make a big deal out of my kicking for the football team, we'll fix his goose. My dad is good friends with everyone who's got any say about things in Ranger. Right now, my dad just wants me to help our team win this game."

"Alright, Frankie. I'm sure you'll get another chance to punt. Did your dad mention anything about your kicking without a shoe?"

"Yes sir. I should've told you. I kick better barefooted."

"Find yourself a seat on the bench. You be ready to kick when we need you," I say, making a mental note to remember about Frankie's dad being good friends with everyone who has influence in Ranger.

Breckenridge has driven down to our twenty-four, grinding out their yardage with a savage ground attack, running alternately over Yung and Davenport, our defensive tackles. A power sweep around left end gains another six. I signal E.P. Robinson, our defensive captain, to call time-out.

Sam and I huddle with Robinson on the sidelines. "You got an idea how we can stop this drive, Coach Aills?" I inquire.

Sam winks at his defensive captain. "Yeah, we got somethin' up our sleeve, but we're gonna save it for later in the game. Right, E.P.?"

"Right, Coach Aills." Robinson smiles, displaying his pleasure at being included in Aills' secret plan.

"Let's try a 6-3-2 defense. Tell McKinney and Cunningham to watch their wingbacks for a pass. Make sure our defensive ends hold their wingbacks at the line of scrimmage."

"Okay, Coach. 6-3-2. Watch the wingbacks for a pass. Hold the wingbacks up at the line," Robinson repeats to us.

The defensive change works successfully. We stop them for no gain, but an offside penalty against us gives Breckenridge a first down at the thirteen.

On the next play the Buckaroos attempt their first pass of the second half. Our linebackers begin to scream, "Pass! Pass!" even before a green-shirted wingback breaks past Champ Pearson and sprints up the right sideline. Breckenridge's quarterback drifts back then floats a pass toward the corner of the end zone. The Buckaroo wingback and the football meet at the three yard line, a split-second before Billy McKinney and E.P. Robinson arrive. The ensuing collision results in the wingback, McKinney and Robinson sliding head first out of bounds while the football rolls into the end zone. Our defensive safety Cunningham falls on the football.

The officials huddle at the sideline. Screaming and shouting, the fans of both teams are on their feet. The Buckaroo band strikes up and begins to play loudly. Finally reaching a decision, the head referee steps away from the other officials. He signals pass interference against Ranger and spots the ball on the three yard line. Buckaroos have possession, first and goal.

"No way!" Sam shouts furiously. "The ball was there before we touched him! If it wasn't a fumble, it had to be an incomplete pass. No way that's the right call."

Our Ranger fans agree. Yells from the visitor's side of the field become even louder and more obscene. Breckenridge scores with a run over left tackle. Their extra point try is good.

Breckenridge   21   Ranger   14

HAMRICK FIELDS THE KICKOFF and returns to the thirty-two. A holding penalty against us moves the ball back to our seventeen.

When Breckenridge's defense takes the field following the kickoff, their big number sixty-six player lines up opposite Sutton, our left guard. A large white bandage is taped to the right leg of the gigantic Buckaroo. He moves with a slight limp.

On three running plays we gain a total of five yards. The huge Breckenridge player is in our backfield on every play.

"Jensen, you ready to punt? Get in there."

Jensen dashes onto the field to join our huddle. His white bare feet contrast conspicuously against the dark green grass.

Murphy chuckles at the sight of our shoeless punter. "If he stays with the team, we need to get him a pair of sneakers to wear when goes on and off the field. That DeLeon field we play on in two weeks is full of sticker burrs."

Thompson's snap is high. Jensen leaps to catch the football. Then, taking two quick steps, he sends the ball sailing high over the head of Breckenridge's deepest receiver. The football dies at the Buckaroo fourteen yard line, fifty-two yards in the air and rolling twelve yards on the ground before it stops. Jensen pauses to excitedly wave at his mom and dad sitting in the stands on his trip back to the bench.

Neither team is able to move the football until midway through the fourth quarter. Breckenridge runs three plays and punts. We run three plays and kick. Jensen's long punts keep Breckenridge backed up deep in their own territory.

Not more than six minutes remain on the clock when I substitute Hamrick for Jones at quarterback, sending Jimmy Comacho into the game for Hamrick at right halfback. Hamrick's quickness yields immediate results. A keeper over left tackle gains eight yards. A pitchout to Comacho gains another twelve, giving us a first down at our forty-six.

A ferocious fight breaks out near the line of scrimmage between Dean Sutton and the big Breckenridge player. Two game officials attempt to break up the fight, but Sutton refuses to quit. He knocks the huge Buckaroo to the ground then jumps on him and keeps slugging away. Three of his Bulldog teammates are required to pull Sutton aside.

Sutton is still in a fighting mood when he arrives at the sideline.

"Coach Warden, somebody needs to get that number sixty-six. If you'll lemme go back in, I'll break his face up."

"What was the fight about, Dean?" I ask, already knowing the answer. Murphy's been screaming at the officials, trying to influence them to penalize the big player for his dirty tactics.

"Coach, he either slugs me or kicks me on every play. He keeps saying he knows some things about my mother. I ain't gonna take no more of his crap. Lemme go back in, Coach. Lemme have another piece of him." Sutton is close to hysteria as he talks.

"Dean, you calm down. Let's see what the officials have decided."

The officials have been in conference at the middle of the field since the fight ended Their huddle breaks up. A single official runs to each sideline.

"Ranger, your player, number thirty-seven, has been ejected from the game for fighting. Breckenridge's player, number sixty-six, is also being ejected. Penalties for unnecessary roughness against each team are offsetting. However, two additional fifteen yard penalties will be assessed against your team, because your player refused to stop fighting after the whistle blew and flags were thrown."

"What? Thirty yards in penalties for fighting? There's no such rule in the book. You zebra people have lost your minds," I shout at the official.

"Coach, that is the decision of the officials. I warn you to control yourself, or additional penalties may be called against your team."

Total bedlam envelopes the Ranger side of the stadium after the officials signal the infractions and step off the penalty yardage against us. Breckenridge fans stand and applaud. The Breckenridge band begins to play a fight song while their cheerleaders do cartwheels along the sidelines.

Murphy steps up next to me. He coughs and spits at the ground in front of us. "Stubby, we're about outta guards. Reckon Alfred can play offense?"

"If you're serious, that's not a bad idea. But let's use Hargrave for the time being. He needs some playing time."

With the loss of down we have the ball on our own twenty, second and thirty-six. Simpson loses control of the football on a pitchout but recovers for a five yard loss. Our third down play is stopped for no gain.

With Jensen in to punt, the snap from center is high again. Frankie is forced to stretch high to catch the ball. Breckenridge's defensive end, charging in from the right side, gets a hand on the football as it leaves Jensen's foot.

The ball lisps blandly, traveling end over end to the thirty-three yard line. A green defender catches the ball in the air and returns to our twenty-two before Stiles and Kenneth Williams can bring him down.

Breckenridge fans display their jubilation–yelling, screaming and stomping their feet. The Buckaroo band begins to play again. Our Ranger bleachers have become deathly silent.

A dive play over center gains three yards. While the Breckenridge team huddles, Sam steps out onto the field and signals for the defense to switch into a 7-3-1 formation.

"Sam, they burned us on that defense in the first half. Don't you remember?" shouts Murphy.

"Yeah, I remember. Don't think I'll ever forget it, not for a long, long time," Sam answers back.

When the ball is centered directly to the Buckaroo tailback, all three of our Bulldog linebackers stand straight up, raising their hands high over their heads. Charles Williams and Champ Pearson, our defensive ends, disregard their responsibilities to defend against an outside run and charge straight into the Breckenridge backfield. The Buckaroo tailback shifts about laterally, looking for his wingback who is slanting across the middle behind our linebackers.

Only a half-second before Pearson and Charles Williams sandwich him in a brutal tackle, the tailback steps forward to throw his pass. The pass floats in a partial spiral into the undefended open area behind our linebackers.

As the Buckaroo wingback slows to wait for the pass, a maroon jersey dashes in front of him to intercept the football. Weldon Cunningham grabs the football, darts to the east side of the field and streaks up the sidelines. After a long chase the Buckaroo fullback catches Cunningham, knocking him out of bounds at Breckenridge's five yard line.

Sam hops up and down, acting like a happy kangaroo. "I knew it would work! I knew it would work! Take that, you dirty, cheatin' bastards!"

Our offense huddles around me while the officials bring up the chains and spot the ball.

"Jones, you go back in at quarterback. Phillips, go in at fullback. Thompson and Elder, listen up. Alfred will be going in for Grey at right guard. He hasn't played that position before. Give him some help. We'll run our fullback over right guard, twice. If we haven't scored, call timeout, and we'll try something else. No offsides or holding, now. We don't want any penalties. Alright, go!"

Our first play nets three yards. Phillips scores on the second try. He goes in standing up, as Thompson, Elder and Steele drive the Breckenridge defenders into the back part of the end zone.

Less than a minute remains when we line up for the extra point try. Thompson's snap hits the ground, bouncing before it reaches Hamrick, the holder. Hamrick scrambles madly, trying to get the ball into position to kick. A green Buckaroo dives at the ball as Will Brownlee's foot connects. The kick veers wide to the left.

Breckenridge 21   Ranger 20

OUR BULLDOG BENCH is stunned. Ranger fans stand quietly with mouths agape. Our cheerleaders, who were excitedly screaming only seconds ago, place their hands against their faces in shocked silence. Meanwhile, the Breckenridge bench and fans are enthralled in wild celebration.

"Damn, damn and holy damn! We had 'em, Stubby. How could we lose after we played so well?"

"I suppose that's football, Sam. Sometimes you lose no matter how hard you play." I feel sick. My stomach is churning. If the game doesn't end soon, I'll probably vomit right there behind the bench.

Showing his frustration, Will Brownlee booms his kickoff into the Breckenridge end zone. The ball is brought out to the twenty.

"All they gotta do is run out the clock. There's only forty seconds left," Murphy observes to no one in particular.

Sam ambles over to join me on the bench. He sighs heavily, plopping down dejectedly beside me, his head lowered.

Hut. Hut. The ball is centered to the Buckaroo quarterback who makes an incredible decision. Instead of dropping down on one knee to kill the clock, he charges into the center of the line where he is met viciously by an unblocked Alfred Steele. The football squirts backward past a surprised tailback who kicks the ball on further toward the Breckenridge goal when he attempts to recover.

A huge pile-up develops at the nine yard line. Game officials dig through the mass of bodies trying to find the football.

After a short conference the officials signal–Ranger's ball, first and goal.

Three Bulldog coaches jump to their feet to stand aghast at the sideline, absolutely dumbfounded by this unexpected turn of events.

"What play you wanna run, Coach?" asks Reed Jones. My mind is in a maze. Not a single play comes to my mind. The scoreboard clock indicates we have less than twenty seconds to score.

"Whatta you think we should run, Reed?" I hear myself ask.

"Coach, we only got one timeout left. We can try Hamrick on the option pass. If our receiver can't get open, Buddy can run out of bounds and stop the clock."

"Good idea. That's what we'll do then. Alfred, you go back in at guard. Just block straight ahead. Give Jones time to make the pitchout. You linemen, stay home. Don't get across the line of scrimmage until after you see Hamrick throw the pass."

Glancing down the sideline, I see Sam and Murphy crouched together, each man resting on one knee. Their mouths are tightly shut. Their faces bear worried expressions. Every Ranger fan is on their feet–cheering, urging their team to victory. Drummers in the band begin to beat to a fast rhythm. The cheerleaders cheer passionately, "Go Bulldogs! Go Bulldogs! Go!"

Hut. Hut. Jones takes the ball from the center, moves along behind the line to draw in the defensive end, then pitches out to his halfback. Taking the pitchout, Hamrick looks downfield, faking a pass. When he sees Breckenridge has stacked the end zone with defenders, he tucks the ball and runs the ball out of bounds on the four.

"We're close enough to kick a field goal, Stubby! Brownlee can easily hit one from there!" Murphy shouts to me above the wild noise of the visiting crowd.

Hamrick ran out of bounds on the right side of the field. With the football this close to the goal line and only fifteen yards in from the sideline, the angle will make it extremely difficult to kick a field goal. A vision of the bad snap on our last extra point try sticks in my mind.

"Let's do it! Let's go with what works! Phillips, go in for Dorsey. If you don't score, son, you'd better jump up and keep on running. I'll be right behind you, because this Ranger crowd is liable to hang the both of us from the goal posts if we mess this up."

Seeing Phillips enter the game, Breckenridge knows exactly what to expect. They set up an eight man line with three linebackers bunched in tightly between the tackles.

Hut. Hut. Hut. Jones takes the snap and hands off to Phillips. Thompson, Steele and Elder surge forward, pushing the charging Breckenridge defenders backward.

Phillips' body momentarily disappears into a sea of green and maroon humanity, then with Alfred Steele leading his way, he emerges on the opposite side of the mound of players. The back of Alfred's maroon jersey is clutched tightly in Eddie's left hand.

Ranger fans cascade onto the football field after the score to celebrate their team's victory. The game officials make no attempt to clear the field for an extra point try. For a few minutes the scoreboard at the end of the field displays the final score:

BRECKENRIDGE 21 VISITOR 26

Then someone turns off the scoreboard lights.

TOTAL EXHAUSTION ENGULFS MY BODY as I sit on the bench watching Sam and Murphy gather up our equipment. My emotional high has drained away. Yelps and screams emit from the visitor's dressing room. Our team is celebrating in the showers before they dress for the bus ride home.

Somehow, I had expected to greatly savor my first win as a head football coach, but the only feeling I can identify at this particular moment is one of overwhelming relief.

Coach Norton once told me, when I congratulated him for a win after one of our Texas A&M games, "Coaches lose games. Only a team can win." At the time I neither understood nor appreciated his profound wisdom.

The exhilaration of the game takes its toll on both players and coaches. The bus is abnormally quiet during the trip back to Ranger. Alfred and I finally reach home sometime around two o'clock. We are both dog tired.

Saturday Morning
August 31, 1949

PRICE MEETS ME AT THE FRONT door of the Pontiac House. He is beaming like a proud father. He shakes my hand warmly.

"Stubby, congratulations. That was a terrific game last night. Were you surprised when we won?"

"No one could've been more surprised than me, Price. I thought we'd lost it for sure."

"Well, you deserve some good luck. You still planning on driving

JOHN CARVER

to Comanche this morning?"

"It all depends on what Juanita has to say when I call her. I was hoping to use the telephone in your office. I'm a little short on funds."

"You know you can, Stubby. You know where the phone is. Make yourself at home. Talk for as long as you want. I need to check with the shop mechanic to find out when the Killingsworth's car will be ready. I'll see you before you leave."

"NUMBER, PLEASE?" the operator requests.

"Operator, I want to place a person-to-person call to Comanche, Texas." This call is on Price's nickel. Besides, on a Saturday morning, there's a chance Juanita might not be at home. I certainly wouldn't want to have her father answer. He would hang up on me.

"May I have the name and number of the person you are calling?"

"Yes, Operator. The number is 969. I want to speak with Mrs. Juanita Warden."

"Hold the line please while I ring."

The line clicks several times. The phone rings on the other end.

"Kimbrough residence," a voice answers. It sounds like Juanita.

"I have a person-to-person call for a Mrs. Juanita Warden. Will you accept the call please?"

"This is Juanita Warden. Please put the call through." I hear Juanita answer.

"Juanita, this is Stubby."

"Hello, darling. I've been waiting on your call. We've already heard all about your game last night. Aunt Phyliss called this morning to give us a play by play account."

"Yes, it was quite a game. It's still difficult for me to believe we actually won. We were bagging the team's equipment, getting ready to leave with our tails between our legs when we recovered their fumble and made that last score."

Juanita quickly changes the subject. "Darling, we're having a terrible time with Dad. When Mother mentioned you might come to see me, he threw a hissing fit. I'm afraid you can't come to the house."

"Juanita, I really need to see you. Is there some place we could

112

meet? We need to talk, face to face."

"I want to see you too, darling. The doctor has ordered me not to drive so I can't meet you in town. Maybe, if you'll drive up the front driveway, I could watch for you and come out to your car."

"Whatever you say, Juanita. I just want to see you today."

"It's ten-thirty now. Can you be here by noon?"

"Yes."

"Alright, darling. That'll be our plan. Drive up the front driveway exactly at twelve o'clock. Please don't honk or make any noise Daddy might hear. I'll come out to meet you."

"You be waiting, Juanita. I'll be there at twelve o'clock sharp. Bye now."

"Goodbye, sweetheart," she says.

THE KIMBROUGH RANCH is about a mile beyond the northern city limits of Comanche, off State Highway 36. A long, narrow lane leads from the highway up to the Kimbrough residence. The roadway is partially paved with limestone gravel. A white wooden fence borders each side of the lane all the way from the highway up to the ranch house.

The ranch house is a large two-story wood structure. A covered wooden porch, surrounded by a three-foot high, wood banister wall, wraps partially around the front and east sides. Suspended on metal chains attached to the porch ceiling, a wooden swing sways gently in the soft summer breeze. The exterior walls are covered with white ship-lap wood siding. Each window is trimmed with louvered wooden storm shutters. The storm shutters and the wood trim around the windows are painted a dark green.

Both the house and yard are immaculately well-kept. A short, white picket fence separates the yard grass from the graveled parking area in front of the house. Flowering rose bushes and small plants line the inside of the fence.

Resting on a high hill, the ranch house commands a magnificent view, overlooking a significant portion of Comanche County. A huge red barn and barnyard surrounded with white wooden fences are situated about a hundred yards east of the house. The rear of the house overlooks the Kimbrough ranch. Cattle graze in grassy meadows, which are crossed-fenced with barbed wire. Enormous fields of red maize and green corn, almost ready for harvest, can be seen in the rich bottom land along the creek which runs through the ranch.

Creeping the Hudson quietly up the gravel entry way to avoid detection, I feel like a sneak thief entering some forbidden region. When I reach the parking section in front of the house, I shut off the motor and wait in silence. After a moment, Juanita emerges through the front screen door. She carefully closes the screen door, then steps quickly across the porch. A swift run to the car and she is in the front seat–her lips pressed against mine.

"Darling, we need to leave before Daddy or one of the ranch hands sees us. Can we go somewhere?" she asks, when our mouths finally part.

Without a word I start the Hudson and drive slowly, and as quietly as possible, back to the highway.

"Stubby darling, there's a roadside park about three miles north toward Rising Star. The park is shaded by a large pecan tree. We can go there," Juanita advises.

Parked beneath the shade of the giant pecan and next to a road-side picnic table, we neck like two aroused teenagers. Juanita is a desirable woman, even in her eighth month of pregnancy.

"Oh, Stubby, I love to kiss your mouth. You taste so wonderful. I've missed you more than you'll ever know," she tells me lovingly.

"Juanita, I want you to come back to Ranger with me. I can't go on living without you near me."

"Sweetheart, we'll be together soon. I promise. It won't be long."

"Juanita, please come with me today. You can have our baby in Ranger. I'll make everything work. We can be together," I plead to her.

Juanita's eyes fill with tears. She scoots up in the car seat and begins to unbutton the front of her thin cotton dress. As the buttons are undone, her braless breasts are exposed, then her bare, swollen stomach.

"Stubby, give me your hand," Juanita tenderly commands, reaching to take my left hand. She places the opened palm of my hand against her bare stomach.

"Do you feel something? Can you feel the baby inside me?"

A slight movement from inside her stomach bumps against my

hand. "Yes, I feel it. Is that our baby?"

"That is Baby Warden. He, or she, is almost ready to be born into our world. Stubby, you and I have a responsibility to make sure this child is born healthy and strong. You're so involved with your coaching job. Here in Comanche, I have my mother, my family and the same doctor who brought me into the world. Do you understand?"

"Of course, Juanita, it's just that I need you so much."

She wraps her arms around my neck, pulling my head down against her chest. "Sweetheart, you go back to Ranger and be the best football coach they have ever seen. I will stay here in Comanche and have you a beautiful, healthy baby. After the baby is born, I'll come back to live with you forever. You have my promise. I will never leave you, not ever again."

Tuesday Morning
September 3, 1949

THE SIZZLING SUMMER HEAT OUTSIDE is severely testing the ability of the two window units to cool the school superintendent's office. A neatly dressed secretary pecks diligently at a typewriter behind her receptionist desk. The secretary is dressed in a bright peach-colored dress with a large white collar, apparently purchased to wear on this, the first day of school. Several minutes pass before she stops typing to glance into G.C. Boswell's office.

"Coach Warden, I'm sure he'll be finished with his phone conversation in another moment or so. I'm so sorry you have to wait."

"I don't mind waiting. I didn't have an appointment, so he isn't expecting me."

In the excitement of being hired, football practice, and the game on Friday night, the superintendent and I never made the necessary arrangements to get me on the school payroll. My financial situation is close to the point of desperation. I was forced to borrow twenty bucks from Price to make the trip to Comanche on Saturday morning.

The secretary leaves her desk and steps to Boswell's office door. She says something inaudible to the superintendent then returns to the reception area.

"The superintendent can see you now, Coach Warden. Go right on in."

Boswell meets me at his door to shake my hand. As usual, he is dressed conservatively, wearing a dark business suit, white shirt and a red tie.

"Coach Warden, that was such an exciting game Friday night. I still can't believe we won. My throat is still hoarse from cheering so loudly."

"Yes, we were quite fortunate to have their quarterback make such an unbelievable error. Our young men competed very well. We wouldn't have been in position to take advantage of their fumble without our superb defensive play."

"Speaking of defense, Stubby. Whatta you plan to do about the Steele kid? Surely you don't intend to keep him on the team."

"No, I don't suppose I can. He'll be nineteen next Thursday, so he's probably played his last high school football game. G.C., is there any chance of getting him a job somewhere in the school system, maybe as a janitor or maintenance helper. He's a good kid, and he really needs some help."

"I don't know, Stubby. I suppose I could check around. We might find something."

"Thanks, G.C. Any job you can come up with would really be appreciated. Alfred's gonna live with me until I can get him situated."

Boswell leans back in his chair and clasps his hands against his chest. "If that's all you need, Coach Warden, I need to get back to work."

"No. Oh, no! I need to talk about getting paid. We discussed my salary, but I forgot to find out when I can get paid."

"Teacher paychecks are issued on the first and the fifteenth. Our first payday will be on Monday, September the sixteenth. You'll need to fill out a few forms so we can get your name and social security number on the payroll. Kathleen, my secretary, can get them for you on your way out."

The sixteenth! That's light years away for a person in my impoverished circumstances. Surely there's some other source of income I can tap into.

"G.C., what about the three hundred dollar bonus you promised for every game I win?"

"Oh, the bonus. Well, Stubby, the bonus applies to real games. The Breckenridge game Friday night was only a practice game. It doesn't count."

Boswell introduces me to his secretary Kathleen Earnest before I leave. She furnishes me with several school employment forms. I promise to fill them out and return them to her.

When I step outside, the smothering heat crushes in on me, adding to my depressed state of mind. I'm still a football coach who's never won a game—at least not one that counts.

CHAPTER SEVEN
THE WEEK FROM HELL

Tuesday Morning
September 3, 1949

MURPHY PROMISED TO MEET me in the field house at ten o'clock this morning. He has films of the Breckenridge game developed and ready for review. I'm anxious to examine in detail how we executed our offensive option plays. I'm running late. My unproductive meeting with Boswell and his secretary took longer than I expected. Hurriedly, I park the Hudson near the stadium entrance and rush beneath the bleachers toward the field house.

In the twilight-like darkness under the stands I never see the punch coming. The sharp pain of something rock hard hitting the side of my face is the last thing I remember. I awake with the rough gravel surface biting against my raw face.

"Ya reckon we killed the little squirt?" someone growls.

"Naw, he ain't dead yet. If I wanted ta kill 'em, I wouldda hit him real hard. Look, his eyes are open. I told ya. He ain't dead."

A big shoe kicks my ribs, taking my breath away. I try to raise up. Another hard fist hits me on the back of the head.

"You stay down there, Mister Smart Guy. We're here to deliver a message to ya."

Another shoe kicks me in the face. I black out again.

"Damnit, Clifford. Quit hittin' on him. This is takin' way too long. Let's give him the message and git," I hear, as I come around again.

"Oh, hell's fire. Why can't we never have any fun? It's gotta be business, business, business, all the time," the other voice complains.

"Listen up, Mister Smart Guy Coach. This here was just a little reminder, so you'll remember who runs things in this town. The big boss man don't want ya to go gittin' uppity cause ya won one lousy football game. Ya got that?"

Still trying to regain my senses, I don't answer quickly enough to suit the voice with the big shoe. The shoe kicks my face again.

"I asked ya a simple question, Mister Smart Guy. I said, do ya got that? Ya want I should keep kicking on ya?"

"No, I believe I understand," I whisper.

Another heavy shoe strikes me in the ribs.

"COACH, COACH WARDEN, PLEASE WAKE UP," I hear Alfred pleading in a frightened tone.

He has my head in his lap. I open one eye slowly. The excruciating pain rampaging through my body helps to clear my mind.

"Are they gone, Alfred?"

Not completely comprehending my question, but anxiously trying to accommodate, Alfred twists his head to look from side to side. "I'm not sure who you mean, Coach. There's no one here but us. Me and Coach Murphy been waitin' for you in the field house. When you didn't show up, I came outside to look for you. I found you here on the ground."

"There were two men. Got me under the bleachers. One of the men was called Clifford."

"Coach, lets us worry about who did this to you later. Can you stand up? We need to get you inside."

"I'll try, Alfred. Give me a hand and hold onto me."

When I stand up, the blood rushes from my head. My knees buckle, and I start to black out again. Alfred puts his arms under me, lifts me up and carries me into the field house.

"STUBBY, YOU LOOK LIKE you're ready for an early Halloween," Sam announces, admiring his handiwork while he wraps a final strip of adhesive tape around my aching ribs.

"Yeah, I suppose I could pass for some kind of spook alright," I reply, trying to match his weird sense of humor.

Alfred sits perched on the edge of a chair next to the training table where Sam's been repairing my damaged body. Showing no appreciation for our witty conversation, his face bears a troubled expression. Alfred has become my guardian angel.

"Lemme take a gander at your masterpiece, Sam. Alfred, can you give me a hand? I need to get to a mirror."

A mirror in the dressing room reveals I'm not injured nearly as badly as I imagined. My ribs are bruised, and my skinned face is frightening because of the white bandage on my left cheek and the orange-colored Merthiolate Sam applied to my facial scratches. My right eye will probably turn black by tomorrow. But everything considered, I don't look all that bad. I survived the beating without any permanent impairments.

"Stubby, you oughta go home. Murphy and I can handle practice this afternoon," Sam counsels.

"No, there's too much to do. With no practice yesterday, we've only got three days to get ready for Albany. Where did Murphy leave the game films? Alfred, can you help me set up the projector?"

—————

Tuesday Afternoon
September 3, 1949

ALFRED AND I SPEND the afternoon reviewing the Breckenridge game film. To my pleasant surprise, Alfred displays a genuine knack for deciphering strategies in my option offense. He also directs my attention to several minor deficiencies in our defensive schemes.

Near mid-afternoon Murphy arrives at the field house. Alfred and I have finished studying the films and are in the process of storing the projector and game reels in the film closet.

"Hey, Stubby. How you doing?"

"Much better now. Sam and Alfred did an excellent job of patching me up."

"I'm sorry I had to run off with you beat up and bleeding, but you remember I coach the junior high team. This was their first day of practice. I had to leave to get 'em started at ten."

"I understand, Keith. You left me in good hands."

"I see you and Alfred have been watching the films. They turn out okay?"

"Yes, the films were excellent. You and the photographer Delbert Capps did a fine job. We discovered a few problem areas where we may want to make some changes. You and I can talk with Sam later this afternoon. Right now, Alfred and I are headed downtown to see if our credit is good at Pearl's."

"You still hungry, Alfred?"

"Coach Warden, you know I'm always hungry."

<hr />

BY THE TIME Alfred and I return from our trip to Pearl's Café, the football team has taken the field. Aills and Murphy have the players lined, side by side, in a giant circle performing calisthenics.

Following the exercise drills, Sam, Murphy, Alfred and I huddle for a moment. I explain to Murphy the changes I want to make in our blocking assignments. The blocking modifications will allow us to compensate for inadequate blocking skills of several individuals who play offensive line positions. I point out to Sam the defensive deficiencies we spotted in the game films. We decide to separate the team into offensive and defensive units while we work on our problems.

"Sam, would you mind if Alfred works with you on defense? He can help teach Barnes the middle linebacker position."

"Sure, Stubby, I'll be glad to have the extra help." From his crouched position Aills wraps a big arm around Alfred's thick neck and squeezes hard. The grieved expression on Alfred's face makes it obvious he's uncomfortable with Aills' manly show of affection.

During the short break, J.L. Barnes runs up to speak with me. Dressed in football pads, Barnes is even more awesome than I expected.

"Hello, Coach Warden. You remember me?"

"Of course, J.L. How did your first day of school go?"

"Everything went great. Starting school at the same time as the other kids was really special. My mama is tickled to death about me being in school today."

"Did the helper show up to work with your dad this morning?"

"Yes sir. He was at our house before six this morning. My dad says to tell you he's satisfied with the whole arrangement."

"That's wonderful, J.L., I'm glad everything worked out so well. Now, you better get down there and report to Coach Aills before he misses you."

"Coach Warden, could I ask a favor?"

"Certainly, J.L. Whatta you need?"

"Could I shake your hand? My family and I wanna thank you for helping us."

Tuesday Evening
September 3, 1949

FINGLER'S O.K. GROCERY is conveniently located at the southwest corner of Sue and Main, hardly a block west of my house. George and Martha Fingler operate a clean, well-stocked store. I have shopped here on several occasions, picking up a quart of milk or loaf of bread when I was in a hurry.

When Juanita and I moved to Ranger last spring, we made the decision to purchase the majority of our food at the A&P and Piggly Wiggly stores downtown. The chain store prices were slightly lower, and every small saving was critical to our delicate budget.

With Juanita living in Comanche and me poised to depart for Corpus Christi, the Warden commissary was almost bare, even before I secured the Ranger coaching job. Now, after several days of feeding my enormous house guest, there's not a crumb of food left in the house. Alfred has even eaten all the mayonnaise and ketchup, making sandwiches with two slices of bread—no meat, no lettuce, no tomato.

The Finglers allow some of their regular customers to shop on credit. Each credit customer is assigned his own individual charge book. Mrs. Fingler, who works the checkout counter, meticulously records each item purchased and keeps a running total of the amount owed by each customer. Charge accounts are generally settled on the first of each month, but in some cases, the Finglers will let their customers pay when they get paid. Alfred and I have come to ask for credit.

Martha Fingler is working the front checkout counter when we enter the store. Her husband George is cutting meat behind the butcher counter at the rear of the store.

"Good afternoon, Mister Warden. Goodness gracious! Whatever happened to your face? Have you been in an accident?"

Martha Fingler has an unusual knack for remembering her customer's names. Juanita and I introduced ourselves to her and her husband the first time we visited their store several months ago. Mrs. Fingler has never failed to recognize Juanita or me and call us by name on any subsequent visit. Her friendliness and their congenial attention to each customer help them survive the stiff competition from the chain stores.

"No ma'am. I got into a scuffle with a couple of tough guys under the football stands this morning. I'm afraid I got the worst of it."

"I'm so sorry, but you look a sight. Are you sure you're all right? Maybe you should see a doctor. Would you like me to call and make an appointment?" she asks helpfully.

"No ma'am. Thanks, but I'll be fine. The colored Merthiolate makes my face look worse than it really is."

While I'm engaged in conversation with Mrs. Fingler, Alfred has begun to wander about the store, enviously surveying the food on the store counters. We are both hungry. I get straight to the point of our visit.

"Mrs. Fingler, I was wondering what I need to do to set up a charge account."

The woman's face expresses her shocked surprise. "Mister Warden! I thought you and your wife were strictly cash customers."

"Yes, we were, up until recently. You may not have heard, but I've been hired to coach the high school football team. The school superintendent informed me this morning that I can't get paid until Monday the sixteenth."

"How about your wife? Isn't she working downtown at the Five and Dime?"

"No ma'am. She's moved back to her parent's home in Comanche until our baby comes."

"Who is the young man with you? Is he a coach, too?"

"No ma'am. He's a friend, Alfred Steele. Alfred is temporarily living at my house."

Mrs. Fingler eyes me suspiciously. If I were her, I would also be reluctant to extend credit to such an obvious deadbeat. Her third degree interrogation is embarrassing. Coming here was a mistake. Having to explain my dismal situation makes me even more discouraged.

"Mister Warden, normally we don't extend credit to anyone who isn't a regular customer. Would you mind if I talk with my husband before I give you an answer?"

"No. No. Of course not, Mrs. Fingler. I don't want to cause a problem. If you are in any way concerned about my repaying you, I'd rather you tell me no."

Mrs. Fingler walks to the back of the store. She and her husband begin a heated conversation. His voice becomes very loud. If Alfred and I weren't so hungry, I would leave. At this moment though, I am willing to beg for food.

George Fingler comes rushing up to the front of the store. A soiled, white grocer's apron is cinched tightly around his waist. He wipes his hand on the dirty apron and extends it to me.

"Coach Warden, you'll have to forgive Martha for being so inquisitive. She's not much of a football fan."

He glances around the store, spotting Alfred wandering between the aisles of food. "Is that the young man who won the game for us Friday night? I'd love to meet him."

"Alfred, can you come up here?" I beckon to my hungry companion.

"Coach Warden, the Breckenridge game last Friday night was the most exciting game I've ever watched. My brother Tony owns the Fingler Food Mart in Breckenridge. All summer he's been beating his chest about how awesome their football team would be this year. You and your Bulldog team sure showed them a thing or two. Now, I won't have to listen to his bragging for another whole year. You can't imagine how much that means. I truly owe you."

Alfred and George Fingler immediately decide they like each other's company. They begin a lengthy question and answer session about the Breckenridge football game. Martha Fingler apologetically returns to the checkout counter and commences to set me up with a charge account.

When the charge account paper work is completed, Alfred and I flaunt our newly found wealth. We stack two grocery carts brim-full with groceries, more food than Juanita and I would consume in a month. My check out bill totals to twenty-seven dollars and some-odd cents.

Alfred and I are happily loading the sacks of groceries into the Hudson when Fingler knocks on the store front window. He motions for me to come back inside the store.

"Coach, Mrs. Fingler tells me some men beat up on you this morning. Do you know who they were?"

"No, I didn't get much chance to see who they were. I was down on the ground with them hitting me all of the time. One of the men was called Clifford. You wouldn't know who that might be, would you?"

"Yes, I think I might know him. Any reason why they wanted to beat up on you?"

"They mentioned something about wanting to teach me a lesson, so I wouldn't get too uppity after winning the football game Friday night."

"Coach, I'm pretty sure I know who those two are. Listen, I have another brother, James. He's a deputy sheriff in Eastland. Would you mind if I called to tell him what happened? James is working with a special commission investigating organized crime in Eastland County. He may want to talk with you."

"Sure, go ahead and call him. Now, if you'll tell me where to find this Clifford fellow, I'd be most appreciative. He and I have some unfinished business."

"Coach, this crime thing is much more involved than your getting even with some hard case who beat up on you. Promise me you'll talk to my brother before you do anything about what happened to you this morning. After you talk to James, maybe I can help you find your Clifford guy."

"Okay, George, I'll wait. Right now, I'm not exactly in the greatest fighting condition anyhow. What'll your brother wanna talk about?"

"You'll have to let James answer that question. His investigation is very 'hush-hush', you know, secretive."

Wednesday Morning
September 4, 1949

A REPETITIVE KNOCKING SOUND interrupts my sleep. Opening one eye, I check the alarm clock next to the bed. The time is 5:45 A.M. More knocking sounds come from the front door. Inaudible noises commence in the next bedroom where Alfred is sleeping.

"Okay! Okay, I'm coming," I call, rolling out of bed.

Wearing only my skivvies, I stumble to the front door.

"Who is it?" I ask.

"Mister Warden, this is your landlady. I need to talk with you."

Mrs. Hines is my landlady who insists on the rent being delivered to her, in cash, on the first of the month. Actually I haven't forgotten to pay the rent, but it's an issue I've been avoiding. I simply have no money to pay her with.

I open the door slightly, peaking through the crack. "Mrs. Hines, you certainly are an early riser. Are you here about the rent?"

"Why else would I be out at this ungodly hour, Mister Warden? I stopped by the house several times during the evening hours, but you're never here. This is the only time I can catch you at home."

"Mrs. Hines, please accept my apologies. Can you give me a moment to put on my trousers? I can explain why I haven't come by to pay the rent."

Scampering back to my bedroom to retrieve my pants, I pass Alfred as he emerges from his bedroom rubbing his eyes.

"Who's that at the door, Coach?"

"It's the landlady. She wants the rent."

"Oh!" Alfred responds knowingly.

Grabbing a dirty shirt and a pair of pants off the floor, I slip into the clothes and walk quickly back to the front door. Still barefooted, I open the door and step out onto the porch. I don't want the landlady to see the sloppy conditions inside the house. Alfred and I are not exactly world-class house keepers.

"Thanks for waiting, Mrs. Hines. I know I haven't paid the rent. There is a good reason. I hope you aren't worried."

"Mister Warden, when you took the house, you agreed to pay me on the first of the month, in cash. You have not honored our agreement."

"Yes ma'am, that is correct, and I apologize. Don't you remember? I told you last week. I got the job coaching football for Ranger High School."

"Yes, I remember. That was the Sunday evening you came by to tell me you wouldn't be leaving, and you intended to keep the house. What does all that have to do with paying your rent on time?"

"At the time I came by, I had no idea the school district wouldn't be issuing me a paycheck until the middle of September. While I was working at the Pontiac House, I got paid every Friday. I thought with my new coaching job I'd be able to pay you on the first, like I always have."

"Mister Warden, are you telling me I have to wait until the middle of September for my rent money?"

"Yes ma'am. If you could please give me until the sixteenth, I give you my solemn promise to pay what I owe you, in cash."

The landlady leans against the porch railing, weighing the pros and cons of my proposal. My bare feet are beginning to ache from the cold morning air.

"Alright, Mister Warden, I'll give you until Monday the sixteenth. Let's have it understood though, you are not to be late again."

"Yes ma'am. You have my word. This situation won't happen again. I truly appreciate your being so understanding."

"I wouldn't be nearly so generous if Phyliss Mitchell hadn't already given me ten dollars to apply against your rent. If you want to thank someone, you should thank her."

Now I know for certain. Juanita's aunt has been subsidizing our rent all along. Oh, Lord, how will I ever repay Phyliss and Price for all they've done for me?

"Yes ma'am. I will thank her. I'll thank her for sure."

Friday Morning
September 6, 1949

A SCHOOL PEP RALLY is scheduled for eleven o'clock this morning on the front steps of the high school. Superintendent Boswell made a special trip to come by football practice yesterday afternoon to request we coaches be present. All classes for grades seven through twelve have been canceled to insure maximum student participation.

When Alfred and I arrive, our Bulldog team members have stationed themselves at the top of the school steps. As we make our way up the steps, the cheerleaders lead the students in a cheer.

"Give us an R!" the cheerleaders plea.

"R-rrrrr!" the crowd responds loudly.

"Louder," the cheerleaders prompt. "Give us an A!"

"A-aaaaa!" the students shout back.

"Louder, louder," the cheerleaders cry, holding their megaphones high. "Give us an N!"

"N-nnnnn!" the students scream.

"Give us a G!"

"G-ggggg!"

"Give us an E!"

"E-eeeee!" Now, all of the students have their hands above their heads. Their screaming voices have become fanatical.

"Give us another R!" the cheerleaders urge.

"R-rrrrr!" the students howl, louder than ever.

"What does that spell?" the cheerleaders shriek.

"RANGER–RANGER–RANGER–RANGER BULLDOGS!"

The cheerleaders lead the students through several yells, exciting them into a crazed frenzy. Then the band starts to play the school song. The cheerleaders hold hands and stand at attention while everyone sings solemnly along with the band. Magically, Superintendent Boswell appears without notice at the top of the steps carrying a megaphone. He raises the megaphone to his mouth and urges the students to give their loyal and vocal support to the home team, then asks them to remember the visiting team and fans are our guests. He reminds the students to always be courteous hosts. Boswell introduces me as the new head football coach and asks me to introduce my assistant coaches and the members of the football squad.

Even before I have finished introducing Coaches Aills and Murphy, the enthusiastic crowd begins to drown out my voice. Opting not to compete with the noise, I simply approach each team member and raise his hand. When I reach Alfred, he steps backward as if to resist, but I grab his hand firmly and hold it up.

"Alfred! Alfred! Alfred!" the crowd cheers gleefully. Alfred appears to be embarrassed but is obviously pleased when the students call him by name.

For a second I consider walking down the steps to the band to raise the hand of Frankie Jensen, then decide to leave well enough alone. In spite of the band director's threat to take the matter to the school superintendent, there's been no further mention of a band member playing on the football team. Jensen showed up yesterday afternoon to practice with the punting team.

While the cheerleaders line up and begin leading the students in another sequence of organized cheer routines, I search through the multitude of people for familiar faces. I'm not surprised to see the familiar faces of school trustees, Blake Tucker, Leo Jackson and Gordon Long. Many adults are scattered throughout the crowd–parents, teachers and avid older fans who have come here in support of the football team.

The cheering ceases abruptly. Roy Lindsey, one of the two male cheerleaders, runs to fetch a huge maroon package near the base of the front steps. An enormous white bow adorns the top of the package. All five cheerleaders grin self-consciously as they circle around the box.

Wanda Clem, a tiny blonde bundle of energy, is the senior female cheerleader. She giggles with embarrassment as the other cheerleaders push her out to act as their spokesperson.

"Coach Warden, would you please come down here? We have a gift to present to you."

Surprised by the unexpected generosity, I bound swiftly down to the sidewalk where the cheerleaders are waiting.

"Coach Warden, the students of Ranger High want to welcome you. We hope your coaching career here will be immensely successful. The students have a gift which we offer as a token of our warm feelings for you," the blonde cheerleader announces.

"Thank you," I reply, not having anything more intelligent to say.

"Open the present! Open it up, Coach!" someone in the crowd urges.

First I remove the big bow and hold it high for the crowd to inspect. The students cheer wildly. Then I begin tearing away the maroon paper.

"Grrrr. Rufff," comes a sound from inside the package. My mind tries to dismiss the irrefutable evidence that this is some kind of animal. Surely they wouldn't give me another mouth to feed.

Concealed beneath the colored wrapping is a large cardboard box. Holes have been punched in the top and sides to allow air to enter. The top of the box unfolds easily. Inside the box lies a tiny, brown and white bulldog puppy. His loose, wrinkled skin is bunched up behind his neck. His nose is large and pudgy. He has a large patch of dark brown fur around one eye. He is easily the ugliest creature I have ever seen. I, of course, instantly fall madly in love with the animal.

"His name is Short Snorter," the cheerleaders inform me.

Reaching into the box, I wrap both hands around the puppy and raise him above my head for the crowd to see. The students scream and shout loudly as I wave the small dog back and forth.

"Be careful, Coach. The puppy has a slight bowel problem," Johnny Marlow, the second male cheerleader cautions.

"I kinda wish you'd told me about that a little sooner," I declare, feeling a glob of oozy wet slime hit the top of my head.

———————

Friday Night
September 6, 1949

OUR GAME AGAINST ALBANY will be the first home game of the season. In anticipation, many of the downtown merchants have decorated their windows in maroon and white colors. On Tuesday, someone strung a banner across Main Street which urges the football team to "Beat the Lions." The Albany game has been the dominant topic of conversation in Ranger all week. Social gatherings have been planned for both before and after the game. Friends have contacted friends, making plans to attend together. Tonight, the football stadium will be filled to capacity. Movie theaters like the Arcadia and Tower will play to an empty house.

Alfred and I arrive at the stadium parking lot around six o'clock. The kickoff is two hours away, but already a number of fans are in the stands. All the parking spaces near the stadium entrance are taken, so we have to hunt for a space to leave the Hudson.

The mouth-watering smell of hamburgers and popcorn cooking in the concession booths whets my appetite. Alfred pauses to gaze longingly toward the food booths.

"Come on, big guy, we'll eat later," I say, clutching his arm and pushing him along.

"Yeah, Coach, I know. We got no money for foolishness. I was just dreaming about how great one of those burgers would taste."

"Me too, Alfred. One of these days you and I will go to a football game and watch from the bleachers. We'll buy ourselves a couple of hamburgers, extra large cokes and some hot-buttered popcorn. We'll really 'pig-out.' Maybe we won't even pay attention to who wins the game."

"That sounds good to me, Coach," Alfred agrees, with only half-hearted interest. His eyes are glued to the burger stands.

"Come on, Alfred. Let's go, before we get arrested for 'visual hamburger molestation.'" I have to shove Alfred to get him moving in the direction of the field house.

ALBANY IS A MEDIUM-SIZED CITY located about sixty miles northwest of Ranger, nestled amongst the grassy, rolling hills of Shackleford County. Like most West Texas cities, Albany's economy is boosted by revenue from oil production, but for most Albany residents, agriculture and ranching are their major sources of income. Albany High has established a long history of fielding well-coached, winning football teams. It's a rare year when the Albany Lions don't represent their district in the state playoffs. Like Ranger, Albany is classified as a Texas One A school.

By seven-thirty our players are dressed out and ready to take the field. Sam has discovered a problem with Comacho's shoes and is hastily replacing the laces. Alfred is re-taping a tender left ankle for Davenport.

Meanwhile, I fret. Keith Murphy is missing.

"Sam, can you think of any reason he should be so late?"

"Nope, last thing he said to me this morning was he'd see me at the game tonight. I can't imagine where he could be. He's always been on time before."

"I suppose we should get the team on the field. Maybe he'll show up before the game starts."

"Yeah, with this being our first home game, the kids are awfully nervous. If we hold 'em in here much longer, they're likely to mutiny."

"Alfred, if Keith isn't here when we finish our warm-ups, you take charge of the offensive linemen. Okay?"

"Sure, Coach Warden. No problem. But I'd sure feel better if Coach Murphy was here."

"So would I, Alfred. So would I."

———————

BY THE TIME my Bulldogs emerge from the varsity field house the Albany Lions have finished their stretching exercises and have broken into small groups. Individual coaches are working with each group, running them through a planned set of pre-game drills. From my viewpoint at the opposite end of the football field, the Albany players look like gigantic warriors. Their bright uniforms of red and white make them seem powerful and unbeatable. In comparison, my scrawny Bulldog players, in their worn-out game uniforms of solid maroon, seem small and vulnerable.

The home side bleachers are overflowing. Many of our fans are roaming the stadium, trying to find a seat. The Ranger High band has arrived. Up in their reserved section at the north end of the grandstands, band members hastily unpack their musical instruments. Our cheerleaders have set up megaphones and cheering paraphernalia in the grassy margin between the sideline and the bleachers, directly in front of the band.

At least a thousand fans are seated in the visitor's bleachers. Red and white pom-poms are sprinkled among the Albany fans. Occupying the north section of the visitor's stands, the Lion band is seated directly across the field from the Ranger band. The two bands are perfectly situated to challenge each other's loud music throughout the game.

While Sam and Alfred supervise our warm-up exercises, I survey the stadium grounds, somehow expecting to find Keith Murphy among the crowd of faces. If necessary, we can muddle through the game without him. Keith and I have drilled the offensive linemen on their assignments so many times they can recite them in their sleep. Alfred is familiar with the players and can help me with our substitutions. Yeah, we'll get by fine. Still, I can't shake an eerie feeling that something terrible has happened. Murphy would be here, if he was able.

"Coach Warden, where is the puppy?"

"What? I'm sorry. What did you say?" The voice belongs to Sue Ewing, one of our Ranger cheerleaders. Lost in worry about my missing coach, I didn't notice her approaching.

"The puppy, Coach Warden, where is he?" she asks.

"At home. I left the dog at home. Was I supposed to bring him to the game?"

The tall blonde cheerleader sighs impatiently, apparently perplexed by my answer. "Of course you were supposed to bring him. That's why we gave him to you. The bulldog puppy is supposed to be our mascot."

"I'm sorry, Sue. I didn't understand that part. Even so, the puppy is too young to be handled by a bunch of different people, and remember, he has that bowel problem."

The lovely young cheerleader's face begins to darken. "Coach Warden, you have ruined everything. Now the team won't have a mascot tonight, and it'll be all your fault," she informs me hatefully.

The girl turns to run back to the cheerleader section in front of the grandstands. There she begins excitedly explaining to the other cheerleaders how I've let them down, pointing and waving her hand accusingly in my direction. The other cheerleaders glare disgustedly toward me.

ELDER, HAMRICK AND THOMPSON MEET with the Albany captains at mid-field. After we lose the coin toss, Albany elects to receive. Since there's not even the slightest hint of wind movement, we choose to defend the south goal.

The capacity crowd rises to sing the National Anthem. The pastor of the First Methodist Church comes on the public address system to deliver an opening prayer. A few minutes later the bands interrupt our pre-game huddle to play their respective school songs. Keith Murphy is still absent.

In anticipation of the kickoff, the home crowd becomes loud and boisterous. After our victory over Breckenridge last week, our Ranger fans harbor great expectations. Bulldog cheerleaders grab their megaphones and spread out down the sideline, facing the bleachers, yelling to the crowd, encouraging their enthusiasm.

Will Brownlee's kickoff sails end-over-end, deep into the end zone. Agonizing grunts of players meeting in hard contact resound across the football field as our kickoff team charges downfield. Albany's receiver lets the ball hit the ground and roll past the back line.

Like a bad omen, a yellow flag back at our forty suggests we were offside. Ranger fans heckle the referees with loud boos, showing their displeasure.

The offside penalty moves the football back to our thirty-five yard line. Brownlee's second kickoff attempt is shortened by a stiff breeze which has suddenly swept in from the north end of the stadium. An Albany receiver catches the ball on the twenty and darts toward the left side of the field. Our defense reacts quickly to counter his movement.

"Reverse! Watch out for a reverse!" Sam bellows excitedly.

Sam's warning comes too late. Another ball carrier, moving in the opposite direction, has grabbed a handoff from the first Albany receiver. Our defense is out of position. Being overanxious, our defenders have abandoned their designated coverage routes to chase after the initial runner. Stiff-arming Brownlee, our last defender, Albany's runner zips unchallenged up the sideline for a touchdown. Albany's extra point try is good.

The stiff northerly breeze quickly becomes a cold windy gale. Paper cups and trash blow across the field. Fans in the bleachers rush for cover underneath the stadium. A chilling light drizzle begins to fall on the two teams lining up for the Albany kickoff. What began as a pleasant summer evening has now become a night to endure.

Perhaps it's the sudden change in the weather. Maybe it's the heavy, damp ball, but neither team is able to move the football with consistency during the first quarter. We run three plays and punt. Albany runs three plays and punts. A strong wind blowing behind the Lions gives them an enormous advantage on the kicking exchanges.

ROBINSON AND PEARSON knock the Lion fullback out of bounds at our thirty, stopping him for no gain on third down. Less than a minute remains in the quarter when the Albany coach sends in his kicking unit to attempt a field goal.

"That's one hellava long kick with a cold, wet ball. He'll never make it," Sam observes wishfully.

"Yeah, no way he'll ever kick one that far. They're stupid for not punting," I add.

With a howling wind behind him, the Albany kicker sends the ball straight and true, right between the uprights.

Sam turns to look at me, shaking his head in disbelief.

"It was still a dumb call," I argue stubbornly.

After the numbers change on the bright red and white Coca Cola scoreboard at the south end of the field, the score reads:

RANGER 0   VISITOR 10

As the teams exchange ends of the field to begin the second quarter, the rain beats down even harder. The wet and cold has everyone miserable. Even our most loyal Bulldog fans have given up and left for home. My rain-soaked players huddle together in misery along the bench.

Seeing the suffering of my young gladiators and yielding to my own agony, I run over to Aills who is kneeling at the sideline. His hunched shoulders and lowered head divulge his own discomfort. "Sam, we got any kind of slickers or rain coats stored in the field house?"

"We had some rain jackets a couple of years ago. I haven't checked lately, but they might still be there. You want I should go look?"

"Yes. Go right now. Bring back anything and everything we have that'll shed water. We'll share whatever we have with the Albany club."

"Share our stuff with the Albany team?" Sam asks, showing his surprise.

"Their kids are just as cold and miserable as ours. Now get going."

The football game becomes a nightmare of trench warfare as the two teams battle back and forth. A steady drizzle of rain continues to pour down until the field becomes a flowing river of mud and water. In their wet and muddy uniforms, at times it is impossible to distinguish our Ranger players from the Albany players.

———

OBSERVING MY ASSISTANT struggling with a heavy bag on the walkway outside the field house, I dispatch Max Wade and Edward Polston, two reserve linemen, over to help Sam with whatever he has uncovered in the way of rain gear. Meanwhile, I collar one of the game officials and request an official's timeout.

I slosh across the field to the Albany bench to speak with Elwood Turner, the Lion head coach.

"Coach, we've located some rain gear. Your team has to be just as wet and miserable as mine. We want to share our rain apparel with you."

"You're right, Coach Warden. My kids are hurting bad. I don't know what to say except, thanks. We accept your generosity."

"If our situations were reversed, I'm sure you'd do the same for us. At this point, the main objective for all of us is to survive this blasted weather while we finish the game."

"I hope you don't expect my team to ease up on you, just because you shared a few rain jackets with us," Turner challenges.

"I'd be terribly disappointed if you did," I defiantly reply.

———

MERCIFULLY, THE FIRST HALF ENDS. With neither team able to get their offense moving, there's been no further scoring by either side. The cold rain continues to fall without any sign of let-up. Except for a few die-hard stragglers hiding beneath the stadium, the bleachers are completely empty. Gone are the school bands and the cheerleaders. Gone are the rabid fans of both teams. Only two miserable football teams, their coaches and six water-logged game officials remain, entrapped by an unwritten law that a football game cannot be postponed, no matter what the weather conditions.

Wading across the flooded stretch between the playing field and the bleachers, I wonder where Mrs. Perlstein is on this dreadful night. Her daughter Rheta Beth plays in the school band. Surely she and her husband must have been present in the stands earlier when the rain started. By now, she's probably safely in bed, sleeping happily, consoled with the indisputable evidence that the drought is over.

At least we didn't have to deal with Mister Gans, the band director, or having Frankie in uniform, ready to march with the band during halftime.

Damn! What could've happened to Murphy?

———————

ALFRED AND SAM beat me to the clubhouse. By the time I arrive, they have issued dry pants and a clean jersey to each team member. Our weary players are changing out of their wet, muddy game uniforms.

"Sam, are you sure we can wear those practice jerseys? Some of the jerseys don't have numbers," I question, concerned that the game officials might find the uniforms objectionable and try to penalize us.

"Stubby, these are the only dry tops we got. Our guys are miserable in their wet uniforms. We're not sending 'em back out there wet and cold. They may get soaked again, but they're gonna start the second half dry," Sam declares forcefully. For a man who, only a couple of weeks ago, was using a sawed-in-half baseball bat to punish these young men, his new protective attitude represents a total reverse of character.

"Okay, Sam, but I'll have to clear it with the game officials."

"If they give you any trouble, you can tell 'em no one'll be able to see numbers after a few plays anyway. There sure ain't nobody left in the grandstands who gives a rat's damn."

"I'll handle it, Sam. You and Alfred get our kids ready for the second half." In his frame of mind, I certainly don't want Sam dealing with the referees.

I find the game officials inside the men's restroom underneath the home side bleachers. They have stripped to their underwear while they wring muddy water from their soggy garments. They agree to allow my team to wear the practice jerseys without numbers, but only after I promise to have my players report to the head linesman each time we make a substitution. These men look even more fatigued and bedraggled than my football players.

Because of the sloppy field conditions, our option offense was almost totally ineffective during the first half. The mud and rain made the football hard to handle. Muddy, slippery footing ruled out all opportunity for fancy ball handling. On most plays our ball carriers were fortunate to make it back to the line of scrimmage.

I decide to switch to a "Standard Tee" offense during the second half, using direct handoffs to our backs instead of having the quarterback make a decision after the play begins. The "Standard Tee" is more of a power style offense and should reduce our chances of fumbling.

SINCE WE LOST THE COIN TOSS we get our choice to kick or receive the second half kickoff. We choose to receive. Although the rain is still trickling down, it is beginning to subside.

With the strong wind behind him, Albany's kicker bangs the heavy football down to our five where it is fielded by Comacho. Disregarding mud and deep puddles of water, he splashes toward the left sideline where Stiles, Hummel and Barnes have set up to form a blocking wall. The wet footing prevents Albany defenders from gaining sufficient momentum to penetrate through our solid barrier of blockers. Comacho is finally shoved out of bounds at Albany's forty-three by the Lion place kicker.

A handoff to Simpson over left tackle and a dive by Hamrick over right guard net us seven yards. The Lion captain calls timeout. Yelling instructions to their red and white defense, the Albany coaches shuffle up and down the sidelines.

Reed Jones trots over to the sidelines. "Coach, they're really stacking up the middle. I don't think our straight running plays will work much longer."

Albany is less than thirty miles from Breckenridge. Surely they had one of their coaches there to scout our game last Friday. I decide to give them an impromptu exam.

"Reed, let's try number thirty-two with an option right. If they bunch up to stop Phillips, you keep the football and run off right tackle. Do you understand?"

"Yes sir. You figure their coaches probably watched our Breckenridge game last week. They'll be expecting Phillips to carry the ball."

"Reed, that's exactly what I mean." Jones may not be the most agile quarterback I'll ever coach, but I may never have one with a keener football mind. He'll make one heckava coach someday.

"Phillips, get in there for Dorsey," I call to the bench.

Hut. Hut. Jones fakes the ball to Phillips, then runs the ball inside right tackle for a gain of six. First down at their thirty.

Hut. Hut. Jones tries a similar play to the left side for a gain of four yards.

Jones continues to call the same play, alternately running to the right, then back to the left until we make a first down at the Albany nine.

Hut. Hut. Jones stuffs the football into Phillips' mid-section, then fakes a run to the right. The outside linebacker takes the bait and rushes in to tackle Jones. Phillips breaks into the secondary after Thompson, Grey and Elder drive back the Albany defense, opening up a hole wide enough to drive a truck through. A devastating block by Stiles downfield clears away the Albany safetyman. Phillips crosses the goal line, dragging a defensive halfback into the end zone. Brownlee's extra point kick is good.

Our quick touchdown revives the Bulldog players on our bench. Forgetting their misery, they rise to cheer our offensive players as they come off the field. Even though the bleachers are empty, someone has hung around to operate the scoreboard. The scoreboard numbers change:

RANGER 7   VISITOR 10

After our score, the game reverts to the monotonous grind of the first half. Neither team is able to mount any kind of drive. Jensen's long punts keep the Lions deep in their own territory.

"Coach, Mister Jackson is up in the stands waving at you. I believe he wants to talk to you," Wayne Hargrave comes to tell me.

Waving his arms wildly to attract my attention, Leo Jackson leans over the walkway railing at the bottom aisle of the unoccupied bleachers.

"Sam, you and Alfred look after things for a minute while I see what Leo wants."

In his long, dark raincoat and yellow plastic sailor cap, Jackson makes a comical sight. He could easily be mistaken for a whaler on an ocean voyage. While I trudge through the flooded grassy fringe once occupied by the cheerleaders, he clutches the wooden railing along the front of the bleachers and leans forward. He begins talking before I can get close enough to hear.

"I said, have you seen Keith Murphy?" he repeats.

"No. We've been wondering why he isn't here. Is there some kind of problem?"

"Keith's wife and mine are close friends. Mrs. Murphy called about thirty minutes ago to find out if he was here at the game. She hasn't heard from him since he left home early this morning. He was supposed to pick her up and bring her to the game. She's very worried."

"Leo, I don't know a thing. The last time anyone saw him was this morning. He told Coach Aills he'd see him at the game. We were concerned when he didn't show up, but with the game about to start, there was no time to check on his whereabouts."

"Mrs. Murphy tells my wife the Leon River is flooding out of its banks. Her car's in the shop, so she can't get into town. Could you help us look for Keith after your game is finished?"

"I'll be glad to help. Are you planning to stay for the end of the game?"

Leo Jackson glances up at the dark, cloudy sky. "Stubby, I've been thoroughly soaked once tonight. Don't think I wanna try for seconds. Why don't you come by my house on Pine Street after the game? Maybe we'll have heard something about Murphy by then."

"Fine, Leo. I'll see you at your house after the game."

As I begin wading back to our bench, Jackson calls to me again. "Coach Warden, I forgot to apologize for making you wade over here. The only dry footwear I could find at the house was these here two hundred dollar rodeo boots." He holds one foot up for me to see. The colorful boot on his foot is knee-high, obviously very expensive, hand-crafted leather.

"Don't worry about it, Leo. My shoes were already ruined. They've been full of water since the first quarter. I'll talk with you after the game."

Returning to our bench, I find Sam and Alfred consulting with Jensen, Comacho and Simpson. The down marker at the side line indicates we have possession of the ball on our end of the field, fourth and long. Our kicking team is preparing to go on the field.

"Stubby, Alfred has an idea he thinks might work," Aills tells me. "Alfred, why don't you explain what you wanna try."

"Coach, their punt receivers have been trying to catch every punt. Instead of playing it safe, letting the ball hit the ground and roll dead, they're trying to get some kind of return out of every punt. That's been working for them because the field is so slippery our guys can't get downfield very fast. What I'm thinking is—if Frankie could punt the ball high and short."

"I like your plan, Alfred. Let's go for it. Maybe we can cause a fumble. I assume you were planning to use our two speedsters, Comacho and Simpson, at the end positions."

"Yes sir. That was the idea."

With deep puddles of water standing at many spots, the playing field is a horrible mess. The once thick and lush grass has been trampled and plowed up by burrowing football cleats.

"Sam, you got any idea how much time we got left?" I ask.

"I'm not sure, Stubby, but there couldn't be much more than a minute or so."

"If Alfred's plan doesn't work, they'll probably run out the clock. Not much chance of us getting the ball again."

"Yeah, this might be the last time we'll have the football. We only got two timeouts left."

Thompson snaps the ball back to Jensen. When Albany's line does not rush aggressively, Frankie hesitates for a second, then takes two short steps forward before his muddy bare foot meets the ball.

As the soggy football spirals high above the field, Comacho and Simpson fly breakneck down the muddy field. Playing deep because he's accustomed to Jensen's long kicks, Albany's punt receiver is forced to run forward to get under the football.

The punted football, the Albany receiver and two mud-caked, maroon-clad rockets all meet in one mighty impact at Albany's twenty-three. An official arrives to untangle the mucky heap. Billy Simpson emerges from the pile holding the ball high over his head. The field judge signals we have recovered the fumble.

The head referee runs over to our sideline. "Ranger, my watch shows we have fifty-two seconds remaining. Your team has two time-outs left."

"Thanks, ref, we appreciate the information."

Alfred, Sam and I huddle with Reed Jones to decide on an offensive scheme for the few precious seconds remaining. We elect to stick with the same "Standard Tee" we've employed throughout the second half.

"Reed, there's plenty of time, so don't get in a hurry. We have two timeouts left. Save one timeout for a field goal try, if you can."

With the horrendous condition of the playing surface, a field goal is absolutely the last thing I want to try. Still, a tie would be better than a loss. Our offensive team breaks their huddle and sets up at the twenty-three yard line.

Hut. Hut. Jones hands off to Simpson who dives for a yard. We line up quickly for another play.

Hut. Hut. Hamrick carries over right guard for two yards. Jones calls for a timeout and comes to the side line.

"Coach, their linebackers are lining up close behind their linemen, expecting us to run. If we fake a handoff to Hamrick, a short jump pass to Rogers might work."

"Yeah, that would be the ideal call. If the pass is incomplete, the clock will stop. If we don't make the first down, we still have one timeout left."

"The ref said to tell you there are twenty-eight seconds left," my quarterback informs me.

"Good. We still have plenty of time."

A slick, wet football is plenty of reason for me to have reservations about trying any kind of pass, but our running game is getting nowhere. We might as well try something bold and unexpected.

Hut. Hut. Jones takes the ball and steps to his right where he inserts the ball into Hamrick's middle. Hamrick wraps both arms around the ball as he crouches low and plunges into a mass of writhing bodies. At the last second Jones withdraws the ball and jumps high, his body turning to face upfield, his arm poised to throw.

Ralph Rogers breaks clear into an open pocket between Albany's linebackers, who have charged forward to tackle Hamrick, and the Lion defensive backs. My quarterback's wobbly spiral is thrown too hard and too high, but big Ralph leaps to snare the ball with one hand. He brings the ball down quickly, holding it close to his body. He is tackled viciously at the seven yard line.

Even before the officials finish moving the chains to mark the first down, Jones has called another play and has our offense in position. Jones takes the snap immediately after the official blows his whistle, signaling for time to begin. A handoff to Simpson nets two yards to the Albany five.

Using our final timeout, Jones trots to the sideline. With no time-outs remaining, the next play will be the game's final play.

While I watch Jones trot toward me, my mind searches for the correct play to call. Perhaps I should try running Phillips over right guard. That worked for us last week, but with their expecting Phillips to get the ball and without Alfred to lead the way, there is little chance it would work. Another jump pass to big Ralph might catch them by surprise. Maybe we should go for the field goal and settle for a tie? What about the three hundred dollar bonus Boswell promised for a win? Do I get half a bonus for a tie?

From somewhere deep inside my brain, my need to win assumes control. "Desperate men must take desperate measures," I remind myself. My promise to myself, that I would never let an emotional decision keep my team from winning, dominates my thought process.

"Comacho," I call to the bench. "Get ready to go in for Hamrick at halfback."

Jones reaches the sideline. "Reed, I want Hamrick at quarterback to run this last play. You stay next to me here on the sideline and watch."

"But why, Coach? I feel fine. I don't understand." From the pained expression on the tall quarterback's face, you would think he's been severely injured.

"Don't argue with me, son. Just stand here beside me and watch."

Comacho steps up alongside me. "Jimmy, you tell Hamrick to take over at quarterback. I want to run forty-four, option right. You understand?"

"Sure, Coach. Hamrick to quarterback, forty-four, option right," Comacho replies. He glances at Jones, sees his agonized face and hastily decides to remove himself from an unpleasant situation. He runs hurriedly onto the field.

Disregarding my command that he stand beside me, Reed Jones trudges dejectedly over to the bench and plops down. His eyes are filled with tears. He lowers his head to keep his teammates from noticing.

A sense of confusion develops among the players on the playing field after Comacho checks into the game to deliver my instructions. First, Hamrick steps out of the huddle to stare apprehensively toward me. Then Elder and Patterson raise up to gaze back at me.

"What's the problem?" asks Aills, noticing Jones on the bench.

"I decided to change quarterbacks. I guess our players out there are having some problem with my strategy."

"How come you made a change? Is Jones hurt?"

"No, I just believe we've got a better chance of scoring with Hamrick at quarterback."

"Well, I think your strategy stinks, Coach Warden. That boy over there on the bench is the number one reason we still have a chance to win this game. You just ripped his heart out."

"Sam, the decision has already been made, so calm down."

Aills stomps away in disgust, putting as much distance between the two of us as possible.

Our maroon team breaks huddle, taking their positions as the officials whistle time back in. Watching the team's complacent movements, I realize I have made a grave mistake. My insensitive and relentless obsession to win may have destroyed my team's fighting spirit. The superb play I have selected is doomed to failure before it begins.

Hut. Hut. Hamrick takes the snap and inserts the ball into Dorsey's mid-section. They move together toward the line. Hamrick attempts to withdraw the football as Dorsey plunges forward, but somehow, the ball sticks to Dorsey's muddy jersey. A fumbled football rolls along the ground in the backfield. Hamrick frantically scrambles to retrieve it.

Time runs out as the referees signal Albany has recovered. A hefty red and white defensive tackle holds the football triumphantly above his head while he races for the sideline.

Final Score: Ranger   7   Albany   10

WHILE ALFRED AND SAM collect our mud-caked equipment, I sit on the bench in tormented anguish, reflecting on the events of this dastardly evening. Never in all my athletic career have I felt so low after a football game. Not only did we lose, but I have severely damaged my relationship with my team and coaches. Even Alfred, my guardian angel, seems upset with me. If I hadn't promised to help look for Keith Murphy, I would jump in the Hudson and leave here forever, ridding myself of the humiliating shame and agony I have found in this town. With the meager amount of fuel in the Hudson's gas tank, I'd be lucky to make it past Eastland.

Gazing morosely across the mutilated and muddy playing field, I recall portions of a famous sports poem:

> *Somewhere the sun is shining...*
> *Somewhere men are laughing...*
> *But there is no joy in Mudville tonight...*

Perhaps for me, the sad poem should end differently:

> *The once mighty Stubby has struck out.*

ALFRED'S MOOD IS QUIETLY THOUGHTFUL as I pull up alongside the curb in front of Leo Jackson's home. He makes no move to open the car door when I cut the lights and turn off the ignition. He has something on his mind–something to tell me, so I wait with him, sitting in the darkness. A light mist falls against the windshield.

"Coach Warden, you're the best friend I've ever had. No matter what you might do, you'll always be my best friend. But, Coach, you were wrong tonight. Winning a football game shouldn't be reason enough to hurt someone that way."

"I know, Alfred. I promise never to be as big a fool again as I was tonight."

We sit in the darkness for another minute. I expect Alfred to finish expressing his disappointment with me.

"That's all I got to say, Coach. You wanna go in?"

"Yeah, let's go in, Alfred."

A PORCH LIGHT flicks on, bathing us in brightness only seconds after we ring the doorbell. Leo Jackson opens the door to greet us.

"Hello, Stubby, Alfred. Thank you for coming. We've been waiting for you. The other men think we should organize a search party to look for Murphy."

"That might be a good idea. We have any clues where to start looking?" I ask.

"Not really. The last time his wife saw him was this morning when he left the house. His school bus was in the shop being serviced. Keith was headed to Ranger to pick it up. You said Coach Aills talked to him this morning. Sam may have been the last person to see him."

From the front entrance foyer we walk down a long hallway to a large room at the rear of the house. Three men are seated in leather chairs arranged in a chatty semicircle to face a massive rock fireplace. The room is totally masculine. The walls of the room are covered with hand-carved wood paneling. Stuffed animal heads and large fish, probably some of Jackson's trophies from past hunting and fishing trips, adorn the walls. An expensive wool rug centered in front of the fireplace covers the wood floor in the conversation area.

Two of the men I recognize immediately as Gordon Long and Blake Tucker. The other man is a stranger.

"Stubby, I believe you know Gordon and Blake. This bald-headed fellow here is my next door neighbor Glen Elgin."

"Yes, we know Mister Long and Mister Tucker very well. Glen, it's a pleasure to make your acquaintance. This is my friend Alfred Steele."

Everyone shakes hands. We talk small talk for a few minutes, getting better acquainted before the conversation shifts to the purpose of our meeting. Thankfully, there is no mention of tonight's football game.

Leo Jackson takes charge of the party, issuing instructions for the search plan.

"Murphy has a sister who lives at Morton Valley. We called her earlier. She said Keith's been promising to come visit her, but she hasn't heard from him today. It's a long shot, but, Blake, why don't you and Gordon drive up that way. He might've decided to run up there to see his sister before the game."

"Stubby, there are two ways to get out to Murphy's farm near Alemeda. Why don't you and Alfred search the road through the Staff community from Highway 80 out of Eastland. That's the longest route to get to Ranger from Murphy's farm. I can't imagine why he'd decide to go that way, but I suppose we should check it out."

Blake Tucker interrupts Jackson. "Stubby, you and Alfred keep a sharp lookout once you get to Staff. That Leon River is sure to be over the road, down in the river bottom. The current will be very swift. Don't try and drive through the flood water under any circumstances."

"Thanks for the advice, Blake. We promise not to take any unnecessary chances."

Jackson continues with his search plan. "The shortest route to Murphy's farm is along the farm road which runs past the Merriman Baptist Church. Glen and I will take responsibility for searching that road. After each group completes searching their designated route, we'll all meet back here. Does anyone have a better plan?"

The Hudson has been running on an almost empty gas tank since I returned from Comanche last Saturday. One of these men would probably be glad to loan me money for gas, but I'm too embarrassed to ask. We break up into groups of two and drive away from Jackson's house. The misty rain is still falling.

THE TEXACO STATION at the south end of main street is closed. I have pulled the Hudson underneath the gas station's front canopy across from the Texas and Pacific Railway depot. Alfred is draining excess gas left inside the rubber pump hoses into the Hudson's gas tank.

"Alfred, you about done? There's a car coming down Main Street."

"Just about, Coach. This is the last one."

I lie down on the seat while the car passes. Alfred squats behind the car to keep from being seen.

"Okay, Coach. That's all the gas we're gonna get here. There's a Conoco station we can try out west of town."

Alfred hops into the Hudson. I start the engine and head west down Commerce Street, out to Blackwell Road and the railroad crossing, next to the Conoco station.

Lord, I never thought I'd stoop to stealing gas. Once I was only an ignorant, insensitive coach with too much pride. Now, I have become a lowly, despicable thief in the night.

We stop again at the Sinclair station on the outskirts of Eastland.

A TALL OIL RESERVOIR TANK with the tiny community's name "STAFF" inscribed in huge vertical black letters appears in the glare of our headlights directly ahead and to our right. We're getting close to the Leon River bottom which Blake Tucker warned us about. We have rolled down all the car windows to make it easier for us to see off to the sides of the road. A roar of fast-moving water comes from up ahead.

"You see anything on your side, Coach?"

"No. I wish we had thought to borrow a flashlight from one of the others. It's so dark, I can hardly see past the edge of the road."

"Coach, you better slow down. I'm pretty sure the road is gonna be under water. We don't wanna accidentally drive off in the river."

When the road grade breaks downward, the deafening roar drowns out the sound of the car engine. My car lights reflect across the ugly black waters of the flooding river. I stop the car at the edge of the swift current, and we climb out of the car to search along the roadsides for some sign of Murphy.

"Good gosh Almighty! That river looks awful scary, don't it, Coach?"

"Yep. I don't think there's any chance anyone could drive across. You don't wanna try it, do you?"

"No way you're gonna get me out in that dark water. I'm a'scared of snakes, and I can't swim worth a flip," Alfred advises me.

"Let's go, Alfred. There's no sign of Murphy here. Maybe the other men had more luck."

We climb back in the Hudson. Since the gravel road is unusually narrow near the edge of the water, I back up the slope carefully, looking for a place to turn around. There's no sense in taking a chance of sliding into the roadside drainage ditch and getting stuck.

"Stop the car, Coach! I think I see somethin', out there in the river!"

"Which side are you looking on?" I ask, searching for the object Alfred has spotted.

"Off to the left, on the downstream side. Ain't that part of a pickup truck sticking up?"

I blink the headlights from bright to dim and back to bright. There's an object of some sort about thirty yards out in the raging river.

"We'd better take a closer look, Alfred." I shove the car into neutral and let it roll slowly back down toward the river. When we get near the water, I swing the car around, pointing the headlights directly at the object.

"Alfred, isn't that Murphy's pickup?"

"Sure is, Coach. It darn sure is. Whatta you think we should do?"

"If Murphy is still in his pickup, we need to get him out before the river gets any higher. I've got a rope in the turtleback that we used to tow cars at the Pontiac House. If I tie it around me, could you hold on to me while I swim to the pickup?"

"Coach, it's too dangerous. Maybe we oughta get help." Alfred's voice is strained. The thought of our wading into the dark, foreboding river is appalling.

"Alfred, the river is rising higher every minute. Anyway, we probably don't have enough gas left to go back for help. If Murphy is out there, he's certain to be washed down river before we can drive into town and back."

We gather up the long tow rope and strip to our skivvies. The cold water rushing against my skin sends a shiver up my back. We slowly work our way out to a point directly upstream from the pickup, taking care to stay up on the flooded roadway. The water is only slightly above my waist, but the force of the furious river makes it difficult to keep my feet beneath me. Securing the rope around my waist, I hand it to Alfred.

"Let me out slowly. I'll jerk on the rope twice to signal when I reach the pickup, then gimme some slack."

"Alright, Coach. You be careful now," Alfred warns in a voice filled with apprehension.

I slip into the deep, murky waters beyond the roadway. Dark objects brush by me. Damn, I wish Alfred hadn't mentioned anything about snakes. My feet no longer touch the bottom. A greasy old tow rope, anchored by Alfred's strong arms, is my only link to life.

The water is deeper and much swifter than I thought it would be. Once I get out away from the roadway, the impetus of the racing river forces me into a horizontal position, facing back upstream. Alfred slowly unravels the rope while I fight to keep my head above the rolling waves of black water. I choke on the filth of dirty water sucked into my nose and throat when I try to inhale.

My legs bump hard into the rigid metal of the rear truck bed of Murphy's pickup. I grab the submerged side rail and pull myself forward toward the cab. The driver's side is facing upstream, indicating the truck was headed toward Eastland when it ran off the road. The driver's window is rolled up, but the silhouette of a body slumped over the steering wheel is plainly visible inside.

The driving force of the river current makes it impossible to open the driver's door, so I work myself back into the truck bed and jerk twice on the rope, signaling Alfred to give me some slack. The truck moves several feet downstream before I can find the passenger side door handle. It's only a matter of time before the rising stream lifts up the vehicle and washes it away.

The passenger door seems to be stuck. Setting my foot against the side of the cab, I pull hard. The door releases and swings open rapidly, ripping my hands from the handle. I flail wildly in the water trying to regain a hold on the cab. My hand finds the side of the door, and I pull myself inside the cab where the water is calm.

Murphy is either dead or unconscious. The deafening roar makes it impossible to determine whether he is breathing. Already having decided it will be impossible for Alfred to pull the two of us back to the roadway, I untie the rope and wrap it around Murphy. Murphy's heavy, wet body is difficult to move inside the cramped cab. Struggling with his limp carcass, I drag sections of his body in short segments toward the open door.

When we clear the cab, I grasp the side rail and pull us back into the truck bed. Re-checking the rope loop tied around Murphy, I jerk on the rope three times, signaling Alfred to begin the laborious chore of retrieving Murphy.

The pickup abruptly lurches several yards downstream, making my heart jump up into my throat.

Resting on one knee inside the sunken truck bed, the swift water comes above my waist and rushes past my exhausted body. Alfred will have to carry Murphy to the dry road before he returns to float the tow rope back out to me. Even if his task takes only a few minutes, this will be a long, anxious wait. Trying to divert my mind away from the intense fear surging up inside me, I force myself to think of Juanita and the carefree days we shared that summer in Stephenville.

CHAPTER EIGHT
REFLECTIONS AND MORE TROUBLES

Stephenville, Texas
Saturday Afternoon
June 2, 1948

THE TRAILWAYS BUS was more than an hour late arriving at the Stephenville bus terminal. It made no difference. I hadn't expected anyone to meet me. After retrieving my luggage, I decided to walk the short distance to John Tarleton's campus. This was my first visit to North Central Texas, and I was anxious to familiarize myself with the city where I planned to spend my summer.

Historical buildings and old houses had never held much interest for me, but while I strolled along the sidewalks through downtown Stephenville to the Tarleton campus, I couldn't help but marvel at how many beautiful old structures had been preserved and were maintained in such good condition. The tall stone courthouse, visible from miles away, with its steep gables and centered with one magnificent steeple, was a timeless masterpiece of architecture. Unique commercial buildings like the First National Bank and Crows Opera House, constructed with natural, hand-carved limestone exteriors, surrounded the ancient courthouse to form the town square. Quaint two and three-story houses along narrow, tree-lined streets had been built many years earlier, probably by successful merchants who desired the luxury of walking home to be with their families for lunch.

Perhaps my walk along the enchanting streets raised my expectations too high. My first glimpse of John Tarleton College was an enormous letdown.

The college campus consisted of a three-story, dark-brick school building, a dilapidated recreation and gym building and four long narrow wooden World War Two vintage barracks which served as dormitories. The exterior walls of the dormitory buildings were faced with a faded, white asbestos siding. The barrack buildings were roofed with grass-green composition shingles. A high stone wall surrounded the front section of the small campus, except at the entrance where two tall stone pilasters were constructed, like bookends, on each side of the road. A wrought iron archway supported by the stone pilasters spanned the entry way. The words "JOHN TARLETON COLLEGE" were spelled out in metal letters between the top and bottom chords of the iron archway.

The tiny agricultural school was a far cry from the majestic buildings and sprawling campus of Texas A&M where I'd toiled on football scholarship for the past three years.

I had come to Tarleton to make up courses in history and economics so I could graduate from A&M after the fall semester. Coach Norton had arranged for me to receive free tuition, room, and board. I would also be able to earn a few extra dollars for teaching two summer school P.E. classes. Because Tarleton was part of the A&M College System, it was one of the few outside schools I could attend and get full credit for college hours transferred to A&M this close to graduation.

An efficient, middle-aged, gray-haired woman in the registrar's office had the school's employment forms prepared and ready for me to sign. Coach Norton's tremendous influence was evident, even there at the Stephenville college. The registrar lady had me in and out of her office and on my way to a room in the men's dormitory in less than ten minutes.

A young man was lying in one of the two single beds when I entered my assigned room. He set aside a comic book he was reading and jumped up to greet me.

"Hello. You must be Onis Warden. I'm Skipper Wilson, your roommate for the summer."

The young man must have been checking the school's records to know my given name. It's not a name I cherish. Even my closest A&M teammates know me only as Stubby Warden.

Skipper Wilson was thin and pale. His light-brown hair and clean-cut boyish face made him look much too young for college. We were actually very close to the same age.

"Good to meet you, Skipper. Please, call me Stubby. Are you a teacher?"

"Not really. I'm more like a teacher's assistant. The school is furnishing me free room and board this summer for cleaning the AG Lab and grading papers for the math classes."

In spite of my curiosity about what constituted an AG Lab and Skipper's specific AG Lab duties, I decided not to pursue the subject. "Skipper, which side of the room do you want? I need to unpack my bags."

"You take the east side, Stubby. I'm satisfied with where I am now."

Skipper returned to his comic book while I unpacked and settled into my summer quarters. Except for the two iron beds, each with a slightly used, black and gray striped cotton mattress, the room held no furniture. One tiny closet with a single clothes-rod was provided on each side of the room. Thin plaster walls, which separated us from adjacent rooms, were painted white. The wooden floor had at one time been stained and sealed with a coat of shellac. Now, the raw wood was exposed with shallow troughs of severe wear, providing pathways in areas of heavy foot traffic.

Seemingly engrossed in his comic book, Skipper watched me closely until I had my bags put away.

"Hey, Stubby, you wanna go down to the gym? They're decorating for a dance there tonight. We might meet some girls."

"No thanks, Skipper. I think I'll just hang around here until supper time. By the way, what time does the cafeteria open?"

"The school doesn't serve an evening meal on Saturday night. If you were expecting a school meal tonight, I guess you're out of luck. Come on. Let's go down to the gym."

The last meal I had eaten was breakfast that morning at the athletic dorm in College Station. In my habitual penniless condition, Skipper's information meant there was no chance I would eat again that day. Afraid I wouldn't like the answer, I hesitated to ask if the school cafeteria served meals on Sunday. Maybe a trip to the gym with Skipper would make me forget my hunger.

"Okay, Skipper, you talked me into it. Let's go check out the girls at the gym."

INSIDE THE GYM long streamers of blue and gold crepe paper decorated the walls and ceiling. A large cardboard sign, hand-painted in blue letters, proclaimed: "John Tarleton College–Get Acquainted Dance."

Several young men and women were circled around a tall, wooden step ladder beneath the basketball goal at the north end of the gym. A girl in shorts was at the top of the ladder, decorating the goal with crepe paper. Skipper pulled me over to the group and began introducing me.

"Hi, everyone. I want you to meet my new roommate Stubby Warden."

Skipper and I stood at the foot of the ladder while he pointed out each person in the group, telling me their name. Suddenly, the girl in shorts who had been up on the ladder above us, jumped down to the gym floor, missing the last few steps and bouncing hard against me. Instinctively, I reached out and caught her in my arms before she fell. Her body was soft and warm.

"I'm sorry, sir. Did I hurt you? I'm not usually so clumsy."

My heart stopped beating for a moment as our bodies touched. Our eyes met like a spark of electric current. I'd never seen such a beautiful girl. Her dark brown hair contrasted against her light, fair complexion, making her skin seem incredibly white and pure. Her tight shorts accentuated her firm, shapely legs. A loose-fitting blouse could not disguise the absolute certainty of a slim waist or the fullness of her bosom hiding underneath. Not even in my dreams had I ever imagined such a girl. When I finally recovered sufficiently to speak, my tongue was thick and pasty.

"No ma'am, I'm fine. It looks like I survived our collision without a scratch. My name is Stubby Warden. I don't believe we've been properly introduced."

"Hello, Mister Stubby Warden. I'm Juanita Kimbrough. Will you be coming to our dance tonight?"

"If you would promise to save a dance for me, Miss Kimbrough, a team of wild horses couldn't keep me away."

She smiled at me. Surely she had felt some of the electric charge exchanged between us. Still, she answered me tauntingly, "If you want to dance with me, Mister Warden, you'll have to stand in line like all the rest. Generally, I only go for tall guys, but if you come to the dance, I might dance with you."

She bounced off to the other end of the gym where the decorating crew was working on the other goal, leaving me to stand alone. Skipper had apparently found himself a date for the evening. He and one of the girls from the social committee were leaving together through the gym front door.

AT TEXAS A&M in College Station there weren't many occasions, and even fewer reasons, to dress up in civilian clothes. Formal dress usually meant wearing my khaki Corps military uniform. My civilian wardrobe consisted of two pair of denim blue jeans and a few white tee shirts. Deciding what to wear to the "Get Acquainted Dance" was quite distressing. I wanted to make a good impression on the Kimbrough girl, so maybe she would dance with me. After much deliberation, I decided to wear a portion of my regular Corps uniform. A long-sleeved khaki shirt with rolled-up sleeves and battalion pants without a cap and no tie gave me a casual, nonchalant look which would've gotten me some serious demerits back at College Station.

The minute I stepped inside the gym, I realized I was overdressed. Most of the guys were wearing blue jeans or slacks with short-sleeved shirts. The girls were dressed in casual summer wear, sundresses, or bright cotton skirts with matching blouses.

My eyes searched the gym floor until I found her. She was dancing with a tall, handsome young man who looked like he might play on the basketball team. They were talking and laughing while they danced. When the music switched to a slower, romantic Glen Miller tune, the young man held her close. The two had obviously danced together before. Their bodies moved in perfect unison to the soft music. Having never been a very good dancer, my hopes for making a hit with her sank lower. I spotted Skipper and wandered over to stand beside him and his date.

Jealously, I watched while my beautiful female fantasy changed partners and began to dance with another tall fellow. She seemed to know everyone, and every good looking young man seemed anxious to dance with her. After an hour had passed, she stopped to chat with a group of other young women. Her latest tall male partner obediently went to fetch her a cup of the punch being served at the south end of the gym.

"Hello, Miss Kimbrough. I was wondering if you might dance with me?"

"Well, Mister Stubby Warden, you are persistent, aren't you? I'd be delighted to dance with you some other time, but right now I'm waiting for a cup of punch."

"Miss Kimbrough, at our A&M school dances the football guys would always bet me I couldn't persuade the most beautiful girl to dance with me. I never once lost one of those bets. Now, dancing with the most beautiful girl at a party has become sort of a ritual for me. I hope you won't be the one to break my streak."

"Mister Warden, that may be the most incredible lie I have ever heard."

"Miss Kimbrough, surely you don't think I could be lying about your being the most beautiful girl here tonight. But the more important question is–have I convinced you to dance with me?"

"How could I ever refuse such a splendid request?" she laughed.

She was like holding heaven in my arms. With her warm body close against me, my feet glided her easily across the dance floor in rhythm to the music. The fresh smell of her soft brown hair pressed against my face overwhelmed my senses. Too soon, the dance ended.

"Thank you, Mister Warden. You are a very good dancer," she told me, as I returned her to the tall male who was waiting impatiently and awkwardly holding two cups of punch.

"It was my pleasure, Miss Kimbrough. None of those beautiful women I danced with at A&M could dance nearly as well as you."

"If you ask me to dance again, Mister Warden, my answer might be more enthusiastic than before."

"Then, you can be certain that I'll be back to ask again."

Although she would occasionally dance with another partner, she essentially became my date for the remainder of the dance. She was a delightful companion who was never at a loss for something interesting to say. We talked and laughed and danced the evening away.

"Mister Warden, would you care to see me home?" she asked, when the dance ended.

"Yes, I'd like that very much. Where do you live?"

"In a private home, about a half-mile from the campus. Do you have a car?"

"No, I came in today, by bus."

"We can walk then. It's not far."

The summer evening was warm and pleasant. An almost-full moon overhead and a soft southern breeze made the perfect setting to end such a wonderful night. Two blocks from the gym she reached to take my hand. We walked together silently, hand in hand, each aware of a deep, strong feeling flowing between us.

"This is where I live," she informed me, as we arrived in front of a large two-story residence. It was one of many private homes in Stephenville where young college women from out of town were housed. The barrack style dormitories were somewhat crude for delicate young ladies.

"Thank you for a wonderful evening, Juanita. Maybe we'll see each other at school on Monday," I said, saddened to see the evening end.

She stood with her hand on the front gate, ready to go inside. "Mister Warden, do you want to kiss me goodnight?"

"Yes, I would like very much to kiss you."

"Then, please quit being so shy. I need you to kiss me, right now."

She came lightly into my arms. Her soft lips pressed against mine. The sweet taste of her mouth as our tongues gently touched, caused my knees to wobble and my mind to reel. Our kiss lasted much too long for a first date goodnight kiss. We were both surprised at the powerful feelings unleashed.

"You kiss very well, Mister Warden. Thank you."

"Can I see you again tomorrow, Juanita?"

"Yes, I'd like that. Would you like to take me to church tomorrow morning?"

"Yes. Sure. Which church do you attend?"

"First Baptist. It's just off the courthouse square. I have to go early to teach a Sunday school class. Can you meet me at eleven o'clock for the main service?"

"Great. I know exactly where it is. It's a date then. I'll see you tomorrow. Goodnight."

"Goodnight, Mister Warden."

She opened the gate and started up the stone-paved walkway leading to the front porch. I waited a moment to make sure the front door was open for her. After she was safely inside, I turned and began walking back toward John Tarleton.

"Stubby! Stubby Warden!" I heard her calling.

She was in my arms again before I could completely turn around. Her mouth pressed against mine. We kissed for a long time. When our mouths parted, she pressed a key ring into my hand.

"Stubby darling, would you mind bringing my car to me when you meet me at church tomorrow?"

"You have a car?"

"Yes, I left it outside the gym. It's a red two-door Ford."

"Why would you leave your car at the gym? Why didn't you drive it home?"

"Because you wouldn't have walked me home if you'd known I had a car, darling," she answered smartly, before she darted back down the sidewalk toward her house.

Walking back to the college campus, my feet barely touched the ground. The most beautiful girl in the world had walked home, just to be with me. And, she wanted to see me again tomorrow. I'd traveled several blocks before I remembered I had no clothes to wear to church.

My stomach growled, reminding me it hadn't been fed.

Friday Night
September 6, 1949

TWO HEADLIGHTS APPEAR on the dark horizon, in line with the farm road leading back to Staff. Alfred has succeeded in retrieving Murphy's lifeless body and has carried him to the dry roadway where we left the Hudson. For some reason he's taking an awfully long time to come back for me. I can see his gigantic body outlined by the car lights as he raises up to wave at the oncoming automobile.

The car pulls to a stop on the road behind the Hudson. Two figures jump out quickly and begin an excited conversation with Alfred. The two figures walk to the edge of the river and gaze toward me.

Alfred picks up the tow rope and begins trudging along the flooded road. One of the figures follows him. The other person kneels down beside Murphy.

The river has been rising fast. As he reaches a point upstream where he'll attempt to float the rope out to me, the water is above Alfred's waist. Leo Jackson is the other figure in the water. In spite of my perilous predicament, I can't help but wonder whether Leo is still wearing those expensive two hundred dollar boots.

Alfred unwinds the rope rapidly, floating it toward me. The buoyancy of the rising waters swings the cab of Murphy's pickup around to face downstream, parallel with the current. Trying to spot the rope amongst the swift, rolling waves, I move to the very rear of the truck bed. At last, I spy the end of the rope, almost ten yards away. The river current has pushed Murphy's pickup too far downstream to be reached with the tow rope.

Attempting to get the rope closer to me, Alfred leaves the safety of the pavement. He steps off the elevated roadway toward me. I can barely pick out his head above the water. The pickup jerks and slowly begins to roll along with the current. The end of the rope is still several yards away. Realizing I'll only get one chance, I muster all my strength and dive head-first into the deadly, boiling waters.

Every muscle in my body strains as I swim hard against the strong current, searching for the rope. My mighty effort makes no difference. The force of the river begins to carry me backward.

My flailing hand finds something coarse and cord-like in the water. In desperation I grasp onto it. My body swings around and comes to a halt. Rolling waters wash over my head. I feel myself being dragged upstream by the round band held tightly in my hands. My guardian angel, overcoming his fear, has come out into the river to allow the rope to reach me. Gripping the rope firmly, I hang on while Alfred pulls me to safety.

"Good gosh, Coach! I thought you was a goner for sure," Alfred professes with relief, when we reach the flooded roadbed where my feet can touch bottom.

"Me too, Alfred. If you hadn't come off the road to get me, I'd be floating down the river right now to my certain death."

Leo Jackson speaks to me. "Stubby, are you sure you're okay? You had us mighty worried."

"Yeah, I guess I'm fine, Leo. I don't think I'll ever want to swim in a river again, though."

The three of us wade through the speeding water along the sumerged roadway toward the two cars. My body begins to tremble. Exhaustion has replaced fear as my adrenaline flow recedes.

"Alfred, how is Murphy? Is he still alive?" I ask, suddenly remembering the reason we risked our lives.

"Yeah, he's alive, but we need to get him to a hospital. Coach Murphy's been shot."

———————

LATE FRIDAY NIGHT we delivered Murphy to the emergency room at Eastland General Hospital. The doctor in charge immediately arranged to send him into surgery. Keith never regained consciousness so we were unable to learn anything about the circumstances leading to his being shot.

Leo Jackson telephoned Mrs. Murphy, making arrangements for him and his neighbor to pick her up and bring her to the hospital. Before they left, I swallowed my pride and asked Leo to help us with our fuel situation. His partner Glen Elgin called a friend in Eastland who brought us five gallons of gas for the Hudson. Alfred and I hardly spoke a word on the drive back to Ranger. We were both too tired to talk.

———————

Saturday Morning
September 7, 1949

A FEW MINUTES AFTER NINE I leave the house. The big guy is still in bed asleep. After our ordeal last evening I don't have the heart to wake him. He'll be hungry when he wakes up, and as he puts it, "He can't cook worth a flip." Maybe I'll treat him to a late breakfast at Pearl's, if I can borrow a few bucks from Price. When I drive into the parking lot, Price is outside talking with a customer. He waves and continues his discussion. Anxious to call Juanita, I go inside to his office. It's been a week since I talked to her.

"NUMBER, PLEASE?" I hear the operator say.

"Hello, Operator, I would like to place a person-to-person call to Comanche, Texas. I want to speak with Mrs. Juanita Warden. The number is 969."

"May I have your name please?"

"This is Stubby Warden speaking."

"One moment, Mister Warden, while I ring for you."

Clicking noises echo on the line. An extended buzzing sound means the phone on the other end is ringing.

"Hello. This is the Kimbrough residence." The voice sounds like Juanita's mother.

"I have a person-to-person call for a Mrs. Juanita Warden. The call is from a Mister Stubby Warden. Will you accept the call?"

"I'm sorry, Operator, but Juanita Warden is very ill. She is unable to come to the telephone. She will not be able to accept the call."

"Mrs. Kimbrough! Mrs. Kimbrough! Please talk with me! What's wrong with Juanita?" I scream into the phone.

I hear a click on the other end. The operator comes on the line. "I'm sorry, sir. The other party has hung up. Do you want me to try again?"

"No thank you, Operator. I'm afraid the Comanche lady's not gonna accept a call from me today."

Mrs. Kimbrough said Juanita was very ill. Oh, Lord, please don't let it be a problem with the baby. Maybe Price will know something.

PRICE FROWNS AT ME from across his desk. He has Juanita's mother on the line. After I related my concern about Juanita and told him about my telephone experience with Mrs. Kimbrough, he hit the roof. Before I could voice an objection, he was in his office calling Comanche.

"Yes, Edna, I understand how you feel, but she is his wife, and it is his baby. He has every right to know what's going on. You were wrong not to accept his call."

An angry expression comes on Price's face as he listens to Mrs.

Kimbrough's explanation.

"Edna, that's a crock, and you know it. Sooner or later, you and Luther will have to accept the fact that she's married, and there's not a darn thing you can do about it."

Price shakes his head. Apparently, his argument is falling on deaf ears.

"Alright, Edna, have it your way. Mark my words, though. One of these days you and Luther will realize how pigheaded you've been not to have seen what a good man you have for a son-in-law. I hope Stubby Warden will be kind enough to forgive you, when you come begging."

Price covers the receiver with his hand while Mrs. Kimbrough gets in the last words.

"You want to talk to her?" he asks me.

"No, I want to talk directly with Juanita," I tell him.

"Edna, listen to me. I will not accept any more of your lame excuses. You get Juanita Warden on the phone. Tell her Stubby insists upon speaking directly to her."

Price hands me the telephone. I can hear people talking to each other on the other end. Juanita's voice comes on the line. She sounds weak and tired.

"Hello, Stubby. What did you do to get Mother so upset? I was asleep. She says you insisted on talking with me."

Oh, what a wonderful family I have married into. Now her mother has twisted the situation around to make me the bad guy. If Price's prediction comes true and Juanita's family does come begging to me someday, I'm not so sure I can ever forgive them. They wouldn't treat a hardened criminal the way they've treated me.

"Juanita, your mother said you were too ill to come to the telephone. Is anything wrong with you or the baby?"

"Stubby darling, I should've let you know, but I didn't want to worry you, not until we knew something. I've been having some problems, a lot of bleeding. The doctor has given me some medicine that he thinks may help. Losing so much blood makes me feel tired all the time. The doctor has confined me to bed. I spend a lot of time sleeping."

"Juanita, is there a chance you might lose the baby?"

"The doctor tells us there's about a fifty percent chance of losing it. He's done all he can do. It's all in God's hands now."

"Juanita, I wish I could be there with you. Maybe I could help in some way."

"Sweetheart, there's nothing you could possibly do that isn't being done. Please don't worry. Remember what we talked about last Saturday. You stay in Ranger and be the best darn football coach you can be. I'll stay here and have you a fine, healthy baby."

"Juanita, I'll pray for you and our baby every day until I see you again."

"I hope that will be soon, darling. I have to say goodbye now. I'm feeling very dizzy."

"Goodbye, Juanita."

Price has been watching me closely during my conversation with Juanita. My pitiful relationship with the Kimbrough family is clearly distasteful to him.

"How is Juanita doing, Stubby? It sounded like she might be having some problems."

"Yeah, Price, it's pretty bad. About a fifty-fifty chance she'll lose the baby. Damn, I wish I could be with her."

"Stubby, if I live a million years, I'll never understand why that family is so strongly against you. If I had a son, I'd want him to be exactly like you."

"And I wish I could've had a father like you, Price."

"Get out of here, before we start hugging each other. Hey, you need some money? I know you haven't been paid by the school yet."

"I could sure put a twenty to good use, if you can spare it."

DESPITE MY WORRIES about Juanita and the baby, the burden of my troubles seems a little lighter as I leave the Pontiac House. The unusual experience of having serious money in my pocket raises my spirits and adds a slight spring to my step.

After I slip into the Hudson's driver's seat, I lay my head against the steering wheel and pray a short prayer.

"Lord, do whatever you want with me, but please don't take Juanita or our baby away. My life would be worthless without them. Amen."

I reach to start the motor, then pause and put my head back down on the steering wheel.

"Oh! And, Lord–P.S. Please help me survive this coaching job for one more week. At least, 'til I get paid. Amen."

CHAPTER NINE
THE SECOND WEEK

O N SATURDAY AFTERNOON, after we finished a late breakfast at Pearl's, Alfred and I drove to Eastland to check on Keith Murphy. We were unable to see him. Following his surgery, the hospital had assigned him to their intensive care ward. No visitors allowed. We talked to Kate Murphy who had been at the hospital all night. She was unable to tell us anything which would give us a clue as to why her husband had been shot. He had not regained consciousness since we left him Friday night. Alfred and I offered to stay and keep vigil while she got some rest. She declined our offer, explaining that her brother was on his way to the hospital from his home in Weatherford.

Before we left Eastland, I considered driving over to the Cisco Country Club and look up Jerry Lowe. One of the orderlies at the hospital informed us that Cisco lost to Big Springs the night before, by a score of 20 to 6. I wouldn't have been surprised to find Jerry on the country club golf course, celebrating his head coach's misfortune. A short minute's deliberation helped me make up my mind; I decided to head back to Ranger.

On Sunday morning I attended worship service at the First Baptist Church on Walnut Street near downtown. It was the first time I'd been inside a church since last July. Not wanting to be recognized by anyone who might want to critique my performance during the Albany football game, I arrived late and chose a seat in the pew nearest the back door. The pastor preached about the evils of alcohol. It was probably a fine sermon, but I didn't pay close attention. I was there for my own personal reasons. No one in church prayed harder than me. I left the service early, during the invitation.

Monday Afternoon
September 9, 1949

A TALL, LANKY RED-HAIRED MAN leans against a dark blue Studebaker pickup as we drive into the stadium parking lot. The man straightens up and walks toward us while I park next to the entrance gate.

"You know that man, Alfred?" After my experience with Clifford and company last Monday, I'm apprehensive about every stranger.

"I believe he's Reed Jones' dad, Coach."

"It might be better if I talk to him alone, Alfred. Why don't you give Sam some help." The upcoming conversation is almost certain to include references to my secret agreements with Lucas Masters. I'd rather Alfred not hear about them.

"Coach, maybe I should wait for you under the stands?" The tone of Alfred's voice denotes his concern for my safety.

"No, you go on inside. Don't worry. I'll be fine."

"You sure, Coach?"

"I'm sure, Alfred. Now, go on."

The red-headed man offers his hand for me to shake as he approaches. Alfred stops beneath the bleachers. He watches us until he's satisfied the man means me no harm.

"Hello, Coach Warden. I'm Radford Jones. Most folks call me Red."

His handshake is firm and sincere. Even though I know this is not a friendly visit, I instantly like the man.

"What can I do for you, Mister Jones?"

"Red. You can call me Red, Coach."

"Okay, Red. What did you come to talk about?"

"About my boy, Reed. He's your quarterback–at least he was until the last play of the game on Friday night." Jones tries to hide his simmering anger behind a cordial voice. He's probably been stewing all weekend.

"I suppose Reed is pretty upset. I treated him badly, didn't I, Red?"

"You know you did, Coach. Reed is heartbroken. He thinks he did something to make you mad at him. He didn't eat a bite all weekend. Just sat around the house, moping. His mother and I are worried sick about him." Some of the anger in Jones' voice wanes after I admit my guilt.

"Red, I don't know what to tell you. Reed didn't do a thing wrong. I just made a dumb call. I have no other excuse. I'm truly sorry your son got hurt, but the plain fact is–what's done is done. All I can do is to ask you and your family to forgive a young coach for a stupid mistake."

"I reckon there's only one question I want answered, Coach. Do you have a problem with Reed Jones being the quarterback of this football team?"

"The answer to your question is no, we don't have a problem. Reed Jones is my quarterback. He'll be the starting quarterback for all of our remaining games."

A frown on Jones' face suggests he's not quite finished with me. There's some other problem, still to be discussed, before he'll be satisfied.

"Coach Warden, are you aware of the agreement I have with Lucas Masters?"

Uh, oh. I was truly hoping we could avoid this unpleasant subject.

"Yes, Mister Jones, I'm aware of your agreement with Lucas Masters."

"Then you understand the serious consequences of not abiding by the promise you've just made–to play Reed at quarterback for the rest of the season?"

"Yes. I'll probably lose my job if I renege on my promise to you."

"Definitely is the word you are hunting for, Coach. You will definitely lose your job if you don't abide by your promise."

"Alright. Yes, I understand your point, precisely."

"Just so we clearly understand each other, Coach. Lucas Masters has been paid handsomely for his services in this matter. I personally arranged for him to acquire, with minimal cash outlay, a one-sixth interest in a producing oil well over in Palo Pinto County. If Lucas does not deliver the agreed service, his interest can be forfeited back to me and my other partners. Lucas will not take kindly to anyone who costs him that much money."

"Like I told you before, Red. I fully understand the agreement."

"Okay then. That's good enough for me. Maybe we'll see each

other at the game in DeLeon this Friday."

"Say, Red! One question. Does Reed know about your arrangement with Lucas Masters?"

"Hell no! And he better not find out from you!"

"Your secret is safe with me, Red, but I wonder how he'd feel if he knew?"

"We'll never know the answer to that question, will we, Coach?"

"No, I guess not, Red."

Shoving a hand into my pants pocket on my way to the field house, the loose change reminds me I have less than seven dollars left from the twenty Price loaned me on Saturday. I wonder how much a one-sixth interest in a producing oil well is worth.

———————

SAM IGNORES MY GREETING when I speak to him. He keeps his head lowered, pretending to be busy sorting through a pile of dirty jerseys. Hard feelings about last Friday night's quarterback incident evidently extend all the way to my assistant coach.

Our football squad is in uniform and on the practice field. Inside the normally bustling room the quietness is nerve racking. Wanting to avoid getting caught in the unpleasantness of the pending verbal confrontation, Alfred suddenly remembers something which needs his attention outside.

"You still mad about Friday night, Coach Aills?"

"Yep," he answers without raising his head.

"Can we talk about it?"

"Ain't nothing to talk about," he answers, keeping his head lowered.

"Sam, we need to get this thing settled between us. What can I do? Do you want an apology?"

"You're trying to make up with the wrong party, Coach Warden. I'm not the one you done wrong."

"You mean you want me to apologize to Reed Jones? Alright, I'm willing to do that."

"Nope, that's not exactly what I think you should do."

Sam's sullen attitude, combined with his short answers, makes him difficult to read. What else could he want me to do?

"Sam, you can't ask me to apologize to the whole team?"

"It's your problem, Coach Warden. If you're not man enough to face up to your team, maybe you oughta be teaching P.E. classes somewhere."

Sam's sarcasm cuts through me like a knife. Without knowing, he has found the soft spot in my armor, driving his sharp sword deep into the bowels of my worst fears.

"But, Sam, I'm the head coach. I'd lose the confidence and respect of every player if I start apologizing for my coaching decisions."

"Like I said, Coach Warden. It's your problem."

"Alright, let's get it over with then. Get the players together under the north goal posts."

Never, in my football career, have I heard of a football coach apologizing to his team for making a bad coaching decision. The possibility of Coach Homer Norton at Texas A&M asking his Aggie team to forgive him for changing quarterbacks would be unthinkable. Football coaches never apologize. It just isn't done.

I try to decide on the exact language to use in my apology, rehearsing my lines while I wait for Sam to return. No matter how I phrase my words, this ordeal will be terribly embarrassing and painful.

Stomping his feet to remove mud from his shoes, Sam comes through the open front door of the field house. The playing field is still wet and muddy, an aftermath of Friday night's rain. He has a strange expression on his face.

"Stubby, the team was already having a meeting. They asked me to leave 'em alone until they were finished. They were deadly serious. Said they'd call us when they're done."

"Whatta you suppose they could be up to, Sam?"

"Only thing I can think of is the quarterback switch you pulled on Friday night. A lot of players were upset after the game. It's a good thing you and Alfred left so quickly. There were some things said you didn't need to hear."

Good God! Not only do I have Lucas Masters and his cronies badgering me and beating up on me, now my own players are meeting to decide my fate. I wonder if a high school football coach has ever been fired by his team.

Sam and I sit side-by-side on a long wooden bench behind the equipment counter, waiting to be summoned by our football team. We don't speak. Our precarious situation makes us both uneasy.

After a half-hour or so, James Burnett, a freshman halfback, sticks his head through the front door. "Okay, Coaches, the team is ready to meet with you. Can you both come out on the field?"

Gathered in a circle, the members of the football squad are sitting under the north goal. The ground there is the driest part of the wet field. Elder, Hummel and Jones are seated in the middle of the circle. They rise to their feet as Sam and I approach.

Deciding to take the initiative, I step through the young men's bodies to the middle of the circle. I am ready to swallow the bitter pill of apologizing to my team.

Dean Elder holds up a hand to stop me before I can speak.

"Coach Warden, this is our meeting. Will you please hear us out before you say anything?" Elder's voice is firm and sober.

"Of course. Please excuse me. I'm always anxious to listen to anything you men have to say."

Jackie Hummel steps forward, in front of Elder and Jones. Apparently, he will be the team's spokesman.

"Coach, there have been a lot of things said among the players about the Albany game last Friday. Some things that were said about you were very uncomplimentary."

"Yes, and I certainly understand…," I begin to answer.

Dean Elder holds his hand up again to stop me from talking. "Coach, will you please just listen? This is very difficult for all of us."

I nod my head, agreeing to keep quiet while Hummel continues. "Coach, like I said, there have been some nasty things said about you. Some of our parents have been particularly critical of you. The football team is concerned you might be upset with us. We players are concerned that you may have heard some of the angry words which were said in the heat of the moment."

The meeting is taking a much different direction than I expected. I glance sideways toward Sam. His facial expression illustrates his total shock at the surprising turn of events.

"The purpose of this meeting is to let you know we respect your right to make decisions needed to coach this team. We put it to a vote. To the last man, every person on this football squad supports you as our coach. Coach Warden, you have our promise. There'll be no more bickering or second-guessing from any of us. We only ask one thing. We want you to stick with us and help us have a winning season."

I survey the faces of Davenport, Bagwell, Cantrell, Pearson, Varner, Tune, Polston, Wade and the other players. There is no sign of the animosity I had anticipated among the young faces. My surveillance stops when I come upon the face of Reed Jones.

"Reed, you have anything to add?" I ask. My quarterback is the person I hurt most. He should have an opportunity to express his feelings.

"Coach, I admit I was one of the players so put out with you on Friday night. But, after thinking about it all weekend, I realize you made the best decision for the team. We stood a much better chance of scoring with Buddy at quarterback. From now on, you're the coach. I'll play, or not play, wherever you want me. Every man on this football team wants to win. We want you to show us how."

An uneasy silence falls over the meeting in the awkward interval after Jones speaks. I wait silently for a moment, wanting to be certain no one else intends to express an opinion. Finally, I break the silence. "Alright then, let's get on the field for practice. Are we gonna kick some DeLeon Bearcat butts on Friday?" I ask, clapping my hands with rekindled enthusiasm.

"Yeah!" the team members yell in unison.

Watching our players scatter across the field, my assistant coach and I stand beside one another in the end zone.

"Well, I'll be damned," Sam mutters under his breath.

"And I'll be double-damned," I repeat, expressing my agreement. "You know, Sam, I think I'm falling in love with these guys."

"Get in line, Stubby. Get in line."

FOOTBALL PRACTICE ON MONDAYS following a game is usually tiresome and boring for a football squad. With a whole week ahead before the next game there's less pressure to get the team prepared for their next opponent. We coaches normally work with individual players, ironing out problems noticed during the game or in game films. Generally, our Monday's practice is rather brief, lasting for only an hour or so. In order to give the players an extra day to recover from injuries and wounds received in the previous week's game, physical contact is minimized.

Because of the time lost during the team meeting, we keep the team practicing later than usual. A blazing, bright orange sun has partially disappeared behind Hospital Hill when we reach the parking lot.

Alfred is the first to notice the note taped across the windshield of the Hudson. He reads the note then hands it to me. The note is handwritten on school stationery and signed by G.C. Boswell.

"What does it mean, Coach?"

"I'm afraid it means more trouble, Alfred."

The note reads: "Coach Warden, please meet Lucas Masters in his office at 2:00 P.M. on Tuesday."

————————

Monday Evening
September 9, 1949

BY SOME ODD COINCIDENCE the house Juanita and I rented last May is next door to the home of a bank president. Willis Ferrol Creager, my closest neighbor, is president of the Commercial State Bank. It is truly ironic that a man in my dire financial straits could be living alongside the man who controls most of the money in the city.

Ferrol and Othel Creager reside in a large two-story house on West Main Street, next to mine. Their house is rectangular and boxlike, not representing any particular style of distinctive architecture. The house is painted white, with dark brown shutters framing each front window. The concrete porch at the front entrance is small and only partially shaded by a gabled arcade which extends out from the second floor. Two narrow steps connect the porch to the front sidewalk. What makes the house unique is that it sits on more than an acre of land, close to downtown. The grounds are pleasingly landscaped with thoughtfully-placed trees and shrubs. A thick green bermuda grass lawn is always mowed and immaculately trimmed. Colorful flowers of many different varieties have bloomed continuously in the Creager's flower beds since last spring.

Othel Creager was the first person who knocked on our door after we moved in. She was bearing a freshly-baked cake and a casserole which were served as the first meal in our new home. With her oldest daughter married and her other two children, LaNita and Bill, in school all day, Mrs. Creager always has time to stop and visit. She and Juanita have become close friends.

Ferrol Creager and I exchange a friendly hello from time to time, but we don't have all that much in common. After all, he's the president of Ranger's only bank. Up until a few weeks ago I was a "grease monkey" working at the Pontiac House.

Pearl tells me Lucas Masters owns most of the stock in the Ranger bank. Perhaps that explains why Ferrol Creager is such a workaholic.

It is almost dark when I pull the Hudson to a stop in my driveway. Othel Creager is sitting outside on the steps of her small front porch. She stands to wave, then begins walking toward us. I glance at the high grass in my yard. In spite of all my promises to the landlady, my lawn hasn't been mowed since mid-August. Mrs. Creager is probably coming over to complain about the unsightly condition of my rented property.

Seeing I cannot avoid conversation with the woman, I slink slowly out of the car. "Hello, Mrs. Creager. How are you this evening?"

She ignores my greeting, getting directly to her point. "Mister Warden, it seems like everyone in town is trying to get in touch with you. My phone has been ringing all afternoon."

"I'm sorry, Mrs. Creager, but I've never given your telephone number to anyone who might want to call me. Can you tell me who it was that called?" I'm puzzled about who would call the Creager residence looking for me. Once or twice Juanita used the Creager's telephone, but we never gave their number to anyone who might try to call us.

"Oh, Coach Warden, don't be so modest! You and Alfred Steele are heroes! All the papers want to get a story from you. The Ranger paper, the *Abilene Reporter* and even the *Fort Worth Press* have all called. I may get my name in the paper just because I live next door to you." Othel Creager's voice is bursting with excitement.

"Heroes? Mrs. Creager, what in the world are you talking about?"

"For saving Mister Murphy. You and Alfred are heroes because you risked your lives to save Mister Murphy. Everyone in town is talking about how courageous you two are."

"Mrs. Creager, we're not heroes. We were both scared to death. We only did what had to be done. I'm not sure either of us would be willing to do it again."

"Oh, Coach Warden! The way you tell it will make the story even more exciting. You're welcome to use my telephone if you want to return the phone calls tonight."

"Thanks for the offer, Mrs. Creager, but Alfred and I are both dog tired and hungry. Would you mind telling anyone who calls that I can't be reached until tomorrow? I'll come over to your house in the morning and get the names and numbers of the people who called."

"That'll be perfectly all right with me, Coach Warden. This is the most exciting thing that's happened since I've lived in Ranger. I feel like I'm part of it, because I know you so well. Maybe I can be your social secretary. Oh, I can't wait to call my sister and tell her."

"Thank you, Mrs. Creager. I appreciate your being so helpful. You're a marvelous neighbor," I proclaim, grateful that she hasn't mentioned my tall grass.

Alfred trails quietly behind me as we walk up the path to the front porch.

"Coach Warden," Alfred says, seemingly in deep thought.

"What, Alfred?"

"I don't wanna be no hero."

"Neither do I, Alfred. All I want to be is a football coach."

THE DOOR BELL RINGS while Alfred and I are washing the supper dishes. Since I am the designated washer, Alfred answers the front door.

"Coach, it's Mrs. Creager. She says it's important she talk with you," Alfred calls from the front room.

I reach for a cup towel and walk to the front door, drying my hands.

"Mrs. Creager, I wasn't expecting to see you until tomorrow morning."

"Mister Warden, I apologize for bothering you again, but I have an important message from Mrs. Murphy. She just called my house. She was very distressed."

"Why would Mrs. Murphy call you, Mrs. Creager? I don't understand."

"She says the sheriff has posted two deputies to guard Mister Murphy's hospital room. They won't tell her anything. She tried to call Leo Jackson, but he's out of town. She said you were the only other person she could trust to come help her."

"But, Mrs. Creager, why are all these people calling you?"

"Mister Warden, Ranger is a small town. Everyone knows you live next door to me," the woman pauses and smiles coyly. "And, I told the operator girls down at the telephone office to forward all your calls to my house. I hope you don't mind?"

"Mrs. Creager, you are truly something special. Thanks for the message. Alfred and I will drive over to Eastland, right away."

"Thank you, Mister Warden, for being such an interesting neighbor. Your life is like a cloak-and-dagger mystery movie. Living next door to you is so exciting. I can't wait to find out what will happen next. Now, I have to call my sister again to tell her what else has happened."

ON OUR WAY INTO THE HOSPITAL we walk past two Eastland County sheriff vehicles, parked beneath the canopy outside the front entrance.

Othel Creager must have called the injured coach's wife like I asked her to do. Mrs. Murphy is waiting for us in the hospital lobby. She runs to meet us.

Kate Murphy is a stout woman, apparently of German descent. Her light eyebrows, pale skin and unpainted lips make her seem plain, but she has a clean, pleasant appearance. I would bet Mrs. Murphy was raised on a farm. With her dishwater blonde hair tied in a tight knot behind her head, she looks like she'd be equally comfortable in the kitchen or in the barn milking a cow.

"Coach Warden, thank you for coming! Neither the sheriff nor his people will tell me anything. I'm worried about Keith. Do you think he's done something wrong?" The woman's voice is panicky. She's on the verge of crying.

"Mrs. Murphy, I'm sure there must be some kind of misunderstanding here. I'm sure we can straighten everything out." I do my best to speak calmly, trying not to reveal how uneasy I feel in the unfamiliar role she has asked me to play.

"They have Keith upstairs on the third floor. Two sheriff's deputies are standing guard outside his door. The sheriff left about a half-hour ago. Maybe you can find out something from the deputies?"

"Yes, that's exactly what I was thinking, Mrs. Murphy," I lie. Actually, I didn't have a clue about whom I should begin talking to. I turn to Alfred. "Would you mind waiting here with Mrs. Murphy while I try to find out what's going on?"

"Sure, Coach. We'll wait for you down here."

While I scale the stairs up to the third floor, I try to think of something I can say to convince the two deputies to tell me why they are so interested in Keith Murphy. I wouldn't be doing this if Mrs. Murphy wasn't so distraught. If the sheriff wouldn't tell her why his deputies are here, there is little chance anyone will be willing to tell me anything.

Two uniformed deputies are stationed in the hallway outside a door midway down the left side of the hall. My sudden appearance at the top of the stairway startles them. The deputies swing around to face me. The leather covers over their belt holsters are unsnapped, exposing the black handles of their pistols. These men are expecting trouble.

"I'm sorry, sir. No one is allowed on this floor. You'll have to go back down the stairs," one of the men warns sternly.

"Excuse me, gentlemen. My name is Stubby Warden. Would you mind if I asked a few questions? Coach Murphy is a friend of mine. His wife is downstairs. We're all very concerned about him."

The deputy advances toward me. "Are you the Stubby Warden who coaches the Ranger Bulldog football team?"

"Yes, Keith Murphy is one of my assistant coaches."

"Hello, Coach Warden. I'm James Fingler. I believe you know my older brother George. He owns Fingler's O.K. Grocery Store in Ranger."

"Yes, I certainly do know your brother. Lately, I've been shopping in his store almost every day."

"Coach Warden, this is my partner Max Crawford. We've been assigned to protect Mister Murphy."

"Protect him? Is he in danger?"

"Coach Warden, I've been planning to get in touch with you. The sheriff's office would like to enlist your help in breaking up a bootleg ring operating in Eastland County. If you will step inside Coach Murphy's room for a moment, I can explain everything to you. Max will stay out here and keep watch."

Inside the darkened hospital room I can see Murphy's body lying on a bed near the center of the room. He is very still, but I can hear his deep breathing. The bed is surrounded by a transparent plastic oxygen tent. A creamy medical liquid flows from a bottle suspended above the bed through a tiny plastic tube attached to Murphy's arm. Murphy does not appear to be conscious.

The deputy explains he is part of a special commission appointed by a federal judge in Abilene to investigate and clean up organized crime in Eastland County. The commission has uncovered evidence of an extensive bootlegging operation, but they've been unable to locate the liquor supply source.

"James, I'd like to help, but this is way out of my league. I don't know the first thing about bootleggers."

"Coach Warden, we don't expect you to arrest the bootleggers, but you do have day to day associations with persons who may know things which could be of interest to the commission. We simply want you to work with us and keep us informed about anything you might hear."

"I'm not sure who it is you think I work with every day that would know anything about bootlegging."

"Coach, don't act so naive. Your teenagers at Ranger High School know more about where to find illegal hooch than all the law officers in West Texas."

"Yes, I suppose that could be true."

"There's a lot of loose talk goes on in the dressing room and on the practice field, among your football players. What I'm asking is for you to let me know about anything you hear which might interest our crime commission."

"Alright, James, I'll agree to be your snitch," I respond jokingly. Actually, I wish there was some way to gracefully tell him no.

Fingler doesn't laugh. "Please don't take this lightly, Coach. What you're agreeing to do could put you in great danger."

"Does your bootlegger investigation work have anything to do with Keith Murphy being shot, and why you need to protect him?"

"Not exactly. Murphy was working with us on another investigation. We're fairly certain he was shot because someone found out he was working for us. He must've been awful close to putting the finger on someone."

"James, you need to tell Kate Murphy something. As you can imagine, she's terribly confused. I don't think she knew anything about the investigation Keith was involved with."

"Okay, I'll talk with her. The sheriff should be back shortly. After he returns, I'll go downstairs and explain everything to her."

"Thanks, James. I'm sure she'll keep anything you tell her in strictest confidence."

Before we leave the room, I step over to Murphy's hospital bed. My assistant coach appears to be in very bad condition. Reaching under the plastic canopy, I take his thick, calloused hand in mine.

"Keith, you better not die on me. We've got too many football games left to play together."

Murphy's hand squeezes mine, ever so slightly.

———————

WHEN I RETURN from my visit with the two deputies upstairs, I find Alfred and Mrs. Murphy sitting together at a small table in the concession cubicle. Judging from the number of candy wrappers and coke bottles on the table, Kate Murphy has discovered Alfred's boundless appetite.

Mrs. Murphy is calmer now. She seems satisfied when I tell her Deputy Fingler will be coming downstairs before long to explain everything to her. Alfred and I take our leave, advising her to call Othel Creager if she needs us again.

As we drive out of the hospital parking lot, Alfred is in an exceptionally good humor and more talkative than usual. He and Kate Murphy had an interesting visit. They uncovered a common interest. She loves to cook, and he loves to eat. He tells me she's invited both of us to her house for dinner after Keith comes home from the hospital. She promised to fix chicken and dumplings, one of Alfred's many favorites.

I try to pay attention to what Alfred is saying, but my mind is filled with thoughts from my conversation with James Fingler.

"Alfred, have you ever bought any bootleg liquor?"

"Not since I was real young, Coach. My mamma caught me and one of my friends drinking it. She like to have wore my pants out, spanking me. My mamma said liquor would stunt my growth."

Fortunately, Alfred can't see the wide grin on my face inside the dark car. I have to choke back my laughter while my mind speculates on what size my enormous friend would be if his mamma hadn't caught him drinking.

"Coach Warden, have you checked the gas gauge? We've about used up that five gallons Mister Elgin's friend loaned us Friday night."

I glance down at the dashboard to verify Alfred's observation. The gas gauge needle is pointing to "E." I have a few dollars in my pocket, but all the gas stations will be closed this late at night.

"Coach, you wanna stop at the Sinclair station on the way outta Eastland? We did pretty good there last time."

Tuesday Morning
September 10, 1949

SUFFERING THROUGH A RESTLESS NIGHT, I wake up early. Dreams about being chased by newspaper reporters and helping the county sheriff raid bootlegger whiskey stills haunt my sleep.

About 5:00 A.M. I give up on trying to sleep and decide to get out of bed. Short Snorter, my bulldog pup who sleeps at the foot of my bed, eyes me warily as I arise and sit up on the edge of the bed. My pants are hanging on a chair near the end of the bed. I slip them on and stumble bleary-eyed into the kitchen.

To save time in the mornings, we measure out the coffee and fill the coffee pot with water the night before. I plug in the percolator and plop down at the dining table, waiting for it to perk. Short Snorter, who is annoyed with me for interrupting his sleep, wanders into the kitchen and scratches on the back door. I open the door to let him out.

A few minutes later Alfred appears at the kitchen door, yawning and scratching his head.

"You up already, Coach?"

"Yeah, I couldn't sleep."

"Me neither. I kept thinking about what we're gonna tell those newspaper reporters."

"We must've had the same dream, Alfred. Did you raid any whiskey stills?"

"Huh?"

"I'm sorry, Alfred. It's too early to be making jokes. Get yourself some coffee. I need to check the Creager's house, to see if their lights are on yet."

FERROL CREAGER IS AN EARLY RISER. He likes to get to the bank early, before the other employees arrive. I have no idea what a bank president would do in the wee hours of the morning before the bank opens. With no secretary to take dictation, I doubt if he writes letters or handles his correspondence. Perhaps he and Lucas Masters meet and count the bank's money.

A light burning inside the Creager's kitchen confirms that someone is awake. Grabbing a shirt, I head across the lawn to knock on their back door. The thick grass is damp from the morning dew.

Responding to my timid knocking, Ferrol Creager opens the back door. He's wearing a long-sleeved white shirt. His shirt collar is unbuttoned, without a tie.

"Stubby, good morning. I couldn't imagine who would be knocking on my door at this time of morning. What are you doing up so early?"

"Good morning, Ferrol. I couldn't sleep. Mrs. Creager told me she has the names and phone numbers of some newspaper reporters who've been trying to contact me."

"Yes, Stubby. You're quite a celebrity. Everyone at the bank yesterday was talking about how you and Alfred Steele risked your lives to save Keith Murphy. Othel tells me you are somewhat of a reluctant hero, but I suppose you should get used to reading your name in the paper for a few days."

"I wish we could escape the publicity, but I can't figure any way to avoid it. If you could get me the names of the people who called, I'll return their calls from the principal's office this morning."

"Sure, Stubby. Come on inside while I find the list for you. You want a cup of coffee?"

THE PRINCIPAL'S OFFICES are on the second floor of the high school. A small waiting room separates the second floor hallway from the main office. A long waist-high counter divides the work zone from the student reception area.

This will be my first visit to the principal's office since last May when I was being interviewed for the Ranger coaching job. I'm not required to teach a regular class during football season so there's no reason for me to spend time here. Fortunately, the students are in class now. I would feel uncomfortable having them see me wandering the hallways.

The principal's office is empty, except for the woman who studied me so curiously before my interview last spring. She seems engrossed in a small mountain of student files which surround the top of her desk. The woman glances up from her work when she notices me standing behind the counter. Her instant smile indicates she recognizes me.

"Hello, Coach Warden. It's so nice to see you again," the woman says cheerfully.

I'm embarrassed. The lady knows my name. I should've asked someone the names of the people who worked here, before I blundered in unannounced.

"Please excuse me, Miss, but I've forgotten your name."

"Mrs. Getts. Mildred Getts. I was here last May, when you interviewed for the coaching position." The woman is much friendlier today than the last time I was here.

"Yes, Mrs. Getts, I remember that day very vividly. As I recall, you were wearing a blue gingham dress."

"Why, Coach Warden, I'm flattered you remember what I was wearing. That dress is my favorite. I love wearing it. Is there something I can do for you?"

Luckily, she changes the subject. I was about to say something stupid, like how much more attractive she looked in the gingham dress.

"Yes, Mildred. I wonder if I could use a school telephone. I need to return some phone calls."

Her facial expression changes to one of shock. "Oh, Coach Warden! How could I be so forgetful? I have a stack of messages for you. It seems like everyone wanted to talk with you yesterday. Our telephones rang all day. Did you see Superintendent Boswell? He promised to stop by football practice to tell you."

"No, I didn't see him. He did leave a note on my car, but it didn't mention anything about phone calls." The secretary's information is a shocker. My impression of Boswell is that he is exceptionally thorough and dependable. His irresponsible behavior yesterday makes me dread today's meeting with Lucas Masters even more.

Mildred Getts sets me up with a telephone in the trustees' meeting room. All the messages she gives me are duplicates of the calls on Othel Creager's list. With the convenience of a private line in the trustees' room, I'm able to return all the calls in about twenty minutes. The reporters from Abilene and Fort Worth are satisfied with asking me a few questions and having me relate my account of the river episode to them over the telephone.

The reporter at the *Ranger Daily Times* insists upon a personal interview with Alfred and me. He also wants to bring along a photographer to take our picture. Reluctantly, he agrees to meet us after football practice this afternoon, arguing that the time will be too late to make Tuesday evening's edition. With my pending appointment at Lucas Masters' office, I won't agree to an earlier time. What I might say at the interview could depend upon whether, or not, I am still employed.

When I leave the trustees' meeting room, I stop to thank Mildred for allowing me to use the school telephone. She has been anxiously waiting to talk with me.

"Coach Warden, I suppose every person in Ranger must know by now how brave you and Alfred were in saving Mister Murphy. Everyone here at the high school is so proud of you. You're our hero."

"Thanks for being so kind, Mildred, but neither Alfred nor I feel we did anything to deserve so much attention. We just did what we had to do, under the circumstances."

"But, Coach Warden, you both risked your lives. Surely, you must agree that you went way beyond what you had to do?"

"Okay, Mildred! Maybe we did do a little more than we had to, but until my football team wins a game, one that really counts, I'm no better off than the unemployed young coach who was here begging for a job last May!"

I leave the curious lady stunned, and with her mouth agape, while I hurriedly exit the principal's offices.

Tuesday Afternoon
September 10, 1949

IF ALFRED WAS HERE WITH ME I would feel much more secure, but I don't want him, or anyone for that matter, to know about my secret dealings with Lucas Masters. I can't imagine the circumstances where my meeting with Masters would lead to violence, but after my encounter with Clifford and his friend last week, I'm distrustful of everyone.

The clock in the window of Pulley's Jewelry Store says it's two o'clock. The big hand of the antique clock points straight up. Dreading the unpleasantness of the ordeal ahead, I open the car door and crawl out. Summoning all my courage, I take a deep breath and stride across the sidewalk.

Unexpectedly, my competitive juices begin to flow. Playing on the offensive line at Texas A&M, I have faced, and defeated, many an opposing player who was bigger and stronger than me. Why should I let myself be so intimidated by a man like Masters? Accepting my own challenge, I step quickly toward the door leading to Masters' office.

The cool air in the stairwell strikes hard against my face. I'd forgotten how sinister this place feels. The wooden stairs creak under my weight as I climb toward the waiting foyer above.

The door to Masters' office is slightly ajar. Pushing the door open, I go inside, without knocking. Lucas Masters is standing in the reception area, waiting for me. He glances at his wrist watch, checking to see if I'm late. He's dressed in his customary dark business suit. The collar of his white shirt is unbuttoned. His solid black tie is loosened slightly.

"Coach Warden, thank you so much for coming. I realize how busy you must be, preparing for the game on Friday night."

Something is wrong here. I have been summoned to meet with the king, and he's thanking me for coming. I answer, as diplomatically as I can, "I didn't mind coming at all, Lucas. Superintendent Boswell left me a note telling me you wanted to meet with me."

"Yes, there are some things we need to talk about. Do you mind if we go into my office?" Masters bows ever so slightly and points with an open hand to the door of his office.

We move into his office overlooking main street. His panoramic view of downtown Ranger is just as impressive as I remembered from my first visit. Masters takes a seat behind his desk. I take a seat in the leather chair on the opposite side, facing him.

"Stubby, I hear you're the man responsible for saving Keith Murphy last Friday night."

"Yes. Alfred Steele and I were able to pull him out of his pickup before the river washed him away."

"I was wondering if you had a chance to talk with Murphy during your incident?" Masters leans forward in his chair to hear my answer.

"No, he was unconscious when we reached him."

"Then you were with Murphy all the time, and he didn't tell you anything about why he was shot?"

"Well, I was with him all the time except for the few minutes I waited in the bed of the pickup while Alfred carried him back to the road. No, he never said a word, as far as I know."

"And you don't think he told Alfred anything while you were waiting in the pickup?"

"No. Alfred would've mentioned it to me if Murphy had said anything."

"So you don't think Coach Murphy talked to anyone on the way to the hospital either?"

"No, we took him to the Eastland hospital in my car. He was unconscious the entire time."

"Stubby, did you or Alfred notice anyone who might've shot him?"

"No. It was pitch dark. We couldn't see anything. It was just pure luck that we discovered Murphy's pickup in the river."

"Alright then. I appreciate your coming to my office, Stubby. I hope your team is ready for the Friday night game."

"We're not quite ready now, but we will be by Friday," I reply, answering automatically without thinking. The meeting can't be finished. We haven't talked about Reed Jones or his dad. What about the other players Lucas was so interested in during our first meeting?

"Very good, Stubby. I'm sure you'll have your team ready to play their best. You're doing an excellent job. Keep up the good work," Masters declares, paying false homage while he dismisses me.

My mind is racing in high gear as I maneuver down the front steps from Masters' sanctum to the sidewalk below. Why was he so interested in Murphy? What about playing time for Reed Jones and Masters' agreement with Reed's father? Why didn't we discuss football? What could Murphy have said to me that would be of interest to Lucas Masters?

Somewhere about halfway to the football field, a peculiar thought strikes me. Maybe Lucas Masters is the crook Murphy was about to put the finger on. No, no way. That would make things way too easy for me.

The Hudson coughs and sputters. The puff of grey exhaust smoke I see in the rear view mirror reminds me to stop for gas.

AFTER FOOTBALL PRACTICE ALFRED AND I parley with the pushy reporter from the *Ranger Daily Times*. He brings a photographer with him, so we oblige them with several different poses. Alfred and I relate our recollection of the river rescue and the events which proceeded. We each attempt to give some credit to Leo Jackson, Glen Elgin and the other men who were involved in the search for Murphy, but the reporter doesn't seem interested in that part of the story. He asks us several times if we have any idea who might've shot Murphy. Although he almost certainly knows about the sheriff's deputies standing guard over Keith Murphy, he doesn't ask us about them.

Wednesday Afternoon
September 11, 1949

TAKING A BREAK from our review of last year's DeLeon game films, Alfred and I stop in at Pearl's Café. Pearl shows us the afternoon edition of the *Ranger Daily Times* while she serves our coffee. The headlines read:

Hometown Heroes!
Bulldog Coaches Brave Flooding River to Save Wounded Comrade

A large picture of the two of us shaking hands covers most of the top half of the front page. An old picture of Keith Murphy is at the bottom of the column. Apparently, the reporter was unable to get past the sheriff's deputies to take a recent picture.

Pearl insists we tell her our story again, in detail. Since she's the person responsible for initiating the friendship between Alfred and myself, and since we are here on credit, we answer her questions courteously and recount the events of Friday night one more time. When Pearl is distracted to the kitchen by her cook, we hastily gulp down our second cups of coffee and leave. Both of us have grown tired of our notoriety.

Friday Afternoon
September 13, 1949

WITH KEITH MURPHY IN THE HOSPITAL the school has assigned another bus driver to transport the football team to DeLeon. Our new driver Leeman Gentry lowers the hood over the engine after making a last minute check of oil and water. The team bus is loaded and ready to go.

Our players chatter excitedly while Sam makes his final inspection around the bus to check for items which may have been left on the ground. After the brief relief furnished by the weekend cool spell, the summer heat has returned with a vengeance. The heat and humidity make the still air inside the bus intolerable. My clothing is soaked with my own perspiration even before I take my seat near the middle of the bus. Alfred will sit up front behind the driver. As usual, Sam will sit in the rear with the equipment bags.

Coach Aills grabs the handrail and pulls himself up the front steps of the bus. He bends over to whisper something into the bus driver's ear. A large grin creeps across Sam's face while he waits at the front of the aisle, until the bus door is closed. As the bus begins to move forward, the big coach raises his fist and pumps his arm twice.

"Watch out, DeLeon! Here come the Ranger Bulldogs!" he calls out. Our bus riders cheer loudly.

———————

DELEON IS A FARM TOWN, located in the northeast corner of Comanche County, about thirty miles from Ranger. While some twenty-five hundred people actually reside within DeLeon's city limits, their school district covers a larger rural region containing a great many farms. When you add the farm children who are bussed in to attend school each day, DeLeon and Ranger High Schools have nearly the same number of students.

The shortest route to DeLeon is over Farm to Market Road 571, most of which is an unpaved dirt road. A longer way through Eastland and down State Highway 6 is paved all the way with blacktop. Either route requires that we cross the unpredictable Leon River.

Our driver chooses to take us the long route. A hard knot forms in my stomach, and my heart skips a few beats when we pass by the tall oil tank at Staff and drive over the section of recently repaired road where we rescued Murphy last Friday evening. Only a shallow current of water now flows within the narrow river banks. The stream seems peaceful and tranquil.

Normally, DeLeon does not field the same caliber of football teams as Breckenridge and Albany, the two teams we've previously faced. The DeLeon game was one of the two games Ranger won last year. This year DeLeon has a new coach and should be much tougher. Last Friday night the Bearcats outlasted Cross Plains 20 to 14.

———————

Friday Evening
September 13, 1949

TODAY IS FRIDAY THE 13th. If questioned, both my assistant coaches would adamantly deny they are superstitious, but Sam has a new rabbit's foot on his key chain, and Alfred cautiously avoids stepping on cracks in the concrete walk while we carry our equipment to the visitor's dressing room.

Never having denied my firm belief in luck, I'm wearing both my lucky socks and my lucky underwear for tonight's game. I will also stand on one foot at the left end of our bench and spit twice before the opening kickoff.

Bearcat Stadium is at the southern end of DeLeon's business district, adjacent to a complex of buildings which houses all of DeLeon's schools–grades one through twelve. A seven-foot high chain-link fence which encompasses the stadium offers an unrestricted view of the playing field, making it possible to watch the game without buying a ticket. The semi-rusted condition of the open-back metal bleachers testifies that it's been a long time since the aged grandstands have seen a fresh coat of paint. DeLeon's football facility has less than half the seating capacity of Bulldog Stadium.

ANXIOUSLY AWAITING the outcome of the coin toss, our team stands at the sideline. Our three captains, Elder, Hamrick and Thompson, are at the center of the field in conference with the game officials and three members of the DeLeon club.

The bleachers are filled to capacity, with people overflowing onto the grassy regions between the playing field and the surrounding chain-link fence. Judging from the crowd noise when our Bulldog team came on the field, I suspect the majority of fans have come from Ranger.

Many DeLeon fans arrived early to position their cars outside the stadium fence facing the football field. Blankets for their children have been spread on the ground alongside their parked cars.

While the playing field grass is thick and green, Keith Murphy's prediction has come true. The football field is full of sticker burrs. In the short intermission between our warm-up drills and these pre-game events Sam's time has mostly been occupied removing stickers from our players' hands with his tweezers.

The officials signal that Ranger has won the coin toss. We elect to receive the kickoff. Our captains come running off the field as DeLeon's school band stands to play the National Anthem. An intense excitement sweeps through both grandstands while the two bands play their school songs. A strong sense of confidence abounds among our players, a confidence which has been missing in our two previous games.

COMACHO FIELDS THE SHORT KICKOFF at our twenty, follows behind fierce blocks by Stiles, Patterson and Sutton, then sprints up the left sideline. DeLeon's place kicker pushes Comacho out of bounds at our forty-six yard line.

Our offensive unit takes the field. Hoping to catch the Bearcats by surprise, we've decided to pass on our first play. If our pass is incomplete, our next play will be an option play to the right. Our third play will depend on the success of the first two.

Hut. Hut. Jones takes the snap and rolls out to his right. Hamrick knocks down a hard-charging DeLeon defensive end with a vicious block. Ralph Rogers, our tall receiver, sets his foot firmly in the turf directly in front of a Bearcat defensive back and cuts sharply toward the right sideline. Jones' wobbly pass falls gently into big Ralph's hands, a second before he runs out of bounds at DeLeon's thirty yard line.

Hut. Hut. Hut. Jones fakes to Dorsey and pitches out to Hamrick for a gain of nine.

Hut. Hut. Jones keeps the football on an option, running over left tackle for a gain of six. First and ten at DeLeon's fifteen.

Two plays later Simpson scores, taking a pitchout down the left sideline and diving into the end zone. Brownlee kicks the extra point.

DeLeon's ball carrier fumbles on the kickoff return after being crushed between the flying bodies of Yung and McKinney. Two option plays and a short jump pass to Ralph Rogers give us another touchdown. Our extra point try is good.

With eight minutes remaining in the first quarter the scoreboard reads:

DELEON 0   VISITOR 14

Even though our staunch defense shuts down DeLeon's offense, we don't score again during the first quarter. Fumbles, unnecessary penalties and our own stupid mistakes are more responsible for our ineptness than aggressive play by the Bearcat club. My Bulldogs are unable to put away the younger and less experienced DeLeon squad, unable to take advantage of our superior athletic talent.

When we regain possession of the football at the beginning of the second quarter, I decide to shake things up. Determined to light a fire under my offense, I insert an entirely new backfield.

Not wishing to press my luck, I decide to leave Reed Jones in the game as quarterback. Hamrick, Simpson and Dorsey take their places on the bench gracefully, without complaint.

A second-string backfield of Comacho, Phillips and Kenneth Williams lines up behind Jones while he barks out the signals.

Hut. Hut. Jones hands the ball to Phillips who hurls over right guard for a gain of five. A pitchout to Comacho on the next play gains eight.

A fake to Phillips and a pitchout to Williams around left end gain fourteen. Williams bulls his way over two Bearcat tacklers, leaving them lying face up on the ground behind him. We score on the next play with a straight handoff to Phillips over right guard. Brownlee kicks the extra point.

Deleon 0   Ranger 21

After our defense stops DeLeon's best drive of the evening, I re-insert my starting backfield of Simpson, Dorsey and Hamrick. The three senior starters are embarrassed at how easily their substitutes were able to score. They take the field, their eyes charged in fierce determination.

The revived starting backfield scores again in seven plays. Hamrick carries four times gaining twenty-six yards. Simpson carries twice for fourteen. In spite of my specific instructions to the contrary, Jones lets Dorsey score the touchdown, carrying the football over left guard. At halftime the scoreboard reads:

DELEON 0   VISITOR 28

As a team, this is by far the best half of football we've played. Our defense has not allowed DeLeon to cross the fifty yard line, and after overcoming costly mistakes in the first quarter, our option offense is running smoothly. We even remember to hustle Frankie Jensen into the dressing room and have him in uniform, ready to march with the band at halftime.

———————

SEVERAL RANGER FANS delay me on my way to our dressing quarters. Our Bulldog fans are in a party mood, already celebrating our victory. Leo Jackson and Gordon Long corral me for a few minutes, talking about the game and congratulating me on the Ranger newspaper story. Even Red Jones runs over to shake my hand.

By the time I reach our dressing facility, many players have removed their shoulder pads and are resting on the floor. A line has formed along the back wall where Sam wields a pair of tweezers, extracting sticker needles from various parts of our young men's bodies.

"Coach Warden, you got a minute?" Sam calls to me when I pass him returning from a visit to the restroom.

"Sure, Sam, what's on your mind?"

"Maybe we should talk outside, Stubby." Sam motions mysteriously toward the front door.

We meet outside in the semi-darkness, beyond the edge of the lighted field.

"Stubby, you given any thought to holding down the score during the second half?"

"No. Why would we wanna let up on 'em? We need this win. I'm not about to take a chance on losing," I answer, thinking how badly I need the promised bonus money.

"Stubby, the DeLeon team has only made three first downs the entire first half. Unless our kids go brain dead and make a bundle of mistakes, there's no way we can lose this game."

"Sam, twenty-eight points isn't that much of a lead. I can recall a number of Southwest Conference college games where coaches got too overconfident with a lead and let the opposing team come back and beat them."

"Stubby, you're the head coach. It's your call. Remember though, we'll be playing these guys again next year. If we whip up on 'em too badly, their coaches will use this game to get their team charged up for us next year. They might field a better team next year. A little motivator like that could make a big difference. You might also consider that our basketball team plays here in their winter tournament this coming January."

"Okay. Alright, Sam. I see your point. Let's score one more touchdown for insurance. Then, you make certain every one of our players gets into the game. If we're still way ahead in the fourth quarter, we might even let DeLeon score."

Sam smiles, pleased that he has prevailed in our discussion. He turns to walk back inside the dressing quarters.

"Sam, one more thing."

"Yeah, Stubby?"

"You don't intend to tell anyone on our team to hold back, do you?"

"Hell, no! Our kids would mutiny on us. This is strictly between us coaches."

DURING THE HALFTIME BREAK we allow the team to relax. With a four touchdown lead it would be futile to talk about second half strategy or urge them to play harder. We'll take care of any problems next week in practice.

A game official appears at the door to notify us we have five minutes before the second half kickoff. Our team members adjust their gear and begin leaving the dressing room. On his way out I catch Reed Jones by the arm and drag him aside.

"Reed, how come you let Dorsey carry the ball? I thought I made it clear; you're not to give him the football!"

"Yeah, I know, Coach. But, Joey blocks his butt off for us on every play, and we had a three touchdown lead. You should've seen the smile on his face after he scored."

"That's wonderful. But from now on, you let me run this team. If I tell you not to give the ball to someone, I expect you to follow my orders."

"Yes sir, it won't happen again. I promise." Jones hangs his head despondently and moves away slowly, his maroon helmet dangling from his hand. A few feet away he pauses, gaining courage for his rebuttal, then turns back to me. "Coach Warden, if it makes any difference, I told Dorsey in the huddle we'd slit his throat if he fumbled."

Jones pulls on his helmet and dashes quickly to our bench before I can respond.

Alfred has been waiting outside the dressing room door, listening to my conversation with the quarterback. He walks over to stand beside me while I watch Jones run away.

"He's right about Dorsey, Coach. Joey is the happiest person on the squad tonight."

"Yeah, Alfred, I noticed."

BROWNLEE'S KICKOFF SAILS to DeLeon's five. At the twelve the Bearcat receiver is smashed down hard by Jack Hummel. In three plays the DeLeon team advances the ball to the nineteen and is forced to punt.

Cunningham catches a partially blocked punt at their forty yard line and returns it to the thirty-five. Reed Jones huddles with me on the sideline while our offensive unit takes the field.

"Reed, don't get in a hurry. Take your time. We want this score, so let's not make any mistakes. You understand?"

"Yes sir. You wanna run some time off the clock before we score?" The quarterback grins knowingly.

"That's about the size of it, Reed. As long as we're making good yardage, you keep the ball on the option plays. That'll kill more time," I advise, before I slap him on the behind and send him into the game.

With Jones keeping the football on every down, we reach the three yard line in nine plays. The quarterback calls timeout and trots to the sidelines.

"Who you want to make this score, Coach?" he asks.

I turn to look at the bench and rub at my chin. "I don't know, Reed. I can't seem to make up my mind. Who would you suggest?"

"Coach, I haven't scored this year, and my mom and dad are here watching the game. Would you mind if I make the score?"

"Alright, Reed, why don't you carry it in this time?"

My quarterback can hardly keep from skipping as he runs excitedly back to the huddle. Jones scores on a quarterback keeper, diving over right tackle. Our extra point kick is good.

Deleon   0   Ranger   35

After we score Sam begins to substitute freely. By the end of the third quarter every one of our players has seen some game action. We even send in Frankie Jensen to play a few downs at defensive safety. DeLeon's offense is more successful against our subs but does not score.

We keep our starters on the bench for most of the fourth quarter, giving our second-stringers an opportunity to log in valuable playing time. Unaccustomed to riding the bench, several of my starters begin to roam the sidelines restlessly, like caged animals.

We have possession of football at the Bearcat forty-five. Coach Aills and Bill Yung approach me.

"Stubby, our linemen are getting stir-crazy sitting on the bench. They wanna know if they can get back in the game."

"No, our younger players need playing time," I respond, too quickly, before I observe the exasperated expression on Yung's face. My starting troops are close to rebellion.

"Bill, you ever carry the football?" I ask, coming up with an idea to quash the insurrection.

"Yes sir. I was a halfback in grade school."

"Okay. Go in for Comacho on the next play. Tell the quarterback to let you carry the ball and run over left tackle."

Yung excitedly dons his helmet and runs onto the field.

"Davenport, Thompson, Patterson, Hummel, Sutton get up here," I call to the bench. I will alternate letting the linemen carry the football for the remainder of the game.

Near the end of the game DeLeon mounts a drive against our subs. They score on their last offensive series. Cantrell breaks through to block the extra point try. We run out the clock after their kickoff. The final score reads:

DELEON   6   VISITOR   35

ALFRED, SAM AND I reclaim the discarded equipment and pieces of football gear strewed around our bench. Only a handful of people remain in the bleachers. With the outcome decided early, many Ranger fans departed before the game ended. Yells and loud screams resound from the visitor's quarters where our team is showering and changing into their street clothes. Before we leave for Ranger, we'll stop at the Veteran's Café in downtown DeLeon to eat a late post-game meal.

For some reason, winning my first regular season game doesn't bring the sense of satisfaction I had expected. I do feel some sense of relief, probably because I expect to receive a three hundred dollar bonus for winning. The bonus money will greatly alleviate my financial difficulties.

Surely, there should be more satisfaction in winning than gaining a financial reward. Perhaps the team we beat was too imperfect. Perhaps we won too easily. Whatever the reason, our victory gives me no pleasure. It does nothing to alleviate the hungry need to win which gnaws at my insides.

CHAPTER TEN
THE BABY

Saturday Morning
September 14, 1949

THE SOUND OF KNOCKING at my front door wakes me from a deep sleep. The alarm clock next to the bed tells me the time is 6:15 A.M. The sudden banging noise frightens Short Snorter. He jumps to the floor and crawls under the bed. Someone on the front porch calls my name.

"Stubby! Stubby Warden!"

"Yeah. Hold on. I'm coming," I call back, while I wander around the bedroom trying to find my trousers.

Alfred and I didn't get home until two o'clock this morning. The stress of the football game and the tiresome bus ride home had taken a heavy toll. My mind and body were totally exhausted. I can't remember undressing. I must've been asleep before my head hit the pillow.

The knocking sound emanates from the front door again.

"Stubby! It's Price Mitchell out here! I need to speak to you! It's important!"

At last, I discover my pants and one shoe on the floor in the hallway. With one leg in my trousers I hop toward the front door. About midway across the living room my right leg finds the other leg hole. I pause to zip the fly and buckle my belt before I open the front door.

"Good morning, Price. What is it that's so important?" I say, making a vain attempt to be cheerful.

"Stubby, Edna Kimbrough called my house a few minutes ago. An ambulance had just taken Juanita to the Comanche hospital. It's pretty serious. I came right over. I knew you'd want to know."

"Oh, no! Did Mrs. Kimbrough tell you what's wrong? Is there a problem with the baby?" Terrible thoughts surge through my mind.

"She didn't tell us much, Stubby. The best Phyliss and I can figure is that the doctor is planning to take the baby by Caesarean section. As you know, Juanita's been experiencing a great deal of bleeding. Phyliss thinks the doctor has decided to take the baby early, before Juanita loses it."

A picture of my young wife lying helplessly on a cold operating table, while indifferent doctors and nurses in clean white uniforms slice open her swollen stomach to remove our baby, flutters through my mind. The thought makes me nauseous.

"Price, I've gotta go to her. Let me get dressed."

"Stubby, you know there'll be hell to pay if you show up at the hospital, don't you?" Price says, reminding me of my deteriorated relationship with my in-laws.

"Yes, I know. Well, they can holler and scream all they want. Juanita is my wife, and I have every right to be there with her. And, Price, just between the two of us, I've about taken all I'm gonna take off the Kimbrough family."

"Good for you, Stubby Warden. Under the circumstances, I know I shouldn't be saying this, but I've been hoping an opportunity would come along for you to stand up to them. Maybe this is it."

"It's not a situation I'm particularly looking forward to, Price. But, if the Kimbroughs wanna cause a stink, I reckon now would be a good time to call their hand. Listen, I'll get dressed. Can I meet you at the Pontiac House?"

"Stubby, I've got too many things cooking to leave work today. If you've decided to go, Phyliss wants to drive down with you. She may stay for a few days, if Edna needs her help."

My car is almost out of gas. It hasn't been washed in weeks. The floorboards are filled with trash, notebook papers and diagrams of discarded football plays. Phyliss Mitchell is the wife of a car dealer, accustomed to shiny new cars that smell fresh and clean. She would gag at the prospect of riding in the Hudson.

"Do you think we could take her car, Price?" I ask hastily.

Price gazes at my dirty Hudson and shakes his head at its unsightly appearance. He smiles as he replies, "Yeah, I think that would be fine. I'll call Phyliss and have her pick you up."

AT A QUARTER AFTER SEVEN the piercing sound of a car horn echoes through the neighborhood. Phyliss Mitchell has parked her two-toned, green and white Pontiac parallel with the street curb in front of my house. She's impatient. Before I can respond, she honks the horn again. I gulp down the last of my coffee, grab my jacket, tell Alfred I'm leaving, then step quickly to the front door.

I jump in on the passenger side, pitching my jacket into the back seat alongside her small suitcase. Phyliss seems nervous. Her face is pale and drawn. Although I have never seen her smoke before, a cigarette burns in the ashtray behind the gear shift.

"Good morning, Phyliss," I say, trying to be friendly.

"Hello, Stubby. You ready to go?" she replies curtly.

"Yes, I'm ready. Do we need to stop for gas or anything?"

Phyliss leans forward and lays her head against the steering wheel. She speaks without looking at me, "Stubby, this is going to be rough. This is my family, but I love you and Juanita like my own son and daughter."

"I know, Phyliss," I acknowledge, not knowing what else to say.

Phyliss raises her head and shifts the car into gear. My head jerks backward, and the tires squeal, as she accelerates down Main Street. Passing through downtown, she crosses the railroad tracks, then turns right toward Comanche.

MESQUITE TREES AND SCRUB OAKS whiz by my window as we speed along the blacktop road. Phyliss has elected to take the long route to Comanche through Eastland, Carbon, and DeLeon. This means we will pass the familiar sight of the Staff oil tank and cross the Leon River again. The speedometer needle is beyond the 70 MPH mark. Phyliss is not in a mood to talk so I lean back and try to catch up on my sleep. Sleep doesn't come, but my thoughts wander dreamily back to my childhood.

MY MOTHER AND FATHER SEPARATED shortly after I was born. My mother tells me that until I was almost one we lived on a small cotton farm, a few miles outside Slaton, Texas. I have no recollection of living there. She and my father were sharecroppers, farming land which belongs to someone else and sharing the profits. After my parents split up, mother and I moved back to Slaton to live with my grandparents.

My father continued to live and work in Slaton after he and mother were divorced. I can remember him stopping by my grandparents' house a few times to say hello when I was very young, but after a while, he quit coming by at all. When I was older, I would occasionally see him riding by on a farm truck or working at the cotton gin. Sometimes he would wave to me. One summer when I was twelve, he just disappeared, without a word to anyone.

After she divorced my father, my mother never remarried. She was an attractive woman with a pleasant personality. But, while numerous suitors tried for her attention, she was never really interested. My grandfather used to say my mother had given so much of her love to my father that there just wasn't enough left for her to love another man.

The house where I lived with my grandparents was a small, two-bedroom, wood frame building located on Farm Road 41, barely inside the highway sign marking the Slaton city limits. Being so far from downtown, we didn't always enjoy the conveniences of city living. We got our drinking water from a well until the city constructed a new water line out to our side of town. I was eleven when my grandfather added a bathroom to give us an indoor toilet.

My grandmother loved roses so she planted rose bushes at every conceivable location–next to the house and along the wood picket fence in the front yard. The front porch of my grandparents' home faced the highway and extended down the entire length of the house. On summer evenings we would sit in the porch swing, drenched in the sweet aroma of my grandmother's roses, and watch the cars drive by. There was never a speck of grass in our yard. Our chickens kept the yard free of grass and other ground vegetation.

My grandparents' house rested on a huge lot with more than an acre of land. We planted a big garden every spring. My mother and grand-mother were both marvelous cooks. They would can all the vegetables we didn't eat or give away. There was an underground cellar in the backyard where we stored the glass jars of canned vegetables and where we'd run to, whenever a dark storm cloud threatened.

Tuesday, Afternoon
September 6, 1941

THE FOOTBALL PLAYER who lined up opposite me outweighed me by more than forty pounds and towered above me by at least four inches. He was a junior at Slaton High School. I was a sophomore. It was my first day of varsity football practice. My friend Bobby Wilkins had talked me into trying out for the varsity squad. The hefty player in his football uniform seemed like a giant gorilla as he gritted his teeth at me from across the mid-field stripe.

"Go! Go! Go!" screamed the line coach.

The big junior charged hard into me. His blunt elbows drove into my nose and face, standing me straight up, then pushing me over backward. His sharp cleats dug into my chest as he ran over me. I felt the wetness of blood begin to trickle from my nose, before I blacked out.

ROY STILLWELL, THE HEAD COACH, stood over me while the trainer wiped my face with a wet towel. Someone had dragged me to the side of the field, away from the blocking drills. Slowly, the stars circling in my head began to dissipate as I regained consciousness.

"Son, how do you feel? You gonna be alright?" the coach asked me with sincere concern.

"Yes sir, I'll be okay. How bad was the other fellow hurt?"

The head coach laughed loudly. "He's got a fairly good chance of surviving. What's your name, son?"

"Stubby. Stubby Warden," I replied.

"Well, young Stubby, someone certainly tagged you with the right name. It's easy to see you're a spunky little kid, but I'm afraid you're gonna be too small to play football. Why don't you turn in your uniform after practice?"

"No sir, I'm not gonna to do that," I told him emphatically. My schoolmates would've teased me unmercifully if I got kicked off the team the first day of practice.

"Listen here, son. Surely you don't want these big guys to keep on beating up on you. You could get hurt real bad out there."

"Coach, the only reason that fellow was able to run over me was because I didn't know what to expect. This is my first day of practice. If you'll let me watch for awhile, I'll learn how to block. I promise he won't ever run over me like that again."

"Okay, Warden, have it your way. But, if you get hurt again, you're off the team. You understand?"

"Yes sir, I understand."

For the remainder of the afternoon I stood behind the coaches, observing how the best players kept their bodies low and used their leg strength for leverage when they blocked. I listened closely to the line coaches when they pulled a player aside to instruct him on improving his blocking techniques.

In the brief intervals between their turns at the blocking drills, several players stopped to ask how badly I was hurt. During the water break my friend Bobby Wilkins came over to apologize for talking me into trying out. His face was smudged with grass stains and his bottom lip was split. He was surprised when I told him I wasn't quitting.

MY GRANDFATHER WAS WAITING FOR ME, relaxing in the front porch swing, when the school bus dropped me off late that afternoon. He was anxious to hear about my first day of football. Seeing my black eye and swollen nose, he rushed me to the back yard to keep my mother and grandmother from becoming hysterical at the sight of me.

After I convinced him I intended to return for the next day's football practice, we tied a bed pillow and one of grandmother's quilts to the trunk of a pecan tree in the garden. He stayed with me until after dark while I practiced blocking on the cushioned tree.

Wednesday Afternoon
September 7, 1941

THE COACHES SEPARATED US into two opposing lines for the blocking drill. I counted off the players in the defensive line, then slipped into the line of offensive players so I'd be pitted against the big junior who had annihilated me the day before. Realizing who would be his opponent in the drill, my extra large adversary began to grin, as players in front of us completed their blocks and took new positions at the rear of the opposite line.

Anticipating a repetition of my catastrophic experience in the prior day's practice, one of the line coaches left our blocking drills to walk across the field and inform Roy Stillwell. They turned to watch while I lined up to block against the big junior.

"You're dead meat, Sophomore. I'm gonna stomp your little bony ass good this time," he threatened with a confident smirk.

I crouched low in a three-point stance. I breathed deeply and gathered all my strength for the coming impact.

"Go! Go! Go!" called the assistant coach.

On the coach's first utterance I sprang forward with all the force my legs could muster. My left shoulder slipped underneath the flying elbows of the surprised junior, sinking deep into the jelly-soft belly above his waist. I felt the breath go out of him while my legs churned, driving him backward. Flashes of bright light blurred my vision before we hit the ground, then came darkness.

I lay there for a few seconds, regaining my senses. Finally, I rolled over and struggled to my feet. The big junior player still lay sprawled out on the ground. One of the coaches rolled him over, grabbed his pants at the belt buckle and began pumping his body up and down to help him get his breath back.

Coach Stillwell caught my arm as I staggered back into the blocking line. Flashing lights were still going off inside my head.

"Son, tell me your name again."

"Stubby Warden," I answered, not sure whether he was asking because he wanted to know my name, or if he was testing me–to see if I knew.

"Stubby Warden. I suppose I'll have to remember that name," Coach Stillwell mused, talking to himself.

"Yes sir. I hope you will," I added.

DURING OUR GAME WITH LEVELLAND in October, our starting right guard broke his leg. By that time the coaches had promoted me to playing with the second-string. Coach Stillwell put me into the game in the second quarter. After that night I started at right guard for Slaton High School in every game until football season ended my senior year.

Thursday Afternoon
February 9, 1944

TWO MONTHS AFTER MY FINAL FOOTBALL GAME at Slaton High, I went by to talk with Coach Stillwell about my football future. When I told him I was thinking about accepting a partial scholarship to play football for the Red Raiders at Texas Technological College in Lubbock, he was furious with me.

"Stubby, don't you know the only college football conference with any credibility in Texas is the Southwest Conference."

"Yes sir, everyone knows that. But, Lubbock is only twenty miles away. I'd be closer to home. My mom and my grandparents could come to the games."

"Listen here, Warden. That may sound good right now. But in the long run, you need to play in the Southwest Conference if you want to coach football in Texas."

"But, Coach Roy, not one single college in the Southwest Conference has offered me any kind of football scholarship. You know my situation. I simply can't go to college without some kind of financial help."

"Whatta you think about Texas A&M College in Bryan? How'd you like to play football down there?"

"Coach Roy, don't joke with me. You know I'd die for a chance to play football for a great school like A&M, but they don't want me. I'm too small to play there."

Coach Stillwell put the fingers of both hands together below his chin and smiled broadly. "It seems like I can remember telling you the same thing on your first day of varsity football practice at Slaton High. You proved to me I was wrong. I believe you would do the same at Texas A&M."

"But, Coach Roy...," I started to object, but he held his hand up to quiet me. He picked up his telephone and held it to his ear.

"Hello, Operator. I want to place a person-to-person call to Coach Homer Norton at Texas A&M College in College Station, Texas. The number is 864."

He must have seen the astounded look on my face. He held his hand over the mouthpiece and whispered, "We're old friends. Went to grade school together.

"Hello, Homer. This is Roy Stillwell.

"Yes, it has been a long time. Yeah, I'm still coaching football here at Slaton High School. Been coaching here for almost ten years now.

"No, we didn't make the playoffs this year. We finished second in our district behind Colorado City. Had a pretty good record though, seven and three.

"Listen, Homer. There's a young man sitting here in my office. He's the best damn offensive lineman who ever played for me. He wants to come to A&M. You got any full scholarships left?

"No, I can't tell you how big he is. You'll just have to take my word that he's good enough to play for you."

Sight unseen, based strictly upon his friendship with Roy Stillwell, the famous Aggie coach arranged for me to receive a full football scholarship. In August the following summer we finally met. Coach Norton was tremendously disappointed. On my first day of A&M football practice Coach Homer Norton told me I was too small to play for him.

I proved him wrong.

Saturday Morning
September 14, 1949

THERE IS NOTHING FANCY about the Comanche hospital. The building is a long, narrow structure with a single gable. The exterior walls are faced with a plain white brick. The roof is covered with light-brown composition shingles. Single hung windows are spaced at equal intervals down each side of the building, apparently providing one window for each hospital room. The hospital entrance is at the end of the building facing the street. A gravel parking lot is located on the north side of the building.

Phyliss swerves into the parking lot and parks the car in the section marked "Visitors Only." She instructs me to lock my door before we walk, side-by-side, across the gravel surface to the hospital.

The front entrance opens into a spacious, but unpretentious, lobby. Situated along the left side of the room and behind an L-shaped, waist-high counter is a combination reception and nurse's station. A wide framed opening on the opposite side of the room leads to a sizeable waiting room.

Phyliss spies several members of the Kimbrough family in the waiting room and hurries toward them. I move to a spot inside the waiting room doorway and stand quietly until Phyliss Mitchell has exchanged her greetings with each of the Kimbroughs. There are nine people in the room. I assume they must be aunts, uncles, cousins or in some way related to Juanita. Several family members notice me but choose to ignore my presence. Juanita's younger brother Gary acknowledges his recognition with a nod of his head in my direction.

Phyliss and Edna Kimbrough hug each other and begin an extended woman's conversation about Juanita's condition. Other members of the family return to private conversations they were engaged in before Phyliss and I arrived.

Luther Kimbrough is resting on a green vinyl couch which is backed up against an outside wall, directly beneath a window. He didn't bother to stand when we arrived. Taking a deep breath, I walk over to speak to him.

"Hello, Mister Kimbrough," I say politely.

Juanita's father noticed me at the doorway and is keenly aware I am in the room, even before I speak to him. Still, he acts surprised at my presence.

"How the hell did you get in here?" he roars nastily.

The conversation between Phyliss Mitchell and Edna Kimbrough terminates abruptly. The soft murmur of people talking ceases. A deathly quiet settles over the room.

"I came from Ranger with Phyliss Mitchell to be here with my wife and baby."

"Well, you're not welcome here, Mister! This is Kimbrough family business! We'll take care of my daughter! You don't belong here, and you're not wanted."

Luther Kimbrough's gruff, unpleasant voice echoes through the room. Every person in the room turns to watch us. A nurse abandons her duties at the reception counter and comes to look inside the waiting room. Seeing the tense situation, she leaves quickly.

This moment has been a long time coming. Being very careful not to raise my voice, I reply the way I have rehearsed many times. I keep my voice tone low, but firm and determined.

"Luther, I'm truly sorry you have decided to make me your adversary. Every person here in this room loves your daughter and is concerned for her life. It's a shame we can't all pull together to help her through this. But, with all due respect, sir, Juanita Warden is my wife, and she's carrying my baby."

I pause for a moment to let what I've said sink in. Edna Kimbrough makes a move toward her husband. I turn my head to glare at her. My fierce scowl stops her in her tracks. Luther Kimbrough stares blankly at me while I continue.

"The fact is, Luther, this is not your business. It is my business, and I intend to be here until my wife and child are ready to leave this hospital. If you'll behave decently, you and your family are welcome to stay. But, if you, or any other member of your family, tries to interfere with my looking after my wife and child, I will personally throw you bodily out of this hospital."

Although his squinted eyes express his extreme hatred for me, Juanita's father offers no response. I wheel around to face other members of the Kimbrough clan. Their faces tell me they are completely stunned by my strong stance. Their silence reinforces my courage. A few seconds pass before I speak to them.

"I mean what I say. I'm not gonna stand for any bull from any of you. Maybe someday we can all be friends, but today, my advice is to stay out of my way."

When no one challenges my authority, I walk slowly out of the waiting room.

"Gary, get your father a glass of water! He's about to pass out," Edna Kimbrough shouts to her son in a hysterical voice.

———————

PHYLISS MITCHELL PEEKS OUT the front door of the hospital, searching for me. Her eyes are puffy from crying. Lines of black mascara are streaked down her face. Using a Kleenex tissue to wipe wet tears from her cheeks, she comes to join me in the shaded grassy fringe next to the parking lot. I'm still stewing after the unpleasant confrontation inside.

"That was quite a speech, Stubby Warden. You've certainly stirred up the Kimbrough family. Things will never be the same between you and them again."

"Please forgive me, Phyliss. You know I didn't want something like this to happen. The last thing I'd ever want is to hurt you or Price, or damage your relationship with your family."

"Stubby, don't misunderstand me. You were absolutely wonderful. Now the Kimbroughs know they have a real man in the family."

We stand together in silence while I try to cool down. Phyliss fishes inside her purse, retrieves a mirror and works on her damaged makeup.

"How is Mister Kimbrough? Will he be okay? With his heart condition…." My strong flow of emotion won't allow me to complete my sentence.

"Yes, he'll be fine. Sometimes I think Luther overplays his heart condition to maintain an upper hand on the family."

"Well, he is Juanita's father. I don't wish him any ill will."

"Stubby, after you walked out, Luther Kimbrough called the Comanche sheriff's office. He plans to have you arrested. You might want to leave. The sheriff should be here any minute."

AN UNCONTROLLED PANIC quickens my heartbeat as the sound of a siren draws closer. Luther Kimbrough has many friends here. His wealth gives him a great deal of influence in county affairs. The chances of him having the local sheriff arrest me is probably very good.

A black and white patrol car pulls alongside the curb in front of the hospital. White letters painted on the front door of the car read "Comanche County Sheriff." A uniformed sheriff's deputy slides out of the car.

"We had a call about a disturbance here at the hospital. You folks know anything about it?" the officer asks us.

"Yes sir," I say, stepping forward to the sidewalk. "Your call was probably about me. My father-in-law and I had a slight misunderstanding about my wife. She's having a baby."

"And what is your name, sir?" the officer asks, taking a note pad from his shirt pocket.

"Stubby Warden. I live in Ranger."

The officer stops writing. His eyes examine me closely. "You're not the Stubby Warden who coaches the Ranger Bulldogs, are you?"

"Yes, I coach the Ranger High football team."

The officer stuffs the note pad back into his pocket and offers his hand. "Coach Warden, my name is Mike Goodman, and I'd like to shake your hand."

The officer's grip is firm and sincere, but I'm totally at a loss trying to interpret the reason for his friendly attitude.

"It's a pleasure to meet you, Mike, but whatever could I have done to make you so anxious to shake my hand?"

"Coach, I live in DeLeon. My son Michael plays football for the Bearcats. With a brand-new coach and a covey of young players, we don't have a very good ball team this year. If you'd wanted, your Bulldogs could've scored sixty points or more on us last night. Instead, you let our boys finish the game with some dignity. You even allowed us to score a touchdown at the end of the game. There aren't many coaches around who would've held the score down like that. A lot of us parents noticed, and appreciated, the way your team played the game."

"Mike, holding the score down really wasn't my idea. My assistant coaches…."

The officer interrupts me before I can explain. "Coach Warden, you needn't be so modest. Just accept my thanks from the DeLeon parents."

"Okay, Mike, I accept. But I hope I never have to ask your DeLeon team to return the favor."

Mike Goodman smiles and nods his head. "Coach Warden, after watching how well your team played last night, I can't imagine your ever needing an opposing team to hold their score down."

"Listen, Mike. I suppose I should explain my side of the story before you talk to Luther Kimbrough."

––––––––––––

A RISING MORNING SUN HAS ELIMINATED my shady spot next to the parking lot. The humidity of the morning heat causes me to perspire freely. Huge drops of sweat roll down my brow while I wait for the sheriff's deputy. He went inside the hospital to talk to the Kimbrough family about twenty minutes ago.

The front door of the hospital rattles as Mike Goodman emerges. I walk over to meet him.

"How did it go, Mike?"

"They won't be giving you any more trouble, Coach. I advised them that the law clearly favors the husband in disputes of this kind. I threatened to lock up anyone who interferes with you and your wife."

"I didn't know that. Are you sure about the law favoring the husband?"

"Coach Warden, I'm just a farm boy dressed up in a cop's uniform. I don't know the first thing about law, but I believe the law solved your problem in this case, don't you?"

"Yeah, Mike, I think you probably did. Thanks."

"Don't mention it, Coach. It's been a pleasure meeting you. I can't wait to tell my son about meeting you. He'll be impressed with me."

The deputy scoots into the patrol car, starts the engine and begins to pull away from the curb. Suddenly remembering a question, I run out into the street and flag him down.

"Say, Mike. On your way to the hospital you had your siren turned on. Did you expect to arrest me?"

"Oh, that. No, it's a new siren, just installed yesterday. This was my first opportunity to test it out."

––––––––––––

A CLOCK ON THE WALL behind the nurse's station says the time is ten minutes after nine. Phyliss and I arrived in Comanche almost an hour ago, and I still don't know anything about my wife's condition.

A heavy-set elderly woman, hunched over a stack of files behind the reception counter, appears to be in charge. She occasionally glances up from her work to issue short, blunt orders to the nurses, sending them scurrying down a hallway to the patient rooms.

"Hello ma'am. Could you tell me where to inquire about Juanita Warden? I'm her husband. I think she is having a baby."

The woman's head jerks up in response to my question. "You're her husband, and you think she's having a baby? You mean you don't know?"

"I'm sorry, ma'am. I'm having a difficult morning. Let me try again. I just arrived from Ranger. My wife was transported to the hospital by ambulance early this morning. She is pregnant. No one will tell me anything. Maybe you can help me."

The woman begins sorting through the stack of files before her. When she finds the file she's searching for, she looks back at me.

"Are you the Onis C. Warden who lives at 435 West Main in Ranger, Texas?"

"Yes ma'am. Can you tell me something about my wife?"

"Mister Warden, there are a few forms you need to sign before your wife can be properly admitted. Can you give me the name of your doctor?"

"No, I'm afraid I don't know who he is. Lady, can't this wait? I really need to find out about my wife."

The woman is perturbed with me for objecting to her check-in routine. She readjusts some papers on her desk while she decides my fate.

"Alright, Mister Warden. We can do most of this later, but I must find out how you intend to pay your hospital bill."

This is a surprise. The bill is my responsibility. I certainly don't mind paying, but I can't understand why the Kimbroughs haven't already taken care of these financial matters.

Score another one for Luther Kimbrough. I'm sure he has intentionally avoided taking care of the monetary details to expose my weakened fiscal condition and embarrass me.

"I don't know. I haven't thought about paying the hospital. How much do you think it'll be?"

"Well, the form your mother-in-law filled out indicates your wife is scheduled for a Caesarean birth. That usually runs about four hundred dollars. It depends on how long your wife has to stay."

"Four hundred dollars! Does that include the doctor's fee?"

"No. The doctor will bill you separately, but all bills will have to be paid before your wife checks out of the hospital. You will need to give me a partial payment today."

My mind quickly calculates how much money I'll have coming on Monday then begins to subtract my rent, my grocery charges, the money I owe to Pearl and Price, the money I need to survive until my next payday. There's no way I can raise four hundred dollars.

"Can you wait until Monday for the deposit? I don't get paid until then."

"Mister Warden, you don't mean to tell me your wife is having a baby, and you haven't planned far enough ahead to pay the hospital deposit?"

"Yes ma'am. That's about the size of it. I'm as broke as a skunk, until Monday."

"Young people!" the elderly woman says to herself. "I don't know what this world is coming to. Alright, Mister Warden, but you have a deposit of two hundred dollars here on this counter on Monday. Do you understand?"

"Yes ma'am. Don't worry. I'll have the money here on Monday, in cash. Now, can you tell me about my wife?"

The lady glances at a chart on the counter. "Mrs. Warden is in the delivery room now. She went in at eight-thirty. She should be coming out sometime around ten o'clock."

"Thank you, ma'am. You've been very helpful. By the way, does your chart give the name of our doctor?"

She studies the chart for a few seconds. "Yes, your wife's doctor is Clyde Blackmar."

"Do you have any idea how much he charges for a Caesarean delivery?" I ask.

"I can't say for sure, Mister Warden, but I imagine his fees will run about five hundred dollars."

Five hundred dollars! Oh, Lord! That's more money than I get for winning a football game. How could delivering a little baby cost that much?

Seeing the grieved expression on my face, the woman tries to console me. "Easy come. Easy go," she explains to me.

"Yes ma'am," I repeat back to her. "Easy come. Easy go."

AN AGED DOCTOR PUSHES THROUGH the double swing door which leads to the corridor running down the center of the hospital building. The doctor is clothed in a white scrub suit which, evidently, is customary operating room attire for a hospital physician. He removes a pair of rubber gloves from his hands while he walks over to the nurse's station. He exchanges a few words with the reception lady before she points toward me.

Since the Kimbrough family has staked out the hospital waiting room as their territory and the torturous heat outside has made waiting outdoors unbearable, the only other convenient waiting place I can find is here in the hospital front lobby. The lobby has no chairs, couches or other places to sit, so I have stationed myself in a vacant corner opposite the waiting room entrance. Using one foot to brace myself, I am leaning against the lobby wall.

"Hello, young man. Are you Onis Warden?" the doctor asks.

"Yes sir," I reply, pushing away from the wall and straightening up.

"Well, Mister Warden, you are the father of a five pound, six ounce baby boy. Congratulations."

"Oh! You must be Doctor Blackmar."

"Yes, Mister Warden, I'm Clyde Blackmar. I have just delivered your new baby."

I grab his hand and begin shaking it frantically. "Thank you, Doctor. Oh, thank you. How is my wife? Is she okay?"

"Your wife is doing fine. We've taken her to the recovery room. You can see her in about half an hour."

A tremendous sense of relief gushes through me. Juanita and the baby have survived. Happy tears fill my eyes.

"By the way," the doctor asks me, "has anyone told you the baby's name yet?"

"No sir. I can't get anyone around here to tell me anything." A quick anger replaces my feeling of relief.

How could Juanita or the Kimbroughs have named my baby without consulting me? I'm the child's father. I've got a right to have some input into naming my baby.

"Warden. I believe the baby's name is Warden," the doctor laughs.

I have fallen for his big joke. He probably plays the same prank on all his new fathers.

The comical doctor excuses himself, still laughing as he heads for the waiting room to talk with the Kimbrough family.

JUANITA LIES ON A PORTABLE ROLLER BED in the recovery room. Her body is covered with white bed sheets. Her eyes are closed. The nurse stationed in the hallway outside advised me to move slowly and deliberately, so I wouldn't confuse her. She is still heavily sedated. I reach beneath the sheets and take her small hand in mine. Her eyes open, sleepily.

"Hello, darling," she whispers.

"Hello, Juanita. How do you feel?"

"A little groggy but not too bad for a woman who just had a baby removed from her stomach." She smiles at her little joke.

"Please don't joke, Juanita. I'm hurting for you too much to appreciate your humor."

"Alright, darling. Have you seen our baby? The nurse told me it's a boy."

"Not yet. I wanted to see you first–to be sure you were okay."

"Will you please go check on him, Stubby? I've been having terrible nightmares about the baby being born with no feet." Her drugged voice is distorted with worry. She pulls my hand to her and squeezes it tightly. She starts to cry.

"Juanita, please calm down. I'm sure the doctor would've told me if there was any problem, but I'll go and examine the baby right now."

I place her hand gently back on the bed and straighten the sheets over her body.

"Stubby darling." Juanita sounds very tired now. Our short conversation has worn her down.

"Yes, Juanita?"

"I'm ready to go home now."

"Yes, I know, but the doctor says it'll probably be a week before he can release you from the hospital. He wants you to be well enough to walk around, before you can go home."

"No, darling," she says drowsily. "The baby and I are ready to go home with you to Ranger now. Can we go soon?"

"Yes, my love. The sooner we can leave this dreadful place, the better I'll like it," I tell her, but she doesn't hear. She has fallen asleep.

"ARE YOU SURE he has all his fingers and toes?" I ask the nurse in the baby room.

"Yes, Mister Warden. He's a perfect male specimen, very healthy and very strong. You have yourself a fine little boy."

The nurse holds my baby up for me to inspect. Not trusting her, I count the fingers and toes on each of his hands and feet.

"Should he be crying like that, Nurse? Maybe something is wrong with him."

"All babies cry when they're hungry, Mister Warden. This young fellow hasn't been fed since he came into this world. We'll be taking him to his mother in a few minutes to let the little guy have his first good meal."

The nurse holds the baby against her bosom and rocks him gently. The baby stops crying.

"Do you want to hold him? He likes to be held."

"No! No, I don't know about babies. I might hurt him," I answer, shocked that she would expect me to handle the baby.

"He won't break, Mister Warden. I promise. Why don't you hold your son for just a minute? It's a wonderful experience, a father holding his son for the first time," the nurse says as she holds the baby out to me.

Reluctantly, I accept the baby and cradle him in my arms. He smiles at me and grasps my finger with his small hand. Holding my son for the first time brings an unexpected realization. This tiny human being is my responsibility. His future depends on me. I am poorly prepared for such a heavy assignment.

"Why is he so red? Should he be so red?" I ask, using great care to hand the baby back to the nurse.

"Your baby was born a little early. He wasn't quite ready to make his entrance into this world. We'll need to keep him in an incubator for a few days. His color will become normal after he adjusts to living in the outside world," the nurse explains.

An enormous joy engulfs me as I walk lightly down the hospital corridor. The exultation and wonderful feeling of happiness which surround me are more satisfying than any football victory I've ever experienced.

I pass Gary Kimbrough in the corridor. The hospital staff has moved Juanita to a regular hospital room now. Gary and a number of other Kimbrough family members are waiting their turn to see her. I stop and shake his hand. He stares after me in astonishment while I stroll happily to the front of the hospital.

IF I WERE A HOSPITAL ARCHITECT, the first room I would design would be a room where fathers of newborn babies could be deposited to keep them out from underfoot. After my visit with Juanita in the recovery room and my inspection of our baby in the nursery, I discover how utterly useless a new father is in a hospital.

Immediately after a baby arrives, the proud father is acknowledged and rewarded with a few ego-building, but meaningless, tributes. Then, the women take control. Women understand the true center of interest is the new mother, not the father. Hospital nurses assume responsibility for all the baby's needs, including feeding, diaper changing and bathing. The mother-in-law and other female relatives stand watch over the new mother, hovering over her and sending any male, who comes within shouting distance of the new mother's hospital room, off on some urgent mission.

A new father quickly finds himself in the ridiculous predicament of being unwanted and unneeded, but at the same time, subject to being severely criticized for his lack of sensitivity if he leaves the premises even for a moment.

Somehow, I suffer through the afternoon at the hospital. With the Kimbrough clan staking claim to the waiting room, most of my time is spent leaning against the lobby walls. Twice during the afternoon, I'm able to sneak unnoticed into Juanita's hospital room for a few short minutes. Both times she is asleep, and both times a nurse comes in to wake her, give her a pill, check her blood pressure and shoo me out.

Trying to appease my mid-afternoon boredom, I wander up and down the narrow corridor between the hospital rooms. I make a remarkable discovery. I find a room without patients and not in use. Slipping inside, I collapse into one of the vinyl cushioned chairs.

About seven o'clock Saturday evening Phyliss finds me in the vacant hospital room. We've hardly spoken since the deputy's arrival broke up our conversation this morning.

"Oh, I see. This is where you've been hiding. Stubby, we're all leaving. Luther is restless and complaining. I guess everybody is about worn out. It's been quite a long day for everyone."

"You mean you won't be coming back to the hospital, Phyliss?" I ask, rising from my chair.

"No. Edna wants me to spend the night at the ranch. I think Juanita probably needs us to leave so she can get some rest. We'll be back early tomorrow morning. Will you be all right, Stubby?"

"Sure. I might sleep here in this room if no one objects. If I can't sleep here, maybe I can sleep in your car, unless you're taking it with you."

Phyliss isn't exactly delighted with the prospect of me sleeping in her new car, but she doesn't protest.

"No, I'll ride out to the ranch with Luther and Edna. Let me give you the car keys."

Looking for her keys, she rummages through her purse. After an extended search, she retrieves her key ring and hands me the keys.

"Stubby, have you eaten anything? You look famished."

"No, but I'm fine. I'll eat something later," I lie.

Phyliss eyes me curiously. "You don't have money to eat on, do you, Stubby?"

"Not exactly, but don't worry, Phyliss. I'll be fine."

Phyliss shakes her head at me. "Stubby Warden, you're too proud for your own good. Here, take this and get yourself something to eat."

Phyliss hands me a five dollar bill.

AFTER THE KIMBROUGH FAMILY DEPARTS, I check on Juanita. She's asleep and resting peacefully. Encouraged by pangs of hunger, I leave the hospital and walk downtown to the courthouse square. On most evenings the square would be deserted by this time, but Saturday is the day farming families from all over the county come to town, to shop and visit with friends. For many Comanche County residents their Saturday afternoon trip to town is the most important social event of the week.

The west side of Comanche's courthouse is encompassed by a wide, asphalt-paved parking area. Most families park their vehicle near the center of the paved area, then both children and adults car hop from one friend's car to another, sharing the latest local gossip.

Durham's Drug Store is on the west side of the square. The store is filled with serious older shoppers and young people who use the soda fountain cubicle as a meeting place. Finding an empty stool at the soda counter, I order two hamburgers, all the way, and a large chocolate shake. Tomorrow is Sunday. All the eating places on the square will be closed. This may be my last meal for a while.

ONE OF THE HOSPITAL NURSES discovers me in the empty hospital room about nine o'clock. She explains that Doctor Blackmar is on his way to the hospital to deliver another baby. They need the room for the new mother.

At five hundred dollars a pop, the doctor is having a very good day. I wonder if I shouldn't warn the expectant father about the good doctor's weird sense of humor.

With my choices narrowed between sleeping on the hard couch in the hospital waiting room or in Phyliss Mitchell's Pontiac, I choose the privacy of the automobile's back seat. I make a poor choice. Continuous traffic in the hospital parking lot keeps interrupting my sleep. The night air is warm and humid. Around six o'clock Sunday morning I wake up, swimming in my own sweat. A horrible sour taste in my mouth makes me wish I'd remembered to bring a tooth brush.

Sunday Morning
September 15, 1949

A YOUNG NURSE DRESSED IN WHITE brings me coffee in a paper cup. The coffee is only lukewarm, but after the rough night I spent in the backseat of the Pontiac, I'm grateful for anything which might help revive my aching body.

"Mrs. Mitchell says you looked like you needed a strong cup of coffee," the nurse informs me.

"Yes ma'am, she's certainly right about that. You don't know how much I appreciate this," I gratefully tell the nurse.

"Mrs. Mitchell and Mrs. Kimbrough want you to come down to your wife's room when you finish your coffee."

"Mrs. Kimbrough wants to see me? Are you sure?"

"Yes sir. They're waiting on you."

The two women, minus Juanita's father and other members of the Kimbrough family who were here yesterday, arrived at the hospital somewhere around eight o'clock this morning. With no Kimbrough family members present to occupy the waiting room, I've been enjoying the luxury of sitting on the hard vinyl couch while I wait.

I sip the coffee slowly, trying to figure why Edna Kimbrough and Phyliss Mitchell would want to see me. Yesterday, I was an unwanted outcast. Today, an angel in white, bearing their truce token, has been sent to request my presence.

The coffee in the paper cup is bitter and too cold to drink now. I deposit the half-empty cup in the metal ash tray next to the couch.

"YOU WANT TO NAME MY BABY after your father? No way! No way in hell I'll ever agree to that!"

"But, Stubby, the baby will have your first and last name. Only his middle name will be the same as my fathers. Onis Jerome Warden. It's a name with real dignity," Juanita argues.

This is the last straw. Since my distasteful episode with Juanita's father yesterday morning, I have tried to maintain a low profile, letting everyone have priority before me.

Now these women want to name the baby, who has filled my being with love and joy, after the man who hates and detests me. How could I live with a child whose name reminds me of my mortal enemy, Luther Jerome Kimbrough. No, I will never allow it.

"No, Juanita, I won't even consider having a baby named Jerome. Besides, it's a sissy name. What would we call him anyway–O.J. Warden?"

"No, darling. We will call him Jerry. Jerry Warden."

"Oh, Yeah! Won't I just love that! Saying your father's name every time I mention my baby."

Phyliss Mitchell has been patiently listening to our heated argument. She and Edna Kimbrough are standing on the opposite side of Juanita's hospital bed.

"Stubby Warden, you are a stubborn, pigheaded man. Can't you see what Juanita is trying to do?"

Her words hurt me deeply. How could my good friend take sides against me so quickly? I glare at her across the bed.

"No, Phyliss! I don't see! All I see is you three women trying to cram something down my throat that makes me want to vomit."

"Stubby, what Juanita is trying to do is bring the two most important men in her life together. If the baby is named after the both of you, maybe you two men will love the child so much you'll put aside your other differences," Phyliss explains. Deep emotion strains her voice.

"Well, I'm not the one responsible for 'our other differences,' Phyliss. Luther Kimbrough never gave me a chance. He has hated me from the minute I first stepped through his front door last Thanksgiving."

I turn to scowl at Juanita's mother. "Edna, you have treated me like dirt, not accepting my phone calls and generally ignoring me. How could you believe I'd ever go along with this preposterous charade?"

Juanita's disapproving glance informs me I've gone too far, but I don't care. I intend to have my say while my temper is up.

Edna Kimbrough begins to cry. "Oh, Stubby, can you ever forgive us? We've been so stupid. I'm so sorry for the way I've acted toward you. I'd do anything, if only we could take it all back and start over again with you."

"Edna, does Luther know about your plans to give my baby his middle name?" I ask Juanita's mother.

"No. Juanita and I thought we should get your permission first. Then we would ask him."

My temper is high. I say words I regret as soon as they leave my mouth. "Lemme tell the three of you this! When Luther Kimbrough gets down on his knees to apologize for the way he's treated me, then maybe I'll consider letting my son have the same middle name as his. Until that happens, you three women can go straight to hell. If you name that baby, Jerome, you can find him another father. I'll not live with the humiliation of having my son named after a man who is so much against me."

———————

PHYLISS MITCHELL HANDS ME THE KEYS to her car. Her red eyes tell me she's disappointed with my actions. All three women were crying when I stormed out of Juanita's hospital room in anger and disgust.

"Stubby, here are the keys to my car. I think it would be better if you went back to Ranger. Luther and Gary will be here shortly. We wouldn't want anything to get started between you two again."

"I suppose I've got a really big mess to deal with now, don't I, Phyliss?"

"Stubby, I understand how difficult this is for you, and I sympathize with your hard feelings. Juanita is only trying to salvage something with her father. She loves the two of you very much. She's caught in the middle. If you truly love her, you should try and understand."

"Phyliss, I wish I could, but what she's asking is simply too bitter a pill to swallow.   Even if I destroy my marriage and lose my child, I just can't go along."

"Stubby, like I told you last night, you're much too proud for your own good.   Why don't you think on it?   Maybe your heart will soften."

"I don't believe I could ever live with what she wants to do, Phyliss, but I will think on it.   I promise."

――――――――――

LEAVING THE HOSPITAL parking lot, the tires on the new Pontiac squeal when I press too hard on the gas pedal.   I need a hot bath and a good night's sleep.   Sleeping in my own bed will be like heaven.   I can't wait to get back home, away from these awful people.

In Ranger, they only beat me up and hurt my body.   In Comanche, they want my soul.

CHAPTER ELEVEN
THE THIRD WEEK

Sunday Afternoon
September 15, 1949

ON MY WAY BACK TO RANGER I decide to stop at the Eastland hospital to check on Keith Murphy. It is eerie how all news about my injured assistant coach has been shut off. There've been no reports about his condition in the newspapers, and I haven't heard his name mentioned since Lucas Masters quizzed me about Murphy during our meeting last Tuesday.

Walking from the parking lot, I observe an Eastland County sheriff's squad car parked near the hospital entrance. I had anticipated finding Mrs. Murphy in the hospital lobby, but she is nowhere in sight. I'm not surprised to discover two deputies on the third floor, guarding Murphy's room. One of the men is Max Crawford, the deputy who was standing watch with James Fingler when I was here last Monday evening.

The new deputy is tall and thin. His dark black hair is combed straight back over his head in thick, wavy layers. He reaches for his pistol when he notices me at the top of the stairs. Max Crawford lays a hand over the new man's holster to constrain his impulsive reaction.

"It's all right, Billy. I know him. He's the Ranger football coach. James said he was okay."

I step down the hallway toward Murphy's door where the two men are standing. "Hello, Max. I see you're working with a new partner. I hope the sheriff is paying you two overtime for working on Sunday."

"Ha! Ha! Fat chance of that, Coach Warden. Us poor, under-paid county employees are fortunate if we get our regular paychecks

plastic tube on the coach's chest and tie a knot in the end of it. Retrieving a dry bath towel from under the bed pan at the end of the bed, I begin to dab at Murphy's gown while he talks.

Murphy tells me how he has been gathering information on a gang of organized car thieves based in Fort Worth. The cars are stolen in Oklahoma, mostly Tulsa and Oklahoma City, then transported by truck to Eastland County. After the cars are repainted, given new serial numbers and Texas titles, they are moved to Fort Worth and Dallas and resold. According to Murphy, more than five hundred automobiles were stolen and resold last year. The thieves apparently selected Eastland County as the ideal place to renovate the stolen cars because of its location along U.S. Highway 80 and because of its proximity to Fort Worth. And Eastland County contains numerous remote regions where the constant coming and going of trucks carrying stolen cars would never be noticed.

"But, Keith, I still don't understand why they shot you."

"Because I discovered the place where they're doing the car renovations. Problem was, I just stumbled onto it. I really wasn't looking for it. They saw me about the same time I realized what I'd found. They recognized me right away. If they hadn't known I was working with the sheriff, I think I might've gotten away. Like I say, someone in the sheriff's office is leaking information."

"Where were you when you found them, Keith?" I find myself asking questions I shouldn't want to have answers for.

"On the Singleton Ranch, about eight miles north of Desdemona."

Now I know too much. I might as well get the whole story.

"Do you know who shot you?"

"Yeah, I'm pretty sure it was Orval Graves or his brother Clifford. I saw both of 'em inside the car repair building."

I would lay odds this is the same Clifford and other tough guy who bushwhacked me under the football grandstands. Sometime, somewhere, we will meet again. Given half a chance to defend myself, I'm confident the outcome of our next meeting will be much different from the last.

Murphy advises me to keep the information confidential, making me swear not to reveal what I know to anyone. Only if something happens to him am I to repeat what he has told me. He doesn't need to tell me that possessing his secret has put my life in danger.

Murphy leans back heavily on the hospital bed. He sighs deeply, like he has been relieved of a great burden. His eyes close. Relating his story to me has sapped his strength. He'll be asleep in a minute or so. I decide to leave quietly.

"Stubby," he whispers, without opening his eyes.

"Yes, Keith." I come back to his bedside.

"I never thought I'd owe my life to that smart ass young kid who wanted to borrow my films last May." Murphy's right hand searches for me.

I take his hand and grip it tightly in mine.

"Right now, Keith, that seems like a million years ago."

———————

THE TWO DEPUTIES GUARDING the hallway are keenly interested about why I stayed so long in Murphy's room. They question me extensively, wanting to know what we talked about. Unable to think of a better explanation, I tell them I spent the entire time praying for Coach Murphy to regain his memory. They watch me curiously when I leave. Most likely neither of them believes my story.

The gas gauge on Phyliss Mitchell's Pontiac is pointing to empty as I pull onto Highway 80. Her new car is a gas guzzler, averaging less than ten miles to the gallon.

Stopping at the Sinclair service station on the east side of Eastland, I spend the last of the five dollars Phyliss lent me last evening. At twenty-five cents a gallon, I barely fill the tank past the one-half mark.

This is the third time I've stopped for gas at the Sinclair station. It's the first time I've paid.

———————

OTHEL CREAGER IS ON HER KNEES working in the flower bed next to her front porch. She glances up to wave at me while I park Phyliss Mitchell's Pontiac in my driveway. She watches me for a short minute, then returns to her gardening. I'm sure she must be wondering how I am driving such a sleek new automobile.

Crawling out of the car, I realize my Hudson is missing from the driveway. A short note is pinned to the front porch screen. It reads:

DEAR COACH
MIS MURPHY CALLED TO INVITE US TO EAT.
SHE IS ALL ALONE OUT THERE BY HERSELF.
SHE IS REAL LONESOME SO I MAY SPEND
TONIGHT OUT THERE. MIS CREAGER GAVE
ME SOME MONEY FOR GAS. WE OWE HER $2.
                    YOUR FRIEND,
                    ALFRED STEELE

Monday Morning
September 16, 1949

"YOUR PAY CHECK WILL BE READY at three o'clock, Coach Warden. We'll have all the teachers' checks ready then. We issue our teachers' paychecks at the same time every payday," Mildred Getts, the receptionist in the high school principal's office, informs me.

"Mildred, the bank closes at three. I have some bills which must be paid today. Is there any way I can get my check earlier?"

"I'm sorry, Coach Warden. Both the superintendent and school board president have to sign the checks. With today being a Monday, we'll be lucky to have the checks ready by three," the lady explains.

Realizing there's no chance of convincing her to speed up the check process, I decide to settle for a favor.

"Mildred, football practice starts at three. Is there someone who could bring my check to me?"

"Certainly. Superintendent Boswell and I both live in that section of town. One of us can bring it to you on our way home from school."

"Thanks, Mildred. Maybe I can get the check cashed after practice."

A subtle grin creeps onto Mildred's face. She's debating with herself about asking me something personal.

"Whatta you have on that devious mind of yours, Mildred?"

"Coach Warden, I've been wondering–is the game you won Friday night one we can actually count?" she teases, reminding me of my callous response to her innocent inquiry during our conversation last Tuesday.

———————

"WHAT'S THE POINT IN HAVING A BANKER for a neighbor if you don't take advantage of it?" I tell myself as I cross the brick pavement of Pine Street, heading toward Phyliss Mitchell's Pontiac.

I'll talk with Ferrol Creager at the bank. Surely he can cash my paycheck for me after I get home from football practice. I need to pay Mrs. Hines and the Finglers tonight. They've been patient, and I'm not up to offering either of them another excuse. Later, I can drive to Comanche and give the hospital their deposit.

"CRACK!" The sound of a backfiring car resonates from an unpaved alley across from the high school. The sound is followed by a whistling noise, then a thud on the brick wall of the Recreation Building in front of me. The shrill sounds interrupt my thoughts of financial matters. I pause in the street for a second, thinking. The sounds have a sequence I recognize but can't quite place.

"Coach, get down!" I hear, a half-second before a huge body comes flying through the air, knocking me to the ground.

My head hits hard on the brick pavement. The force of my unexpected impact with the enormous flying body sends me skidding head first over the rough pavement, scraping skin from my elbows.

"CRACK!" The backfire sound occurs again. This time I realize why I recognized the whistling noise. That is the sound of a bullet whizzing through the air close by. The bullet strikes the pavement a few feet away and ricochets into the side of the green and white Pontiac.

"Coach, we gotta get behind the car!" The voice belongs to my guardian angel Alfred. He grabs me by the arm, and we race for the safe haven behind Phyliss Mitchell's Pontiac.

A third shot rings out. An angry bullet smacks the car hood, carving a large ugly scar in the shiny green metal.

Alfred and I squat low behind the car, hardly breathing, not knowing what to expect next. Responding to the gunshot noise, several students wander out onto the front steps of the high school.

"What are you doing here, Alfred? I thought you were spending the night at the Murphy farm," I ask, as we crouch behind the car.

"I did, Coach. But this morning I helped Mrs. Murphy drive the school bus," Alfred explains. "We had to get her some gas so she could get back home. I was fixin' to come looking for you when I seen them two fellows getting a rifle out of their pickup."

The high-pitched screech of tires spinning against street pavement stimulates my curiosity. I peek over the back of the car to see the back end of a dark green Ford pickup speeding away. The pickup has no license plate.

Alfred slumps down to sit on the ground, leaning his back against the rear fender. He tilts his head backward against the car, showing his relief. "Who was that, Coach? Who'd want to shoot you?"

"I can't say for sure, Alfred. But I've got a good idea who it might be," I reply while I gently investigate the swelling lump on my forehead. It feels soft and spongy.

"You don't reckon it was that Clifford fellow again, do you, Coach?"

THE RANGER POLICE STATION is downtown, on Main Street, next door to the Arcadia Theater. No one has actually pointed it out to me, but I know it's there. Juanita and I have passed by the dark, unlit recessed entrance many times on our way to the movie. Yet, in the five months I have lived in Ranger, I have never seen a policeman or a police car. Perhaps that is why I'm so astonished at how soon the Ranger Police arrive after the shooting incident.

A small throng of students and teachers have crowded around us when the police car drives up. Once the students verified that neither Alfred nor I had been shot, they lost interest in us, perhaps disappointed that we escaped unharmed. The bullet holes in the car become their main focus of attention. Several older students assume the role of tour guides, ushering the younger children to the car to observe and run their fingers over the jagged bullet holes.

The police officer takes charge immediately. He disburses the crowd, assuring the students that everything is under control and the excitement is over. He urges everyone to return to class.

Alfred and I wait impatiently while the students leave, anxious to explain about the shooting incident. The police officer recognizes us and quickly introduces himself. The officer is Eugene Brownlee. His son Will is my place kicker. Before he begins his investigation, Brownlee wants to talk football and about the DeLeon game. Brownlee reminds me that Will has not missed an extra point in either of our two regular season games. We replay the DeLeon game for a few minutes before the police officer finally retrieves a note pad from his car. He asks for the correct spelling of each of our names, then makes notes about the time the shooting took place and the precise location of the gunmen. He acts disappointed when we are unable to accurately describe the two gunmen or give him a license plate number. With the sketchy information we are able to furnish him, he tells us not to be optimistic about the police making an arrest. He warns us to be careful before he drives away.

Driving the bullet-riddled Pontiac to the football field, I find myself crouching down behind the steering wheel. Alfred also slumps low in the passenger seat.

"STUBBY, IS THIS GITTIN' TO BE A HABIT? Seems like every Monday morning, I've gotta come in here and patch you up," Sam humorously complains, as he applies Merthiolate to my bloody elbows.

"Every other Monday, Sam. This only happens on the Mondays after we win a football game." I grimace at the stinging pain. The fiery orange liquid burns like the devil. I grasp the table top tightly and try not to flinch when he begins stroking on a second coating.

Only sissies flinch.

Monday Afternoon
September 16, 1949

"I THOUGHT YOUR CHECK WOULD BE LARGER," Ferrol Creager comments, sounding like he's disappointed.

"So did I, Ferrol. I was expecting to be paid another three

hundred dollars."

"Stubby, are you sure you can get by on this kind of pay? You've been coaching for more than three weeks now. Surely you were making more than this working at the Pontiac House."

My paycheck is for half a month's salary—one hundred seventy-five dollars, less social security and some teacher deductions which I wasn't expecting. The total amount of my check is $164.83.

Superintendent Boswell personally delivered my paycheck to me at the field house after practice. He knew I'd be expecting the three hundred dollar bonus for winning the DeLeon game. I was pretty hot when I discovered the bonus was not included on my paycheck. Boswell explained I would get the extra money, in cash, on Wednesday. Apparently, my bonus money has to be collected from several influential football boosters. It doesn't come directly from the school district. I suspect Lucas Masters is the largest contributor.

"If they keep their promise, I should get another three hundred on Wednesday, Ferrol. I can get by on this until then," I reply, avoiding his question about how much I was making at the Pontiac House. My banker neighbor might be shocked to learn this coaching job pays twice what I was making there.

———————

MRS. HINES SEEMS TO BE IMMENSELY RELIEVED when I stop by her house to pay her the thirty dollars of rent I owe. Martha Fingler acts disappointed when I pay her only thirty dollars against my grocery bill, but she accepts the money without complaint. I think about promising to pay the balance of my bill on Wednesday, then decide against it. I've made too many promises lately which I haven't been able to keep.

Because Alfred rode the school bus with Kate Murphy this morning, the Hudson is still out at the Murphy farm. I check the gas gauge on Phyliss Mitchell's Pontiac. With any luck I can make it to Comanche and back. If I put a hundred down on the baby deposit, I'll have $4.83 left for gas.

My puny hundred dollar deposit won't please the demanding hospital reception lady, but that's the least of my worries. Phyliss Mitchell is gonna strangle me when she sees the bullet holes in her new car.

Monday Evening
September 16, 1949

DARKNESS CLOSES IN as I pass the Comanche city limit sign. A once dazzling amber sunset is now practically obliterated by a maze of silver clouds on the horizon. Even though I stopped to fill the gas tank at the Sinclair station in Eastland, the needle on the gas gauge is already down to the one-half mark. I head straight for the hospital.

The archaic, overweight receptionist is not on duty when I arrive at the hospital reception counter. In her place is the attractive young nurse who brought me coffee yesterday morning.

"Hello. Could you please help me? I'm supposed to leave a deposit with you. My wife is here. She just had a baby."

The young nurse recognizes me. She notices the bandages Sam taped around my elbows. "Hello, Mister Warden. Oh, my! Have you been in an accident?"

"Yes. Well, sort of an accident. I discovered that brick pavement is much tougher than the skin on my elbows."

"Do you want someone to take a look, Mister Warden? You might need a tetanus shot."

"No, I'm fine. My assistant football coach in Ranger cleaned my wounds and disinfected me thoroughly with Merthiolate before he put on these bandages."

The young nurse takes my hands and lifts up my arms to inspect my bandages closely. Apparently they pass her rigid standard of approval.

"Your assistant did a good job, Mister Warden. You have a good chance of healing satisfactorily. Now, how much deposit do you want to make?"

The young nurse doesn't argue when I hand her the hundred dollar deposit. She records the deposit in a black ledger book and makes me a receipt.

"Mister Warden, do you want to see your wife and baby?" she asks, handing me the receipt.

"No, I need to get back to Ranger," I answer. The strong emotion from my encounter with the three women on Sunday morning still lingers. I'm in no mood for another confrontation. I came here only because I promised to deliver the deposit money today.

"I'm sure your wife wants to see you, Mister Warden. It's after visiting hours for the nursery, but I can arrange for you to see your new son, too."

The nurse is almost begging me not to leave. Comanche is a small town. Probably, there are very few secrets here. I'm sure, by now, everyone at the hospital knows about my difficulties with my wife and my in-laws. That's why she's trying to be so helpful.

"No, thanks. Not tonight. I really need to get back."

"Mister Warden, please don't leave without seeing your wife. She needs you so very much."

The young nurse is close to tears. I reach out and place my hand on hers.

"Thanks for caring, young lady. I appreciate your concern, but there is too much anger inside me to see her right now."

———————

ABOUT FIVE MILES OUTSIDE COMANCHE I pull the car off the highway and stop. The sincere concern of the young nurse at the hospital has dampened my angry resolve. The hatred and animosity inside me begin to subside.

The words of Phyliss Mitchell echo through my mind. "Stubby Warden, you're too proud for your own good."

Everything I want and need in my life is back there at the Comanche hospital. The only woman I'll ever love is there. The young nurse said my wife needs me. The boy child, who filled my heart with joy and happiness when I held him in my arms, is waiting there. Is my pride so important that I can turn away from the two people I love so much, just to prove my masculine point?

I crank the engine and turn the car around on the highway, heading it back to Comanche.

———————

"OH, STUBBY, THE NURSE TOLD ME you had left," Juanita sobs. Her eyes are filled with tears. She has been crying.

I walk over to stand beside her hospital bed. She raises her body and pulls me down to kiss her lips. Her mouth is warm and sweet.

I take her head in my hand and wipe the tears from her cheeks. She trembles slightly at my touch.

"I came back, Juanita. I had to tell you. I don't care what you name the baby. I want the two of you with me. Nothing else matters, not anymore."

"Stubby darling, the baby's name is not important to me either, but your son must have a father. When the doctor releases us, we are ready to go home with you, if you still want us. Then, we will follow you wherever you say, even if you want to live in Corpus Christi."

"I want you, Juanita. Oh, God, how I want the two of you to be with me."

"Stubby, please promise not to ever leave me that way again. I was so afraid. I thought I'd lost you."

"I promise, Juanita."

"ONIS JEROME WARDEN."

The young nurse at the front desk jumps, startled by my statement. She didn't notice me approaching.

"What, Mister Warden? I'm sorry. I didn't hear what you said."

"Onis Jerome Warden. You can tell the lady in the nursery we have a name for our baby. She can put a name on his bassinet now."

"EEEEEK!" the young nurse screams out happily. She runs down the corridor, looking for someone to tell.

Tuesday Morning
September 17, 1949

"STUBBY, THESE LOOK LIKE BULLET HOLES," Price says to me.

"You're right, Price. They are bullet holes. What I want to know is can you fix them before I have to return the car to Phyliss?"

Price and I are in the front driveway at the Pontiac House. He is inspecting the holes absorbed by Phyliss Mitchell's new automobile in yesterday's shooting. He stands up, resting his chin on his fist while he ponders the situation.

"Who the hell would want to shoot you, Stubby? I don't understand...."

Price generously doesn't continue his thought, but he's right. Why would anyone want to shoot a dirt-poor football coach? Surely the shooting was not a simple retaliation for my winning another football game. Having Clifford and his friend beat up on me should be plenty of punishment for winning a football game.

No, the shooting incident is somehow connected to my visiting Murphy at the Eastland hospital on Sunday afternoon. Murphy was right about there being a leak in the sheriff's office.

"Price, at this moment I fear the wrath of Phyliss Mitchell, after she sees this car, more than I'll ever fear any cowardly gunman trying to bushwhack me."

Price considers my statement for a moment. Not necessarily teasing, he replies, "You know, Stubby, I've never been shot at, but I have felt the sting of Phyliss Mitchell's wrath. Given a choice between the two, I'm pretty darn sure I'd choose getting shot at."

WITH A REGULAR SEASON WIN under our belts, the daily grind of our football workouts finds a groove. After almost a month of constant, tenacious drilling, our players are acutely familiar with their assignments on every offensive play, and they understand precisely what we expect from them, on both offense and defense.

I'm not satisfied. I insist upon running the plays over and over until every team member, including the subs, performs his job perfectly. Sam, Alfred, and the entire team become bored with my unchanging routine, but no one complains. We spend each practice perfecting our execution. As a football team, we improve a little each day.

On Wednesday after practice, G.C. Boswell brings me the three hundred dollar bonus. As promised, the bonus is in cash, three–one hundred dollar bills. The three bills appear to be brand new, crackling when I fold them to fit my wallet. This is the most money I have ever possessed at one time. The feeling of having so much of my own money is intoxicating. Sadly, the feeling will be only temporary. All the money has been spent long before I receive it.

After I pay my bill at Fingler's Grocery and settle up with Pearl for the numerous meals Alfred and I have eaten on credit at her place, less than half the bonus money is left. Price argues with me, but I prevail by repaying him thirty dollars. I owe him more than twice that amount.

Not trusting his own paint and body man, Price has the bullet holes repaired at Scott's Paint and Body Works in Eastland. They do a terrific job. The holes are almost invisible when the car is returned on Wednesday afternoon. Only a professional would ever notice the slight difference in paint match.

On Wednesday night, finally having money for gas, Alfred and I drive out to the Murphy farm to retrieve my Hudson.

Wednesday Night
September 18, 1949

THE MURPHY FARM is about twelve miles south of Ranger on a dirt side road, off Farm Road 571. The farm house sits at the base of a small mesquite-covered hill which hides it from the main road.

This locale is referred to by old timers as the Alemeda Area. At one time this part of Eastland County had its own school district. Up until 1947, when the Alemeda Area joined the Ranger School District, the children living on farms here attended the Alemeda School. The unused Alemeda school building is still standing and in good condition.

We catch a glimpse of the building's brick exterior when we turn onto the dirt road leading to Murphy's farm. The abandoned school building seems so isolated and lonesome, like it misses the laughter of happy children who once filled its hallways.

A last piece of setting sun disappears from the horizon as we pull up alongside my maroon Hudson, parked in front of the farm house. A light burns on the front porch.

"Why don't we go inside, Coach? We should say hello to Mrs. Murphy," Alfred urges.

"You go in, if you want, Alfred. I think I'll head on back to town. You can bring my Hudson when you're ready to come in."

"Come on in, Coach. You'll hurt Mrs. Murphy's feelings if you don't say hello."

"Alright, but I can only stay for a moment," I reluctantly agree.

The front door is open, allowing the cool evening breeze to ventilate the house. Only a wire-screened door is closed to keep out bugs. Alfred knocks lightly on the screen door. Kate Murphy emerges from the kitchen. She appears to be expecting company. The expensive dress underneath her decorative pink apron is obviously meant for special occasions.

"Hello, Alfred. Hello, Coach Warden. Please come in. Our supper is about ready."

A cloth-covered table in the dining area has been set for three, complete with plates, silverware and drinking glasses. Centered on the table is a vase filled with fresh wild flowers.

"What's going on, Alfred? She acts like she's expecting us to stay for dinner."

"Mrs. Murphy is a great cook, Coach. Just wait 'til you taste her homemade rolls," Alfred responds, avoiding a direct answer to my question.

From all appearances this evening is a planned event, not a simple, impromptu evening visit. These two people have contrived to get me here for this meal. Because of the hazardous mutual knowledge I now share with her husband, I had hoped to avoid further personal contact with Mrs. Murphy, for fear of saying something which might lead her to suspect how much I know. Nevertheless, I don't want to disappoint Alfred. I have little choice other than to go along with their scheme.

Alfred and I watch while our hostess fills the table with bowls of steaming fresh vegetables, placed around a heaping platter of fried chicken. A basket of homemade rolls, covered with a blue table towel, sits next to a dish of freshly churned butter. The last time I sat down to such a splendid meal was at my grandparents' house on the Easter Sunday before I left for college at A&M.

"Alright, gentlemen. Please take your seats. We are ready to eat," Mrs. Murphy announces. Alfred steps behind her chair. Surprising me with his good manners, he holds her chair while she seats herself.

For a few minutes we eat in silence, enjoying the excellent food. Mrs. Murphy initiates a conversation by speaking to me. "Coach Warden, Alfred tells me your wife will be bringing your new son home soon. I imagine you must be quite excited with the prospect of having your family living with you again."

"Mrs. Murphy, would you mind calling me Stubby? After all we've been through these past weeks, I feel like we're good friends. Let's not use last names."

"Fine. I'll agree to call you Stubby, but only if you will call me Kate."

"Alright, Kate, we have a bargain. And, to answer your question about my wife and baby–yes, I expect they'll be coming home soon, probably next week, unless we run into unexpected complications."

"You know what, Stubby? I have some wonderful baby clothes stored away, from when my children were young. Perhaps, when your wife and baby come home, I could bring some of the baby clothes to her. Children that age grow so fast they hardly ever wear out their clothes. Most of the baby clothes I have saved are just like new."

"That would be very thoughtful, Kate. I'm sure Juanita would appreciate the baby clothes. I'd like for you to get to know my wife. She's a wonderful person. You'll like her."

Alfred keeps unusually quite, not participating in the table talk. Contrary to his normal behavior, he has stopped eating. He watches us while Kate and I carry on our conversation.

Kate Murphy is an intelligent and exceptionally interesting woman. During the meal she smoothly changes the topics of conversation from baby clothes to local politics to high school football. She seems knowledgeable about each subject. She expertly maneuvers our friendly conversation to her farm while she serves a mouth-watering dessert of coconut pie and strong coffee.

"Yes, Stubby, it takes a lot of work to keep this farm running profitably. With Keith in the hospital, I really don't know how I'm going to manage."

"Maybe you could get someone to help you. Maybe you could hire someone to help out temporarily?" I suggest, remembering how I solved the problem for Buster Barnes.

"Yes, that might help, but what I really need is someone who can be here full time. Someone I can depend on."

She seems to be waiting on me to offer a solution to her problem. We sit silently at the table while she anticipates my answer. Several ideas cross my mind. Then it strikes me. Now I understand what this whole scenario is about.

"Alfred, maybe you could move out here and help Kate. Sounds like she really needs someone like yourself."

"What? Me? Why sure, Coach. I'd be glad to help her out, if you say it's okay. Maybe I could drive the school bus to Ranger every morning and keep helping you with football."

Alfred tries to act surprised by my suggestion. A sly grin gives him away.

"My, what a wonderful idea, Stubby. That'll be the perfect solution to my problem. How did you ever come up with such a simple and imaginative solution?" Kate gushes.

"Just lucky, I guess," I answer aloud, with false modesty.

Sometimes I'm simply amazing, I think to myself.

––––––––––

AFTER SUPPER I offer to help with the dishes, but Kate refuses my offer, insisting that washing dishes is woman's work. I don't argue. It's been a long day, and I'm ready to leave. Alfred decides to stay and talk with Kate. Probably, they want to celebrate their triumphant evening after I'm gone. I thank Kate for her hospitality and promise to let her know when Juanita and the baby come home.

On the drive into Ranger I laugh to myself about the great lengths Alfred and Kate went to obtain my blessing of their plan. Even though the two of them had already decided Alfred should move to the Murphy farm, their concern for my feelings is touching. They are two very special people.

Actually, Alfred's decision to move will alleviate several potential problems. With Alfred, Juanita and the baby all living with me in one small house, I was on the verge of having a severe shortage of bedrooms. And, Juanita might have been less than delighted about sharing her house with such a hungry, and possibly permanent, house guest.

Living on the farm with Kate Murphy, Alfred will be appreciated and well-fed. The two of them always seem to have something to talk about. Kate promised to try to get Alfred on the school district payroll for driving the bus. If that happens, he'll have some money of his own. No one knows better than I how important having your own money can be, for ego and peace of mind.

No matter how well Alfred's leaving works out for everyone else, I'll miss having my guardian angel around.

———————

Thursday Morning
September 19, 1949

SHORT SNORTER SCRATCHES AT MY BED COVERS. He wants to be let out. I roll over to look at the clock on the table beside the bed. The time is a quarter past six. My eyes close. I begin to drift back into sleep. The dog scratches at my bed covers again. "Okay, dog! Be patient! I'm getting up. Gimme a minute to wake up."

"Grrrrrr," Short Snorter retorts. He's impatient with me. I also suspect he seriously resents being referred to as a dog.

I sit up in bed, trying to recall where I left my trousers. When Short Snorter growls again, I decide to look for the pants later. He follows me as I stagger, half-asleep, toward the back door.

Alfred is sitting at the kitchen table, staring blankly at the coffee percolator which is beginning to perk.

"Good morning, Alfred. You must've been out late last night. I didn't hear you when you came in," I say, opening the door to let the puppy outside.

"Yeah. Me and Mrs. Murphy got to talking about Coach Murphy getting himself shot and being in the hospital. She's worried sick about him. She's afraid whoever shot him will try to kill him again."

"I suppose they might try, but with the sheriff guarding him, I don't think she has anything to worry about," I say reassuringly. If Kate knew how unreliable the sheriff's department actually is, she'd really worry.

"It all makes me so mad, Coach. If I ever find out who it was that shot Coach Murphy, I intend to hurt him, real bad."

"Then I'll let you have him after I get through with him, Alfred, or maybe you can have Orval, and I'll take Clifford."

It was out before I could stop myself. I could bite my tongue for being so stupid. Alfred's quick glance tells me he picked up on my loose comment.

"Coach, you don't think it was them two Graves boys, do you? Yeah, it makes sense. Them two fellows is meaner than a couple of rattlesnakes. I'll bet Clifford is the one who beat you up."

"Alfred, forget what I said. It could put you in great danger. We sure can't have Kate Murphy suspecting it was those two who shot her husband. I want your promise not to tell anyone what we suspect about the Graves boys, at least not until we can find out who they're working for."

"Alright, Coach, I promise. But I want a crack at 'em when the time comes. Okay?"

"Okay, Alfred. We both share similar ambitions when it comes to getting even with Orval and Clifford Graves."

The coffee pot finally stops perking. Alfred pours us each a cup of coffee while I let Short Snorter back inside. The taste of the hot coffee brings an edge to my sleep-dulled senses.

"Coach, my bag is packed. I'll be spending the night at the Murphy farm tonight."

"Yeah, I thought you'd probably be leaving today. Good luck, Alfred."

"Thanks, Coach."

Thursday Evening
September 19, 1949

TONIGHT I STAYED LATE at the field house, wanting to review film of last year's game with Stamford one more time. I've already watched the film several times, but with Alfred gone, there's no reason to hurry home and cook supper. The Stamford game tomorrow night will be our second home game. I'm determined to do everything necessary to make it our first home win. In past years Stamford has been a football powerhouse, dominating their district and giving an excellent account of themselves in the state playoffs. However, since their head coach moved on to greener pastures two years ago, their football program has struggled. They have lost their first two games this year.

Stamford is in Jones County, about forty miles north of Abilene. A bus trip from Stamford to Ranger would take more than two hours. Remembering how uncomfortable the rock-hard seats in our school bus can be, I'm grateful we play them at home this year.

The current Stamford football coach has scrapped their traditional single wing, opting for a more up-to-date offense. His new offense uses a "Straight Tee" backfield alignment. Although their new coach is progressive, the game films reveal that his blocking schemes are not always compatible with his backfield sets. Many times I observe an opposing linebacker in the path of the play who is left unblocked or a defensive lineman who is blocked in the wrong direction. If our defensive team plays its customary hard-nosed game, Stamford shouldn't be able to move the football on us with any consistency.

Around nine o'clock I finish watching the films, satisfied my Bulldog squad is prepared to face the Stamford club. A slight chill in the night air makes me shiver as I fumble with the front door lock. The moon has set, leaving the football field and stadium covered in darkness. The nearest light is a street lamp several blocks away.

I left the Hudson parked in the parking lot outside the stadium. The shortest distance to my car is along the gravel pathway underneath the home side bleachers.

I take the long way, skirting around the grandstand and keeping the playing field to my back, ready to run at the slightest movement.

Friday Night
September 20, 1949

SOMETIMES, BEFORE A FOOTBALL GAME, an aura of supreme confidence develops in a football team. Players can sense, long before the game, that they will prevail. In the team's collective mind they become unstoppable and unbeatable. This is the kind of feeling which has been building all week in my Bulldog team. With each successive practice we become more convinced that this is a team of destiny. This football squad is blessed with players of exceptional talent. And, a special kind of chemistry has developed between the team and their coaches. By game time our young men are excited and ready. Their spirited anticipation acts like a charge of electric current flowing through the football team. Our warm-up drills are so sharp and crisp, I wouldn't be surprised to see sparks fly when the football is exchanged between players.

THE REFEREE BLOWS HIS WHISTLE, signaling the game to begin. Stamford's kicker booms the ball to our five where Billy Simpson receives. Returning the ball up the left side line behind Stiles, Hummel and Patterson, Simpson reaches the twenty-eight before he's tackled.

While our offense runs on the field, I glance toward the pep squad area. The cheerleaders are taking turns parading Short Snorter back and forth in front of the grandstands. Ranger fans have concocted some sort of arm-waving motion to show their worship of the bulldog pup. They stand and wave their arms up and down each time the small dog passes by. Short Snorter seems to be enjoying the attention.

Before the kickoff Jones and I agreed on which plays he would call in this first offensive series. If we had returned the kickoff past our thirty-five, he would call a pass on first down. Since we're starting from the twenty-eight, he'll keep the ball on the ground.

Hut. Hut. Jones fakes the ball to Dorsey, then moves to his right behind our linemen. Stamford's defensive end gives up his outside coverage and comes in to tackle Jones. The pitchout flutters out to Hamrick as he breaks around right end. Twelve yards downfield Hamrick is pulled down by a blue and white defensive halfback.

Hut. Hut. Jones calls the exact same play. This time the Stamford end stays outside, defending against a pitchout. Jones cuts inside the end for an eight yard gain.

Hut. Hut. We run the same play again. Again, the defensive end comes in to tackle Jones. A pitchout to Hamrick gains nine yards.

Hut. Hut. We run the play again. Our quarterback has apparently decided to keep calling the same play as long as it works. Once again the defensive end stays with his outside coverage and Jones runs inside. He gains only three yards.

Stamford's defensive backs have moved up close to the line of scrimmage, trying to shut down our running game. I try to signal Jones to call a pass but can't get his attention.

Hut. Hut. Jones takes the snap and drops straight back. Ralph Rogers brushes by a blue and white defensive back and sprints down the right sideline. We've caught the Stamford defensive backs by surprise. They race back, trying to recover.

Jones' wobbly pass is short. A blue and white defender, chasing after our wide-open receiver, stops to intercept the pass. Rogers charges back to tackle him at their seventeen.

"Holy Crap! Rogers was wide open. If Jones could pass worth a damn, we had a touchdown for sure," Sam growls disgustedly, kicking at the turf along the sideline.

"Yeah, that's the problem with passes. Three things can happen. Two of them are bad," I tell my assistant, stupidly repeating an old cliché. We don't need to talk about Jones' inadequate passing arm in front of our players.

Jones comes running off the field with several other members of the offense. He stops to face me.

"I'm sorry, Coach. The ball slipped out of my hand just as I let it go."

"It's okay, Reed. We're doing pretty good with our running game. Whatta you say we stick with running the ball for a while?"

"Alright, if you say so, Coach."

Jones walks over to the bench. He pauses there, watching the fans in the bleachers for a few seconds. Then he comes back to stand beside me.

"Coach, the ball really did slip. I can throw a football more than twenty-five yards."

"I believe you, Reed. Look, it's okay about the interception, but let's keep the ball on the ground this next series."

The quarterback gives me an exasperated expression and returns to the bench, shaking his head. It's impossible to tell whether he is more upset with me or with himself.

Stamford takes possession deep in their own territory. They line up in the same "Straight Tee" formation they used in last year's game. If they haven't added anything new, our defense should contain them easily.

Stamford tries a direct handoff to their fullback over right guard on their first play. Barnes meets him at the line of scrimmage for no gain. Their second play is a pitchout around left end. Charles Williams makes the tackle behind the line for a loss of four. Sam, Alfred and I huddle at the sideline to discuss how we will return their punt.

"Oh, hell! Where did that guy come from?" Ed Polston yells from the bench.

We glance up to see a lone blue and white player rise up. He has been lying in the grass, hiding out along the sideline opposite the football. Our defensive backs have not noticed him yet. After faking a handoff to his fullback, Stamford's quarterback has drifted back, looking downfield.

"It's a hideout play!" Sam screams to the defense. "Somebody cover the hideout man!"

Too late. The Stamford quarterback releases his pass before our defensive backs can recover. The ball is thrown perfectly, floating gently down into the outstretched arms of the blue and white receiver who is racing up the sideline.

Our deep safety Weldon Cunningham is the last Bulldog defender with any chance of running down the Stamford hideout man. Taking advantage of a favorable tackling angle, Cunningham somehow catches Stamford's ball carrier and shoves him out of bounds at the seven yard line, saving us the embarrassment of having Stamford score on their first offensive series.

"Damn! How could that happen? Didn't the U.I.L. outlaw that play a couple of years ago?" I ask Sam.

"I guess not. If they did, the refs don't seem to know about it. I don't see any penalty flags."

"Damn," I repeat.

WHILE THE OFFICIALS MOVE THE CHAINS upfield, we make some quick substitutions, inserting Wade, Yung and Davenport, beefing up our defensive line to enhance our goal line stand.

"Coach Warden, Mrs. Hopper wants to talk with you. She's over there with the cheerleaders," Jimmy Cantrell informs me.

"Who is Mrs. Hopper? I don't know anyone by that name."

"She's the cheerleaders' sponsor, Coach. You know, the lady who arranges for their transportation to ballgames. Mrs. Hopper's daughter is the cheerleaders' mascot."

"Jimmy, tell her I can't talk now. We're trying to stop Stamford from scoring."

"She's awfully mad, Coach, and she's got a real mean temper. You oughta talk with her before she does somethin' crazy."

"Alright. Alright, I'll go talk with her," I say, yielding to young Cantrell.

"Alfred, tell Coach Aills I gotta leave for a minute. You two can decide on our defensive alignments."

Leaving the sideline, I hurry over to the cheerleader section. The cheerleaders have gathered about an attractive blonde woman, giving her their adoring, undivided attention. The woman is in her early thirties. Her clothes are stylish, but for a Friday night football game, she is blatantly overdressed, wearing a custom-tailored, two-piece dress, complete with feathered hat, gloves and patent-leather, high-heeled shoes.

When I approach, the lady rushes out to meet me, leaving the circle of cheerleaders. She is obviously upset.

"Stubby, you have to do something about your bulldog," the woman demands. Her authoritative and presumptuous attitude stuns me. She calls me by first name, without our ever having been introduced.

"I'm not sure what you mean, Mrs. Hopper. Has he done something wrong?"

A loud roar from Ranger fans in the grandstands drowns out the woman's answer. In anticipation of some action on the playing field the home crowd rises to its feet. I turn to look, but the woman grabs my arm and jerks me back around to face her. Mrs. Hopper is not at all interested in what is happening out on the field.

"I'm sorry, Mrs. Hopper. I didn't hear all of what you said."

The lady is furious now. Her voice is sharp and angry. "I said, your dog relieved himself on my daughter's saddle-oxford shoes! That's what he did! My daughter was so embarrassed. She was crying her heart out. Her father's taken her home to wash her feet and get her another pair of shoes. She'll miss the entire first half on account of your bulldog."

"Well, of course I'm very sorry about your little girl, Mrs. Hopper, but what do you expect me to do? As you can see, I'm rather busy right now, coaching a football game." I smile, trying to make light of the situation.

Up in the home side bleachers excited fans jump to their feet and begin to chant, "Defense! Defense! Hold that line!"

The woman's blazing glare adamantly declares that she's in no mood to laugh about the incident.

One of the female yell leaders, Betty Jo Penn, leaves the group of anxious boosters to lend her support. "Coach Warden, little Kaye isn't the only one your dog tried to pee on. He's been sneaking up on all of us and heisting his leg. We can hardly get off a yell, for fear we'll get a leg wet down."

"Ohhhh!" Ranger fans moan. The moan is followed by loud cheering and exuberant celebration. Rumbling sounds of a thousand feet stomping on the wooden deck delay my response to the cheerleader and her sponsor.

"Mrs. Hopper, Betty Jo, I'm truly sorry about the problem with my bulldog. Please accept my apologies. Maybe I should keep him at the bench for the rest of the game."

——————

AFTER TYING SHORT SNORTER'S LEASH to the bench, I return to the sideline. Our offensive team is back on the field. The football is positioned just outside our goal line.

Hut. Hut. Jones hands off to Phillips who rips through the blue and white defense for four yards.

"Alfred, what's happening?" I inquire.

"Oh! Hi, Coach. I sent Phillips in for Dorsey. I knew you'd want to get the ball away from the goal line before we started running option plays again."

"Alfred, tell me what happened! Did they score on us?"

"Naw, we held 'em. Stopped 'em twice after they drove down to our one-foot line. Barnes, Wade and Davenport just put a plug in the middle of the line. It was the finest goal line stand I've ever seen, but I reckon you would've had to see it to really appreciate it. Wish you could've been here."

"Yeah, me too," I despondently concur.

"Hey, you guys! You better move down to this end of the bench! That little bulldog will pee on you when you're not looking," Wayne Hargrave advises the defensive players returning from the playing field–after their sensational goal line stand.

IN THREE CARRIES Phillips moves the football out to our twelve yard line, giving us a first down. I send Dorsey back in at fullback with instructions for Jones to begin running the option plays again.

Alternately running the options to opposite sides of the line, Jones moves the ball down the field with little opposition from Stamford's defense. Hamrick runs the ball into the end zone after only ten plays. Brownlee's extra point try splits the uprights. With three minutes left in the first quarter, the red and white Coca Cola scoreboard reads:

RANGER 7   VISITOR 0

Brownlee's kickoff is returned to the twenty-two where the blue and white offense begins their second possession of the game. After being fooled by the trick hideout play, our defense gets down to business. On each Stamford play one of our linemen manages to get into their back-field to either disrupt their execution or make the tackle. The Stamford club is forced to punt from their own eighteen, losing four yards on three offensive plays.

Comacho receives the punt and returns the ball to the Stamford forty-four. A clipping penalty against us eliminates the nice return. After stepping off a fifteen yard penalty, the game officials place the ball on our thirty.

Sticking to our option plays, we grind out good yardage, running first to the left, then back to the right side. However, with each successive play our gains become less and less as Stamford's defensive backs begin to cheat up again, playing close behind their linebackers. We barely make a first down in three plays.

"Stubby, we need to call another pass play. Their backs are moving up to stop our running game," Sam advises me.

My assistant coach is right. Even if we throw an incompletion, a pass will make the Stamford defensive backs more cautious. A completed pass would definitely shake up their defense.

"Comacho, get up here," I call to the bench.

While the game officials move the chain following our first down, I give the speedy halfback specific instructions about how I want the pass play executed.

"Jimmy, you check in for Hamrick. Tell the quarterback to call sixty-eight, pass right. I want the right end Rogers to run downfield twenty yards, make a button hook, stop and wait for the pass. You understand?"

"Yes sir. I sub for Hamrick. Reed calls sixty-eight, pass right. Ralph, button hook, stop, twenty yards downfield, so we don't get intercepted again," the young halfback replies, grinning as he repeats my instructions.

As Comacho reaches our huddle, the officials whistle for time to start. He taps Hamrick on the shoulder. They exchange a few words before Hamrick breaks quickly from the huddle and runs to the sideline.

My maroon team remains huddled for an extended duration.

"What's taking 'em so long, Stubby? You call somethin' new?" Sam asks.

"Darned if I know. It's just a simple pass play. We've practiced it a hundred times."

"Holy crap! We're gonna get a delay of game penalty if they don't hurry."

Our players break from the lengthy huddle. While his linemen take their positions, Jones lingers behind, gazing at us on the sideline. Finally he walks through the backfield and gets in position to take the snap from center. The line official vigilantly checks his watch while he places one hand on his penalty flag. An instant before the official grabs for his flag, Thompson snaps the football.

Jones fakes the ball to Dorsey, then back-peddles into a blocking pocket between Simpson and Comacho. Rogers charges down the right sideline, not bothering to stop twenty yards downfield as instructed. Stamford's defensive backs scramble to get back.

Jones waits patiently in the pocket provided by Comacho and Simpson. When our tall receiver runs past the deepest blue and white defender, Jones flings the oval shaped ball with all his might.

A wobbly spiral pass becomes more of an end over end pass by the time it reaches the outstretched hands of Ralph Rogers at the Stamford twenty. No matter, Ralph catches the ball easily and trots untouched into the end zone for a touchdown.

Fans in the Ranger bleachers celebrate wildly, stomping their feet and proudly waving maroon and white pom-poms. Jones runs forward to the line of scrimmage and stops. With his hands resting on his hips, he turns to stare toward our bench. His pass, wobbly spiral that it was, traveled more than forty yards in the air.

My quarterback is waiting for a reaction from me. I snap to attention and salute him to acknowledge his accomplishment. Reed smiles broadly and salutes me back before he runs downfield to hug Ralph Rogers.

"Well, I'll be dogged," exclaims Sam, standing a few feet away, after watching the exchange of salutes between the quarterback and myself. "I've never seen him throw a ball that far before. What got into him anyway?"

"I don't know, Sam, but something has him motivated tonight."

BROWNLEE COMES LIMPING to the bench after he kicks the extra point.

"Hey, Will! What's the matter? Are you okay?" I ask him.

"I don't know, Coach Warden. It feels like I pulled somethin'," our kicker grimaces. He is obviously in pain.

"Can you do the kickoff, Will? Maybe we should let McKinney kick."

"No, I'll be fine, Coach. Lemme stretch a minute."

Brownlee drops to the ground and begins touching the toes of his shoes. After a few seconds of the stretching exercise, he rises to his feet and limps onto the field. The kickoff team has lined up with our maroon defenders spaced at equal intervals across the thirty-five yard line.

Brownlee positions the football on the kicking tee and assumes his kickoff position. Will signals the referee. The referee blows his whistle and waves his arm. Halfway to the football our limping kicker stumbles and collapses. Bulldog teammates on the field rush to his aid.

Sam and I dash onto the field while the game officials push a crowd of players back.

Brownlee lies writhing on the grass, his face contorted with pain. Sam kneels beside him to examine the kicker's leg.

"Stubby, I think his leg is broken. You better get a stretcher out here," Sam advises me in a calm, but worried, voice.

RANGER FANS RISE and give a standing ovation to our injured kicker as the ambulance drives from the field. Doctor Watkins, our team doctor, is aboard the ambulance, riding with Brownlee. He'll examine Will's leg at the Ranger hospital where they have the proper X-ray equipment.

A game official comes to our bench to advise me we are being penalized five yards for being offside on the kickoff.

"That's not right!" I shout at him. "You can't penalize us! We had a player injured!"

"Coach, several members of your kicking team passed the forty before the ball was kicked. That is the infraction we are calling. If you persist, we can also give you another penalty for unsportsmanlike conduct. That would be another fifteen yards."

"Okay. Okay. But, you're wrong about the offside penalty," I say, getting in the last word.

The official jerks a yellow penalty flag from his back pocket and throws it on the ground.

"Coach, that remark cost your team fifteen yards. Wanna try for thirty?"

"Hey! I said okay! Don't I have a right to disagree with your call?" I'm really mad now. This idiot has let his authority go straight to his head.

The official reaches for his penalty flag on the ground, apparently with the intention of throwing it on me again.

Sam steps out gracefully to place a huge foot on the flag, preventing the game official from retrieving it.

"Stubby, shut up! Before we have to kick off from the end zone."

Aills glares at the man dressed in black and white. "Okay, Danny, you won the argument. How 'bout we play some football?"

Sam removes his foot from the penalty flag, stoops down to pick it up and hands it politely to the official. The man leaves without saying a word. The big coach huffs conspicuously to display his irritation as he turns and tramps away.

BILLY MCKINNEY MIGHT be an exceptional defensive back, but he hasn't kicked off in a game this year. After all the penalties are assessed, the football is placed at our twenty. This is one heck of a situation to be breaking in a new place kicker.

McKinney's short kick is received at the fifty and returned to our forty yard line.

As we near the end of the first quarter, Stamford has made only one first down, and that was on the hideout play. In fact, if you take away the hideout play, the blue and white team would have a negative total yards gained. Stamford's running game has been totally ineffective against our solid defense.

Having possession of the football inside our territory for the first time tonight, Stamford's coach must realize his club needs to score on this possession if they plan to get back in the game.

A new quarterback enters the game for Stamford. I suspect they have one quarterback who best executes their running game and another quarterback who is a more proficient passer.

"Sam, tell the defense to watch for a pass."

"Yeah, I already signaled Robinson to call a 5–3–3. Maybe I should put in another defensive back. With a new quarterback in the game, I'd bet my last dollar they're gonna pass."

"No. Let's wait and see what kind of formation they pass from, then we can adjust to it."

Stamford's offense lines up in a "Tee" formation. Their two ends are split out, leaving a wide gap outside their tackles. One Stamford halfback lines up behind each of the split ends in wingback positions. Their fullback takes his normal position behind the quarterback, probably staying in the backfield to act as a lone blocker for the passer.

Taking the snap, Stamford's quarterback swivels and fires a pass to his left wingback. After the football was centered, the wingback dropped back behind the line of scrimmage. With the split end blocking for him, the wingback gains eleven yards before Kenneth Williams, our defensive halfback, drags him down from behind.

"What kind of pass is that, Stubby? That looked more like a lateral to me," Sam questions. He sounds confused.

The Stamford coach is very progressive. Only one other time have I seen this passing formation. That was year before last, when my A&M team played Baylor University in Waco. It worked extremely well against us, until halftime, when Coach Norton devised a defense to stop it. We shut down Baylor's passing game in the second half.

"Sam, call a timeout. Get Robinson over here to the sideline."

E.P. Robinson trots to our sideline while two freshmen players, Bagwell and Cantrell, run a case of water bottles to our defensive huddle on the field.

Sam, Alfred and I meet with our defensive captain on the sideline. On a note pad I quickly sketch the defense we will use against the unorthodox Stamford passing formation.

"Look, E.P., our defensive end and our outside linebacker move up directly in front of their receivers. Our defensive halfback plays a few yards back. He's our insurance in case they complete the pass. After the ball is centered, the defensive end knocks out their split end and our linebacker charges across to take out their wingback. We play a three-man defensive line with Barnes behind them as a single linebacker. Cunningham will play semi-deep at the safety position."

"Alright, Coach. I think I understand. I'll call timeout again if we have a problem."

"Have Barnes key off the fullback. One weakness with this defense is a quick handoff to the fullback on a running play. Tell Cunningham to look for the running play first, then go help the side where the ball is thrown."

"Barnes keys on their fullback. Cunningham looks for the run first, then goes to help. Okay, I got it," the scrappy defensive captain repeats.

The referees whistle time back in. Stamford breaks from their huddle and sets up in the same widened passing formation. Across the field on the Stamford sideline their coaches are thinking they've found a weakness in our defense. I cross my fingers, hoping the Stamford coaches won't surprise us with some wrinkle I haven't seen before.

When the ball is snapped, Stamford's quarterback swivels to his right to discover his split end lying on the ground. The Stamford right end has been flattened by Champ Pearson. A blue and white wingback behind him is on his knees, trying to recover from his collision with our outside linebacker Robinson.

The Stamford quarterback panics. He turns to look to his left, only to find his two receivers on that side down on their knees. A second later Davenport comes crashing over the Stamford fullback to smash him to the ground.

After another incomplete pass and a handoff to the fullback, which Sutton and Yung stop for no gain, Stamford decides to punt. The quarter ends as they kick the ball out of bounds on our six yard line.

IF OUR BULLDOG TEAM controlled the game during the first quarter, we own it in the second quarter. After the Stamford punt, a sustained drive from our own six leads to our third touchdown of the night. Following our score, Sam begins to liberally substitute second-string defensive players into the game. On their third possession Stamford makes their second first down–against our second-string. We score again right before the half.

With our extra point kicker at the hospital we miss on both extra point conversions. The score on the end zone scoreboard changes while I untie Short Snorter and begin the short run to the dressing room.

RANGER 26   VISITOR 0

ALMOST ALL OUR PLAYERS got playing time in the first half. With little doubt about the outcome of the game, the mood of the dressing room is happy and playful. Cheerful player talk and laughter echo through the field house.

Herb Williams lies stretched out on a training table while Sam retapes his ankle.

"Sam, have you seen Alfred?" I ask.

"No, not since he went with Jensen to help him change into his band uniform. Anything I can do?"

"Not really. I just like to know where my coaches are," I reply.

Actually, I am worried. It's not like Alfred to take off without checking with me. Oh, hell! That's not all of it! Lately, I worry about everyone associated with me.

ALFRED IS STILL MISSING when a game official comes to advise us the second half will start in three minutes. Players gather up their gear and head out the door to the playing field. Sam waits behind, until the players are all gone.

"You ever see anything of Alfred, Stubby?"

"No. We might have to play the second half without him. I can't imagine where he could've gone," I answer, with sincere concern.

A wry grin indicates Sam is not all that concerned about Alfred. He has something else on his mind. I already know what he's thinking.

"Okay, Sam. You don't have to say it. Yes, I'll try to hold the score down in the second half. You just be sure all our players get some playing time."

"Stubby, did anyone ever tell you you're psychic? You just read my mind," Sam chuckles, slapping me on the back as we leave the field house.

BILLY MCKINNEY'S KICKOFF to begin the second half is short, reaching the Stamford thirty. Stamford's ball carrier is immediately slammed to the ground by Polston and Tune.

With our reserve players playing defense, Stamford mounts their first drive of the evening, gaining three consecutive first downs before we stop them on a fourth down try at our twenty-six.

Our second-string offense is taking the field when I spot Alfred walking slowly toward the bench from the south end of the bleachers. He stops and gazes into the stands, then continues to our bench. He looks very grim.

"Alfred, where've you been? We've been worried about you."

"I've been waiting on Mrs. Murphy, Coach. She was supposed to meet me at halftime by the concession booth. She never showed up."

"Didn't she ride in with you to the game?" I ask.

"No, I bummed a ride with the Woods family. They live right down the road from the Murphy farm. Mrs. Murphy was planning to drive in after she put the cow up. Coach, I'm worried about her."

"Maybe she had car trouble or a problem with the farm animals. I'm sure she's all right. If she isn't here when the game is over, we'll go look for her," I say, trying to reassure Alfred.

"You're right, Coach. I'm probably making too big a deal about her not showing up. How we doing in the ballgame?"

———————

OUR SECOND-STRINGERS have driven the football down to Stamford's three yard line. Alfred and I turn our attention back to the game in time to watch James Burnett take a pitchout from sophomore quarterback Jim Cole and dance into the end zone.

We've missed on our extra point kick after our last two touchdowns. I decide to try something different.

"Bill Yung. You wanna carry the football again this week?" I call to the junior lineman on the bench.

"Yes sir, I sure do," Yung replies, jumping to his feet. A group of suddenly attentive starters also quit their seats, hoping to participate in the party.

"Alright then, get in there. Tell Cole to give you the football. Run the same play you ran last week in DeLeon."

"Yes sir," Yung responds, buckling on his helmet.

"And, Bill–if you don't score the extra point, you owe me twenty laps around the football field on Monday," I declare, to motivate him.

Yung hesitates, his mind meticulously calculating the possibility of owing me twenty laps.

"If I score, will you owe me twenty laps, Coach?"

Uh, oh! I started this. I can't back down now. "Okay, Bill, if you score, I'll do twenty laps for you."

Yung tears out across the field toward our huddle.

Hut. Hut. Cole takes the snap and hands the football to Yung. A stubborn wall of blue and white uniforms converge on our husky ball carrier as he charges into the line. Several Stamford players fly backward into the end zone when Yung bursts across the goal line. Yung proudly hoists the football above his head for me to see. Our starting players on the bench cheer loudly for him.

Even though our subs finish out the remainder of the game, Stamford is unable to score. We purposely avoid scoring again.

The final score posted on the big scoreboard reads:

RANGER 33   VISITOR 0

SHORT SNORTER SITS TIED to the end of the bench, clearly distressed because he's no longer the center of attention. Alfred, Sam and I are picking up around our bench when the Stamford football coach approaches us.

"Are you Coach Warden?" he asks.

"Yes. What can I do for you?" I answer curtly, thinking he has some complaint about the football game.

"Coach Warden, I'm Carl Cook. I coach the Stamford High team. I'd like to compliment you on a terrific job of coaching tonight."

The Stamford coach is a young man, only a few years older than myself. He is smartly dressed, wearing a tie and sport coat. With his short-cropped, light-brown hair and fair skin, he could easily be mistaken for one of his players.

"Well thanks, Carl." His compliment is flabbergasting. My football team just thrashed his team soundly. I can't think of anything else to say.

"Coach, you mind if I ask a question?"

"No, of course not. What's on your mind?"

"How did you come up with a defense against my wide-out passing formation so quickly? We've been working for weeks perfecting that passing formation, so we could use it against someone. You came up with a defense that shut us down completely after seeing it only one time. I'm curious how you knew what to do."

"Hey, Coach Cook, I'm not a football wizard. But I had the privilege of playing for one at A&M. Homer Norton designed that defense, when Baylor used your passing formation against his A&M team year before last."

The Stamford coach sighs with relief. "Whew! Then maybe our passing formation might work against some other coach. I was afraid we might've wasted half the season learning a passing offense that was useless. Thanks, Coach Warden. If we play you again, I hope to give you a more competitive game."

The young coach leaves to walk back across the field. He's a nice guy, but until he learns more about running a "Tee" offense, he's gonna be a losing coach.

"Oh, hell! Stamford's not on our schedule next year. Someone has to help the guy out," I tell myself.

I run out on the field to catch him. He quickly agrees to call me next week and let me explain about the flaws in his blocking schemes.

KATE MURPHY'S BRIGHT HEADLIGHTS blind us as she swerves into the stadium parking lot. Most of the cars are gone now. Alfred and I were heading for the Hudson to go look for her.

Recognizing her familiar blue Ford, Alfred runs ahead to meet it. He leans inside the driver's window. They begin a hurried exchange of information.

Alfred turns to me when I arrive at Kate's car.

"Coach Warden! Mister Murphy's disappeared from the Eastland hospital!"

Chapter Twelve
The Homecoming

Friday Night
September 20, 1949

KATE MURPHY PARKS HER FORD beside the Hudson and kills her engine. The three of us sit inside her dark car while she relates the details of her strange evening.

Around eight o'clock, as she was preparing to leave for the football game, a sheriff's deputy knocked on her door. He demanded she come with him to the Eastland hospital. At first he wouldn't give her a reason, only telling her there was a problem with her husband. When she refused to accompany him without an explanation, he admitted Keith was missing.

After Kate and the deputy arrived at the hospital, she was informed that it was Sheriff Williams himself who had discovered her husband missing. The sheriff had gone to the hospital to personally check on Murphy, shortly after seven o'clock when his deputies changed shifts.

The sheriff was furious with everyone, mercilessly cursing his deputies and the nurses on duty. Kate says the sheriff seemed mostly upset because the deputies had wasted so much time protecting her husband then had him disappear right from under their noses. As far as she could tell no search effort was being made to find her missing spouse.

No one noticed Murphy leaving the hospital, but the sheriff advised Kate that there's a definite possibility of foul play. Murphy was much too sick to leave on his own.

Sheriff Williams and his deputy took Kate to an office in the

Eastland courthouse where they questioned her for almost an hour. They were suspicious she might've helped Murphy leave the hospital.

"Kate, does the sheriff think someone kidnapped Keith?" I ask. "The story you tell makes it sound like your husband has escaped from the sheriff's custody rather than being snatched from his protective care."

"I don't really know, Stubby, but after the way he and the deputy questioned me, the sheriff must believe someone helped Keith leave the hospital. There was no mention of kidnapping."

Not wanting to add to Kate Murphy's worries, I don't mention my suspicion that someone in the sheriff's office is responsible for her husband's disappearance. I cannot imagine Keith Murphy leaving the hospital without the use of force. When I visited him last Sunday, he was in no condition to be going anywhere for a long, long time. It's unlikely he can survive for any extended length of time without proper medical care.

"Kate, is there anything we can do? Alfred and I are willing to help search for Keith, if you can give us any idea where we might find him."

"No. I've gone through my mind a thousand times, trying to think where he might be. I simply don't have any idea where to look for him."

"Kate, perhaps the best thing to do is go home, so you can be near a telephone. Maybe the sheriff will find him. I'm sure the authorities will call you if anything new develops."

Kate and Alfred drive away while I place Short Snorter in the Hudson's front seat beside me. I didn't want to tell her, but I have a good idea where to look for Keith Murphy. Tomorrow, I intend to pay a visit to my two friends, Clifford and Orval, out at the Singleton Ranch.

———————

Saturday Morning
September 21, 1949

"HELLO? HELLO, EDNA. This is Stubby," I announce into the telephone.

"Good morning, Stubby. We've been expecting your call," Juanita's mother replies. Her voice sounds unusually cordial.

I'm calling the Kimbrough ranch house from Price Mitchell's office.

"How are Juanita and the baby?" I ask. Even after my happy reconciliation with Juanita, I'm not prepared to call my son, Jerry, not just yet.

"They're both doing fine. The doctor should release Juanita from the hospital after he makes his morning rounds. They want to keep little Jerome in an incubator for a few more days, though."

"I want to come to Comanche and bring them home with me. Isn't there some way the doctor could release the baby today? We have a very good hospital here in Ranger."

"Stubby Warden, you've waited all this time. Surely you can wait a few more days, so your infant son can leave the hospital with his doctor's blessing," she scolds.

"I'm sorry, Edna. I'm just anxious for them to come home to me."

"I understand. Why don't you call back this afternoon? Juanita should be here, and by then, we should know more about little Jerome. You two can decide when you should come to get them."

"Okay, Edna. I'll call back later this afternoon. Please tell Juanita I called."

———————

LITTLE JEROME? I thought the three women agreed we would call him Jerry. Price walks into the office while I am stewing over Edna's reference to my son.

"Stubby, I saw you drive in. Did you talk with Juanita?"

"No, but I did talk with Edna. She thinks Juanita will be released from the hospital today. Looks like it may be several more days before the baby can come home."

"Did you talk with Phyliss? Is she planning to stay until next week, too?"

"I'm sorry, Price. I didn't think to ask about Phyliss. I still have her car. She's stuck down there afoot until I take her car to her."

Price laughs with deep amusement. "Stubby, you are severely underestimating my number one wife. Phyliss Mitchell has never been stuck anywhere, not unless she wanted it that way."

"Yeah, it's only sixty miles. I guess she could catch the bus to Ranger."

Now, Price is laughing so hard he falls back into a chair on the opposite side of the desk.

"Phyliss Mitchell ride a commercial bus! Stubby, you gotta stop this! You're making my sides hurt."

Price thinks I'm joking, so I go along. I wonder how Phyliss would get back to Ranger without driving her car or taking the bus, but I don't dare ask. Price would only break out into more hysterical laughter.

When Price finally stops laughing, I ask him how to find the Singleton Ranch. His jovial mood turns sober very quickly.

"The Singleton Ranch! Why would you want to know about the Singleton Ranch?"

"There's a couple of fellows I want to see. I understand they work out there. Orval and Clifford Graves, you ever hear of 'em?"

"Yeah, Stubby, I know exactly who they are. You'd be smart to leave them alone."

"I'll be careful, Price. I just wanna check out the place. I won't start anything, if they don't."

"Stubby, if you know what's good for you, you'll stay away from that place. Everyone calls it the Singleton Ranch, but do you know who the real owner is?"

"No. Does it really matter, Price?"

"Yes, it really matters. It matters a lot. Lucas Masters owns the Singleton Ranch."

A LONG MOVING VAN RUMBLES PAST ME as I maneuver slowly along the narrow, winding asphalt pavement of State Highway 16, driving south from Highway 80. The truck driver eyes me suspiciously while he passes. When he pulls back onto the right lane ahead of me, he adjusts his side view mirror so he can watch me following behind. After a few minutes he loses interest and guns his engine, smothering the Hudson in a trail of black smoke.

The moving van has stopped in a driveway facing a wide iron gate, constructed from second-hand drill pipe. The gate is rusty and unpainted. A small white sign with black letters next to the gate reads simply "Singleton Ranch." I'm disappointed with the entrance to Lucas Masters' ranch. I expected something much more elaborate and obtrusive. There's not even a "No Trespassing" sign to warn unwanted intruders to keep away.

When I drive by, the truck driver has unlocked the gate and is pushing it open. He stops beside the half-open gate, staring after me until my Hudson tops the next hill and disappears from his sight. A few hundred yards further down the road I pull off the road and park.

The dashboard clock reads 1:18. I decide to wait ten minutes to make sure the truck driver hasn't followed me.

When the Hudson was moving, the breeze from the autumn-like air kept the inside of the car comfortable, but now, sitting in the still air of the parked car, the afternoon heat quickly becomes unbearable. After what seems like an hour, but with only eight minutes actually passing on the clock, I slip out of the car. My shirt is spotted with sweat marks. My underwear is bunched and sticking to my legs.

A five-foot high barbed-wire fence extends down both sides of the highway. Strips of land about 50 feet wide have been cleared inside the fence lines. Beyond the cleared sections, thick stands of cedar trees intermingle with short, scrubby mesquite trees. The heavy cedar growths make movement of any kind more than a hundred feet off the road impossible to see. The cedars could also serve to muffle any unusual noises from curious ears. The landscape here makes ideal cover for illegal activities of the car theft ring. Now I understand what Murphy meant when he said he simply stumbled upon the auto theft repair operation. He probably didn't see or hear anything until he was right on top of it.

Before I scale the barbed wire fence, I raise the hood of the Hudson, giving me an excuse for being stopped alongside the road. If someone questions why I'm here, I can claim I had car trouble and went to look for help. I leave the car windows rolled down but take the keys with me.

Zigzagging through the clumps of cedars and mesquites, I become disoriented before I'm two hundred yards from the road. The sun is directly overhead, making it useless for keeping my bearings. Sharp needles from unrecognizable, cactus-like bushes prick through my britches and sting my legs. The cedars block off any breeze but still absorb and radiate the midday warmth. The suffocating heat out here is even more fervent than inside the parked car. Perspiration fills my eyelashes and pours down my face. The hot sun blasts down on my uncovered head, but I trudge on diligently through the cedars, without the faintest idea of what I'm searching for.

After twenty minutes of wandering aimlessly around in the thick cedars, I am miserable, totally lost and thoroughly convinced this poorly planned excursion to the Singleton Ranch is not one of my better ideas. My pants are torn, and my arms are raw and bleeding from scraping against the sharp thorns on the mesquite limbs. I'm ready to quit. I would head back to the road and the Hudson if I knew for sure which direction to go.

Unexpectedly, a break appears in the cedar growths, and I spy a dirt lane ahead. Intermittent banging noises from somewhere down the lane draw my attention. I move cautiously through the trees along the edge of the roadway toward the banging sounds. The dusty lane leads to the edge of a wide clearing where I discover a small city of metal buildings. The cleared area is an abandoned strip mine, probably dug during the Thurber coal mining era. The complex consists of five buildings located down in the excavated depression of the ancient open mine. Two of the buildings are quite large. Possibly, these buildings are used to store the stolen cars–maybe before and after their renovation. The other buildings are smaller. One building appears to be a bunkhouse and mess hall. A trickle of smoke rises from a metal stack on the roof. The other two buildings are long and narrow with double-wide, garage-type swinging doors on each end. These two buildings could be used for repainting the automobiles, installing new license tags and replacing the engine serial numbers. I slide down the embankment for a closer look.

If they are holding Murphy here, he'd most likely be in the bunkhouse. Crouching low, I run to a large boulder at the base of the embankment near the bunkhouse. I wait quietly, watching for any movement.

Except for the shrill banging noise coming from inside one of the large buildings, the encampment seems deserted. It's Saturday afternoon. Perhaps most of the workers have knocked off for the weekend to visit the beer taverns only a few miles north in Strawn and Mingus.

A side door on the bunkhouse swings open, and two men appear. The screen door slams loudly behind them. I duck behind the big rock.

"Hey, Clifford! You plan on takin' out that big Mexican gal again tonight?" one of the men calls out to the other.

"Hell no! That bitch tried ta slice me up with a butcher knife, just 'cause I called her a fat sow. The woman is plumb crazy. She's way too sensitive for my taste."

"Ya wanna go up to Strawn and pick us up one of them Amish women? They all come in ta town on Saturdays. I hear they don't wear nothing under them long dresses."

"Joe, you got about as much chance of making it with one of them Amish girls as a snowball does in hell."

"Yeah, maybe. But, some of 'em are awful good lookers. I'd sure like ta git a peek at what they wear under them long dresses."

"Ta hell with women! Let's go have some real fun. Let's drive up ta Mingus, get drunk on our asses and beat hell out of some ignorant cowboys," Clifford exclaims.

"Yeah, that oughta be real fun," Joe agrees, without enthusiasm.

"Yeah, ta hell with women. Who needs 'em anyways?"

The two men cross the open graveled stretch between the buildings and enter the largest building adjacent to the one emitting the banging sounds. A minute later Clifford appears, pushing open one side of a double-swing door. An aged, beat-up, gray and white pickup follows closely behind the opening door. Joe is driving. When the pickup clears, Clifford pulls the door shut, then jumps in on the passenger side. The spinning rear tires of the old pickup sling chunks of gravel against the bunkhouse wall as the vehicle digs out toward Mingus.

I watch the pickup's tailgate disappear behind the cedar trees along the dirt road before I make a dash for the rear wall of the bunkhouse. By keeping the bunkhouse between me and the other buildings, I should be able to peek inside, safe from detection by prying eyes.

Crawling on my all-fours along the wall, I stop under a small window. I raise up slowly and peep inside to discover a kitchen area. A long dining table with wooden benches on each side is centered in the room. A wood-fired cook stove abuts the far wall. Next to the cook stove is a linoleum-covered counter for food preparation. Apparently the kitchen has no running water. The counter is without a sink or water faucet.

Seeing no one inside boosts my courage. I rise to my feet and step to the back door. I open the screen door gently, taking care to keep springs from squeaking, and slip inside to the kitchen.

The kitchen is separated from the bunk room by a thin partition wall. A door connecting the two rooms is slightly ajar. I move quietly to the door and gaze through the crack in the half-opened door. Two-tiered single beds are positioned perpendicular to the bunk room walls in boot-camp military style. A naked light hangs from the ceiling above a square wooden card table at the center of the room. Several metal folding chairs surround the card table. At first glance the room appears to be unoccupied. Then I spot an unmoving, covered figure lying in one of the lower bunks. If the body in the bed is Keith Murphy, he is almost certainly dead.

———————

THE SOUND OF A TRUCK ENGINE roaring into the yard outside breaks the silence. Men begin yelling to one another out in the compound. I start across the room to Murphy but hurry back into the kitchen when I hear talking and footsteps at the front door.

A man opens the door and calls into the bunkhouse.

"Hey, Clifford! Joe! Come out here! We need some help unloading these cars."

When no one answers, the man stomps into the room. He walks over to the figure lying on the bed and slaps it hard on the shoulder.

"Hey, Pedro! Where the hell are Joe and Clifford? We need some help."

The figure in the bed rolls over and sits up slowly. It is a young Mexican. He rubs his eyes, trying to wake up.

"Oh, Señor Robbins. Meester Joe and Meester Clifford, they are not here. I think they went to Mingus to look for some women." The young Mexican speaks with a heavy accent.

"Those good-for-nothing bastards. They knew we had another load coming today, but they couldn't wait to go chasing after them sleazy Mingus bar maids. You can bet they'll be singing a sorry tune after Mister Masters takes a bite out of their no-good, lazy asses!" the man bellows at Pedro.

"I donno, Señor Robbins. I donno anything about that."

"Pedro, you get your ass out there and help unload the truck."

"But, Meester Robbins, I don't feel so good. Meester Joe and Meester Clifford, they feed me the bad tequila last night."

"I don't give a rat's damn how you feel, you measly little weasel. I need some help. Now get your butt outside, before you get me riled."

"Yes sir. Sí, Señor Robbins. I will come, right away."

Young Pedro slips on a pair of leather sandals and steps quickly to the front door ahead of Robbins. When the front door slams, I breathe a heavy sigh of relief, realizing how close I came to waking the Mexican boy and being discovered. With all the activity outside I decide to give up my search for Murphy before my luck runs out. I leave through the bunkhouse back door and scramble up the embankment to the safety of the cedars.

————————

A GREEN AND WHITE PICKUP TRUCK sits parked directly behind my Hudson alongside the highway. Behind the wheel of the pickup is a heavy-set, shirtless man in dirty overalls. The man is badly in need of a bath. His exposed hairy body is covered with dark blobs of grease and oil. A rifle barrel protrudes through the driver's window.

"Hello," I call to the man as I approach the front of his pickup. The green and white truck looks familiar. I'm sure this is the same vehicle I saw speeding away from the high school after the shooting incident last Monday. Chances are even better the rifle is the one used to shoot at me.

When the man doesn't respond, I try again. "Hello, there. Can you help me? I'm having a bit of car trouble."

"Hey, Mister. Don't try and feed me a line of bull. I ain't buying no car trouble story. Ya think I'm stupid or somethin'? I know who you are. You're that runt football coach from Ranger."

Although we've never had a formal introduction, I'm positive this man is Orval Graves. I have been looking forward to this opportunity. The two of us have a score to settle.

"Yes, you're right about that. I'm Stubby Warden, the Ranger football coach. But, I truly do need some help with my car. Could you give me a push?"

While I'm talking, I walk on past his open window and stand slightly behind the door. The burly man is forced to rotate his body around to face me. He yanks the rifle inside the cab and bangs at the pickup door with his shoulder until it swings open.

He makes a terrible mistake, by opening the door to slide out of the cab. Clutching the rifle in his right hand, he barely has one foot on the ground when I hit him squarely on the end of his nose with my clenched fist. His neck snaps backward, and the bony gristle of his nose collapses under the solid force of my knuckles. His front teeth slash fiercely through his top lip before they dig into my fist and yield inwardly.

The collision of my fist with the man's face causes a bone to pop in the top of my hand, but the sharp pain does not diminish the incredible rush of euphoria I experience from challenging and conquering my enemy.

Orval's eyes express his total shock and surprise, a second before they roll upwards into his head. His flailing left hand tries to grab onto the cab seat as his legs crumple. His left shoulder hits hard on the running board while he falls to the blacktop road beside the pickup. A yellowish green mucus, mixed with blood, runs out the nostrils of his broken nose. A loose tooth falls from his bleeding, open mouth.

"Okay, Orval. If you wanna be stubborn, I suppose I'll have to admit it. I was lying about the car trouble," I say to the grizzly, limp body.

Orval's right hand still clutches the rifle. I reach down and grab the weapon.

"You know, Orval, we still aren't even, not yet. I wanna leave you something special–somethin' to remember me by."

My thumb pushes the button above the trigger guard to release the safety while I raise the rifle.

"CRACK! CRACK! CRACK!" the rifle resounds as I empty it into the hood of the green and white pickup. The bullets rip through the metal and ricochet off the engine, leaving huge, ugly holes.

"There. Now we're close to being even, big fellow. You can tell your brother Clifford I'll be around to settle up with him, too," I advise the unconscious, still body.

I pull back the lever on the rifle to eject the last shell casing from the chamber, take the gun by the barrel and slam the wooden handle against the metal railing surrounding the bed of the pickup. I fling the broken pieces into the cedars inside the fence line.

Stepping over Orval's lifeless body, I reach inside the cab and take the keys from the dashboard. I start to throw the keys into the cedars but change my mind, having a better idea. I unscrew the gas cap on the side of the pickup and drop the keys, one by one, into the gas tank.

A groan from the bleeding, dirty carcass lying on the ground hints that Orval is returning from his unexpected trip into the Land of Nod.

———————

SEVERAL MILES DOWN THE ROAD my hands begin to shake uncontrollably. I pull the Hudson over to the side of the road and stop. My rapid flow of adrenaline has slowed now, and the rapturous feeling of victory has given way to a conscious realization of my perilous predicament. Once Orval discloses that I was snooping around the Singleton Ranch, my life will be in even greater danger than before.

Damn! I didn't find Murphy like I'd hoped. All I did was burrow myself a lot deeper into this car theft mess. Why didn't I take Price's advice and stay away from the Singleton Ranch?

Acute pain in my hand keeps me from dwelling on my hard-headed stupidity. Remembering the elbow bandages left in the rear floorboard, I bind my aching right hand with pieces of the gauze wrapping. I removed the bandages yesterday afternoon before the Stamford game. My hand is already swollen to twice its normal size.

———————

EPSOM SALTS DISSOLVED in the wash basin's warm water does little to soothe my throbbing hand.

"Coach, don't you know to hold a shotgun shell or a round piece of wood in the palm of your hand when you hit someone's face with your fist?" Alfred chides me.

"Yeah, now I know. But I didn't have time to do much planning. He was sitting there in his pickup waiting for me."

Actually, I've never had much reason to hit on people's faces, not until I accepted this Ranger coaching job. Somewhere, probably at A&M, I've been told about keeping something solid in your hand during a fist fight to keep from busting up your knuckles.

Alfred reaches into his pants pocket. "See here, Coach. I keep this piece of iron bar with me all the time, just in case of emergency. You won't never catch me with busted-up knuckles. They can hurt worse than losing the fight. I'll get you one to carry in your pocket."

"Okay, Alfred. But I'm afraid it may be a while before I can use it," I reluctantly reply. I raise my hand out of the warm water. The slight movement causes me excruciating pain.

Wiping her hands on her apron, Kate Murphy comes to the kitchen door. "How is our champion prize fighter patient coming along, Alfred?" she asks with a grin.

"Oh, he's alright, ma'am. Coach is gonna be fine, but don't it seem like we spend a heck of a lot of time keeping him patched up?"

"HELLO, JUANITA. THIS IS STUBBY," I state, speaking into the mouthpiece of the pay telephone.

"Oh, Stubby, I've been waiting and waiting for your call. Mother said you would call again this afternoon."

"I'm sorry, Juanita. I drove down to a place near Desdemona to look for Keith Murphy and ran into some trouble. I just got back to Ranger."

Darkness is closing in on the brick street which runs past the phone booth outside the Telephone Office. My unscheduled stop at the Murphy farm to attend to my injured hand took longer than I expected. Alfred and Kate wouldn't allow me to leave until my hand was thoroughly soaked in Epsom salt to reduce the swelling, and properly bandaged. Over my objections, Kate insisted I wear a foolish-looking cloth sling to keep my hand elevated. She was right of course. The sling has relieved the hurt in my hand immensely.

"Stubby, the hospital says you haven't paid them a deposit, like you promised. They won't let us have our baby until we pay their bill. What are we going to do?" Juanita's voice is full of emotion.

"I don't understand. I paid them a hundred dollar deposit last Monday night. The reason I drove all the way down there was to keep my promise. I told the reception lady I'd bring her a deposit on Monday. The receipt is right here in my wallet."

"Mrs. Willard, the woman who runs the business office, says you promised to bring two hundred dollars for the deposit, but she never saw you. Do you remember who you gave the money to?"

"Yes, it was the young nurse working the nurse's station Monday evening. You probably know her. She acted like she knows you. I didn't ask her name, but it may be on the receipt she gave me. Hold on while I look."

Holding the telephone receiver in my left hand, I remove my right hand from Kate's sling to retrieve my billfold. The exercise causes a sharp pain to shoot down the back of my hand.

"Here it is. Her signature is hard to read. It looks like P. Kimbrough. Is she kin to you?"

"Yes. You must've given the money to Patsy Kimbrough. She's my cousin, but I'd rather not admit to it."

"Why? She seemed like a nice young woman, and she was so worried about whether I was going in to see you. Actually, I'm not sure I would've come back, if she hadn't been so concerned."

"It's a long story which I'd rather not get into. Let's just say her family has a reputation for lying and stealing. She hasn't been to work at the hospital since Monday. Our money is probably gone."

"Do you mean to say the hospital won't honor the receipt she gave me? If she took their money, that should be their problem, not mine."

"I don't believe they'll be very sympathetic. You were supposed to give the deposit money to Mrs. Willard."

"That's ridiculous. How was I supposed to know the place is full of thieves? I didn't see any signs posted, warning me not to give money to your outlaw kinfolks."

"Stop it. You stop right now, Stubby Warden. You know I can't do anything about my relatives. Now calm down, before you say something nasty about my family and start a fight. I'll talk to Mrs. Willard tomorrow to see what she says. Meanwhile, we need to decide what we have to do to get our baby."

"Okay, Juanita, I'm sorry. It just seems that every time I come to Comanche, something bad happens to me. Did Mrs. Willard tell you how much we owe the hospital?"

"Mrs. Willard thinks it'll be about nine hundred dollars."

"Nine hundred dollars! No way! Maybe that includes Doctor Blackmar's five hundred dollar delivery fee."

"Yes, I'm sure it does. Mrs. Willard says she told you that you'd need to pay the doctor before she could check us out of the hospital. She wasn't too happy about releasing me this afternoon."

"Juanita, can you talk to the doctor? Surely he has some kind of easy-payment plan. Nobody could ever have five hundred dollars–not all at one time."

Juanita laughs softly at my comment. "You might be surprised, sweetheart. But, yes, I'll call him Monday. Clyde Blackmar has been our family doctor for years. I'm sure he'll agree to let us pay him later."

"That'll be a big help. I should get a three hundred dollar bonus on Wednesday for winning the Stamford game. Can you talk to Mrs. Willard? Maybe she'll take the three hundred and let us pay the rest later?"

"I don't think so, Stubby. She was very explicit about being paid the full amount."

"How about your father? Is there any chance he might make up the difference?"

This is a question I didn't want to ask. An awkward pause interrupts our conversation while she considers her answer. When she responds, her voice is weak and strained.

"I'm sorry, darling. I've already asked him. He says this is your business."

What kind of man could be so insensitive and vindictive? What does he hope to gain by punishing his loving daughter and innocent grandbaby, just to embarrass me? Luther Kimbrough is a strange and petty man. His unforgiving attitude will hurt the people who love him much more than he'll ever hurt me.

"I kinda suspected he'd take a position like that. I'm sorry you asked him. He's a hard man to figure, your father."

"Stubby, let's not get off on Daddy. In a way he's right, though. This is our business. Little Jerry is our responsibility."

The telephone operator comes on the line to interrupt us. "I'm sorry, sir. Your time is up. Please deposit another twenty-five cents if you wish to continue your call."

I fish my last quarter out of my pants pocket with my left hand

and deposit it in the coin slot. The telephone makes a dull, ringing sound as the quarter drops through into the coin box.

"Thank you. You have another three minutes," the operator tells me.

"Juanita, you still there?" I ask.

"Yes, darling, I'm still on the line."

"That was my last quarter, so we don't have much time. When does the doctor think the baby will be ready to come home?"

"It should be either Wednesday or Thursday of next week, depending on how much weight he's gained."

"When will you know for sure?"

"I think I can get an answer from Doctor Blackmar when I talk to him about his fee on Monday."

"Good. I'll call you Monday night after football practice. We can decide when I should come to Comanche to bring you home. Talk to Mrs. Willard. Try to convince her to either give us credit for my deposit, or let us pay the rest of what we owe later."

"Alright, darling. I'll talk with you Monday. Did I tell you I love you?"

"You didn't need to, Juanita. I already knew."

Monday Morning
September 23, 1949

"YOU'VE NEVER HAD A checking account before? That's hard to believe, Stubby," Ferrol Creager remarks.

"I guess I never needed one before. I've always operated strictly with cash. Not until recently did I discover how foolish I am to pay my bills with cash," I tell my neighbor, the bank president.

"Well, we're glad to have you for a customer. Let me have my secretary get the forms we need to open your checking account."

The Commercial State Bank is located at the east end of the downtown business district at the southeast corner of Main and Rusk. The two-story bank building is a unique structure, and by far the most impressive building in Ranger. Custom-cut marble and limestone walls rise from broad sidewalks to frame the wide glass windows, extending from the ground floor up to the second floor ceiling. Along Main Street, massive, fluted limestone columns protrude out from the exterior walls on each side of the broad windows. Huge, thick, double-glass doors accent the two main entrances—one off Main Street and one off Rusk. This may be the only bank in Ranger, but there's plenty of room inside to hold all the town's money.

While Ferrol Creager talks with his secretary, I survey the bank interior. Both the bank's front doors open into a spacious marble lobby. Two male bank tellers labor inside enclosed metal cages which are supported by a long marble-top counter facing the lobby. Bank secretaries and lesser bank officials work in a carpeted section behind a knee-high, wooden dividing partition adjacent to the bank lobby.

A sign painted on the glass door to a private office in the corner of the secretarial area reads "President." Ferrol Creager was behind this desk in the open work sector when I arrived. It's my guess he enjoys working out here, where he can be seen and can visit with his customers.

"Here we are, Stubby. All I need is your signature and social security number. We know all about you, so my secretary can fill in the other blanks," Ferrol tells me, as he slips into the chair behind his desk.

"Is that all there is to it? Can I write a check on your bank now?"

"Well, you need to make a deposit, but after that, you're all set. Do you want us to have some personalized checks printed or do you plan to use our bank drafts?"

"Do the personalized checks cost extra?"

"Yes, there's a small charge for that service. A dollar fifty for your first two hundred personalized checks."

"The bank drafts, how much do they cost?"

"Our bank draft checks are absolutely free. Many of our customers, who don't write a lot of checks, use our drafts. They prefer to save the expense of personal checks."

"For the time being, I think I'll use the bank drafts. Maybe you could show me how to write a check with one?"

Ferrol Creager patiently explains the proper way to fill out a draft check so it will be honored by the bank. He graciously accepts my five dollar deposit to open up the account. I explain that I'll make another deposit on Wednesday when I receive my bonus money for winning the Stamford game. Treating me like his most valued customer, he shakes my left hand warmly and walks me to the Main Street entrance when I leave.

My grandfather used to say there was no better feeling than having money in the bank. Ferrol Creager's kindness and personal attention to my account make me appreciate his wisdom.

A cold front which moved in over the weekend brought a welcome break from last week's late summer heat wave. The crisp morning air outside the bank reminds me the seasons have changed. Fall is here. Summer is gone. The scorching-hot summer weather is almost over. For a brief moment I forget the pain in my right hand while I savor fond memories of college football games, played and won on cool autumn afternoons.

"GOOD MORNING, MRS. GETTS. Has anyone called for me this morning?" I ask the friendly lady in the principal's office.

"Oh! Hello, Coach Warden," she says, looking up from behind her desk. She inspects the sling on my arm curiously but decides not to ask about it. "No, are you expecting a phone call?"

"Carl Cook, the Stamford football coach. He promised to call me at ten this morning. I guess he forgot."

She glances at her watch. "Coach Warden, it's only five minutes after ten now. My, my, aren't you the impatient one this morning. Give the poor man some slack. After the way your Bulldogs beat up on his team Friday night, he may be having second thoughts. I'll wager he's thinking about calling you right now."

"Mildred, I would never bet against a woman's intuition. Okay, I'll wait around for a few minutes. Can I use the telephone in the trustees' meeting room, if he calls?"

"You surely can, Coach. You can wait in there. The door is unlocked."

Waiting in the privacy of the trustees' meeting room is preferable to the tiny waiting room off the school hallway where passing students can gawk at me. For some reason I feel guilty sitting out there, like I'm about to be punished for doing something wrong. Juanita would say I have a guilty conscience.

Chasing after the young Stamford coach last Friday night was a dumb move; one I already regret. Who am I to be handing out coaching advice? I have won a total of three games during my coaching career, and one of those was a meaningless pre-season game. Carl Cook is older and probably much more experienced. I'm sure he's decided he has better things to do than listen to advice from a green, rookie Ranger coach.

Mildred Getts opens the door and peeks inside. "Coach Warden, your Carl Cook is on the line."

"But, I didn't hear the phone ring."

"The phone in here is switched to ring at my desk. It's a little gadget we use so the trustees won't be disturbed during their meetings."

"Oh!" I reply, marveling at the up-to-date technology. I wonder how the gadget works.

"Mister Cook is waiting on the line, Coach Warden," Mildred reminds me.

"Oh, yeah. I got it," I respond, reaching for the phone.

"Hello, Coach Cook. How are you this morning? I'm so glad you called."

The Stamford coach apologizes for not calling me promptly at ten o'clock as agreed. He tells me he's been in an emergency session with his school trustees to explain why he is fielding a losing football team. The trustees gave him an ultimatum—win or resign. Carl Cook is married with two young children. He says he has no prospects for another coaching job. His voice breaks occasionally as he speaks. He sounds very distraught.

Sometimes the pressure on a football coach to win can be overwhelming, changing good men into demons who abuse players and abandon their values. The pressure is always to win now and forget the consequences.

My recent experiences have made me acutely aware of how the need to win can make a coach completely lose sight of goals he set out to accomplish and why he became a coach in the first place. With two consecutive victories my job is temporarily secure, but I could be facing the same ultimatum as Carl Cook a few weeks from now. No matter how much I love this job and the game of football, I have picked one hell of a way to make a living.

On Sunday afternoon I spent several hours studying the Stamford game films which Delbert Capps dropped off at my house late

Saturday night. In anticipation of this call from Carl Cook, I kept precise, detailed notes so I could specifically point out plays where his blocking assignments were wrong or difficult to execute. Many times, one or more of my Bulldog defenders were left unblocked, allowing them to plug up the hole or make the tackle.

After his apology and initial show of emotion, Carl Cook switches personalities. He becomes all business. His telephone manner is lively and precise. While I walk him through the items in my notes, I'm mildly amazed at his astute football mind. His questions are informed, short and to the point. He is quick to understand and acknowledge my suggestions. His vivid memory of each offensive play in our game astounds me.

After some twenty minutes of sharing information we conclude our telephone conversation. Cook thanks me again for waiting on his call and wishes me good luck. I tell him to call me anytime I can help.

Mildred Getts smiles at me when I wave to her on my way out. A male student has her engaged in a lengthy conversation about his skipping class to attend an FFA stock show.

A preferred bank customer, a new coaching friend who appreciates my help, terrific weather—I'm having a great day.

Ignoring the pain in my injured hand, I remove the sling from my arm and pitch it into the back seat of the Hudson. Who cares about a little pain when you feel this good.

———————

Monday Afternoon
September 23, 1949

WILL BROWNLEE USES A PAIR OF CRUTCHES to navigate the steps leading up to the field house. His right leg is confined inside a heavy plaster cast. The cast bears the signatures of several persons who have signed their names in ink. Will is a good student and a school favorite. By week's end his cast will be completely covered with signatures of schoolmates wishing him a speedy recovery.

With the distraction of Keith Murphy's disappearance, my Saturday morning excursion to the Singleton ranch and the Stamford game film, I completely forgot to inquire about Will's broken leg.

"Sam, did you get a chance to go by Brownlee's house to see how badly he was hurt?"

"No, I thought you were gonna check on him. You knew Anne and I were leaving to visit her parents after the game Friday night. I told you last week I'd be out of town this weekend."

"Yeah, I knew you weren't in town. I was just hoping maybe we didn't screw up as badly as I think we did."

"If you didn't check on him, we have definitely screwed up, Stubby. Big time."

Brownlee negotiates across the room to a spot facing his open locker. He begins removing his uniform and other football gear, setting the items on the floor. A hush falls over the locker room as his teammates watch.

Sam's face is grim. I step around our work table and walk across the room to talk with my disabled kicker.

"Will, how's the leg? I see you needed a cast," I say, trying to strike up a casual conversation. Brownlee pauses while he considers whether to acknowledge my question, then continues unloading his locker without responding.

"You got a problem, Will? Maybe we should talk," I try again.

"My dad says I've gotta quit the team. I'll turn in my uniform as soon as I sort my things out," Brownlee mumbles softly. His quiet voice is almost inaudible.

"Why would your dad want you to quit? You're one of our most valuable players. This football team needs you."

"That's what I told my dad. He said if I was so important, why didn't one of the coaches come by my house to see how bad I was hurt. We're poor folks, Coach. The hospital bill for setting my leg was more than fifty dollars. My dad'll have to work overtime at the police station to pay the bill."

"Your father had to pay for the cast? That's not right. I'm sure the school must have insurance to cover the cost." Actually, the question never came up before. I make a mental note to ask Superintendent Boswell about medical expenses.

"I don't know anything about that, Coach. Doctor Watkins didn't charge us nothing, but the Ranger hospital wouldn't lemme go home Friday night until my dad signed a paper agreeing to pay their bill."

"Listen, Will. Let me see what I can do about getting your father reimbursed for the hospital bill. We don't want you to quit. Coach Aills was out of town last weekend. I'm the one who dropped the ball and forgot to check on you. I assure you it wasn't because I don't care about you or don't consider you a valuable member of the team. Please accept my apology and stay with the football team. I want you to stay. The team needs you."

Brownlee contemplates my plea for a short minute. He lowers his head and studies my bandaged right hand. The locker room is incredibly silent.

"I'm sorry, Coach. My dad told me to check in my equipment and quit. I gotta do like he says."

"Will, let me talk with him. I'm sure I can convince him to change his mind. He's so proud of you being our kicker," I say, remembering Eugene Brownlee's beaming face last Monday when he reminded me of his son's kicking accomplishments.

"You can talk to him if you want, Coach Warden, but he told me to quit, and that's what I gotta do. I'll check in my gear to Coach Aills after I go through it."

Sam doesn't speak when I come back behind the work counter. His facial expression depicts his disappointment with me.

So much for having a good day. My right hand has begun to ache like the devil.

─────────

ON MONDAY EVENING I call Juanita to find out how she fared in her financial negotiations with the doctor and with the Comanche hospital. She informs me that Doctor Blackmar agreed to let us pay off his bill at fifty dollars a month. The hospital is less compassionate. They want all their charges to be paid in full before they'll release our baby from the hospital. They don't intend to give us any credit for the missing deposit money.

"Did Mrs. Willard say how much the hospital bill will be?" I ask, trying to hold back my anger.

"She says the bill will be about four hundred dollars, plus or minus."

"Plus or minus what? Doesn't the woman know how to figure a bill? What kinda operation are they running down there? Can't they tell you exactly how much we owe?"

"Don't be harsh with me, sweetheart. I'm just repeating what she told me. You can discuss the bill with her on Thursday morning when you come to pick us up. I'm sure she can be convinced to settle for four hundred dollars, if we have it."

"Juanita, I don't think I can raise four hundred dollars. Three hundred's probably the best I can do."

"Then somehow, we'll have to convince Mrs. Willard to settle for three hundred, won't we? Stubby, I intend to take my baby and go home with you to Ranger on Thursday morning. Nobody is going to stop me. Do you hear me? I'm going to get my baby on Thursday! Nobody is going to stop me!" Her voice is firm and determined, but tears are on their way.

"Yes, Juanita, I understand perfectly. I plan to be there to help you."

Wednesday Evening
September 25, 1949

IT'S SURPRISING HOW EARLY it gets dark. It's only a few minutes past seven, and already the Creager's yard is cloaked in darkness.

A light burns in their kitchen. I knock on the back door of the Creager's house. Sounds of footsteps echoing down the hallway precede a jiggling of the back door handle.

"Hello, Stubby. How are you?" Ferrol Creager asks courteously from inside the screen door. He seems surprised to see me.

"Ferrol, I need to ask a favor. I'm leaving early tomorrow morning to pick up Juanita and the baby in Comanche. I plan to pay the hospital with a check. Can I leave some money with you to deposit in my bank account tomorrow morning? I wanna be sure the money is there, in case they call to see if the check's good."

"Certainly. I'd be delighted to make your deposit for you. Why don't you come inside? Let me find something to write on, so I can give you a receipt."

Ferrol Creager ambles down a long hallway while I step inside. I hear him rummaging around somewhere in the front of the house.

"Here we are, Stubby," Creager says when he reappears, "I found a bank receipt book in my desk. Othel will be excited to hear about Juanita and the baby coming home. She's been worried about them. Will you be bringing them back to Ranger tomorrow?"

"Yes. At least I hope so. The hospital's giving us a hard time about a hundred dollar deposit I gave them last Monday."

"Hard time? I don't understand. Don't you have enough money to pay the hospital?"

"Well, the hospital bill should be around four hundred dollars. With my three hundred dollar bonus for winning the Stamford game, everything would've been fine, but the hospital seems to have lost the hundred dollars I gave them for a deposit."

"Stubby, this sounds serious. They may not let you have the baby if you can't pay their bill. You need a loan?"

"Ferrol, with my lousy credit, no one would loan me a hundred dollars. I'll work something out with the hospital."

"You say you've got three hundred. Why don't you let the bank loan you another hundred? I can add it to the money you have and deposit four hundred dollars into your checking account first thing tomorrow morning."

"How much interest will you charge me?" I ask defensively, not certain whether I should jump at his offer.

"Your total interest plus the bank's initiation fee will be two dollars. That is, if you pay the loan back in less than thirty days."

"A hundred dollar loan would sure help. You sure the bank'll loan me that much?"

"Stubby, the day my bank won't allow me to loan that kinda money to a good solid customer like you is the day I'll start looking for another job."

"You're joking me, Ferrol. But, thanks, I'll take the loan."

"Not really, Stubby. You're a good risk. There's not a doubt in my mind that you'll pay back every penny you borrow."

––––––––––––

WALKING IN THE DARKNESS across the wide stretch of lawn separating our two houses, I can hardly believe my good fortune to have such fantastic neighbors as Othel and Ferrol Creager. The bank loan Ferrol promised will make things go a lot easier at the Comanche hospital tomorrow morning.

Wow! The bank charges two bucks for loaning out a hundred dollars for thirty days. That's more than a half-day's wages at the Pontiac House. It's no wonder they have so much money.

Thursday Morning
September 26, 1949

THE NARROW ROADWAY leading up to the Kimbrough ranchhouse seems menacing and foreboding, giving me second thoughts about agreeing to pick Juanita up here. All my experiences at this unfriendly place have been extremely unpleasant.

I can probably handle a light conversation with Juanita's mother and Phyliss Mitchell, but I dread the possibility of another meeting with Luther. It will be almost impossible to avoid seeing him.

I park the two-toned Pontiac in front of the white picket fence and turn off the engine. I wait inside the car for a minute, hoping Juanita will come running out the front door to greet me. When she doesn't appear, I slide out and walk to the front porch. The front door is opened; only the screen door is closed. I knock on the wood casing surrounding the doorway.

"Hello. Is that you, Stubby?" Edna Kimbrough's voice inquires from down the hallway.

"Yes, Edna. It's Stubby. I came to pick up Juanita. Is she ready?" I try to sound cheerful and friendly, but this is very difficult.

"She's not quite ready. Why don't you come in while she finishes packing?" Edna offers when she reaches the door. An apron covers her dress.

"I'd just as soon wait out here. It's a nice day. Maybe I'll sit in the swing."

"Stubby, please come inside. I've baked some sweet rolls and put on a fresh pot of coffee, just for you. Leaving Ranger so early, I'm sure you didn't have time for breakfast."

"Alright, Edna. A cup of coffee sounds pretty good."

The front door opens into a small foyer. A wide mirror hangs on the right wall above a heavy wood table covered with a starched white linen cloth. Fresh wildflowers protrude from a huge blue vase, centered on the table below the mirror. A long, multicolored throw rug in the middle of the foyer covers the wooden floor. The Kimbrough's only telephone is mounted at eye level on the wall opposite the mirror. The telephone is an antique, box-like apparatus encased in a wooden body. A round metal mouthpiece extends out the front. The receiver hangs from a metal bracket on the left side, connected to the wooden box by a short black chord.

Juanita's mother leads me down a darkened hallway from the foyer to the kitchen. Phyliss Mitchell is sitting at the kitchen table. She and Edna have, apparently, been waiting for me.

Sweet rolls, fresh coffee—a sixth sense somewhere deep inside warns me to be wary. These Kimbrough females, I have learned, can be devious and conniving. I wonder what these two women have been discussing. Almost certainly, I have been the subject of their conversation.

"Good morning, Stubby. I'm so glad to see you. How is everything in Ranger?" Phyliss asks me.

"Things are going great," I answer with a lie. "My Bulldogs have won two games in a row. Looks like we'll have a winning season."

"I'm so happy that things are going so good for you, Stubby. Have you seen Price? How is he faring without a wife?"

"I talked with him last Saturday. He's doing fine, but I'm sure he'll be happy when you come home."

"I hope you brought my car. I'd like to ride back to Ranger with you and Juanita today."

"I thought you might want to come with us so I drove down in your Pontiac. It's still good as new," I reply, telling a second lie. It's best she doesn't know about the bullet holes, at least not now.

"Here, Stubby, you sit at the head of the table," Edna offers accommodatingly. She pours me a cup of steaming coffee and sets a dinner plate bearing a large cinnamon roll on the kitchen table before me. Warning signals go off in my head. These women are up to something. They are buttering me up for some reason.

The two women nervously watch me devour the sweet roll and gulp down the coffee. Edna was right. Anxious to get underway, I skipped both my coffee and my breakfast this morning.

Edna fills my empty cup with a second serving of coffee. She offers another roll, but I decline. No sense in getting myself too much in their debt—not before I find out what this is all about.

While Edna returns the coffee pot to the stove, Phyllis Mitchell leans forward, looking directly into my eyes from across the table. "Stubby, would you mind talking with Luther before we go? He wants to see you."

So, that's what the royal treatment is all about. They've been softening me up, lowering my resistance, making it easier for my enemy to defeat me. "Why would he want to see me? And what makes you think I'd want to see him? He's got nothing I want. Once I get my wife and baby away from this awful place, I don't ever plan on coming back."

"Oh, Stubby! Please don't say that! I want to see my grandchild. You have to let me see my grandbaby," Edna cries, bursting into tears.

Gazing hard at me across the table, Phyliss ignores Edna Kimbrough's emotional outburst. "Stubby, this is important to Juanita. And, it is killing Luther's soul to have us ask you to meet with him. Can't you give a little and meet him halfway? It would mean so much to all of us."

I owe this woman and her husband more than I can ever repay. Only because of their generosity and support have I survived. Saying no to her might seem callous and unappreciative, but how can I agree to give in to my adversary? No, it's asking too much.

"Phyliss, it's too much to ask. Why can't we leave this thing alone? I'll take Juanita and the baby. Luther Kimbrough and I never have to see each other again. There'll be no more confrontations or harsh words between us. Everyone can be happy again."

"Stubby, it's not that simple, and you know it. Look at Edna. Her heart is breaking. Think about Juanita. Do you think she could ever be happy, totally cut off from her family because of this preposterous man's thing between you and her father?"

"I'm sorry, Phyliss. All I came to do is pick up my wife and baby. I don't want any more trouble with the Kimbrough family. There's no telling what might happen if Luther and I get into it again."

Phyliss Mitchell looks at me sternly and with disgust. "Stubby," she challenges, "if you're man enough to face him, Luther is waiting for you out in the barn!"

LUTHER KIMBROUGH EYES ME WARILY from inside the horse
stall while I open the corral gate and meander across the hoof-marked
barnyard terrain. He lowers his head, pretending not to notice me as
he tacks on an iron shoe to the back hoof of a splendid black mare. I
stop outside the stall and lean over the railing.

"Nice horse. You always shoe your own horses?"

"No. Normally I have the blacksmith come out. I'm planning on
riding this here mare in the Coleman Rodeo Parade tomorrow afternoon," Juanita's father remarks coldly, without looking at me.

"I reckon there's some things you need to do yourself. You need
some help?"

"Yeah. You could hold her steady, while I nail this shoe on."

I open the stall gate and grab the leather bridal reins on the horse's
head. The horse is gentle as a lamb. She noses my shirt pockets looking for a treat. I'm sure she's been shod many times, without anyone
holding her steady.

"Alright, I got her. Go ahead."

Luther Kimbrough taps the shoe on quickly and expertly. When
he's done, he drops the horse's leg gently and turns around to face me.
He holds the shoe hammer menacingly in his hand.

"I guess you've come to pick up Juanita?"

"Yes, that's why I'm here–to take her and the baby back to Ranger
with me."

"I hear you're a hundred dollars short, that you don't have enough
money to pay the hospital bill."

I expected him to use my lack of money on me, to try and embarrass me. My first inclination is to tell him I have the money, and that
he can go straight to hell, but this is a Kimbrough family show. I'll
play along and see where this is leading.

"That might be the case," I respond, verbally sparring with him.

"I hear you agreed to give the baby my name."

"Only your middle name. He's named after me."

"You gonna call him Jerry?"

"Yes, that's the plan."

"Edna would sure hate to see the baby get off to a bad start, you
know–not getting paid for."

"How about you, Luther? How would you feel about it?"

"I suppose I'd hate it, too."

"Yeah. I guess we'd all hate it," I say, taunting him. The man is ready to offer me money. I don't intend to make it easy for him. With the loan from the Ranger bank, my financial bases are covered. If this meeting is about money, I have control, not Luther Kimbrough.

"You need a loan?"

"Yeah, who doesn't?"

"What I mean is, do you want me to loan you the money to pay the hospital?"

There, now it's out. He's made his offer. He is the first to reveal weakness. He has succumbed to the will of the women. If I choose, I can show him up, make him look small, easily winning this battle in our on-going feud.

With easy victory within my grasp, my desire to defeat him vanishes. After all these months of despising Luther Kimbrough, I suddenly realize what a sad person he is. He is petty and inconsiderate. He holds onto his family with fear instead of love. His acquaintances respect him but don't truly like him. He represents everything I hope not to become. What would I gain by beating him? It would only cause more hard feelings and pain. I change my mind, deciding to let him win this battle. I will accept his offer.

"What kind of interest would you want?"

"Oh, I don't know. How about five dollars a month?"

"That sounds awful high. How about two dollars a month?"

"If that's what you're willing to pay, I suppose I could agree to those terms. You wanna shake on it?"

When I was a green freshman at A&M, I made the mistake of extending a limp, relaxed, unsuspecting hand for an upperclassman to shake. He promptly crushed it and brought me to my knees in agony. It was a mistake I have never repeated. The possibility of Luther Kimbrough pulling such a childish stunt registers in my mind, a split-second before my right hand meets his. I push my hand hard into his to keep him from getting a grip advantage.

My hand hasn't completely healed from its solid encounter with Orval Graves' nose. I only removed the bandages before my shower last evening.

The ritual in this foolish man's game is not to flinch or show pain.

My opponent's grip is like a powerful vice. I return his strong grip with every ounce of hand power I can muster. We stand facing one another, eye-to-eye, each exerting his maximum force upon the other.

After what seems like an eternity, my father-in-law jerks his hand back sharply. My own hand is throbbing with pain, but I do not rub it or give him any indication of how much he's hurt me.

"You've got a nice grip there, Mister."

"So do you, Luther—a real nice grip."

"Come on, Stubby. Let's go up to the house. I'll get you some money to bail my grandson outta the hospital."

His words stun me. My mind must be clouded because of the aching pain in my hand. Luther Kimbrough has never called me by name before.

JUANITA WATCHES US FROM THE BACK PORCH while we plod up the dirt trail from the barn. When she hears our voices engaged in conversation, she claps her hands and runs inside to tell Edna and Phyliss.

EDNA KIMBROUGH'S EYES are filled with tears as she stands in the front yard watching us load Phyliss Mitchell's Pontiac with baggage and baby things. The handkerchief in her hand is soaked from her tears. She's been crying, off and on now, ever since Luther and I returned from the barn.

When the car is finally packed, Juanita and Phyliss go to her, exchanging affectionate hugs and goodbyes. I start the car's engine and turn around in the driveway.

The extended goodbyes have advanced to a prolonged crying session when Luther appears on the front porch and steps down into the yard. He hugs Phyliss, gives Juanita a kiss, then wraps an arm around his wife's shoulders. Juanita's parents stand together in the yard behind the picket fence, continuing to wave as we drive down the gravel roadway to the highway. It is a sight I thought I'd never see.

PHYLISS AND JUANITA HOP from the car before I can come to a complete stop in the Comanche hospital parking lot. They scurry hurriedly up the sidewalk onto the front porch and go inside.

There's no reason for me to hurry. Before the baby can leave, diapers will need to be changed, information on the baby's formula must be supplied, last minute instructions on the baby's feeding times must be dispensed, and the baby must be dressed in his "going home outfit." All this will be efficiently accomplished without any input from the father. My only duty is to settle the financial matters.

Anticipating a long, boring wait, I take my own good time. I park the car, lock the doors and stroll deliberately across the parking lot and into the hospital.

The hospital lobby and waiting room are empty. There is no sign of a nurse or patients in either of the front rooms. The entire hospital staff seems to be congregated in the nursery to watch Little Jerry being readied for his trip home. Since no one is available to discuss my hospital bill, I grab a magazine and take a seat in the waiting room.

"HELLO, MISTER WARDEN. I understand you're taking your son home this morning," the young nurse says, as she walks up to me.

"Yes. Yes, we are." I'm at a loss for words. This is the same young nurse who took my deposit money and skipped out. What is she doing here? Why isn't she in jail?

"Mister Warden, I believe I owe you an apology. I'm afraid I have caused you a great inconvenience."

Great inconvenience–that's hardly an accurate definition. She stole my money, and except for an exceptional run of luck, could've prevented me from getting my wife and child out of the hospital.

"Inconvenience is not exactly the word. Aren't you some kin to my wife, Juanita?" I want to run to the front door and scream, "Thief!" I want to call the police. I should take her by the neck and strangle her, but her innocent demeanor keeps me from taking immediate violent action against her.

"Yes, she's my cousin. My name is Patsy Kimbrough."

"Patsy, it seems Mrs. Willard never received the hundred dollar deposit I gave you. What did you do with the money?"

"Oh, Mister Warden, I'm so sorry! Mrs. Willard told me all about the mix-up when I came back to work this morning. I've been out of town. I had to leave Comanche unexpectedly, because of a family emergency. This is the first day I've worked at the hospital since the night you gave me the deposit."

"Patsy, what happened to my money? Did you take it?" I say, trying not to reveal the anger inside me.

"No. Oh, no! Please don't say that! I was afraid you might think I took it. Juanita's family has always accused mine of being dishonest, but we're not. We're just poor. Sometimes we simply can't pay our debts, but I would never steal your money, Mister Warden." The young nurse is crying now. Huge tears begin to roll down her cheeks.

"What happened to my money then, Patsy? What did you do with it?"

"I put it in Mrs. Willard's cash drawer, right under the receipt book. I showed her exactly where it was when she jumped on me this morning."

"You mean the money has been right there, all along?"

"Yes. I never took your money. I'm not like that. Please forgive me, Mister Warden."

The youthful nurse begins to cry profusely, out of control. I stand up and pull her into my arms. She continues to sob on my shoulder.

"It's all right, Patsy. It's all right. There's nothing to forgive. It was all just a big mistake."

A nurse emerges through the door leading to the hospital hallway. Seeing me holding the young woman in my arms, she retreats quickly back through the door.

IN THE REAR VIEW MIRROR I can observe Juanita in the back seat, cuddling Little Jerry to her chest while she and Phyliss coo and ogle over him, talking baby talk.

"The head nurse told us you were up front in the waiting room hugging my cousin," Juanita accuses me from the back seat, without warning.

Her sudden accusation causes a ripple of guilt to shoot through my heart. My hands tighten on the steering wheel while I search for the right words to logically explain my behavior with the young nurse.

"She was crying, Juanita. I was trying to console her. She was feeling guilty about her part in misplacing our deposit money."

"Well, Mister Warden, the next time you decide to console some pretty young girl, you had better hold her hand and keep your distance. I don't want my husband going around hugging other women."

Relieved to discover she's only jesting with me, I tease back, "Alright, Juanita, you have my promise. I won't go around hugging other women, at least not in public."

"If Mrs. Willard gave you credit for the deposit, then you didn't really need Daddy's loan, did you?" Juanita asks, changing the subject.

"No. But, let's not tell him. In a couple of weeks, I'll pay him back. Your father seems to enjoy having me owe him money." I haven't told Juanita I already had plenty of money in the Ranger bank. There's little point in bringing it up now.

Juanita leans forward from the back seat and kisses me on the back of my neck.

"Phyliss," she says, "did you know I'm married to a very wonderful man?"

"Yes, I've known about him all along," Phyliss answers, joining in on the adoring praises.

None of today's events makes sense. Somehow, by hiding my strength, giving in to Luther Kimbrough–letting him loan me money I didn't need–I emerged the winner. It doesn't add up. In my competitive world of football, admitting even the slightest hint of weakness will get you your brains beat out. Someday, when I have more time–maybe after the football season is over–I'll sit down, sort out all the pieces of this puzzle and try to understand how I came out the winner.

I push down harder on the foot-feed. The car surges ahead. If I hurry, I can be back in Ranger for football practice at three o'clock.

Damn. Four bucks–wasted–borrowing money I didn't need.

CHAPTER THIRTEEN
THE JAIL

Thursday Evening
September 26, 1949

WILL BROWNLEE'S FAMILY resides in a small wood frame house located south of town on Highway 80. Their tiny farm is a narrow, infertile strip of land bounded by the highway on the east and by the Texas and Pacific Railroad on the west.

When Superintendent Boswell delivered my bonus money on Wednesday afternoon, I questioned him about the school's policy on paying for players' injuries. I wasn't surprised to learn the school system does not carry football insurance, nor is there an official school policy for handling injured players' medical expenses. In the past, if a boy got hurt, his family absorbed the expenses. Fortunately, Boswell explained, no one has ever been injured seriously. At least no one has violently objected to the school trustees about paying their own medical costs.

Doctor Watkins, a young physician recognizing an opportunity to promote his medical practice, volunteers his services to the team free of charge. His only compensation is free admission to the high school football games. Apparently, he loves football and cherishes the questionable notoriety of being referred to as the "Team Doctor."

When I told him about the situation with Will Brownlee, Superintendent Boswell offered to contact a few influential supporters. He seemed confident he could raise the fifty dollars needed to reimburse the Brownlee family for Will's hospital expenses.

This visit to the Brownlee's place is one I'd just as soon not make, but I have put it off too long already. I need to tell them about the school's promise to reimburse their medical expenses. I'll also try to apologize for not coming by last weekend to check on Will's injury.

An unpainted picket fence separates the Brownlee's barren front yard from the highway right-of-way. Evidently, visitors to the Brownlee property are expected to park in a widened gravel drainage swale between the highway pavement and the picket fence. An afternoon thundershower has made the side slopes of the drainage ditch wet and slippery.

Against my better judgement I decide to chance it and park in the graveled channel. Wind sheer, caused by the passing of a large truck, rocks the Hudson while I pull slowly off the road and slide down the bank to a stop. Fearing for my vehicle's safety, I double check the Hudson's rear bumper to make sure it clears the highway pavement. Satisfied my car is temporarily secure, I open the gate and enter the Brownlee property.

A covered wooden porch extends out across the front of the small house. Several straight, ladder-backed wooden chairs lean against the front wall. The family obviously enjoys sitting on the front porch to watch the cars drive by, like we once did at my grandparents' house in Slaton. The front door is open. A latched screen door keeps out unwanted visitors while allowing the cool evening breeze to filter inside. The front rooms of the house are dark. However, kitchen sounds coming from the back of the house testify that someone is home.

I knock on the front wall next to the door. "Hello! Hello, Mister Brownlee!"

"Just a minute," a voice responds from somewhere inside.

"It's Stubby Warden–Will's football coach," I announce loudly to forewarn them.

A light flicks on in the front room, and a thin, aging woman appears at the screen door.

"Coach Warden! What brings you out here?" The woman recognizes me. She must be Will's mother. I'm relieved to hear the friendly tone in her voice.

"I came to talk with you about Will. Is Mister Brownlee home?"

"Yes sir. He's down at the cow shed, feeding the pigs and tending to his other chores. He has to milk the cow, so he may be a while. You can walk down and see him if you don't wanna wait."

I had hoped to make this a short visit. I'm anxious to get home to Juanita and Little Jerry. There are a thousand things Juanita and I need to talk about.

"I was hoping to talk with both of you, Mrs. Brownlee. I want to apologize for not coming by to check on Will last weekend and to tell you the school is making arrangements to reimburse you for his hospital costs."

"You better go down to the cow shed and talk with Gene, Coach Warden. He's the one who was so upset, because of the extra hours he'll have to work to pay off the hospital."

MY MIND REPLAYS Mrs. Brownlee's words as I hike along the muddy path to Brownlee's cow shed. Could it be Will's father is more upset over the fact he has to work overtime than he is about my not coming to visit Will? If that's the case, maybe with my promise to have the school pay him back, he can be convinced to allow my kicker to return to the team. When I think about it, quitting the team seems like pretty drastic action to take in retaliation, even for my pathetic conduct. Mister Brownlee's ultimatum will hurt his son as much as anyone.

Approaching the wood fence which encloses an open side of the metal cow shed, I find Eugene Brownlee squatting on a short wooden stool. His head is bent low, and his right shoulder is pressed firmly against the cow's rear leg. The sound of the cow's milk splashing against the metal pail reminds me of many happy times I helped my grandfather with evening milking chores.

"Mister Brownlee, I don't mean to interrupt your milking, but could we talk about Will and football for a minute?"

The man ceases his milking and turns halfway around on his stool to face me. "Coach Warden, what're you doing out here?"

"Your wife sent me. She said you were busy with your chores but wouldn't mind if I came to talk with you. I hope it's okay."

"Sure. I'll be finished here in a few minutes. Why don't you tell me what's on your mind?" He lowers his head and pushes it against the cow's stomach, resuming his milking duties.

"Well, there's really two things I need to say. First–about Will's hospital bill–I've talked with the school superintendent. He has promised to reimburse you for all medical expenses related to Will's injury."

Brownlee stops his milking and turns around again. "You mean the school's gonna pay the hospital bill? Do they know how much it was?"

Damn! I should've checked on the amount of the hospital bill before I talked with Boswell. What if Will was wrong about the hospital cost? It's too late to worry about that now. I charge blindly ahead.

"Will told me the hospital charges were around fifty dollars. He said Doctor Watkins provided his services free of charge."

"Yeah, that's about right. You know how many hours I'd have to work overtime at the police station to earn that much money?"

"No sir. I suspect it might take you quite a few extra days to earn that much," I answer sympathetically. It would be more than two weeks' take-home pay for me when I worked at the Pontiac House. I hope Brownlee makes more than that.

"You're dern tootin', Coach. Quite a few days."

"Listen, Eugene. I hope you don't mind me using your first name?"

"Most of my friends call me Gene."

"Okay, Gene it is then. Gene, I'm concerned about Will's quitting the football team. He tells me you're upset with us coaches because we didn't come out to check on him last weekend."

"Yeah, I was upset. I was kinda angry about everything–Will getting hurt, the big hospital bill. Then, when nobody came to check and see how bad he was hurt, I got real mad. Except for a couple of his teammates, not one person from the school ever called."

"Gene, I don't know any other way to say this, except plain and simple. Checking on Will was my responsibility, and I simply didn't do my job. He's your only son. I can't expect you to understand or forgive me for being so thoughtless, but for Will's sake, I wish you'd consider letting him rejoin the team."

Brownlee finishes with his milking. He gently removes the milk pail from beneath the cow, covers it with a white cloth and sets it on a shelf inside the cow shed.

"Why would you want him back? He can't help you. By the time he can kick again the season will be over," he says, turning back to look at me.

"Gene, if you would consider letting him come back, I want him to act as our team manager, that is, until he's well enough to play again. Coach Aills and I really need some help. Besides, I'm very confident we will win the district championship and get into the playoffs. There's no telling how long the team might be playing. We'll need Will kicking for us in the playoff games."

"You'd let him kick for the Bulldogs in the playoffs? What assurance do I have you'll make the playoffs?"

"Trust me, Gene. This football team will be in the playoffs. I want Will to be there to kick for us."

"WHY MUST I ALWAYS overload myself?" I lecture myself on the path back to the Brownlee's house. Telling him the school would pay the hospital bill was sufficient argument to persuade Will's father to change his mind. Now I've promised my football team will be in the playoffs.

Well, at least he agreed to let Will come back as our team manager. Chalk up a win for me.

Damn. Why must I keep fighting battles I could easily avoid by exercising just a little more good sense?

"SHHH...THE BABY IS ASLEEP," Juanita warns me, putting a finger to her lips behind the screen door. I was about to begin stomping my muddy feet on our front porch.

Juanita opens the door quietly and steps out on the porch to greet me. She reaches for my hand, pulling it against her chest. "Coach Warden, it's after eight o'clock. Did you have to work late on my first night home? I hope this isn't a bad habit you've picked up while I've been away," she reprimands me, using an alluring smile to soften her criticism.

"Mrs. Warden, you know a coach's work is never done. We never quit. We just run out of daylight."

"That may be, darling, but even big boys should stop playing their silly little games and come home when it gets too dark to play. Otherwise, they might miss their supper, and other erotic things."

"Missing my supper would be terrible, Mrs. Warden. My question is–what could possibly be more erotic or exciting than supper?" I say, reaching out to pull her to me. Her arms wrap around my neck as she arches her back, anticipating my kiss.

Suddenly, she pushes me away and steps back. "Ooh! Stubby! What's that smell? Where have you been? You smell worse than the Kimbrough barn yard."

"I've been in a cow shed talking to Will Brownlee's father, trying to convince him to let his son stay on the football team. I suppose I should've paid more attention to where I was stepping." In an instant our romantic mood has disappeared.

She holds her nose in mock nasal distress. "Pew Wee! Darling, you need to take a bath before you come to the supper table."

"I thought women liked a man with the fresh smell of the outdoors. That's what all the radio commercials advertise. You mean it doesn't excite you?" I say to provoke her, trying to hide my disappointment at not receiving her kiss.

"You must have me mixed up with some country girl, sir. To me, you smell like plain old cow manure. Coach Warden, you go bathe while I finish cooking your supper," she giggles in amused response.

I slip off my soiled shoes and leave them on the porch. My young wife continues to hold her nose while she hurries inside to the kitchen.

"STUBBY, WHAT HAVE YOU BEEN EATING? There was almost no food in the house. If Phyliss hadn't been here to take me grocery shopping, you wouldn't be getting much of a supper tonight," Juanita scolds at me when I join her in the kitchen after my shower.

"Well, some days I grab a sandwich at Pearl's before our afternoon practice. For the past week or so I've been staying late to review game films. By the time I get home, I'm too tired to cook. Sometimes I'll eat a peanut butter sandwich and drink a glass of milk. Since Alfred moved out to the Murphy farm, I haven't had much reason to cook."

"No wonder you look so thin. Now that I'm home, I'll see that you start eating right again. Who is this Alfred fellow?"

"Juanita, so much has happened since you left for Comanche. I have lots of things to tell you."

WHILE I EAT MY FIRST HOME COOKED SUPPER in over a week, I tell Juanita about Alfred, my secret meetings with Lucas Masters, and Murphy's shooting and disappearance. Juanita sits quietly on the opposite side of the table and listens attentively, spellbound by my tales of intrigue. Occasionally she reaches out to touch my hand, but she doesn't interrupt until I'm through talking. Not wanting to frighten her, I don't tell her about being beat up, shot at or about the car theft ring. If I told her everything that's happened while she's been away, she might pack up the baby and head for Comanche. I'm not ready to gamble on that. The stories I do tell her are more than enough for her to absorb on her first night home.

After I finish, Juanita picks up my plate and deposits it in the kitchen sink, then begins to clear the table and put things away. She's disturbed by everything she's heard but not sure how she should respond.

When she passes, I grab her arm and pull her down in my lap. She comes to me willingly, pressing her soft, warm lips to mine. I finally get the kiss I've been yearning for.

"Stubby, how could all this have happened? Are you in any danger? Are we in danger?" she asks. Her eyes are filled with tears of anxiety.

"No, I don't think so. Keith Murphy was shot because he was working for the sheriff, not for coaching football."

"Are you sure you want to keep a coaching job where someone else dictates which players you play?"

"No. But I think I can change all that, in time."

"But, Stubby–what about your principles–all the things we talked about–how you would never compromise or let anything keep you from winning."

"Sometimes things don't turn out like we plan, Juanita. Sometimes, you have to make the best of what's available. That's what I'm doing–making the best out of what I have. I'm gonna win, in spite of all the obstacles they put in my way."

"Darling, you know how much I love and support you. But, are you sure this job is what you want? There must be other coaching jobs, in other places–where you won't be confronted with so many problems–where you can be respected for doing a good job."

"There aren't that many coaching jobs. Remember, a month ago I was prepared to move to Corpus Christi and teach P.E. classes. No, I'm staying here. This is where I want to coach. I'm not leaving unless they fire me and run me off. And as long as my football team keeps winning, they'll have one heck of a time getting rid of me."

"Alright, darling. If you're certain this is what you want, then it's settled. This Warden family will make our stand, right here in Ranger, Texas–come hell or high water, no holds barred." She wraps her arms around my neck and kisses me passionately to seal our pact. Her lips have a salty taste, from her tears.

SHORT SNORTER AMBLES INTO THE BEDROOM while Juanita and I prepare to retire. Wanting to be petted, he scratches at the bed covers.

"Your bulldog pup seems to have adopted Jerry. He's been sleeping beside the baby's bassinet ever since we came home from grocery shopping this afternoon," Juanita tells me from the bathroom.

"Yeah, I'm jealous. Usually he sticks close to me. I was wondering why I wasn't getting any of his attention." I lean down from the bed and scratch the young bulldog's ears.

Juanita turns off the light and slips into bed beside me. I reach to pull her close. I slide my hand under her nightgown, feeling the warm bare skin between her legs.

"Sweetheart, there's no point in either of us getting excited. We can't do anything about it," she whispers in my ear.

Juanita takes my hand and slides it up on her stomach, just below her belly button. Her skin feels rough and uneven. The ends of her stitches are stiff and stick into my fingers. I'm not sure what she has in mind, but my desire for her has rapidly diminished. This is not what I hoped for.

"Can you feel where they made the incision to take the baby?" she asks softly.

"Yes, I can feel it."

"The doctor says we should refrain from any sexual activity until the incision is healed and the stitches are removed."

"How long will that be?"

Juanita pecks my cheek with her lips before she returns my hand back to my side of the bed. "The doctor said it will be about six weeks. You'll have to be patient."

"I've missed you so much, Juanita. Six weeks is a long time. Do we really have to wait so long?"

"The doctor told me you'd be impatient. He said to tell you ice cold showers will help a lot."

That Doctor Blackmar is quite a joker. Somehow, his weird humor is always lost on me.

WITH ALL MY FAMILY here close to me, under my roof, I should be content and sleep soundly. I don't. I have a fitful night. I keep waking up, patting on Juanita to make sure she's actually here in my bed, that I'm not just dreaming.

Short Snorter also has a rough night. He can't decide whether to sleep next to my bed or in the baby's room. Finally, after watching Juanita nurse Little Jerry at his two o'clock feeding, the bulldog heaves a heavy sigh and chooses the baby's room.

I truly am jealous this time.

Friday Morning
September 27, 1949

WITH COACH MURPHY INCAPACITATED, Alfred and Sam have volunteered to coach the junior high football team. The younger team only plays a seven game schedule, so they should be finished several weeks before our varsity season ends.

Surprisingly, after two games, the junior high squad is undefeated and unscored on. Alfred has asked me to come watch them practice. He and Sam tell me their players are big and exceptionally talented.

They believe this could be the finest group of Ranger football players to ever come along.

Football practice for the junior high team begins at ten o'clock in the morning, lasting for only an hour and a half. After a restless night, I finally fell asleep sometime about daybreak, then overslept. It's half past ten now. I'll be lucky to catch the last hour of their practice.

"Whrrrrrrrr," a siren shrieks from behind me. I check my speedometer. No way I could be guilty of speeding, not on these muddy potholed roads which lead to the football stadium.

Blinking red lights atop the squad car behind me reflect in my rear-view mirror, urging me to pull over. Curious about why I'm being detained, I coast to a stop, turn off the engine and get out of my car.

The patrol car is a county sheriff's vehicle. Billy Hancock, the young deputy who was helping guard Keith Murphy's hospital door, is the driver. Sitting beside him is the familiar face of Orval Graves. A large white bandage covers his nose.

"That's him, Billy! That's the little bastard who hit me with a wrench! Go ahead! Arrest him, like you promised," Orval yells, getting out of the squad car.

"What's the problem, Officer? Why did you pull me over?" I ask, trying to stay composed. Inside, I'm steaming.

Fortunately for Orval, he elects to stay behind the patrol car door while the young deputy approaches me. If Mister Graves gets close enough, I'll let him have another dose of the same medicine that damaged his bandaged nose.

"Coach Warden, this man has sworn out a warrant for your arrest. He claims you beat him with a metal weapon."

"Come on, deputy! You don't believe that! Yeah, I hit him. But I hit him with my fist. He was threatening me with a loaded gun."

"I'm sorry, Coach. I have a warrant. I gotta arrest you. I hope you'll come peaceable," the deputy says, placing a hand on his holstered gun for effect.

"Look, Billy. You know me. I'm not about to leave town. I'm overdue to monitor my junior high team's football practice. I've got a game tonight to prepare for. Can't I come by the sheriff's office later and get this settled?"

"I'm afraid not, Coach Warden. Put your hands behind your back. I need to handcuff you."

ORVAL SNEERS AT ME through the wire cage separating the squad car's front seat from the prisoner's section in the back.

"How ya feel now, smart guy? We tried ta teach ya a lesson by busting ya up a little. But you can't take a hint. No, you gotta be a wisenhiemer and come out to the ranch, snooping around. Well, we'll fix your wagon, won't we, Billy?"

"Shut up, Orval! He knows too much already. If you tell him any more, we'll have to kill him for sure," the deputy rebukes his ugly companion.

The youthful deputy must be in cahoots with Orval and the other car thieves. He was on duty at the hospital. He could've been involved in Keith Murphy's disappearance. Most likely, he's also the one responsible for information leaking out of the sheriff's office.

I should've put up a fight. Here in the back seat of the sheriff's patrol car, with my hands cuffed behind my back, I am easy prey for whatever they have in mind.

THE TIRES OF THE SHERIFF'S SQUAD CAR squeal as the young deputy swings sharply into the driveway behind the jailhouse and slams to a stop. He and Orval leap out. Without speaking, they open the back door of the car and signal for me to slide out. I think about putting up a fight here, then decide to take my chances inside. Surely there will be someone working in the jail who's not involved in the car theft operation.

Orval and Billy hustle me out of the car and through a rear entrance. Orval pushes me from behind and growls at me when I stop to look around inside.

"Let's move it, smart guy. We ain't got all day. We need to get this over with. Me and Clifford got big plans for the weekend."

We climb a winding staircase up to the third floor where three individual jail cells face onto a hallway. The prison-like cells are separated from each other and from the hallway by walls of thick steel bars. Each chamber is furnished with one badly-stained, unsanitary ceramic toilet and a single metal bed covered by a thin cotton mattress. None of the cells has a window. Sunlight from a single steel-barred window at the end of the hallway is the only noticeable connection to the world outside. All the cells are empty.

"Which one you want, fellow? You can have your choice. Looks like you're the only tenant," Orval snarls, prodding me from behind.

"You can't lock me up–not without a hearing–not without letting me make a phone call. I've got rights."

I've never been arrested before. I don't know exactly what my rights are, but the way these two are treating me, definitely isn't according to the law.

"Ha! Ha! He thinks he's got rights," Orval cackles to Billy Hancock, then he turns back to me. "Don't talk to me about rights, ya little pipsqueak, not after you went and broke my nose, hittin' me when I wasn't ready. Git your smart ass into one of them cells, before I break both your legs and kick the living dookie out of ya."

Orval shoves me through the open door of the middle cell, sending me skidding across the dirty concrete floor. I roll over to face him while he locks the door behind me.

"Could you at least remove my handcuffs? They're hurting my hands."

"Screw you, Mister Smart Guy! Hey, don't worry. You won't have to wait long. We'll be back soon. Then it won't make no difference to ya whether you're wearing handcuffs or not."

Orval and Billy traipse down the stairs to the first floor, leaving me alone in the cell. The sound of their cruel laughter resonates up the stairway while I inspect my gloomy cell and consider my dire circumstances.

The Eastland County Jail is a three-story, brick and stone structure located one block north of the courthouse square. I drove by the jail once, when I was on my way to Cisco to visit Jerry Lowe. The jail is an interesting old building, built during the "New Deal" Roosevelt Administration.

In my wildest dreams, I never imagined I'd be a resident here.

MY TWO CAPTORS PROMISED to return promptly to finish with me. I can't be sure what they have planned, but I'm certain it will be unpleasant. When they don't return immediately, I begin to wonder what could've detained them.

I hear noises on the floors below, but no one answers my repeated calls for help. After a while, I quit calling and stretch out on the lumpy mattress of the narrow metal bed.

With my hands cuffed behind my back, it is impossible to find a comfortable position. By lying on my back, rolling up on my shoulders and using a few contortionist-like moves, I'm able to slip the handcuffs below my hips. A few more acrobatics and I manage to bring one leg between my cuffed hands, then the other. My strenuous maneuvers are tiring. I roll over to lie on my back, exhausted.

Time passes slowly as morning fades into afternoon. My stomach growls from hunger. After oversleeping, I declined Juanita's offer to fix me breakfast. Now I wish I'd taken time to eat. Maybe I could've avoided Orval and Billy altogether.

Our game tonight is against Burkburnett. It's a home game so I won't definitely be missed until sometime around seven. Juanita isn't planning to attend the game because of the baby. When I don't come home, she'll think I got tied up with my game plans. Alfred and Sam will wonder why I didn't make their junior high practice but won't really get concerned until I don't show up before game time.

Damn! Why do these car ring people keep knocking us coaches off on game days? If they must do away with me—why couldn't they pick some other day of the week?

Hours drag by. Afternoon becomes dusk. A single incandescent light mounted in the ceiling of the hallway flicks on. I spend a few moments contemplating whether the light comes on automatically or if someone downstairs has manually turned it on. Maybe I should start calling for help again. Finally, I discard the idea, deciding to save my energy. I should know by now, no one's going to help me.

By now, fans are arriving at the Ranger football stadium. Sam and Alfred are beginning to wonder where I am—why no one's heard from me. I pray my assistant coaches have the good sense not to panic.

Our football team is ready. We have prepared all week to face the Burkburnett High Bulldogs and their single wing offense. My Bulldogs can win without me, if they'll stick to our game plan and play to their potential. Sam is a good motivator. He'll keep the team charged up.

Holy smoke! Who am I fooling? I don't want my football team to win without me being there. Somehow, I've gotta get out of this mess alive.

I jump up, run to the front of the cell and begin yelling for help again. My calls get the same response as before–none.

REALIZING AGAIN THAT no one will be coming to rescue me, I plop down despondently on the edge of the bed. With time on my hands and nothing to do but think, my thoughts stray to unhappy memories of the distressing events which occurred after my grandfather's death.

IT WAS A SATURDAY NIGHT when my mother called me at the athletic dorm. I could hardly hear her voice. Half-naked Aggie football players were out in the hallways, hollering and screaming–celebrating our victory over Rice Institute. Coach Norton had promised to give us the next Monday off, if we won.

Many of my teammates were planning to use the long weekend to drive up to Texas Women's College in Denton to see their girls. Being broke, as usual, and not having a steady girl, the day off meant nothing to me except a long weekend alone in the empty dorm.

The news of my grandfather's death hit me like a lightning bolt. He was my anchor, my source of strength, my biggest fan and my best friend. I didn't know at the time, but my life would never be the same again.

I packed a bag and hitchhiked to Dallas. I can still remember the cold November rain, biting at my face as I waited there in the darkness along the highway. I thought I'd never catch a ride.

From Dallas I rode a Greyhound bus to Slaton. My bus ticket was purchased with money generously contributed by my A&M teammates.

My mother met me at the Slaton bus station. She was accompanied by a middle-aged man whom I immediately distrusted. I was suspicious of his motives. He claimed to be a free-thinking evangelist who was raising money and recruiting volunteers for a hospital he was building in Brazil. He kept patting my mother's arm, telling her that her sorrow would soon pass. He kept reminding her about the deplorable conditions in Brazil and how her presence could make such a difference there. My mother seemed to be completely mesmerized by the man. Her strong religious convictions and her naive, trusting nature made her an easy target. It was only a matter of time before he'd be hitting on her for a sizeable donation.

Maybe it was the long bus trip. Maybe I was overly sensitive because of my sorrow. Maybe I was jealous for my mother's attention. But, by the time we arrived at my grandparents' house, I was thoroughly disgusted. Why should my mother be concerned about people in Brazil, especially during a time of such great sadness for our family?

"Mother, tell your friend to get lost. I don't want him coming in the house with us."

"Onis, you have no right to tell me who I can, or cannot, bring into the house," she objected.

"Mother, he's a shyster. Can't you see he's only after your money? If you won't make him leave, then I'll do it for you."

"Hey, young fellow, who you calling a shyster? I've never asked your mother for money. Can't you see she's in pain? Someone should teach you some manners," the self-serving preacher threatened from the front seat, mostly to impress my mother.

I reached across the back of the front seat, grabbed him by the shirt collar and pulled him violently toward me, so that we were nose-to-nose. "Listen, you slithering, sanctimonious creep. You keep out of this. This is between my mother and me. One more word and you'll be talking without your teeth."

Seeing I was deadly serious, he quickly retreated.

"Alright, young fellow. Calm down. Calm down."

I released his shirt collar and shoved him away from me. My mother began to cry.

"How can you be such an insensitive child, Onis? Can't you see I need someone to help me, in my time of sorrow? Please don't cause a scene."

Her tears and my inclination to obey her softened my resolve. "Alright, Mother. But, if he lays a hand on you again or asks anyone for money in my presence, I'll break every one of his fingers."

Despite my reservations, I reluctantly agreed to let him come into the house. I should've stuck with my initial mandate.

MY GRANDMOTHER MET US on the front porch. She was weak and exhausted from crying. Her face was white and drawn, almost ghostlike. The death of my grandfather had sucked out the last of her youth. I couldn't believe she had aged so much in such a short time. She had seemed so happy and full of life when I left for college only a few months earlier.

We buried my grandfather on Monday morning. The services were held at the tiny Methodist church where he and my grandmother had attended every Sunday since before I was born.

The church was filled to capacity. A multitude of mourners stood outside on the church grounds during the service. My grandfather had many friends. I doubt if there was a person in Slaton he didn't know.

After the funeral we returned to my grandparents' house. Several neighbor ladies had prepared food for the family and for those who wanted to come by and pay their respects. The money-hungry missionary was there, too—but not to pay his respects.

I was visiting with one of my cousins when I noticed a commotion on the front porch. My blood was boiling as I excused myself and went to check.

Out on the front porch, a small crowd had gathered about the beguiling evangelist. He thumped his Bible loudly, waving it menacingly at my grandfather's friends while he fanatically pitched for contributions to build his church hospital. A hat was being passed among his flock of listeners.

"What the hell's going on here. Don't you have any decency? This isn't the time or place for this. We just buried my grandfather—my mother's father," I angrily screamed at them.

The preacher turned to face me, obviously perturbed that I'd interrupted his fund raising effort. "Butt out, little fellow. This doesn't concern you. Your mom...."

He never completed the sentence. I punched him hard on the side of his face before he could finish. He staggered for a split second before I grabbed him and rammed his head against the front wall of the house. He was out cold when I picked him up and threw him over the porch railing into the yard.

My mother screamed in anguish and ran to the yard. She dropped to her knees, taking the preacher's head in her arms. Her face reflected both her sadness and her disappointment when she glanced up at me. Her eyes told me; I'd done wrong.

I hitch-hiked back to College Station. It took me two days. Coach Norton was mad as hell about my missing two days of football practice. But he still started me at offensive right guard, when we played SMU the following Saturday.

MY MOTHER CALLED ME three weeks later to tell me my grandmother had passed away. She said my grandmother just wasted away after my grandfather died.

My mother told me she'd decided to accept the evangelist's invitation to go with him to Brazil. She was leaving as soon as she could sell my grandparent's property. She planned to use the proceeds to help build the new hospital. I argued strongly, telling her she should wait, take time to get over her grief, not to make such a monumental decision until she had a clearer perspective. When she wouldn't listen, I begged her to reconsider, but her mind was made up. She was committed to a new life and ministering to natives in the Brazilian rain forests.

I didn't attend my grandmother's funeral. I didn't have the money to make the trip, and I could never have handled watching the self-righteous evangelist gloat over the prospect of getting his greedy hands on my mother's inheritance.

My mother writes occasionally. The evangelist, along with the funds donated for the new hospital, disappeared shortly after they arrived in Brazil, but she made connections with another missionary group and decided to stay. We haven't spoken, not since the day she left for Brazil. Maybe she's found her purpose in life. I hope she's happy.

THE HALLWAY LIGHT outside my cell flickers, then goes dark. Orval and Billy must finally be coming to get me. My heart skips a beat, then begins to pump faster. I wonder why they would turn the light out before they come. Maybe they have someone new with them to do the actual killing and don't want me to see his face. My mind runs wild with imaginary fears.

The beam of a moving flashlight reflects up the walls of the stairway. I hear the faint sound of footsteps ascending the stairs. I flip the metal bed over and drag it into a corner of the cell. I'm not gonna make this easy for them. It's late in the game, but this time I intend to put up one hell of a fight. I double up the mattress and put it in front of me. There's not much chance it'll stop a bullet, but it's all I have to protect myself.

The lighted flashlight reaches the top of the steps. A ray of light dances around the room.

"Coach Warden, are you up here?"

The voice sounds like James Fingler, the sheriff's deputy who asked me to help him find bootleggers. Why would he be here? Surely he can't be involved with the car thieves. I don't answer, keeping hidden behind the fortification of the bed.

The flashlight moves down the hallway, first searching the cell next to the stairs then moving to my cell. The light stops on the overturned bed.

"Coach Warden, is that you? It's James Fingler. I came to let you out of jail. You're safe now."

"If I'm safe, how come you turned out the lights?" I ask from behind the bed.

"Coach, I'm sorry if I scared you by turning the lights off. I was trying to keep from climbing those damned circular stairs twice. Maybe I should've come up here first and warned you. Sheriff Williams is in a penny-pinching mode this month. He's trying to save money on the electric bill. We hired an electrician to put the jail lights on a timer. Somehow, the electrician got the light timer crossed up with the prisoner alarm system. If we open the cells after dark, without turning off the lights, the prisoner escape alarm goes off."

"Where are Orval Graves and Billy Hancock?" I ask cautiously, desperately wanting to be convinced he means me no harm. His story about the lights might be true, but it sounds fishy. I'm not about to be duped again, not by anyone connected to the sheriff.

"Billy Hancock? So that's how you got locked in here. Do ya know what they were planning to do with you?"

"Orval said they were gonna take care of me when they came back. I'm sure they had plans to kill me. Last Saturday, I went out to the

Singleton Ranch searching for Keith Murphy. Orval caught me. He and Billy seem to be up to their necks in this car theft business. I suppose they think I know too much."

"Well, I'll be.... I never would've suspected Billy. I guess now we know who's been leaking our information. The sheriff's deputy told me someone saw an Eastland County vehicle in DeLeon. I'll bet it was Billy."

"DeLeon? I don't get it."

"Oh, yeah! Orval and Clifford Graves are in the Comanche County jail. That's how I knew you were here. Mike Goodman, a deputy who works for the Comanche sheriff, called our Sheriff Williams' house. Sheriff Williams is in Fort Worth this weekend so Mrs. Williams had him call me. The deputy claims to know you. Told me they had a fellow in their jail who was bragging about having the Ranger football coach locked in the jail at Eastland."

"Orval and Clifford are in jail?"

His story sounds plausible. How else would he know about Mike Goodman, the deputy who interceded for me at the Comanche hospital? I'm still not totally convinced. This amazing series of events is difficult to believe.

James Fingler points the flashlight at the cell door lock and begins fumbling through a ring of keys.

"Yeah, according to your friend, Clifford's been sniffing around this big Mexican girl in DeLeon. Apparently, Orval and Clifford went by her mother's house, trying to get her to leave with them. When she resisted, they roughed her up and forced her to go. The Mexican girl's mother called her son, then called the DeLeon Constable's office. Her son and a pickup truck load of his Mexican buddies chased Orval and Clifford down. There musta been one heckava ruckus. Mike Goodman said it took four sheriff's deputies and two constables to break it up. The Mexican girl and her brother are in the Comanche hospital. The rest of 'em are in the Comanche County jail."

"Orval mentioned he and Clifford had a big weekend planned, when he and Billy were locking me up. I guess it didn't turn out like he figured," I summarize for the deputy, while I rise up to peek over the bed.

James Fingler's story is too incredible to be a lie. I crawl out from behind the protection of the bed and turn it upright. Now that I can see there's no danger, I'm somewhat embarrassed by the ridiculous fortress.

The deputy finally finds the right key and inserts it into the lock. The cell door swings open. A tremendous sense of relief sweeps over me as he points the flashlight onto my face.

"You look like you've had a long, hard day, Coach. Come on downstairs, and I'll remove those handcuffs. Then I'll give you a ride back to Ranger."

Fingler leads the way while we traverse down the dark circular stairway. He holds the flashlight behind him to light my way. On the first floor we stop at a fusebox where he trips a switch. Suddenly, the jail lights up. We see can see each other's face for the first time.

"Wait here a minute, Coach. I'll get the keys to those handcuffs."

The deputy steps briskly to a desk near the foot of the stairs and retrieves another ring of keys. I hold out my hands while he sorts through the new key ring.

"Coach Warden, you're a very lucky man. If Orval and Clifford hadn't been so anxious to see that Mexican gal, you might be lying in a shallow grave now. Lucky for you they were planning a big weekend. Lucky for you today is Friday."

"Yeah, I'm pretty lucky alright," I agree after some consideration, thinking of the football game I missed.

———

THE SQUAD CAR coasts to a stop, at almost the same spot where Billy Hancock put me in handcuffs some twelve hours earlier. The Hudson sits parked by the side of the road, right where I left it.

I jump out and run to look inside my car. My keys are still in the ignition.

Deputy Fingler wears a worried face when I return to say goodnight and thank him again for getting me out of the jail.

"Coach, you almost got yourself killed today. There's something I gotta tell you, so maybe it won't happen again. Can I trust you to keep what I say strictly to yourself?"

"Of course, James. I would never divulge anything you tell me in confidence."

"Keith Murphy is alive and safe. Sheriff Williams had him moved to Abilene because we didn't have sufficient manpower to protect him.

Murphy is in the protective custody of the Texas Rangers. As soon as he's well enough, he'll testify to the Special Grand Jury. After they issue their indictments, we should bust this car theft operation all to hell."

"Good Lord! I wish I'd known sooner. I could've avoided a potful of troubles."

"That's why I'm telling you now, Coach. I'm hoping you'll stick to coaching football and let us lawmen chase the crooks."

"You'll get no argument from me on that, James. I've played all the cops and robber games I ever wanna play."

———————

I KNOW I SHOULD GO HOME to Juanita. She may be worried about me. But my curiosity about the outcome of the Burkburnett game demands to be satisfied. I start the engine and head toward the football field.

Bulldog Stadium is deserted. The football field is dark, not a light shines anywhere. The football game was over hours ago. Not a solitary soul remains to tell me who won the game.

Sam lives a few blocks away. I've never been invited there to visit, but I'm almost certain I know which house is his.

———————

"OKAY! OKAY! I'M COMING! Hold your horses! You don't need to knock the friggin' door down!" Sam shouts gruffly from behind the door. He obviously resents having his sleep interrupted.

"Sam, it's Stubby. I need to talk with you," I call from his front porch.

Locks unlock and latch handles are pulled back. Suddenly, the door swings open. Sam is clothed in a long red nightgown which extends down to his ankles. I would never have believed this if I wasn't here to see it. I try not to smile or show my amusement at my assistant coach's choice of nightwear.

"Stubby, what are you doing here? Why aren't you in Comanche with your wife and baby?"

"Comanche? Why would I be in Comanche?"

"With your sick baby. We found your note taped to the door of the field house."

"Note? Sam, I never left any note. What did it say?"

"Said you wouldn't be able to attend the football game because you had to rush the baby to Comanche for an emergency operation. Stubby, if you didn't write the note–then who did?"

"Sam, I don't know anything about a note, but my baby's fine. I've been in jail. Just got out. Tell me who won the football game."

"Jail? Why would you be in jail? Did ya do somethin' wrong?"

"Sam, it's a long story–one you won't believe, even when I tell you. I've gotta know–who won the football game?"

"We were all worried about you and your baby. Instead of talking game strategy at halftime, the whole team got together and prayed for the baby. We prayed for you, too," Sam continues, ignoring my question about the game.

"Hmm. You know, it might only be a coincidence, but that was probably a short time before James Fingler showed up to break me out of jail. Sam, I need to know–did we win the ballgame?"

"Good grief! Someone had to bust you outta jail? You mean your baby's okay, and you've been locked up in jail? What on earth for?"

"Please, Sam! I'm dying here! Tell me who won the game. It's late. We can talk about me tomorrow."

"Sure, Stubby. Yeah, we won alright. It was a hellava game. Tied nothing to nothing at the half. Our offense couldn't seem to do anything right. In the third quarter, the offense got revved up and scored twice. We blew 'em away, when we scored two more touchdowns in the fourth. Since we didn't have a place kicker, we had to run for all the extra points. Took four tries, but we finally made the last one. Our defense played their best game of the year, kept Burkburnett down in their end of the field all night."

"Damn!" I say, expressing my unhappiness.

"Stubby, are you sure you're all right? You act like we lost. Hey, we won!"

"Yeah, Sam, I know. You guys won without me. Damn!"

Sam's face signifies he is totally bewildered by my dismal attitude. "I reckon I'll see you tomorrow morning then. Okay, Stubby?"

"What? Yeah. Okay, I'll see you tomorrow."

Watching me walk down the sidewalk to the Hudson, Sam waits beside his half-opened door. When I start the engine, he shakes his head in disbelief, mutters something to himself and shuts the door.

Damn! How could they have won, without me?

IF SOMEONE LEFT A NOTE explaining that Juanita and I had to leave town because of an emergency, you can bet Lucas Masters put them up to it. Yeah, that'd make the perfect excuse for my coaching absence. And the baby story would eliminate any reason for someone going to check with Juanita about my whereabouts. Apparently no one even suspected I was in trouble. No search parties. No report to the police.

Even Juanita wouldn't have missed me until tomorrow morning. Meanwhile, I could be lying dead in a shallow grave, while any trail left by my killers was getting stone cold.

Maybe I should be thankful to be alive, but at this moment, my predominate thought is how I'm gonna get even with Lucas Masters.

"OH, STUBBY, IT'S YOU," Juanita observes sleepily, as I wiggle into bed beside her.

"Yes. It's me, Stubby–your husband. Were you expecting someone else?"

"How did your game go? Did you win?" she asks, still half-asleep and failing to pick up on my weak attempt at humor.

"Yeah, we won. Twenty-five to nothing."

"That's wonderful. I'm so happy for you, darling. You deserve to have lots of good days, like today."

"Yeah, it was a terrific day alright."

"Stubby, I hope you'll sleep better tonight. You kept patting me and waking me up last night. I kept dozing off all day today. I could hardly stay awake."

"Sure, honey. I'm sure I'll sleep like a baby tonight. I've had a long day."

I close my eyes and lie back on my pillow, expecting sleep to come easily.

My eyes pop wide open, reminding me I've been in bed all afternoon.

Chapter Fourteen
The Fifth Week

Monday Afternoon
September 30, 1949

"WELL, HELLO, STRANGER," Pearl welcomes me, when I step through the front door of her café. From the way she greets me, you might think she hasn't seen me in weeks. Actually, I was in here last Wednesday.

"Hi, Pearl. How are things going for you today?" I ask cordially, slipping onto a stool at her lunch counter.

"Probably a lot better than for the Ranger High School football coach," she replies. "Have you seen the papers?"

"No. I was hoping you saved the Abilene Sunday paper. I wanted to check the high school football scores."

"Darlin', you know I wouldn't dare throw the papers away until I was certain you'd read through them. I stacked them on the end of the counter. You want some hot coffee?"

"Sure, Pearl. Coffee would be great. Thanks for saving the papers," I say, sliding across several stools to reach for the stack of newspapers.

"All the teams in your district won last Friday night–Comanche, Eastland, Hamilton, Gorman and Dublin. Plus, they all have winning records. I'd sure hate to be in your shoes for the next few weeks, Coach Warden," Pearl joshes me, as she pours my coffee.

I shall never cease to be amazed at Pearl. The woman is a perpetual fountain of information. She works constantly. I've never caught her reading a newspaper, and yet, she always seems informed about any subject I want to discuss.

Today though, I'd rather she hadn't told me about the teams in my district. I get a certain kick out of checking the football scores in the paper. Even if I'm not familiar with the coach or anyone playing on the team, there's a kind of special nostalgic thrill in discovering which city won their high school football game. Knowing all the teams in my district won last weekend, before I open the sports pages, somehow takes away some of the fun.

"Stubby, I heard you missed the football game Friday night. Are you having problems with the new baby?" Pearl asks while I scan through the sports section for the high school scores.

"No, the baby is fine. I was in jail," I answer inattentively, absorbed in searching for the high school scores.

Pearl's head pops up from behind the cake display.

"Darlin', I've warned you about lying and about the consequences. Now, tell me the real reason you weren't at the game."

I had no intent of starting something with Pearl, but from her livid reaction, it's quite obvious she hasn't heard about my jail experience. This is too good an opportunity to pass up.

"Like I said, Pearl, I was in jail," I tell her nonchalantly.

She stares at me intently, trying to make up her mind if I'm joking. Finally, she shrugs her shoulders and goes back to her cleaning, convinced I'm pulling some cheap gag on her. In her mind she is refusing to bite on my bait.

I decide to let her stew. Her curiosity will eventually get the best of her.

District 8-A is composed of six teams. Because the cities in the district are small and don't represent many readers, the coverage in the Abilene and Fort Worth papers is generally rather limited. If our district or one of its teams is mentioned, it usually amounts to only a line or two.

Nonetheless, this year District 8-A is recognized by the sportswriters as one of the toughest in the state, with every member team having sufficient talent to contend for the district title. I scan quickly through the scores.

Hamilton	20	San Saba	7
Comanche	33	Coleman	13
Dublin	14	Grandbury	7
Gorman	19	Cross Plains	14
Eastland	21	Albany	14

Good Lord! Eastland has beaten Albany. Eastland always fields a good football team. Looks like they'll be double tough this year.

Hamilton won. We play them in four weeks. Hamilton is the pre-season favorite to win the district.

Comanche won. We play them this Friday night. I suppose we have our work cut out for us. Pearl's analysis is correct. None of our district games will be an easy win.

Checking through the other game results, I find several which have special interest for me.

Slaton   28   Post   21

After all these years, Roy Stillwell is still coaching at Slaton High. I'll bet he's feeling no pain this morning.

Stamford   18   Munday   6

Holy cow! Stamford finally won a football game. That has to be the most points they've scored in a game this season. Maybe my telephone advice to Carl Cook helped his offense. Perhaps he'll get to keep his job, at least for another week anyway.

Graham   39   Cisco   6

Hmmm. That's four losses in a row for the Cisco Loboes. By now, the new Cisco head coach is up to his neck in hot water. My ex-roommate Jerry Lowe is probably enjoying watching his boss take the heat.

I finish my coffee and leave a nickel on the counter. Football practice starts in forty-five minutes. I need to hurry.

"You're not gonna tell me, are you?" Pearl calls from the kitchen.

"Tell you what?" I say, reaching for the front door handle.

"Where you were Friday night," she answers. Her gnawing curiosity is plainly showing now.

"Pearl, I already told you. I was in jail." I wave goodbye and step swiftly through the door.

"Stubby Warden, you rascal! Come back here! You come back here this minute! You can't run off and leave me like this," I hear her cry, while I dash for the Hudson.

The café front door swings open, and Pearl runs out onto the side walk as I drive away. She points a forefinger at me and wags her hand to shame me.

Wednesday Afternoon
October 2, 1949

IT IS ALMOST DARK when the last player finishes dressing and departs from the field house. The grandstands cast an enormous dark shadow across the football field as I lock the door and walk to the parking lot.

At my insistence we practiced long past our customary quitting time. Sam and Alfred were ready to send the team to the showers when I interceded. The team's complacency during the practice session had me concerned. I sent the squad back on the field and had them run each of our offensive plays over and over, insisting that each player carry out his assignment perfectly.

The extra practice didn't help. It only made my players more lethargic and irritable. After practice, Sam and Alfred were anxious to leave, probably perturbed with my dogged tenacity. I stayed to lock up.

G.C. Boswell is waiting for me in the stadium parking lot. I've never understood why he chooses to wait for me out here instead of coming inside. Perhaps he feels intimidated by the presence of the football players–the way I feel walking the high school hallways. Perhaps he feels the varsity field house is my private sanctum–not to be invaded unless specifically invited.

"Good evening, Stubby. My goodness, you certainly kept the boys practicing late tonight. Are you expecting a tough game Friday night?"

"G.C., there aren't any easy games on our schedule. Comanche will be as tough as anybody we've faced. I'll work our kids until mid-night if that's what it takes to get 'em ready." I answer his friendly question much too harshly, letting my frustrations spill out.

The superintendent takes my comment seriously. "Coach Warden, surely you wouldn't keep the boys out that late. They have homework.

Some of the farm boys have chores to do after they get home."

"Relax, G.C. I've had a long and disappointing day. Maybe I over-stated my case. Yeah, I'm anxious about the Comanche game, but at this point in the season, more practice isn't gonna make us play better. What I need is to find some way to keep the team focused on this week's game instead of basking in the glory of last week's win."

"I'm sure you'll figure out something, Stubby. You always have before."

Boswell pauses. His eyes wander across the parking lot. He has something on his mind, something unpleasant he needs to get off his chest. This visit is more than a casual delivery of my bonus money.

"Stubby, I think we should talk. Some of your football benefactors–the ones who contribute to your bonus–were concerned about your not being present to coach the game Friday night."

It was inevitable that someone would eventually approach me on this subject. It seems like everyone in Ranger is preoccupied about my absence during the Burkburnett game. So far, only Deputy James Fingler knows all the details. Hoping to avoid revealing my knowledge of the car thieves, I've been careful not to divulge any specific facts about how I wound up in jail.

My story is that I was arrested because of some outstanding traffic tickets. No one has challenged me on the story, although I seriously doubt if anyone actually believes it.

Boswell's eyes refuse to meet mine directly. His steady gaze is fixed on a point behind me. This is not a task he enjoys. I wonder who could've complained so strongly to make him accept such unpleasant duty.

"When you say some–do you mean several donors, or do you mean Lucas Masters?"

"Alright, Stubby. Lucas Masters is the person most concerned." Boswell finally looks directly at me. His eyes don't disguise his uneasy anxiety.

This discussion is beginning to stink badly. It was two of Lucas Masters' cronies who were responsible for my missing the game. Masters knows that. What kind of rotten trick is he up to now? Maybe my generous benefactor has decided not to pay for games won–when his hired goons have the head coach locked in jail.

"G.C., you're not trying to tell me, if I'm not present at the games we win, they don't count, are you?" I counter angrily.

"Coach, please don't take this so personal. I'm just the messenger. Lucas says he's willing to do what's right, but he wanted me to ask if you thought it was fair to pay you a bonus for a football game you didn't actually coach."

Slowly the rationale for this discussion becomes crystal clear. This is just another of Lucas Masters' ploys to intimidate me and let me know he is still in control. Boswell is a straight shooter. I need to stay cool and respond to his question sensibly. No need to take my animosity out on him.

"I don't have a good answer, G.C. I simply assumed I'd always get the bonus, as promised, when my team wins. I had our young men prepared to win. I spent the entire day last Sunday, watching films and studying the Burkburnett offense. Coach Aills and I worked with our defense every day last week, teaching them techniques for stopping the Burkburnett single wing attack. But perhaps Lucas is right. A head coach should be present at every game. If Lucas and the other donors want to keep my bonus money this week, I'll understand."

"Coach, no one has suggested we not pay your bonus. Lucas only asked me to get your response to his question. I hope you understand why I had to ask?"

"I understand only too well. Maybe I should go by Lucas' office and explain everything to him in person."

"Stubby, that's not a good idea. Let me handle this. We don't want to put your bonus arrangement in jeopardy. If Lucas wants to talk with you further, I'll let you know." Boswell is obviously troubled by my offer to personally meet with Masters.

"Alright, Mister Superintendent, I will respect your good judgement. But you can tell Mister Masters that, unless he has other plans, I don't expect to be missing any more football games."

LEANING AGAINST THE HUDSON, I fold the three crisp one hundred dollar bills and stick them in my shirt pocket while I watch the superintendent walk to his car. Collecting the bonus money lifts my low spirits.

Hell's bells! Why should I let myself be intimidated? If I continue to be rewarded like this, I can handle Lucas Masters' silly mind games–at least until the end of the season.

JUANITA AND LITTLE JERRY ARE WAITING ANXIOUSLY on the front porch when I arrive home. She picks up the baby and hurries to meet me while I gather up my playbook and practice notes.

"Hello, sweetheart. How did your day go? It's awfully late. Jerry and I were beginning to worry," Juanita says, giving me a peck on the lips.

"I guess you could say I've had better days. Gimme some time to calm down some before you ask too many questions, unless you like hateful answers."

"Here, Stubby. Why don't you hold your son? He'll make you feel better. Let me carry your things."

Juanita is right. The baby is like soothing medicine on my tortured soul. Holding my small son in my arms makes all my troubles seem unimportant. Little Jerry smiles at me when I caress his soft cheek.

My worries about the complex problems of the day have almost evaporated when Juanita drops her bombshell.

"Stubby. Jerry Lowe called the Creager house for you this afternoon. Since you weren't here, I took his call. He wanted to tell you the Cisco head coach has resigned. The Cisco school board has given Jerry the head coaching job for the remainder of the season."

"Jerry Lowe is the head football coach for Cisco High School! Well, I'll be damned! I guess the stinky stuff has really hit the fan in Cisco," I laugh.

"Stubby Warden, watch your language! You should know better than to curse around the baby."

"Oh, yeah, I gotta watch that. I just can't believe Jerry Lowe is the Cisco head football coach. We play them in three weeks, you know."

"Yes, Jerry mentioned that. Darling, Jerry said the telephone operator informed him she has instructions to forward all your calls to the Creager house. Why would she tell him that?" Juanita asks inquisitively, as she trails behind Little Jerry and me.

Thursday Morning
October 3, 1949

"IT'S HARD TO BELIEVE I haven't spoken with Jerry Lowe since the end of August–since before our Breckenridge game. My closest friend lives and coaches only twenty miles away, and yet, I've been too occupied with coaching duties to check on him. Cisco's football season may have degenerated into a total disaster, but I never doubted Jerry would land on his feet. Perhaps I should be feeling sorry for his head coach," I muse to myself, as I drive along 8th Street on my way to the Cisco High practice field.

A lone workman, riding a tiny tractor, is mowing at the opposite end of the practice field. I rub my eyes to make sure I'm not seeing things. The man atop the small mower is dressed in work clothes, wearing a pair of overalls. The workman is my friend Jerry Lowe. Recognizing my car, he waves at me, raises the mower blades and steers the tractor toward me.

"Stubby Warden, if you aren't a sight for sore eyes," Jerry exclaims, shutting off the tractor's engine.

"Hi, Jerry. It's good to see you, too. Juanita tells me you're the head football coach now. Congratulations."

"Stubby, before you start shaking my hand too heartily, you should know the school board only gave me the job until the end of the season. If we don't start winning, I'll be gone."

"What happened to the old head coach? Why did he resign?"

"He had no choice. It was either resign or get fired. I told you about his skipping some of the 'two a day' practices. Well, he didn't do much better after the football season started. Eventually, some of the school board found him out. When we kept losing, they gave him an ultimatum. He chose to resign."

"Jerry, how are you gonna turn your team around this late in the season? You've been getting your socks beat off every week. I read the newspapers."

"That's why I called you, good buddy. I was hoping you could help me. Remember your offer to help me with the offense last July when I got the assistant's job? As long as old flower butt was head coach, I didn't much care whether we won or not. Now I'm the man in the spotlight. How about giving me some help? Whatta you say?"

"I'm not sure what you're asking, Jerry. Are you offering me a coaching job? I already have a good one."

Maybe I shouldn't turn him down too quickly. Only a couple of months ago I'd have jumped at the opportunity to be his assistant. Like Carl Cook, the Stamford coach, I could be losing and facing a win or resign ultimatum myself a few weeks from now.

"No. No, Stubby. I know you'd never leave your Ranger job. Heck, you're winning, and you've got everything under control over there. Look, I hear you're having great success with that 'Tee Option' offense our ex-teammate invented. Could you teach the offense to my Cisco kids? Now that I'm the head coach, I intend to concentrate on what I do best–defense."

"Gee, Jerry, I don't know. My Bulldogs begin district play this Friday night. I don't know where I'd find the time."

"Come on, good buddy. I really need your help. If I lose this job, you might have to hire me as your assistant coach."

The prospect of having Jerry as one of my assistants is more than enough to convince me.

"Okay, I'll do what I can."

"It won't take all that much time. I promise. I'll have my team practice on Saturdays, Sundays–whenever it's more convenient for you. You can help on those days, can't you?"

"Saturdays, maybe. But, not on Sundays," I object meekly.

Jerry Lowe is a smooth negotiator. I've always been a sucker for his velvet-coated arguments. And, in spite of his self-serving ways, I truly do like him.

Damn! Now I've promised to teach his football team my "Option Tee" offense. Jerry is a genius at defense. What if his Cisco team were to beat mine when we play in three weeks? Oh, Lord, have mercy on me! The only thing worse than losing a football game to Jerry Lowe would be having him for an assistant coach.

Friday Afternoon
October 4, 1949

THE COMANCHE GAME will be our first district game–the first major step toward our goal of winning the District 8-A championship and advancing into the state football playoffs. After three consecutive victories a spirit of expectancy for the Bulldog football team begins to surface among Ranger citizens. Still smarting from the disappointment of last year's losing season, the city is anxious and ready to support a winning football team.

Freshly painted banners proclaiming "We Love Our Bulldogs" spring up along Main Street. New signs, declaring their support for the Bulldogs, appear in downtown merchants' windows. Maroon and white streamers fly from almost every moving car. Car windows are painted in white shoe polish with signage which urges the team to "Beat the Indians–Go Bulldogs!"

Come Friday night, more than half Ranger's population will travel to Comanche to watch the game. Since I must ride with the football team, Juanita has made arrangements to ride with Price and Phyliss. They'll drive to the Kimbrough Ranch first. Edna has offered to babysit Little Jerry while the others attend the game. To everyone's surprise, Juanita reports Luther is planning to attend the game with them. Although we had an amicable parting last week, I have little doubt that Luther will be fervently rooting for the Comanche team.

COMANCHE'S FOOTBALL FIELD is only a few blocks west of the courthouse square, off U.S. Highway 67 toward Brownwood. Leeman Gentry, our bus driver, expertly maneuvers our bus across the rough graveled terrain behind the home side bleachers, pulling to a stop only a few feet from the players' entrance gate.

Unlike our home field, which still exhibits scars carved into the grass surface during the muddy Albany game, the Comanche football field is in excellent condition. Thick, dark green bermuda grass blankets the playing field. The metal grandstands have been recently painted in bright silver.

Comanche's football stadium seats about fifteen-hundred, about two-thirds the capacity of Bulldog Stadium. Tonight, these bleachers will be filled and overflowing. Football fans will be lined, elbow to elbow, along the four-foot high chain-link fence which separates the playing field from the grandstands.

People are already at work in the concession booths, preparing for tonight's sellout crowd. The simmering aroma of hamburgers cooking on the concession grills whets my appetite.

Remembering Alfred's addiction to the hamburger smells, I glance back to see if he has also picked up on the smell of frying hamburgers. Alfred has stopped beneath the grandstands. His eyes are closed, and his head is tilted backward. A contented smile is affixed upon his face as he breathes in deeply.

There's plenty of time before the game. We're in no hurry. I pause to inhale another long, deep breath of my own before following my players into the visitor's dressing facility.

—————

Friday Night
October 4, 1949

WHILE THE TEAM STANDS ATTENTIVELY along the sideline, I search the stands for Juanita. Finally, as Comanche's band finishes playing their school song, I spot her. She, Price, Phyliss and Luther are sitting about ten rows up in a reserved section of the home-side bleachers, almost on the fifty yard line. I wonder what strings Luther could've pulled to wrangle such good seats. Such excellent seats could never have been purchased on short notice.

Luther doesn't impress me as a rabid football fan. There's no telling how he got those tickets, or how much he had to pay. And he did it to show off for Price and Phyliss.

—————

FORTUNATELY, WE WIN the coin toss. Our captains, Elder, Thompson and Hamrick, elect to receive. With Brownlee injured, we are at a severe disadvantage when we kick off.

My receiving team flocks around me while the Ranger band blares loudly, making it almost impossible to hear inside our pre-game huddle. I repeat the instructions twice, to make sure everyone understands. We decide to return the ball up the middle of the field, hoping to surprise our opponents.

Sam collars Patterson, Sutton and Hummel before they run onto the field. He gives them a few last words of instruction, then slaps them on their buttocks and sends them onto the playing field.

"I reminded them not to bunch up on the return and to keep moving together upfield. Let our ball carrier use his blockers like shields to avoid the tacklers," he explains, seeing my inquiring stare.

"Good idea. I hope this works, Sam. We could be starting our first play from the ten if it doesn't."

"Don't worry, Stubby. It'll work," Sam assures me. His hands are behind his back, hiding fingers which are almost certainly crossed for luck.

Comacho fields the kickoff at the five, takes a couple of short steps in the direction of the right sideline then cuts back sharply to get behind a human wall our blockers have formed at mid-field. Our wall of blockers moves steadily upfield, repelling each Comanche defender who tries to penetrate. Comacho is brought down from behind at the forty-eight, only a step away from breaking past their last defender.

This is our most successful kickoff return of the year. A steep incline of Bulldog fans behind us rises to cheer in wild celebration at our excellent start. Ranger cheerleaders begin cartwheeling along the sideline while our band launches into an ear-splitting fight song.

"I knew it would work! I knew it would work!" Sam yells to me.

"Yeah! Me too! There was never a doubt about it," I yell back to him.

In the dressing room before the game, we decided to try a pitchout to Simpson around the left side on our first play, if we got a decent kickoff return.

Hut. Hut. Jones takes the snap. He moves down the left side behind the offensive line. The defensive end charges in, leaving Simpson wide open. Jones' lateral flies high over Simpson's head.

Two Comanche defenders run past a surprised Simpson to recover the football at our thirty-six.

"What the hell! How could that happen? Nobody even touched Jones," Sam bellows, sounding both irritated and astounded by our sudden change in fortunes.

"I couldn't see exactly what happened, but we better get the defensive team ready. Now Comanche will really be fired up. They weren't expecting us to give them a quick, easy turnover."

We huddle with our defense on the sideline, instructing them not to let the unexpected turnover affect their play. I remind my players they have shut down much better teams than this Comanche Indian club and to play their defensive positions the way we've practiced.

My pleas not to let the early turnover affect our defensive play go unheeded. Our Bulldog players seem dazed and confused by their sudden plight. The Indian quarterback, finding our defense out of position, drops back and throws a perfect pass to his black and gold flanker back streaking down the left sideline. Touchdown Comanche.

Our defense recovers to block their extra point try. With less than a minute expired on the game clock, the scoreboard reads:

COMANCHE 6 VISITOR 0

Our defensive players stagger off the field with an air of disbelief. This Bulldog squad hasn't been behind in a game since we lost to Albany four weeks ago. The swaggering overconfidence I noticed in my players earlier this week has quickly changed to panic. This football team had convinced themselves they were invincible. Now, they suddenly realize they could easily lose this game.

Comacho receives Comanche's kickoff at the six and returns it up the right side to the twenty-four. While the receiving team runs off the field, I catch Reed Jones.

"Reed, are you okay?" I ask.

"Yeah, Coach, I think so. My side was hurting some during the warm-up exercises, but I'm fine now."

"You wanna sit out this series? If you're hurting, maybe we should let Buddy run the offense for a while."

"No sir. I'm the quarterback. The team is depending on me to get us back in the game. Please lemme stay in."

"Alright, Reed, you're the quarterback. Get in there."

OUR OFFENSE CAN'T SEEM TO GET IN GEAR. On the first play Jones gets his feet tangled up with our left guard Patterson and loses two yards. Jones' handoff to Hamrick on the second play is bobbled. Hamrick recovers the ball in the backfield for a loss of four.

Hut. Hut. Jones keeps the ball on an option right for a five yard gain on third down. After three offensive plays, we have a net loss of one yard. Fourth and eleven from our own twenty-three. We send Jensen in to punt.

Jensen's booming punt travels more than forty yards, going out of bounds at the Comanche thirty-six. Our defense recoups from the trauma of their first series to stop the Indian offense. In three plays Comanche gains only two yards.

We obviously have the superior team, and we're only six points down. There's no reason to panic. We can still come back and win. All we need is to execute our plays.

With Davenport and Charles Williams charging savagely toward him, the Indian punter barely manages to get his kick away. The football rolls to our thirty yard line. We gain seven yards on the punt exchange.

Jones glances inquisitively toward me before he starts onto the field. I point my hand in the direction of Comanche's goal line, making it clear I expect him to move the team in that direction.

This time, on our second possession of the game, the offense begins to roll.

Hut. Hut. Jones carries the ball over left tackle for a gain of five.

Hut. Hut. A pitchout to Hamrick around right end nets us eight yards and a first down.

Comanche's defense, responding to our success at running the football, begins to bunch up near the line of scrimmage. The Indian defensive backs move up close behind the linebackers. Two running plays net us only eight yards.

"Comacho, get in there for Hamrick. Tell Jones to run sixty-eight, pass right. Hurry now, before we break our huddle."

"Yes sir. Sixty-eight, pass right," Comacho calls back to me as he dashes onto the field, still trying to snap his chin strap.

Comacho taps Hamrick on the shoulder and enters the huddle. Hamrick glances up at the scoreboard clock, then hightails it toward us at the visitor bench.

Hut. Hut. Jones takes the snap, fakes to Dorsey and nimbly drops back into a pocket between his two halfbacks. He waits patiently behind the impenetrable blocking of Simpson and Comacho while Ralph Rogers sprints downfield, slanting toward an open space behind Comanche's defensive backs.

Rogers breaks clear behind the last defensive back. Jones draws back and throws the ball. His wobbly pass is short. The ball flutters end-over-end, landing in the hands of a waiting black and gold defender. Big Ralph sinks to his knees in disbelief. He was at least ten yards beyond Comanche's nearest defender.

After a frantic chase, the Comanche interceptor is brought down at our forty-five by Reed Jones who threw the interception.

Watching us self-destruct each time we have the ball motivates the Comanche team and their fans. The home side bleachers come alive. Indian fans stay on their feet yelling and stomping their feet. Total bedlam breaks out in the home side bleachers as their Indian team, taking advantage of the turnover, begins to advance the ball steadily toward our end zone.

From the three yard line the Indian quarterback rolls out to his right, fakes a pass, and runs in untouched for the touchdown. This time their extra point kick is good.

Comanche   13   Ranger   0

In spite of my begging, my pleading, and finally, my threat to make the entire team walk back to Ranger if we lose, our offense is unable to move the football, or to even make another first down, for the remainder of the first quarter. Only Jensen's long punts and inspired defensive play keep us in the game.

BLAMING MY BALL CARRIERS for our offensive woes, I substitute Kenneth Williams, Comacho and Phillips into the backfield on our first possession of the second quarter. For a brief time the change helps. With Comacho carrying twice around right end, we make our second first down of the night.

A fumble by Phillips on the next play gives Comanche the football on our forty-six.

"Eddie, what's the matter with you, son! Can't you hang onto the ball?" I scream angrily at my normally sure-handed fullback, when he returns to the sidelines.

"I'm sorry, Coach. I never got a good hold on the football. Reed handed me the ball with the end turned up."

"Come on, Phillips! You can't blame the quarterback for your mistake. Next time, you hold onto the ball, or I'll have you running wind sprints next week 'til you drop. You understand?"

"Sure, Coach. You're right. The fumble was my fault. I won't fumble again."

After my confrontation with Phillips, Alfred strolls to the bench to talk with him. A few minutes later my huge assistant walks over to stand beside me at the edge of the field.

Getting another golden opportunity because of our fumble, Comanche is again advancing methodically toward our end zone.

"Coach Warden, I talked with Phillips, Hamrick and Simpson. They all tell me they're having trouble with Jones' handoffs. I think somethin' is wrong with Reed tonight. He's in some kind of pain."

"You could be right, Alfred. I talked with him at the beginning of the game. He said his side was hurting."

I pause for a minute, watching the game and considering the consequences of removing Jones from the game, then give Alfred my decision.

"I don't wanna take him outta the game, Alfred."

"I'm just telling you, Coach. Thought you needed to know."

"Thanks, Alfred. I appreciate the information. I'll have a talk with Reed before I let him go back in."

Our defense is tiring. They've been on the field most of the game. With all the offensive turnovers and our lack of first downs, they've had almost no rest. They need a breather. Their exhausted condition becomes evident as Comanche easily drives the football downfield.

When Comanche nears our goal line, our defense stiffens, valiantly holding the black and gold squad at the two yard line for three plays. Our ferocious defensive effort comes too late, only prolonging the inevitable. On fourth down the Indian quarterback sneaks in for the touchdown. The extra point kick is wide.

Comanche   19   Ranger   0

While we watch Comanche's kickoff, I talk with Reed Jones. He assures me again that he is fine. He says the pain in his side returned for a time but has now dissipated. My quarterback is as tough as they come. Disregarding all my coaching instincts to replace him, I send him in again to run the offense.

———————

"COACH WARDEN, I NEED TO CHANGE UNIFORMS. It's almost halftime," Frankie Jensen informs me.

I glance at the scoreboard clock. Less than two minutes are left until the half. Comanche has the football in their end of the field.

"Okay, Frankie, you better get going. Tell the band to do their best. Maybe Ranger can win the halftime show."

"I sure will, Coach. I'll tell 'em to play, 'to beat the band'–to beat the Comanche band," Frankie mimics, picking up on my sarcastic remark about the traditional fierce competition between opposing school bands during their halftime presentations.

Seeing Jensen leave for the dressing room, Sam steps over to talk with me.

"Stubby, we could be in bad trouble if we need to punt before the half," Sam declares, reminding me of our fragile kicking situation.

"I know, Sam. Maybe we'll get lucky. Maybe Comanche will make a long drive and run off some of the clock for us."

My attempt to make light of our precarious position is lost on my assistant coach. He is seriously concerned.

"Stubby, with Jensen in the band and with Brownlee's leg broke, we ain't got a soul on the team who can kick the football more than thirty yards."

"How about McKinney? If we get in a bind, we can let him punt. At least he won't fumble the ball."

"I don't know, Stubby. I don't like it. Let's hope we don't have to punt."

Our tough defensive play stops Comanche short of a first down, forcing them to punt. Comanche's punter kicks the ball out of bounds at our twenty-two. Less than a minute remains in the half when our offense takes the field.

Hut. Hut. Jones keeps the ball over right tackle for two yards. Comanche calls timeout.

"Stubby, did you talk with McKinney about punting? It looks like Comanche wants another crack at scoring on us before the half. If we don't make this first down, we're gonna need a punter."

"Yeah, Sam, I talked with Billy. He thinks he can handle the kicking role for one punt. I reminded him his main objective is to avoid a blocked punt. He promised to catch the football and drop down on one knee if he experiences trouble."

Hut. Hut. Jones hands the ball off to Phillips. Our fullback is stopped for no gain. Comanche uses another timeout. The clock ticks down to less than twenty seconds.

Hut. Hut. Jones fumbles the snap. He falls on the ball for a two yard loss. Comanche calls timeout again. The Indians have only one timeout left.

"Lord, let us get this one punt off. Just let us make it to the half without them scoring again," I overhear Sam praying.

I say a similar prayer myself.

McKinney lines up some fifteen yards behind Thompson to take the snap.

Hut. Hut. Two lines of determined young bodies collide. Grunts of agony roll across the field. Gilbert Thompson topples over into our backfield. The snap from center is high, sailing through McKinney's raised, clutching hands.

The ball rolls into the end zone as time runs out. A speedy, black and gold Indian player gallops past McKinney to recover the football. Touchdown Comanche.

No one seems to notice or even care when the Indian quarterback fumbles the ball on the extra point try. A wild party is underway at the Comanche bench. It's halftime, and they have put the game away.

Comanche   25   Ranger   0

"COACH WARDEN! COACH, OVER HERE," a voice calls to me from behind the chain-link fence. The sound of a familiar voice jolts me back to the present. While I was watching the Ranger band assemble under the goal posts, I was trying to recall a similar time, back in Slaton or at A&M, when my team was behind by this many points at the half. We never were.

The voice belongs to Mike Goodman, the Comanche sheriff's deputy. I hop over the wooden visitors' bench and run to greet my deputy friend.

"Mike! Hello! Hey, what're you doing here? Doesn't your boy have a game tonight?" I ask, while I reach across the short fence to shake his hand.

"Yeah, Coach. DeLeon plays at Throckmorton tonight. It's a game our boys should win. Sure wish I could be there. I'll have to miss it, though. Sheriff Bonner wanted me to be here for extra security. We had some problems with that Coleman bunch last Friday night."

"Mike, I owe you another thanks. Your phone call to the Eastland sheriff last Friday saved my neck. I don't know how I'll ever repay you."

"No problem, Coach. I'm glad I could help. It's my pleasure to call you a friend. Say, what's wrong with your team? These don't look like the same kids who played in DeLeon three weeks ago."

"I'll be darned if I know what's wrong with us, Mike. We can't seem to do anything right tonight."

"Well, I hope you play better in the second half."

"Thanks, Mike. I'd better get to our locker room."

"Coach Warden, about those two brothers we had locked in our jail–Clifford and Orval Graves."

"Yeah, what about 'em."

"The judge set bail for them yesterday–five thousand dollars each. Some fellow from Ranger put up their bail. We released them from jail this afternoon. I thought you'd wanna know."

CLIFFORD AND ORVAL are out of jail. They'll probably come looking for me again. Mike Goodman advised me to be careful. He said they are two mean hombres, I tell myself, turning the corner to the visitor's dressing facility. My thoughts are abruptly interrupted when I bump into Alfred. His wide white eyes are stricken with panic.

"Coach Warden, come quick! Reed Jones is pissin' blood! He's passed out on the restroom floor!"

SAM IS KNEELING beside Reed Jones when I enter the restroom. Most of the Bulldog squad has crowded around their fallen quarterback.

"Okay, everyone step back!" I command, using my most authoritative voice. "Reed will be fine. Everyone step back and give him room to breathe."

Obeying my orders, the players move back a few steps. I crouch down next to Sam.

"What's wrong with him, Sam? Did he say anything?" I whisper lowly.

"Darned if I know, Stubby. He was laying here on the floor when I came in. Maybe we should get him to a hospital."

"I've already sent Alfred to get the ambulance. Reed told me his side was hurting him before the game. You think it could be something he ate?"

"It might be, Stubby, but I'm afraid it's somethin' a heckava lot more serious than a stomachache."

NEWS OF OUR QUARTERBACK'S CONDITION spreads through the stadium like wildfire. By the time the ambulance arrives, a huge crowd of Ranger fans has congregated outside the dressing building. Several of our team members take charge, shoving the crowd back while the ambulance crew transports an unconscious Jones through the maze of people and places him in the rear of the ambulance.

Radford Jones and a woman who I assume is Reed's mother push through the multitude of curious people. The woman is sobbing.

"Coach Warden, what's wrong with my boy?" the quarterback's father demands.

"We don't know, Red. The ambulance is taking him to the Comanche hospital. A doctor should be on his way there now to examine Reed."

"You think it would be okay if Blanche and I ride in the ambulance with our son? She's terribly worried about him."

"I don't know why not. You want me to go with you?"

Radford Jones steps back to look me straight in the eyes. "Coach, you can't leave. You've got a game to play here. Me and the Missus, we'll take care of Reed. You and the rest of the team go out there and win us a football game."

THESE ARE NOT THE CIRCUMSTANCES I would've chosen to test my theory about Buddy Hamrick being the best quarterback to run my "Option Tee" offense, but this is the way the hand has been dealt me. Now is as good a chance as I'll have to find out if he can handle the job.

Because of the confusion with the ambulance and the crowd, the game officials give us an extra five minutes before beginning the second half. I assemble the team around me in the dressing room.

"Alright, men, you all know we're a better team than that bunch of Comanche clowns. Maybe our problem during the first half was at quarterback. Maybe you guys thought these Comanche kids had read your newspaper clippings and would lay down and roll over. Now we all know better. Is anyone here ready to throw in the towel and go home?"

"No!" the team screams back at me. Their response is deafening.

"Okay, then. Let's go out there and score some touchdowns. Twenty-five points isn't enough to beat us. How about it? Can you men score four lousy touchdowns in the second half?"

"Yeah!" the players yell back. Some of the players jump up to shove on each other and butt helmets. These kids are ready to play. I need to wrap this up and get them on the field.

"Buddy, when we get the football–you're the quarterback. Comacho, you take Buddy's position at right halfback. You men on defense–not one stinking first down for the Indians in the second half. You hold 'em, and we'll win this game for Reed. Okay, now go!"

The tiny building trembles as the entire team charges for the front door. Several players bounce against the door jambs when they barrel through, knocking off a section of wooden trim.

After the team clamors out of the building, Sam bends down to pick up a broken sliver of wood and places it carefully up on the window sill.

"Stubby, you ever see a football game where a team came back from a twenty-five point halftime deficit?"

"No, I never have. Have you?"

"Nope. But someone, somewhere, must've done it before. Don't you think?"

"Yeah, Sam. I'm sure some team must've done it before," I answer, trying to sound confident.

––––––––––

IN SPITE OF THE LOPSIDED SCORE, our Ranger fans don't seem discouraged. They are loud and vocal with their support while the team warms up on the sidelines.

Searching for Juanita, I gaze across the field to inspect the home side grandstands. I'm disappointed to find four vacant seats where she and my in-laws were sitting when the game began.

Maybe they gave up on my team and returned to the ranch. I wouldn't blame them. This hasn't been much of a football game. Luther will enjoy telling Edna about the poor showing by my Bulldogs. He's probably bragging to Price about how the Comanche boys are better coached.

Damn, I would've loved to have won this game.

With Brownlee on crutches, Billy McKinney handles the second half kickoff. His kick is a line drive to an Indian receiver on the twenty-eight yard line. Yung and Barnes crash through to bring him down at the thirty-five. Comanche's ball carrier staggers dizzily on his way to their huddle.

Displaying his conviction that the game is out of reach, the Indian coach starts an entirely new offensive team to run his first series of plays. I ponder whether his intent is to hold the score down, like we did in our DeLeon and Stamford games. Good grief, I hope not. That would make our loss even more embarrassing.

Our revitalized defense makes this new offensive team pay for their coach's insolence. In three plays we push them back six yards. Pearson and Sutton are in their backfield, clobbering their quarterback on every play. The Comanche coach is visibly unhappy with his new quarterback's performance. He shouts angrily at the Indian quarterback while their punting team goes in to kick.

Simpson receives the punt. He dodges through several waves of black and gold tacklers, then runs out of bounds near the mid-field stripe.

Buddy Hamrick pauses next to me at the sideline before he enters the game. He seems nervous. He stomps at the ground several times with his cleats.

"Coach Warden, I'm scared. What if I mess up, like I did in the Albany game?"

I place my hands on his shoulder pads and turn him around to face me.

"Hey, Buddy. Our team is twenty-five points behind. No one expects us to win. I don't expect us to win. All you gotta do is go in there and execute our offense the way I know you can. I don't want you to worry about winning. You understand? I don't want you to worry about winning."

"Okay, Coach. I'll do the best I can, but I wish Reed was here to play quarterback."

"Me too. But he's not here. Listen, Buddy, don't try to carry the whole load out there. If you get in trouble, call timeout and come to the sideline. We'll give you all the help we can. Now get in there!"

––––––––––

HAMRICK FUMBLES THE FOOTBALL on his first snap from center. The ball rolls around in our backfield with Hamrick and Dorsey chasing after it. Our entire bench breathes a sigh of relief when Dorsey finally recovers for a five yard loss.

"Now, ain't that a fine way to start. We sure as hell ain't gonna win this game playing like that," Sam grumbles.

"It's just not our night, Sam. We can't seem to do anything right," I gloomily concede.

Hut. Hut. Hamrick takes the ball and moves to his right behind the line. He laterals to Comacho–too soon. Comanche's defensive end reaches out to slap the ball to the ground. Comacho reacts quickly to recover the ball for a six yard loss.

"Holy crap!" Sam hollers. "Stubby, tell me when this thing is over. I can't bear to watch any more." My disillusioned assistant wanders over to the bench and slings a dirty white towel over his head. I resist a very strong inclination to join him.

Our steadfast supporters in the visitor's bleachers behind us become restless. A number of Ranger fans rise to their feet and begin gathering up their belongings, preparing to leave the stadium.

Hut. Hut. Hamrick takes the ball, fakes to Dorsey and moves to the right behind his line. He fakes a pitchout to Comacho, then tucks the ball under his arm and runs inside the Indian defensive end. Elder knocks the outside linebacker off his feet with a crushing block. Hamrick scrambles up the sidelines to the Comanche thirty-four where he is finally shoved out of bounds.

Hearing the loud cheers from the Ranger bleachers, Sam peeks out from beneath his towel. Ranger fans, who were about to leave, stop and begin returning to their seats.

"What happened? How'd we get the ball all the way down there?" Sam asks, jumping to his feet.

"Maybe you should keep your head under the towel, Sam. Buddy Hamrick just made a first down and our longest run of the season."

Hut. Hut. Hamrick runs the same play, only to the left side. Stiles levels the outside linebacker while Hamrick freezes the defensive end, by faking a lateral to Simpson. Hamrick keeps the ball and streaks to the sideline. Comanche's safetyman pushes Hamrick out of bounds at the four.

"Phillips, where are you?"

"Right here, Coach. You want me to go in for Dorsey?" the young fullback asks expectantly, running up beside me.

"Eddie, you tell Hamrick to run thirty-two right, then run an option keeper to the right. You got that?"

"Yes sir. Thirty-two right, then keeper right."

"Eddie, if you fumble, I'll feed you to the linemen for breakfast next week."

"Don't worry, Coach. You won't see me fumble again, not in this game–maybe, not ever."

Phillips scores on the power play over right guard. Patterson, Grey and Thompson shove the black and gold defenders back, almost to the goal posts.

Hamrick uses the same play for the extra point. Phillips rushes into the end zone again, standing up.

Comanche   25   Ranger   7

RESPONDING TO OUR SPURT OF OFFENSIVE VITALITY, the Comanche coach reverses his earlier strategy and sends his first string offense back into the game. With the security of his team's over-whelming lead he chooses to stick to a conservative running game–one which will eat up the clock and reduce their chance of turnovers.

Our defensive team makes the Indian running backs pay dearly for every second run off the clock. Sharp, popping sounds of our tacklers' hard collisions with Comanche ball carriers resound across the field on every play.

Our aggressive defensive play contains Comanche's offense, but our offense bogs down again. We are unable to mount any kind of sustained drive against the Indian's first string defense. Because of Jensen's booming kicks, we continue to gain a few yards on each exchange of punts.

Only seconds remain in the third quarter when we regain possession of the ball at mid-field.

"Buddy, we need to shake up their defense. Their backs have been coming up quickly, trying to stop our running game. We need to call a passing play," I advise my quarterback before he enters the game.

"I've been thinking the same thing, Coach. Ralph says he's pretty sure he can get open."

"Alright then, on your first play call sixty-eight, pass right. We'll see what happens. No interceptions, though. If Ralph isn't open, throw the ball away. You understand?"

"Yeah, Coach. I got it."

Hut. Hut. Hamrick takes the snap, fakes to Dorsey and drifts back into a blocking pocket between Comacho and Simpson. Big Ralph races past Comanche's defensive halfback then cuts diagonally across the field toward the goal line.

Hamrick fires the ball downfield just as his blocking pocket collapses. Several Indian defenders come crashing in on him, an instant after he releases the pass.

"Oh, no! Buddy, you threw it too far! Ralph'll never catch that ball!" I scream in anguish, but to no one in particular.

Reaching the peak of its long arch, high above the field, the pass appears to be far beyond the reach for our speeding receiver.

Seeing the ball is overthrown, Ralph Rogers lowers his head and quickens his pace. At the ten yard line he leaves his feet, diving after the descending football. The football falls gingerly into his huge outstretched hands. Ralph's long, thin body bounces hard as he bangs onto the grass surface and slides through the end zone. The official following the play raises both hands to signal a touchdown.

"Did you see that, Coach Warden? Buddy must've thrown the football sixty yards," Alfred howls with joyous excitement.

"Oh, yeah! I saw it! What a play! What a catch!" I yell at the top of my lungs. The boisterous roar of the Ranger crowd behind us affirms that I'm not alone in appreciating the fantastic reception.

On the extra point try Hamrick gives the football to Dorsey over right guard. Dorsey fumbles.

Damn! I forgot to tell my new quarterback about my firm decree—to never let Joel Dorsey carry the football.

Comanche 25   Ranger 13

BULLDOG CHEERLEADERS AND THE SCHOOL BAND have been silent for most of the third quarter. With the Indian team leading by four touchdowns, there wasn't much to cheer about. Now, after our dramatic passing play, the noise on the visitor's side of the field begins to grow. Our cheerleaders lead their Bulldog fans in a loud yell of support, while drummers in the band thump their musical instruments in ear-splitting unison.

After McKinney's kickoff is returned to their forty, the Indian offensive team enters the game with renewed determination. Comanche players realize Ranger has pulled within striking distance. Their once insurmountable lead has been reduced to only two touchdowns.

Regaining their momentum, the Indians drive across mid-field into our territory. My Bulldogs become even tougher and meaner with each yard the Indian team gains on our side of the mid-field stripe. We finally stop Comanche at the thirty-five, forcing them to punt. Their punter lays down a perfect kick, rolling out of bounds on our four yard line.

"Alright, men! Now everyone knows you're the best team here tonight. Let's take the football and ram it down their throats. No fumbles. No missed blocks. Everybody do your job. Now break. I want a touchdown, and I want it on this possession," I impel my offense, while we huddle together near our bench.

My Bulldog team has become possessed with a desire to win this football game. The faces of my young gladiators display their grim resolve as they run onto the field.

Hut. Hut. Hamrick barks the signals. His earlier insecurity is gone now. His voice is cool and confident. He takes the snap and laterals smartly out to Comacho for a gain of six yards.

Groaning sounds of young men exerting their strong bodies in maximum effort resonate from the field as we steadily move the ball toward the Comanche goal.

Five yards. Eight yards. Twelve yards. Urging his troops to rise up and stop us, the Indian coach runs frantically along the sidelines. The panic in the coach's voice is contagious. His defense becomes reckless, abandoning their defensive assignments, trying to outguess our quarterback on the option plays. In twelve plays we run the football from our own four to the Comanche six. Hamrick is in total control. He calmly barks out his signals with confidence and authority. On first and goal Hamrick takes the snap and runs over right tackle for our third touchdown of the half. Dorsey leads the play, putting a punishing block on the Indian middle linebacker.

Comacho runs through a gaping hole at right tackle to score the extra point.

Comanche   25   Ranger   20

Ranger fans are overcome with delirious anticipation, screaming and running around behind the chain-link fence which separates the pathway in front of the bleachers from the playing field. At halftime not one person in the stands could possibly have expected this Bulldog team to make such a miraculous comeback–to be in position to win. Our fans had only hoped to see us keep the score respectable. Now, victory is in sight.

Every person in the stadium is on his feet for our kickoff. Comanche fans are furious, pleading with their team to maintain possession of the football. Ranger fans are screaming for us to get the ball back. Our Bulldog band is playing furiously and as loud as they can play.

Only two minutes remain on the scoreboard clock when McKinney gets off his best kickoff of the night. Robinson and Cunningham smash through a wall of Indian blockers to viciously tackle the ball carrier.

"Hey, E.P.! Save your timeouts. There's plenty of time," I shout to Robinson, our defensive captain, out on the field.

Robinson nods his head, indicating he understands.

"You sure about that, Stubby? There's not much time left," Sam questions me.

"Yeah, Sam, I'm sure. We'll need all our timeouts if we get the ball again. If they make a first down, I'll have Robinson use the timeouts then."

An Indian run off right tackle nets three yards. Their fullback plunges up the middle for another four. On third and three we smother their halfback for a one yard gain.

"Hot damn! Now we got 'em, Stubby. It's fourth and two. They've gotta punt. No way they'll go for the first down," Sam cries out while he stalks the sideline.

I check the scoreboard clock. Less than a minute remains in the game.

"What would you do, Sam? Would you go for it, or punt?"

Sam ceases his mad pacing and grins at me. "Darned if I know. I'm glad it's the Comanche coach who's gotta make the call and not us."

I think about his statement for a second, then reply, "You're right, Sam. I'd sure hate to be in the Comanche coach's shoes right now."

"Oh hell yes! Wouldn't we just hate ta be sittin' on a five point lead with less than a minute left? That'd be an absolutely terrible predicament," Sam bellows in a crazed kind of laughter.

"Yeah, that'd be about as bad as it gets," I add, sharing his strained laughter.

COMANCHE'S QUARTERBACK lets the clock run down to less than forty seconds before he calls a timeout.

"What the hell are they up to? Stubby, I'll bet they're planning to go for the first down."

"I think you're right, Sam. Let's get our defense back in there."

While Sam and Alfred send our first string defense back into the game, I go to the bench and kneel down beside Hamrick.

"Buddy, if we get the ball again, Comanche will be expecting you to pass. I want you to keep running the ball outside for as long as you can. Get out of bounds when you can. Use your timeouts to stop the clock when you can't. Forty seconds doesn't seem like much time, but it's all we need if we use the time wisely."

"I think I understand, Coach. They'll be playing back, defending against a pass. That should make it easier for us to move the ball on the ground," Hamrick analyzes, beginning to sound like a seasoned veteran.

The Comanche coach decides to gamble and go for the first down.

Taking the snap, the Indian quarterback lunges over his right guard. Somehow, Barnes slips through from his middle linebacker position to get a hand on the quarterback's foot, dropping him for no gain.

The clock stops for the change of possession. Only thirty-five seconds remain on the scoreboard clock.

Hut. Hut. Hamrick fakes to Dorsey and keeps around right tackle for a gain of nine. Our timeout stops the clock with twenty-four seconds left.

Hut. Hut. Hamrick pitches out to Simpson who scampers around left end and out of bounds at the twenty-six. Sixteen seconds are left on the clock. I signal Hamrick to call timeout. Hamrick hurries to the sidelines.

"Buddy, there's not enough time left for us to score on the ground.

We've gotta pass. We still have one timeout left. Let's call a jump pass to Ralph over the middle."

Hut. Hut. Hamrick takes the snap, fakes to Dorsey plunging over right guard, then jumps high in the air with his arm cocked to pass, looking for Ralph Rogers.

Comanche was anticipating we would try to pass to our towering receiver. Their outside linebacker and defensive end have blocked Ralph Rogers to the ground before he can cross the line of scrimmage.

Hamrick comes down on the run, rolling out to his right, being chased by three Indian defenders. Rogers picks himself up and dashes toward the goal line, waving his arms in the air.

Hamrick is trapped at the right sideline. The three black and gold defenders block Hamrick's view. He is unable to see his tall receiver downfield.

Suddenly, from out of nowhere, a maroon-clad body comes flying horizontally down the sideline. One, two…, three surprised Indian players go sliding out of bounds, leaving Hamrick free to pass. As Hamrick fires his pass, the figure of Gilbert Thompson raises up from among the pile of bodies.

Big Ralph leaps high in the air to snare Hamrick's pass with one hand. He pulls the ball against his chest and falls to the ground at the two yard line. Every Bulldog player on the field is trying to call time-out when the last second ticks off the scoreboard clock.

Comanche and Ranger fans commence a screaming frenzy. Both school bands are blaring loudly. Comanche coaches run frantically onto the field. Sam and Alfred have to restrain our excited players, shoving them back to our bench. Everyone is trying to find out whether or not the game is over.

Huddling near the goal line, the officials consider their decision. After a few seconds they break up. One official runs to our bench.

"Coach, our official watch shows we have two seconds left in the game. You have no more timeouts."

Hamrick runs to the sidelines while the game officials clear fans from the field for our final play.

"Buddy, here's the play. You keep the football. Try a quarterback sneak over left guard. Tell Hummel, Patterson and Thompson to block straight ahead. You go behind them."

Hamrick's face is wrought with anxiety. I should have some soothing words of wisdom to calm him down, but my heart is pumping too fast. My emotions are too strong. I can only tell him exactly what I'm thinking.

"Buddy, this is the situation we've been working for all night. Let's score this touchdown and go home."

"Okay, Coach Warden. We'll celebrate all the way back to Ranger."

PANDEMONIUM BREAKS OUT in the Ranger grandstands when the referee raises his hands to signal a touchdown after Hamrick's quarterback sneak.

The game officials call timeout while they attempt to remove Ranger fans who have run onto the field after the touchdown. A young Ranger fan dashes out on the field and grabs the game ball. The officials chase him for a few yards, then give up.

Several Comanche players lie exhausted and crying on the end zone grass. Their cheerleaders and teammates hasten on the field to console them. Hundreds of people mill around in the end zone and along the sidelines, waiting to race onto the playing field.

Finally, the game officials surrender to the will of the crowd, blowing their whistles to end the game. The extra point play means nothing. My Bulldogs have already won the game. Seeing the officials signal an end to the game, our Bulldog players sprint from the bench to join in the riotous celebration taking place among their Ranger teammates on the field. Players, cheerleaders, band members, fans and coaches meet to hug each other and roll in the grass with glee and in sheer, delirious happiness.

AFTER CONGRATULATING MY QUARTERBACK and shaking several hundred hands, I glance around, searching for Gilbert Thompson. Without his amazing block Hamrick could never have completed that last pass to Rogers. I spot Gilbert standing alone at the center of the field, seeming oblivious to all the howling people surrounding him.

"Gilbert Thompson, you big lug! You were the real hero out there tonight. We couldn't have won without you," I say, grabbing his shoulder pads to pull him down and hug his neck. Then, swept up in the lunatic emotion around us, I pull his face to me and kiss his cheek. Gilbert jerks back sharply. His wide eyes express his obvious distress.

"Coach Warden, I really like you, too, but please don't kiss me again. Our teammates will think we've turned queer."

I can hardly contain my laughter. I love this quiet, unassuming young man. I will probably never have another football player who contributes so much and asks for so little.

Gilbert watches me apprehensively after I move on to join my team in their exhilarating gaiety.

———————

MY WOBBLY LEGS cause me to realize how my energy has been sapped by the dramatic excitement of the game. I walk over to the sideline to watch my players and Ranger fans as they continue to celebrate out on the field. Standing there alone, I find myself immersed in feelings of fulfillment which I'd always hoped would come from winning. It is a feeling of pure, absolute joy, not for myself, but for my courageous young men. They have achieved something tonight which they'll look back on with pride for the rest of their lives.

Juanita slips up beside me, interrupting my happy thoughts. Her warm hand slides gently into mine.

"Congratulations, Coach Warden. That was quite a game."

"Juanita, where've you been? Your seats were empty after the half. I thought you'd gone home."

"We've been up in the press box with the president of the Comanche bank. Those were the bank's seats we were sitting in. Ever since your team scored their first touchdown in the second half, Daddy's been telling him what a terrific coach you are, how you never give up."

"Your father, bragging on me? I can't believe that."

"It's true, darling. Right now, he and Price are making the rounds in the parking lot, informing all of Daddy's friends that the Ranger coach is his son-in-law."

"That won't win him many friends in Comanche. Someone's liable to take a swing at him."

"Stubby, you should know my father will never win a popularity contest. Until tonight, he's never cared a thing about football, but he can't resist an opportunity to brag about his family. Besides, the Comanche fans are all in a state of shock. No one can believe Ranger actually won."

"Yes, it has to be one of the most thrilling high school comebacks of all time. I'm utterly exhausted from the team's effort."

Juanita rises up on her tiptoes to kiss me on the cheek.

"You didn't look so tired out there–kissing Gilbert Thompson. Were you trying to make me jealous?"

"Oh, Juanita! I don't know what came over me. I love all these kids so much. I suppose I got caught up in the excitement. Gilbert was so embarrassed. I'll have to apologize to him on Monday," I tell her, trying to explain my irrational action.

"Don't worry, darling. He'll get over it. I kissed him, too."

"You did? What did he do?"

"I think he kinda liked it."

"Now I'm the one getting jealous."

"I kissed Alfred and Sam, too."

"You did? Well now, when does the head coach get kissed?"

"Anytime he wants. Anytime...."

My lips interrupt her in mid-sentence. I lift her off the ground and pull her close to me. Her arms wrap hungrily around my neck. We stand in front of the Comanche grandstands, kissing passionately like two young lovers.

CHAPTER FIFTEEN
THE SIXTH WEEK

Friday Night
October 4, 1949

REMEMBERING MY AGREEMENT with Buddy Hamrick to "celebrate all the way back to Ranger," I reject requests from several team members who want to ride home with their families. My football team won by sticking together. Every player will remember this game with a deep sense of satisfaction for the rest of his life. I want each player to also remember sharing the ecstatic thrill of victory with his fellow teammates during the bus ride home.

The school has made arrangements for the football team to eat a light meal at the Chief Café near downtown after the game. A gnawing anxiety about Reed Jones prompts me to forego the meal and visit the hospital while my players and coaches dine.

Being without my own means of transportation, my in-laws make hurried arrangements to get me to the hospital. Juanita, Phyliss and Luther accept an offer from Norman Caffey, the bank president, to drive them home while Price shuttles me to the hospital. After we visit the hospital Price will drop me off to ride the team bus back to Ranger, then meet the others at the Kimbrough Ranch.

Price parks in the parking lot, and we walk briskly across the sidewalk to the hospital front door. A uniformed nurse is tending the nurse's station in the front lobby of the hospital.

The nurse is Patsy Kimbrough, Juanita's cousin. When she recognizes me, she jumps from her chair and rushes around the counter to hug me.

"Mister Warden, it's so wonderful to see you again," she says, wrapping her arms around my neck and lightly kissing my cheek.

"Price, this is Patsy Kimbrough, Juanita's cousin," I explain, trying to justify the attractive young nurse's affectionate greeting.

"Yes, her kissing cousin, no doubt," Price observes with an amused grin, noticing my discomfort at receiving the young woman's embrace.

"It's nice to see you, too, Patsy," I tell the young nurse while I gently remove her arms from around my neck. "Patsy, can you help me find a Reed Jones? He's the quarterback on my football team. Your ambulance crew brought him here about an hour and a half ago."

"Certainly, Mister Warden. You should know I'd do anything for you," she replies seductively. Then, becoming more businesslike, she reaches for a clipboard on the reception counter. "Let me have a look at our list of incoming patients."

Returning to her chair behind the counter, the affectionate nurse studies the list of names on the clipboard. She frowns, as if reading causes her great pain.

"Yes, he checked in at 9:14 P.M. Doctor Malone examined him and sent him immediately into the operating room for emergency surgery. Your Mister Jones is in the recovery room now."

"Patsy, would it be possible to see him? His teammates are concerned about him. Our bus is about to leave for Ranger. I'd like to give them a report on his condition."

"The recovery room is right down the hallway. I'm sure you remember where it is. How are Juanita and your baby boy doing?"

"Thanks, Patsy. Juanita and the baby are doing fine. Listen, we're in kind of a hurry. Maybe we can talk later."

"DOES JUANITA KNOW about her kissing cousin?" Price joshes me, as we walk together down the hallway.

"Yes. But, if it's all the same with you, Price, I wouldn't mind if we kept the little scene out there strictly between us men."

"Stubby, my lips are sealed forever," Price laughs.

RADFORD JONES MEETS US at the recovery room door. Glancing inside, I can see my afflicted quarterback stretched out on a portable rolling bed. A white sheet covers his body, but his bare, long legs hang out beyond the end of the bed. Reed's mother is standing alongside the bed holding her sedated son's hand.

"Hello, Red. How is Reed? The nurse up front told us he had to have emergency surgery," I whisper quietly.

"As far as we know, he's doing fine. The doctor said his appendix had completely burst. We were lucky to get him into the hospital so quickly, otherwise he might've died."

"Red, he must've played the entire first half in terrible pain. He's gotta be the toughest kid I've ever known."

"Yeah, he's always been that way. When he was young and got hurt, he'd never cry like other kids. He's a mighty tough cookie alright."

"Can I see him? I'd like to tell him about the game."

"Sure, Coach. By the way, how much did they beat us?"

"We didn't lose, Red. We won!"

"You did? Well, I'll be darned. Boy, we must've missed a hell of a football game."

"Yes, Red, you most certainly did. It was one hellava game."

REED SLOWLY OPENS HIS EYES as I approach his moveable bed.

"Hi, Coach," he says drowsily.

"Hi, Reed. How do you feel?"

"I'm feeling okay. How'd the game come out?"

"We won–scored a touchdown on the last play of the game."

"I'm glad. Now I won't feel so bad about letting the team down. Coach, I'm sorry I didn't play well. I should've told you I was hurting."

"Hey, Reed, don't worry about it. You just get well as fast as you can. You're our quarterback. We need you back."

The quarterback's grim face brightens, then changes to a smile.

"You mean that, Coach? You really want me back?"

"Not just me, Reed. The whole team wants you back. After the game your teammates voted unanimously to dedicate the game and the game ball to you. Coach Aills plans to paint the score on the ball. We'll give it to you after everyone signs it."

In the hallway outside the recovery room Blanche Jones hugs my neck and kisses me. Radford Jones shakes my hand vigorously. His face is beaming with pride.

Price grins and shakes his head as we stride down the hospital hallway.

"I know, Price. But can I help it if all the women wanna kiss me tonight?" I whisper to him.

Price begins to walk faster. When we get near the hospital door, he begins to run. By the time we are outside, he is bursting with hilarious laughter.

"HERE YOU ARE, COACH WARDEN. I had the cook make you a ham sandwich. We figured you wouldn't be back in time to eat with the team," Alfred says thoughtfully, handing me a sandwich wrapped in wax paper before I board the school bus.

"Thanks, Alfred. I'm hungry enough to eat a steak, raw."

"How was Reed? Is he gonna be all right?"

"Yes, he had an appendicitis attack. The doctor had to operate. Apparently his condition was almost fatal, but I think he'll be fine now."

Inside the bus my Bulldog team continues to celebrate their comeback victory—yelling at passing cars and screaming wildly. When I report that Reed Jones is okay and out of danger, they whoop with joy, then break out into a song, singing an unpublished version of "For He's a Jolly Good Fellow" which would make their mothers blush.

The rowdy jubilation continues until we pass through downtown DeLeon where our happy young people holler loudly at several unsuspecting old men gathered on a street corner. Then the physical exertion of the game and the exuberant post-game celebration begin to take its toll. By the time we reach DeLeon's city limits, most of my Bulldog players are either asleep or quietly resting.

Alfred has to wake me up when the bus stops to unload us at the stadium gate in Ranger.

Saturday Morning
October 5, 1949

SIPPING LUKEWARM COFFEE, I slap at my face, trying to stay awake, while I wonder whatever could have possessed me to agree to coach an eight o'clock Saturday morning practice for Jerry Lowe's football team. The Lobo squad is suited out and on the practice field, circled in a ragged formation while they perform stretching exercises. I gulp down the last few drops of cold coffee, climb out of the Hudson and head across the field.

Jerry hands a clipboard to his assistant coach and runs to meet me.

"Good morning, Stubby. We're all set to go. How did your game go last night?"

"We won." I consider relating the details about last night's exciting victory but decide against it. My cloudy mind isn't up to a full recount of the Comanche game. "How did you guys do?"

"Lost to Weatherford—14 to zip. Our defense played well, but as usual, our offense stunk it up."

"Well, that's what I'm here for. Let's see what we can do to fix your offense," I proclaim decisively. I'm in no mood for friendly conversation.

After Jerry sets his offensive team, I walk his ball carriers slowly through several basic plays to show them how the "Option Tee" works. Satisfied the Lobo ball carriers have a fundamental understanding of my offense, I send them to the other end of the field with Jerry's assistant coach to continue practicing while I explain blocking assignments to the linemen.

"Stubby, this 'Option Tee' is a lot easier to understand than I expected. You think there's a chance my team could use it in our next game?" Jerry asks, while we stand waiting for his backfield to return to work with the linemen.

"It's not a difficult offense to learn, Jerry. The key is having a smart, quick quarterback to execute the plays."

"I guess that answers my question. None of my boys can walk and chew gum at the same time."

We set the backfield and offensive line in full-fledged formation to work together, walking them slowly through their assignments again and again. Finally, I'm satisfied the players understand their jobs well enough to run a few plays at full speed.

Jerry's assessment of his offensive players is not far off. His quarterback is uncoordinated and slow to learn. I patiently explain the quarterback steps to him over and over until, at last, he begins to get the hang of it.

"Stubby, it's eleven-fifteen. These kids are worn out. Maybe we should call it a day," Jerry suggests to me.

"But they're just beginning to understand what I want 'em to do. How about letting us practice for another half-hour?" I protest.

Neil Brooks, Jerry's assistant coach, hearing my stubborn plea, intercedes for his exhausted players.

"Coach Warden, these guys played a ballgame last night. Let's turn 'em loose. Jerry and I understand what you want. We can work with them all next week."

"Alright, but you be sure to work on the linemen's blocking assignments. That's just as important as the quarterback's timing."

"Sure thing, Coach. We'll have this offense down pat by next Saturday. I promise."

"HEY, STUBBY! Carolyn Sue is home from college for the weekend. She's meeting me for lunch at the country club. You wanna come?" Jerry asks while he gathers up football equipment from the practice field.

"Maybe another time, Jerry. I'm hot and sweaty, and I'm certainly not dressed to go to the country club."

"Suit yourself, good buddy. But you can shower here, and I'm sure no one would mind what you're wearing. Carolyn Sue would be delighted to see you. She'd enjoy hearing about your Ranger coaching job."

"Tell her Juanita and I will take a rain check. Maybe we can get together after football season. Say, Jerry! We've been wondering about your love life. You two still plan to get married?"

"I guess it depends on whether I keep this head coaching job. Carolyn Sue insists on living here in Cisco—won't even consider living anywhere else."

"That's a tough assignment for someone in our nomadic profession,

Jerry. In this crazy business you can be the hero one season and fired the next."

"Yeah, I know. That's why I appreciate your help, Stubby. If I get to keep this job, I plan to marry that gal next January. I was hoping you'd stand up with me–you know–be my best man."

"I'm ready anytime, Jerry. You name the date. I'll be there."

Tuesday Morning
October 8, 1949

MY GRIP TIGHTENS on the Hudson's steering wheel when I notice the sheriff's squad car parked in the stadium parking lot. Recalling my last morning encounter with an Eastland County sheriff's vehicle, a hard knot forms in my stomach.

I decide not to be intimidated. Ignoring my fears, I drive straight for the parked car.

The patrol car's driver, seeing my Hudson coming toward him, opens his door and begins waving to me. The driver is my deputy friend James Fingler.

"Good morning, Coach Warden. How are you on this fine day?" the deputy greets me cordially, when I stop alongside him. Then, seeing my strained expression, he adds, "I reckon you weren't expecting a sheriff's squad car to be waiting for you. I hope I didn't frighten you."

"No, not really. I gotta admit though, that since my stay in the county jail, I do get a little tense when I see a sheriff's vehicle. What brings you over to Ranger?"

"Coach, I came to tell you Keith Murphy is well enough to testify. A Special Grand Jury will convene in Abilene tomorrow morning at eleven o'clock."

"That's wonderful news, James. Does Mrs. Murphy know about Keith?"

"I'm sorry, Coach. That's all I'm allowed to tell you."

"But she's worried sick about her husband. Someone needs to let her know he's alive and well. If you people won't tell her, then I'll tell her myself."

"Coach Warden, you gave me your promise I could trust you. You promised to keep what I told you about Keith Murphy in strict confidence."

"Yes, I did. But how can you continue to keep this from Kate Murphy? She's got a right to know about her husband."

"I'll have to ask you to trust us, Stubby. Sheriff Williams knows what he's doing. Someone tried to kill Murphy once. If they knew where he was, they might try again."

"Okay, James. I don't agree, but I'll go along."

"I'll tell you what, Coach. After you and Murphy finish with your testimony to the Grand Jury, I'll release you from your promise. You can tell Kate Murphy about her husband then."

"Me? Testify before the Grand Jury! I don't understand."

"Oh, yeah. That's the main reason I came by–to serve you with this subpoena. The Grand Jury wants you in Abilene tomorrow morning, to testify," the deputy informs me, handing me an oversized, official looking envelope. My name is printed in dark black ink across one end.

"But I don't know anything. What can I tell them that Keith Murphy doesn't know? Besides, I have a football team to coach. I need to be here."

"I'm sorry, Coach. I wish we could've given you more notice. The subpoenas were issued late yesterday afternoon, after the doctor gave his blessing for Murphy to testify. You have to go. If you don't show up, a warrant will be issued for your arrest."

———————

FOR THE REMAINDER OF THE DAY I can't seem to shake off the deputy's threat–that I could be arrested for not showing up to testify before the Grand Jury. Unanswered questions cloud my mind. There's no logical reason for me to testify. What could I know that would be useful to their investigation?

The distraction of my upcoming court appearance and my befuddled mind causes me to glide mindlessly through the afternoon football practice, like I'm in some sort of trance. After only an hour of practice, I realize I am confusing both my coaches and the football team with my bizarre behavior. I dismiss practice early.

Tuesday Afternoon
October 8, 1949

A FAMILIAR BLUE FORD SEDAN sits parked in my driveway. The car belongs to Kate Murphy. I park the Hudson parallel with the front street curb so not to block her exit. Kate and Juanita will be shocked to see me home so early.

When I enter through the front door, the two women are sitting in my living room, chatting in friendly female conversation. My unexpected appearance surprises them.

"Stubby, what are you doing home so early? Are you sick?" Juanita asks with concern.

"No, I'm fine. I canceled football practice so I could get home early and see what you women do with your afternoons. Hello, Kate. Finding you here is certainly a pleasant surprise."

"I dropped by to see your baby boy and to bring Juanita some baby clothes. Juanita and I have been talking about our men, both our big ones and our little ones."

"Wow! No wonder my ears have been burning. I hope Juanita hasn't told too many embarrassing stories about me."

Kate Murphy glances at her watch. "I suppose I should go. With all our woman's talk, Juanita hasn't started your supper."

"Please don't leave on my account, Kate. You and Juanita continue with your stories while I change clothes. My supper can wait. Normally I don't get home this early."

"No, I really need to go. If football practice is over, Alfred will be needing a ride home. Our school bus has been acting up. The bus mechanic wants Alfred to leave it in town tonight so he can check it out."

"Kate has invited us to come out and eat with Alfred and her on Sunday after church. We can finish our conversation then," Juanita advises me.

"That would be wonderful. Kate is easily the best cook in Eastland County. I'll look forward to sitting at her table," I respond enthusiastically, remembering the delicious, lip-smacking meal she served me once before.

"Alright then. Alfred and I will expect you for dinner on Sunday.

We will see you then," Kate reiterates, picking up her purse.

Juanita and I stand together on the porch waving goodbye, watching Kate scoot into her car. She starts the engine and begins to back out the driveway.

To hell with my promise to James Fingler. She needs to know about her husband. I leap from the porch and run to flag her down.

"Kate, I have some news about Keith. He's in Abilene, in the protective custody of the Texas Rangers. He is alive and well."

"Stubby, how did you find out about Keith?" Her face is white and strained, visibly expressing her alarm. Her widened eyes reveal her fear.

"From James Fingler, one of Sheriff Williams' deputies. I promised not to tell you, but I couldn't keep the secret. I thought you needed to know."

"Oh, thank goodness. Stubby, you haven't told anyone else have you?"

"No. Certainly not. I promised not to tell anyone, not even you."

"Stubby, promise me you won't tell another soul. Keith's life is already in too much danger."

———

STANDING IN THE GRAVEL DRIVEWAY, feeling very foolish, I watch Kate Murphy back up and drive away, wondering how long she has known about her husband. She kept her secret very well, not even telling Alfred.

Juanita calls to me from the porch, reminding me to pull the Hudson into the driveway before I come inside.

———

Wednesday Morning
October 9, 1949

UNTIL NOW, WAITING CONSPICUOUSLY OUT HERE in the hallway next to U.S. District Court No. 2, I'd never noticed the faded and tattered condition of my double-breasted blue suit. I bought the suit second-hand, for five bucks, in Stephenville, only two summers ago, so I wouldn't embarrass Juanita when I accompanied her to church.

The court bailiff has advised me I'll be the next person to testify. My nervous anticipation causes my mouth to produce a sour-tasting saliva. Finding no convenient place to spit, I swallow hard.

Several men emerge from a doorway directly down the hallway from the main courtroom entrance. Three of the men, dressed in western attire and wearing wide brimmed cowboy hats, are obviously Texas Rangers. The man they are escorting is in a wheelchair. The man is Keith Murphy, my assistant coach.

I stand up and walk swiftly toward the group of men. "Good morning, gentlemen. I wonder if I might say hello…."

Before I can complete my sentence, two of the Rangers have shoved me against the wall, pinning one of my arms behind me.

"Hey, you're hurting me! I didn't mean any harm! I just wanted to speak with Keith Murphy," I complain loudly.

"Shut up, Mister, or I'll break your friggin' arm," the Ranger threatens. "Joe, you frisk him! Make sure he's clean!" the Ranger instructs his companion.

My tormentor's companion stoops down and begins checking my pant legs for weapons.

"What's that in your pocket?" he asks, after searching up each of my legs.

"It's only a steel cylinder," I answer guiltily, hoping I won't have to explain that it's used to reinforce your knuckles in fist fights.

"Let's see it," the Ranger demands.

The first Ranger releases his hold on me, just enough to allow me to reach into my pants pocket. I hand the piece of steel to the Texas Ranger who was searching me.

"Yeah, I know what this is used for. You get into lots of fights, do you?"

"Not really," I answer through the side of my mouth. The right side of my face is pressed hard against the wall.

"Okay, Mister, what are you doing here? Why were you after the man in the wheel chair?"

"I'm here to testify before the Grand Jury. The man in the wheel chair is Keith Murphy. He's a friend of mine."

"The Special Grand Jury in Court Number Two?"

"Yes. Is there another Grand Jury taking testimony today?"

"Don't be a smart ass! Now get your butt back down the hallway and leave our witness alone, before we put you under arrest."

"ONIS C. WARDEN! MISTER ONIS WARDEN! The jury is ready to hear your testimony now," the bailiff calls out from the court-room entryway.

"Here I am! I'm ready!" I respond, rising quickly from the hallway bench. The bailiff holds the door open while I enter. Except for two men sitting behind a table facing the judge's bench, the court room is empty. The two men appear to be lawyers.

The courtroom is small and inauspicious with seating for only about thirty spectators. The bare, pictureless plaster walls are painted a yellowish white. The Judge's bench and a low partition wall around the juror's box are constructed with an inexpensive wood paneling. Even that has been painted a drab milk-chocolate brown.

"Take a seat up near the front, Mister Warden. The judge and jurors will be in shortly," the bailiff advises.

Jurors begin to trickle into the courtroom from a side door even before I can find a seat. In less than a minute all the jurors are seated within the jury box.

Glancing back over my shoulder, I realize I'm the lone witness in the courtroom. The spectator seats behind me are unoccupied.

"All rise," the bailiff calls out, announcing the judge's arrival.

"MISTER ONIS C. WARDEN, would you please come forward to be sworn in?" the court bailiff requests, reading from a loose-leaf ledger book.

"Yes sir," I answer and step smartly to the witness box.

The judge raps his gavel to silence a murmur of conversation among the jurors, then peers down at me from his leather chair, high above the witness box.

"Mister Warden, this Grand Jury has been convened to investigate and to possibly issue arrest warrants in connection with suspected criminal activity in Eastland County, Texas. Any testimony you may give will be in strictest confidence. You will be under the same rules as if you were in a court of law. Do you understand?"

"Yes sir."

"Mister Warden, do you understand you will be subject to the same penalties for perjured testimony before this Grand Jury as you would be in a regular court of law?"

"Yes sir."

"Mister Warden, do you promise to tell the truth, the whole truth and nothing but the truth, so help you God? Place your hand on the Bible before you and say 'I do.'"

"I do."

The Texas Ranger who frisked me in the hallway enters the court-room from a side door next to the juror's box. He approaches the two attorneys behind the table and whispers something to them. The attorneys both nod their heads in agreement.

One of the lawyers rises to his feet and strides boldly toward the witness stand. The lawyer is probably in his mid-sixties. His pin-striped black suit and long, but neatly groomed, white hair make him a striking figure in the courtroom.

"Mister Warden, my name is H. Lloyd Dumont. I am the elected district attorney for Taylor County. The man sitting at the desk behind me is Todd Rainwater. He is also an attorney and my assistant. Today, the two of us are here representing the great State of Texas. Do you wish to make an opening statement before we begin your testimony?"

"No sir, I guess not. I'm really not sure why I'm here, but I'll try to answer all your questions, if I can."

"Mister Warden, do you wish to be represented by an attorney today?" the elderly attorney asks accusingly.

"No. Should I be? I was subpoenaed to testify. Am I under investigation?"

"That will be determined by your testimony. If you have nothing to hide, then you won't need an attorney, will you?"

"No. I won't," I answer, very decisively.

The two attorneys take turns asking me questions about where and when I was born, my marital status, my education, my employ-ment history, how long I have coached football in Ranger and how a young man, like myself, with almost no coaching experience, was able to land such a prestigious job. I answer each question honestly, even revealing my losing record at Gulf State.

"Mister Warden, do you know a man by the name of Lucas Masters?" the older attorney asks me abruptly.

"Yes, he's the president of the Ranger school board."

"Don't you know him in some other capacity?"

"I've been told he owns a great deal of real estate in Ranger. He's probably the richest man I know."

"Come on, Mister Warden. Aren't you on his payroll? Doesn't he pay you to perform certain unholy duties for him?"

This lawyer is crafty and dangerous. His actions resemble a hunter stalking his prey, waiting for some slip of the tongue or mental mistake which will allow him to include me as a pawn in his investigation. He will use anything I might say to tie me to the crime organization he is after. He is out for my blood. I need to be very careful with my answers. Surely he can't know about my secret agreements with Lucas Masters.

"If you are talking about a bonus I receive for winning football games, I believe Mister Masters is one of the major contributors to my bonus arrangement. The bonus is certainly no secret. It was part of an agreement with the Ranger school trustees when I accepted the job. The school superintendent collects the bonus money from several donors and gives it to me on Wednesday, after my team wins a football game. I've never tried to hide the fact that I receive a bonus for winning football games. In fact, receiving the bonus is a tremendous motivator for me."

"Oh, I see–you only get paid for winning. Do you know the people who make the donations to your little bonus fund?"

"No. I've never asked. Actually, I'd rather not know. Like I said, the school superintendent collects it and delivers it to me after a win."

The two attorneys huddle, conferring at their table. Grabbing his note pad, the younger attorney excitedly points to some written notation. They whisper to each other. Then the older attorney whirls and fires his next question.

"Mister Warden, have you ever made agreements with Lucas Masters to play certain members of your football team over other players?"

This is the question I've been praying he wouldn't ask. Maybe he knows something. Maybe he's just fishing. I have already considered the consequences of my answer. I know the penalty for perjury is severe, but too many people would be hurt by my telling the truth—Juanita, Price, Phyliss, Sam, Alfred, all my Bulldog players. I'd rather go to jail than to admit what I've done.

"No. I have never made any such agreements with Lucas Masters or anyone else."

The attorney glares at me. He knows I'm lying. I wait for him to point at me and demand my arrest. Instead, he asks another question.

"Mister Warden. You have two friends, Orval and Clifford Graves. Aren't they also employed by Mister Masters?"

His question is a complete surprise and so unexpected. I take a minute to recover before I answer. How could he think Clifford and Orval are my friends? This lawyer is too slick and experienced to believe that. No, he has something else up his sleeve. Perhaps he's setting a trap to be sprung later. I warn myself to proceed cautiously.

"Yes. I mean, no. They are certainly no friends of mine. I do know who they are."

"Are they also in the employ of Mister Masters?" the crafty old lawyer probes cunningly, using a trick question.

"Yes, I believe they are. But, like I told you before, I am not employed and have never been employed by Mister Masters."

"Then how do you know them?"

Maybe this is what the lawyer has been setting me up for. Until a few minutes ago, I was a most reluctant witness. However, with the threat of being guilty by association, I'm ready to tell everything—like they say in gangster movies—"to spill my guts." I explain to the jury how Clifford and Orval beat up on me after my team won the Breckenridge game, and how they tried to shoot me after my hospital visit with Keith Murphy. I tell the jurors about discovering the small village of buildings on the Singleton Ranch and about my confrontation with Orval on the road. Finally, I tell them about being locked up in the Eastland County jail by Orval Graves and the sheriff's deputy Billy Hancock.

Both the jurors and the two lawyers listen intently during my long narration of the strange events which have occurred since I became the Ranger football coach. The aging attorney's final questions suggest he may have gotten what he wants. Perhaps he has given up chasing after me.

"Mister Warden, are you acquainted with either a Louis or Anthony Vargas?"

"No sir. I don't know anyone by those names."

"You might know them as the Vargas brothers. They own and operate a chain of used car lots in Fort Worth and Dallas."

"Yes, I've seen their car advertisements in the Fort Worth papers. But I've never met either of them or had any dealings with either of them."

"Do you have knowledge of any kind which would directly link Lucas Masters to the Vargas brothers or to their organization?"

"No. All I know is what Keith Murphy told me at the Eastland hospital. He was in pretty bad shape at the time."

"Thank you for your time, Mister Warden. You will be contacted by the Eastland sheriff, if an indictment for your arrest is issued by the Grand Jury."

"My arrest! Why would you issue a warrant for my arrest?"

"We both know the answer to your question, Coach Warden. You will have to wait and see what the Grand Jury decides."

Wednesday Afternoon
October 9, 1949

MY TESTIMONY BEFORE THE GRAND JURY and the trip back to Ranger took longer than I expected. Emergency stops at service stations in Baird and Cisco to refill my overheating radiator were absolutely necessary. My Hudson won't survive many more long trips like the one to Abilene.

Most of the players are suited out and on the football field when I arrive at Bulldog Stadium. Alfred is waiting on the sidewalk outside the field house front entrance.

"Superintendent Boswell came by looking for you, Coach. He seemed awfully upset."

"Really. Did he say what he wanted?"

"No, but he left a message for you. He said you were to go directly to Mister Masters' office as soon as you got back from Abilene."

How could the superintendent have known I was in Abilene? I

didn't mention the subpoena to a soul, not even Juanita.

A MIXTURE OF STEAM AND SMOKE rolls out from under the Hudson's hood as I slam the car door and begin the dreaded journey up to Lucas Masters' offices. My aged, but usually reliable, car has had a long, exhausting day.

Taking a deep breath, I summon all my courage before I begin my ascent up the darkened stairway toward Lucas Masters' sanctum.

LUCAS MASTERS' RECEPTION ROOM is unoccupied. When I notice the open door to Masters' private office, I decide not to wait to be invited in.

Masters is sitting behind his desk. His back is turned to me while he stares out the window. He seems to be deep in thought.

"Lucas, did you want to see me?" I ask in a low voice, not wanting to startle my generous benefactor.

Masters whirls around in his swivel chair.

"Oh, Coach Warden! Excuse me. I didn't hear you come in. I was reminiscing about all the good times here in Ranger." Masters' voice has a hint of sadness. He looks tired and weary. I've never seen him so vulnerable.

"You go back a long way, Lucas. I'll bet some of your memories are humdingers."

Masters' face breaks into a wry smile, and his eyes brighten in response to my observation.

"Stubby, I could tell you stories that would make your hair stand on end. The oil boom days, those were the good times. A man could make a fortune with the stroke of a pen, or lose one by drilling his well in the wrong spot. Sometimes a hundred feet one way or the other made the difference between fabulous wealth, or a dry hole and going broke."

"I suppose those were wonderful times. Too bad they're gone. Ranger was a much different place in those days."

"Yes, Stubby. The really good times are behind me. I suppose you know why I wanted to see you?"

"I figured you want to know about my testimony before the Grand Jury in Abilene this morning."

"Hell, I'm not worried about what you told the Grand Jury, Stubby. You don't know enough to cause me to lose a minute of sleep. Murphy is the one I'm worried about. Did you see him there?" Masters asks candidly.

"Lucas, I'm not sure you and I should be having this conversation. I don't know how I got mixed up in all this cloak-and-dagger stuff. I never intended to. All I ever wanted was to coach football here in Ranger."

"You might find this hard to believe, Coach, but I never intended to get in this deep myself. Sometimes you get hooked up with the wrong people. Then you find you can't get out."

"After all the grief you've put me through, Lucas, I don't know why I should believe you, but I suppose I do."

"Tell me about the Grand Jury. It's important I know."

"Can I have your word you'll leave Murphy alone, and that you'll call your hired goons off of me?"

"You have my word."

"Okay. Yes, Murphy was there. He's being held in the protective custody of the Texas Rangers. It would be a very dumb move on your part, or any of your hoodlum associates, to go after him. I almost got my arm broken just trying to say hello to him."

"Do you think he was able to testify?"

"Yes. I'm sure he told the Grand Jury everything he knows."

"He knows about the car operation out at the ranch, doesn't he?"

"Yes, and probably a great deal more."

"Did my name come up during your testimony?"

"Yes, but the prosecutor brought it up, not me."

"Things don't look too good for me, do they?"

"Lucas, I didn't tell them a thing they didn't already know. My guess is they had me there to confirm a few minor details. I'd be very surprised if the Grand Jury doesn't issue a warrant for your arrest before they're through. There's also a chance they may issue a warrant for my arrest, too."

"If you're talking about our agreements regarding the football players, I wouldn't be too concerned, Coach. The Grand Jury is after the syndicate bosses in Fort Worth. They'll probably settle for me if they can't nail the big guys, but I'm small potatoes compared to the enormous crime operation they're actually after."

"Lucas, all this is way too much for a small town boy like myself to grasp. How did I ever get mixed up in this stinking mess?"

"I ask myself the same question every day, Stubby. I had it all. Now, it appears I'm about to lose it."

A DARK STORM CLOUD has moved across the sky, blocking out the bright October sun. The weather is changing. In only a few hours the temperature has dropped maybe twenty degrees.

A shiver runs up my spine, causing me to hunch my shoulders and rub on my bare arms to try and stimulate my circulation. My thin, short-sleeved summer shirt offers little protection from the sharp cold wind which has begun to blow up Main Street.

Lucas Masters' words ripple through my mind while I climb into the Hudson and start the engine. "I had it all. Now, I'm about to lose it."

Those same words will apply to me if the Grand Jury elects to indict me. I could lose everything–my job, Juanita, my baby son, my friends.

A sickening gray smoke emits from beneath the hood of the Hudson when I stomp down hard on the accelerator. I don't have time to worry about what might happen to me. My Bulldogs have a football game to play on Friday night, two days from now. I need to get them ready.

HAVING BUDDY HAMRICK AT THE HELM of my offense opens up numerous offensive opportunities. Unlike Reed Jones' wobbly offerings, Buddy's passes are crisp and bulletlike. Until now, we've stuck to a running game, using only three basic passing plays. All of those passes were designed for one receiver–Big Ralph Rogers. Buddy's excellent passing skills allow me to add an entirely new collection of passing plays to our already potent offensive attack.

Alton Stiles, our starting left end, hasn't touched the football in a game since the season began. He and my two starting halfbacks, Billy Simpson and Jimmy Comacho, seem particularly pleased at having more active roles in the offense.

"Great pass, Buddy! Throw me one like that in the Eastland game, and I'll score a touchdown," Stiles declares, offering praise to his quarterback while he trots back to our offensive huddle, following a nice reception downfield.

"That's good, Alton. Then I'll count on you for at least one touchdown Friday night," Hamrick challenges, goading his receiver.

"How 'bout you, Comacho? Can I count on you to catch a touchdown pass Friday night?" Hamrick taunts our young Mexican halfback.

"You chunk the football where I can catch eet, Meester Quarterback. I'll get you a touchdown every time," Comacho answers, putting extra heavy emphasis on his Spanish accent.

After only a few days of practice Hamrick has taken complete charge of this team. His teammates have accepted his authority without the slightest hint of opposition.

My new offensive director's speed and quickness allow me to insert a quarterback run-pass option into our offense.

If Eastland's coach has been scouting us, and I'm almost certain he has, he'll have prepared his team to defend against a hard-nosed running game. We have some surprises in store for him, come Friday night.

Friday Evening
October 11, 1949

THE YELLOW SCHOOL BUS sways back and forth after our bus driver swerves sharply to avoid a jagged pothole. The turbulent movement causes several half-dressed Bulldog athletes to howl and groan, as if they were on some sort of carnival ride.

It's only ten short miles from Ranger to Eastland, about a fifteen minute ride on the old school bus. At Sam's strong suggestion we had the team suit up before we left the Ranger field house. Each man is wearing his dark maroon game pants and a white tee shirt. Sharing the seat beside each player are his shoulder pads and maroon game jersey.

According to Sam, the visitor's facilities at Maverick Stadium are cramped and less than sanitary. Actually, that's the way we find visitor's facilities at most of our away games.

After the game we will load the team directly onto the bus and leave immediately for our own dressing facility back in Ranger where players will shower and change into their street clothes. This plan will reduce the possibility of confrontations between our team and Eastland fans. We will also save a few of the precious dollars budgeted for athletics by foregoing a post-game café meal.

My young men's verbal reactions divert my attention from the opened playbook in my lap. Gazing out the bus window, I see a crudely painted sign positioned alongside the Ranger city limit marker. The sign reads:

Last one leaving for Eastland
Please turn out the Lights!

After our dramatic "come from behind" victory in Comanche last week, the city has worked itself into a frenzy over the success of this Bulldog football squad. Anticipation of our game against Eastland has been building all week. The roadside sign pretty much expresses the city's sentiment. Every man, woman and child who lives in Ranger will be at Maverick Football Stadium tonight—at least in spirit, if not in person.

This rivalry between the two neighboring cities is not always friendly. Sam tells me that only a few years ago the annual Ranger–Eastland football game was played in the afternoon, on Thanksgiving Day. The game was usually marred by a few fist fights, but after having a near riot break out during the final minutes of the last day game, officials of the two schools moved the game date back to October. Their reasoning being, that playing the game earlier in the season would lessen its importance on the district race. The game is now played on Friday night, perhaps with hope that the rabid football fans will be less inclined to pick a fight in the dark.

Both teams are undefeated in district play. Eastland hasn't lost a game this season. The winner of tonight's ballgame will have an upper hand in the quest to represent District 8A in the state playoffs. The loser will definitely have a "tough row to hoe."

––––––––––––

A QUEASY FEELING COMES OVER ME during pre-game warm-up drills. All week long I've been anxious to try out my revitalized offense. Now, a few minutes before the opening kickoff, I begin having second thoughts. The importance of winning this game presses in heavily on me.

A thousand things which could go wrong race across my mind. My quarterback is inexperienced and untested. Maybe Hamrick's performance in the Comanche game last Friday was a fluke. Can he play at a winning level for an entire game? What about my new corps of receivers? How reliable will they be against a tough and aggressive Eastland secondary?

When I was playing for Coach Norton at A&M, he used to refer to my stomach condition as "a bad attack of intestinal butterflies." The best known cure is hard physical contact with a player from the opposing team.

Not having that option, I decide to make a quick visit to the restroom under the visitor's bleachers. The toilet facilities in our visitor's dressing quarters are even worse than Sam had described. Alfred and Sam have everything under control. For the moment I am expendable.

––––––––––––

LEANING AGAINST THE CONCRETE MASONRY WALL, I close my eyes and strain hard, trying to relieve myself into the concrete urine trough at my feet. My nervous condition is not at all unusual. I've seen men stand, in pain, before a urinal for long periods prior to a football game, unable to pee a drop. Your mind tells you your bladder is full and about to burst. Your tense body refuses to cooperate.

"Well now, if it ain't the little dude coach from Ranger."

I know who the voice belongs to, even before I open my eyes. It is Clifford Graves. He must have seen me leave the field and followed me in here.

I zip up my pants quickly and pivot around to face him.

"Look, Clifford, I don't want any trouble. Lucas Masters and I agreed to call off this thing we have going between us."

"This ain't got nothing to do with Mister Masters. This is personal. Ain't no one ever done to me and Orval–what you've done. I'm gonna beat ya to a bloody pulp, then slice ya up and feed ya to my dogs."

His malicious threat adds to my feeling of weakness. My knees begin to wobble. My unsteady legs are on the verge of collapsing beneath me. I glance around the room for a place to run. There is none. The only exit is through the door behind Clifford.

"Clifford, you don't wanna start something here. Someone's liable to come in, any minute. My football team knows I'm here. You could get yourself in very big trouble," I threaten, trying to buy some time. I back away from my menacing adversary until I feel the damp, unmovable masonry wall against my back, blocking my retreat.

Clifford giggles insanely and cries out, as if there were someone else in the restroom with us. "Hey, look! Now tha little shrimp coach is scared." Then his voice tone changes to an animal-like rage, "Say your prayers, Mister Smart Guy. You're about to meet your maker."

Remembering Alfred's steel cylinder, I reach into my pocket and grasp it tightly in my hand. Clifford may make good on his threat to kill me, but I intend to get in a few licks myself. Bracing myself against the wall behind me, I crouch low, waiting for his coming assault. My shaking knees are slightly bent.

Clifford runs at me like a charging bull. My swinging fist grazes his chin but does not slow his enormous body from crushing me against the wall behind me. His mighty blows pound on my body, then the top of my head as I sink to my knees on the floor.

For an instant the big man stops his relentless battering on my body. He's breathing hard. Maybe he's tiring. He obviously thinks I'm beaten. Maybe he has stopped to savor his conquest. For whatever reason, his hesitation gives me an opportunity to regroup and counterattack.

With all my strength I swing my fist upward between Clifford's widespread legs.

Knowing I would always be short and stocky, my grandfather told me many times that a big man's weakness is below his belt. The best way for a small guy to defeat a bigger man is with a sharp blow to the testicles or to his knee.

"Uh! Oh, no!" Clifford gasps in pain, grabbing for his crotch.

Pushing up from off the floor, I slam my steel-filled, clenched fist up hard under his chin. His teeth make a clicking noise as his jaws snap together. A split-second later I kick him in the left knee with the steel-reinforced toe of my cleated shoe.

My shoe strike to his leg causes the big man to drop down, with one knee resting on the floor. Grabbing him by the back of the head, I smash my right knee into his face. Blood spurts from his broken nose when I shove him sideways and release his head.

My knee would've finished off an ordinary man, but Clifford is a tough nut. He doesn't go down easily. He pushes himself back up to his knees, trying to stand up, making an easy target for my ferocious punch to the side of his face.

Streamers of bright red blood fly from his mouth as his battered head snaps backward. His wide white eyes roll upward into his head before he collapses, falling forward onto the concrete floor.

As I stand over Clifford's unconscious body, I remember another of my grandfather's favorite sayings: "The bigger they are, the harder they fall." A lone teenage boy wanders into the restroom. Seeing Clifford's unmoving, bloody body lying on the floor, he turns around and runs back outside.

"I hate to break this up when we're having so much fun, Clifford, but I've really gotta go now. Maybe we can get together and do this again some other time," I tell the unconscious body on the floor.

Before I leave, I place my foot against Clifford's heavy carcass and shove him, face up, into the shallow urine trough. The wetness and the acrid smell of urine should bring him around shortly.

"COACH WARDEN, WHERE'VE YOU BEEN? The game's about to start. We've been looking all over for you," Alfred questions me anxiously, when I return to the football field.

"Been taking care of some unfinished business, Alfred. I'm ready to play now."

"Yeah, when nature calls, we've gotta answer," Alfred says, grinning at me and nodding toward the restroom facility beneath the visitor's bleachers.

Gingerly, I inspect the swollen bumps left on my head by Clifford's hard fists. My butterflies and queasy stomach are gone now. A good dose of hard physical contact will cure a case of pre-game jitters every time.

THE EASTLAND SCHOOL BAND BLARES OUT, and an excited crowd roars behind us as we huddle on the sideline. The eyes of my players tell me they are pumped sky high. Usually this would be a good omen. Our normal running game gives my linemen and blocking backs plenty of opportunity to take out their powerful emotion on the opposition's defense. However, with more passing plays, our revised offense will require more prudent control of their feelings.

We lost the coin toss. Our defense will start the game. That should give our offense time to calm down.

McKinney's kickoff is short, allowing Eastland's receiver to return the football to the Maverick forty-two before we can bring him down.

"Holy crap! They've already got field position on us. Can't we ever start a game without having our backs to the wall?" Sam complains while our defensive team takes the field.

"I guess not, Sam. Maybe that's the only way we know how to start. Remind me to work on our kickoff defense next week."

Sam spins around to question our team manager resting on the bench. "How's your leg coming, Brownlee? You gonna be ready to kick any time soon?"

"I don't think so, Coach Aills. My leg don't seem like it's ever gonna get well," our injured kicker replies, gazing despondently down at his heavy leg cast.

Our defense responds to the challenge. In three plays Eastland can gain only six yards. With fourth and four they elect to punt. Simpson returns the punt to our twenty-three.

"Good gosh Almighty, look at the size of that Eastland defense, Coach Warden. I wonder where they find fellows so big?" Alfred asks innocently.

Alfred's question reminds me of his story about his mamma

spanking him for drinking liquor and stunting his growth. All sorts of comical replies gyrate through my mind. My confrontation with Clifford relieved all my tension and worry about the football game. Now, everything seems funny to me. Tonight, my changeable emotions are taking me for a wild ride. I turn away, so Alfred won't see the amusement in my face when I answer.

"Yep, you're right, Alfred. These Eastland kids are a lot bigger than any team we've faced. They must outweigh us by at least ten pounds per man," I reply, using the most concerned voice I can muster.

Eastland lines up with seven men on their defense line. Like I suspected, the Eastland coach has been scouting us. He's anticipating that we'll stick to our usual ground-oriented offense.

Hut. Hut. Hamrick takes the snap and drops straight back. Several Eastland defensive linemen break through and charge toward him. Hamrick fires a pass to Comacho in the flat near the side line. Twenty-two yards upfield Comacho is run out of bounds.

On the next play Hamrick hits Stiles on a down and out pass at the left out of bounds stripe. The completed pass gains twelve yards.

Hut. Hut. Hamrick takes the snap and fires a bullet to Simpson who's lined up at a flanker position. He snares the pass, dodges a tackler and runs for another twelve yard gain.

Eastland calls timeout. Their defense is completely confused. They were expecting us to run. Now, using three passing plays, we've completely wrecked their game plan, gaining three consecutive first downs and moving the football down to their thirty-one yard line.

Across the field the Maverick coaches are talking frantically with their defensive captains.

Our new air-oriented offense has surprised everyone–even our fans. Ranger cheerleaders stand idly along the sideline, totally absorbed in the game action, neglecting to lead their fans in a supportive yell. Ranger school band members sit spellbound in their reserved section, not playing a note during the timeout.

"Stubby, I'll bet that's the last we'll see of their seven man line," Sam muses.

"I think you're right, Sam. And I'll wager they'll be looking for another pass. Maybe we should give 'em something else to think about. Get Phillips up here."

When the young fullback runs up alongside me, I grab his arm and give him some hasty instructions. "Eddie, tell the quarterback to run forty-six, option right. You personally tell Elder I wanna see their outside linebacker lying on his back after the play."

"Yes sir. Forty-six, option right. Outside linebacker laying on his back," Phillips repeats to me, snapping on his chin strap.

I grab onto him again before he runs away.

"One more thing, Eddie. You block the middle linebacker after Hamrick fakes the handoff to you."

"Yes sir. Middle linebacker on his butt," Phillips repeats, showing me a toothy grin.

Hut. Hut. Hut. Hamrick fakes the ball to Phillips and moves to his right, protected by his wall of maroon blockers. Faking a pitchout to Comacho, he keeps the football and follows behind Elder's bruising block on the outside linebacker. He cuts to the sideline and carries to the one where he is knocked out of bounds.

Back near the line of scrimmage, Elder and Phillips raise their arms triumphantly to show me the two Maverick linebackers are lying on the ground.

We score on a quarterback sneak to the left side. Phillips scores the extra point on a power run over right guard.

Eastland 0   Ranger 7

After our quick touchdown the Maverick coach makes a number of prudent adjustments. This Eastland team is no pushover. They are unbeaten this year. One of their wins was a victory over Albany, who defeated us on our home field. The Mavericks are big, tough and well-coached. We were lucky to catch them in the wrong defensive formations and score so easily.

AFTER BRIEF INITIAL SUCCESS our passing game breaks down. A backfield motion penalty, two dropped passes, hurried throws and an interception contribute to my decision to return to our more reliable ground game.

Eastland's oversized defense begins to dominate and wear us down. During the second quarter our offense becomes totally inept, unable to rush for a single first down. Neither Jensen's long punts nor inspired play by our defense can keep the Eastland club from gaining yardage on us with each exchange of possession.

Time expires with the Mavericks in possession of the football on our twenty-four and driving steadily toward our goal.

———————

"STUBBY, OUR KIDS ARE RUNNIN' ON EMPTY. Eastland has us beat. It just don't show up on the scoreboard yet," Sam observes, as we jog off the field at halftime.

"Yeah, I know, Sam. We need to think of something to turn the momentum back in our favor."

Sam's observation is right on target. Many times I've seen a small scrappy team, like this Bulldog squad, holding a halftime lead over a larger and more physical team, only to have the larger team come back in the second half and stomp them badly. All the signs were there in the second quarter. We couldn't move the football offensively. Near the end of the half our defense was tiring badly.

"Sam, can you and Alfred take care of things for a few minutes? I need to check on my wife and baby."

"Sure thing, Stubby. Be thinking about what I said, though. We gotta do somethin', or we're gonna get our butts kicked in the second half."

———————

RADFORD JONES DETAINS ME as I climb the bleacher steps toward the section where Price, Phyliss, Juanita and my baby are seated. I argued against them bringing Little Jerry out in the cold night air, but Juanita explained, "He is a coach's son, and he needs to get accustomed to spending time sitting in the bleachers, watching his father pace the sidelines and scream at the game officials." Who could argue with such perceptive logic?

"Hello, Red! I'm surprised to see you here. I figured you'd be home taking care of my quarterback tonight."

374

"Coach, me and the Missus wouldn't let a little attack of appendicitis keep us away from this game. I got lots of business friends over here in Eastland. They've been bragging to me all year about how good their football team is. We had to be here to razz 'em, after our Bulldogs whip their butts."

"How is Reed? Has he come home from the hospital yet?"

"Reed's doing fine. Came home from the hospital late Thursday afternoon. We left him at home with his grandmother tonight. He should be back in school by the middle of next week."

"I'm glad to hear that, Red. You tell him Coach Aills has his game ball ready. We'll present it to him officially when he's up and around."

"I'll do that, Coach. It'll mean a lot to him."

"Listen, Red, I'll talk with you later. I need to check with my wife before the second half starts."

———————

SPYING MY FAMILY MEMBERS up in the bleachers, I wave at them and begin climbing the steps toward them.

The idea hits me like a ton of bricks. Coach Homer Norton used an identical strategy on his A&M team during halftime at the 1941 Cotton Bowl. That was before my time, but students at A&M still talk about how he tricked his team into winning. I turn around and run back to Radford Jones.

"Hey, Red. Have any of my players come by to see Reed since he came home?"

"Naw, he hasn't seen any of his friends. We didn't get Reed home from the hospital until real late yesterday afternoon. The trip from Comanche wore him out. He went straight to sleep."

"That's great. That's just what I need. Thanks, Red."

Radford Jones and his wife gaze after me in absolute bewilderment while I dash swiftly up the bleachers, taking the steps two at a time, toward Juanita, Price, Phyliss and my infant son. We might have a chance to win this ballgame, if I can find a sheet of paper. Surely, someone in this stadium has one lousy sheet of paper.

"A WOMAN'S PURSE IS A MAGICAL INVENTION," I tell myself, loping down the stadium steps on my way back to the playing field. There's no telling what secrets she may have hidden in all those private compartments, secured with metal zippers and tiny leather straps.

Printed in lavender blue ink at the top of the sheet is the message: "Written with Love, From the pen of PHYLISS MITCHELL."

I have no idea why a woman would carry a sheet of her personal stationery around with her. Perhaps she was planning to write a letter during some boring part of the game. No, that would be too logical. There must be some more diabolical reason—one a man could never comprehend.

No matter what her motive, Phyliss may have helped me win a football game. I carefully fold the page of stationery paper and place it into my back pocket.

ALFRED AND SAM HAVE ASSEMBLED the team in a grassy stretch at the south end of the visitor's bleachers. Many players openly show their exhaustion, lying stretched out on the grass. They are tired and listless. The heart has gone out of my team. Continuous battle against a larger Eastland squad has worn them down.

"Alright, men, listen up! I've just finished talking with Reed Jones' father." My announcement commands immediate attention from my players. Several players roll over and sit up, anxious to hear more of my news.

"How is he, Coach? Is he gonna be okay?" Charles Williams asks.

"His father gave me this letter Reed wrote to the team. Lemme read it to you. You can each judge for yourself how he's doing."

Now every one of my Bulldog players is sitting up, eagerly waiting to hear me read the letter. I reach into my back pocket and pull out the folded sheet of paper. Unfolding it very deliberately, I begin to read:

"To my Bulldog Teammates:

"The doctors discharged me from the hospital today, telling my parents there was nothing else they could do about my condition. They tell me I may never be able to play football with you again.

"You guys on the football squad are the best friends I have in this world. You know how much I love football. Nothing, not even my health, is more important to me than seeing our Bulldog football team have a winning season. Even though I can't be with you on the field tonight, I will always be there with you in spirit. My last request is that you play this game for me the way I would play it for you, if our situations were reversed.

"Your loyal friend and teammate, signed, Reed Jones."

The fraudulent message from Reed Jones works like a charm. My young men act like they've been plugged to an electric supercharger. When I finish, they leap up and chatter excitedly. Dean Sutton requests permission to say a prayer for our fallen quarterback. After the prayer E.P. Robinson suggests we dedicate the game to Reed. I reluctantly agree, after the players overwhelm me with their dogged insistence.

"STUBBY, I WONDER if I might have that letter. I'd like to save it for the team," Sam requests, as we walk along together toward the visitor's bench.

"Sure, Sam. It's an important document, for sure," I reply, handing him the blank sheet of paper.

Sam stops abruptly and holds the sheet of paper up to the bright blur of the stadium floodlights.

"This paper is blank! There never was no letter, was there?"

"No, Sam, there is no letter. It was all a hoax to motivate our players."

"Coach Warden, how could you sink so low? This is the meanest, vilest trick I've ever heard of a coach pulling on his team."

"Yeah, I know, Sam. I'm already having second thoughts. Maybe I should get the team together and explain."

"It's too late for that, Coach! The fat's in the fire now! We'll have to live with what you've done," Sam pronounces angrily.

My assistant coach storms off in a huff, leaving me to walk alone. Some ten yards away, he suddenly whirls around and walks back to me.

"You suppose we could use the same trick again next year, Stubby?" Sam questions slyly, an insidious grin is glued on his face.

"Maybe. Let's see if it works in this game first," I answer, very much relieved to have a willing partner sharing in my crime.

WITH RENEWED ENTHUSIASM our maroon-clad troops square off against the red and black Maverick club. Out on the field, Bulldog teammates exchange violent greetings by slapping each other on their shoulder pads and butting helmets.

Our players' eagerness to begin the second half is contagious. Seeing our players' rejuvenated attitude, Ranger fans, who have remained strangely quiet throughout the first half, rise to their feet, clapping their hands and cheering loudly. The rhythmic vibration of a base drum beating in a thunderous, irregular cadence adds to the electrified air of excitement which has suddenly brought Ranger supporters to life.

Eastland's kickoff soars high in the air. Cracking sounds of padded bodies colliding and groans of powerful, determined young men meeting in solid contact resound across the football field. Comacho returns the football to our thirty-eight yard line where he meets with a swarm of red and black uniforms. The Maverick team has also returned for the second half with new vitality.

"Buddy, let's keep the ball on the ground and try to establish our running game. If we make a first down, we might try the quarterback option pass. Let me decide. I'll send in a sub to tell you when to pass."

"Ralph says they're using two men to cover him. Maybe we can use him as a decoy to get Comacho or Simpson open deep."

"Good idea. Comacho's the fastest. Set him out at left flanker. Have him go deep, while Ralph slants across the middle in front of their halfbacks. Now go!"

Three running plays—a pitchout to Simpson around right end and two quarterback options with Hamrick keeping the ball—net us twelve yards and a first down at the fifty.

"Phillips, get up here," I call out in the direction of the bench.

"Yes sir," the red-headed fullback responds, grabbing for his helmet.

"Eddie, tell Hamrick to call sixty-one, option pass left, on second down. He already knows which formation to use."

"Yes sir. Sixty-one, option pass left, second down," Phillips repeats, while he snaps on his helmet. He nervously jumps up and down on his toes in anticipation of entering the game. I slap him on his hindside to get him going.

On first down Hamrick runs an option left, faking a pitchout to Simpson, then keeps the ball over left tackle for a gain of four. Our passing game has been non-existent since early in the first quarter. Expecting another running play, Eastland's defense draws in tight. Two red and black defenders, a linebacker and a halfback, line up directly in front of Ralph Rogers.

Hut. Hut. Hut. Hamrick takes the snap and fakes a handoff to Phillips then rolls out to his left. Ralph Rogers fights his way past the two Maverick players and cuts across the middle of the field.

"Pass! Pass!" the Eastland linebackers scream, holding their hands high while they move back quickly to cover their defensive zones.

Comacho streaks down the left sideline until he runs beyond the projected path of Ralph Rogers, then cuts diagonally upfield.

As our two receivers cross paths, Eastland's safety is faced with a choice of helping cover our towering right end or trying to catch up with Comacho. The Maverick safety is well-coached. Every long pass we have completed this season has been to Big Ralph. The Maverick defender has been told our quarterback can't throw deep. He runs to help cover the most obvious receiver.

Hamrick fakes a pitchout to Simpson. Simpson pretends to catch the football then proceeds to demolish Eastland's defensive end with a vicious block.

Hamrick stops near the left sideline and waits for Comacho to clear the Maverick defenders downfield. Fierce blocking by Elder, Hummel and Patterson on our offensive line holds back a tide of red and black jerseys trying to break through.

After what seems an eternity, Hamrick draws back and flings the ball in a high spiraling arc. Comacho clears Eastland's safety and is picked up by the Maverick left halfback. They race neck and neck toward the end zone.

At the goal line Comacho and the Maverick halfback leap high for the ball. The red and black defender is taller and stronger. He tips the pass with one hand while he pushes Comacho to the ground with the other. The football bounces high in the air, careening away from the two players.

Comacho hits hard on the ground, rolls over and begins scrambling on his hands and knees, chasing after the descending football. Gathering his feet beneath him, he dives at the last possible second. The football disappears beneath Comacho's maroon uniform.

Two game officials following the play sprint into the end zone. They glance anxiously at one another, each hoping the other will make the call. Fans in both the home and visitor bleachers jump to their feet, howling at the officials, trying to influence their decision.

Every man on the Bulldog bench has leaped to his feet and rushed to stand at the sideline. Many of my players are holding their arms in the air, convinced we have scored a touchdown. Across the field Maverick players signal the pass was incomplete.

"Did he catch it, Coach Warden? I couldn't tell."

Even though I'm only a few feet away, Alfred has to yell his question at me.

The two officials stand in the end zone discussing their decision. Meanwhile, wild pandemonium has consumed both grandstands. This will be a tough call for the officials. Because of the violent history associated with football games between these two cities, a decision against either team could put the referees in serious jeopardy. Their decision might determine the game's outcome.

"I don't know, Alfred. But, if he didn't catch it, surely the referees will have to call pass interference. Their guy was all over Comacho."

Comacho jumps up, holding the football above his head. The other two game officials join their comrades in the end zone conference.

"Stubby, this could get real nasty if they rule against the home team," Sam observes, yelling in my ear.

"Sam, if anything happens, you and Alfred get the team into the bus as fast as possible. Shut the doors and leave for home. I don't want our players involved in an ugly fracas."

"You can count on me, Stubby. We don't want no part of any fighting. I saw that last Thanksgiving Day game between these two schools. You never saw so much blood. Some of the men were still trying to fight while they were being loaded into ambulances."

The officials break up their conference. The field judge steps forward and raises both arms, signaling a touchdown.

Eastland's reaction is loud and abusive. Foul, abusive language and catcalls can be heard all the way across the field. Many Maverick fans leave their bleacher seats to prowl the sidelines and shout obscenities at the officials.

After retrieving the football from Comacho, the four game officials acknowledge their fear of the unruly Eastland fans by hanging close together while they place the ball for the extra point try.

The going rate for officiating a Class One A high school football game is something like six dollars a game. The men wearing black and white striped uniforms are being grossly underpaid tonight.

Knowing we don't have a reliable extra point kicker, Eastland throws up an eight man line to defend against our running play. Our extra point try is stopped cold.

"Hey, Jimmy! Did you really catch that pass before it touched the ground?" Hamrick asks his young Mexican receiver as they return to our bench.

"Yes sir, Meester Buddy. I sure deed. Like I told you in practice—you throw the football to Jimmy—he will geet you a touchdown every time." Comacho flashes a wide, beaming smile. The speedy sophomore halfback is terribly pleased with himself. If he didn't actually catch the football, he'll never tell.

While the scoreboard numbers change, our Bulldog defense huddles to discuss our kickoff strategy:

EASTLAND 0   VISITOR 13

FOLLOWING OUR KICKOFF, Eastland mounts a long drive. Our staunch defensive play makes them earn every yard, but the Mavericks systematically move the ball toward our goal line. Using a relentless ground attack, they grind out a succession of first downs in small chunks of three and four yards at a time. With less than two minutes left in the third quarter Eastland's fullback bulls his way into our end zone. The Maverick extra point try is good.

Eastland 7   Ranger 13

The Eastland score does little to appease unhappy Maverick fans. While they are still mad and upset about the official's decision which gave us our touchdown, they seem even more frustrated by the lackluster, uninspired performance of their team.

Until tonight, this big Maverick team has soundly defeated everyone they've played. A lot of civic pride is at stake here, and a lot of big talk preceded this game. The home crowd was expecting a big win. Now, the best they can hope for is to squeak out a narrow victory. Maverick fans are irritated and disappointed. Their abusive language is almost equally directed toward the game officials and the Eastland coaches.

Sam, Alfred and I talk to our players every time they come off the field, trying to keep them focused on the game and not on the deteriorating situation among Eastland fans.

Coke bottles, rocks and miscellaneous objects come flying out onto the playing field from the home stands at irregular intervals. Twice during Eastland's touchdown drive, the officials stopped the game to clear foreign objects from the field of play.

Fortunately for us, the majority of object-throwing has occurred on the opposite side of the stadium, causing the Eastland home team to dodge various articles being thrown by their own fans. Nevertheless, we caution our players to keep their headgear on, even when they're off the field.

Sam, Alfred and I discuss the possibility of us coaches also wearing a helmet but decide it might only encourage our bombardment. At this point Ranger fans have not retaliated by throwing objects onto the field. Realizing that attitude could change without warning, the three of us stake out positions very close to the sideline. We each keep our shoulders hunched high around our necks.

———————

THE HEAD REFEREE CALLS timeout and runs over to our bench.

"Coaches, I'm afraid this game is getting out of hand. We are seriously considering calling the game and forfeiting the contest to Ranger," the referee advises.

"How does that count in the district standings? Does it count the same as a win for us?" I ask impulsively.

"I don't know, Coach. You'll need to consult with someone else about that. Right now, I'm more concerned about the safety of my crew and the young people on the field."

"What do you think, Sam? Will it count as a win?" I ask, turning to my assistant coach.

"Yeah, it probably does. No, I'm not sure. How the hell would I know! I've never been involved in a forfeit before," Sam replies uncharacteristically, indicating his total lack of experience with forfeits.

"If we don't know for sure, then I don't wanna take a chance," I advise Sam.

I turn back to the head referee. "What does the Eastland coach have to say? Won't he object?"

"We're gonna let you make the decision, Coach. The Eastland coach obviously can't control his fans, so he doesn't get a vote. We will inform him of your decision."

"Good God, man! Have you lost your mind? You want me to make the decision? Hey, you're gonna get us all killed! This place'll go berserk when you inform the home crowd that the visiting coach made the decision for Eastland to forfeit the game."

"That's the way we're gonna handle it, Coach. It's your call."

"Okay. Okay. Wait a minute. How about letting me talk with the Eastland coach? Surely he and I can come up with something better than instigating a riot."

"Like I said, Coach, it's your call. I'll give you five minutes to work something out."

———

A SHOWER OF FALLING OBJECTS pelts the ground around me as I near the Eastland bench. A flying green coke bottle, landing less than five feet away, impels me to run faster.

Wendell Siebert is the Eastland head coach. We've never been introduced, but I recognize him huddled with one of his assistants beneath an oversized parka jacket at the sideline. Their faces are grim. My impromptu visit has caused a fresh new rain of flying objects and more despicable insults from the home fans standing along the sidelines. The two Maverick coaches are not at all pleased to see me.

"Coach Siebert, I'm Stubby Warden, the Ranger coach."

"What the hell ya want, Coach? If you're here to complain about our fans, there's not a darn thing I can do about 'em. Can't you see we're the ones taking the brunt of their wrath?"

"The head referee tells me he plans to forfeit the game to Ranger. When I objected, he gave me five minutes to work something out with you."

"Forfeit! Oh my God! All hell's gonna break loose if the referees declare a forfeit."

"That's exactly what I believe will happen. I have a suggestion. What would you say to meeting me and my Bulldog team in the middle of the field to shake hands in a show of friendship and good sportsmanship?"

"I don't think that'll work. My kids are pretty worked up. Some of 'em are ready to fight. We could end up with our two teams in a bloody brawl."

"I can control my Bulldogs, Coach. Surely you can control your team. This is important. We came here to play football. What did your team come for?"

"To play football."

"Then we'll meet you at mid-field."

Running back across the football field, I travel in a zigzag pattern, keeping my hands up to protect my head from flying bottles. At mid-field I approach the four game officials who are clustered in a semi-circle around the football where they halted the game.

"The Eastland coach and I have agreed to have our teams meet at centerfield and shake hands. We'd be obliged if you gentlemen would join us. Maybe we can get this mob calmed down."

———

WHILE TWO LINES OF YOUTHFUL ATHLETES file by each other shaking hands, the voice of Eastland's school superintendent comes on the loudspeaker system to plead with the crowd to follow the example of sportsmanship shown by the coaches and players, begging fans of both schools to behave themselves.

The Maverick head coach and I exchange a warm handshake at mid-field, smiling and waving to fans on each side of the field. Then we go to shake hands with each game official. The two school bands, picking up on the spirit of sportsmanship, take turns to softly play their respective school songs.

For a few brief moments fans from both cities are treated to a break from the hard feelings which have developed in past football games. Getting caught up in the spirit of the occasion, I make a mental note to get back with Wendell Siebert next week to insure this game be played under more friendly terms next year.

Eastland's coach motions he wants to clasp hands one last time before we return to our teams waiting for us on the sidelines. He smiles broadly to the Eastland crowd while he stands beside me and raises my hand in the air. Applause from Eastland's bleachers is polite, but not enthusiastic.

"Coach Warden, you're a good man. Not many coaches would have the courage to try a crazy stunt like this. It may have done some good."

"Thanks, Wendell. But it wouldn't have happened without your cooperation. My team came to Eastland to play football, not fight."

"You Ranger coaches may be good sports, but your football team is a bunch of cheating, cry baby wimps. And my kids are gonna kick their lily-white asses in the last quarter," the Eastland coach informs me spitefully. He shoves my hand sharply back toward me, then turns his back and heads for his bench.

I was thinking about suggesting something like: "Maybe we could get together with our wives after the football season." I guess that's out now.

OUR UNSTABLE TRUCE with the Eastland fans remains intact until midway into the final quarter. Neither team has been able to move the football. Jensen's long punts keep the Mavericks at bay, forcing them to begin each possession from deep in their own territory.

"Stubby, our kids are taking a hellava beating out there. Sutton, Williams and Davenport are worn to a frazzle, wandering around between plays like three zombies. I don't think they can hold on much longer," Sam advises, telling me something I already know.

"Maybe we should give those guys a rest. We got anyone who can sub for them?"

"Not anyone who can stand up to the three giants they're going up against. Hell, we ain't got no choice. They'd probably collapse and pass out on us if we took 'em out of the game."

Eastland's coaches have spotted the defensive weakness which Sam has pointed out. A huge Maverick fullback crashes over left tackle for a six yard gain. Davenport and Charles Williams make the tackle, but only by desperately hanging on until Barnes can shake free to help. After the play our three defensive players pick themselves up slowly and stagger back to their defensive positions.

"Sam, Davenport and Williams are dead on their feet. We've gotta give 'em a breather. How about sending in Wade or Polston?"

"No, we better stick with who brung us, Stubby. If we're gonna win, it'll have to be with the guys who got us here," Sam argues, reversing his earlier position.

———————

TAKING ADVANTAGE OF OUR WEARY DEFENSE, the Eastland drive gathers steam, ripping off gains of five and six yards on each carry. Sensing a last minute victory, the home stands come back to life. Maverick fans begin to yell, scream and stomp their feet. Eastland's band plays continuously, lowering their volume while their quarterback barks out the signals, then blaring out noisily when the ball is snapped. Maverick cheerleaders use their megaphones, urging their team to drive for the score.

A slashing run by Eastland's fullback carries the football down to our eighteen yard line. Kenneth Williams calls a timeout when E.P. Robinson, who made the tackle, is unable to get to his feet. Pearson and Barnes help an exhausted Robinson to his feet and assist him while he limps to the sideline.

While Sam tends to a groggy Robinson, I counsel with Barnes and Pearson, explaining how to execute my plan for a desperate defensive gamble.

"It's called a safety blitz. With Robinson out, they'll almost certainly try running their fullback over right tackle again. Tell Cunningham not to move up until their quarterback begins calling his signals.

When the ball is snapped, he goes 'kamikaze' style over right guard, straight for their quarterback."

"That'll leave us wide open for a pass, Coach," Pearson perceptively points out.

"I realize it's a big gamble, Champ. But, if we don't make something happen, they're gonna score anyway. Our defense is too tired to stop 'em."

"You're right about that, Coach Warden. We're all too tired to spit," Barnes agrees.

"OH, LORD, please don't let 'em pass," Sam prays beside me, while the two teams square up out on the playing field.

"Don't worry, Sam. I've got their coach figured out. He's gotta go with a running play. That's what's been working for them."

Hut. Hut. Hut. The Maverick quarterback takes the snap, fakes a handoff to his fullback, then fades back to pass. Eastland's right end runs past Varner, the reserve player who replaced Robinson at linebacker, and cuts sharply toward the zone left uncovered by our blitzing safety.

"Oh, hell! They're gonna pass!" Sam yells to me.

"No! No! That's all wrong! They're not supposed to pass. How could they be so stupid?" I scream. A nauseating feeling engulfs me while I visualize our victory slipping away.

Weldon Cunningham crashes through a struggling mass of humanity at the line of scrimmage, untouched. Expecting to meet with violent contact, Cunningham pauses to glance around and get his bearings. He seems dazed by his unchallenged entry into the Maverick backfield and at not finding anyone there to tackle.

Eastland's right end breaks into the clear. Our nearest defender is ten yards away. The Maverick quarterback spots him and draws back to pass.

"Crack!" The tooth-rattling impact echoes across the field after Cunningham hammers their quarterback, at the same instant he releases the pass.

The football flutters harmlessly across the scrimmage line, straight into the arms of a surprised Donald Varner. Varner cradles the football against his chest and falls to the ground.

Our interception causes an immediate outburst of objections from the Eastland coaches. They cry to the officials that we were offside, that we used an illegal defense. Sam, Alfred and I watch their antics with amusement, realizing that, except for the fickle finger of fate, they could be us.

Bulldog players on the field have mobbed Cunningham and Varner. Our entire defensive team is rolling around on the grassy field, hugging each other in ecstatic joy. Ranger fans in the visitor bleachers are on their feet screaming with delight.

"Coach Warden, sometimes I think we gotta be the luckiest team on earth. It seems like we always get some kinda lucky break at the end of every close game," Alfred says to me.

"I prefer to call it great coaching, Alfred. What you just witnessed was a masterpiece of great coaching."

Hearing my boastful reply to Alfred, Sam coughs loudly and turns his head away.

———————

EASTLAND USES THEIR LAST TIMEOUT after Hamrick takes the snap and falls to the ground. The field judge runs over to inform us of the situation.

"Coach, we have thirty-five seconds left on the official game watch. Your team has the football, third down and twelve."

"That's too much time to run off in one play. I guess we gotta punt," Sam surmises.

"No, we can't take a chance on a blocked punt. Get Phillips up here." The referee waits for Sam and me to finish our conversation, then offers some advice.

"Coaches, my crew and I will be leaving the very second the game is finished. I suggest you and your team get to your bus and get out of town as quickly as possible. This Eastland bunch is a keg of dynamite waiting to go off."

———————

PHILLIPS RUNS INTO THE GAME with my instructions for ending the game. Hamrick is to take the snap and fall down on the next play, then let the clock run until the officials flag us for delay of game.

A five yard penalty for delay of game will move us back to the ten yard line, leaving about ten seconds on the clock. On fourth down Hamrick will take the snap and run back into the end zone, holding the football tightly to prevent a fumble when he's tackled for a safety.

"Sam, let's get our equipment sacked up. Alfred, go find Leeman Gentry. I want the bus running and waiting at the gate. Let's get ready to leave as soon as our people come off the field."

Not a single player tarries or causes a delay when we hustle them from the visitor's bench to the bus. Not one Bulldog player ever sees the final score on the big scoreboard:

EASTLAND 9 VISITOR 13

ONCE WE GET BEYOND THE GLARE of the stadium lights, the mood inside the school bus becomes happy and playful.

Alfred lumbers back to sit down beside me. Taking a cue from the cheerful players, he is in exceptionally good spirits.

"We're riding high now, aren't we, Coach Warden? Our team's in first place. We've got everything going for us now."

Bagwell and Hargrave lower a side window to yell "Yea Ranger" at a couple of teenage boys. They quickly shut the window when the two teenagers stoop down to pick up rocks alongside the road.

"Yep, Alfred, we're riding high alright. We've got it made now. Everybody loves a winner."

The stones, thrown by the two Eastland youngsters, pelt loudly on the back of the old bus, bidding us adieu as we speed away from Maverick Country.

CHAPTER SIXTEEN
THE SEVENTH WEEK

Saturday Morning
October 12, 1949

HEY, STUBBY! STUBBY, WAKE UP!" Jerry Lowe shouts in my ear, while he taps on my shoulder through the open car window.

"What? Oh, Jerry, it's you," I stammer, raising my head off the Hudson's steering wheel.

"Are you okay, Stubby? We saw you drive up. When you didn't get out of the car, I thought I'd better come check on you."

"Yeah, I'm fine. Missed a couple hours of my beauty rest last night."

"My team is ready, Coach. We won our game last night. First win of the season for us. My boys were here bright and early this morning, raring to go. They kinda like this winning thing you're trying to teach us."

"Who did you play? I've forgotten."

"Throckmorton. Beat the socks off 'em–21 to 7."

"That's wonderful, Jerry. I'm really happy for you. Get your team set up and have them walk through the plays I taught you last Saturday. I'll be with you as soon as I change shoes."

"Sure thing, Stubby. But, hurry. My guys are really pumped."

Sitting groggily in the front seat, I slip on my cleated shoes and wonder why the Cisco kids should be so excited about beating a team like Throckmorton. I'm surprised a small Class B school like Throckmorton is even on their schedule. I don't believe they have won a game this year. I know for sure they lost to DeLeon, who we beat pretty badly.

Holy smoke! Who am I to be judging them? A win is a win. Winning beats the heck out of losing–no matter who it is you beat.

My coffee cup on the dashboard is still half-full. The last thing I remember is taking a sip of coffee just outside the Ranger city limits. I must have slept the rest of the way.

It's a good thing the Hudson knew where we were going.

JERRY'S ASSISTANT Neil Brooks and the Lobo team welcome me to their early morning practice like a rich uncle. Somehow they have concluded that my arrival to help them last Saturday is connected with last night's victory. They listen intently to my every word, afraid they may miss out on some tidbit of my amazing wisdom.

By the time I reached the practice session, Jerry and Neil had walked their team through most of the plays I taught them last Saturday. We decided it's time to see how well they can execute the "Option Tee" in a full speed scrimmage.

We divide the players into offensive and defensive teams. Neil and I take charge of coaching the offensive team. Jerry is the defensive genius. He takes the defense.

I challenge my friend to come up with a defensive alignment which can stop my offense.

"HEY, STUBBY! I think my kids are getting the hang of your offense," Jerry calls from the opposite side of the line, after our quarterback rushes for a six yard gain against his defense.

"Yeah, they're looking a lot better," I shout back to him, without genuine enthusiasm. The Lobo quarterback made a mistake on the play. He had the defensive end frozen. A pitchout to his halfback could've gone all the way for a touchdown.

If one of my Bulldog quarterbacks made as many mental mistakes as Jerry's quarterback has this morning, I might be tempted to have Sam bring out *Jelly* again.

We continue scrimmaging for about an hour until the Lobo players begin to visibly tire. To their credit, not a single player complains.

Taking timeout for a water break, we send the team running to the water faucets at the opposite end of the practice field. We allow the thirsty players to gorge themselves for a few minutes, then bring them back. Jerry's quarterback has a fair throwing arm. I want to add a couple of passing plays to the offense.

———————

A FIERY-HOT MORNING SUN beats down from directly overhead when Neil points to his wrist watch.

"Coach Warden, it's almost twelve. What say we call it a day? Our guys have learned about all they can absorb in one day," the Lobo assistant coach pleads to me.

"Sure, I agree. How about running one more passing play before we quit?"

"Coach, these guys are bushed! Some of 'em may collapse before they make it to the dressing room."

"Alright, send them to the showers. But next week, I want you to work on those passing plays. When I meet with you next Saturday, I want to hear you completed some passes off the 'Option Tee.'"

"Coach Warden, we play your Bulldogs this Friday night!"

"Oh yeah, I guess you do."

———————

THE SHERIFF'S PATROL CAR turns into the practice field parking lot while I sit in the Hudson's front seat, changing shoes. My friend James Fingler is the driver.

"Whrrrrrrr," the squad car's siren sounds off, causing my heart to jump up into my throat.

Prompted by the shrill siren noise, several Lobo players loitering outside the dressing facility step out on the practice field and curiously gaze toward us. The deputy pulls his car alongside the Hudson and rolls down his window.

"Good morning, Stubby. I heard you were over here, moonlighting as a Cisco football coach. Can't you get enough work in Ranger?" the deputy jokes.

"Just helping out a friend, James. Say, did you have to use the siren? You almost scared me out of my wits. The young men down there will think I'm being arrested."

The deputy laughs loudly, like he has pulled off some big joke.

"I thought that might shake you up. I've never known anyone who gets so spooked by a siren."

"It all depends which side of the siren you're sitting on, James. The law can be very intimidating when you're on the outside looking in."

"Come on, Stubby. You've never been in trouble with the law. There's no logical reason for you to be afraid, is there?"

"I guess not. Maybe I'm overly sensitive. I'll work on it."

"Listen, Stubby. The reason I came to look you up is to let you know the Special Grand Jury issued their arrest warrants yesterday."

My heart stops beating. My breath gets lodged in my throat. This must be the bad news I've been expecting. The deputy used the same tactic when he subpoenaed me to testify–joking with me, then handing me the subpoena document. I glance around the seat of his car, my eyes searching for an arrest warrant.

"Do you have a warrant for my arrest, James?" I ask meekly. My voice is quivering. I can't seem to get a deep breath.

The deputy looks at me pitifully.

"Coach, you are a complete mess when it comes to the law. You really should get some help. Why would the Grand Jury issue a warrant for your arrest? You're a football coach. You don't steal cars, do you?"

"No! No, I've never stolen a car in my life. And I've never bought any bootleg whisky either," I add quickly, giggling aloud with nervous relief.

Suddenly, I'm able to breathe again. "Alfred Steele and I confiscated a little gas for my car, when we were out hunting for Keith Murphy. I hope that doesn't count."

Hearing my humorous response, Fingler laughs and shakes his head.

"Coach Warden, you're quite a comic. You really had me going. For a minute there I thought you were serious."

"Yes, I love a good joke, especially when it's not on me. You were about to tell me about the Grand Jury warrants?"

"Oh, yeah. The Grand Jury granted us a search warrant for the Singleton Ranch and issued arrest warrants for your two buddies,

Clifford and Orval Graves. Sheriff Williams and six Texas Rangers raided the ranch early this morning. We've got Clifford and Orval locked up in the Eastland County Jail. Billy Hancock was out there with them. We got him and three other mean-looking hombres in jail, too."

"Clifford and Orval, arrested. James, that's the best news I've heard in a long time."

"According to Sheriff Williams, they didn't put up a fight. But they were sure beat up when the sheriff brought 'em in. Both Clifford and Orval have broken noses. That Clifford, he smells terrible, like he's been sleeping in somebody's outhouse. I don't reckon you'd know anything about their sorry condition, would you, Coach?"

"How about Lucas Masters? Did the Grand Jury issue a warrant for his arrest?" I ask, ignoring the deputy's question. No one, except me, knows about my confrontation with Clifford in Eastland last evening. I'd just as soon keep it that way.

"No, not yet. But Billy Hancock is ready to sing like a canary. He wants to tell everything. Sheriff Williams thinks he can get the Grand Jury to convene again on Monday. The sheriff plans to run Billy over to Abilene to testify. After Billy tells what he knows, I'm certain we will get a warrant issued for Masters' arrest."

"What about the Vargas Brothers and the Fort Worth Crime Syndicate?"

"I don't know. They're mighty slippery. We haven't been able to directly connect them with the car thefts or with the Singleton Ranch operation. Maybe Masters will testify against them. Right now, that's pretty iffy. We may have to settle for Masters."

"I thought you wanted to bust up the crime ring. Arresting Lucas Masters won't do any good. The syndicate will just move on to some other location and set up for business all over again."

"Yeah, you're probably right. But we do the best we can. Sometimes that means just being a nuisance for the real bad guys and settling for the small-time crooks."

ON MY TRIP BACK TO RANGER, I take a short detour to drive past the Eastland County Jail. From the outside, the building looks peaceful and serene. Locked somewhere inside are Clifford and Orval

Graves, my deadly enemies. I say a short prayer–thanking God I'm not locked in there with them–vowing never to do anything wrong again or let anyone influence me to do wrong.

––––––––––

Monday Night
October 14, 1949

A HALF-FULL MOON peeks faintly over the horizon as I turn into the driveway. Normally, I get home earlier on Mondays, but watching Jerry Lowe last Saturday gave me some ideas about improving our defense. Sam and I stayed late to talk about how we might use some of Jerry's innovative defensive schemes.

Juanita is waiting on the porch. She runs excitedly up alongside the car, before I can pull to a stop.

"Sweetheart, thank goodness you're home! Othel was just over here, looking for you. She's terribly worried. You've got to go down to the bank with Ferrol Creager. He's meeting Lucas Masters there. Stubby, be careful! Ferrol is wearing a gun!"

––––––––––

A DARK, MOTIONLESS FIGURE lurks in the shadow of the buildings across Rusk Street, while Ferrol Creager unlocks the bank's side door. When the bank door swings open, the figure steps out of the shadows and hurries quickly across the street. The mysterious figure is Lucas Masters.

"What's the gun for, Ferrol? Don't you trust me? For Pete's sake, I thought we were friends," Lucas objects acidly.

Strapped to Ferrol Creager's waist is a heavy leather belt and holster. The holster contains a menacing, pearl-handled, thirty-eight pistol. During our drive to the bank, I watched Ferrol load the pistol. The pistol is ready to fire, if necessary.

"I suppose I trust you, Lucas. It's the low-life characters you run with who bother me," Creager replies.

"Don't worry then. I'm here alone. You got the papers ready to sign?"

"Yes. They're there on my desk, ready for your signature."

"You got the cash ready?"

"It's in the safe. You'll get it after you sign."

Lucas Masters strides swiftly to Ferrol Creager's desk in the open work area overlooking the bank lobby. Finding a neatly-stacked pile of papers, he sits down, takes a fountain pen from his shirt pocket and begins applying his signature to each document.

"These deeds will need to be notarized, Ferrol," Masters says, without looking up from the papers.

"Yes. I'll have my secretary take care of that first thing tomorrow morning."

After he signs the last document, Masters pushes his chair back away from the desk and breathes a heavy sigh, like he has completed some monumental task.

"There, that's the last one. Now where's the money?"

"Give me a minute to look these over. I want to be sure everything is in order. Then you'll get your money," Creager replies, sounding very much like a banker approving a routine bank transaction.

While Creager studies the papers, Lucas turns to me, acknowledging my presence for the first time since he entered the bank.

"Stubby, what are you doing here? I didn't know you had an interest in the banking business," Masters asks. His question is cynical, but his tone is gentle. This is not the same man who has bullied people in this town for years.

"I'm just an interested bystander, Lucas. I came to help keep the peace, that's all."

"There are a lot of people who will be glad to see me leave this town. I suppose you're one of them."

"Is that what this is all about? No, I can't say I'll be particularly glad to see you go. We've had our differences, but I was beginning to think we were coming to an understanding."

Lucas grins, then begins to laugh.

"Coach, if you aren't the damnedest optimist I've ever known. I've had you beat up, shot at and thrown in jail, and now you tell me we were coming to an understanding. You make it sound like you have beaten me."

"You're the one leaving town, Lucas, not me."

Masters roars with laughter and slaps his knee. "Okay. Okay, Stubby. You win. I certainly can't argue with you over who's leaving town."

––––––––––

WHEN FERROL CREAGER IS SATISFIED the papers are in order, he walks to the bank vault behind the teller cages and begins spinning the combination lock back and forth. After a complicated sequence of turns, he steps back, grabs the large circular handle and pulls the vault door open.

Reaching inside the vault, Creager retrieves a small brown suitcase, then shuts the vault door, twisting the lock knob to reset the combination.

"Here you are, Lucas. Two hundred thousand, all in small bills, just like we agreed."

Creager swings the suitcase up on his desk and snaps open the lid. The small handbag is filled with neatly stacked bills in denominations of tens and twenties.

"You wanna count it?"

"No. I trust you, Ferrol. In all the years I've known you, I've never seen you make a mistake counting money."

"Then I guess our business is finished. Good luck, Lucas. You know I wish you nothing but the best."

"Thanks, Ferrol. Maybe our paths will cross again someday. I can't think of anyone I'd rather have looking after my money."

Masters turns to me and shakes my hand.

"Stubby, I'm truly sorry for all the grief I've caused you. Under different circumstances we might've been good friends. You're sure one hellava football coach."

"Thanks, Lucas. Coming from you, that means a lot to me."

"You and Ferrol take good care of my town."

"We will. I promise. But, where will you go? What will you do now?" I ask, strangely concerned about my adversary's welfare.

"I'm not really sure yet. Maybe I'll cross the border into Mexico or Canada and hide out for a while, until this all blows over. Then I might head for Venezuela. I hear there's more oil down there than we ever dreamed about here in West Texas. With all that oil, there has to be a place for an old wildcatter like myself."

"You take care, Lucas, and watch out for the sheriff. He's after you."

Masters and Creager walk to the bank door. They shake hands warmly. Then Masters slips through the door into the darkness, carrying the small suitcase.

"I guess we didn't need the gun after all," I say to the bank president with great relief, as he locks the bank door behind Masters.

"This may not be over yet, Stubby. Let's wait in here for a spell. I want to make sure some of Lucas' pals aren't hanging around– waiting to rob the bank after he leaves," Creager tells me, while he mysteriously surveys the dark street outside.

———————

WHILE CREAGER GAZES INTENTLY through the bank window, I sit quietly beside his desk. My mind is inundated with questions about the bizarre event I have just witnessed.

"Ferrol, what just happened here? What were you and Lucas up to?"

Creager leaves his post at the window and comes over to the desk. He shuffles through the stack of documents Masters just signed and hands one of the pages to me.

"Don't worry, Stubby. It was all very legal and strictly on the up and up. What you observed was the bank's purchase of all of Lucas Masters' real estate holdings. It was a good deal for the bank. We paid him about fifty cents on the dollar."

"Oh, I see. Kinda like a fire sale, because Lucas has to leave the country to avoid being arrested."

"That's it exactly, Stubby. You're very perceptive. Look at the description on the deed I handed you. The description will tell you which property we purchased."

"Lot 1, Block 5W of the Ranger Township, as platted by the Texas and Pacific Railway Company. Ferrol, I don't understand all this legal mumbo jumbo."

"Sure you can, Stubby. Come into my private office. I've got a map of Ranger. I'll show you how to locate each property."

On the wall inside Creager's office is a Surveyor's Map of Ranger. The title at the bottom reads:

Township of Ranger, Texas
Surveyed and Platted by the Texas and
Pacific Railway Company, September 1882.

I study the map closely while Ferrol explains how to find the properties described on the deeds.

"You see how the blocks are divided, Stubby? The blocks west of the railroad are followed with the suffix W. The blocks east of the railroad are followed with an E."

"Sure, that makes sense."

"Alright then, see how all the blocks on the north side of Main Street are odd numbers? The blocks on the south side of Main are even."

"Oh, I see. And the lot numbers begin with the lots nearest the railroad–1, 2, 3 and on up."

"You see, I told you there was nothing to it. Now, let's see if you can find the property on the deed I just handed you."

I read the description on the deed again and move my finger along the map to the lot and block which corresponds with the description.

"Hey, that's the P & Q Realty Building. Pearl's Café is on the ground floor of that building."

"That's correct, Coach. Pearl will be paying her rent to the bank next month."

I pick up another deed and locate the property on the map. The property is the Paramount Hotel, directly across the street from Pearl's Café.

"Lot 4, Block 5W. That's the Arcadia Theater. You mean Lucas owned the Arcadia Theater?"

"Lucas owned the building and the property. The Interstate Theater Chain has been leasing the building from him. Their lease expired several months ago. The bank will need to work out a new deal with them."

Spotting a specific lot and block on the map, I begin sorting through the deeds again. I need to verify my darkest suspicions. Yes, there in the stack is the deed I'm searching for–Lots 11 and 12, Block 2W–the Pontiac House. So that's the reason Price Mitchell was so fearful of Lucas Masters.

"Ferrol, what will happen to these people who leased from Lucas? Will the bank continue to lease to them?"

"I really can't say, Stubby. Lucas didn't always own a property strictly for profit. He had plenty of income from other sources. He owned property for power and the control his ownership gave him over the business people he leased to. Some of the tenants in these properties haven't paid full rent for years. A bank couldn't survive doing business that way. The bank will be looking to make a profit on these properties."

"What will happen to the people who own businesses on the properties that don't show a profit? Surely the bank won't kick them out."

"Banking can be a heartless and ruthless business, Stubby. The bank's stockholders will insist their tenants pay full rent, on time, every month. Every property will be expected to show a profit for the bank. Many businesses located on these properties won't be able to pay a fair rental rate. Of course no one can predict the future, but what you may have witnessed here this evening is the demise of down-town Ranger as we know it today."

Wednesday Afternoon
October 16, 1949

A HANDWRITTEN SIGN scotch-taped to the front door of Pearl's Café reads:

Coffee   10 cents
Refills   5 cents

I hesitate for a second before I open the door, trying to decide whether I'm willing to pay a dime for a cup of coffee, just so I can find out about last weekend's high school football scores.

"Good morning, Stubby," Pearl greets me meekly. Her voice lacks the perky friendliness I have come to expect when I enter her establishment.

"Hello, Pearl. How are you today?" I say, taking a seat at the service counter. The newspapers I want to read are stacked neatly at the end of the counter.

"Not so good. I guess you saw the sign on the front door," Pearl replies, abandoning her dish washing duties to walk up to the counter and talk with me. Her eyes are red and puffy. She's been crying.

"Yes, I did. What's the deal?"

"The Ranger bank has purchased this building. They notified me yesterday that they'll be raising my rent to seventy dollars a month–effective the first of next month. Can you believe they could be so heartless? Doubling my rent, right outta the blue."

"No, that certainly doesn't sound fair. Is that the reason you're raising the price on your coffee?"

"I gotta do something, Stubby. I barely make a living out of this place as it is."

"Pearl, I'm not sure raising the price of your coffee is the right solution. Won't you lose a lot of customers?" I already know the answer to my question. I almost didn't come in myself after I read the sign.

"I already have. You wouldn't believe how many of my loyal customers got up and walked out this morning when I told 'em coffee was a dime a cup. That's why I put the sign on the door–to save me the embarrassment." Huge, glistening tears well up to fill Pearl's eyes. She wipes her eyes with her apron, then begins to sob.

"Hey, Pearl, please don't cry. Listen, the bank president is my neighbor. I'll talk to him. Maybe he can do something about your situation."

"Oh would you, Stubby? If I lose this place, I don't know what I'd do. There's nobody in this town who would give me a job, and I'm too old to start over somewhere else."

AFTER I SLIDE INTO THE FRONT SEAT of the Hudson, it dawns on me I forgot to check the football scores. I never even got a cup of coffee. Pearl was so distraught and anxious to lay her troubles on me, she forgot to serve me coffee.

Thirty-five dollars divided by five cents. That's seven hundred cups of coffee a month Pearl will have to sell at a higher price to pay the extra rent. I'm no economist, but even I can see she'll never be able to make up the higher rent payments by raising her coffee price.

If Pearl can't pay the higher rent, the bank will force her out, closing my favorite café. Then, the bank won't be receiving any rent from the property. Pearl works long hours and operates her café very efficiently. If she can't make a go of it paying the higher rent, probably no one could.

Ferrol Creager told me a bank has to be heartless. It seems to me they can also be downright stupid.

―――――――――

Thursday Afternoon
October 17, 1949

"COACH WARDEN, Reed Jones and his dad are over there at the sideline. You wanna talk to 'em?" Alfred tells me, interrupting our offensive huddle.

I raise up to look over the players surrounding me in the huddle. Radford Jones and my incapacitated quarterback stand expectantly along the sideline, just off the playing field.

"Not really, but our players will wanna talk to Reed. Let's put practice on hold. Tell Sam to get out the two game balls. The team can present them to Reed while he's here."

―――――――――

A CHAOTIC SITUATION DEVELOPS at the edge of our practice field. My eager, concerned young men crowd around Reed Jones. Every player is trying to shake his hand and ask about his health at the same time.

Sam patiently monitors the disorderly turmoil until he's satisfied each player has had an opportunity to say something to Reed. Then, handing a football to two of the senior captains, he declares the party is over. It's time to present the footballs and get back to practice. Aills advises the players they can lollygag later, on their own time.

Yielding to Coach Aills' overpowering influence, Elder and Hamrick keep their presentations short and sweet. Both captains say about the same thing–telling Jones how happy they are to see him up and around and expressing their hope that he'll be able to play football with the team again.

─────────────

WHILE SAM HUSTLES THE TEAM back onto the field, I linger behind to speak with the two Jones men. With all the commotion, I never had a chance to say hello. Reed is all smiles, holding a game ball under each arm.

"Reed, thanks for coming by. You doing okay?"

"I'm doing fine, Coach. I should be back in school on Monday."

"That's terrific. We don't want you to get behind in your schoolwork."

"Coach Warden, Bill Yung and Jackie Hummel dropped by to see me last Sunday. They were talking about a letter you read to the team."

"Yes, what about it?" I reply with a smile, trying not to look as guilty as I feel.

"Coach, I never wrote a letter to the team."

"Did you tell Yung and Hummel that?"

"No, I was afraid I might mess up their minds, if they found out."

"Reed, the letter was a desperate coach's ploy to motivate his football team. Eastland had us on the ropes. The team needed a shot in the arm. I used their strong feelings for you to give them a reason to win. I hope you don't mind."

"Then, that's the reason the team gave me the Eastland game ball?"

"Yes. After I read the fictitious letter, your teammates were convinced you were deathly ill, about to die. The team said a prayer for you and dedicated the game to you."

"Coach Warden, you always have the right answer for every situation. Someday, when I get a job coaching football, I'd like to come back and have you teach me every trick you know."

"You've got yourself a deal, Reed. But only if you agree to keep what you know about the letter under your hat. We wouldn't want to mess up the team's minds now, would we?"

Reed Jones smiles sheepishly and nods his head affirmatively.

Radford Jones has been standing a few feet away, listening to my conversation with his son. He has something on his mind, something other than reminiscing about my creative football tactics in the Eastland game.

"Son, why don't you go watch the practice for a few minutes. I need to talk with Coach Warden in private," Radford Jones instructs his son.

"Yes sir. I'll be over there with Will when you're ready to leave."

Reed Jones, carrying a football under each arm, steps gingerly out onto the football field to stand next to Will Brownlee, who is on crutches. The two exchange a few friendly pleasantries before turning their attention to the team scrimmaging on the field.

"What's on your mind, Red?"

"I reckon you've heard about Lucas Masters leaving town?"

"Lucas Masters? Why would he leave town?" I say, attempting to sound like his information is news I haven't heard before.

"Don't be coy with me, Coach. You know dang well why he left. Lucas and I are business partners–at least we were until Monday night. He came by my house to settle his affairs with me after he met with you and Creager at the bank."

"Okay, Red, let's assume I know all about Lucas. What's on your mind?"

"I wanna know if you intend to honor the agreement you made with Lucas about playing my boy at quarterback."

"I honor all my agreements, Red. But Reed can't play. He's still recovering from a serious operation."

"I'm talking about when he comes back. Is he still the quarterback on this team?"

"Red, I've already told you. I honor all my agreements. If Reed recovers sufficiently to play, without hurting our chances of winning, I'll have him in the games as our quarterback."

"As your starting quarterback?"

"Don't push me, Red. I already told you. I will honor my agreements, whether Lucas Masters is in town or not."

"Okay, Coach. Just treat my boy right."

"There's one thing I'll never understand, Red."

"What's that, Coach?"

"Reed is a fine athlete. There are plenty of other positions he

404

could play on this football team. It wasn't necessary for you to make a deal with Lucas Masters for him to play. Why did you do it?"

"Maybe it's because I don't trust football coaches. Football coaches have a godlike power to play–or not play–a boy, but they aren't always good judges of a kid's talent. I know a lot of kids who've spent their senior year riding the bench while a lesser athlete played. Sometimes a coach will look at his prospects and decide to build for next year, playing his young players instead of his seniors. A father who truly wants to see his son play can't leave the decision up to the whims of a football coach whose primary motive may be keeping his job."

"That could be, Red. But what about the young men who lose their playing time because another player's father bought their position."

"Coach, most of these kids will never play another down of organized football after they graduate from high school. If they have a good experience their senior year, they'll look back on their high school years with pride and pleasure. If they have a bad experience, they might spend the rest of their lives fighting off feelings of inferiority, agonizing over a situation which they had no control over. I didn't want my son to leave Ranger High with those kinda feelings."

"Then you'd make the same deal again, even knowing Reed is good enough to play for me. Red, are you sure it was really worth it?"

"You're darn right, Coach. If I had the same choice, I'd do it again–in a New York minute. Making sure my son would be a starter his senior year was worth every penny, and then some."

G.C. BOSWELL WAITS for me in the stadium parking lot as I leave the afternoon practice. Normally he brings my bonus money on Wednesday afternoon. The superintendent is generally prompt and reliable. His absence yesterday caused me some concern.

"Stubby, I apologize for not coming yesterday afternoon. Lucas Masters has disappeared. No one knows where he's gone," Boswell blurts out when I get close.

"Yeah, that's what I heard. What about my bonus money? Do you have it?"

"I'm sorry, Coach. Leo Jackson is out of town on a hunting trip. Gordon Long and Blake Tucker are the only ones I could run down and get to contribute."

"Don't act so worried, G.C. You can get Leo's money when he comes back. I'm sure he's good for it. How much do you have for me?"

"Twenty dollars."

"Twenty dollars! You mean that's all you could raise!"

"That's all I could come up with, Stubby. Leo sometimes kicks in a twenty when he's in a good mood. Lucas always makes up whatever difference I need for your three hundred."

"G.C., I know for a fact that Lucas Masters has left town. He won't be coming back. Does that mean I won't be getting my three hundred dollar bonus for any other games I win?"

"That's about the size of it, Stubby. There's no money in the school budget to cover your bonus. Without Lucas, I'll be lucky to raise fifty dollars a game for you."

Damn! First Pearl, and now me. I wonder how many others will be negatively affected by Lucas Masters' untimely exit.

Sometimes you never really appreciate a person until after he's gone.

Friday Evening
October 18, 1949

"BOOM! BOOM! BOOM!" The loud impact of the palm of Wayne Hargrave's hand beating against the window gently rocks the old school bus.

Hargrave is impatient. He lowers his window and sticks his head out.

"Come on, Coach Aills! Me and Gerald want to bulldog us a Lobo! We didn't leave nothing out there! Hurry up!" Hargrave slams the window shut while Bagwell giggles uproariously at Hargrave's clever play on words.

Unfazed by Hargrave's stimulating persuasion, imploring him to hurry, Sam continues his meticulous inspection around the bus. Finding everything to his satisfaction, he grabs the hand bar at the front of the bus and swings himself up onto the lower step. He takes a long look at the bus passengers to verify everyone is properly seated, then gives a thumbs-up signal to Leeman Gentry.

Not everyone is as jovial as Bagwell and Hargrave. Kenneth Williams and Alton Stiles, sitting in separate seats across the aisle from me, are glum and serious. They haven't spoken a word since they climbed into the bus. Both Williams and Stiles are seniors. This will be their last chance to claim a victory over Cisco. The Loboes have defeated Ranger in this traditional meeting for the past two years.

———————

DESPITE A FEW ANNUAL FIST FIGHTS, the football rivalry between Cisco and Ranger has never been the rowdy, and often bloody, affair which occurs yearly when Eastland and Ranger meet. Possibly, the game is less violent because it has little impact on either team's race for the state playoffs. Cisco is only slightly larger than either Ranger or Eastland, and yet, somehow, Cisco High has been classified as a Class Two A school, requiring them to compete in a higher football classification against much larger cities.

Nevertheless, the Cisco–Ranger game is played each fall with strong emotion on the part of Ranger fans. After the oil boom ended, much of what little money was left behind in the county wound up in Cisco. Cisco is perceived to be a rich man's town–a city of country clubbers who spoil their children with fancy clothes and new cars. Ranger, on the other hand, is perceived as a blue collar, working man's town, with a population made up mostly of roughnecks and ruffians.

In many ways Ranger residents enjoy, and even promote, their city's wild and wooly image, but oh, how they love to beat their rich, sophisticated neighbors in football. Somehow, winning the annual football game proves to Ranger citizens that they are better off than their Cisco counterparts.

There's something almost sadistic in this city's attitude about winning the annual game. The high feelings have spilled over into our football workouts this past week, keeping practices spirited and players eager for the upcoming competition. Just winning the game will not be sufficient to satisfy my team. My Bulldogs want to win big and stomp the Lobo kids into the ground, making them pay for the unforgivable sin of having wealthy parents.

I suspect there's very little truth to the myth of Cisco's flagrant wealth. Most people who live in Cisco work hard for a living and probably have just as tough a time making their ends meet as the people who live in Ranger. The truth makes no difference. The perception is there among my players, and that perception has made it easier for me to keep them motivated. I have used it to my advantage–to insure a victory tonight.

———————

JERRY LOWE COMES RUNNING across the playing field while the field judge bends down to position the football prior to the Lobo kickoff. The official rises and indignantly places his hands on his hips, showing his annoyance at the unorthodox behavior of Cisco's head coach.

Jerry reaches our bench, breathing hard.

"Stubby, I wanna shake hands and wish you good luck."

"Sure, Jerry," I respond, extending my hand. "Good luck to you, too."

"And may the best man win," Jerry adds, shaking my hand hastily. He drops my hand abruptly and turns to run back across the field.

"No! No, Jerry! May the best team win! Best TEAM win!" I yell after him, wanting him to correct his statement.

Jerry glances back over his shoulder and waves at me. He's too far away to hear me above the crowd noise.

"Why is the Cisco coach so friendly, Stubby?" Sam questions gruffly, ambling up the sideline to stand beside me and watch Jerry Lowe run back to the Lobo bench.

"We were college roommates. We played football together at A&M."

Sam solemnly studies the congregation of black and gold uniforms gathered on the other side of the field. I can sense the wheels in his mind turning slowly.

"That don't sound like a good reason. Stubby, I don't like it. He must be up to somethin'. We ain't supposed to be friendly with the other team's coaches before the game. What'll our kids think?"

"HERB WILLIAMS, MOVE BACK! You're offside!" I yell to the tall, lanky Bulldog lined up with our front wall of blockers.

Hearing my warning, Williams glances down and moves his left foot back behind the mid-field stripe, a half-second before Cisco's kicker boots the kickoff.

The football sails high in the air, drifting down into the waiting arms of Jimmy Comacho. Tucking the football under his arm, Comacho cuts quickly to the left side of the field, getting behind a protective shield formed by the bodies of Williams, Patterson and Sutton.

Three Lobo players come crashing into our wall of maroon blockers. Comacho is knocked backward by the lunging tacklers but does not go down. He reaches out with his free hand to touch the ground and steady himself.

Regaining his balance, Comacho swerves around the gigantic pile-up and dashes through a seam in the defense at mid-field.

"He's in the clear! He's going all the way!" a player howls from our bench behind me.

Comacho streaks past a diving Lobo defender, shifting into high gear as he breaks open.

"Go, Jimmy! Take it all the way!" I yell excitedly.

"Hey, Coach, don't get too worked up. I think we were offside," Sam notifies me. His voice is accented with gloom.

Looking across the field, I spot a yellow handkerchief lying on the ground near the forty yard line.

"No way! Williams got back in plenty of time! No way we were offside," I scream at a referee running past us.

The official stops abruptly and turns to face me. A wry, perverted smile is pasted across his face.

"Sorry, Coach, but you're yelling at the wrong man. You oughta be complaining to the head linesman. He's the one who threw the flag on you. However, if you'd like to repeat your remark, I can add on another fifteen yards for unsportsmanlike conduct."

"Say, aren't you the hard ass who worked our Stamford game? I thought I made it clear to your official's organization that we didn't want you working any more of our games."

"The fellow scheduled to work your game called in sick. I'm a last minute sub. Now, you want the penalty or would you like to apologize for calling me a hard ass?" The deranged referee stares menacingly at me. He places a hand on the yellow flag in his back pocket to emphasize his authority.

"We sincerely apologize, ref. Everyone knows you're not a hard ass. You're really just a sweet, lovable guy who's terribly misunderstood. Now, don't you have more important things to do than harass Coach Warden?" Sam intercedes. "Your buddies out there are ready to step off the penalty against us. Shouldn't you be helping 'em?"

The sensitive referee grins, amused by my assistant's commentary. "It's good to see you again, Coach Aills. I always enjoy working these Bulldog games, mainly because you Ranger coaches are such good sports."

"Yeah. And we love you too, Danny Boy. Maybe we'll invite you over for dinner after the season," Sam replies sarcastically.

The referee laughs openly, slaps Sam on the shoulder, then runs away to huddle with the other officials about the offside penalty.

"Sam, you didn't need to butt in. I could've handled that guy. He was just bluffing. There's no way he would've called an unsportsmanlike penalty on me. I didn't cuss him or say anything really bad to him."

"Sure, Stubby. As any fool could see, you had everything completely under control."

"JIMINY CHRISTMAS! Why do we have to start every cotton-picking game the same way? Can't we ever start a game without somebody screwing up?" Sam agonizes, while he stomps up and down in front of the bench.

Players sitting on our bench keep their heads down, fearful they might become the object of the big coach's wrath. After a flurry of loud protests following the penalty, hardly a sound now comes from our bench or from the visitor's bleachers behind us. The offside penalty, which erased Comacho's outstanding kickoff return and our score, has taken the wind from our sails.

BULLDOG PLAYERS CONGREGATE along the sideline while Ranger fans in the visitor's bleachers rise to their feet in anticipation of a second Cisco kickoff. Because of the five yard offside penalty, the football is teed up on the Lobo forty-five.

"Thud!" The dull sound of the Lobo kicker's toe meeting the football summons the players to action. Our front linemen are mad and upset. They rush up angrily to meet the charging Loboes. Herb Williams knocks an onrushing Cisco player off his feet with a bone-crushing side-body block. A second Cisco player stumbles over them and falls to the ground.

Simpson receives the kickoff. He catches Cisco's defense off guard by running straight up the middle of the field. Expecting us to return the football to the outside, the Lobo's coverage is concentrated out along the sides of the playing field. Solid head-on collisions by Elder and Sutton clear away the few black and gold uniforms coming down the middle of the field.

Simpson sidesteps a lunging Lobo at the forty yard line and shifts into overdrive. Jim Patterson's ferocious block levels the Lobo kicker as Simpson runs past at the forty-five.

Ranger players climb up to stand on our bench, jumping up and down, screaming at the top of their lungs. The Ranger bleachers come alive, bursting out with loud whoops and howls of approval. The Bulldog band blares out in an ear-piercing fight song.

Over on the Cisco side of the field I can see Jerry Lowe and Neil Brooks engaged in heated debate. Their wild mannerisms attest to their confusion and frustration.

A yellow handkerchief lies on the grass near the forty yard line.

"Oh, hell! Not again! What is it this time?" I cry, lowering my face into cupped hands. The situation has become embarrassing. My football team is supposedly well-coached. Now, my friend Jerry Lowe, his assistant and their entire team have watched us blow two easy touchdowns because of penalties.

The head linesman picks up his yellow handkerchief and runs over to talk with us.

"Coaches, all four men on your front line were offside on the kickoff."

"What! All of 'em offsides! That can't be," I object.

"Coach, after the five yard penalty the penetration line for your receiving team moved back to the forty-five. All your blockers were in front of the forty-five when the ball was kicked."

"No! That can't be right! You've gotta be wrong. He's wrong, isn't he, Sam?"

"No, he's right. Our guys were offside," Sam dejectedly declares.

———————

CISCO AND RANGER FANS grow impatient. Some ten minutes have passed since the game began, and we haven't completed the opening kickoff yet. Repulsive boos and catcalls rebuking the Ranger club and their coaches burn our ears.

We huddle with the receiving team at the sidelines before a third kickoff try.

"Alright–Elder, Sutton, Hummel, Patterson, Williams–pay attention! Their kickoff will be from the fifty. That means our receiving zone is moved back to our forty yard line. You can't cross the forty until after the ball is kicked. Better yet, why don't you all stay behind the forty until after the play is over?"

The booing, the filthy catcalls and my anxiety about having another offside penalty called against us affect my coaching judgement. My timid instructions do not reflect the hard-nosed, persistent aggressiveness we have stressed in practice.

———————

DEAN ELDER TROTS over to talk with the head linesman while our other players take their positions to receive a third Lobo kickoff. Elder and the official begin an animated discussion, pointing to various yard line stripes across the playing field.

"Sam, I don't think our captain trusts us. Looks like he's decided to check things out for himself."

"You can't blame him, can you? It was our fault they lined up wrong. We should've explained to our front line blockers about the receiving zone moving back after the penalty."

"Are you insinuating I ought to spend less time arguing with the referees and concentrate on coaching the football team?"

"That'd be a tremendous relief to everyone, but you said it, Coach Warden, not me." Sam sighs heavily, shrugging his shoulders to confirm his indignation.

ELDER, WILLIAMS, SUTTON and Patterson fall back to form a wedge at the fifteen after Hamrick fields the football near the back of the end zone.

Hummel's body flies by, bowling over a black and gold uniform who has slipped in behind the wedge, clearing a path for Hamrick. A block by Comacho seals off an attempt to penetrate the wedge from the right side.

Moving upfield to our thirty-five, the blocking wedge begins to break up as our linemen peel out to block. Hamrick slips through the frantic grasps of two Lobo players and scampers to the left sideline. A hip fake at the fifty leaves the last Lobo defender diving at air. Hamrick cuts back to the middle of the field, then gallops into the end zone.

An eerie silence follows Hamrick's titillating return as our spectators survey the playing field for penalty flags. Finally, the visiting crowd explodes. Ranger fans go berserk while Bulldog cheerleaders careen in cartwheels along the sideline. Drums beat and trumpets blare as the Ranger band clamors loudly.

"Well, I'll be a cotton-picker! We finally started a game off right," Sam bellows.

"I knew we could do it. All it takes is great coaching. Isn't that right, Coach Warden?" Alfred chimes in from his seat on the bench behind us.

"Ha! Ha! Ha! Alfred, you're a real comic tonight," I counter in mock annoyance.

Alfred and Sam glance at each other, then burst into hilarious laughter. I join in with them. It's easy to laugh now. We have scored a touchdown—on the first official play of the game.

OUR AMAZING SERIES OF KICKOFF RETURNS sets the tone for the first half. After our kickoff, Pearson recovers a fumble by Cisco's quarterback on their third offensive try.

Hamrick's perfect execution of the option plays keeps the Lobo defense confused and frustrated. We score again in three plays. Comacho carries for the extra point.

With only three minutes expired on the game clock, the scoreboard displays:

CISCO   0   VISITOR   14

A REPEATING SEQUENCE develops for the remainder of the half. We score. We run for the extra point. We kickoff. They receive. They run three plays and punt. We drive the ball down to their goal line and score again.

During the early part of the first quarter Cisco attempts to implement their "Option Tee" offense. The Lobo quarterback never executes proficiently, and our defense, being familiar with the offense, is never fooled. We stop them for no gain on almost every play.

Realizing the "Option Tee" is ineffective against our defense, Cisco abandons the "Tee" and switches to a peculiar offensive formation—something similar to a single wing formation.

Jerry Lowe must've concocted the outlandish formation while he was a Cisco assistant coach in charge of the offense. My friend has never claimed to be an offensive wizard, but his unorthodox offensive formation is worse than pathetic. It's easy to understand why the Loboes are having offensive problems. This new offense is so elementary, my Bulldog defenders figure it out without any input from the sideline.

Only numerous offside and motion penalties by our eager, overzealous players keep the first half from being a total rout.

When the whistle blows to end the first half, the score stands at:

Cisco   0   Ranger   35

COACH AILLS SMILES KNOWINGLY when we meet outside the visitor's dressing facility.

"You about ready to let up on your A&M friend?" Sam asks.

"Sam, this game has gotten out of hand. I never intended or wanted to beat his team so badly. We've gotta hold the score down in the second half. I don't want us to score again."

"Stubby, I'm not so sure we can keep from scoring. Even if we put in all our subs, we'll have to play a few starters. With all our injuries, we haven't got all that many spare players."

"Sam, what if we play the offense on defense and the defense on offense? That oughta slow us down. Surely we can't score if we use our players that way."

"Offense on defense. Defense on offense. Are you serious?"

"I'm as serious as I've ever been, Sam. Put all our subs in the game and let 'em play both ways."

"Stubby, remember the Comanche game. They thought we couldn't overcome a twenty-five point lead, but we did. Our faces will be mighty red next week if we do somethin' stupid and lose this game."

CISCO FOOTBALL FANS HAVE BEEN SUFFERING through a long, losing season. The Lobo's win over lowly Throckmorton has, thus far, been the highlight of a dismal season. When the game started, the home stands were only half-full. Now, after watching their team be thoroughly humiliated during the first half, only the Cisco band, the Lobo cheerleaders and a handful of die-hard supporters remain.

When I announced my plans to reverse our offensive and defensive positions during halftime, my Bulldog players reacted like I was serving up extra large helpings of free ice cream. Both the starters and our subs are excited about playing the second half. Every player has his own reasons. The offensive players want to prove they can play defense. The defensive players want to prove they can play offense. My subs are just anxious to prove they can play–period.

COLE FAKES THE PITCHOUT to Cantrell, then follows behind a crushing block delivered by Al Tune on Cisco's outside linebacker. Ten yards downfield, the Lobo safety tackles our second-string quarterback to save a touchdown.

"Sam, how can this be happening? Our reserves shouldn't be able to run the football better than our starting offense."

"I'll be damned if I understand it, Stubby. I think we've created a monster we can't control."

"Maybe we should have our quarterback take the snap and take a knee on every play?" I suggest half-heartedly.

"You know we can't do that, Stubby. This might be the last chance some of our kids get to play this season. We can't take an opportunity like this away from 'em. Your A&M buddy will just have to take his lumps."

"Yeah, he wouldn't want us to do it anyway. It would be too embarrassing for him."

I walk over to the bench and plop down despairingly beside Alfred. I close my eyes tightly and bury my face in my hands.

The Ranger crowd squeals with delight as Gerald Bagwell catches a pitchout from Cole and runs in for another touchdown.

TWELVE SECONDS REMAIN on the scoreboard clock when Jerry Rushing takes a direct handoff from Cole and rips over left tackle for eight yards down to the Lobo three yard line. Seeing me waving frantically from the sideline, after he calls a timeout, my sophomore quarterback trots over to me.

"Jimmy, I want you to take the snap and fall down. Do not score. Let the clock run out. Do you understand?" I command forcefully.

"But, Coach, Rushing hasn't scored his touchdown yet. Every one of our backs has scored except for Jerry. This might be the last chance he'll get this year."

"No more scoring! If you can't follow instructions, then I'll put someone in there who will!" I bark impulsively.

"I'll do whatever you say, Coach. But Jerry's gonna be disappointed. I already told him this was his turn to score."

THE GAME ENDS with Cole taking the snap and falling to the ground. Young Rushing kicks angrily at the ground, glancing toward me in aggravated frustration.

While my team rallies to celebrate the victory, I rush across the field to talk with Jerry Lowe. He and Neil Brooks are collecting their gear, preparing to leave for their dressing room. Several Lobo players sit dejectedly on the bench, their heads hung down. One player is crying.

Neither Jerry Lowe nor his assistant turns to greet me. They are both obviously angry and upset.

"Jerry, hey, I'm sorry about the score."

Jerry throws the equipment bag to the ground and spins around to face me. His hands begin to shake. His anger causes his voice to quiver when he speaks.

"Coach, if we hadn't been close friends for so long, I'd whip your ass all over this field. There was no call for what you've done to my team tonight."

"You can't mean that, Jerry. That was just a football game out there. Who won or lost, whatever the score, shouldn't affect our friendship."

"There was no need for you to run the score up on my team like that. Look at these kids. They're totally devastated. Because of you and your demented obsession with winning, I'll probably lose my job."

"Jerry, I swear I tried, but I couldn't keep my team from scoring. I played my subs both ways the entire second half. I switched my offensive starters to defense and my defensive starters to offense. I don't know what else I could've done."

"Have your quarterback take a knee, punt on third down. I can think of a lot of ways not to score."

"If that's the kind of competitor you've become, Jerry, then I feel sorry for you. You've got no business coaching football. Your young men deserve a better shake than to have their coach ask an opposing team to lie down for them. That would be even more embarrassing for them than losing by a big score."

Neil Brooks has been listening quietly to my heated discussion with his head coach. He butts in, interceding in our bitter exchange.

"Jerry, he's not lying about playing his subs. He had three fresh-men–Cantrell, Tune and Wade–playing both offense and defense. And, I remember wondering why he moved Burnett and Varner to the offensive line. They both played defensive linebacker positions the first half."

"Yes, and my sophomore quarterback did fall down instead of scoring there at the end of the game. Jerry, how about it? I'm truly sorry about the score. Please accept my apologies and let's shake hands."

"Okay. Apology accepted. I don't feel much like shaking hands, though."

"Fine. But we're still friends. Your team has three more games. We need to get them ready. I'll see you at your practice field, bright and early tomorrow morning."

"I don't know, Stubby. My kids are awfully upset. I'm not sure how many will show up to have you coach them, not after the way your Ranger team beat up on us tonight."

"Jerry, you tell any of your young men who didn't mind losing tonight that they can stay home tomorrow morning. We only want football players who can't stand to lose. That kid, who was crying on your bench, you tell him I want him to be there, for sure."

I glance up at the scoreboard while I jog back across the football field. The scoreboard reads:

CISCO 0 VISITOR 62

I shake my head–in shame and disbelief.

CHAPTER SEVENTEEN
THE EIGHTH WEEK

Saturday Morning
October 19, 1949

A NERVOUS HUSH DESCENDS over the Lobo practice field as I approach the circle of players warming up at midfield. Each young man is suited out in full pads, ready for our scheduled Saturday morning workout.

"Good morning!" I say boldly.

Several Lobo players acknowledge my friendly greeting by grimacing silently at me from beneath their black helmets but continue their stretching exercises without speaking. Even though he stands only a few feet away, Jerry Lowe also ignores my verbal peace-offering, pretending to be absorbed in conversation with his quarterback.

When no one returns my overture of friendship, I stroll silently off the practice field to wait, self-consciously, at the edge of the cinder running track. I was prepared for a cool reception this morning but not for this total rejection. Coming here this morning, after my Bulldogs defeated this team so handily last night, was a mistake. I should've stayed home. I have no business being here. This is not my team. Why should I care whether they win or lose?

Damn! My problem is, I do care. I want to help these kids win another football game. I want Jerry Lowe to succeed. He's my friend–maybe the best friend I'll ever have. I want him to keep this job.

Neil Brooks emerges from the equipment building. Seeing me standing alone, he immediately runs over to welcome me.

"Good morning, Coach Warden. We're all set. Unless you have something else in mind, I was thinking we should continue to work on the 'Option' running plays," Jerry's assistant suggests, without true sincerity.

"Good morning, Neil," I answer, returning his greeting and trying not to show my profound relief at having someone finally speak to me. "No, I wanna try something new. Let's put the 'Option' on a back burner for the time being. I've been racking my brain, trying to figure why this team can't get untracked offensively. There's plenty of talent here. The problem must be in the way we are using our people. Do you realize your team only attempted two passes last night?"

"Yes, I know. And I remember your telling me you wanted us to try more passes. But, to be honest, after your Bulldogs returned those three consecutive kickoffs for touchdowns, Coach Lowe and I totally lost our cool. I'm not saying Ranger shouldn't have beaten us, but Jerry and I have to shoulder the blame for our team's poor performance. We did a horrible job of coaching. We got so stupid we reverted to using that crazy single wing gizmo Jerry invented. We haven't scored using that offense all season."

"Neil, I believe I've been pushing this team in the wrong direction by teaching them an offense which relies mostly on a ground game. An offense that depends on the run works wonderfully for my Bulldogs, but it's just not right for this Lobo squad. I think I knew it last Saturday, but I'm so hard-headed it wouldn't sink in."

"Coach Warden, you can't ask us to give up on the 'Option Tee.' No, Coach! We can't do that. These kids are gonna lose all their confidence in us, if we switch offensive formations on them again."

"No. No, I don't mean give up on the 'Option Tee.' What I have in mind is changing the philosophy to be more pass-oriented. We'll use an 'Option' ground attack to set up your passing game."

"I'm sorry, Coach. You're way ahead of me."

"Let's go talk to Jerry. Darnit, I oughta be kicked for not seeing this last week."

Neil nods his head to agree, but his eyes tell me he has serious questions about my sanity.

"I DON'T THINK SO, STUBBY. How can you be so sure a passing offense will work for us?" Jerry argues. My friend's resentment about last night's score is evident in his stubborn resistance to my suggestion.

"Look at it this way, Jerry. Whatta you got to lose? Your quarterback can't handle the 'Option' running plays. Maybe he'll improve, but right now, he runs the 'Option' like he's got two left feet. And we all know you'll never win any games with that preposterous single wing offense you tried last night."

"Okay. Okay. Now you've hurt my feelings. Maybe my innovative single wing formation isn't so fantastic. But there's no call for you to be so brutally blunt," Jerry laughs, his normal good humor showing through.

"Okay, Jerry. No more cracks about your creative offense. But pay attention to my logic. Your quarterback is a better-than-average passer. You've got several good receivers. Your offensive line is not exceptionally quick, but they've got good size. If we mix in a few running plays with a solid passing game, your Loboes should be able to move the football against anybody."

"TAKE A LOOK. The defense is set in a five-three, expecting another pass. What play would you call now?" I quiz the Lobo quarterback in our offensive huddle.

"Forty-two, option right."

"Perfect. Let's see how it works," I tell the quarterback, then I swivel to speak directly to the right tackle. "I wanna see the outside linebacker on his butt. Do you understand me, son? On his butt!"

"Yes sir, I understand. I'll knock him on his skinny little ass," the big tackle grins.

Neil shoots me an approving smile while I instruct his quarterback about reading the defense. Our team has just completed a third consecutive pass against Jerry Lowe's defense. These offensive players have responded to the modified, air-oriented offense like ducks to water.

"Hut. Hut." The Lobo quarterback takes the snap, fakes to his fullback, then moves to his right behind his linemen.

"Run! Run!" the outside linebacker screams as he scrambles back toward the line of scrimmage.

Expecting a pass, the defensive end has already committed himself to rushing the passer. The quarterback's pitchout to his halfback catches the end flat-footed, fooling him completely.

"Crack!" A ferocious, bone-crushing block sends the outside linebacker skidding across the grass, while the halfback gallops past.

Jerry's defensive back pushes our ball carrier out of bounds twelve yards down the field.

"Was that block alright, Coach?" the right tackle asks, seeking my approval when he returns to the huddle.

Feeling a need to exert my authority, I answer the player through gritted teeth.

"You call that a block, son? I've seen harder licks between little girls at a Sunday school picnic!"

"But, he's my little brother, Coach! My mama will kill me if I hit him any harder."

"Your brother! Oh! Well! Good job. Yes, it was a fine block."

Several players in the huddle lift a hand to their mouths to hide their amusement. Neil Brooks begins to snicker, then hastily raises up to inspect the alignment of the defense.

Their laugh is on me. I really don't mind. It beats the cold resentment I was met with earlier–by a long shot.

––––––––––

NEIL BROOKS WIPES A BEAD OF SWEAT from his eyes and checks his wristwatch, preparing to remind me of the time. I beat him to the punch by instructing him to dismiss practice and send his team to the showers.

A bright October sun has burned away the early morning clouds. The resulting humidity has caused everyone to become soaked with their own perspiration.

Our practice, just completed, has been–by far–the most productive of our Saturday morning meetings. The two Lobo coaches and I are extremely pleased, and actually somewhat astonished, at how easily their team adjusted to an air-borne offense. Excited about the team's improved prospects, Jerry, Neil and I remain behind to talk while the hot, sweaty players sprint for their dressing room and a refreshing shower.

"Who do you guys play this week?" I inquire.

"Stephenville. They'll be tough, only lost two games this year," Jerry advises.

"Have you seen 'em play? I wonder what defenses they use?"

"No. With only me and Neil coaching, there's no one available to do any scouting."

"We've got a film of last year's game somewhere. They'll probably be using the same defenses. Stephenville has the same coach as last year," Neil Brooks informs us.

"See if you can find the film, Neil. We'll take a look at it. We might discover something that'll help you on Friday night."

"Sure thing, Coach Warden. Hey, why don't I go and look for the film? You and Jerry need to talk. I'll see you next week."

"Okay, Neil. Thanks."

Jerry and I hardly speak while he walks along beside me toward my car. Our ugly debate after last night's game has damaged our friendship.

We linger for a moment in front of the Hudson. I want to apologize and make things right between us again, but somehow, I can't find the words. Jerry's always been the talkative one. I wait for him to initiate conversation which will allow us to mend our relationship.

When my friend makes no effort to talk, I decide it's time to leave. Maybe time will heal the wounds we opened last evening.

"I need to go, Jerry. If Neil finds the film, call the Creager house and leave a message. I'll drive over one night next week and watch it with you," I suggest, breaking the long silence.

"Yeah, I'll do that. Thanks for coming this morning," Jerry replies absently. His mind seems a million miles away.

"See you later then."

"Yeah. See you later."

Jerry waits at the edge of the parking lot, facing the Hudson, while I open the car door and slide in. I fumble with the keys, hoping he'll run to me and say something to break down the senseless barrier which has sprung up between us. Finally, I start the engine, back up and turn around.

My friend stands grim-faced, like a statue, at the edge of the parking lot. He continues to watch after me until I drive out of sight.

Sunday Noon
October 20, 1949

THE HUDSON COUGHS and spits out a puff of black smoke before the engine dies, as Juanita, Jerry and I return home from church services. When the car refuses to restart, I shut off the ignition and coast down Main Street, gaining enough speed to swing into my driveway and glide to a stop.

While Juanita gathers up baby paraphernalia, I notice Ferrol Creager trudging along behind a manual fertilizer spreader in his yard next door.

"Juanita, you and Jerry go on inside and change clothes. I need to talk with Ferrol. I'll be along in a jiffy."

"Please don't be too long, Stubby. I have dinner in the oven," Juanita pleads. She remembers how long one of my "jiffies" can last.

WATCHING ME TRAMP ACROSS his yard, my banker neighbor leans the fertilizer spreader against his house and reaches for a multi-colored bandanna tucked in his back pocket. Creager greets me with a grin while he wipes perspiration from his sweaty brow.

"Hello, Stubby. How was church? As you probably noticed, Othel and I played hooky this morning, so I could work in the yard."

"Church was fine, but the sermon wasn't too uplifting. Brother Perkins preached about giving again. Apparently us folks at First Baptist aren't quite as well off as you First Methodist people. Our church is short on funds. We might not be able to meet our financial obligations. We may have to ask the Methodists to loan us their financial advisor."

Ferrol laughs at my reference to his respected status concerning monetary affairs at the Methodist Church.

"I never seem to enjoy sermons about giving either, Stubby. All I do during the week is worry about other people's money. I attend church to nourish my soul, not to listen to more money problems. Your preacher's right, though. With Lucas Masters gone, there'll be a significant decline in First Baptist's income. Lucas didn't always attend church services, but he was always their most generous donor. His leaving will affect First Baptist and a lot of other people."

"That's what I came to ask about, Ferrol. Pearl Fraiser tells me your bank plans to double her rent. Isn't that a little steep?"

"Yes, I definitely agree. Raising our tenant's rents like that is ludicrous. In my opinion, it's not in the bank's best long-term interest. But, the bank's board of directors wants all the properties to begin showing a profit."

"I thought you and Lucas Masters owned controlling interest in the bank. Who are these directors you're talking about? Surely they can't be Ranger people. Ranger folks would know better."

"Stubby, at one time Lucas and I did own control of the bank. Lucas actually owned most of the shares. He offered his bank stock to me before he left, but I could only come up with enough cash to buy a few shares. He sold the majority of his shares to Martin Ratcliff and his partners."

"Martin Ratcliff. Isn't he the president of the Cisco bank?"

"One and the same. Talk about a cold fish–he's got no heart. And he's mean as a sidewinder. He's in the banking business strictly for the bucks. Yeah, Martin Ratcliff has control of Commercial State Bank. He's the one who insisted on our doubling the rents."

Damn! Ranger rids itself of one dictating tyrant and here comes another. And this tyrant may be worse than the first.

———————

Monday Morning
October 21, 1949

A THIN CLUSTER OF CLOUDS blocks out the morning sun as I round the end of the stadium bleachers. Alfred has been waiting for me, squatting on anxious haunches atop the rock wall outside the varsity field house. He leaps down, shoving his hands deep into his trouser pockets. He lowers his head between hunched shoulders and strolls slowly toward me. From his troubled expression I suspect he will be the bearer of unwelcome news.

"Hi, Coach," Alfred says, turning to walk alongside me.

"Good morning, Alfred. You look worried. Is anything wrong?"

"Coach Warden, Sheriff Williams came out to see Mrs. Murphy at the farm last night. The sheriff's known where Keith Murphy was, all along."

I stop abruptly, turning to place both hands up on Alfred's shoulders.

"Alfred, that's wonderful news. Is Keith all right?"

"Yeah, I reckon he's okay. The sheriff came to tell us Coach Murphy will be coming home this week, probably on Thursday."

"So, Keith will finally be coming back home. It'll be good to see him. I'll bet Kate is excited."

"Coach Warden, she already knew. Mrs. Murphy knew her husband was safe all the time. Why didn't she tell us? She had to know we were worried about him, too."

"Kate had to keep it a secret, Alfred. Her husband was in great danger at the Eastland hospital. The people who tried to kill him might've been able to trace him and try again if they'd known Sheriff Williams was responsible for having him moved."

Alfred frowns and gazes straight into my eyes.

"You knew too, didn't you, Coach?"

"Yes, I knew. I'm sorry I couldn't tell you, Alfred. But I gave my word I wouldn't tell anyone. I couldn't even tell my wife."

"That makes it twice as bad then."

"Twice as bad. Whatta you mean?"

"Me and Mrs. Murphy. After I found out she'd known about Coach Murphy all the time, we had a fight. I got real mad, so I packed up and moved out this morning. I was hoping I could move back in with you."

Monday Afternoon
October 21, 1949

SAM GLANCES UP expectantly when I enter the field house. He and Brownlee stand half-hidden behind a heaping stack of grimy game uniforms worn in last Friday night's game. Their grim faces delineate their aversion to the distasteful task as they sort jerseys from pants, getting them ready to launder.

"Stubby, you heard anything about J.L. Barnes? Al Tune and Jim Cantrell told us he wasn't in class today. You think he could be sick?" Sam questions me from behind the equipment table.

"No, not a word. Maybe he was hurt in the game Friday night."

"He didn't mention anything about being hurt. He looked fine when he left here. I don't have a clue why he wasn't in school."

"I've got a good idea why he's staying home. If he's not back in school tomorrow, I'll drive out and check on him."

Monday Evening
October 21, 1949

JUANITA'S FLASHING EYES signal her disapproval as she glares at me from the kitchen door. She gestures for me to meet her outside, in the back yard. I leave Alfred on the floor of the living room playing with Little Jerry and Short Snorter.

"Stubby, how could you? How could you bring him home without talking to me first?" Juanita scolds at me when I arrive at the back steps.

"It's only for a couple of nights. He and Kate had a spat. I'll have everything fixed up between them in a day or so; then he'll be gone."

"We don't have room. Where will he sleep?"

"In the baby's room. There's a full size bed in there. We can move Jerry's cradle into our bedroom, or we can let Jerry sleep in the bedroom with Alfred. Alfred won't mind."

"Alright, we'll move Jerry's cradle into our bedroom. I don't want your friend seeing me in my night clothes. But this can't last. If he's not gone after two nights, you can both find yourself another place to stay. Do you understand me, Stubby Warden? Two nights–that's it."

"Sure, Juanita, I understand. Two nights. No problem. I'll have everything patched up with Kate by then."

Alfred is lying on his back, holding Little Jerry on his chest when Juanita and I arrive back inside. Short Snorter crawls up close to affectionately lick Alfred's face. My bulldog pup is delighted to have his huge friend back home.

Two nights. Surely I can get things patched up between Kate and Alfred by then. Fortunately, Juanita doesn't know about Alfred's enormous appetite. I can explain about that later.

Tuesday Night
October 22, 1949

THE HUDSON DIES AGAIN when I let up on the foot-feed to slow down and turn onto the dirt lane leading to the Barnes' farm house.

"Coach, hold the clutch in 'til we get off the highway. Then you can try and start it up again," Alfred advises.

J.L. Barnes was absent again today, from school and from football practice. I'm almost certain his absence is connected to Lucas Masters' leaving town. Alfred and I have driven out here to talk with the Barnes family.

Holding down on the clutch, I let the car coast until we clear the highway pavement. The Hudson engine chokes and shakes violently when I pop the clutch too quickly. Then the engine catches and starts again, roaring loudly as the car surges forward.

BUSTER BARNES HEARD US COMING. He waits on the front porch, watching while we park the Hudson in the yard alongside his pickup.

"Hello, Buster," I call to him as Alfred and I climb out of the car.

"Coach Warden, I thought that looked like your car. Sounds like you're having engine trouble."

"Yeah, I need to get my car worked on, but it seems like there's never a time when I don't need it. Is J.L. here? I'd like to talk with the two of you."

"Naw. The only ones here are me and the younguns. J.L. drove his maw over to Olden to see her sister. Maw's sister's got a touch of the flu."

"I'm sorry to hear that. How've you been?"

"Not real good, Coach. You know your man didn't show up to

work with me last week?"

"No, I wasn't aware of that. Mister Masters is the man who's responsible for furnishing you with a helper. But, it's late October. Don't you have your crops harvested yet?"

"Not quite. We still got thirty acres of cotton to pick. Then we gotta plow it under."

"I suppose that's why J.L.'s been absent from school the past two days. You must be keeping him home to help get your cotton picked."

"Yep. Without a helper I can't get much work done. I can't just let my cotton crop lie out there in the field and rot."

"Buster, Lucas Masters has been paying your helper, the one I promised to help you get your crops harvested. Mister Masters had to leave town rather suddenly. We have an important game against Hamilton coming up Friday night. Is there any chance J.L. could be back in school by the end of the week? We really need him to play for us."

"Coach Warden, if you'll remember, our deal was you'd furnish me a helper and J.L. could play football. My deal was with you. I don't know anything about your arrangements with this Lucas Masters fellow. As far as I'm concerned, you reneged on our deal. Football's just a game. Keeping my family fed takes priority over any football games. When all our crops are in, J.L. can go back to school. If he still wants to play football, you can have him back then."

"I can't argue with you, Buster, because you're absolutely right. Tell J.L. we dropped by to see if he was okay. We'd like to have him play for us Friday night, but only if it doesn't affect getting your crops harvested."

Damn! Lucas Masters' untimely departure has blown another hole in my plans.

Wednesday Morning
October 23, 1949

"UGGGRRR. UGGGRRR. UGGGRRR." The Hudson tries hard, but it won't turn over. The wear and tear of recent trips to Abilene and Cisco and the chill of the cold fall morning have sapped the life from my car.

"I don't think it's gonna start, Coach. We better think about walking," Alfred suggests. Tiny clouds of steam emanate from his mouth when he exhales.

"I'm afraid you're right, Alfred. Come on. We'll walk to the football field. I'll have Juanita call the Pontiac house to come tow it in. Maybe they can get it fixed today."

Wednesday Afternoon
October 23, 1949

"TWO HUNDRED DOLLARS! Price, that's more than the car's worth. I can't afford to pay that much."

"I'm sorry, Stubby. That's what it'll take to repair your engine. The rings are shot. The valves need grinding. Your motor oil is as thick as mud and as black as coal tar. When was the last time you changed the oil?"

"Sometime last summer, when I was working for you here at the Pontiac House. I'm almost certain I changed the oil last summer."

"You really need to take better care of your car, Stubby. Your next one will last a lot longer if you'll have it serviced regularly. Your best choice here would be to buy another used car. I can give you fifty dollars trade-in if you wanna junk this one."

My faded maroon Hudson sits parked alongside the street curb outside the Pontiac House, looking lonesome and unloved. The usually reliable old car has served me faithfully through the toughest days of my life. Sending it to the junk yard would be like abandoning an old friend.

"Fix it, Price. I don't care about the cost."

"Okay, Stubby, it's your call. The engine repairs will take about a week."

"I don't care. Just make sure nobody treats my car badly."

"Hey, Stubby, it's just a machine. You shouldn't get sentimental about an old car. It'll only cost you money, believe me!"

"Yeah, I know. It's just a damned old car," I agree sadly, blinking back a tear forming in my eye.

Wednesday Evening
October 23, 1949

ALFRED AND I CAUTIOUSLY OPEN THE FRONT DOOR
and sneak inside like two cowards, half-expecting to have dishes
come flying toward us from out of the kitchen. Little Jerry sleeps
quietly in his playpen centered on the living room floor. Short Snorter,
lying close beside the playpen, opens one eye. He seems interested in
our strange behavior but not interested enough to move.

Sounds of cooking come from within the kitchen.

"Alfred, you better stay out here. Lemme try and soothe things
over."

"Okay, Coach. But, be careful. I don't wanna sleep at the football field tonight."

"Me neither, Alfred. It's too darn cold to be sleeping on a hard
concrete floor."

VOWING TO DEFINITELY make a trip out to Murphy's farm
tomorrow and settle the argument between Kate and Alfred, I timidly
slip into the kitchen. A mouth-watering aroma fills the room.
Apparently unaware of our arrival, Juanita stirs diligently at the pot of
stew simmering on the gas stove.

"Hi, hon. What's for supper?"

"Hello, darling. I didn't hear you come in."

"We tried to be quiet. Didn't wanna wake the baby."

"We? Who is we?" Juanita asks despairingly, a scowl quickly
erasing the loving smile from her face.

"Alfred. Me and Alfred."

"Stubby Warden! You promised—only two nights! You promised
me!" Juanita cries unhappily.

"Yes, but the car broke down this morning. I had no transportation to get out to the Murphy farm, to get their argument settled."

"You should've gone last night. Why didn't you go last night? You
could have settled it then," Juanita rebuts unsympathetically.

"Juanita, don't you remember? Last night Alfred and I drove out to talk with J.L. Barnes' dad. With the car acting up, we barely made it back to town."

"Out, Stubby Warden! You and your big friend get out of my house! You made me a promise! I warned you about the consequences if you didn't keep your word."

"But, Mrs. Warden, you can't mean that! It's freezing cold outside! Surely you wouldn't want two frozen football coaches on your conscience. What would you tell our baby when he grows up? Would you want our son's only memory of his father to be that he froze to death in the Bulldog field house?" I plea with exaggerated desperation, trying to change her inflexible attitude by making her laugh.

Juanita frowns indignantly, shaking her head slowly to demonstrate her firm determination. A slight smile begins to creep across her face. She turns back to stir at the pot on the stove. Her soft laughter hints that she may be yielding.

"Okay, Coach Warden, you can stop your begging now. I've suspected all along you'd be bringing Alfred home again tonight. I've already prepared an extra large helping of supper for him. But seriously, darling, this house is too small for all of us. Promise me that tonight will be the last night he stays here."

"I promise. You have my word on it. And, while it's on my mind, have I told you how much I love you today?"

"Yes, I think so. But I wouldn't mind your telling me again. Lonely, love-starved coaches' wives are always desperate for a man's attention," Juanita professes. She lays her big wooden spoon on the counter and melts softly into my arms.

Thursday Morning
October 24, 1949

THE COLD MORNING AIR nips at my bare cheeks as Alfred and I walk along an unpaved section of Walnut Street on our way to the football field. A sharp wind slices through my loose clothing, making me wish I'd worn a heavier jacket. Alfred's face bears an expression of severe pain.

A beat-up brown pickup passes us, then slides to a stop on the gravel roadway a few yards ahead. C.D. Jensen sticks his head out the window and begins to back up toward us.

"Coach Warden! What are you and Alfred doing out here? Don't you know it's almost freezing?"

"My car's in the shop for repairs. We decided to walk. I'm afraid we made a bad decision."

"Get in, before you catch your death. I'll run you wherever you wanna go."

Alfred grabs the door handle of the pickup and holds the door open while I climb in. Jensen's pickup has a stick shift in the floor. I have to straddle the gear shift as I slide over to take the middle seat. The arrival of Alfred's huge body in the cab's narrow front seat makes it necessary for C.D. and me to shift around and squeeze against each other.

"We're headed for the football field. You can drop us off in the parking lot. We really appreciate this, C.D."

Jensen shifts into low gear and stomps on the gas. Anticipating the sudden takeoff, I brace myself. Alfred is caught by surprise. His head bumps against the window above the back of the seat as the pickup jerks forward. Jensen's spinning wheels leave the smell of burning rubber and a trail of dust behind.

"Hey, Coach, no problem. I was headed this way anyway, looking for you."

"Looking for me?"

"Yeah, Coach. Frankie's come down with some kind of flu virus. Doctor Brazda gave him a shot and told him to stay in bed. It don't look like he'll be able to play tomorrow night."

Alfred gingerly massages the back of his head, then grabs my knee to brace himself as Jensen swings sharply onto the dirt road leading up to the football stadium.

Thursday Night
October 24, 1949

"COACH WARDEN, I don't think this is such a hot idea. Maybe we oughta turn around and go back to Ranger. If Mrs. Murphy wanted me back, she would've lemme know by now. She knows where I've been staying," Alfred argues as I wheel the used Chevrolet, on loan from the Pontiac House, onto the dirt road leading up to Murphy's farm.

"Okay. So all that means is that Kate Murphy is a very stubborn woman—she might even be more stubborn than you. Alfred, we need to get this thing settled between you two, before I end up sleeping in the field house."

"I don't know, Coach. I don't see how this is gonna work, not with her husband coming home today. No siree! I just don't see how it's gonna work at all."

Alfred's strong reservations about continuing to live at the Murphy farm after Keith Murphy comes home is probably the key to the problem between him and Kate. Over the past two months Kate and Alfred have shared a warm and close mother-son relationship—a kind of caring relationship which Alfred may never have experienced before. Now, the return of Kate's husband threatens to change all that. Alfred is obviously having a difficult time dealing with having another man come into Kate's life.

Somehow, I intend to get Alfred's situation resolved tonight. I don't plan to spend the cold winter nights sleeping at the field house, not when having Juanita's warm body pressed softly against me in my own bed is the alternative.

Nearing the farm house, I recognize Keith Murphy sitting in a high-backed, wooden rocking chair on the front porch. Several blankets are wrapped around him to protect him from the cool evening air. An old black hat is slouched down over his head. Only his unshaven face is uncovered. Seeing Murphy causes a lump of sadness to lodge in my throat. He seems so weak and pitiful—certainly a far cry from the muscular, virile man I knew only two months ago.

I steer my borrowed Chevy up onto the grass yard fronting the farm house porch and park. Murphy's bleak face begins to beam when he sees us getting out of the car. He waves meekly but does not rise to greet us.

"Keith, we were hoping you'd be here. How are you?" I call to him, slamming the car door shut.

"About as well as can be expected. Come up on the porch where we can talk. I wanna know all about our football team. Kate tells me you're in first place."

"Well, we're tied for first place with Hamilton. We play them tomorrow night. If we can win that one, we should be a cinch to make the playoffs," I advise, stepping up on the porch to shake Murphy's outstretched hand. His hand is cold and limp, like shaking a damp dish rag.

There are a thousand things I need to talk over with Keith Murphy. I want to know details about the night he was shot, about Sheriff Williams moving him to Abilene, about his testimony before the Grand Jury. We could spend the entire evening having him fill me in on things I desperately want to know. It would be so easy to take a seat beside him and visit for hours, but I am a man with a purpose. I am here on a mission of significant importance–to save a place for myself in my own warm bed.

I grab two straight-backed chairs and shove one on each side of Murphy's rocker.

"Here, Alfred, have a seat. Why don't you fill Keith in on our football season? You two will have to excuse me for a minute while I say hello to Kate."

"I think she's in the kitchen, Stubby. She promised me a home-cooked meal. All I've had to eat for the past two months is hospital food," Murphy laughingly informs me when I head for the front door.

"Alfred, Kate tells me you've been staying here to help her while I've been away. I really appreciate your taking care of things around the farm. Kate thinks the world of you. We both do," I overhear Murphy tell my huge friend, as I open the door to go inside.

"Ah, Coach Murphy, it wasn't no trouble. I was more than glad to help Mrs. Murphy. She's a fine lady," Alfred replies modestly.

———————

I DISCOVER KATE MURPHY IN THE KITCHEN beating fiercely on a large bowl of cake batter. Apparently, Keith will also get a freshly-baked cake with his home-cooked meal. My mouth drools while my mind fantasizes about one of her double-layered cakes topped with dark chocolate icing and sprinkled generously with whole pecans.

"Hello, Kate."

Kate Murphy winces, startled by the sound of my voice. She

glances up from the bowl of batter. A tiny spattering of white batter decorates one side of her face.

"Oh, Coach Warden! You scared me. I didn't hear you drive up."

"We just arrived a couple of minutes ago. Alfred is with me. He's out on the porch talking with Keith."

My announcement about Alfred accompanying me causes tears to form in Kate's eyes. Her mouth quivers with sadness when she speaks.

"Stubby, I don't know what got into him. When he heard Keith was coming home, he began to fret. Then he acted mad at me because I hadn't told him about Keith being alive. Next morning, he packed up and moved out. I understand he's staying with you."

"Yes, that's what I came to talk about. I was hoping we could patch things up so Alfred could come back. I know you need his help. Keith doesn't look like he's in any condition to be doing farm work."

"Oh, Stubby, I don't know what I'm going to do. I've been so worried about Alfred. And now Keith comes home. He's so sickly and needs so much attention. How am I gonna do the farm work, drive the school bus and take care of Keith all by myself?"

Tears stream down Kate's face as she begins to weep, then cries openly. She clutches my jacket and pushes her face against my shoulder.

"There, there, Kate. Hey, there's no need to cry. This thing with Alfred is all a big misunderstanding. He wants to come back just as much as you need him to come back," I say to console her, gently patting her on the back.

"Do you really think so? Oh, Stubby, I miss him. He's become like a son to me. Keith and I need him so much."

"Lemme handle it, Kate. Leave everything to me. I'm sure we can make everything work out."

———————

ALFRED AND KEITH ARE ENGAGED in a lively conversation about Murphy's plans for the farm when I arrive back out on the front porch. Alfred grabs the front of his chair and scoots himself up closer to the injured man, hanging onto Murphy's every word.

"Yeah, Alfred, with the right equipment we could make a real show place out of this farm. All it would take is some good planning and a lot of hard work."

"I wouldn't mind working hard, Coach Murphy—not if we had a goal, not if we was building somethin' we could be proud of," Alfred offers anxiously, while I slip silently into the straight-backed chair on the opposite side of Murphy.

"John Deere. Now those folks know how to make a real farm tractor. Whatta you think about John Deere tractors, Stubby? Don't they make the best farm tractor around?"

"Why, yes. I guess so. I don't know much...."

"See there, Alfred! Even Coach Warden agrees with us. I tell you what. Why don't you and I ease over to Eastland this Saturday morning and check out the John Deere tractors?"

"That'd be swell, Coach Murphy. Boy, oh boy! If we had us a John Deere tractor, we could have this farm fixed up in no time," Alfred responds excitedly.

During my absence my young friend has become totally hypnotized by Keith Murphy's persuasive optimism. Murphy's body may be weak, but his mind is still as sharp as ever. Like a sly old fox, Murphy has convinced Alfred he's needed on the farm and has a future here. Alfred has fallen completely under Keith Murphy's spell.

Sitting attentively, I listen while Alfred and Murphy make plans for the farm—talking about what crops they should plant next spring, what fertilizers to use and about the best time to sell their crops in order to reap maximum profits. Murphy does most of the talking. While he explains his visions for each segment of the farm, Alfred's eyes scan dreamily over the farm land surrounding the house. Alfred seems to be visualizing each field abundantly covered with tall green crops, waiting to be harvested.

The absorbing conversation continues for almost an hour, until Kate Murphy comes to the front door to announce supper is ready. Seizing an opportunity to leave gracefully, I beg out of sharing their supper, explaining I need to finish some preparations for tomorrow night's game.

I say my goodbyes hastily, promising to come back soon for another visit. I remove Alfred's bag from the Chevy and set it inside the front door, leaving my three friends on the porch discussing another idea for managing the farm.

Alfred hardly notices my departure.

Friday Afternoon
October 25, 1949

SAM PAUSES to lean against the field house front door. He heaves a deep sigh, gathers his strength and staggers inside.

"Sam, you look terrible. Are you sick?" I ask.

"I don't know what's wrong with me, Stubby. I started feeling kinda putrid right after lunch."

I walk over to my assistant coach and lay my hand against his forehead. His skin feels like it's on fire.

"You've got a high fever. You feel dizzy?"

"Yeah, and my head feels big as a watermelon. My stomach feels like I'm about to throw up any minute."

"Sam, you need to go home and get in bed. I'll bet you've caught the flu bug that's been going 'round. Mildred Getts told me this morning that half the kids in high school have come down with it."

"Stubby, you know I can't go home. We got a game to play tonight," Sam proclaims, his portly body weaving back and forth, as if he's about to topple over.

"You don't have any business being out on a cold night in your condition, Sam. How about letting me drive you home? You can take a couple of aspirins and lie down. If you get to feeling better, your wife can bring you to the game later on."

"No, I'll be fine. I need to...." Sam cups both hands over his mouth and sprints for the toilet area.

Closing my eyes, I try to block out the indecent sounds of misery and pain while I wait outside the restroom. Sam has both arms wrapped around a toilet bowl, puking his guts out.

Friday Night
October 25, 1949

SURVEYING THE PALE, ANEMIC FACES among my Bulldog players, my heart swells with pride. These valiant young men are so dedicated and so fiercely loyal. At least half these kids missed classes today, many climbing out of their sick beds to come here and play football for their school.

The Ranger school band plays faintly and slightly off-key in the background. Only a semblance of our regular band is in attendance tonight. A majority of the band members stayed home, sick with the flu. The home side bleachers are laced with empty seats.

How can a whole town come down with the flu? And why did it have to happen on the night of our most important home game of the season?

"WE COULD SURE USE FRANKIE JENSEN TONIGHT, couldn't we, Coach Warden?" Alfred remarks, stating my inner thoughts exactly after we watch Billy McKinney's punt attempt hit the ground and roll out of bounds at our forty-five yard line.

"Yes, things would be a whole lot better if he were here. But he's not here. We can win anyway. We'll just have to play smarter."

"You bet, Coach Warden. That's what we'll do. We'll outsmart 'em," Alfred agrees, trying to encourage me.

Actually, there's little hope of our defeating the Hamilton Bulldogs tonight. They are well-coached, and they outweigh us by almost ten pounds per man. Hamilton was picked as the pre-season favorite to win the district championship, and they have not disappointed their supporters, coming into this game undefeated.

Without Frankie Jensen's long punts and J.L. Barnes to anchor our defense, things would be bad enough. But now, with half our players either missing or suffering from the flu, we are seriously outmanned.

Out on the football field, Hamilton's quarterback takes the snap, dances back and lofts a long, high pass. Downfield, a lanky red and black receiver leaps high over the outstretched arms of Cunningham and Cole to gather in the football. The Hamilton receiver's strength and momentum carry him into the end zone, dragging our two Ranger defenders along with him.

Groans of despair from the Ranger stands indicate the home crowd's disappointment with their team's poor performance.

I wish Sam was here. He'd help me think of something.

HAMILTON SCORES THEIR THIRD TOUCHDOWN near the end of the second quarter. Cursing under my breath about my bad luck, I pace recklessly up the sideline while our kick-receiving team takes the field.

Distracted by evil thoughts and feeling sorry for myself, I bump hard into Alfred, who innocently steps back into my path. Our collision knocks me to the ground, sending me skidding onto the playing field. I lie there for a moment, collecting my composure. From my embarrassing position I can observe the scoreboard changing at the south end of the field:

RANGER 0   VISITOR 19

"I'm sorry, Alfred. I should watch where I'm going."

"No, Coach, it was my fault. I was looking for Mister and Mrs. Murphy. They said they might come to the game."

Alfred's information activates a brain cell somewhere deep inside my head, reminding me of a stunt Coach Norton once used to motivate a lethargic A&M football team.

"Keith Murphy! Here at the game? Alfred, see if you can find him. Bring him down to the dressing room. He could be just what we need," I exclaim, jumping to my feet with renewed enthusiasm.

LIKE WAR-WEARY SOLDIERS, fatigued and sickly Bulldog players line the bare walls of the varsity dressing room, sitting dejectedly on the floor with heads lowered. Several players simply collapse and stretch out horizontally on the floor, utterly exhausted. Sounds of someone vomiting in the restroom add to the feeling of absolute despair in the room. The flu and the thorough beating applied by the Hamilton club during the first half have this football team in total disarray. My Bulldogs have given up on winning the game. For most of these players their only goal is to survive the second half and go home.

No matter how sick or how exhausted, I will not allow this team to use that as an excuse to accept defeat so easily. What these kids need is a cause–a reason to forget their ills–something to give them new incentive to fight on and play hard.

Keith Murphy and I meet outside the field house for a brief conference before he makes his entrance. I want to make sure he understands the role he's to play.

———————

ALFRED GUIDES MURPHY'S WHEELCHAIR through the front door and pushes him to the center of the room. The unexpected arrival of the crippled coach causes a sudden ripple of noise and activity. Players leap to their feet and hurry over to greet him, patting his shoulders and shaking his hands.

The flurry of players crowding around Murphy allows me to exit the building unnoticed.

———————

MY TEAM CONTINUES TO CIRCLE around Murphy when I re-enter. A murmur of polite conversation circulates throughout the dressing room.

I pick up a wooden chair and fling it across the room. The cracking noise of the flying chair shattering against the concrete block wall abruptly interrupts the friendly conversation. Several Bulldog players jump aside to avoid pieces of the wood chair ricocheting off the wall.

"What tha hell's going on here–some kind of ladies' tea party? Doesn't anyone here care we're losing a football game?" I scream in anger.

"I'm sorry, Coach Warden. Maybe I picked a bad time. I wanted to say hello to my boys," Murphy apologizes, trying to console me.

"Boys? Where do ya see any boys? All we have here is a bunch of weak-kneed, panty-waist girls! You won't find any boys here–you certainly won't find any men in here!" I bellow in loud revulsion.

My players are completely stunned by my raging anger, backing away from me like I've suddenly gone stark raving mad. The room becomes deathly quiet. You could hear a pin drop while I stare grim-faced at the players standing around the room.

"You're wrong, Coach. These boys are all fine young men, but they're sick. You can't expect them to play hard when they don't feel well. Surely you can't expect them to win—not when they feel so bad," Murphy argues, defending the players.

I reach for the edge of the equipment table and flip it over, strewing shoulder pads, towels and rolls of adhesive tape across the floor. Several players wince, fearful for their safety. I kick a metal pail sitting next to the table and send it sailing across the room.

"Coach Murphy, if you think so much of this bunch of mamas' cry babies, you can have 'em! They're all yours! Me, I'm tired of watching them whine and make excuses while they get their asses kicked! I'm sick to my stomach from coaching these sissy girls! My junior high pup team has more real men than this sorry congregation of wimps!"

"Alright, if you feel that way, Coach Warden! Go ahead! This team doesn't need you! We'll show you! We can win without you!" Murphy yells back at me. His voice is overflowing with hostile emotion.

"You take 'em then, Coach Murphy! There's not a winner in this room! They're every one a pack of gutless losers! Just the sight of this bunch of cowards makes me wanna vomit!" I shout, before I storm out the doorway.

LOUD ANGRY VOICES reverberate from within the field house while I wait uneasily on the steps outside, hoping my lunatic psychology will restore my team's broken spirit. The heated roar of voices from inside tells me I have, at least, created a strong reaction.

Ranger team members burst suddenly through the doorway, yelling loudly. Several players bump against me as they brush by, totally ignoring my presence. Their loathsome attitude toward me is my reward for an outstanding acting performance, informing me that my actions have produced the desired effect. My entire team is furious with me. I can only hope they despise me enough to forget how bad they feel. Hopefully, their hate will help them overcome their fear of the Hamilton Bulldogs.

A FUMBLE BY HAMILTON'S QUARTERBACK gives us a quick turnover and possession of the football on their thirty-six yard line. Murphy grins knowingly and signals me a thumbs-up from his wheelchair stationed alongside our bench.

To accentuate my disgust for the team, I have taken a kneeling position on the sideline, some fifteen yards away.

Alfred and Murphy huddle in a brief conversation. Then, Alfred rushes down to speak with me.

"Coach Warden, whatta you want us to do?" Alfred asks, showing his exasperation. He obviously doesn't appreciate my weird psychology.

"Use the 'Option' running plays. Concentrate on the left side. We've had more success running against their left side."

"Okay. That's what we'll tell Hamrick to do. But, Coach Warden, why can't you come tell him?"

"Let's see how this goes, Alfred. If we get back in the game, I'll come back then."

"Okay. But this sure ain't much fun–with everybody being mad at each other," Alfred objects despondently. He runs back to the bench shaking his head.

OUR EXTRA POINT TRY is stopped short by a determined red and black defense, after Hamrick sneaks in for the touchdown. Nevertheless, putting our first points of the evening on the scoreboard causes a stir of activity among home fans. Ranger cheerleaders line up quickly to organize a rousing yell of approval. Drums in the band begin to beat noisily. Perhaps the revived spectator enthusiasm is because our fans remember our ferocious comeback in the Comanche game.

Hamilton receives our kickoff and returns the football to their forty. Using the same strategy which worked so well for them earlier, they begin pounding away at the middle of our defense. Their hard-nosed running plays between the tackles ate us up and wore us down in the first half.

Alfred comes running toward me at full speed.

"Coach Warden, J.L. Barnes is here at the game. He wants to know if it's okay for him to sit on the bench with the team?"

"Sit on the bench? Like hell he will! Where is he?"

"Over there, at the end of the bleachers. You wanna talk with him?"

J.L. BARNES STANDS SHYLY behind the short rock wall at the north end of the home side bleachers. His dirty overalls and faded denim shirt tell me he's put in a full day of laborious farm work. His pair of badly worn work boots suggest he came straight to the game, without taking time to change shoes.

After running most of the distance between us, I slow down to a fast walk, trying not to reveal my elation at having my defensive star show up.

"J.L., what are you doing here?"

"Hi, Coach. My daddy let me off. We got all the cotton picked, loaded and put up in the barn, so he said I could come watch the game."

"J.L., we need you to do more than watch! We're getting our tails kicked out there! Can you play?"

"Yeah, I can play–if you still want me. I thought you'd be mad, because I missed practice this week."

"Let's get you suited out. I'll be mad later."

HAMILTON'S QUARTERBACK calls timeout as J.L. and I arrive at the Ranger bench. Hamilton has driven down to our eighteen yard line. With a third and two situation, their quarterback trots over to the sideline to confer with his coach.

"J.L., you need to warm up before you go in?"

"Naw, I been loading cotton since six this morning. I reckon I'm plenty loose."

"Alright, go in for Varner at middle linebacker. Look for a run up the middle. They don't do anything fancy. Generally, they just use a direct handoff to the ball carrier. Watch their quarterback. He's the key."

———————

A SHARP TWINGE OSCILLATES through my gums after a mighty collision between Barnes and the Hamilton fullback rocks the stadium. The clamorous report reminds me of an occasion when I was one of the parties participating in a similar tooth-rattling encounter.

Ranger fans squeal with delight as they watch Charles Williams chase down the loose football and recover it at the twenty-five. When the lively action ends, H.V. Davenport hastens back to help a slightly-dazed Barnes to his feet. A few seconds later the game officials signal a timeout to allow Hamilton's fullback to be carried from the field.

I've been separated from my team much too long. I step quickly up the sideline and catch Hamrick as he prepares to enter the game.

"Buddy, these Hamilton guys are too big and too strong for us to run against. Let's switch to a short passing game–jump passes, button hooks, short down-and-out passes. You understand? Don't try to throw anything long. Keep your passes short. And no interceptions."

"Sure, Coach Warden, I understand. Are you still mad at us?"

"No, I can't stay mad at you guys. Someone, besides your mamas, has to love your ugly mugs."

"I'm glad you're not mad anymore, Coach."

"Get in there, Hamrick! You throw an interception, and I'll have you running laps 'til your legs fall off."

"I love you too, Coach," Hamrick shouts, grinning back at me while he scampers onto the playing field.

———————

USING SHORT, QUICK PASSES our offense begins to gel, moving the football down the field with remarkable consistency. With gains of four and five yards on each pass, we advance within scoring range of Hamilton's goal line.

Taking the snap at the Hamilton eighteen and rolling out to his right, Hamrick apparently disobeys my instructions to stick with short passes by sending his receivers, Comacho and Rogers, running deep toward the end zone. Hamrick stops near the right sideline, waiting for one of his receivers to break open.

"Damnit! I told him to use short passes," I yell venomously to Keith Murphy in the wheelchair beside me.

"Maybe he don't understand what you mean by short passes, Stubby. Remember, Buddy can throw the football better than fifty yards in the air," Murphy replies in defense of the quarterback.

"When he finishes running laps next Monday, he'll darn sure know what I mean, when I say short."

Comacho and Rogers cross paths near the goal line. Hamrick draws back, pump-fakes the pass, then tucks the football under his arm and races down the sideline. Diving over a would-be red and black tackler at the five, he lands hard, but still holding onto the football, inside the end zone.

"Where the hell did he come up with that play? We've never run that play before," I question Murphy, astounded by our success.

"Well, at least it wasn't a long pass. You won't need to punish him now," Murphy chuckles.

"You're right, Keith. It definitely wasn't a long pass. I suppose we can forgive him for scoring on a play I didn't design," I concede, sharing his amusement.

Phillips runs in the extra point try. At the end of the third quarter the scoreboard reads:

RANGER 13 VISITOR 19

SENSING ANOTHER COME-FROM-BEHIND VICTORY, the home fans remain on their feet through the first minutes of the fourth quarter. Our fans scream wildly at every tackle and with every yard gained which favors Ranger. The excited, cheering crowd acts like a stiff wind behind our backs. Encouraged by our two, third quarter touchdowns, my maroon team responds positively to the loud noise of the supportive home crowd.

With Barnes at middle linebacker, Hamilton finds little success running inside. Changing strategy, they attempt to run outside. Cantrell, Polston, Wade and Burnett smear their outside runs for losses. Our revitalized defense forces Hamilton to punt on every possession.

Despite our inspired defensive play, our offense is unable to mount another offense drive until late in the game. With two minutes remaining, a long punt return by Kenneth Williams gives us possession in excellent position at the Hamilton forty-six.

———————

"HEY, STUBBY! I gotta leave. Kate is worried about my being out in this night air," Keith Murphy informs me.

"Sure, Keith, you go on. Kate knows best. We've waited too long to get you back home to have you get sick on us. I hate to see you leave, though. We might pull this game out yet."

"I hope you do. Alfred can tell me all about it when he gets home tonight."

"Thanks for the help, Keith. Without you, we wouldn't have had a chance to win. It's great to have you back."

"Anytime, Coach Warden. Anytime. Good luck now."

Watching Alfred wheel Murphy over to meet Kate at the edge of the grandstands saddens my heart. I wonder if Keith will ever coach or drive a bus again.

———————

"LISTEN UP, BUDDY! Let's keep the ball on the ground for this first series. If we make a first down, you call a deep pass on the next play. Use the sixty-seven, option pass left," I say, issuing commands to my quarterback.

"Right, Coach. We run the ball, then throw deep. We've been setting 'em up for a deep pass all along, haven't we?"

"You're absolutely right, smart guy. Now, let's see if you can execute as well as analyze," I challenge.

Three "Option" running plays to the left side net us a first down at Hamilton's thirty-four. Before calling the next play, Hamrick steps away from the huddle and glances toward the sideline to make certain

I haven't changed my mind. I nod my head affirmatively.

Hut. Hut. Hamrick takes the snap, fakes to Dorsey and shuttles back into a blocking pocket formed by Comacho and Cole. Ralph Rogers bumps the outside linebacker and cuts toward the right sideline.

Hamrick pumps the football in the direction of Big Ralph, then rotates his body to face the left side of the field. He fires a pass to Alton Stiles who is waiting all alone in the left corner of the end zone. Stiles clutches the football to his chest and falls to the ground, making an easy catch seem terribly dramatic.

Our touchdown sends the Ranger grandstands into hysteria. The flu-riddled band blares while people scream and stomp their feet. Despite sickness and adversity, their beloved Bulldogs have pulled out another miraculous victory. A successful extra point try is all we need to secure another win.

Finally realizing we don't have a reliable place kicker, Hamilton throws up a nine-man defensive line. Phillips runs into a brick wall. Our extra point try is stopped short.

Ranger   19   Hamilton   19

"WHY NOT KICK IT DEEP, COACH? There's only a few seconds left. Let's settle for a tie. That's a whole lot more than we hoped for at halftime," Alfred pleads with me.

"No, we can still win this game. An onside kick. We can get the ball back and score again," I tell him stubbornly. A twinge of guilt, nourished by our thwarted extra point try, weighs heavily on me. After seeing Hamilton's nine-man defensive line, I should've signaled for a timeout and switched to a passing play.

The kicking team hurriedly musters about me before the kickoff. With our regular place kicker on crutches, we've not been inclined to waste valuable practice time working on onside kicks. In Texas high school football an onside kick is rarely used. Some of my players may have never seen one.

I quickly explain that the football must travel ten yards before we can legally make a recovery. Billy McKinney nods his head as if he comprehends. Several of my players act confused, probably wondering why I'm not satisfied with a tie.

———————

MCKINNEY KICKS THE FOOTBALL perfectly. The oval shaped ball rolls end-over-end until it reaches the fifty, then bounces high in the air. Hamilton's front linemen scramble madly for the football while my maroon-clad warriors charge boldly into the mass of bodies.

Several players of both teams touch the football, before it squirts away—straight into the arms of a Hamilton halfback who has run up to join the frantic struggle.

The red and black halfback seems shocked, surprised at finding the sought-after football fall suddenly into his arms. A split-second later he regains his senses and streaks for the Ranger goal. Kenneth Williams runs him down and pushes him out of bounds at our two yard line.

In the space of a few seconds my team's role has changed from dominating aggressor to hanging on by a thread, praying for some miracle to salvage a tie.

Opposing players at the Hamilton bench raise their arms in triumph, hopping up and down, shouting with glee at their good fortune. Our Ranger grandstands have become deathly quiet. Their coach's stupid obsession with winning has erased their team's amazing comeback.

"Good grief! How could that happen, Alfred?"

"I don't know, Coach Warden. Maybe we weren't supposed to win tonight. Maybe fate was just teasing with us."

For two running plays our defense stubbornly denies Hamilton's fierce charges. Finally, on their third try, Hamilton's fullback plummets over a writhing heap of bodies into the end zone. Their extra point kick is good.

Time runs out as Cole is tackled on the forty after the Hamilton kickoff.

Bleary-eyed Bulldog players come running off the field with heads hung low. My disappointed players, obviously blaming me for the loss, avoid me like I carry some sort of plague. They have every right. To a man, every member of this squad gave their all tonight, reaching deep for the courage and strength to match a stronger and superior opponent, only to have my passion for victory snatch away their reward. My ever-gnawing need to win has caused my team's defeat.

Alfred and I slowly collect the equipment around the bench, not talking, not wanting to face the players in the dressing room. My head aches. My body joints are stiff. I feel a fever coming on.

The scores posted on the scoreboard beyond the south goal posts add to my pain:

RANGER   19   VISITOR   26

Saturday Morning
October 26, 1949

"STUBBY! STUBBY DARLING, wake up! Jerry Lowe wants to talk with you. He's at the front door," Juanita's voice beckons to me from somewhere far away, somewhere in outer space.

"What! Oh, Juanita! Honey, I don't think I can make it to the door. What time is it anyway?" I answer drowsily, trying to lift my head off the pillow. My bed seems to be spinning inside the bedroom. My face feels hot and dry.

"It's a few minutes after two. Sweetheart, I know you don't feel well, but Jerry is terribly excited. I think he's going to explode if you don't come talk with him."

"Okay, okay, gimme a minute. Maybe I can make it, if you'll let me lie here for just another minute," I answer. My body is a mass of pain. My head hurts. There's no way I'm getting out of this bed, not until I feel better. Jerry Lowe's news can wait.

"Stubby Warden! You can't fool me with that line! You have to get up right now! We can't leave poor Jerry standing out on the porch all night."

My mind spins like a top when I push my aching body up and slide around to sit on the edge of the bed. This blasted flu has hit me like a sledge hammer. I feel miserable. I'll never understand how my sickly players made it through a football game tonight.

Juanita hands me my bathrobe. I slip my arms through the sleeves and wrap it around me gingerly. After a moment of deliberation, I stand up and stagger barefooted across the room and down the hallway, bumping against both sides of the doorways when I pass through.

Midway across the living room a sudden wave of nausea hits me. I open my eyes wide, trying to keep from throwing up on the carpet.

Through the front door window I see Jerry clap his hands and rub them together, then cup his hands against his mouth and blow through them. I open the door and slide outside, keeping my back against the exterior wall for support. Beneath my thin bathrobe my bare legs immediately alert me to the chill of the cold night air.

"Hi, Jerry. I apologize for taking so long. Don't come too close. I'm not feeling well. I think I've caught the flu."

Jerry is high as a kite. He completely ignores my apology and my warning, oblivious to my pain and agony.

"Stubby, we won! We beat Stephenville!"

"You don't say? Hey, that's terrific. What was the score?"

"Twenty-seven to twenty. Stubby, my Loboes are in first place! Breckenridge lost tonight. Can you believe it? We're in first place!"

"That's wonderful. Look, Jerry, I feel terrible. I need to get back to bed. Can we talk about your game later?"

"Sure. Sure thing, Stubby. I'm sorry to bother you so late, but I had to come by and let you know you're a genius. You were right about the new offense. Our air game caught 'em with their pants down. We really wore 'em out with our passes."

"You mean the passing offense really worked then? And, in a real game? Well, I'll be damned."

"Get some rest, Coach. I'll tell you all about it tomorrow morning."

"Tomorrow morning? Jerry, there's no way I'll be well by tomorrow. You think you could get along without me? I really need to stay in bed until I shake this flu bug."

"Yeah. Sure. You stay in bed. Neil and I know what to do now. I'm sure we can get by one Saturday morning without you. Take it easy and sleep in tomorrow."

"Good. But, Jerry, you and Neil keep working on the 'Option' running plays. If you wanna keep winning, you'll need to develop a reliable running game."

I hear Jerry starting his car engine shortly after I close the front door. As he backs out my driveway, the glow of his headlights shines through my front windows. The lights dancing across my living room wall cause my delirious mind to imagine a crazy scenario.

What if Jerry keeps his coaching job, and I get fired? Jerry's Lobo team has only won two games all season, and yet, somehow he's in first place. My team's lost only two games. We're tied for second and, most likely, out of the playoffs.

Why do things come so easy for men like Jerry? No matter how irresponsible his behavior, he always comes in first, while conscientious chumps like me struggle—so desperately—to come in second. Life is really not fair.

Another wave of nausea sweeps over me, interrupting my brooding thoughts of self pity. I bolt for the bathroom.

Chapter Eighteen
The Winter Wait

Monday Afternoon
October 28, 1949

A SIGN TAPED TO THE FRONT DOOR of Pearl's Café
reads:

By Customer Request–
Coffee is again 5 cents a cup.

I pause for a few seconds on the sidewalk outside the café, contemplating about the new sign. A strong blast of cold wind whips up the
back of my jacket, encouraging me to get inside.

Pearl is working behind the lunch counter. Seeing me enter, she
abandons her culinary chores and rushes around the counter to greet me.

"Oh, Stubby, I'm so glad to see you. How can I ever thank you?
What you did was absolutely wonderful," she declares, laying her head
against my chest and hugging me tightly.

"I'm glad you feel that way, Pearl. But what could I possibly have
done to deserve such loving admiration?" I reply, laughing to hide my
embarrassment and surprise.

Pearl releases her hold on my body and shoves me backward,
continuing to grasp my arms. She looks straight into my eyes.

"Didn't you see the sign on the door, sweetie? You've saved my
business."

"Saved your business? Pearl, I swear I don't know what you're
talking about."

"Don't try and play innocent with me, Coach. Ferrol Creager
dropped in to see me early this morning. He said, because of your

intervention, the bank has decided not to raise my rent. He even apologized for the inconvenience the bank had caused me. Can you believe it–the bank president apologizing to me? Oh, Stubby, how did you ever make them change their minds?"

"He told you that! Pearl, it's not true! As much as I'd like to take credit for your good fortune, it's simply not true. Sure, I talked to Ferrol, but he never agreed to reduce your rent."

Relaxing her grip on my arms, Pearl walks back to the other side of the serving counter. I slide onto a stool facing her.

"You shouldn't be so modest, darlin'. Why would he tell me you were responsible for changing his mind, if it wasn't true?"

"I don't know, Pearl. I truly don't know."

"Well, I believe the bank president. And I still think you're absolutely wonderful. You want some hot coffee?" A happy smile has replaced the tears and worry which clouded Pearl's face during my last visit to her café.

IN SPITE OF A BITING COLD WIND, downtown Main Street is bustling with activity. Only a few high school students were absent when classes began this morning. It seems that, over the weekend, the Ranger community has completely recovered from the sickness which literally brought us to our knees. The epidemic of influenza that struck this town like lightning last week has departed as quickly as it arrived.

After a rugged weekend bout with what Juanita refers to as the "three-day flu," I awoke this morning feeling quite chipper. Except for wobbly knees and a very sensitive stomach, I feel fine.

Football practice begins in less than an hour. Even after Friday night's disappointing defeat, I have a burning desire to know the results of other games in our district.

Pearl and I talk small talk for a few minutes. She seems perturbed when I reach for the stack of newspapers, realizing I am more interested in the sports news than her latest town gossip. Shrugging her shoulders, she marches back to the kitchen to chat with her cook while I scan through the sports pages. In the Sports Section of the *Abilene Reporter* I find a synopsis of the latest standings and game results for each district:

District 8A

	Conf.		Overall	
	W	L	W	L
Hamilton	3	0	8	0
Eastland	2	1	7	1
Ranger	2	1	6	2
Comanche	1	2	5	3
Dublin	1	2	5	3
Gorman	0	3	4	4

Friday's Results

Eastland	27	Dublin	20
Comanche	20	Gorman	6
Hamilton	26	Ranger	19

No surprises here. Hamilton and Eastland have the best teams in our district. Except for my Bulldogs, all the other teams have now been eliminated. Well, at least we're not out of the district race, not yet anyway. Eastland and Hamilton still have to play each other. If Eastland could win that game, and if we can win our two remaining games, we could still share a piece of the district title with Eastland and Hamilton. That's a whole lot of ifs.

District 6AA

	Conf.		Overall	
	W	L	W	L
Breckenridge	2	1	6	2
Weatherford	2	1	5	3
Cisco	1	1	2	6
Mineral Wells	1	2	5	3
Stephenville	1	2	5	3

Friday's Results

Cisco	27	Stephenville	20
Mineral Wells	27	Graham	7
Weatherford	28	Breckenridge	26

Oh! Now I understand about Jerry's Loboes being in first place. Jerry was stretching the truth a bit. Actually, his team is tied for first with two other teams. All the teams in District 6A have at least one loss. Jerry's Cisco team has a long way to go, but who's to knock it–being tied for first place ain't bad. Wouldn't my Bulldogs love to be in their position?

Before I can leave, Pearl returns from the kitchen to thank me again, despite my repeated denials of responsibility for the Ranger bank's benevolence.

––––––––––

SNOW FLAKES COVER THE WINDSHIELD of the borrowed Chevy which I left parked against the curb, a few doors down from Pearl's Café. A bone-chilling north wind ripped through the city early this morning, bringing a shower of light sleet. Now the sleet has turned to snow. Practicing football in cold weather, and on a snow-covered field, can be pure unadulterated hell for both players and coaches. Nevertheless, I have no intentions of canceling today's practice. After losing to Hamilton last Friday night, I don't intend to reward my team by letting them have a day off.

Before I head to the field house, I stop by my house to pick up long underwear.

––––––––––

AGONIZED SCREAMS OF DISTRESS emit from the gang showers. The blatant screaming causes a sly grin to creep onto Sam's face. He hunches his back and concentrates on the pair of shoulder pads he and Brownlee are repairing. He makes no move to go and determine the cause of the shower anguish.

An unclothed Billy Simpson rushes into the equipment room. Tiny droplets of shower water stream down his bare skin. A small white towel is cinched about his waist.

"Coach Aills! There's no hot water in the showers! Can you check and see what's the matter?"

"I already know what the problem is. The problem is–you people lost a football game! We don't provide hot water in the showers for losers!"

Unruffled by the curt answer, Simpson grins and tries again. "You're kidding, aren't you, Coach Aills? You wouldn't make us shower without hot water. We'd all catch our death of a cold."

"No, I'm not kidding! And you can tell your buddies in there that they'll get hot water, when they win—not after they lose!"

Simpson waits impatiently, his chilled body trembling as he shifts from one foot to the other, trying to decide whether the big coach is joking. Finally, he leaves. Yells of obscene profanity follow Simpson's return to the showers.

"Sam, aren't you overdoing this a bit? Some of these kids haven't fully recovered from the flu. If they get sick again, we're liable to catch hell from their parents," I argue, thinking a dose of common sense might persuade my assistant to reconsider his diabolical behavior.

"We ain't furnishing no hot water to losers!" Sam declares firmly, ending all discussion.

A FEW MINUTES after the last player leaves the field house, Sam and Alfred emerge from the dressing room. Alfred grins profusely, like a big gorilla. Both men are nude except for towels wrapped around their waists.

"Here you go, Stubby," Sam says, handing me a clean towel. Sam's offer of the towel baffles me, then I realize what he has in mind.

"What! Oh, no! No, Sam, I just got over the flu. I'll take my shower when I get home."

"Your players took their punishment without putting up much of an argument. Now it's time us coaches stepped up to the bar."

"No, Sam! Really, I can't! What you're asking is utter insanity! No, I won't do it. It's too damn cold."

"Are you gonna join us, or are you too chicken-hearted?" Sam challenges.

"Yeah, are you man enough to join our little party, Coach Warden? What are you—a mouse or a man?" Alfred chimes in.

"Oh, crap! I suppose I'm a man," I reply, knowing I'll regret my answer.

Sam and Alfred watch with great amusement, standing and

shivering at the shower entrance, while I slip out of my clothes.

"You ready now, Coach?" Sam asks.

"I'm as ready as I'll ever be. You realize, this is stupid? You two are absolutely insane. You know that?"

"Alright, go!"

"YAAAAAAAAAA!"

Three towels drop to the floor as three crazed football coaches run butt-naked into ice cold showers, screaming wildly at the top of their lungs.

Tuesday Morning
October 29, 1949

"NO CHARGE! Price, I don't understand. We agreed I would pay you two hundred to repair the engine," I argue with Price Mitchell, as we talk inside his office.

"Stubby, after the way you stood up for the merchants of this town, taking on the bank, I can't charge you for repairing your car. I wouldn't feel right," Price tells me.

"Stood up to the bank? Price, all I did was ask Ferrol Creager how the bank could justify raising rents the way they did. Actually, I only asked about the rent at Pearl Fraiser's place. We never discussed the Pontiac House."

"That's not the way I heard it. Creager's telling everyone his board of directors totally capitulated after you interceded for us."

"HELLO, BEAUTIFUL," I say to flatter the Hudson when I slide behind the steering wheel and pat the dashboard affectionately.

"I've really missed you, baby. From now on I'm gonna treat you right. And that's a promise. You can count on it," I add, gently inserting the key into the ignition.

The engine kicks over and fires up on the first try, then begins to purr like a kitten, every cylinder hitting in perfect precision.

My Hudson has missed me, too.

WHEN FERROL CREAGER notices me in the bank lobby, he quickly offers an excuse to the customer sitting beside his desk, rises and walks swiftly to greet me.

"Stubby, what a pleasant surprise. I don't think you've been in my bank since you came in to pay back your loan."

"Haven't had a good reason to come in, Ferrol. Juanita handles our money now, so she does our banking. Actually, she's a much better money manager than I am."

"Yes, women can generally make a dollar stretch further than us men can. So, what brings you in? Is there something I can help you with?"

"Ferrol, there's a story going around that I'm responsible for the bank changing its mind about raising rents on the properties you acquired from Lucas Masters."

"Yes, that's the story I've been telling, and it's quite true. After I informed my board of directors about our discussion and your concern for our tenants, they sent a man from the Cisco bank over to inspect each of the properties. Apparently, the Cisco fellow agreed with you. Martin Ratcliff called me at home last Sunday evening, instructing me to visit with each of our tenants on Monday morning and rescind their rent increases. Ratcliff seemed alarmed that you'd take time to get personally involved."

"The Cisco bank president was worried about what I think? No, I can't believe that."

"Stubby, he specifically instructed me to make you aware we had changed our policy concerning the rent increases. Didn't Juanita mention I came to your house Sunday evening? She said you were too sick to talk. I'm sorry. I should've followed up, to make sure you got my message."

"Ferrol, now I'm totally confused. I've never met Martin Ratcliff. Why is he so concerned about what I think?"

"All I can tell you is he seems to be very impressed with you. He tells me you are personally responsible for salvaging the Cisco High School football season. Isn't it true they hadn't won a game, until you volunteered to help them?"

"Well yes. But...."

"Are you sure you've never met him, Stubby? Martin Ratcliff knows all about you. Aren't you supposed to be best man in his daughter's wedding?"

OUTSIDE THE BANK I sit dumbfounded behind the wheel of the Hudson, talking to myself.

Maybe there actually is a God up there–a God who watches over us and rewards us for our good deeds. Man, He sure works in mysterious ways.

UNEVENTFUL WINTER DAYS PASS SLOWLY while the football season winds down. With the outcome of the district title and gaining a spot in the playoffs no longer in our hands, my players grow weary of long, grueling practices in cold, unpleasant weather. My dogged insistence on perfect execution by every player adds to their frustration.

Neither of the two teams remaining on our schedule has much incentive to defeat my Bulldogs. Both Dublin and Gorman have been eliminated from contention for the district title. After entering district play with winning records and great expectations, both teams now find their football seasons in shambles. With only school pride to play for, our final two opponents lack the competitive fire which drives me and my Ranger team.

On Friday night we travel to Dublin to derail a halfback nicknamed Clarence "Freight Train" Randolph. Before he runs against our stingy Bulldog defense, Randolph is the district's leading ball carrier. With Barnes keying on him every play, we apply a painful brand of brakes to the "Freight Train," allowing him to rumble for less than 70 rushing yards and making him pay dearly for every yard. A fumble and an interception allow the Lions to roll up a first quarter lead, then my Bulldog offense gets on track and comes roaring back.

Final Score: Dublin   25   Ranger   34

After a promising pre-season, Gorman's football club has faded badly, losing all of their district games. My Bulldogs and a cold, blustering winter evening only add to their woes, making the Panthers yearn for the beginning of basketball season and the comfort of a warm gym.

The contest between Ranger and Gorman is the final regularly scheduled game for both teams. Our senior players, realizing this could be the last football game they'll play together, meet before the game and dedicate themselves to one final victory. My emotionally-aroused Bulldogs establish control of the game on our first offense possession. We score three touchdowns in the first quarter. The outcome of the game is never in doubt.

During the second half I try to hold the score down by using second-string players at every position. My compassionate gesture has little effect. Even our reserves score at will. The Panther offense never mounts a serious scoring drive.

Final Score: Gorman 0   Ranger 51

Monday Morning
November 11, 1949

"COACH WARDEN, a Wendell Siebert from Eastland has been trying to reach you. He's called several times," Mildred Getts advises me, when I arrive at the principal's office to check my mail.

"Wendell Siebert. He's the Eastland football coach. I wonder why he'd wanna talk with me?"

"Eastland plays Hamilton this weekend. Maybe he wants you to help him get his team prepared."

"It'll be a cold day in hell when I go outta my way to help that jackass. He and his assistant coaches treated us very badly the night we played the Mavericks."

"Don't you read the papers, Coach Warden? Hamilton lost to Dublin last Friday. If Eastland wins their game against Hamilton, we'd be district co-champs with Eastland. Since we defeated Eastland, that means our Bulldogs would represent the district in the playoffs."

"Dublin beat Hamilton! District co-champs! Hey, that's fantastic news. Mildred, please get my good friend Wendell Siebert on the line for me."

———————

"HELLO, COACH WARDEN. It's so kind of you to return my call," the Eastland coach says cordially, like we're old friends. Apparently he's forgotten the bitter feelings and harsh words which were exchanged when our teams clashed only a few weeks ago.

"Hello, Wendell. My secretary tells me you called," I reply curtly, trying to sound annoyed and inconvenienced at having to return his call. He may not remember his display of disgraceful animosity, but I certainly do.

"Yes, I called to ask a favor. As you probably know, my Mavericks play Hamilton this Friday night."

"Your season's not over yet? My Bulldogs played their final game last Friday. I'm surprised you're not finished," I interrupt, purposely trying to intimidate him.

"Normally we would be done by now. Our game with Hamilton was originally scheduled to be played in September, but because of a conflict with the Jaycee's Rodeo that weekend, we requested a change in the game date. The Hamilton coach was kind enough to agree to move our game to this weekend."

"Oh, I see. A rodeo has priority over your high school games. I'm glad we don't have that situation here in Ranger. I don't think I could handle playing second fiddle," I respond cattily, insinuating I'm in complete control of my football domain.

Ignoring my snide remark, Eastland's coach continues, "My purpose in contacting you is to request your help. Because of our full schedule, we haven't been able to scout the Hamilton club. Your team has played Hamilton, I was hoping you might be willing to share a few tips which might help us prepare for them."

"Why would you think I'd be willing to help you, Wendell? After the way you people treated us the night we played? Surely you recall how indignant you acted when I asked for your help in controlling your fans?" I question him angrily, verbally unloading my bruised feelings.

"Coach Warden, I'm amazed a fine coach like yourself would still be upset about things which occurred in the heat of a hard-fought football game. Please accept my apologies. This game with Hamilton is much too important. We shouldn't let any past animosities affect our goals. Don't you realize how significant this game is for us? Surely you understand that, if we win, Eastland will share the district championship with Ranger, but your team will represent the district in the playoffs."

"Yeah, I know all that. Alright, for the sake of our teams, I suppose I can put aside my ill feelings. I'll do what I can to help you," I concede, finally giving in to his request. I've made my point. Maybe he'll think twice about treating me or my team badly again.

———————

Monday Afternoon
November 11, 1949

NOT WANTING TO BE CAUGHT in an embarrassing situation where I might be forced to explain the Maverick coach's presence, I decline Siebert's offer to meet me in Ranger. I'm fairly certain our sharing information about a common opponent is perfectly legal, but somehow, I can't overcome the feeling that I'm conspiring with the enemy.

After lunch, I drive to Eastland, taking along our Hamilton game film and some personal notes I recorded the week after the game.

Coach Siebert and I meet inside the Eastland High School gymnasium. As we watch the game film, I point out how we shut down Hamilton's running game by having our middle linebacker key on their quarterback. I also explain how we had more success running the football to our left side and suggest his Maverick team use short, quick passes to keep the Hamilton defense off balance. After about an hour of viewing film and reviewing my notes, our coaches' skull session concludes.

"Coach Warden, you've been a great help. From what I've seen here, I believe we can give Hamilton one heckava game this Friday night."

"Actually, Wendell, you should win. You've got home field advantage, and I truly believe you have the best team we've played this season. With the size of your kids, you should match up very well against Hamilton, on offense and on defense."

"I hope you're right, Stubby. I promise we'll do our dead-level-best to win."

"After playing your Mavericks, in your home stadium, I have no doubt that your football team and this entire town will be doing their dead-level-best to win. With so much on the line Friday night, Hamilton will be lucky to get out of here alive. I'm certainly glad we don't have to play you at home again, at least not for a while," I state jokingly.

"Yeah. Hey, Stubby, I suppose I should apologize for our fans. Truly, they're not always so bad. They just seem to get especially riled when we play Ranger. What say we get together after the season and talk about some things we can do to keep our football games from getting so out-of-hand? Maybe you and the Missus could meet me and the wife for dinner some evening?"

"Wendell, that's a terrific idea. I'll call you after the season is over," I answer enthusiastically.

"I wonder why I never thought of it," I mutter sarcastically to myself while I walk to my car.

Thursday Morning
November 14, 1949

"STUBBY, I CAN'T BELIEVE you're afraid to go. Half the population of Ranger will be there. How can you not go?" Juanita chastises me, finding fault with my decision not to watch the Hamilton–Eastland game.

"I've discussed it with my coaches, Juanita. We think attending the game would be a bad idea. It might jinx us. Sam and Alfred have decided to stay home, too. Besides, my heart couldn't stand the strain. I might expire right there in the Maverick grandstands, if Hamilton were to win."

"Admit it, Coach Warden. You and your assistants are all chicken-hearted cowards. After all your big talk about football coaches being so mean and tough, while underneath, the three of you are actually all spineless cowards."

"Okay, Juanita, maybe you're right. I admit it. I'm scared to death. I'm afraid we won't make the playoffs, and then, I'm afraid we will. I've never taken a team to the state playoffs before. I don't even know how to go about scheduling a game with the team we might play."

"It's a good thing you men don't have the babies. You'd be out of a job, Coach. With your kind of courage, there would never be any boy babies to grow up and play football."

"I couldn't agree with you more, hon. It's plenty tough, just being the boy babies' football coach."

Friday Night
November 15, 1949

"GOOD NIGHT, DARLING. I think I'll go on to bed. Are you sure you want to wait up? The game won't be over until after ten. By the time they eat and drive back to Ranger, it'll be close to eleven o'clock."

"I think I'll stay up a while longer. Vonceil Hopper and the cheerleaders promised to come by and tell me who won. I wouldn't be able to sleep anyway, not until I know about the game."

HONKING CAR HORNS out on Main Street precede rapturous screams of delight, then a thunderous knocking on my front door. The loud noises frighten Short Snorter. He leaps from the couch and waddles quickly to the protection of the hallway. Anticipating good news, I lay aside my playbook and hurry to the door.

"Coach Warden, Eastland won! We're in the playoffs!" the cheerleaders howl when I open the front door.

"Eastland won? Well, I'll be darned! What was the score?"

The cheerleaders on my porch are much too excited to answer. Several girls run wildly out into the street to yell at passing cars. The young women are ecstatic, out of control, jumping up and down, screaming in thrilled exultation.

After a few minutes of sharing in their victory celebration, I begin to fear their uncivilized screams and the mad chaos surrounding my house will wake my neighbors.

My initial attempts to calm the young women go totally unheeded, but eventually, I convince the cheerleaders to relocate their celebration to some more appropriate location. Reluctantly, they finally agree to leave, but before returning to their car each girl insists on congratulating me on the football team's success by hugging me and kissing my cheek.

The tires of the long Cadillac squeal and the car weaves from side-to-side, as the cheerleaders' vehicle makes a sharp U-turn to head back down Main Street. Watching the car filled with screaming females drive away, I realize no one ever told me the score. I wonder if a single one of the girls actually remembers the score.

Oh well, who cares? It's been a night to remember. I'll visit Pearl's Café tomorrow morning, find out the final score and read all the details.

———————

"WHAT WAS ALL THE NOISE ABOUT?" Juanita asks sleepily, as I slip into bed beside her.

"The cheerleaders and Mrs. Hopper came by to tell me Eastland won the game. We've been out on the porch. All the girls insisted on kissing me before they'd leave."

"Oh. Well, goodnight, darling. You can tell me all about it in the morning."

———————

"WHACK!" Something smacks me in the face, interrupting my deep sleep.

"Whack!" The object hits me hard in the face again. This time I come fully awake. Juanita stands over me, my night slipper in her hand.

"What! Juanita, what are you doing?" I complain groggily, as she draws back to hit me again.

"Stubby Warden, I've warned you about hugging and kissing other women! Now you're going to pay!"

"Juanita, stop that! You really hurt me! Besides, I'm an innocent man. It was their idea, not mine. You're the only woman I love."

"You've sinned, and you have to pay," she chastises, laughing as she draws back to hit me again.

Reacting swiftly, I lunge up to grab her arm as she swings the night slipper, and pull her roughly to me.

"Love me, Juanita. Love me, right now. I need you so much. I can't wait any longer," I demand, reaching around her waist to pull her closer to me.

Juanita kneels to tenderly kiss my lips. "We've waited much too long, darling," she whispers, letting her nightgown slip from her shoulders and fall to the floor.

Oh, how amazingly unpredictable, this woman I have married–half-angel, half-tiger–the light of my life.

Chapter Nineteen
The Controversy

Monday Morning
November 18, 1949

A LONG LINE OF STUDENTS seeking information about game tickets and other playoff related activities extends through the waiting room and out into the hallway. Ringing telephones and the lively clicking of typewriters at work articulate the busy hum of this morning's excitement inside the principal's office.

"Oh, Coach Warden, thank goodness you're here!" Mildred Getts cries. Her belabored voice reflects the frantic circumstances. "You've had several phone calls. It seems like everyone wants to talk with you this morning. The Ballinger coach called. He wants to arrange a meeting to decide about the bi-district game site. Superintendent Boswell needs to see you. His secretary says to tell you it's urgent. A reporter from the Abilene paper left his number. He wants to do a follow-up story on Coach Murphy's shooting."

"Mildred, I'd better talk with Boswell first. Get me a list of the people who called. I'll return their calls after I meet with the superintendent."

"Tell Mister Boswell I could use some help. Maybe he can send Kathleen over. It's been absolutely chaotic here this morning."

Leaving Mildred in a state approaching total panic, I walk across the street to Boswell's office. The situation in the superintendent's office is similarly hectic.

Several people who I don't recognize are waiting in the reception area. Boswell's secretary has a telephone receiver pressed against her ear. She looks unusually harried. Giving me a half-hearted smile, she motions for me to go on in.

Boswell is also on the telephone. When he sees me, he lays a hand over the speaker.

"Have a seat, Stubby. I'll be with you in a minute," he says, gesturing toward a chair opposite his desk.

I take a seat and wait silently while he finishes his conversation. After a few minutes he excuses himself and hangs up.

"Good morning, Stubby. I'm sorry you had to wait. It's been like this all morning. I've never seen people in this town so excited."

"Mildred Getts said you wanted to see me. I suppose we need to decide about the bi-district game site."

"Yes, there are a number of things we need to consider, but first, give me your opinion on where we should play."

"I wanna play the game at home, here at Bulldog Stadium. Where else would I want to play?"

"Well, there are a number of things we should think about. From all indications, we can expect the largest turnout of Ranger fans for any game this season. And there should be an equally large number of Ballinger fans who attend the game. Our stadium is much too small to hold that large a crowd, and our parking facilities will be woefully inadequate."

"G.C., surely you're not proposing we play the game in Ballinger?"

"No, we have another choice. Under Interscholastic League rules, Ballinger must agree to a mutual site if we insist. The Abilene High School stadium is an excellent facility. It will accommodate more than twice as many fans as either Bulldog Stadium or Ballinger's stadium, and the parking facilities are very good. Arrangements can be made for each school to share in the concessions sold at the game."

"G.C., please, let's not make this an economic decision. We want to win this game. Our best chance of winning is to play the game here, at home. I definitely think we should try for home field advantage."

"Look at the big picture, Stubby. By playing in Abilene, our school system should benefit much more financially. Besides, if we choose to flip for choice of fields, we might lose. We could end up playing Ballinger on their home field. I hear it's very tough to win there."

"I want to play at home, G.C. When we win, the school system will benefit even more, by sharing in the proceeds of another playoff game."

"Coach, you're not thinking straight. You could be making a very poor decision. Please consider the consequences."

"I've already thought about it. I want to play here. Don't you worry. Everything will work out fine. I'll win the coin flip–guaranteed."

LEAVING THE SUPERINTENDENT'S DOMAIN, I return to the principal's office in the main building. The earlier confused commotion has diminished. Mildred Getts has the phone numbers ready for me.

My first call is to Ballinger. The Bearcat coach has been waiting on my call. He also prefers to flip for home field advantage rather than play on a neutral field. We agree to meet in Abilene at one o'clock to determine where the game will be played.

It's essential to get the game site decided quickly. A thousand things need to be done before game time. Tickets will need to be printed and distributed. Newspapers need to be notified. Travel plans for the visiting team have to be arranged. The home team needs to prepare their concession operations for the anticipated large crowd.

Boswell and I ride together to Abilene to meet with the Ballinger people. I don't object when the superintendent volunteers to take his car. It would be embarrassing to have Ballinger's delegation see us arrive in my Hudson.

We meet on the front steps of the Taylor County courthouse, the building where I testified before the Special Grand Jury only a few weeks earlier. Boswell is a personal friend of the district judge and invites him to do the honors of flipping the coin. Ballinger's coach agrees to let me make the call.

"Heads," I call confidently, while the coin spins in the air.

The judge catches the coin and slaps it to his wrist.

"I'm sorry, Ranger. Looks like it's a tails," the judge informs us.

"No, that can't be. Lemme see," I object in disbelief. A hard knot lodges high in my stomach as I lean to inspect the coin on the judge's wrist. Boswell's lips are pressed together tightly. His worst fears have come true.

"We choose our home field in Ballinger. How about a game time of two o'clock on Thursday afternoon?" the Ballinger coach offers, trying to subdue a smirking grin creeping across his face.

"Thursday is Thanksgiving. An afternoon game should be warmer and more pleasant. Yes, that should be acceptable. What do you think, Coach Warden?" Boswell replies courteously, recouping from his shock of my losing the coin toss.

"Yes, I suppose I can live with that," I answer, choking back my disappointment. I'm sick to my stomach. I can't breathe. How could I have been so arrogant and stupid? I need to lie down somewhere.

"Fine then. We will call you tomorrow morning to make arrangements for our game tickets," Boswell diplomatically advises the Ballinger delegates. I'm thankful he takes charge of the conversation. Suddenly, I am in a very ugly mood.

We shake hands politely with the Ballinger delegation. Boswell lingers on the steps for a few minutes, talking with the district judge. An overwhelming premonition of defeat prevents me from any display of social grace. I head for the car and wait there, pouting.

Our trip back to Ranger is quiet. Boswell hardly speaks to me. That's fine with me. I don't feel like talking anyway.

Monday Afternoon
November 18, 1949

"HELLO, COACH," a familiar voice addresses me from inside the dressing room. I'm in a sour mood, still smarting from my bad luck at losing the coin toss.

"Hello, Reed. Haven't seen you in a while. How you doing?" I reply, my mind questioning why he should be here.

"I'm fine. My doctor says it's okay for me to play football again. I dropped by to give you my release slip. I hope you'll let me play again."

"Reed, you haven't worked out with us in weeks. We're in the midst of the state playoffs. Every game we play from here on could be our last. I doubt if there'll be many opportunities for you to play."

"Coach, I'm still in good condition. I've been exercising every day. This is my team. I really want to play again."

"Lemme think about it, Reed. Maybe I'll feel different later.

Right now, I'm in a really bad mood."

"Coach, at the Comanche hospital you told me to hurry and get well because you needed me. You said I was your quarterback."

"Okay, Reed, don't push it. I've said a lot of things since I took this job that I've come to regret. Let me think about it."

A moment of weakness after the Comanche game and the ghosts of secret agreements with Lucas Masters have come back to haunt me. After achieving my goal of making the playoffs, how can I be having such a horrible day? Good Lord, what else can go wrong?

WILL BROWNLEE HAS BEEN WALKING without crutches for over a week. I catch up with him in the parking lot before practice.

"Will, how's the leg feel? We've been hoping you'd be well enough to play in the playoff games. Is there any chance you can kick for us?"

"I don't think so. My leg still hurts me if I walk on it too much."

"How about suiting up today and trying a few kickoffs, just to see how it feels?"

"Sure, if you say so, Coach Warden. My dad would sure like to see me kick in the bi-district game."

"I'd bet my last dollar you can do it, Brownlee. Trust me. You'll do just fine."

WALKING TOGETHER along the edge of the playing field, Alfred and I discuss our plans for a Thanksgiving meal after Thursday's game.

"How is Keith? I suppose he's happy to be home for Thanksgiving?"

"Coach Murphy is gittin' along fine. He spends a lot of time studying seed catalogs. We got big plans, come spring."

"I'm glad to hear that. Will they be at the game on Thursday?"

"I don't think so. It's a long trip. Mrs. Murphy thinks it's too far for her to drive."

"She's probably right. It is a long trip, probably too long for Keith. I'm sure Kate will have a wonderful Thanksgiving meal waiting for you when you get back from Ballinger."

"Yeah, I'm kinda glad we play Thursday afternoon. I don't think I could eat a thing before the big game."

"Alfred—you, me and Sam, we'll all be skin and bones if we keep on winning."

Seeing my conversation with my assistant coach is finished, Buddy Hamrick hands the football to Jimmy Cole, leaving him in charge of their passing drills. Hamrick trots over to speak with me.

"Coach Warden, could I see you for a minute, in private?" Hamrick asks, when he gets close.

"Sure, Buddy. What's on your mind?"

"I wanna talk about Reed. He tells us his doctor's given him the green light to play football. Are you gonna let him come back and play quarterback?"

"I haven't decided yet, Buddy. Reed hasn't practiced in weeks. You're the one who got us to the playoffs. What do you think I should do?"

"Coach, I've talked it over with most of the other guys. We all agree. Reed should be our quarterback. He's a senior, and he's missed most of the season. This could be his last game."

"I'll agree with you on one thing, Buddy. If Reed plays quarterback, there's a darn good chance it'll be the last game of the season for everyone. If I do something stupid and lose, it could be the last game I coach for Ranger High School. No way I'm gonna jeopardize my job, just to satisfy the whims of a bunch of emotional schoolboys."

"Just think about it, Coach. That's all I wanted to say."

"No. You've made up my mind for me. It's totally out of the question."

"HE LOOKS PRETTY GOOD, don't he, Coach?" Alfred exclaims enthusiastically, as we stand and watch Will Brownlee walk back to attempt another kickoff. Brownlee walks with a slight limp.

"He's not really booming the football, but it beats anything we've seen around here lately. He needs to work, Alfred. It's been a long time since he's kicked."

Brownlee signals his receivers downfield and begins his short-step approach for another kickoff. The impact of his right foot hitting the football echoes across the field. The ball sails high, traveling some forty yards before reaching the peak of its trajectory.

"That one sure looks good. If he can kick like that on Thursday, this team'll be a whole lot better," Alfred observes.

"For sure, Alfred. One heck of a lot better. I'll never know how we made it to the playoffs without him."

"It was great coaching, Coach Warden. Don't you remember?" Alfred grins.

"Oh, yeah, and a little luck," I add, laughing at Alfred's new found humor.

———————

Tuesday Morning
November 19, 1949

EVEN THOUGH LOSING the home field advantage still gnaws at my insides, the townspeople have easily shrugged off their disappointment of not hosting the bi-district game with Ballinger. Downtown, along Main Street, the city is afire with anticipation of the upcoming football game. Any automobile or pickup which does not proudly display maroon and white streamers or a "Beat Ballinger" message on its rear window can be quickly identified as being from out of town.

Everywhere signs and banners have sprung up in support of the Bulldog football squad. Our game is scheduled for Thursday, Thanksgiving afternoon. Being on a holiday, not a single store will be open for business. There's even been talk about closing down one of the two hospitals to allow hospital staff members to attend the game.

Ballinger is some 120 miles from Ranger, about a two hour automobile drive. In spite of the distance, more Ranger fans will attend this game than any home game we've played this season.

Superintendent Boswell left a message in my box asking me to drop by his office. Entering his offices, I say hello to his secretary Kathleen, then take a seat while Boswell finishes a phone call.

After a few minutes the secretary nods her head at me, indicating the superintendent is off the phone and available. I jump to my feet quickly and enter his office before his telephone rings again.

"Good morning, G.C. You wanted to see me?"

"Yes. The Ballinger coach called this morning. According to him, they have the option of selecting game officials because they won the coin toss. I didn't object. At the time he sounded convincing. I didn't think anything of it. Then, I thought maybe I should check with you, to see if he's right."

"G.C., I don't know the rules all that well, but this doesn't sound right. Ballinger has a notorious reputation for administering their special brand of 'home cooking' against visiting teams. Can't we call the Interscholastic League and find out if he's right?"

"Yes, I'll call them today. Surely we should have some say in selecting the game officials."

"I don't trust these Ballinger people. My impression is they'll try just about anything to get a leg up on us."

Boswell seems amused at my statement. He smiles and taps his fingers on his desk.

"And we wouldn't. Is that what you're telling me, Stubby?"

"I hate to lose more than anyone. You already know that. But recently, I've discovered there are some things even I wouldn't do to win."

Tuesday Afternoon
November 19, 1949

JERRY LOWE AND HIS ASSISTANT COACH Neil Brooks appear unexpected and unannounced at the edge of the football field. Jerry waves to attract my attention. My offensive team is running half-speed through each of our "Option" plays against a simulated Bearcat defense composed of second-string players. I am meticulously instructing each of my blockers on how to determine his assignment against the defense we expect Ballinger to use on Thursday.

The arrival of the two Cisco coaches places me in an awkward predicament. They are obviously expecting me to walk over and acknowledge their presence. I decide to abandon my coaching duties, advising Alfred and my quarterbacks which plays they should run again. Leaving the huddle, I trot over to meet Jerry and his assistant.

I haven't spoken with Jerry since the night he came by my house to tell me his team had beaten Stephenville. However, from reading the newspaper, I know his Loboes finished in third place, losing to Breckenridge on the last night of the season. His season is finished. I can't imagine what would bring him here to visit me, particularly during an important practice session.

"Jerry, Neil, how are you two? It's about time you came to one of my practices," I say, mustering up my most friendly tone of voice.

"We came to help, if you need us. We figure we owe you," Jerry offers.

"I read where your Loboes finished in third place. That should give you a real boost for next year," I say, ignoring his offer to help, buying some time while my mind tries to decipher what he's up to.

"Third place ain't so bad, good buddy, not from where we started. We won two and tied one out of our last five. Might've been three wins, if we hadn't played your Bulldogs," Jerry laughs, wrapping an arm around my shoulder and squeezing me tightly.

"Yeah, I guess you finished better than expected. You think they'll keep you on as head coach?"

"They'd be absolute fools not to keep him, Coach Warden. After all, he's got a direct connection to the smartest offensive coach in Texas, and Jerry's the best defensive coach," Neil Brooks surmises, asserting himself into the conversation.

"Neil, what happened with your Lobo team was all your and Jerry's doing. All I did was push you in the right direction."

"That's not the way we see it, good buddy. That's why we came to offer our help. We'll do anything you want. Carry the water bucket, wash socks–whatever you need. We owe you one."

"I appreciate the offer, Jerry. But right now I really need to get back to my practice. We'll be finished here in a half-hour or so. If you've got some time, why don't you two stick around. Juanita would love to see you. If you'll wait, you're invited for supper."

Walking back to the offensive huddle, I rack my brain, trying to think how I might use the two coaches who have so graciously volunteered to help me.

I suppose there was a time when I would've been grateful for their help, but why would I want Jerry or Neil to help me now? It's one thing for me to help them and quite another for them to want to help me.

PARKED ALONGSIDE MY FRONT CURB is a dark blue Studebaker pickup. I recognize it immediately. The vehicle belongs to Red Jones, who is sitting patiently in the driver's seat reading a newspaper.

Cursing silently under my breath, I park the Hudson and walk back to Jerry's car. He and Neil have pulled into my driveway behind me. I advise them to go on inside.

"You need some help, Stubby? Sometimes these parent problems can get kinda messy," Jerry offers, eyeing the tall man sitting in the pickup.

"No, I can handle him. You and Neil go on in. Tell Juanita I'll be there in a minute or so."

Jerry and Neil amble slowly toward my front door, watching curiously while I stride over to Red Jones' vehicle. They pause on the porch for a few seconds, waiting for the red-haired man to crawl out of his pickup. Seeing Jones extend his hand in friendship, Jerry turns and knocks on the door. I hear Juanita's screams of surprised delight before she ushers them inside.

"Hello, Red. What's on your mind?" I say, turning back to my unwelcome visitor.

"Coach, I apologize for bothering you. I didn't know you'd be having company."

"That's my college roommate and his assistant coach. They understand. You wanna talk with me?"

"Yeah. You see the slip from the doctor? Reed says he gave it to you."

"Yes, I saw it. What about it?"

"Then you know it's okay for Reed to play in the Ballinger game?"

"Red, I said I saw the note. What's this all about?" I'm tired of playing his foolish word games. I know what he wants. I intend to make him tell me.

"I been wondering if you intend to play my boy–honor our agreement, like we talked about."

"Red, our conversations are getting to be incredibly redundant. I've told you before. I plan to honor my agreement with Lucas Masters, even though he's no longer around. But I don't intend to play a kid who can't perform. Reed hasn't practiced in weeks. He's rusty and out-of-shape. Red, I can't play him, not if he might jeopardize our chances of winning. Our other kids deserve better."

"That's exactly why I'm here, Coach Warden. I'm releasing you from our agreement. You do what's best for the team. If Reed can't cut the mustard, you keep him on the bench. We Joneses don't want to be responsible for your losing."

"Red, what can I say? Are you sure about this? I wouldn't want you to change your mind at the last minute."

"I'm sure, Coach. Yeah, I'm dead sure. You do whatever you need to do to win that game on Thursday."

"You can have my word on it, Red. I'll do everything that's humanly possible to bring home a winner. Hey, thanks for stopping by. Your support means a lot to me."

JERRY AND NEIL are waiting on the living room couch when I come inside. Appetizing smells of supper cooking radiate from the kitchen where Juanita is preparing our meal.

Short Snorter has taken a position next to Little Jerry's playpen, apparently ready to defend his tiny playmate from the two unfamiliar intruders.

"How'd it go, good buddy? That man give you a problem about playing his kid?"

"No. No problem at all. Actually, he offered to let me sit his kid. This is a strange town. Someday, maybe I can tell you everything that's happened here since I took this coaching job. Did Juanita make a fuss about me bringing you two home without calling?"

"You'd better talk with her, Stubby. It looks like Neil and I are welcome to dine here tonight. We're not so sure about you."

Wednesday Morning
November 20, 1949

AFTER SUPPER LAST EVENING Jerry and Neil stayed to talk until almost midnight, bringing us up-to-date with accounts of their final games. Jerry seems confident the late season surge by his Lobo team will insure his return as Cisco High's head coach. If his contract is renewed, Neil has agreed to stay on as his assistant.

They were both excited about their prospects for next year. Even after they were out the front door, we stood on the porch in the cold night air and talked for almost half an hour. I promised to call them if I needed their help in preparing for the playoffs.

It was almost one o'clock before Juanita and I finally retired. Tired as I was, I couldn't sleep. In spite of Radford Jones' offer to release me from my commitment to play his son, I continue to wrestle over the enigma of my quarterback situation. My Bulldog team has proved time and time again it can be extremely sensitive, subject to emotional letdowns, sometimes needing a strong psychological boost to shock the team into playing at a winning level.

My quarterback dilemma weighs heavy on my mind when I awake.

Even though it's almost eight o'clock before I drag myself out of bed, I delay leaving for school, staying to discuss my quandary with Juanita over a late cup of coffee.

"Darling, I can't tell you what to do. You should know your team better than anyone."

"My heart tells me one thing; my head says no. This quarterback decision is driving me nuts."

"Darling, women almost always go with their heart when they have difficult decisions to make. I'm not sure what a football coach should do."

"Juanita, my football team is so emotional. The least little thing can affect their play–change the team's whole personality. Sometimes my players can be awesome and fearless, each one a lion. Then, at other times, they can be amazingly sensitive, getting their feelings hurt so easily."

"Your football team may have assumed the personality of their coach, darling. I believe you've just described yourself, to a tee," Juanita laughs, standing up to kiss my cheek and send me off to work.

———————

Wednesday Noon
November 20, 1949

THE BIGGEST PEP RALLY of the season is scheduled today during the noon lunch break at the high school front steps. The rally will involve not only every student from every school, it will also include a majority of the city's adults.

By the time I arrive, the mass of assembled people extends beyond the campus grounds, spilling out into the street which fronts the high school.

My football team stands grouped together on the landing at the top of the steps, facing the crowd. The young men are dressed casually, most wearing denim jeans and their maroon letter jackets. They seem ill at ease, embarrassed by the attention they've received since making the playoffs.

My players' faces exhibit a variety of grim expressions, revealing the intense pressure each feels inside. The upcoming contest will be the first time any of these young men has participated in a post-season football game.

Our cheerleaders lead the crowd in an ear-splitting yell while I ascend the steps, two at a time, to stand with my team.

"R-rrrrr! A-aaaaa! N-nnnnn! G-ggggg! E-eeeee! R-rrrrr!"

"Ranger, Ranger, Ranger Bulldogs!" yells the crowd in a sort of deranged, deafening unison.

An unprecedented enthusiasm and sense of anticipation have swept through the city like a cyclone, bringing a spirit of civic pride to every Ranger student and adult. Perhaps nothing can bring a small town together like a winning football team. An entire city has banded together here today, in support of twenty-seven dedicated young gladiators who will represent them on the playing field.

The spirited cheerleaders lead excited, frenzied fans through a series of well-known yells. The crowd's screams become louder and louder and more energized with each successive yell. I can sense an electric-like current of exhilaration flowing between the fans and my Bulldog players. It is a tingling sensation I have experienced before, during bonfire pep rallies at A&M prior to our games with Texas University.

As the crowd's enthusiasm peaks, the school band begins playing a familiar fight song. Both cheerleaders and fans sing the words passionately. The fierce, loud singing and music will be heard from several blocks away.

Superintendent Boswell climbs the front steps after the fight song ends. When he reaches a point high enough to be seen by the crowd, he stops and turns to address the fans. He offers his best wishes to the team, then begins a monotonous oratory, reminding the students to always be good sports. Loud boos and catcalls from the crowd cause him to cut his speech short.

The pep rally ends with the cheerleaders rushing up the steps to hold hands with members of the football team while the band plays our school song. Proud tears stream freely down the faces of both students and adults as they sing fiercely and passionately about the school they love.

The strong emotion all around me is contagious. Hoping no one will notice, I discreetly brush away a tear forming in my eye.

———————

Wednesday Afternoon
November 20, 1949

"FOR A KID who hasn't practiced in a month, Reed looks pretty sharp," Sam observes, as we stand together on the practice field watching our ends and backs run through a series of routine passing drills.

"Yes, he seems to be stronger and more confident. The long layoff may've helped him become a better football player."

"You gonna play him at quarterback?" Sam asks.

"I honestly don't know, Sam. My tendency is to stick with Hamrick. He's the one who got us here. I haven't made up my mind completely, not yet anyway."

Hamrick, Jones and Cole are taking turns alternating at quarterback in our passing drill.

Hamrick takes the snap from center, drops back and fires a bullet pass to Herb Williams, causing me to doubt my sanity.

How could I even consider not playing my best athlete at quarterback?

"COACH, COULD I TALK to you for a minute?" someone asks, after I open the door of the Hudson and slide into the driver's seat. The unexpected voice startles me, causing my hands to tighten their grip on the steering wheel. My adventures with Clifford and Orval have left a residue of fear inside me which I may never overcome.

The voice belongs to Reed Jones.

"Sure, Reed. What's on your mind?" I answer, releasing my grip and exhaling heavily.

"My dad says he talked with you yesterday."

"Yes, he came to my house. We had a rather friendly visit," I respond defensively, not wishing to reveal the content of my conversation with the elder Jones.

"He says he told you it was okay with him to play Hamrick at quarterback on Thursday."

"Yes, that was about the gist of our conversation. We also talked about you. I told him he should be very proud of the fine young person he's raised."

"Coach Warden, Buddy's the team's quarterback now. I want you to play him at quarterback against Ballinger."

"Reed, you need to talk with Hamrick. The two of you need to get together on this. Buddy tells me he wants you to play quarterback."

"He does? Buddy wants me to play quarterback?"

"Yep, that's what he said. Perhaps I should check with Jimmy Cole. Someone has to play quarterback on Thursday. Maybe he'll want the job."

"You're kidding me, Coach. You'll make the decision on who plays. We all know that."

"That's right, it'll be my decision, Reed. Was there ever any doubt about it?"

"No sir, I just thought I should let you know how I feel."

"Reed, a coach can't make decisions based on how his players feel. Otherwise, he'll end up teaching P.E. classes somewhere. You remember that when you become a head coach."

"Yes sir, I will. Thanks for the advice."

I pitch my jacket into the back seat and start the car engine. Letting the engine idle, I sit in somber thought, watching the tall, lanky quarterback stroll away.

Damn, I love these unselfish kids. Well, at least my quarterback dilemma is resolved. Now I know what I intend to do.

Thursday Morning
November 22, 1949

THE YELLOW SCHOOL BUS rumbles across the gravel parking lot and slides to a stop alongside the entrance gate. Our team is lined up outside the stadium fence. Each player's gear is packed and stashed on the ground close by.

The bus is late arriving. It's almost nine-thirty. We were scheduled to leave at nine.

Leeman Gentry opens the bus door and jumps out, apologizing.

"I'm sorry I'm late, Coach Warden. The old lady here didn't wanna start this morning. Had to use my car battery to jump her off."

"The game starts at two. Can you get us there in time to suit out and run through our warm-up drills?"

"Sure thing. No problem. I can make up a lotta the time on the road. I know a shortcut."

"No shortcuts, Leeman. We can't afford to get lost. Superintendent Boswell suggested we take Highway 80 through Abilene. That way, Ranger fans will see us if we have trouble."

"Okay, Coach, we'll do it your way, but I could save some real time by taking Highway 183 through Brownwood."

Our players load their gear quickly while Sam makes his usual inspection round. Since we are running late, he completes his survey in record time.

Satisfied that nothing has been left behind, Sam jumps aboard and taps our bus driver on the shoulder, giving him a thumbs-up.

"All aboard the Bearcat, Butt-Kicking, Ballinger Bullet," he shouts to the team. Our players yell their approval and briefly applaud Sam for his humorous originality.

The old bus sputters, chokes and spits out a cloud of smoke before it settles down and begins to run smoothly. The bus engine's smoke and noise are familiar, a pattern similar to the way my Hudson acted before it quit on me.

I cross my fingers and pray a short prayer, asking for divine assistance to aid the old bus in making the long trip to Ballinger without breaking down.

IN SPITE OF MY FEARS, our school bus is running smoothly by the time we reach Highway 80. Ranger fans, packed in long caravans of cars which bear maroon and white streamers, wave at us when they pass. Better than half the population of Ranger will be in Ballinger by the time we arrive there. Ranger has a long history of monumental events, but today is the biggest day in recent memory.

Today is also a big day for Juanita. Putting past differences aside, most of Juanita's family will attend our bi-district game to support me—even Juanita's father.

Phyliss and Price arrived early this morning to pick up Juanita and Little Jerry. Their plan was to stop in Comanche and pick up Luther and Edna. Juanita's brother Gary and his wife will meet them in Ballinger. Even Juanita's older brother Joe may drive down from Abilene to attend the game.

BOASTING A POPULATION NEAR 5,000, Ballinger is located on U.S. Highway 83, about 70 miles south of Abilene. Like most West Texas towns, the city's economy is dependent on oil, ranching and agriculture. The Ballinger High football club is a perennial powerhouse in their district. Last year, the Bearcats advanced to the state quarter-finals before being eliminated. This year's team is just as good and has the experience of participating in last year's playoffs.

OUR BUS TRIP takes a little more than three hours. It is almost one o'clock when we pass the Ballinger city limits, enter the downtown business district and roll down Hutchins Avenue. The sidewalks along Ballinger's major streets are completely deserted with every shop closed. We have no problem finding Bearcat Stadium. We simply follow a long line of automobiles decorated in black and red.

Leeman Gentry accelerates past a congested conglomeration of automobiles in search of parking spots, and deposits us at the entrance gate near the visiting team's facility. Even though there's still an hour to go before game time, the grandstands are already filled to capacity. Football fans have spilled out onto the grassy expanse surrounding the playing field. Shrill sounds of off-key music reverberate across the stadium as the two school bands warm up their instruments.

FINDING OURSELVES CRAMPED and miserable inside the visitor's dressing quarters, we move the football squad outside to sit on the grass while we discuss last minute strategy. A few minutes before we take the field, I light the fuse which, I hope, will rocket my team to victory.

"Alright, listen up! Here's the starting offensive lineup."

Left End–Stiles, Left Tackle–Hummel, Left Guard–Patterson, Center–Thompson, Right Guard–Sutton, Right Tackle–Elder, Right End–Rogers, Left Halfback–Hamrick, Fullback–Simpson, Right Halfback–Comacho, Quarterback–Jones.

My choice for starting quarterback triggers a ripple of enthusiastic chatter among the players. A happy roar of approval follows as players stand to slap on Reed's shoulders.

"Okay. That's enough girl-talk. Let's get on the field and have some Bearcat meat for lunch!" I shout to the excited young men.

Our overzealous, yelling players stumble over each other in their eagerness to take the field.

"Tough decision, Stubby. I never thought you'd have the courage to do it. I hope it won't cost us the ballgame," Sam tells me while we trot onto the playing field, following behind our Bulldog team.

"Wasn't so tough at all, Sam. I simply picked the best man to quarterback this team for this particular game. Win or lose, we both know it's the right decision."

———————

I COULDN'T HAVE ORDERED more perfect weather for today's game. A bright sun has burned away most of the morning clouds. The air is cool and crisp. A light southerly breeze occasionally ripples the goal line flags at the corners of the end zone, but wind will not be a factor in this game. It's a perfect day and perfect football weather. A Ranger victory will make this pleasant fall afternoon even better.

Gazing across the field, watching the Bearcat team complete their warm-up drills, the finality of this game sinks in on me. Both these teams have been practicing and playing since mid-August, in order to be here to compete for the Texas State Class One A Championship. When this game is over, one team will be finished for the season. All their hard work and high hopes will be dashed in a matter of two short hours. The winning team will advance to another similar game of finality to be played next week.

Somehow, it all seems so senseless, and yet, it brings people together, uniting entire cities in a common purpose. High school football is truly a social phenomenon.

———————

ELDER, JONES, HAMRICK, PATTERSON, ROBINSON, Stiles, Sutton, Thompson, Charles Williams and Kenneth Williams meet with the Ballinger game captains at mid-field for the coin flip. We've decided to have all our seniors serve as captains for the remainder of our season.

With Will Brownlee back in uniform, we seriously considered the benefits of electing to kick off if we win the toss. That would allow our defense to be on the field first, giving our offensive team and Reed Jones additional time to rid themselves of any pre-game jitters. Jones hasn't played in a game since his appendicitis attack in Comanche. An offensive fumble at the beginning of the game could prove disastrous.

We dismissed the idea of choosing to kick off, deciding against giving up an opportunity to gain possession of the football, but I cross my fingers, hoping Ballinger will win the toss.

The game officials signal that Ballinger has won the toss. They choose to receive. That's terrific. Now we can begin the game with our defense on the field and without giving up our choice of receiving or kicking off at the beginning of the second half.

Our ten senior captains slap on each other's pads while they gallop back to our sideline. They understand. We got exactly what we hoped for. Judging from their happy faces, you'd think they had won the coin toss.

———————

BROWNLEE'S BOOMING KICKOFF sails to the twelve where a Bearcat receiver gathers it against his chest. Yung and Patterson crash through a wall of red and black blockers to slam the ball carrier down at the twenty-four.

A penalty flag is thrown by one of the officials near the point of tackle.

"No! No!" I scream at the officials, "There was nothing wrong with that tackle. You people can't penalize us for hitting too hard."

"I think the penalty's on them, Coach Warden. Probably for holding," Alfred advises, resting a hand gently on my shoulder. His voice sounds unusually calm and collected.

Play is halted momentarily while the game officials discuss Ballinger's violation. When their huddle breaks up, the field judge signals a holding penalty against the Bearcats.

Our defensive captain Robinson checks with Sam, then accepts the penalty.

"Sam, isn't that our buddy Danny Pitcock officiating. How in blue blazes did we get stuck with him again?"

"I wouldn't know, Stubby. But, ole Danny Boy is the one who threw the flag. I guess we ain't got no complaints so far."

"I don't like it. He causes problems for us every time he works one of our games."

"Yeah, he's a bad one alright. Wants to argue with our head coach all the time," Sam quips in a half-hearted attempt at humor.

"Okay, so I have a personality conflict with the guy. I still don't like him," I persist, ignoring Sam's semi-humorous observation.

Despite the penalty he called against the Bearcats, the referee is bad news. I kick myself for not objecting more forcefully when Boswell informed me Ballinger's coach had prevailed in their argument about selection of the game officials.

———————

THE HOLDING PENALTY against Ballinger pushes them back to their twelve. Our defense responds like we had hoped, holding the Bearcats to only four yards gained in three rushing plays.

Hamrick returns Ballinger's punt to their forty-four. Our first offensive series will begin inside our opponent's territory. I confer hastily with Jones before he enters the game.

"Listen up, Reed. We've got terrific field position. Be patient. Stick with your 'Option' running plays. Even if we don't score on this possession, we've got their backs to the wall. Let's not make any mistakes that'll let 'em off the hook."

"Sure, Coach, I understand. With our defense and Jensen's punts we should be able to keep Ballinger down on their end of the field. If we make them start from deep in their own territory on every possession, it'll be a lot tougher for them to score."

"Exactly. Now, don't get anxious. We've got all afternoon. Ballinger doesn't have a high-scoring offense. If our defense does their job, two touchdowns should be all we need to win."

Slapping Jones on his backside, I send him scurrying toward our team's huddle and turn back to Sam. His face is as white as one of Juanita's sun-bleached sheets.

"Sam, are you okay? You look terrible."

"Just got a bad case of butterflies. I've never coached a playoff game before, you know."

"Neither have I, Sam. Neither have I," I say, repeating myself, wishing he hadn't reminded me of my inexperience.

———————

THREE CONSECUTIVE RUNNING PLAYS against a hard-hitting, six-three Bearcat defensive alignment grinds out a single first down.

After we penetrate their thirty, our offense bogs down. Ballinger's defense becomes unmovable, holding us to three yards gained in three attempts.

Too far out to attempt a field goal, we're forced to punt. Jensen's kick sails out of bounds at the Bearcat four yard line.

"Now, this is the right way to begin a football game. Stubby, maybe we oughta start every game by kicking off," Sam tells me smugly, pleased with the play of his defense.

"If you'll guarantee we can have the opposition start every possession from inside their fifteen, I'd be inclined to go along," I grin back. Our pre-game jitters are gone now.

———————

BALLINGER'S COACH elects to use a game strategy similar to mine. His team continues to run the football, pounding at the middle of our defense, unwilling to risk a pass, hoping we will make the first mistake. Three offensive plays and the Bearcats punt again.

The game becomes a war of nerves, a kind of poker contest between two coaches. Each football team sticks with an ultraconservative game plan, hoping their opponent will make some mistake which will turn the tide in their favor.

For the remainder of the half, the football game ebbs back and forth. Neither team is able to mount any kind of sustained drive.

Remarkably, the football game is free of any penalties which might give either team an edge. Benefiting from Jensen's long kicks, we restrict Ballinger's offense to their side of the mid-field stripe.

The magnificent struggle between two teams of almost equal skill and ability keeps the holiday crowd electrified and on their feet. With my Bulldogs constantly knocking on the door, needing only one Ballinger mistake or some lucky break to help us score, neither the home fans nor their Ranger visitors are able to relax and enjoy the fine day.

When the first half ends many zealous supporters have never taken their seats.

AN UNRULY MOB OF PEOPLE blocks our exit from the playing field. Ranger players are forced to wade through layers of closely bunched football fans to reach our dressing rooms. Numerous familiar faces pat my back and shout words of encouragement while I shoulder my way through the elated multitude.

A hand reaches out to grasp my arm firmly as I approach the entrance to the visitor's dressing facility.

"Coach, could you spare a minute to speak to an old friend?" a deep, rasping voice asks.

I twist around to face a man in a knee-length black overcoat. A dark knit ski cap is pulled down low over his head. Only a portion of his bearded face is visible.

Even behind a heavy beard and mustache, the face is unmistakable. The man is Lucas Masters. He lifts a finger to his lips, imploring me not to call out.

"Please don't say my name. I prefer not to be recognized," Lucas whispers softly. His voice is so low I can barely hear him over the crowd noise.

"What are you doing here? Someone's certain to recognize you. The Eastland sheriff's still looking for you. And I'm sure your face must be posted in the sheriff's office here in Ballinger."

"Couldn't stay away. You know how I love Ranger football. When I heard we were in the state playoffs, I had to come. This is a great day for Ranger. You've done one hellava job with our football team."

"Thanks, Mister, ahhh…Mister M. Coming from you that means a lot."

"I see you're playing the Jones kid at quarterback. You don't have to play him on my account you know. All our deals have been canceled."

"I'm not playing him because of any agreement with you. I have other reasons."

"Fine. Handle it your way. I wanna wish you luck, Stubby. I guess my town's in good hands. Take care of it, you hear?"

"Good luck to you too, Lucas," I say, forgetting his request not to call him by name. "Hey, you be careful, too."

"I'm always careful, Coach. I'll be watching to see how you run my town. Maybe I'll see you around," Masters warns, before he turns to run toward the crowd of people.

"Hey, you owe me some bonus money!" I call after him, but Masters doesn't hear. He has already disappeared into the mob of football fans, leaving me to agonize over unanswered questions.

Where is he hiding out? If Lucas crossed the border like he planned, how did he get back here to attend the football game?

Hell, I don't have time to worry about Lucas Masters. Right now, I've got a football game to win.

―――――――――

A NERVOUS CLATTERING OF FOOTBALL CLEATS echoes through the dressing facility as Bulldog players stomp loudly into the visitor's building, each searching for an empty spot on the floor to rest while we discuss second half strategy.

Grim, battle-scarred faces chronicle the fierce determination of my players. It's incredible how these young men have matured during the past three months. No longer are they green, inexperienced kids who need to be prodded into playing their best. I won't need any tricks today. Each player understands the strenuous, individual effort which will be required of himself in order for us to leave here with a victory.

"Looks like we've got a Mexican-standoff out there, Stubby. You got anything up your sleeve to get us moving in the second half?" Sam asks.

"No, I guess not. We'll have to beat this Ballinger club by playing flawless football. Let's stick with our ground game and good defense. This game may go down to the wire. The outcome will probably be decided by which team makes the first mistake."

During the first half we didn't attempt a single pass. Maybe my game plan is too conservative, but I don't intend to give this game away by being too anxious or making some stupid mistake.

―――――――――

THE SECOND HALF becomes a replay of the first. We receive Ballinger's kickoff and return the football to our thirty yard line. In three running plays against a rock-solid, unyielding Bearcat defense, we can gain only six yards. Jensen gets off a high-booming punt which hits and rolls out of bounds on the Ballinger nineteen.

The game returns to the scenario of the first half. Ballinger runs three plays and punts. We return the punt, run three plays and punt.

––––––––––

A LOUD, MOANING WAIL originates from beneath a heap of bodies near mid-field after Simpson carries over right guard, lunging behind Thompson, Sutton and Elder to gain the short yardage needed for a first down.

Maroon bodies, along with black and red uniforms, topple sideways off the entanglement of humanity as Gilbert Thompson rises up from somewhere deep down in the pile. Thompson lets out another bloodcurdling scream when his huge shoulders propel out the top of the stack.

Shoving his way through the heap of players, Thompson comes running toward the bench, holding onto his right hand. His contorted face is laced with deep lines of intense pain.

Sam and I run out to meet him.

"Coach Warden, they broke my thumb! They broke my thumb!" Gilbert screams to me as we approach.

"Okay, Gilbert, calm down. Let Coach Aills take a look. Maybe it's not broken. It may only be dislocated."

"No, Coach, my thumb is broken. They broke my thumb. Those dreadful Ballinger fellows broke my thumb."

"Sure, Gilbert, and we'll make 'em pay for hurting you. Now come over to the bench and let us have a look," I advise sympathetically.

While Sam examines Gilbert's hand, I make some hasty substitutions. Thompson has played at center for almost every offensive down since the beginning of the season. I send E.P. Robinson in at center and instruct Donald Varner to take over our left linebacker position on defense.

Sam comes to report the results of his examination. He is grinning from ear-to-ear.

"How's his thumb, Sam? Is it broken?" I ask, wondering why my assistant should be so amused about Thompson's injury.

"Stubby, his thumb is fine. It's his middle finger that's broken. I had to put a splint on it to keep it straight. Thompson's through for this game."

"His middle finger? Are you sure? Gilbert was screaming about his thumb being broken. Surely he knows the difference between his thumb and his middle finger."

"It's the middle finger on his right hand that's broke alright. Both his thumbs are fine," Sam chuckles, shaking his head in mock disbelief.

Giggles from the bench attest that someone else finds something funny about poor Gilbert's injury. Somehow I don't get the joke.

LATE IN THE FOURTH QUARTER we finally get the break we've patiently waited for. A Ballinger offside penalty backs the Bearcats up to their own twenty. A plunge by their fullback over left guard is stopped for no gain. Ballinger calls timeout.

"Sam, I've got a feeling they'll try a pass. Signal the defense to switch to our five-three alignment and watch out for a pass."

"I'll do better than that. Kenneth Williams, get up here," Sam calls to the bench.

Sam and I quickly explain to Williams about our premonition. I hold onto my speedy senior's arm, giving him a last bit of advice before he enters the game.

"Kenneth, you play defensive rover. Stick with Hallmark, their right end. He's their quarterback's favorite receiver."

"Yes sir. Rover. Stick with the right end. I got it."

HUT. HUT. Ballinger's quarterback takes the snap and drops back to pass.

"We were right, Stubby! It's a pass play, for sure," Sam shouts.

Ballinger's right end darts past Varner, feints to the inside, then cuts upfield.

Streaking up the right sideline, the Bearcat end finds himself all alone, apparently undefended.

Ballinger fans rise to their feet, roaring with anticipation as the quarterback cocks his arm and releases his pass toward the wide-open Bearcat receiver.

"Where the hell is Williams? I told him to stick with their right end!" I yell with worried anger.

The football arches high above the playing field. The trajectory is true, but the pass is thrown short.

The Bearcat end slows down at the fifty, waiting for the ball to arrive.

As the football descends, a maroon uniform comes flying across the field, leaping high in front of the Ballinger receiver to intercept the football.

The maroon defender is Kenneth Williams. He lands on his feet running, sidesteps a Bearcat tackler and returns the football to the Ballinger twenty-eight before being run out of bounds.

Our visitor's bleachers erupt with hysteria. Ranger fans scream hoarsely in ecstatic delight. Thundering noise from beating drums fills the stadium with deafening sound. Bulldog cheerleaders run to the edge of the field, using megaphones to shout words of encouragement to their team.

A dull second half of football is suddenly overflowing with excitement. Not a single person in Bearcat Stadium remains in his seat.

A pitchout to Comacho and two option keeper plays by Jones net us nine yards. We have the football at the Ballinger nineteen. Fourth down and one.

The game officials call timeout, and a referee comes running over to our sideline.

"Ranger, your team has registered its first penetration of your opponents twenty yard line. If the game ends in a tie, the winner will be determined by penetrations. Your team is now ahead by one penetration," the referee advises.

"Thanks, ref. Hey, how much time is left? Is the scoreboard clock right?"

"There are less than three minutes left in the game. The scoreboard clock is very close to the official time."

Sam, Alfred and I huddle close to discuss our options.

"Here's the situation. If we try for a first down and don't make it, Ballinger will get possession of the ball on their nineteen. If we punt, Jensen can kick the ball out of bounds–hopefully, inside the ten. The way our defense has been playing, I don't believe Ballinger can score on us, not in the time we have left. We gotta keep them from penetrating inside our twenty. Ten yards could make a big difference."

"I agree with you, Stubby. Let's have Jensen kick. Our defense will hold. I guarantee it," Sam concurs.

———————

SAM, ALFRED AND I each hold our breath while the two teams line up for our punt. With Thompson injured, Robinson will make the deep snap to Jensen, a feat he's not performed in a game this season.

Suddenly visualizing all the things which could go wrong, I begin to change my mind about my decision to punt. Visions of the ball sailing over Jensen's head race through my head.

I signal timeout to stop the play, but it's too late.

The snap to Jensen is a perfect spiral. Jensen catches the football, takes two steps forward, then softly punts the ball toward the corner of the end zone.

Ballinger's receiver runs over to retrieve the punt, then stops and steps back, expecting it to travel into the end zone. The football strikes the ground at the five and rolls end over end, hitting the flag at the very corner of the end zone before it rolls out of bounds. A hush falls over the stadium while the game officials discuss where to place the football.

"Where did it go out of bounds? Did it cross the goal line?" I call to Sam, somehow expecting him to see something I couldn't.

"It was hard to tell from here. The official was right there. He should've seen it. It was awful close to the corner."

The officials break from their huddle and place the football on the one-half foot line. Seeing the ball placement, the Bulldog crowd squeals with delight. Ranger students run deliriously back and forth in the narrow runway along the front row of the visitor's bleachers while our band blasts out a fight song.

With only two and a half minutes remaining, the only way Ballinger can win this game is to complete a long pass or force us into making a mistake. Unwilling to risk a pass from their own end zone, Ballinger decides to punt on first down, hoping we'll botch the punt return.

Hut. Hut. The snap from center bounces on the ground before it reaches Ballinger's punter. Hummel and Pearson break through to trap the Bearcat punter while he juggles the ball, trying to get off his kick.

We have scored a safety.

Ranger fans are frantic with joy. A safety is not exactly what they had hoped for, but it's been a long, anxious afternoon. A score of any kind is welcome, particularly this late in the game. Ranger fans abandon the grandstands to run out on the playing field and hug Bulldog players, beginning an early victory celebration. It takes several minutes to clear the field so the game can continue.

A game official comes to the sideline to sternly warn us about our fans.

"Coach, if you can't control your fans, we will have to penalize you."

"Don't worry, ref. We'll keep 'em under control," I promise solemnly.

Actually, there's nothing I can do to stop my fans from celebrating. I plan on joining them in a few minutes.

———————

A SAFETY IS WORTH only two points, but against the stingy Ballinger defense, it represents a significant accomplishment. With two points on the scoreboard we no longer need to worry about penetrations. Now, we only need to keep Ballinger from scoring.

An even more gratifying reward for our scoring the safety is that we get possession of the football, hopefully with good field position. Following the safety, Ballinger must "free kick" to us from their twenty.

———————

BALLINGER'S PUNTER KICKS the football high, sending it soaring down to our thirty-eight. Comacho makes the reception and is tackled immediately by a desperate, hard-charging Bearcat defense. The scoreboard clock shows a minute and fifty seconds remaining.

Ballinger has two timeouts left. They use a timeout to stop the clock after each of our first two running plays. On third down the Bearcat defensive end gets a hand out to knock down a pitchout from

Jones to Simpson. Ballinger recovers the loose football at our twenty-nine.

Jones comes to the sideline with tears in his eyes. A minute and twenty seconds remain.

"I don't know what happened, Coach Warden. I waited for him to commit inside before I decided to lateral. I don't know how he got a hand on the ball."

"It's okay, Reed. We're still gonna win. Don't worry. Our defense will hold them."

Damn! Less than a minute has elapsed off the clock since we scored the safety, and now Ballinger has possession of the football, seventy yards closer to our goal line. We were better off before we scored.

HUT. HUT. Ballinger's quarterback hands off to his halfback. Barnes and Robinson meet him head-on. Four yard gain.

Hut. Hut. A quarterback keeper over left guard is stopped for no gain as Davenport and Sutton smother him at the line of scrimmage.

Hut. Hut. The Bearcat quarterback pitches out to his fullback. Two black and red blockers lead the power sweep around their left side. Charles Williams clears away the two blockers, allowing McKinney to knock the ball carrier out of bounds. Two yard loss. Fourth down and eight.

A heated shoving match develops out on the playing field between a Ballinger lineman and E.P. Robinson. Players from both teams step in quickly to break up the fracas. The Bearcat player involved in the brief slug-fest continues to protest to the line official long after Robinson returns to his defensive position.

Like Sam guaranteed, our defense is holding. Less than thirty seconds remain on the scoreboard clock. In the bleachers behind us the Ranger crowd begins to howl, "Fourth down! Fourth down!"

"They've gotta go for it, Coach Warden. They ain't got no other choice. There's not enough time left for 'em to kick and get the ball back," Alfred analyzes. His tense voice is almost an even match for my nervous pacing.

"You're right, Alfred. Sam, send Kenneth Williams back in as rover. Tell the defense to watch for a pass."

Hut. Hut. The quarterback drifts back, watching patiently while his two ends crisscross ten yards upfield. The crossing pattern confuses our defensive backs. One Bearcat end breaks open after three Bulldog defenders follow the other player.

Seeing his receiver break free, Ballinger's quarterback lofts a long pass in his direction.

Downfield our defenders realize their mistake. Cunningham races back across the field, diving to knock down the pass an instant before the Bearcat receiver can gather it in. Our visitor bleachers become a wild, excited mass of hysterical pandemonium. Stomping feet, clapping hands, screaming voices, loud whistles and beating drums indicate the happiness of Ranger supporters.

The game is over. We've won. All we need to do is to run out the clock.

"Hey! What the heck's going on out there? Ballinger's running back to huddle, like they still got the football. The referees are bringing the football back to the line of scrimmage," Sam bellows. He sounds both astonished and concerned.

"Maybe there was a penalty. You see a flag?"

"No! No penalty! What the heck's going on here? The officials are saying it's fourth down."

"No! No! That's not right! That can't be right!"

Out on the playing field the few Ranger players who remain are milling around, questioning one another, totally confused. After the last play a majority of our defenders retreated to the bench, expecting our offense to take the field.

I run out onto the field to ask the game officials to clarify their strange ruling.

Danny Pitcock meets me halfway, dashing over to personally confront me.

"Hey, Pitcock! You've got the down wrong! Ballinger's already used their four downs. We should get possession of the football."

"You're wrong, Coach. Don't they teach you dumb hicks in Ranger how to count? Now, get off the field, before I flag you for unsportsmanlike conduct."

"But, you've made a mistake about the downs! Check with the Ballinger coach! He should know how many downs they used!"

"The Ballinger coach knows perfectly well what's going down here. Get off the field, Coach! This is your last warning!"

"Danny, please listen to me! This is important! The outcome of the game may be hanging on your decision here. Take time to check. Don't make a mistake like this. A bad call here could haunt you for the rest of your life."

"I'll count to three, Coach. If you're not off the field by the time I reach three. One. Two...."

"Okay. Okay. I'm leaving. Don't penalize my team."

COMPLETELY MORTIFIED by the referees' decision to reward Ballinger with an illegal fifth down, our players glance with bewildered faces toward our sideline, somehow expecting us coaches to intercede and correct the game officials' horrible blunder. Sam and I yell at the players to get ready, to get their heads back in the game.

Ballinger's quarterback barks his signals quickly, taking advantage of our confusion. Several of our defensive linemen are standing straight up, still questioning the absurd ruling, when the ball is snapped.

The quarterback drifts back, watching his receivers run easily past our befuddled defense. He fires a bullet pass to his right end who is wide open and undefended fifteen yards downfield. Cunningham and Kenneth Williams recover from their dazed stupor to chase him down and push him out of bounds at the two.

Hordes of Ranger fans storm the sidelines, protesting loudly, as the game officials place the football and signal a first down for Ballinger. Our Bulldog players try to call for a timeout, but they are ignored by the officials.

A plunge over right guard by the Bearcat quarterback scores their touchdown.

Ballinger's extra point try veers off wide to the right. With hundreds of angry, howling Ranger people swarming about the end zone, an intimidated and frightened Bearcat place kicker totally loses his concentration.

Ballinger   6   Ranger   2

SCREAMING, ENRAGED SUPPORTERS of both football teams completely surround the playing field while Sam, Alfred and I try to calm our players. Absolute fan insanity reigns all around our bench. The football game isn't over yet. Eighteen seconds remain on the clock. We try to convince our team we have a chance of winning. Maybe we can still pull out a win.

While the two teams square off for the Ballinger kickoff, Reed Jones steps up beside me.

"Coach Warden, the only chance we have of winning is to complete a long pass. Buddy's our best passer. Why don't you let him finish the game?"

Jones is right. His logic makes good sense. I carefully consider my quarterback's suggestion before I answer.

"No, I don't think so. This is your team, Reed. From the look of things, this'll probably be the last game you ever play for Ranger High. I want you to savor these last few plays. They may have to last you a lifetime."

"But, Coach...."

"No buts, Reed! Do like I say!"

"Thanks, Coach Warden. We'll give it our best shot. I promise."

THE BALLINGER KICKOFF and the two incomplete passes we attempt before time runs out seem to take place in some other dimension. The "stranger than fiction" events which occurred here this afternoon couldn't possibly have taken place in a real world. I watch the game end through tear-filled eyes, not feeling sad for myself, but for my courageous young men who have put forth such a gallant effort, only to be beaten by four stupid and arrogant game officials.

ABSOLUTE CHAOS DEVELOPS after the game ends. Infuriated Ranger fans bound onto the playing field, loudly cursing the game officials and anxious to slug any person who might be a Ballinger supporter. Fist fights and shoving matches break out on the football field and in the parking areas behind the home side bleachers.

Fearing for the safety of the game officials, several Ballinger policemen arrive to escort them from the stadium. Encircled by a large crowd of crazed, howling Ranger fans, the Ballinger police are forced to literally fight their way to reach the four men who, seeking refuge, are cowering beneath the home side bleachers.

Numerous blows are exchanged as the police officers guide the referees to the safety of their patrol cars. Bulldog fans reek with the shock and hurt of losing. The four men have committed a sinful error. Aroused Ranger visitors have no intentions of letting the men's foul deed go unpunished.

The nasty mood of the mob causes me to become more concerned for my players' safety than about losing the football game. We instruct our players to proceed directly to the visitor's dressing facility, grab their street clothes and head straight for our bus. The prospect of the heated turmoil evolving into a vicious bloody riot is more than a possibility. It seems almost certain.

———————

LEAVING SAM AND ALFRED to watch after our disappointed young men while they retrieve their clothing, I rush back to the visitor's grandstands. I want to find Juanita and her family, to verify they are safe.

My concern for their well-being grows when I discover Juanita and Phyliss alone, waiting beside a concession stand underneath the visitor-side bleachers.

"Juanita, are you okay? Where is Jerry? Where are Luther and Price?"

"We're all fine, darling. Mother and Gary's wife took the baby to the car. But we're worried about Daddy. Price and Gary went to look for him. He's over there in the crowd on the Ballinger side, chasing after the game officials. Daddy was terribly upset about your losing the game."

"Your father, upset about my losing? What about his heart condition? He might have a heart attack."

"Stubby, don't you worry about that tough old bird. Luther

Kimbrough will outlive us all," Phyliss counsels to dispel my concern.

"Listen, I need to get back to my team. We plan to load our kids on the bus and get out of here, before this thing erupts into a full-blown riot. Are you sure you ladies will be safe?"

"Darling, you take care of your boys. We women will be fine. We'll be leaving just as soon as we get my adolescent father under control."

I kiss Juanita tenderly and give Phyliss a hug. As I turn to leave, Gary and Price round the corner of the bleachers, towing Juanita's father between them. Blood trickles from the right side of Luther's mouth. The front of his shirt is torn open. From the looks of him, he's been in a fight.

"Luther, are you hurt?" I inquire, amazed at the sorry sight of Juanita's father.

"No, he's okay," Price answers. "It was me and Gary who almost got killed, dragging him out of there."

"I got that bad one for ya, Stubby. I socked him right in the kisser," Luther tells me, shaking loose from his two captors.

"Who? Who'd you hit, Luther?"

"That one you was arguing with."

"You mean the referee–Danny Pitcock?"

"Yeah, that's the one. I think I busted his jaw. It sure felt like a good lick."

SAM TAKES A QUICK HEAD COUNT, making sure everyone is safely inside the bus. He nods to me, indicating all our players are accounted for, then taps Leeman Gentry on the shoulder. Our objective is to get the bus underway, removing our team from the explosive situation surrounding the football stadium.

From the bus window I can see two Ballinger police cars transporting the four besieged game officials as they attempt to drive through an angry Ranger mob. Several men plant themselves directly ahead of the police vehicles, preventing the cars from moving forward, while other fans beat furiously on the patrol car roofs.

A woman, whom I immediately recognize as Eddie Phillips' mother, stoops down beside the rear of the second police car. Reaching into her purse, she withdraws what appears to be an ice pick. I watch in awe as she drives the point of the ice pick into the side of the tire. Completing her task on the back tire, she moves ahead to the front of the police car, then plunges the sharp pointed weapon into the front tire.

"Hey, Gilbert!" Gerald Bagwell calls to our injured center who is sitting quietly in a front seat opposite the bus driver. "Come back here and give those low-down, rotten cheaters the finger! Let's show 'em what we think of 'em! Come on, Gilbert!"

"No, Gerald. I do not think we should stoop to their low, dishonorable level. Let them stew in the juice of their own making," Gilbert answers in his simple, precise language.

Laughter resounds throughout the bus as my players respond to Gilbert's comment. The laughter somehow eases their pain. The easy resilience of these young people sometimes amazes me.

From my seat at the center of the bus I inspect Gilbert Thompson's bandaged hand. The middle finger is held straight, sandwiched between two long wooden splints and wrapped in heavy white tape.

His bandaged middle finger, protruding away from his hand, could easily be misconstrued by devious minds to be a monstrous obscene gesture.

Now I understand what all the grinning was about, after Sam discovered it was Gilbert's middle finger which was broken.

TEARS FLOW FREELY inside the bus as my players anguish over our loss. A few players attempt to lower their windows, wanting to shout to relatives or verbally express their harsh feelings. Sam and Alfred move quickly to warn the players against inviting retaliation by Ballinger supporters. We definitely want to avoid any incidents involving our football squad.

In a matter of minutes we clear the throng of angry people at Bearcat Stadium and reach the open highway. A roadside billboard, requesting that we come back soon to shop in Ballinger, "A City of Friendly and Caring People," whizzes by my window after Gentry shifts into high gear.

Alfred lumbers back down the aisle to check on me.

"Coach Warden, you doing okay?"

"Yeah, Alfred, I suppose we should be grateful that we got away without any of our players being hurt."

"I been thinking, Coach. You know, we deserved to win that game. I'll bet, right about now, the Ballinger coach isn't feeling too good about the way he won. How will he ever explain to his team what he let happen today?"

"I don't know, Alfred. When it comes to winning verses losing, a football coach can justify just about any behavior."

"That's not right, Coach. A football coach should set an example for his players. The Ballinger coach may have won today, but his players will never have real respect for him, not the way your players respect you."

———————

GAZING MINDLESSLY out the window while Alfred ambles back to the front of the bus, I ponder over his astute observation. Remembering an old sport's passage written by Grantland Rice, a strange feeling of tranquility settles over me:

> *For when the One Great Scorer comes to write against your name,*
> *He marks—not that you won or lost—but how you played the game.*

CHAPTER TWENTY
THE FINAL EPISODE

DURING THE WEEK following our ill-fated Ballinger game, I assist G.C. Boswell in filing an official protest with the Interscholastic League, documenting the fact that Ballinger was allowed an illegal fifth down which directly resulted in our loss. We support our argument with newspaper articles and sworn testimony from many reporters, school officials and unbiased elected public officials who attended the game. We have high hopes we can have the outcome of the game reversed.

On Thursday morning, Boswell receives a phone call from Rodney Kidd, Director of the Interscholastic League. Kidd is sympathetic to our plea but advises Boswell that league rules prevent him from reversing any decisions made by game officials on the field of play. He promises to reprimand the four officials for their incompetent actions.

A Ballinger loss to Littlefield two weeks later ends all speculation about our getting back into the playoffs. Several newspaper reporters who attended the Ballinger–Littlefield contest call to tell us the Bearcats seemed to have lost their desire to win. Adverse publicity and the turmoil following their bi-district game had taken its toll on the Ballinger club.

Friday Afternoon
December 20, 1949

A LIGHT-RED TINGE in the overcast sky hints at a chance for snow. Cold winter weather, along with the ice and slick streets which come with it, is not my favorite time of year, but to most people who reside in this dry, thirsty country, any form of moisture is always welcome. Already the wind has picked up. Leafless trees in the school yard bend stiffly in the brisk breeze.

Parking my Hudson among a multitude of empty spaces facing the high school, I turn up my collar and pull my light jacket tightly around my body. No students are visible on the barren campus. School was dismissed for the holidays at noon today.

The note in the envelope was from Superintendent Boswell. It read simply:

"Coach Warden:

"The school trustees request your presence at three o'clock."

No explanation or reason was given. Sam worried over the note, telling me this was the way the last coach was fired.

A biting chill in the air encourages me to take the front steps two at a time.

THE PRINCIPAL'S OFFICE is empty, but I can hear muffled sounds of men talking inside the adjacent trustees' meeting room.

I take a seat on the couch in the same small waiting room off the hallway where I waited to be interviewed for the head coaching job only last spring. So much has happened since then. That day seems so very long ago.

Clicking sounds of short, quick footsteps out in the school hallway announce the arrival of Mildred Getts even before she appears in the doorway. The secretary's arms are loaded with a huge stack of papers. She seems to be in a hurry. Her face is flushed and sweaty. At first Mildred seems startled to find me here. She quickly regains her composure.

"Coach Warden, it's so nice to see you. You should come in to see us more often." The woman's voice is strained. She acts like I'm a stranger. She's trying much too hard to be friendly.

"Mildred, I was here yesterday morning to get my teaching schedule for the second semester. Don't you remember?"

"Oh, yes. Of course, how could I be so forgetful? Coach Warden, are you here for the school trustees' meeting?"

"I'm not exactly sure, Mildred. Superintendent Boswell left a message for me at the field house, requesting that I be here at three o'clock. I'm here like he requested."

"The trustees have been in their meeting since before two. I hope you got your message right. No one mentioned anything to me about their wanting to see you."

The woman is obviously lying. The trustees would never arrange to meet with someone without notifying her.

"I guess I'll just wait until someone comes out then. I don't know what else to do."

"Yes, Coach Warden, I believe that would be the proper thing to do. I wish I could tell you more. You're certainly welcome to wait until we can find out something."

Taking a seat behind her paper-covered desk, the curious woman watches me uneasily for a few seconds. Her nervous demeanor betrays her discomfort with the odd situation. She shuffles through some papers on her desk, then turns to her typewriter and begins furiously pecking away.

The clock on the wall behind the secretary indicates the time is five after three. Minutes pass slowly. Listening to the rhythmical clicking of the typewriter, my thoughts drift back to the warm afternoon last May when I sat here on this same couch, so naive and with such great fear of events to come. If I could have foreseen what my future held, I would surely have bolted down the school hallway and out the front door along with the students. Knowledge of the pain and agony which lay ahead would've been more than I was prepared to deal with.

The chain of events set in motion on that eventful day changed the course of my life. The innocent, idealistic young man who waited here, anxiously hoping for a coaching job, is gone forever.

The door to the trustees' meeting room swings open. Sounds of chairs sliding against the concrete floor emit from within the room. Blake Tucker's head appears from behind the door. His face is without expression.

"Coach Warden, we're ready for you now," Tucker informs me sternly.

I stand up and stride toward the room. Something weird is happening here. My coaching contract doesn't expire until the end of May. With the football team's improved record, I've felt very confident I'd be given an opportunity to coach the Bulldogs for another year. Now, I feel like a man who's been invited to witness his own hanging.

Each of the seven school trustees remain standing when I enter the room. Their solemn, frowning faces reflect an unfriendly, negative attitude toward me. There are no smiles or handshakes for me. My heart sinks. My mouth has become very dry. Several of these men I had counted as my friends. Why should they greet me with such a sober, adversarial attitude?

Good God! They're gonna fire me! My knees start to wobble. Rockets of anguish shoot off inside my head. I search for an unoccupied chair, something to lean on, to support me. The thought of starting over, searching for another coaching job, makes me nauseous.

Superintendent Boswell is the first to begin clapping. The other men quickly join in. The clamoring sounds of clapping hands, echoing off the walls inside the small room, become deafening.

Mildred Getts rushes from the principal's office to stand at the meeting room doorway. She smiles brightly and claps along with the trustees. All the men are smiling and laughing now.

The clapping and laughing sounds die down while each man comes forward to shake my hand. Mildred is sobbing when she runs to hug my neck.

"Stubby, please forgive us for our crude little joke. We trustees figured a cold shock treatment would be the most impressionable way of expressing our gratitude for your wonderful work this past football season. We also want you to know how much we admired the professional way you handled the turmoil and adversity during the season."

I try to respond, but Boswell stops me by raising his hand. "Coach Warden, the board has authorized me to offer you a five year extension to your existing coaching contract. Our offer includes a raise of one hundred dollars per month for next year, with increases of five percent every year thereafter. We hope you'll seriously consider accepting our offer. We want you to be our football coach."

My feelings of joy and relief are exhilarating, but my first reaction is not to jump at their generosity. There are so many changes which need to be made. Changes which some of these trustees might find objectionable. Some might even deny that problems exist.

Never again will I agree to play certain players over others.

What about Sam and Alfred? They should be compensated for their efforts. Our winning season could never have been possible without their help.

The expectant faces of Boswell and the other trustees tell me this is not the time to negotiate. To bring up unpleasant issues now would only spoil their party.

There'll be plenty of time to discuss problems and changes at a later date. Right now, I must be satisfied to simply savor and enjoy this rare moment and to share the friendly company of these men who have acknowledged my accomplishments and appreciate the heartache, tears and effort necessary to achieve them.

"Superintendent Boswell and distinguished members of the school board–your offer is more than generous, and I gratefully accept. Thank you for your faith in me and for your loyal support this past season. I can assure you I will continue to use every ounce of my strength and energy to make Ranger Bulldog Football a program you can be proud of–a program in which each young man who participates will be glad he did."

My short speech gives rise to another round of applause. The meeting breaks up with everyone trying to shake my hand, pat my back and talk to me at the same time. My tears of joy are impossible to hold back.

Friday Evening
December 20, 1949

CLANKING NOISES OF POTS BANGING AGAINST PANS and the marvelous smell of cooking food emanate from the kitchen where Juanita is preparing our supper. Little Jerry frolics happily in the playpen at the middle of the living room floor. He appears to be keenly interested in the brightly colored dog and cat figures bouncing on the string above him. Short Snorter lies, half-asleep, beside the playpen, but keeping a close watch on every move the baby makes.

A few light snowflakes were beginning to fall when I drove home from the trustees' meeting. By now, the ground outside should be completely covered with snow. Juanita has been hoping for a white Christmas. We have plans to purchase a tree tomorrow and decorate it tomorrow night.

Outside the house I hear sounds of children laughing.

Drawing back the drapes and looking out my front porch window, I observe several neighborhood children running around in my yard. My curiosity about their laughter compels me to open the front door and step out into the cold evening wind.

The children have several rolls of toilet paper which they are pitching up into the branches of trees in my yard. The tall hedge row along the east side of our yard is already heavily decorated with the white bathroom tissue.

Juanita steps onto the front porch and slips her arm under mine.

"What's going on?" she asks, laying her head against my shoulder.

"I'm not exactly sure, but I think our yard is being decorated by the Ranger west-side kids."

One of the smaller children darts by our porch. The young boy is Michael Dean whose parents live a few doors away. The young child is surprised to see Juanita and me standing on the porch, enjoying the decorating festivities. He stops and turns to face us.

"Hello, Mister and Mrs. Stubby. Isn't the snow great?" Michael starts to run away, then stops and comes back to clarify the children's actions. His frail, small voice is remarkably intense as he solemnly explains, "We only toilet paper the yards of people we really like."

Juanita laughs and whispers to me playfully, "Darling, isn't it wonderful to be loved so much?"

"Sometimes I think it may be more important than winning football games," I reply, my mind replaying the exhibition of warm appreciation at the trustees' meeting.

"Darling," Juanita scolds, "everyone wants to win. It's how you win that counts. Real satisfaction comes from having people respect your achievements. Being loved and respected is what makes life worthwhile."

Short Snorter pushes open the screen door and waddles out onto the porch. He surveys the decorated yard, finds it boring and the cold weather not to his liking. He scratches at the door, wanting back inside. Juanita holds the door open for him, then follows him inside, returning to her kitchen.

The cold wind chills my skin, but a genuine sense of belonging warms my insides. Recalling Buford Dinger's words during our encounter on that lovely summer evening only a few months ago, I pray silently to the dark sky.

"Lord, I truly love this town. I love these people. Let me live here with my family forever. Amen."

EPILOGUE I

IN 1953, THE RANGER HIGH BULLDOGS captured the Texas Class One A Football State Championship, defeating Luling by a score of 33 to 25. Onis C. "Stubby" Warden was the Ranger football coach.

In September 1996, Bulldog Stadium in Ranger was renamed O.C. Warden Stadium.

Even though he was a football genius, Stubby Warden never won another State Championship. He made a fatal coaching mistake–he fell in love with his players.

EPILOGUE II

IN 1958, Damon Rupe, the famed Houston wildcatter, discovered an enormous oil field in Venezuela, bringing in the largest producing well ever recorded. Rupe had a silent Texas partner, whose name was never revealed.